KT-448-582

Stormlord Rising

GLENDA LARKE

Papers used by Orbit are natural, renewable and recyclable
products sourced from well managed forests and certified
in accordance with the rules of the Forest Stewardship Council.

Mixed Sources

FSC

Orbit
An imprint of
Little, Brown Book Group
100 Victoria Embankment
London EC4Y 0DY

An Hachette UK Company
www.hachette.co.uk

www.orbitbooks.net

ORBIT

First published in Great Britain in 2010 by Orbit

Copyright © 2010 by Glenda Larke

Excerpt of *The Drowning City* by Amanda Downum
Copyright © 2009 by Amanda Downum

A CIP catalogue record for this book
is available from the British Library.

ISBN 978-1-84149-812-6

Typeset in Minion by Palimpsest Book Production Limited,
Grangemouth, Stirlingshire
Printed in Great Britain by Clays Ltd, St Ives plc

for
Taylah Griffiths
This one is for you, with love

The Quartern

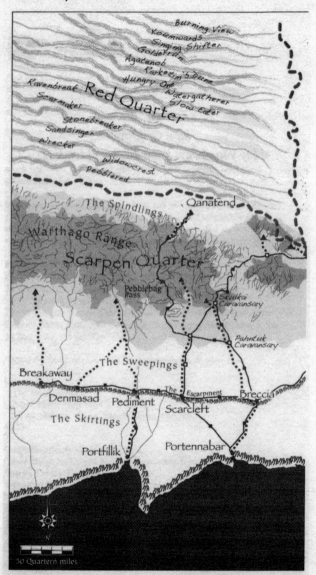

The Quartern

Burning View
Koumwards
Singing Shifter
Golden Ob
Agatenob
Parketim Dune
Hungry Ob
Watergatherer
Glow Eater
Ravenbreak   Red Quarter
Scarmaker
Stonebreaker
Sandsinger
Wrecker

Widowcrest
Pebblered

The Spindlings   Qanatend

Warthago Range
Scarpen Quarter

Pebblebag
Pass

Skulka
Caravansary

Pahntuk
Caravansary

The Sweepings

Breakaway

Denmasad   The Escarpment   Breccia
Pediment   Scarcleft
The Skirtings

Portfillik   Portennabar

N

50 Quartern miles

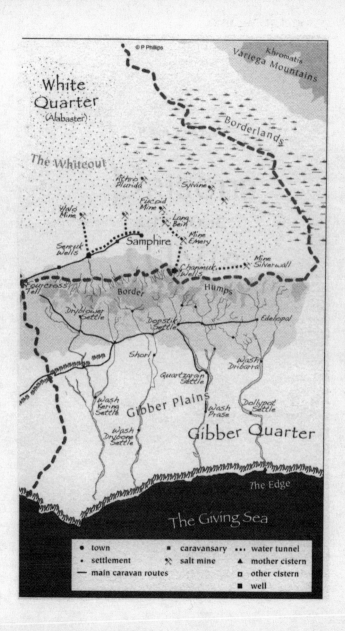

Acknowledgements

This book owes much to others. They know who they are, but they deserve to be named here. Phillip Berrie gave his usual invaluable comments as a beta reader. So did Karen Miller who, in spite of her own writing commitments, still found time to give insightful comments. Then there's Donna Hanson, who has the wonderful knack of seeing mistakes that everyone else misses. Alena Sanusi not only keeps me on track grammatically but supplies me with much needed moral support and good company in the local coffee shop during my breaks from writing. I don't know what I would do without her. And I mustn't forget the Voyager Purple Zoners, who always have answers to my questions – thanks folks.

And then there are all the professional people involved in bringing a book to publication. Most definitely I wouldn't get anywhere at all without them! At the top of the list there are my two wonderful editors, Stephanie Smith in Australia and Samantha Smith in the UK. My heartfelt thanks also goes, as always, to my agent, Dorothy Lumley.

PART ONE

The Bondage of War

1

The man lying next to Lord Ryka Feldspar was dead.

His eyes stared upwards past her shoulder, sightless, the vividness of their blue already fading. For a while blood had seeped from his wounded chest onto her tunic, but that had slowed, then stopped. She did not know his name, although she had known him by sight. He'd been a guard at Breccia Hall. Younger than she was. Eighteen? Twenty?

Too young to die.

The man on top of her was dead, too. He was a Reduner. His head lay on her chest and the beads threaded onto his red braids pressed uncomfortably into her breast, but she didn't dare move. Not yet. Around her she heard Reduner voices still; men, heaving bodies onto packpedes, talking among themselves. Making crude jokes about the dead. Coping, perhaps, with the idea it could so easily have been them. Death or survival: even for the victors, the outcome was often as unpredictable as the gusting of a desert wind.

Reduners. Red men from a land of red sand dunes, flesh-devouring zigger beetles and meddles of black pedes. Drovers and nomads and warriors who hankered after a past they thought was noble: a time when rain had been random and

3

they ruled most of the Quartern with their tribal savagery. A people who had recently returned to a time of slave raids, living under laws decided by the strength of a man's arm and dispensed with a scimitar or a zigtube.

Ryka had been a scholar once, and she spoke their tongue well. She could understand them now as they chatted. "Those withering bastard rainlords," one was saying, his tone bitter and angry. "They took the water from Genillid's eyes while he was fighting next to me. Left his eyeballs like dried berries in their sockets! Blind as a sandworm."

"What did you do?" another asked, a youngster by the sound of him.

"For Genillid? Killed him. That was Sandmaster Davim's orders. Reckon he was right, too. What's left for a dunesman if he can't see?"

"I heard he went around the men afterwards and killed everyone who was likely to lose a hand or a leg as well. No place for a cripple on the dunes, he said."

Ryka felt no pity. They had taken her city. Killed her people. Cloudmaster Granthon Almandine, the Quartern's ruler, its bringer of water and its only true stormlord, was dead, she knew that. His son, Highlord Nealrith, the city's ruler, had been taken and tortured. He'd died in a cage swung over one of the city gates. She knew that, too. She'd heard Jasper Bloodstone had killed him to save him the agony of a slow death.

Poor Jasper. She'd seen the respect and affection in his eyes when he'd spoken to the Highlord.

Gentle, kindly Nealrith. She had grown up with him, gone to Breccia Academy with him, attended his wedding to that bitch, Lord Laisa. *Oh, Sunlord receive you into his sunfire, Rith. You did not deserve your end.*

"Did we get all them bastards?" the same youth asked.

"The rainlords? Reckon so. I hear exhaustion finally sapped

their powers, leaving them defenceless. My brother killed one of them rainlord priests. Still, not even a sandmaster can tell one from an ordinary city-grubber. They don't look no different."

"I heard some of them are women."

The first man gave a bark of laughter. "One thing's for sure, we can slaughter any force that has to use women to fight a battle!"

Ryka wanted to grit her teeth, but couldn't risk even that slight movement. *Blast Davim's sun-blighted eyes.* The tribes of the Red Quarter had been leaving their violent past behind until he'd come along to twist their view of history.

Sandmaster Davim, with his vicious hatreds and his brutal desire for power, had taken away that scholarly life of hers. He'd shattered the Quartern's peace, mocked the cultures not his own, destroyed the learning, all in a couple of star cycles. His men had killed her father. Watergiver only knew what had happened to her sister and her mother. And Kaneth?

No, you mustn't think he is dead. You mustn't lose hope.

Strange even to think of the life she'd had because it was all gone now, spun away on the invaders' swords and the shimmering wings of their ziggers, like sand whirled into the desert on a spindevil wind. A wisp of her hair tickled her cheek. She ignored it. She mustn't move. Not even a twitch. She had to live through this, for the baby. For Kaneth.

Sunlord, I know I don't really believe in you, but let him be alive, that wonderful, gentle bladesman-warrior of mine. Father of my child. She longed to raise her head and look for him. Perhaps he lay somewhere beneath her, still alive. Or dead. Her hand longed to move to cover her abdomen where their son stirred. She knew his water and thus his maleness. *Oh, Kaneth, we had so little time . . .*

The memory of her last moments with him replayed over and over. The battle in the waterhall. His last conscious act had been to protect her with his body. Could she have done more? Done something differently? She had used the last of her power to stop his bleeding, to dry the horrible wound exposing the bone of his scalp as he floated face down, senseless in the cistern. She had kept pure the bubble of air around their faces so they could both breathe. But mostly she'd just had to float there, eyes almost closed, hoping the invaders would leave the waterhall so she could pull Kaneth out of the water and take him to safety.

A futile hope, easily splintered. The Reduners had slung them both out of the cistern. They had dumped Kaneth, unconscious – or dead – on the floor; the sound of his body thudding onto the paving echoed in her head still. She'd landed on top of him a moment later. It had taken all her courage to allow herself to fall like a dead body. Not to stretch out a hand to break her landing. Not to open her eyes, not to touch him, not to look to see if his wound was bleeding again.

More waiting then, more futile praying that the Reduners would leave the waterhall, more begging a boon of a Sunlord she didn't believe in. A little joy, too, when she'd felt the baby stir within her.

She'd tried speaking to Kaneth, whispered words of encouragement and love, but he had not replied. She thought she'd felt the movement of his breath faint against her cheek, but she couldn't be sure.

Several runs of the sandglass later, the guards had received fresh orders. She'd heard and understood: "Take the dead outside. Load them onto a pede and dump them outside the walls."

Her heart had leaped within her. A chance. A chance for both her and Kaneth – if he lived. *Please let it be so . . .*

More rough handling when she was thrown over a man's shoulder and carried, her face bumping against his back, only to be dumped once more onto this heap of the dead. She wasn't outside the city walls; she knew that much. Cracking open an eyelid, she'd recognised one of the Breccia Hall court-yards. Hampered by her confounded short-sightedness blur-ring the details of anything more than ten paces away, she saw enough to know the last bastion against the invaders had fallen. They had lost the city to the Reduners.

And so it was that she now lay motionless, cushioned by lifeless bodies, her clothes drying out in the heat of an after-noon sun, as she listened and awaited her time to move.

Sunlord, but she was tired! She needed to eat, and eat well. Without food she had no energy, without energy she had no water-power, no way of fighting back. Her sword was gone and she doubted she could have lifted it anyway.

Some more desultory conversation, laughter, and then a voice answering an unheard question. "No. That's the dead burning outside the city wall you can smell."

The words sent fear stabbing into her bowels. They were burning bodies.

"Are we eating them now?" someone asked, amused.

"You sand-tick, Ankrim! The sandmaster ordered all the dead burned as soon as possible. Easier, I suppose, than burying them, when we have all those bab palms to fuel the pyres."

"Nah. More to teach a lesson to the living, I reckon. Here, let's get this pede loaded."

She stopped listening. *Burned! Sandblast the bastards – if Kaneth was unconscious, then . . .* Being taken outside the wall began to sound like a rotten idea.

The packpede was loaded, but no one approached the heap of dead Ryka was on. The nearby voices were gone, leaving only far-off screams and shouting. She risked opening her eyes. No one. Cautiously, she raised her head and looked around. She was in front of the main entrance to the pede stables adjoining Breccia House, and as far as she could see, there was no one in sight. As she climbed down, bodies squelched under her sandalled feet and the odours of death intensified. Rot, shit, piss, blood. She gagged.

Boys, some of them. Not all soldiers, either . . .

In death, there was little difference between those who had their skin stained red by desert dust, and the fair-skinned Scarpen folk like herself.

Her feet reached the gravel surface of the courtyard and she stood up. She was sore all over, and stiff. She moved like an old woman. After another swift glance around to make sure she was unobserved, she poked through the piled corpses. The Reduners she ignored, and those wearing a guard uniform. Kaneth had never been one for uniforms. "If I am going to fight, I want to be comfortable," he'd said as he chose his oldest tunic and trousers. She'd joked that he looked like a brass worker from Level Twenty, but she had followed his lead and worn clothes more suited to a labourer than a woman of her class.

She couldn't find him. Tall, broad-shouldered, muscular, long-limbed – he was hard to miss. And that sun-streaked fair hair he kept tied at the nape, it would stand out among the Reduners.

Again she searched, even more carefully. He wasn't there. There had been a second pile of bodies, but it had disappeared. If he'd been among those . . .

Panicking and weak and thirsty, she swallowed back a surge of dizzying nausea.

"Looking for something?"

The voice, and the accompanying sound of a weapon being drawn from its scabbard, dulled her fear for Kaneth, smothered it in more immediate terror. Her heart skipped, pounded. Slowing its beating by force of will, she turned to face the speaker. A Reduner man, for all he spoke the Quartern tongue with a strong Gibber accent. He'd just stepped out of the stables. Slim, athletic, armed, his red skin streaked with dust and blood. His dark red braids were untidy with beads missing or broken. His sword was blood-drenched.

The darkness of his eyes contained no hint of mercy, no hint of anything. She guessed he was at least ten cycles younger than she was, but he carried himself with assurance. His belted robe was elaborately embroidered, so she knew why: he came from a wealthy and important family.

Probably learned his Quartern tongue from Gibber slaves, she thought, her bitterness deep. Reduners had been raiding the Gibber, almost with impunity, for more than four years. Kaneth and his men had done their best to curtail such raids, but their success had been limited.

"My husband," she said, keeping her voice level and respectful – but not meek; she would not grovel, even though she knew she was a finger's breadth away from death. Or worse.

He held his scimitar up and took a step towards her, the blade pointed at her chest. She did not move.

"Find him?" he inquired, his tone deceptively mild if the sword was to be believed.

"No."

"You're supposed t'be in the big room." He waved his free hand towards the hall. "In there. How did y'get out?"

The point of the scimitar came within a whisker of her left nipple. She refused to look down and held his gaze instead. "A woman will risk much to serve her husband."

Something flared in his eyes then, but she wasn't sure she could read it. "Not in my experience," he said, his lip curling in cynicism. "These folk," he added, indicating the heap of bodies, "came out of the waterhall. Your husband – guard, was he? Fighting up there?"

"He was up there," she said, "but he wasn't a guard. He was a brass worker from downlevel. He went to help." She did not have to feign grief; she knew it was written on her face and captured in her voice, for anyone to see and hear. "He brought me up here for safety. He knew nothing about fighting."

"Then I think you can be certain he's snuffed it. Everyone in the waterhall died."

No, they didn't. I'm here.

She didn't move. Every piece of her being concentrated on not showing fear. Reduners valued courage and despised weakness, even in their women. Not, of course, that he would think twice about lopping off her head with his blade if it pleased him. "Doubtless you're right," she said, fighting her nausea, "but I would like to know one way or the other."

"What's your name?"

I shan't make you a present of that, you bastard. If he realised she was a rainlord, she was dead – and someone among the Reduners might know the name of Ryka Feldspar. "Who wants to know?"

He stared at her, as if he couldn't believe his ears. "My name's Ravard," he said finally. "But what should count with you, woman, is the weapon I hold t'your body. *What's your name?*" The blade tip brushed her nipple this time, then traced a pattern up to her throat.

"Garnet," she said, appropriating the name of the cook in Carnelian House and then adding another gemstone at random: "Garnet Prase."

"Dangerous for a woman t'be out on the streets after a battle," he remarked with heavy mockery. "You never know what nasty thing might happen. There's men wanting their rewards for a battle well fought, and they'll take them anyhow they please."

10

"So your men are out of control already?" she asked, and then bit her tongue. Why could she never learn to keep silent when it counted!

His eyes narrowed. "You play a dangerous game, woman, with your Scarpen arrogance. Perhaps you care nothing for yourself." The sword point dropped to her abdomen. "But what about the brat you carry?"

This time she couldn't control her shock. "How—?" she began, and then closed her mouth firmly, though her hand dropped to cover the roundness of her belly, as if she could protect her son from his weapon. *If only I had my water-power—*

"I have eyes in me head," he said. "Suggest you keep a still tongue in yours, Garnet, 'less you want t'lose your life and your man's get, as well. I'll take you to the other women in there. Tonight you sleep with a man who's not your husband, or you'll lose more than your man. Think on it."

He turned her roughly and started her walking in front of him towards the Hall's main door. She hugged her arms about her to stop the trembling.

A complete stranger works out I'm pregnant at a glance? It took Kaneth nearly half a cycle to wake up to it! This fellow was strange.

When she slipped in a patch of blood on the gravel, he grabbed her by the arm, wrenching her upright before she hit the ground. "Careful, sweet lips," he said in her ear. "We want you undamaged, don't we?"

She gasped in pain. The sword cut on her upper leg – not deep but raw and throbbing nonetheless – had opened up.

He hadn't noticed it before because the slash in her trousers was almost covered by her tunic, but he saw the fresh blood now and gave an exasperated grunt. "Why didn't y'tell me you were hurt?"

"It's nothing."

He pulled up the hem of the tunic and looked at the wound. A makeshift bandage around her thigh had long since come loose and fallen off. "Hmph. Maybe not, but needs covering nonetheless, t'stop that bleeding."

He left her where she was and went back to the heaped up dead. With his scimitar, he slashed at a dead man's tunic and brought back a piece of the cloth. She wanted to take it from him, but he ignored her gesture and knelt to wrap it around her thigh himself, over the top of her trousers. She braced herself for an intimate touch, a leer or a sneering remark, but all he did was bandage her.

As he tied off the ends, he said, "When you get a chance, wash the wound 'n' put a clean cloth 'bout it. Even a small cut like that can kill you, if it gets dirty."

Perhaps that would be best anyway, she thought. *To die.*

The thought must have been reflected on her face, because he said harshly, "Listen t'me, you water-soft city groveller. Living's what counts, understand? Your man's dead. Probably your whole withering family's been snuffed. Your city's fallen. Your rainlords are rotting in the sun. Soon there'll be no more water in your skyless city. Take your chance with us. We've not got rainlords, but our sandmasters and tribemasters can sense water on the wind. Our dune gods protect us." He pointed to her abdomen. "That young'un of yours? It can grow up Reduner, a warrior or a woman of the tribe. Reduners don't make no difference 'tween folk. Out there on the dunes, we're all red soon enough. Being alive? That's all that matters. That's *all*."

She stood facing him. Wasn't there more to life than that? Yes, of course there was – but you had to be alive to achieve it. *Sandblast it,* she thought, despairing. *How did we Breccians ever come to this?*

She nodded to the man. "Yes," she said. "You are right."

"Now, get going, Garnet. I don't have time t'waste on you."

12

Kaneth, I will be strong. I promise, for the sake of our son. You're on your own, wherever you are. And so, dammit, am I.

And then, just a whisper in her mind, to a man who was probably dead: *I love you.*

2

Ravard handed Ryka over to a Reduner bladesman guarding the double doors of Breccia Hall's public reception room. The man pushed her roughly inside and closed the doors behind her.

Though the area was large, it was crowded. And noisy with crying. Her heart sank as she looked around and absorbed the significance of what she was seeing. Women. No men. Women, yet no small children. Every head turned her way to see who had entered, eyes fearful. And she was standing in a patch of half-dried blood on the floor.

Waterless hells.

There was a gasp from a group sitting on the floor, and a figure came flying to grab her in a tight embrace, sobbing, gasping, shuddering, pouring out her woe. Beryll, but not her pretty, carefree tease of a little sister. Not any more.

"Beryll," she whispered, "quietly, quietly. I can't understand what you are saying! Calm down."

But she wouldn't be calm. "Ryka, Mother! They killed Mother! They didn't give her a chance. She – she—"

Ryka had been expecting it, but still the stab of grief pierced deep, then twisted painfully with the bitter rage that followed it.

14

Her eyes swollen, her chest heaving, Beryll wailed between gulping sobs, "I wanted us to escape with the others down the underground passageway, but she said she'd wait until Father came back. He never came. Then we heard he was dead, but she still wouldn't go. And I couldn't leave her, could I? Anyway, there was the Lady Ethelva and the ceremony of the taking of the Cloudmaster's water and Mother thought we ought to be there, so we went to the House of the Dead and we couldn't come back safely because of the ziggers until Lord Gold brought us with the Lady Ethelva afterwards. Oh, Ryka, it was awful. Lady Ethelva seemed so – so old, all of a sudden. Like she'd all shrivelled up. It was so horrid. And we didn't know whether you were all right, or if Papa really was dead, and then the Reduners broke through . . ." Her face went white, just with the remembering.

Ryka led her away from the door to a more private spot near the wall. Her sandals left sticky footprints on the floor.

"But Mother really is dead? Are you sure?" She was having trouble absorbing the reality behind the words.

"They – they slit her throat. Like they were slaughtering an animal."

Oh, sweet water save us. "You *saw* it?"

Beryll's frame shuddered in her arms as she nodded. "Her and the Lady Ethelva. Oh, Ryka, they killed so many! The guards and the men first, in the fighting when they broke in through the gates. Then they rounded up the women, servants and all. They took the older ones out and – and just killed them. Just like that. They said it was because Stormlord Jasper didn't surrender himself. There were so *many* dead. So many of the older ones had thought they'd have a better chance if they didn't go down the tunnel. There wasn't room for everyone anyway . . ." Her voice trailed away in misery.

Ryka tried not to change words into images. The words

were bad enough. Blindly, she patted her sister on the back; aching, she kissed the top of her head.

When Beryll had calmed, she changed the subject. "Listen, you mustn't call me Ryka. If the Reduners know they have a rainlord, I'm dead. Our only chance of getting out of this alive is to hide who I am. Call me Garnet."

Beryll lifted her puzzled gaze to look at her sister's face. "What? Garnet? Why?"

"Just in case they know there is a rainlord called Ryka Feldspar."

"Oh. Would they know that?"

"I doubt it, but I don't want to take the risk." There was also a slight risk a Reduner warrior might see her and recognise her as a woman who'd fought in the waterhall, but she didn't think there was much danger of that, either. Those still alive were under the impression she had died; certainly none of them knew she was a rainlord. To make herself less recognisable, she untied her hair, shaking it loose over her shoulders and around her face.

She looked around short-sightedly, seeking familiar faces, neighbours from her level perhaps, anyone who might give away her identity, but saw no one she knew. "Is there anyone here who will recognise me?" Beryll shook her head. "I don't think so. I don't know these people. They were from the other levels. They took refuge here when the city was attacked."

As far as Ryka could tell, no one was looking at her with recognition. Dirty, sweaty, bloodied and dressed as she was, she was not surprised. She hardly looked like an upleveller rainlord. Besides, she was not well-known, not like Kaneth or the Cloudmaster's family, the Almandines. She was a scholar who fulfilled her duties as a rainlord by teaching at Breccia Academy and taking her turn to check on the mother wells and patrol the water tunnel between the city and the Warthago Range.

"We are going to be slaves, aren't we?" Beryll whispered.

"Beryll, I'm a rainlord, remember? We just have to wait for the right time, for when I am strong again and can get us out of here."

"Can't you do it now? I don't want to stay here! They – they murdered children, Ryka. *Children*. All the really young ones."

And left the older ones and the young women, Ryka thought, but she didn't give voice to the words. Instead, she said, "I don't have any power left. I haven't eaten in so long. Or slept. Is there any food here? If I had something to eat . . ."

"I don't think so. After the Reduners herded us in here, they seemed to forget all about us. No one has brought us any food. But then, they killed the servants. Except for the pretty ones. Ethelva sent them down the tunnel before the Reduners came." She brushed hair out of her eyes with a trembling hand. "I wish – I wish I had gone, too."

"Where is everyone from our level? Why aren't they here?"

"Most of them went down the tunnel. Level Three and Four people had first choice. Maybe they're still hidden there. Where's Kaneth?"

"He was injured. I don't know what happened to him."

"Oh." Beryll started to cry again, in juddering sobs. Helplessly, Ryka patted her on the back. *Oh Beryll*, she thought, *things could get a lot worse even than this*.

Miserably, she looked around. Nealrith had brought as many of the city folk as he could within the walls of the level, but it had been an illusory safety. The city's two top levels, where the waterhall and the Cloudmaster's residence were located, had lasted longer than the stepped levels of the lower city, but in the end it had made little difference. *We rainlords failed these people.*

The Scarpen's only hope was that Jasper Bloodstone had escaped with Nealrith's wife, that spitless bitch Laisa, and their daughter, Senya. Perhaps Jasper and Senya could start a new line of stormlords.

Perhaps the other cities will prevail. Perhaps they will stop this Reduner sandmaster. Perhaps in the end it will be that bastard Taquar Sardonyx who will stop him . . .

"Listen Beryll, you must tell me all you have seen. The Reduners – the leaders. Who are they?"

Slowly, Beryll calmed enough to speak again. "Well, there's Davim. He's the sandmaster. He's horrible." She was trembling still, and stark fear shone in her eyes.

"How will I recognise him?"

"He wears a red robe that's got all this red embroidery down the front and lots of gemstone beads – no one else has as much. He's maybe about Kaneth's age. There're some others who have some embroidery. Like the man who translates for those who don't speak the Quartern tongue. His name is Ravard, I think."

"Ah. I suspect I've met that one."

"I – I don't know about any of the others. Someone said the man in charge of all the killing is older. They call him the Warrior Son, but I don't know which one he is. They all look alike to me anyway. And it's better if you don't stare at them. They don't like you to stare." She clutched at Ryka's arm. "Be careful, Ry. You can't argue with them. They don't like that, either."

Time passed so slowly. Ryka circled the room, looking for a way out, but the doors were locked and the openings for light and air were high above their heads. There was a small water-room tucked away at the far end, its facilities too few for so many people. There was always a queue, and the place stank because there was only a trickle of water. No one seemed to have any food, and most had not eaten anything in over a day. The wailing of grieving women and terrified, hungry youngsters – not one of them under nine or ten – was a constant noise, grating on her nerves because no one had the means to comfort them.

In the end, Ryka fell asleep lying on the floor in Beryll's arms.

It was dark when she woke to the sounds of commotion. Slamming doors in the distance, fear-saturated muttering, renewed weeping. Everyone scrambled to their feet. Beryll clung to Ryka's arm. The central double doors were flung open and a line of Reduner warriors, some bearing torches, entered behind two of their leaders. One was the man who had brought her there: Ravard.

Staring at the other, Beryll hissed in her ear, "That's him. Sandmaster Davim!"

Her first thought was, *But he's so young!* The next: *Watergiver, damn his eyes. The man has no soul.* There was nothing in his gaze that spoke of pity or compassion and much that rejoiced in the misery he saw before him.

Silence spread to cover the room, as if the sandmaster's gaze compelled all sound to cease. Even the children were silent. He stood in front of the doors, Ravard at his side, his warriors arrayed behind him. He wasn't a tall man, but there was no doubt he commanded.

He nodded to Ravard and the younger man stepped forward. He said, "I speak for Sandmaster Davim of Dune Watergatherer. The sandmaster rules here now. Kneel before him."

The room stilled. For a moment no one moved. No one even seemed to breathe. Then, when Davim's stare bored into the women closest to him, they fell to their knees. Gradually others around the room followed.

"I won't!" Beryl whispered. "He's the one who ordered Mother killed! And Lady Ethelva."

Ryka grabbed her by the arm and yanked her down as she

herself knelt. "Oh yes, you will," she murmured. "Your job is to stay alive until I can get you out of here. Pride means nothing. Living is what's important. And don't forget – my name is Garnet." She glanced around and was relieved to see no one remained standing.

Davim spoke then, in his own tongue. His voice snapped into the silence, confirming Ryka's every fear. She was probably the only person in the room who understood the language, but the others weren't left wondering for long. Ravard translated all the sandmaster said.

"Sandmaster Davim wishes t'tell you everyone here will serve his men, or die. You are Reduner women now. He is going t'honour one of you with his personal choice."

Beryll shuddered and turned her face into Ryka's shoulder once more. "Oh Sunlord save me," she whispered. "Ryka, he wants me, I know it. He looked at me in *such* a way before." Her trembling wouldn't stop.

"Hide your face," Ryka said softly. But even as she spoke she knew it was too late. The sandmaster was threading his way through the kneeling women towards them.

He pointed at Beryll and said, "Stand."

Ryka stood, pulling Beryll up with her. At Davim's shoulder, Ravard's dark eyes were fixed on hers, but there was no expression there. The sandmaster reached out and pulled Beryll away from her. He cupped her chin with a hand and forced her face up. "Her," he said to Ravard in his own tongue.

"The sandmaster has done you a great honour," Ravard told Beryll. "You'll share his pallet tonight. If you please him, he'll spare your life."

"Does the sandmaster not want a real woman in his bed," Ryka drawled before Beryll could react, "instead of a mere child?"

Davim's sharp eyes switched from Beryll to her.

He knows what I said, Ryka thought. *He many not speak the Quartern tongue well, but he understands.*

As if to confirm that thought, Ravard did not translate.

Davim's arrogant gaze slid up and down her body, assessing. Critical. "Ugly she-pedes don't please the bull when there are prettier pede-heifers to hand," he said in his own tongue, his tone mocking. He grinned at Ravard, who grinned back.

Not wanting to let any of the Reduners know she could understand them, Ryka was careful not to react. Beryll, still held by the sandmaster, darted a despairing, frightened look at her.

Ravard translated Davim's words.

"Bulls are blind in the dark," Ryka replied, looking past Beryll to hold the sandmaster's gaze with her own. "And all she-pedes are black in the depth of night." She gave what she hoped was an enticing smile. "Touch, on the other hand . . ."

"*Whore!*" one of the Breccian women spat at her from behind.

Davim, laughing, said to Ravard, "The ugly bitch thinks to seduce me! Who wants stringy pede meat if he can have the tender venison of a young desert deer?" He turned his attention back to Beryll. "Come with me, eager to please," he said. "Or die."

Ravard translated – and Beryll spat in the sandmaster's face.

A split second later, she dropped to the floor. For one frozen moment, Ryka didn't understand. Refused to understand. She saw Davim's merciless rage as he wiped the spittle from his face with the back of a hand. Only when her gaze dropped to Beryll where she lay spasming on the floor, did she see the glistening red of the slash across her neck. With unbelieving eyes she stared at the welling blood, matched by scarlet drips along the sandmaster's dagger blade. She hadn't even seen him draw it. Behind her, someone screamed.

21

With an agonised cry, Ryka fell to her knees to gather Beryll into her arms. In her dying moments, the girl flailed. A horrible sucking sound came from her throat. Her eyes closed as she desperately tried to draw breath. And then she was gone.

No!

For a moment, Ryka remained where she was, stunned, disbelieving. When she looked up again, Davim was already turning away, uninterested. Shock turned to blinding rage. She wanted to rip out his throat. She groped for the power to kill him, but because she was drained and starving, nothing came.

He didn't see the uncontrolled fury, didn't see her naked desire to kill. And that saved her. She had the fleeting moment she needed to dampen down her emotion.

In agony, she touched her sister's face with trembling fingers. *Beryll. Oh, Watergiver, why? Oh, Sunlord. Oh, Beryll.*

She'd kill him. Then, common sense prevailing, *This is not the time to try, Ryka. Not yet. Oh, Watergiver have mercy. Beryll!*

"Find me a pretty young woman, Ravard," Davim was saying. "*Young*, the way I like them. And kill the stringy meat. She does not please me."

Terror ripped through her. *I've run out of time.* She flicked a glance to the row of Reduner warriors. The nearest, one of those bearing a burning brand to light the room, had propped his chala spear against the wall. *I'm dead, but maybe I can take Davim with me*, she thought, eyeing the spear. *If Davim dies, maybe the Scarpen has a chance . . .* She tensed herself for a leap past the sandmaster to the weapon.

Ravard laughed easily. "That's because you have experience and can teach the young to please you. Me, I need the stringy old ones to teach me how to be pleased!" He stared at Ryka in open appraisal, halting her intention to move. "Kill her? Certainly, if that is your wish, but I'd rather sharpen my, er, sword on her experience."

Davim frowned and stared hard at Ryka. She dropped her gaze submissively, still pretending she did not understand their conversation. He shrugged. "As you wish. If she gives you any trouble, hand her over to the chalamen. They can use her for target practice for *their* spears."

The Reduner warriors chuckled, leaving Ryka in no doubt that the double meanings were intended.

Ravard nodded, grinning. "Take her to my rooms," he told one of the warriors, "and lock her in."

3

Scarpen Quarter
Scarcleft City,
Scarcleft Hall, Level 2

Lord Taquar Sardonyx looked up from his desk, frowning. It was late, it was cold, and he had been about to go to bed. In fact, he'd been wondering whether to ask his steward to fetch him a woman. That pretty new servant girl, for example. Eighteen, wistfully innocent and adoring – she would do. And yet . . . he glanced at the painting he had mounted on the wall. Terelle's painting. A waterpainting once, until the earthquake had separated the paint from the water. Now it lacked a little of the life it must have once had, but still the figure leaped at him out of the paint.

Taquar, Highlord of Scarcleft, driving a pede.

She had captured everything he liked to think he possessed: the aura of power, the ruthlessness, the strength, the commanding stature, and of course the sensuality. But more than that, she had painted something of herself into the work: her fear of him, her fear of her attraction to him. Every time he looked at it, he cursed the earthquake that had enabled her to escape. Watergiver, what a lover she would have made! All she'd needed was the awakening, and he could have stirred her senses so easily. Stupidly, he had thought her not ready. And now, whenever he took another woman to bed, he thought of what he had missed, and cursed again. Innocence and the promise of initiating a maiden's sexual awakening – it intrigued him every time, and rarely disappointed. A victim either learned to match his passion or shivered in fear. Either way, he enjoyed the result.

He'd sent people out looking for her, of course, once he realised she had escaped. Unfortunately it had been a day before they had cleared away enough of the rubble along the passage to her room to see that she was not dead or trapped, but missing. Even then, he'd assumed she was still in the city. Now, five days later and thanks to his seneschal's investigations, he knew better.

It was infuriating. How would he ever entice Shale Flint – or Jasper Bloodstone as the wretched lad was called now – back to Scarcleft City if he found out Terelle had fled?

Scarcleft was a wounded city still, and it riled Taquar that the most serious damage was to his own hall on Level Two. He was tired of the noise and dust of cleaning up and the preparations for rebuilding. He was infuriated by the grumblings of discontent from Level Thirty-six, the lowest level, where the waterless lived. How *dare* they protest the slow reaction to their plight! As if they had any rights at all. He would have killed the lot of them long ago, if some of the merchants and tradesmen and artisans had not made it clear they needed the labour of the waterless from time to time.

Definitely, he needed a little solace in his bed. He was reaching to ring for his steward, when a knock sounded at the door.

The visitor the servant ushered in a moment later took Taquar by surprise. He rose to his feet, trying to conceal the extent of his astonishment. "*Laisa?* My dear, this is a surprise! A pleasure of course, but – er – unexpected." Even as he spoke he was taking in her grubby appearance, the fatigue about her eyes, the tension around her mouth. Her long blonde hair was dusty and tumbled out of its jewelled clips, her skin bare of any artificial powders or paints. She was still beautiful, of course. She had the kind of looks that weren't ruined by a little grime or lack of sleep; a brilliant, cool beauty that improved rather than diminished with age. Looks that suited a harsh land and matched a nature that revelled in luxury. Laisa was a sensual woman, yet pitiless.

And he had never seen her so dishevelled. What the salted damn had happened?

"What brings you here? And looking like this?" he asked, keeping his tone carefully neutral.

"Don't pretend you don't know what happened to Breccia City," she said. "You can't really be unaware the desert beast has slipped the leash you tried to put around his neck!"

"I don't know what you mean." And he didn't, but he could guess, and the guess left him cold. *Davim.* That spitless sand louse of a Reduner. He must have moved his forces from Qanatend to Breccia City. Why couldn't he have waited for things to fall into place of their own accord?

The answer came all too soon. *He must have found out I don't have Shale.*

Aloud, he said, "Suppose you tell me, my dear." He nodded to the servant. "Bring us some of the best imported wine and sweetmeats, man." When they were alone again, he waved at a chair in front of the fire. "Sit down, Laisa."

She flung herself into the chair, saying, "What the sand-blasted hell happened here, Taquar? Why is part of your city in ruins and much of the lowest level burned? Did Davim attack Scarcleft too?"

He shook his head, and went to stand with his back to the fire. "Hardly! No, it was the earthquake. You didn't hear? I sent word. It happened a few days after Gratitudes."

"We have been otherwise occupied," she said, her voice

brittle with irritation. "We were attacked five days after Gratitudes. Nealrith sent word immediately."

"I see. None of your messengers arrived, and neither did mine to you, apparently. Davim's to blame for that, I suppose. He must have Breccia ringed. You were lucky to get through yourself."

The look she gave him was scathing. "I did not take the road and anyway, give me some credit. I do have enough water-sense to dodge men out looking for people escaping the city. So what was this earthquake? I've never heard of one doing this much damage."

"The damage was fairly localised, fortunately. Some damage to the hall. And a fire on the thirty-sixth level, but that place is no great loss. Far from it, in fact. Gave me an excuse to clean out some of the water-wasters. But tell me about Breccia's troubles."

"*Troubles?*" She shot him a look of scornful fury as she warmed her hands at the fire. "Is *that* what you'd call it? The city has *fallen*, you withering sand-brain! Nealrith is *dead*. So is Granthon. And doubtless most of our rainlords as well: Ryka and Merquel Feldspar, Kaneth Carnelian, Lord Gold and most of the rainlord priests, for a start. The Scarpen is without a competent stormlord."

Baldly, concisely and without histrionics, she told him all that she knew about the siege and how she had escaped with her daughter and Shale Flint. Except, he was quick to realise, the most important fact: the exact whereabouts of Jasper Bloodstone. The tale didn't take her long; she finished just as the servant came in and left the tray of refreshments.

He poured her some wine, imported from across the Giving Sea, saying: "Let me see if I understand you: Breccia City's rainlords decided to die fighting – a piece of monumental stupidity on their part. Typical of Kaneth Carnelian, of course, to indulge in heroically futile gestures, but I expected better of some of the others. Doubtless the city will have been thoroughly subdued in the time it took you to cross the desert to my gates."

"Doubtless," she agreed.

"Sandmaster Davim now controls both Qanatend and Breccia and has access to whatever water the two cities have. At a guess, you are now about to offer me the estimable young man, our only stormlord, in exchange for – what, I wonder?"

She took the proffered drink in its imported goblet of blown glass, and he had to admire her aplomb. Newly widowed and having just ridden several days across a desert, dispossessed of all her wealth and much of her status, and still she could look at him coolly across her glass of wine and say, "What did you hope from all this, Taquar? Were you really so sun-fried as to bargain with this Reduner nomad and think he would do your bidding?"

He shrugged indifferently. "It could have worked. But he is an impatient, arrogant hothead. And greedy with it. I promised him free rein in the Red and White Quarters in exchange for water when and where he wanted it, but apparently it wasn't enough for him. I must assume he found out Shale ran to Nealrith?"

"Cloudmaster Granthon made sure he knew."

"Which prompted him to renege on my alliance with him, of course. I assure you, these attacks on the cities of the Scarpen were not my idea. Oh, I thought to threaten the other cities with the idea of Reduner attack, yes – but I want to rule a wealthy nation, not a huddle of ruined buildings and groves."

Laisa turned on him, her anger vicious. "You were out of your sand-stuffed mind! Do you think a rainlord can control a sandmaster, one whose thinking is as twisted as a spindevil wind? He dreams of returning to a Time of Random Rain, when the dunes managed without rainlords. You unleashed a force you can't control, you fool! And now we all have to suffer for it."

He felt the heat of his anger flood his face, but kept his temper under control. "I don't fear for Scarcleft. Unlike the late unlamented Granthon and Nealrith in Breccia, or Moiqa over in Qanatend, I believe in ziggers and a trained army. Every young man of this city can handle a pike and a scimitar or a sword. They can drive a pede or fight from its back. They can handle ziggers. They don't get their water allotments unless they undergo the training sessions once a year. Davim would never take Scarcleft – but that is neither here nor there. You were wise to get Shale out of Breccia City. The idea of Davim getting his hands on our last stormlord at this stage does not bear thinking about."

"Pity you didn't *think* before you began all this," she retorted.

He ignored that. "The question is, what do you want in exchange for Shale?" He rubbed a finger around the top of his glass reflectively. "Of course, I could force you to tell me where he is, but bargaining is so much more civilised, is it not, my dear?"

She leaned back in her chair, both hands cradling her goblet. "And more rewarding, I think. You won't find my terms too arduous. Put simply: I want to be the wife of a highlord, with all the, er, panoply that entails, and I want my daughter to be the wife of the Quartern's one and only stormlord. That's basically it. The details can be negotiated later."

Taquar almost laughed. "Not quite the grieving widow, are you?"

She did not deign to reply, merely helping herself to a sweetmeat instead.

"What in all the waterless sands of the Quartern makes you think I would *want* to marry you, Laisa?"

She took the insult in her stride, shrugging. "I don't really care whether you want to or not, Taquar. I want the *position*. As Nealrith's wife, I've grown used to being pampered. I like the power I have as a rainlord, but I also like the extra that comes with being the wife of a city's highlord. I don't want to give it up. I'd be willing to let you have all the freedom you need, to do whatever it is you've always done. In return, I can run your household, be your hostess, share your bed if you want, or not if you don't."

He chuckled. "I do not need a hostess, or another seneschal when I have Harkel Tallyman, and I have plenty of women for my bed."

"Harkel? I heard you were so enraged that he let Jasper escape to Breccia, you threw him in your deepest pit."

"I am a civilised man. He was ensconced in the tower for a while, deprived of all his normal luxuries. After half a cycle both he and I were fed up with the situation. He missed his luxuries; I missed his organisational skills. He is my seneschal once more, and vastly more subservient." He paused, suddenly thoughtful. "However, you do tempt me. My original idea was to keep Shale hidden. To have everyone thinking I was the one who shifted the storms, that I was the stormlord. Not possible now, of course, seeing everyone knows about the lad. But I will need someone to keep him in line. He is not going to take kindly to doing my bidding . . . Take on *that* job, and I might think about it."

She waved a careless hand. "I can manage a young man of his age."

"And then there is one slight problem you have neglected to mention, my dear. You are selling me a carpet with a flaw in the weave."

"I beg your pardon?"

"Oh, come now, Laisa. When I lost Shale to Breccia, I decided it wasn't such a bad idea. The Cloudmaster could teach him all he knew about making and breaking clouds. Once he'd learned, I had the means to entice him back.

"I did hear that he was cloudshifting, so I put the plan into operation. But then I heard a few wind-whispers from our fellow rainlords. Shale Flint, or Jasper Bloodstone if you prefer to call him that, has only been shifting storms, and has needed Granthon's power to lift the water vapour from the ocean in the first place. He cannot do it on his own. Moreover, as far as I can tell – and I may be wrong of course, because I cannot always sense far distant clouds the way a stormlord can – no rain has fallen anywhere in the past few days. Which, I assume, means since Granthon died. Tell me, do I have the truth of it?"

Unfazed, she said, "Unfortunately, you do. However, Jasper told us you were the one who stole Granthon's storm. That makes you a very powerful rainlord, Taquar. It seems to me, you have neglected to mention to other rainlords the extent of your abilities. I have the feeling there is a good chance, if you back Jasper with your power, the young man will be able to do what is needed. Of course, it won't be enough water for everybody, but that can't be helped."

He sipped his wine, thinking. "Unhappily, the reason I stole a storm was because I couldn't make one. As it turns out I didn't do too good a job of moving a cloud a long distance, either. I lost the cloud I stole, remember? Let's face it, Laisa, I may be a damn fine rainlord, the best there is in fact, but I am nowhere near being a stormlord."

"Together the two of you may achieve something. Jasper's talents at moving water and sensing water are phenomenal. And he can extract vapour from pure water, just not from a salty sea. Anyway, we don't have a choice. We have to try. *You* have to try. Otherwise there's no rain and we are all in trouble. How long will Scarcleft's water last, Taquar?"

"Not long enough. All right, I'll try. And at least we don't have Granthon or Nealrith's highly developed moral sense to deal with any more, do we, m'dear?"

"Exactly. But we do, unfortunately, have Jasper's. Extraordinary just how moral he is, considering he comes out of the Gibber. He can hardly have learned ethics from you, either, can he? However, with his nicely developed sense of duty, I think he can be persuaded it's necessary to work with you. He won't like it, but he'll do it."

"You have it all worked out already, it seems." He sat back in his chair, absently swirling his wine, while he considered her proposal. It was some time before he added, "One other thing before we seal the bargain, something I have idly wondered . . . I want an honest answer to a query."

Laisa raised a questioning eyebrow. "You trust me to be honest?"

"There's no reason not to be, now Nealrith is dead. Who is Senya's father?"

She laughed then, with full-throated amusement. "So you have wondered? I'll give you an honest answer: I don't know. It could have been either of you. I doubt she's dark enough to be your daughter, but I could never see anything of Nealrith in her, I must admit. But you – everything I've heard seems to indicate you don't leave a trail of bastards behind you. Is it possible I could be the only woman who ever bore yours? It seems unlikely. Does it matter anyway?"

He shook his head. "Not really. Stormlord children would have been an asset, but apart from that, I have never hankered after brats, especially not one as spoiled as Senya. You are going to have to rein her in, Laisa, if she is going to reside in my household."

With an airy wave of the hand, she dismissed that problem. "That won't be a problem now that Nealrith's not here to spoil her."

"Very well. It won't harm me to have a decorative wife, I suppose – will it?"

There was more than a note of warning in his tone, and she raised her eyebrows in acknowledgement. "I know where my interests lie, Taquar. But tell me, what happens now you have Jasper again? Where does that leave Sandmaster Davim? Is he still going to go on the rampage around the Scarpen?"

He rose to put another couple of seaweed briquettes on the fire. The Scarpen sun may have seared the land by day, but at night the cold had an edge to it. "No. I think I can bridle him, if I have Shale. Jasper. Davim knows I'm no Granthon, and no Nealrith either, with silly scruples about bringing water to everyone. I shall tell him he will not receive any water at all – random or otherwise – unless he holds to his end of the bargain. He can have the White Quarter, and I will assist him if any of the other dunes in the Red Quarter prove restless under his rule. He wants his Time of Random Rain, true, but until he has the logistics of that worked out, he needs predictable water."

"At the moment he is stealing it," she said. "He is draining the Qanatend mother wells dry, and doubtless he intends to do the same thing to Breccia."

"That water won't last forever without a rainlord replenishing it. We can bargain with him. He needs us. Any trouble, I will see to it the dunes will not receive *any* rain. As long as I have Jasper, and Davim fears the power I have over water as a consequence, he will behave. In exchange, I get to call on his troops if I need them to quell a rebellious city or a recalcitrant Gibber settle on my own. And so, Laisa – it seems we have a bargain. Now tell, where is Jasper?"

"Not far from here. I killed the pedeman shortly after we left Breccia, and I drugged Jasper's water." She laughed. "He made it so easy for me – he even gave me his water skin to carry when he was organising his rather spectacular departure

33

from the city. Senya is keeping an eye on him at the moment. He's been befuddled out of his mind for a couple of days now, and I fear he will wake up in a fury when he realises I led him here and not to Portennabar."

He laughed and stood, holding out a hand to her. "Then let us go find them, my dear. I cannot wait to see the look on that Gibber grubber's face when he sees me again!"

Laisa stood, rising a little too close to him for normal social conventions. He took the hint and pulled her into his arms, kissing her roughly, deliberately bruising her arms and lips, kneading her breasts with a shade too much force. When they parted, she was still smiling.

Softly, full of menace, he said, "One thing, m'dear – do not *ever* treat me as you treated Nealrith. Never. Or you will regret it."

Her smile didn't waver – but he thought her confidence did.

Which was exactly what he wanted.

4

The Scarpen to the White Quarter
Caravanner routes

The two waterpainters left Scarcleft on the morning after the earthquake, just as dawn was breaking over a tattered city. Crumbled walls, collapsed roofs, broken pipes and cracked cisterns, water gushing into the streets, fires raging through the lowest level – they'd seen it all on their way to the city gate.

And they were the only two people alive who knew who was to blame.

Only one of the two looked back as they left, and she cried, shedding water-wasting tears that no one else in the Scarpen ever shed unless they had something in their eye. She cried because she knew people had died that night – died because she had inadvertently killed them; she cried because she wasn't going to Breccia towards the only friend she had in the world.

Oh, Shale. I'm sorry.

And then, because she hated people who whined about their fate, she dried her tears and looked resolutely ahead. She was Terelle Grey, nineteen years old, and one day she would be truly free. She swore it. Perhaps she'd even find Shale again.

Russet Kermes had not hired a guide or a pedeman. Terelle had naïvely assumed her great-grandfather knew what he was doing; after all, he had once made the trek from his home in the Variega Mountains of Khromatis, through the White and Gibber Quarters to the Scarpen Quarter. He'd spent years travelling the Quartern in search of her mother, Sienna. He must have ridden myriapede hacks as well as the huge packpedes capable of carrying up to fifteen people.

However, soon after they left the Scarcleft livery in the aftermath of the earthquake, she was forced to revise any assumption about his competence. He had bought a single myriapede, and piled it with their supplies on the back four segments, leaving the first two segments for the two of them. He took the front, sitting cross-legged on the padded cloth saddle as pede drivers and riders did, but as they headed along the trail up the scarp heading directly north, he had trouble organising the reins. The pede sensed his incompetence and indicated its irritation by clicking its mouthparts and flinging its long feelers around.

"Never be driving pede before," he confessed when Terelle, seated behind him on the beast, asked him how much experience he had. "Always be passenger in caravan, or hiring pedeman. Offered tokens, but nobody be going White Quarter now. Dangerous. Reduners be raiding the 'Basters and killing caravanners. So – we go alone."

Terelle felt her mouth go dry. *Dangerous?* "Do you know the way?"

He pointed ahead with his riding prod. "There be trail. We follow."

"Aren't we heading north now? The White Quarter is to the east, isn't it?"

"I be knowing the way!" he snapped. "Waterpainters *never* forget a route. We turn north-east at second caravansary."

She wanted to ask if he knew how to harness the pede, or any of the one hundred and one other things that must have

36

been necessary to cross a desert safely, but before she could frame the question, he said, "If anything wrong, ye can be painting our way out of the problem, no?"

"No, I can't. I'm not painting any more. At least, not in order to shuffle up the future."

He twisted in the saddle to look back at her in open surprise. "What ye mean? Of course ye will! Why ever not?"

"Because we can't tell what will happen! Artisman, people *died* when the earthquake came. They died just so I could walk free of my prison." The horror of it was still fresh in her mind, as raw as the moment it had occurred.

A mother rocking her dead child in her arms, keening her loss . . .

No, don't remember. Some things are better forgotten.

But there was no escaping what had happened. True, she had not been the one who had painted the wreckage of Scarcleft Hall with her scrambling over the ruins; that had been Russet. Nonetheless, she had been the one who'd made the quake possible. Russet no longer had the power to shuffle up the magic into his paintings; he could not move water through the motley undercoat and the layers of paint any more, nor couple it with his waterpainter's power and fix the future of whatever it was he had painted.

She could, though. When Highlord Taquar Sardonyx had sent the waterpaints to her prison room, she had even tricked the magic and done what was supposed to be impossible. She had influenced her own future. How could she have known that shuffling up her shadow would also give power to Russet's concept of an earthquake?

Behind them, the lowest level of the Scarcleft still burned. If she turned, she would see the smoke. "Sunlord help me, how many innocent people did we kill, the two of us?"

Still looking at her, Russet shrugged. The pede moved steadily ahead in spite of his inattention. "Who cares if folk died? Scarpen folk only. Not be our people. They imprisoned you to use you. Deserved to die!"

Furious, she glared at him. "You are *sun-fried*! Taquar imprisoned me, not some poor boy asleep in his bed who'll never wake up because a wall fell on him. What kind of monster are you?"

He shook his finger at her. "*Ye* matter! They *not* matter. Ye are Pinnacle heir. Must be going home. Quartern folk no more than sand-ticks beneath your feet. Ye be not even knowing them."

"Do you think that makes me feel one sand grain better?" she asked, incredulous. She took a deep breath. "I am *not* shuffling up, not ever again." She pressed her lips together in what she hoped was a determined line.

Russet scowled. "Foolish frip of a girl! We could die." When she didn't reply, he looked behind them, as if he expected to see someone following. "Best we leave this trail. Taquar might be finding out we left city and sending enforcers after us."

She looked at the stark brown dryness of the fissured land to either side. "Strike out across the desert? We'd be lost in minutes!"

"Not if I be painting me riding into Fourcross Tell, and ye use waterpainting skills to make that the future." He was intent on her now, still paying no attention to the pede. "We try it."

"Taquar's far too busy coping with the earthquake," she said. "We'll take our chances following the track."

"Ye defy me, girl? After all I be doing for ye?"

Her knuckles whitened on the handle driven into the segment in front of her saddle. "I owe you *nothing*! Not since you painted me into your pictures to take away my freedom to determine my own future." Worse, every time she had tried to defy the magic of the shuffled up paintings, she'd been sick. He'd done that to her. To her mother, too. Sienna had been ill for a long while, probably because she'd tried to resist her painted future, until she had died giving birth to Terelle.

Murderer.

With sudden resolution, she met his gaze squarely, ignoring the disquietening fanaticism in the glare of his age-rheumed eyes as the pede lurched and scrambled up the steepest part of the escarpment trail. "I don't want to be here. I escaped from Highlord Taquar to go to Shale, not to you. I am only here because you painted my future and I cannot fight the magic of your art. But don't ask me to like it. Or to feel loyalty to you. Or even to obey you."

"Be for your own good."

"My good – or yours?" she snapped.

"Ye be kin! Ye could lead a nation."

Watergiver help me, he's crazed. "That's my misfortune, not my obligation! You can't think your people would welcome me simply because my mother was the heir."

Forced to turn his attention back to manipulating the reins, he didn't reply. Her stomach roiled, protesting her rebellion, and she suspected he would not forgive her. However, he did not turn off the caravan trail, and that was her first small victory.

Instead, he started to teach her the spoken language of Khromatis.

The journey was a nightmare, yet a nightmare painted on a background that stirred Terelle's soul. The wide skies, the strange orange light of dawn, the burning white sun of midday and the crimson dusks; the shadowed scarps, the gnarled trees clawing their way into barren soils, the weathered rocks and sculpted cliffs: she remembered it from her childhood's single journey, but then she had seen it with a child's eye. Now the artist in her saw the beauty of the land's raw roughness. It murmured to her, stirring a restless desire to record it, to capture it, to make it her own.

But there was no time to paint the scenery, and the nightmare was always there, riding with her: her great-grandfather was a murderous old man who didn't care that he had killed people to pursue his quest for power. Worse, she couldn't free herself. She was chained to him by the paintings he had done when he still had the power to make them come true. She would never be free until she stood on a green slope next to running water; the scene he had painted all those years ago.

It was a lonely journey. All trade between the quarters had ceased because the White and Gibber Quarters had been under periodic attack from Sandmaster Davim's marauders. Where once there had been a thriving trade route, a deserted trail was now often covered by wind-blown dust unmarked by any pede prints. Where once there had been Alabaster salt and soda traders and gypsum merchants, where once pede caravans of Reduner drovers had passed, laden with minerals and gems from the Gibber Quarter, or herding a meddle of pedes for sale, now there was nobody.

The first caravansary along the route was a huddle of deserted buildings just a day's ride from Scarcleft. The cistern was still half full, even though the windmill normally drawing water from the Scarcleft tunnel had been shut down and disconnected.

"Used to be caretakers here," Russet muttered. "Reeve too, to stop water theft from tunnel. Must be leaving after Qanatend taken by Reduners. Afraid Reduners come this way."

"I don't understand," she said to Russet. "Why did the Reduner sandmaster attack Qanatend? Reduners benefited from trade with the Scarpen as much as everyone else. They bought our bab oil and our beads and Gibber gems, our cloth and bab-weave canvas for their tents – so many things. They sold us pedes and animal pelts and dyes and wild herbs."

"Street gossip say Davim be thinking to return people to old time of noble warrior. Nomads, raiding and stealing and hunting. Hear he says dune gods be angry because tribesmen deviated from nomadic ways." He shrugged. "Foolishness of ignorant man hungry for power."

And you? Terelle thought. *That describes you, too, you frizzled old driveller.*

They lost the trail half a dozen times the next day when the hardened ruts left by generations of pede feet disappeared under sifted dust. Russet's remedy was simple. He gave the pede its head and hoped it at least knew where it was supposed to go. Sooner or later, the trail would magically reappear under the points of the animal's feet and Terelle would breathe a sigh of relief.

Late that night they arrived at the second caravansary. It was larger than the first, but equally deserted. Fortunately there was a small grove of fruiting bab trees, so they ate well and the pede gorged itself on the fallen fruit until it could eat no more.

The language lessons continued until they went to bed.

The trail divided at the caravansary, one branch veering off to Pebblebag Pass and Qanatend, a second heading northeast towards the White Quarter and a third due east. "Goes to Pahntuk Cistern," Russet remarked about the latter in the morning. "Route to Breccia."

She thought nothing of that until later in the day when they were following the middle trail up into the foothills of the Warthago Range. The way was steep, the views spectacular. Ahead were the savage peaks of the range scarifying the sky with their clawed edges. When she looked back, she could see for miles across The Sweepings, the rugged gullies they had crossed now no more than insignificant cracks on the landscape. Maintenance shaft towers cast their shadows across the land in lines, one to the west, one still ahead of them, marking the water tunnels to Breccia and Scarcleft respectively.

And far below, a spindevil whirling up the dust in his dance . . .

No. Not a spindevil.

She clutched at Russet's shoulder. "Artisman. Look behind."

He reined in and turned.

"That's not a spindevil wind," she said. "That's dust from pedes."

They sat in silence, watching, their shock growing. There were so *many*.

"They can't be after us. I don't think there are that many pedes in the whole of Scarcleft."

"No," Russet agreed. "Look. Not following us. They crossed our trail. Be riding south from Pebblebag Pass towards Breccia."

"Who—?" she began, then stopped. "Reduners."

He nodded. "Interesting. Pedes plenty; men not so many, I think. But too many of both to be trade caravan."

Shale. "We must warn Breccia!"

He gave her a contemptuous look. She flushed, acknowledging it was a silly idea. She and Russet were further away from Breccia than the Reduners, and they were two unskilled riders mounted on a slow hired hack.

"Be too late anyway, I think," he said. "They be looking like supply caravan."

He flicked the reins again and the pede ambled on.

"What do you mean?"

He was silent.

"You think Reduners have already attacked Breccia!"

Russet looked over his shoulder at the caravan, squinting against the light to see better, and shrugged indifferently. "I think maybe we be lucky. "I think we be missing the main army. They already in Breccia." She stared at him, appalled. "Besieging, maybe." "Oh, Sunlord – *no.*" *Shale.*

"Not our business."

He flicked the reins, but the pede maintained its leisurely pace. He jabbed it with his pede prod, and it reluctantly moved a little faster. Terelle watched behind. *Sunlord save them*, she thought, and reached for her water skin to pour out a little water to give force to her prayer.

They crossed over the Breccian tunnel several runs of the sandglass later and breathed a little easier. Folds and gullies in the land soon blocked their view and they saw no more of the pedes or their dust.

Another night passed, so cold the stoppers froze in the necks of their water skins. The chill didn't stop the sand-ticks and sand-fleas though; Terelle rose in the morning itching all over. Another blisteringly hot day followed. Harnessing, saddling and packing their innately lazy mount every day took almost an hour because it would not cooperate. The terrain worsened and the distance they travelled each day decreased. It took them two days now to ride between the deserted caravansaries.

After that, the language lessons became more sporadic. Russet was morose. Terelle would even have welcomed a return of his malicious humour; anything would have been better than hours of riding behind his hunched and silent back. Then, one day, when he seemed slower than usual rising from the sleeping platform in an empty caravansary, it occurred to her it wasn't just bad temper making him so taciturn. He was tired and old and the journey was wearing him out.

Uncharitably, she thought it served him right, but she did take over most of the driving after that, learning to manipulate the reins and the prod and to battle the recalcitrant pede. Russet sat behind her, sunk in his own thoughts, rousing himself only to teach her a few more words in the language of Khromatis.

Her arms and shoulders ached. To dismount after hours of

riding meant loosening stiff muscles and joints as if she was teasing out knots. No wonder Russet had been so tired. Still, she had no affection for him. Nothing could erase the knowledge that he had murdered her father and caused her mother's death. It was the pull of Russet's waterpainting that was sending Terelle to the White Quarter, not any genuine wish of hers to find out her history, or meet what was left of her family.

Russet had told her that his son-in-law was the Pinnacle of Khromatis, but the old man had not set foot in his country for twenty years. His son-in-law could just as easily be dead. Anything could have happened. All Russet's dreams for power could be so much dust in the wind. And what did it matter to her? She was Gibber born, Scarpen bred; she didn't want to go to Khromatis. She wanted to make sure Shale was all right. She wanted to explain about the letter Taquar had forced her to write. She wanted to be certain Shale had not done anything foolish because of that letter. What if he surrendered himself to Highlord Taquar again because she had begged him to do so in writing—?

But no, Cloudmaster Granthon would never have let him do that, surely.

What if Sandmaster Davim and his Reduners took Breccia City? Had already taken it?

No, don't even think that.

Sleep, whether wrapped tight in blankets on the ground or barricaded inside a mud-brick caravansary, offered relief from those tangled thoughts she had of Taquar and Shale, but dreams brought nightmares which might even have been real. Her sister, Vivie, trapped under the ruins of Opal's Snuggery. Garri the snuggery gatekeeper lying dead in the courtyard, hit by a falling balustrade. Madam Opal herself crushed under a fallen roof . . . Terelle would wake, cold and shivering, wanting it all to be untrue. Wanting to wake up and find everything was all right.

But it wasn't. She and Russet had caused an earthquake and people had died because of it. Vivie could be dead in truth; she didn't know and had no way of finding out. *I will never shuffle up the future again,* she thought. *Never. Waterpainting power is wrong.* To secure the future for your own benefit was wrong – because you never knew who would suffer to make that future real.

Their journey continued, apparently interminable. Russet had a fall from the pede and was badly bruised, which necessitated staying days at one of the caravansaries while he recovered. Their supplies ran out and they were reduced to living solely on the bab fruits they found in the caravansaries' groves. The pede liked nothing better, but Terelle found it a boring diet. Fortunately, now there were no travellers, each of the caravansaries still had plenty of water in their cisterns.

With a normal caravan, fifteen days would have found them entering Samphire, the main Alabaster city. It took them almost double that before they even reached the border between Scarpen and the White Quarter, a place called Fourcross Tell where all four quarters met.

The caravansary there, on the heights of a crumbling plateau, was not deserted as the others had been. The keeper and his family were, however, readying for their departure to return home to the Gibber.

The keeper's wife, a spare woman with straggling grey hair and a harassed expression that could have been permanent, was only too glad to explain why. "We was attacked this morning, by a small band of them withering red marauders, the beaded bastards," she said. "Took everythin' they could find, they did. They're ridin' into the White Quarter, seizin' water – anythin'. They spared us till now 'cause we served Reduner caravans well in the past, but we've decided we don't want t'risk it no more. Got to think of them." She indicated the two children clinging to her travelling breeches. Their worried faces, wearing expressions that were miniatures of their mother's, peeked out through uncombed hair.

Her husband looked Terelle up and down in pity. "You'll be ripe for their pluckin', girl. Watch how you go. You're welcome t'whatever we've left behind. We won't be comin' back. Get the young'uns up on the beasts," he added to his wife. "We've lingered long enough."

"You think they'll be back? The Reduners?" Terelle asked.

He gave a bitter laugh. "Oh, yes. They made that clear. This part of the Quartern belongs t'them red savages now."

Terelle and Russet watched as the family urged their mounts down the hill slope into the Gibber, the two pedes – prodded into fast mode – scudding up dust that hung in the air long after they'd gone.

"Are we going to be safe?" Terelle asked as they shared a meal that evening while the sun slipped behind the Warthago Range. "Shale told me Davim and his tribe wanted to take over the White Quarter. We might be riding into the middle of a battle."

Russet thought for a moment. "Best we pass Samphire by, no?"

"How do we do that?"

"Cross Whiteout."

"The Whiteout? I've heard of that. It's a salt plain."

"Flat. Easy ride. No Reduners be finding us on Whiteout. Cross straight to salt marshes. That be the border to Khromatis."

"I've heard stories about the pans. Trackless, they say. Just heat and salt and nothing else in all directions. I heard the white sends folk mad. How will we find our way?"

"I crossed it once. Can be doing it again." Russet stood abruptly and walked to the open doorway. He pointed across the courtyard to the gateway. "Look! See that white line

46

bordering the sky? Those be the clouds over Variega Mountains in land of Watergivers. That be where we be heading. Keep clouds in sight, can never lose selves."

She squinted. The caravansary was high on the range dividing the southern quarters of the Gibber and the Scarpen from the northern two – the White and the Red – and the view to the east and north-east was extensive. The plain far below stretched without interruption to the distant line of pinkish white, illuminated by the last long rays of the setting sun. "Why can't we see the mountains themselves?" she asked, doubtful.

"Far, far away. Later ye see the white tops."

"White? Are they made of salt then?"

"Be topped with snow," he said, and she heard his familiar mockery of her ignorance.

"Snow? What's that?"

"A form of water. Like – like shavings of white ice."

She tried to imagine a world where there was so much water it coated the hilltops with ice shavings, and failed.

"That family leaving much food behind. Pack it all," he said. "And all water pede can carry. Make sure it drinks well too, before we be leaving." He already sounded invigorated, as if the hint of his homeland had infused him with energy.

Terelle did as he suggested, stripping the bab palms of their ripe fruit the next morning in the washed-out light of pre-dawn and cutting them into strips so they would dry easily. She filled every water skin they had to the brim, sealing them with candle grease after stoppering them tightly. Russet found some extra dayjars, and she placed those in the side panniers of the pede as well. When they'd finished, Terelle regarded the loaded pede dubiously.

"That's a heavy load for a myriapede," she said.

"Downhill," Russet said. "Then flat, mile after mile. Each day weight less as we drink and eat, no?"

"The pede will need to drink a lot, and often, out there. How many days will it take to cross the Whiteout?"

"Less time than be taking to finish the water," he replied.

Unsettled, she wondered if he really knew. In the snuggery, she had heard tales of the White Quarter, of travellers dying on the salt, their bodies found years later, mummified and dried solid. Pickled. What kind of people were they, these Alabasters, who apparently did not have red blood in their veins? Who could live in a land where the very ground beneath one's feet was made of salt?

In the first few miles after Fourcross Tell, the land was not all that different from the areas they had already crossed: stunted trees dug into the soil with grotesquely twisted roots, gullies scarred the land in memory of long ago streams. Even the dust felt the same. Later in the day, though, as they descended to the plains, the vegetation changed and she felt as if she was leaving everything sure and familiar behind. The trees disappeared, replaced by low bushes and creepers snaking over the ochre-coloured earth. When they stopped to rest, Terelle fingered the leaves of one plant and found it dusted with salt.

It was hot by then, stifling. The air hung so still it felt heavy on her shoulders, and thick to breathe. When she licked her lips, she tasted salt. When she touched her hair, it was stickily coated.

"We stay here while sun high," Russet said. They dismounted and he sat in the shadow cast by the pede. Wearily, he pulled his embroidered head wrap loose, and drank from his water skin. His earlier vigour seemed to have been vanquished by the heat. "We go on later; be cooler."

Terelle nodded and strung up bab matting for shade by tying it to the pede on one side and a single saltbush on the other. She sat down next to Russet, using the pede as a backrest. Even under the cover, the heat was intense enough to shrivel the skin. Carefully she smoothed some of the pede

48

ointment on to her face; Vivie would have approved. The pede flicked one of its feelers backwards and touched her cheek in a tentative gesture.

"What is it, girl?" she asked. "You can't be thirsty already." She gently prodded the belly between the segments; the moisture-saturated tissues were soft. She gazed into its myopic compound eyes, and wondered whether it had a name or not. The liveryman had called it Number Twelve – indeed, it had the number etched into its rear segment. It wasn't a hand-some creature, all carved and polished and sewn with embroidery like a lord's animal. It was just a plain, working hack. Still, she tried to do what was best for it. Russet had said pedemen kept the crevices between carapace and skin cleaned of grains of sand and such, so every evening she groomed the pede carefully and checked every segment groove for sand-ticks, every one of its eighteen pairs of feet for injury. When she found abraded spots on its skin, she smeared on the lanolin supplied by the livery.

Encouraged by Terelle's words, the beast curved its front end around, poked its head into the shade cast by the cloth, then rested the base of its head on the ground at her feet. If a pede could look soulful, then that was what it did. Terelle chuckled. "Oh, I see – you're just hot too, eh? Fine, Number Twelve, you stay right where you are. We can share the shade." The creature settled its first segment mantle down over its eyes – the only way it had of closing them – and dozed. Next to her, Russet was already sleeping.

Terelle glanced around. Nothing moved in the midday heat, so she too closed her eyes.

She was awoken by a scream.

She leapt up, whirling around to find the danger. The pede raised its head and flicked its feelers. Russet was clutching his leg and moaning.

"What is it?" Terelle asked, trying to slow the thumping of her heart.

"Something be stinging me." Hurriedly, he pulled the cloth of his wrap back from his calf. A single spot of blood oozed just above the ankle.

"Snake?" She cast around where he had been lying, but nothing moved.

"Only one hole."

"Sand-leech?"

"More painful. Scorpion."

"That – that's not – not so very serious, is it?"

"Not if ye be treating it," he replied between gritted teeth. "Reduners use herbal concoction."

"We can go back to the caravansary—"

"Don't be stupid. We be going on. Get the water skin. Must be washing leg." He took the water and waved her away, indicating with a gesture that she should dismantle the shade cloth and reload the pede. She did as he asked; she knew better than to argue.

They set off once more, in silence, and she concentrated on persuading the pede to whatever speed it was capable of – which never seemed to be as much as she had seen other pedes do. Whenever she looked behind at Russet, he was staring straight ahead, expressionless.

When she slowed their mount some hours later, thinking to stop for the night because the sun had almost set, he spoke again. "No," he said, "go on."

"I won't know what direction. I can't even see the ground properly." *And I'm tired. And you are sick.*

"See well enough once star river shines. Go on."

She did as he asked. A little later he brusquely pointed out a particularly bright star in the sky and said, "Be keeping that on your left."

He was silent for a long time as they continued. Every now

and then she turned her head to check if he was still there, to find him hunched up and motionless behind her. In the silver-blue light she could not tell if the bite was bothering him. She felt a pang of guilt at her lack of compassion, but he was forcing her on this journey, sunblast it! He had no right to expect anything of her except rage.

It was pleasant travelling in the cool of the night; at least at first. Later the slight breeze they generated with their passing chilled her skin like slivers of ice. She drifted off, dozing on the saddle, but roused with a start when he spoke.

"We camp now."

His voice sounded small and thin in the silence of the night, as friable as ancient sun-bleached rock. She reined in, dismounted and went back to help him. Even so, he fell out of the saddle rather than climbed down, and then collapsed, unable to stand.

"Give me my pack and be fixing a meal," he said, and there was still enough authority in his tone to have her obey without protest. If he did not ask for help, she knew it would only anger him to offer it. She stifled a sigh.

By the time he was wrapped in his blanket, she had a fire alight, using dry twigs and leaves for fuel. The salt coating the soil and plants spat in the flames with green and blue sparks, the sound animating the quiet of a salt-encrusted world. She made some soup out of the shredded dried meat and bab root she had obtained at the caravansary. She had to wake him when it was ready, but he ate gladly enough, then slept again. After she'd had some of the soup herself, she went to groom the pede. It was eating the low plants with enthusiasm and took no notice as she followed it around brushing out its segment joints. When she'd finished, she hobbled the animal by linking its antenna together. No pede moved far or fast when it didn't have the free use of its feelers.

Just before she turned in herself, she felt the pull of her

journey as sharp as a knife beneath her ribs. The pull of the future Russet had painted for her.

My mother could resist, she thought. *Why can't I?* And she remembered once again the offhand words Vivie had uttered about Sienna: *She was always ill.*

Resistance came with a price.

5

Scarpen Quarter
Breccia City,
Breccia Hall, Level 2

Beryll.

She was dead. One moment Ryka had been so relieved to find her little sister alive and unhurt – and then she was gone. Those blue eyes had lost their light like a candle suddenly snuffed.

Ryka's stomach heaved in rebellion. *No.* She clamped a hand across her mouth. Not Beryll. *She was so young.*

She swallowed the bile in her throat. *Sweet Sunlord, why? Beryll, you could have recovered from rape, but there's no coming back from death . . . Why, oh, why couldn't you see that?*

She mustn't think about it. Mustn't dwell on it, or she'd lose her edge. Beryll was dead; accept it. But Kaneth? She had to believe he was still alive. His son moved within her body, and him she must keep safe, no matter what it took. She inhaled, a deep calming breath to push away the paralysing grief. *Think, woman. Start planning. You are Ryka, rainlord.*

She glanced about Ravard's quarters. *Watergiver damn, I recognise this. It's Nealrith's private reception room.* Her next astonished thought was tinged with fear. *Who the sunblast is this Ravard fellow that he warrants getting the Breccian Highlord's quarters?*

Davim, obviously, would be quartered in the Cloudmaster's rooms, if he wanted them. She'd already known Ravard must be important from the way he dressed and the way he had bantered with Davim, even defying his orders to kill her. But to be assigned the Highlord's apartments?

Davim's son? No, not possible, surely. Ravard must have been twenty or so, and Davim didn't look much older than Ryka herself. His sons, if he had any, would still be children.

She shivered and wrapped her arms around her upper body. Night had fallen, and the rooms were cold. The shutters had been left open, and no one had brought fuel for the night braziers. Limping because the wound in her leg pained her, she stepped out onto the balcony and looked over the balustrade for a way to escape. Her distance vision was blurred, but the burning torches helped her recognise where she was. Below was the walled forecourt open to the sky in front of the main doors of the Hall. Now there were guards camped there and fires burned on the paving. The smell of cooked meat wafted upwards. She wasn't surprised. She knew many Reduners hated the idea of sleeping within solid buildings.

Oh, the smell of that food . . . Sunlord, but she was hungry!

Quelling all thought of eating to concentrate on her escape, she raised her eyes to the defensive wall surrounding the first and second levels. It was being patrolled by Davim's men; she could see their shapes against the sky. If she tried to escape via the balcony, she would just be climbing down into an ants' nest of Reduner warriors – and still be on the wrong side of the wall. There was no freedom for her that way. For a moment despair overwhelmed her.

Her father, her mother, Beryll. All gone. Her friends, her city, her whole way of life; too much, too soon. It numbed her, and she couldn't afford to be numb. Watergiver's heart, she had to fight. For Kaneth. For their son. For their land.

Closing the shutters behind her to keep out the cold of

night, she stepped back inside and examined the apartment with more care by the light of the single tiny oil lamp they had left for her. If the mess was any indication, the place had been searched and looted. No, more than that: it had been the scene of a fight. The head of a Scarpen-made spear was buried in a cupboard door, the shaft missing. The tip of a sword blade lay on the floor. The rest of the weapon was nowhere to be seen. A chair was smashed, the pieces lying where they had fallen.

She tried the door she had entered by, only to find it firmly barred from the outside. When she crossed to one of the other two doors, she found it led to Nealrith's private study. The floor and desk there were strewn with parchment and scrolls. A dark splash of blood had sprayed across the wall and then dribbled downwards in parallel lines.

The second door opened into Nealrith's bedroom. The bed was unmade, and a Reduner cloak had been flung carelessly over the end. The wardrobe and a trunk made of bab wood had been emptied, although some of the contents seemed to have been discarded on the floor. The entrance to a small water-room was hidden behind a carved screen. There was another door as well, bolted top and bottom. She opened the bolts, only to find it was somehow locked or barred on the other side as well. She guessed Laisa's bedroom lay beyond.

Ryka wanted to sit down and give in to despair. Instead, she began to search methodically, looking for anything that could be helpful. In the study she salvaged some paper and a graphite stick for writing, a piece of twine, a tinderbox, flint and steel. In the water-room she drank deeply from the dayjar; in the reception room she examined the broken sword point. It was, she decided, too short to be of any use to her as a weapon. She thought about digging out the spearhead, decided Ravard might notice it had gone and so left it where it was, a symbol of a battle lost. Her gaze alighted on the wood of the broken chair with more hope. The shards were long and sharp; the wood hard. She found a number of pieces that might have potential as makeshift daggers, and secreted them in various places around the rooms, tucking one under the pallet of the bed.

In the bedroom she picked through what was left of the clothes to find something clean and small enough for her to wear, finally selecting a tunic and a pair of trousers probably dating back to Nealrith's adolescent years. In the water-room she used the water closet, then eyed with interest the porphyry bathtub big enough to sit in, the full copper, the seaweed briquettes in the fireplace underneath, and the soap. She hadn't had a proper bath in over a star cycle. She and Kaneth had done their best to cut water consumption, wiping themselves clean with wet cloths – but right now she couldn't think of any material thing she wanted more than a soaking hot bath. And why conserve water anyway? Whatever there was would only go to the city's conquerors.

She started a fire under the copper and when the water was warm, she ladled it into the porphyry tub. After a quick listen at the door to the outside passage just to make sure there was no sign of Ravard's approach, she returned to the water-room, stripped off and stepped into the glorious decadence of a hot, soapy bath.

Ryka woke before dawn, ravenous and in a state of unfocused terror. Fatigue and tattered emotions had plummeted her into the oblivion of an exhausted sleep in one of the large woven chairs in the reception room, covered by a blanket taken from Nealrith's bed.

Even before she was properly awake, she was on her feet. She had *slept*. How could she have fallen asleep? She'd been devastated by Beryll's death. So scared of the Reduner returning and demanding the use of her body. Worried sick by Kaneth's disappearance, by the unthinkable idea the Reduners had thrown his unconscious body on a funeral pyre and burned him alive.

And she had slept like a child. What sort of woman was she? Furious with her weakness, she stood in the dimness of the room lighted by a single guttering oil lamp, shivering. And then realised – *this was not the lamp she had been using.*

Her nebulous fear coagulated into something more immediate. She wasn't alone.

She drew in a sharp breath. Someone stood beside the open door to the bedroom. She stared. A Reduner. Not Ravard. Someone else – a man standing with folded arms, a favourite stance of a dune warrior on guard. Guarding the door from – her? She stared past him to the room beyond. A man lay sprawled on the bed, on top of the covers and still dressed. Another lamp at the bedside showed a face smoothed by sleep into youthful innocence.

She knew better than to trust her eyesight. "Ravard?" she asked softly, raising an eyebrow in query at the guard. His face was impassive, but his eyes glinted, promising action if she moved towards the door.

"*Kher* Ravard," he agreed, his tone chiding because she had not used the honorific.

She allowed herself the hint of a smile. So she worried Ravard enough he didn't feel quite safe and had to have a guard at his door? Good. She wanted to keep him off balance. Then her smile faded. He had come, found her asleep in the chair and then left her alone. Strange, unsettling man.

Who could this Ravard be?

Kher, she knew, meant the equivalent of lord. It was a title carried by only a handful of any dune's elite, including the tribemasters, the men who commanded one of the encampments of that dune. No more than ten men, fifteen at the outside, even on a large dune like the Watergatherer.

Three of these tribal leaders were particularly important; they were the sandmaster's blood sons or adopted sons and they would all be water sensitives. The least of them was the Drover Son, who was charged with the care of the dune's pedes, their capture, training and sale. The second in importance was the Warrior Son, who trained and commanded all the dune's armed tribesmen. The most important was the Master Son, who would one day be sandmaster unless there was a closer blood relative with water sensitivity to take his place.

When a sandmaster didn't have three blood sons, or if his sons were still children, or if they were water-blind, then it was common practice to adopt sons. This arrangement was sometimes lasting, sometimes temporary.

Ryka wrinkled her forehead, trying to recall anything else that might be useful to know. There were at least two others who would be addressed as kher as well, the Shaman Kher and the Trader Kher, but neither of them, she decided, would be given Nealrith's rooms for their use, even if they were in Breccia. No, Ravard must be a tribemaster at least, sandblast his eyes.

Cold and frightened, she turned away from the guard and limped to open the shutters and walk through to the balcony. He made no move to stop her. Dawn light was already in the sky, and the wall and its sentries were outlined against a pale background streaked with rose pink, promising a lovely sunrise over a devastated, suffering city. She dropped her gaze to the huddled sleeping warriors below; their fires extinguished, they were barely visible in the darkness of the courtyard.

"Kaneth," she whispered, "where are you? Please be alive. I need you to help me protect our son. He is all that matters. He must have a future, even if we do not . . ."

She waited for the sun to rise and the day to begin,

dreading the new griefs it would harbour. Hunger gnawed at her insides, not just for food but for the renewal of her power. In her weakened state, she could feel neither the water within living things nor the bodies of water within the city; she had no more perception than an ordinary citizen. She'd never been the best of rainlords, but she hated being so water-blind, so cut off from her surroundings. To add to her physical misery, her muscles ached from the fighting of the previous two days and the healing wound on her leg was stiff and sore.

When there was movement in the rooms behind her, she did not move. She heard Ravard murmur something to the guard, but could not sense his water, so when he stepped up behind her and draped his cloak over her shoulders, she jumped.

"Cold at this time of the morning," he said. "You shouldn't be standing out here so ill clad."

She did not turn to face him. "Thank you," she said, her voice flat.

"Glad t'see you slept," he added.

"Better than remembering the horror of yesterday."

"War and horror are twin brothers."

"*We* did not ask for this war."

He shrugged. "Weren't none of my doing, neither." When she didn't reply, he added, "I'll not force you t'share my nights, y'know. I get no joy from that. But I need a woman t'warm me. Last night I was too tired, but that won't last. If it's not you, then I'll choose another."

"And what happens to me then?" she asked, already knowing what the answer was likely to be.

"You go back to the general pick. Take your chances when the warriors choose a woman. Many of 'em share and some are none too fussy what they do with a woman. You're better off with me, but it's your choice."

She turned to face him then, tilting her head in question as she asked with genuine curiosity, "Why me?"

His mouth quirked up. "I like a feisty woman. Women of courage breed warriors. The tribe needs good strong blood, like yours. Pretty faces mean nothing. Not t'me."

Well, thanks for that, you oaf. "I've got to be ten years older than you."

Ravard continued to smile. "An advantage. I seek learning from the experienced."

"What do *you* offer *me*?"

He laughed out loud. "I'll be waterless! You have the cheek of a sand-tick, woman. All right – I'll tell you. The alternative you know, and it's not pleasant. With me, there's only me. No one else will dare t'touch you. And best of all, your child – girl or boy – will come under my protection. Not just now, but always. On that you have m'word."

"What proof do I have you'll keep your word?"

His face darkened and his jaw tightened. It was a moment before he replied. "I am Tribemaster Kher Ravard, son of the sandmaster. My word is my honour."

Son? Watergiver help me. He would have water competence equivalent to a reeve! A chill coursed down her spine. He could resist any attempt she made to kill him by taking his water.

Damn, damn, damn. "I apologise. How could I know that?"

"Don't make the same mistake twice. Grown men have died for less insult t'the son of Davim."

"I am not a fool. Very well; I accept your offer. I will, er, warm your bed." *You withering waste of water.*

"Willingly?"

"Yes, in exchange for your protection for me and my child. But I would ask a small boon."

"Boon? I don't know the word."

Ryka was gambling, she knew. "A favour. Yesterday I lost

my husband, my sister, my parents, my city. To lie with you so soon would be to dishonour them. Give me ten days to grieve. It is our custom."

His eyes narrowed. "You dream."

"The difference between a reluctant and a willing woman in your bed is worth the wait."

He considered and then shrugged. "Three. You can have three days and nights to grieve. Starting now."

She allowed a short silence before she nodded. *And you'll be dead before then, you arrogant louse. You think a woman forgets the father of her son so readily?* "I sleep alone three more nights, and then come willingly," she agreed. *Blighted eyes, this has to be the strangest ravishment ever.*

Before he could answer, a loud knocking came at the door. Ravard stepped back into the reception room to deal with the visitor, and Ryka turned away to look down at the fore-court once more. The warriors were awake, eating food brought to them from the kitchens by Scarpen women. She looked on the scene with pity; even with her poor eyesight she could see the women looked wretched and that most had torn clothes. She averted her eyes, rather than watch.

Ravard came out onto the balcony once more. "My father calls me. You stay here, in these rooms. I'll be back on the fourth day. I expect to be welcomed."

"I hope you intend to feed me in the meantime. I had nothing to eat at all yesterday, and not much the day before, either."

"Oh. Of course. I hadn't thought of that. I'll have something sent up."

As he turned to go, she asked, "Are you really Davim's son?"

He paused to answer. "Not blood son, no, but his son for all that. If not, you would have died on the floor together with the girl you so foolishly tried t'protect."

Once again she gambled, hoping he would not see anything odd in her knowledge. "You are the Warrior Son?"

He smiled once more. "No, Garnet. I am the Master Son."

He departed then, leaving her in shock. *Master Son!* He was heir to Davim, to the leadership of the whole Watergatherer Dune. Not only would she be unable to kill him the rainlord way, but his importance meant she would be under scrutiny, too. She leaned against the balcony railing, and dropped her head into her hands, giving in to her despair.

Barely half the run of a sandglass later, still before any food had been brought to her, Ryka saw Ravard again. He was in the forecourt talking to several guards, giving orders. A few moments later, a number of prisoners were brought out of the building. Most of them were boys, varying in age from about nine or ten to fourteen or so. Scattered among them were some older men. She squinted hard, cursing her inadequate eyesight, and thought she recognised Breccia Hall livery.

Skilled men, I bet, she thought. *The kind of people they need as slaves. Cooks, perhaps. Or pede grooms.*

Anxiously she scanned the men, looking for others she might know. And spotted one she had not thought to see again: the pikeman Elmar Waggoner. At least he was easy to recognise; there was no mistaking his face with its twisted scar from the chin across his left cheek to his forehead. She drew in a sharp breath. He had been one of their academy teachers and later one of Kaneth's men, the pikeman who had fought at his side against the Reduner incursions into the Scarpen. He had been with Kaneth when they snatched Jasper from Highlord Taquar and the seneschal of Scarcleft. And he had fought alongside her and Kaneth in the waterhall. She'd thought him dead, but he must have been one of the few who'd escaped in the final few moments after the roof was breached.

She shook her head in disbelief. The man led a charmed life. *Possibly because he's a damned fine warrior. Smart, skilled and withering lucky, the ugly bastard,* she thought affectionately.

Fingers gripping the balcony balustrade, she stared at him, willing him to look up. He did not notice, apparently fully concerned with the man standing next to him, half slumped, dressed in a hall servant's livery. The fellow swayed as if injured; a rough bandage had been wrapped around his bald head. Which was odd, when she came to think of it. They killed their own badly wounded; why by all that's wet would they leave a wounded Scarperman alive?

The prisoners were lined up at the foot of the steps leading to the massive main doors of the Hall, from which Davim emerged a moment later. He halted on the top step to survey the people arrayed before him, then beckoned to Ravard. The young man took the stairs two at a time to his father's side. The two men had a conversation, after which Ravard turned to address the prisoners, his voice strong and clear. Ryka had no trouble hearing him from where she was.

"You're now slaves of the dunes," he began. "You have a choice. You can submit t'slavery, or you can die now. Your women folk had the same choice. Most chose t'live. If you work hard and display loyalty to your masters, one day you'll earn your freedom. If you choose t'serve, tomorrow you will be taken to the dunes – refuse, and you die here, today. Now."

He nodded to the row of watching guards. Five of them came to the bottom of the steps, where they drew their scimitars. Davim stayed where he was, but Ravard descended to the forecourt, where he seized one of the prisoners, a half-grown boy, by the scruff of the neck and pushed him down onto his knees. When he spoke again, the words were still loud enough for all the slaves to hear. "Say this, lad: 'I swear obedience t'my new masters. I swear loyalty t'Davim, sand-master.'"

The boy looked around wildly, seeking aid from the crowd of slaves. One of the guards slapped his face with the flat of his scimitar, drawing a thin line of blood. The boy started to stutter the submission, but Ravard had to prompt him several times before he could get the words out.

Ryka watched, unable to drag her eyes away from the sickening fascination of the scene. One by one the other boys in the front row followed the example of the first, but she knew sooner or later someone would choose death. It came with the tenth prisoner – a lad of perhaps fourteen or fifteen who refused to kneel. He was not given a chance to draw another breath. His throat was slit and his blood pumped out on to the paving, dark and viscous.

Yet still Ryka could not look away. It seemed right that she was there to bear witness to such bravery, even as her heart ached and her logic told her it was better to go on living – to live so one day you could fight back.

Elmar was the first adult to be asked to swear fealty. Ryka's fingers tightened their grip on the balustrade. She expected him to choose death. *Elmar, a slave?* It was unthinkable. He was one of the bravest men she knew, never showing any fear of death. Anxiously she strained to hear his answer.

Before he gave it, however, Davim intervened, calling out in Reduner, "Why do we want this man? With a scar on his face like that, he must have been a warrior."

Ryka felt sick.

Ravard replied in the same language, "He's a worker of metals. He told me the scar's from a splash of liquid metal. We need his skills, and he says he'll work for us."

"And the man standing next to him?" Davim asked.

"That's the fellow I mentioned earlier," Ravard said. He

had to speak loudly so Davim could hear, but Ryka guessed it didn't worry either of them because they assumed no one except the Reduners understood their tongue. "The one who survived the fire and can't remember who he is. He has a wound on his head, in addition to the burns, which probably explains the loss of his wits."

Ryka stiffened and leaned forward. Nausea swamped her, trailing a futile hope. The man didn't look like Kaneth.

At Ravard's words, several of the guards shifted uneasily, and exchanged glances. Davim, his interest sharply focused, took several steps down the stairs to see better. Ryka could not take her gaze from the wounded man. He remained where he had been, his stillness remarkable in one who had obviously been so badly hurt. He waited as if he was uninterested in the outcome, his arms hanging loosely at his sides. There was nothing in the relaxed way he stood to tell Ryka it was Kaneth, yet her heart started to pound.

Oh, what I wouldn't give to have decent eyesight!

"Bring him here," Davim told Ravard.

Ravard gripped the man by the arm and urged him to mount the steps to the sandmaster. At that moment, Ryka heard the door to Nealrith's reception room open and looked over her shoulder. A young woman she didn't know entered carrying a tray laden with food. Bobbing her head quickly in Ryka's direction, she deposited the tray on the table and scuttled towards the door where a guard waited.

Ryka, no longer interested in food, quickly turned her attention back to what was happening outside. She heard the door close, but her focus was elsewhere.

"Food," a voice behind her said.

She jumped, her heart pounding wildly as she whirled to see that, although the woman had left, the guard had not. He stood close behind her, pointing at the tray. "Eat. Kher Ravard say."

The smell of freshly cooked bab bread wafted her way. "All right. I will," she told him with an impatient nod, still not interested.

He frowned, not moving, worried perhaps that she was refusing to eat at all. To distract him, and because she wanted to know the answer, she pointed down into the courtyard and asked, "The man down there in front of Sandmaster Davim – who is he?"

The guard, his frown deepening, approached the balcony railing. She pointed again, to where Davim stood with Ravard, both staring at the man with the bandaged head. She could no longer hear anything they said to each other, but the man was unwinding his bandage in apparent answer to a request.

"Half-face," the guard said, his words guttural, as he struggled to speak an unfamiliar tongue. "Born mother fire. Dune god sire."

She stared at him blankly, wondering what he meant. Mothered by a fire and fathered by the dune god? Ah, one of the stories found in Reduner myths, if she remembered rightly.

He struggled on. "Half-face. Kher Shaman. Dune god son." When she continued to look blank, he gave up trying to explain. "Eat," he repeated. "Kher Ravard say."

"Yes, yes, all right. I will." She stepped towards the tray and stuffed some bread into her mouth.

Satisfied, he left then, and she turned once more to the tableau on the steps. Davim was reaching out a hand to cup the cheek of the wounded man. He spoke, Ravard translated, and the man sank to his knees apparently uttering his promise of allegiance. Ravard said something more and the man rose.

As soon as he turned to descend the stairs, the warriors drew back out of his way, and Ryka saw his face for the first time. Half of it was horribly and freshly scarred. All his hair had burned away to leave him bald and the skin of his head unnaturally red. A rough twist of fresh scabbing tissue crossed his skull – but in spite of his injuries and the relaxed way he walked, she had no trouble recognising him now. He may have worn the livery of a Breccian Hall servant, but he was Kaneth Carnelian, rainlord.

6

Scarpen Quarter
The Skirtings between Breccia and Scarcleft cities
Scarcleft City, Scarcleft Hall, Level 2

Jasper woke in the cool of the pre-dawn, with a savage headache throbbing at the back of his eyes and a foul taste on a coated tongue. Thoughts jostled, unpleasantly confused. He frowned, sorting through the muddle in his head for something coherent, for something that made sense of how he felt.

He was on his way to the sea, he remembered that much. Breccia had fallen. He had killed Nealrith, rather than see him suffer. Cloudmaster Granthon was dead. And he, Jasper Bloodstone, was the only stormlord the Quartern now possessed, even though his water sensitivity was flawed and incomplete. Making clouds from sea water was beyond him, which meant people would thirst and die.

He blinked, looking straight up at the fading stars in the sky. Somewhere under his bed-roll, a stone dug into his back, so he shifted position – and saw someone looking down at him.

Taquar. Taquar Sardonyx.

But that couldn't be right. Taquar lived in Scarcleft on The Escarpment, west of Breccia City. But he, Jasper, was going to Portennabar on the south coast with Laisa and Senya.

His frown deepened. There was something. A memory. Hadn't he protested at one stage about going in the wrong direction? He groaned. Why couldn't he remember?

He blinked, focussing. And sat bolt upright. It *was* Taquar.

The man was looking down on him, with a half smile on his lips and a sardonic glint in eyes reflecting the light from the lantern he held high.

"Good morning, Shale," he said softly. "It is good to see you again."

Jasper scrambled to his feet, senses muddled, thoughts lagging behind what his eyes told him was true. Senya stood behind Taquar with the smug, superior expression on her face that he hated so much; her mother stood further back holding the reins of a pede. *What's going on?*

And then he knew.

His gaze flew to Laisa.

She shrugged. "Sorry."

"Why?" he asked. "*Why*, damn it?" Bitterness consumed him. How could he have been so stupid as to trust Laisa? Kaneth had even *warned* him about her!

"It's for the best."

He refused to look at Taquar, but pointed to him as he yelled at Laisa, "After what that withering bastard did to us? He *encouraged* Davim! And now Breccia's fallen, the Cloudmaster is dead, your own husband tortured so badly that—" He choked. He'd slit the throat of the man he was proud to call a friend. The kind of man he wished had been his father. "*Why?*" he cried again.

Laisa shrugged. "To be on the winning side, why else? I didn't want to be harried from city to city by Davim's marauders, always wondering whether I'd be dead before the end of the next star cycle." She sighed, more a sound of regret than exasperation. "Jasper, look at it this way. In Scarcleft you will be *safe*. Davim is not going to take Scarcleft the way he took Breccia City and Qanatend. Taquar has defences: ziggers, pedes, more trained men than Breccia City ever had. He can protect you, and he can take the battle to Davim in a way Nealrith never could, if it proves necessary."

It was well she did not wait for a reply because, although he heard the words, his head felt as if it was filled with sand.

"And with Taquar to help," she continued, "perhaps you can be a stormbringer. He was strong enough to steal Granthon's storm, remember? He can help you extract clouds from the sea."

Senya interrupted. "How else are we going to get water? You can't do it on your own! If it weren't for Taquar, if we'd gone to Portennabar, we'd all be waterless, with you being as much use as a pebble in a dayjar."

Her contempt riled Jasper beyond measure, and his distaste made his head ache even more. With difficulty, he reined in his rage. "Where are we?" he asked.

It was Taquar who answered. "Two hours' ride from the walls of Scarcleft." The words mocked him. Mocked his brief taste of freedom.

He looked at the Highlord then, locked his gaze onto the man's grey eyes set in a face as swarthy as his own.

"You aren't going to Portennabar, Shale," Taquar said with quiet certainty.

Deliberately, Jasper began to relax the muscles of his back and neck, to ease the tightness of his shoulders, in an attempt to appear in command of himself. If only his damned head would cooperate. "No? And if I insist? What will you do: use those ziggers on me?" He gave a derisive snort and nodded at the zigger cage strapped to the back of the pede Laisa held.

Drugged, he thought, *those two spitless women drugged me.* That was the only explanation for his confusion. He felt like killing them both. His drinking water, of course. Laisa had carried it for him while he covered their escape by fighting the Reduners outside the walls of Breccia. He'd had to show Davim's men that he'd escaped the city so they would not kill the hostages in their attempt to force his surrender to the sandmaster.

He still didn't know what had happened after that. Perhaps they had killed the hostages anyway. Perhaps all the Breccian rainlords were dead, not just Nealrith and Cloudmaster Granthon. Maybe even Ryka and Kaneth. His heart lurched. *Please let them at least be safe . . .*

But he had no way of knowing.

"Laisa's right," Taquar said. "On your own, no one gets water. With me, we have a chance. You are stronger and more experienced than you used to be, and I have been working on vapour extraction in the years since I saw you last. But we will talk of this again later, in Scarcleft." He snuffed the wick of his lantern now that the sky was pink with dawn.

"I'm not going back to be imprisoned by you all over again. You're sandcrazy to think I will! And what did you do to Terelle? Kill her the way you killed Amethyst?"

"I didn't kill Terelle, I assure you. She is free, living her own life. And who mentioned a prison? You will live in Scarcleft Hall with Laisa, Senya and me, an honoured guest. The Quartern's stormlord. You'll have whatever you need. My word on it."

"Your words are not worth as much as the air it takes to say them. How do I know anything you say is the truth?" *Terelle. Ah, please let that be the truth.* Jasper's heart thudded under his ribs as he dared to think of her, dared to hope she was alive and free.

Taquar shrugged. "Then think of the Quartern. Without me, you will never bring clouds to the Warthago, or anywhere else, either."

The horrible thing was he was probably correct. *Without help, will I be able to lift a single drop of fresh water into the sky from the ocean?* He could move clouds all over the sky afterwards; he could send them wherever he wanted – but that initial pulling of the vapour out of the salty waters of the Giving Sea was, as far as he knew, still beyond his flawed powers. They had been planning to go to Portennabar because Nealrith and Granthon had hoped being close to the sea would make it easier for him. Even Taquar had once suggested it as a possible solution. Jasper had always been dubious.

In no mood to be conciliatory, he glowered at Laisa. "You think the Quartern will be best served by having its only stormlord under the thumb of the man who as good as invited Davim to attack us?"

"Come now, Jasper. Think," she said in answer. "Taquar's reason for keeping you hidden no longer exists. If he was the only one who knew who you were and where you were, *then* he had power. His aim was to make us believe *he* was the stormlord." She smiled at Taquar, her glance gently mocking. "The irony of that, of course, was that it wasn't necessary. Granthon made him heir – if he'd waited, he would have had the power of a ruler legitimately, even if he couldn't be a proper stormlord."

She handed the pede reins to Senya and came forward to lay her hands on Jasper's shoulders. He was uncomfortably aware of her, of her perfume, of her sensuality. He was taller than her now, but she made him feel awkward, clumsy, and very young. He schooled his face into an expressionless mask as the first rays of the sun cast morning shadows across The Skirtings.

"But that has all changed," she said. "All Taquar wants to do now is keep you safe in Scarcleft and help you create storms. He needs water just as much as the rest of us, after all. If we abandon the other three quarters, the two of you may manage to supply all of Scarpen."

He was silent, hiding his rage behind the mask. She so

72

easily dismissed the rest of the Quartern and all its people as if they were of no import. Faces skimmed through his memory: the Alabaster salt trader, Feroze Khorash, who had offered aid when he needed it; the Gibber folk of his childhood. People like them would die of thirst, if Laisa and Taquar had their way.

He shook off her hand and bent to pick up his cloak and put it over his shoulders. The sun might have risen, but there was little warmth to the air yet.

Laisa added with unusual gentleness, "If Taquar wants to sever the power of the stormlord – you – from that of the Quartern ruler – himself – then let him. It's no bad thing, you know. People will not protest his rule. They are afraid, and they know Taquar is the strongest leader we have. It will not diminish your standing; you are a stormlord: *the* stormlord. You will be revered, you'll have everything you want."

He stared at her, wondering what her motive was, and hating her because she could forget Nealrith so soon. Because she could forgive Taquar so easily. Because in a terrible, ghastly way, she too was *right*.

He looked away from her, back to Taquar and said levelly, "I know what you plan. You want to give the north to Davim and his tribe to do what they want with. And you think you're going to rule in the south in a way the Scarpen and the Gibber have never been ruled before. As a – a –" he searched his memory for the correct word "– a tyrant. The cities of the Scarpen and the towns and villages of the Gibber will have no autonomy, no freedom. And what will be left of the Gibber anyway, if it is sent no water?"

Laisa arched an eyebrow. "*Autonomy?* Where did a Gibber grubber learn a word like that?"

Senya sniggered.

He did not look at either of them, but kept his gaze pinned on Taquar as he continued, although he addressed Laisa, not the Highlord. "I read a lot." His voice was steady, uninflected. He wondered if Laisa guessed how inadequate her scorn made him feel. "Let's assume for a moment that Taquar and I, in combination, can indeed create some clouds as you believe. Tell me, Laisa, just what do you suggest I do when Taquar tells us to withhold water from one of the Scarpen cities, as punishment for an indiscretion on their part?"

She gave him a withering glance. "They would still be better off than if they were captured by Davim! The whole of the Scarpen is better off, including yourself, if you work with Taquar while living in Scarcleft – can't you *see* that?"

Taquar, still holding his stare, said urbanely, "I will send a message to Davim telling him I have you. I will insist his men return to the Red Quarter now and stay there unless invited back. And Davim has to do it, or risk having us send no rain to the Red Quarter."

"That won't worry him," Jasper pointed out. "He *wants* to return to a Time of Random Rain!"

"Yes, but in his own time, and his own way. Gradually, so his people have time to adapt. He wants to make sure we will send rain. He still needs the aid of a stormlord; he has made that clear to me."

When Jasper didn't reply, Taquar continued, "Besides, I can tell him we not only have the power to send him rain – or not – but we could also ensure they get no *random* rain – if we so wish. You and I could divert natural clouds from the dunes, just as we could create clouds for them." He gave a malicious smile. "That won't have occurred to the red drover, but I intend to make it clear in due course. If he defies us, if he tries to seize our cisterns to bring us down or to steal our water, he risks ultimate unimaginable disaster for his people. I can still bring him to heel, believe me."

"You underestimate him."

"I don't think so. I can threaten him with you. Imagine

74

what a single stormlord could do to his dune. You could drain his waterholes, empty his water jars, steal the water."

"Not so easy. I can't get at water enclosed in a jar! In theory, I might be able to steal all the water in a waterhole and dump it a few hundred paces away, I suppose, but I'd have to be a great deal closer than this."

"You could steal water from a waterhole by turning it into a cloud. After all, it's not salty," Laisa said.

He contradicted her. "Not necessarily. I can't make vapour from muddy or dirty water, either."

"The threat is all I need," Taquar said, impatient. "I doubt Davim knows the details of your abilities! Anyway, reverting to the other part of your argument, do you really think the poor of the Quartern have ever had choices about the way in which they live? Freedom means nothing to someone who has to think about where his next full dayjar is coming from!"

"Are you telling *me* what it's like to be poor?" Jasper asked, incredulous.

"Yes, because you have evidently forgotten. You aren't the only one who was once a dirt grubber, you know. Although in my case it was more often the midden heaps of Breakaway. That's where I started and I'm damned certain I don't want to end there. When did your Gibber family ever care about who ruled in Breccia City? What did they care about *autonomy*? As I recall, in your village, they thought rainlords were gods!" Taquar's sneer stabbed at him, all the more hurtful because it was true.

Feeling himself under assault, he was silent.

Laisa had not finished with him, either. "And anyway, let's be honest, Jasper. Do you really *want* to be the ruler of the Quartern? Can you imagine the responsibility? You are hardly more than a child. In the past there have been as many as ten or so stormlords at any one time, dividing the duties of cloud-shifting and cloudbreaking. You will have to do the work that was once shared between many. Why would you want to burden yourself with the additional task of governing?"

He thought of replying to that. Of telling her even an incompetent ruler would be better than Taquar. Of telling her he had an inkling – no, he had a vision of a better world. Of a place where the Gibber urchins could get an education, where a snuggery girl could rise above her fate, where a rich upleveller couldn't pay for extra water so he could have an extra child or two even as lowlevellers thirsted. But he knew when he was beaten. The trick was to put yourself in a position of strength before the fight began; he had learned that much from Kaneth and Ryka.

He forced himself to calm. "No, of course I don't want to be the ruler of the Quartern. You're right – it would be more than I could do. More than I would want to do." He switched his gaze to Laisa. "How wise of you, Laisa."

The look she gave him was sharp, wondering how he dared to mock her, not quite certain if he did. She said, "Anyway, what are we doing out here discussing this in the middle of The Skirtings? Let's go to the city and have a civilised meal and a bath, and thrash out the details of an agreement between you and Taquar in more pleasant surroundings."

"Indeed," Taquar agreed. "Much more pleasant – and once there, I will tell you all I know about what became of Terelle."

They waited for Jasper's reply. He looked from one to another, sickened, hating their cynical manipulation, their selfishness. But what choice did he have? In the long run, what mattered was the Quartern – and its water supply.

He nodded, unable to speak, and thought of Terelle.

In the end, it was just Taquar and Jasper who had the discussion. Jasper had washed – using as little water as he could, even though the servant attending him had offered to heat an entire bath full to the brim – and changed into the clean clothes provided. A lavish meal was delivered to his room, and he found to his surprise he was ravenously hungry. When he thought back, he realised he had no memory of eating much on his journey from Breccia. When he was finished, a servant led him to the Highlord's sitting room. Neither Laisa nor Senya were anywhere in evidence.

"I thought we might do better without them," Taquar said. "Women tend to complicate things. Please sit down and allow me to pour you something refreshing. Do you drink amber now? You must have endured quite an ordeal over the past few days and I imagine a drink might be welcome."

Jasper sat, but did not reply to the question. "Where's Terelle?" he asked instead.

Taquar shrugged indifferently and poured two goblets of amber. "I've no idea."

Dragging in a deep breath, Jasper curbed a desire to slam a fist into the man's face. "I know you had her – you forced her to write that note to me. You said you'd tell me what became of her. Do so."

"I don't know where she is. Nor do I have any interest now you are here." He handed one of the goblets to Jasper.

You wilted bastard. You're playing games with me. He took the goblet, but did not drink. "In the letter you sent, you threatened to kill her. To torture her, if I did not return."

"And you were supposed to believe it. But really, I am not the monster you think me to be. Having written the note, the little whore was free to go. After a while, she did." He turned to look at the portrait of himself on the wall. "She left me that, a memento of our times together, the little jade! Quite a fine painting, don't you think?"

The feeling smothering Jasper was so intense he could hardly breathe. It was every searing event he had ever endured: the moment when Citrine had been thrown into the air and skewered on the chala spear; the moment when he had seen carvings on a pede and known its owner was the man who had killed her; the moment he had drawn his blade across Nealrith's neck; the moment one of Davim's bladesmen had uttered Mica's name only to die. It was the last time he had seen Terelle, when Harkel Tallyman, Scarcleft's seneschal, had said so casually: "Kill her."

Silent, struggling with the intensity of his feeling, he stared at the painting and saw all Terelle had put into it: the despair, the hate, the fear of the power intimidating her. Worse, he also saw Taquar's sexuality, his attractiveness, through her eyes. The allure. Terelle had looked at this man and part of her had been mesmerised by him.

Jasper's bitterness stirred. *Is that what attracts a woman? Sensuality coupled with a callous indifference to others? An attractive body coupled with the reality of power?*

He battled his jealousy, knowing it was ridiculous. *No, not Terelle. Never Terelle.*

Yet the pain of those thoughts ebbed but slowly. Expressionless, he looked at Taquar. "Yes," he said. "It's a very fine portrait. And you are lying. What happened to her?"

Taken aback, Taquar blinked.

Good, I've disconcerted him.

"You saw the damage to part of the city as we rode in."

"The earth shook and walls fell down, you said. What did you call it? An earthquake? What has that to do with Terelle?"

"She escaped that night. She was here in the Hall. You're right; I had no intention of letting her go. I thought if I had her, I had a way of ensuring your cooperation. Believe me, the last thing I ever wanted to do was hurt her."

"Did she have her paints?" Jasper asked suddenly.

Taquar blinked in surprise at the question. "Yes, she did. So?"

"Nothing. Nothing that matters now anyway." But inwardly he smiled. He knew now what had brought down the outer wall of Scarcleft Hall. Terelle had not escaped by accident – she had painted her way free. "I am sure you tried to find her afterwards," he said. "Where did she go?"

"It was a day before I realised she was even missing. We were somewhat preoccupied in the aftermath of the earthquake," Taquar said, his irritation surfacing.

"I can imagine. But I still know you tried to find her. Are you saying she escaped your clutches leaving not a single clue behind?"

"Not exactly. Harkel found out she went to that old man – the waterpainter. What was his name again?"

"Russet Kermes."

"Russet, that's right. The two of them left Scarcleft on a pede, immediately after the quake. No one saw which way they went. By the time we found out, there didn't seem to be much point in searching."

Jasper considered, wondering if he should continue to needle the Highlord, or if he now had an approximation of the truth. He was inclined to think so. A spike of grief jabbed at his heart, then receded to a dull ache. The odds were he would never see her again. Russet had wanted to take her to his home, way beyond the borders of the Quartern. Terelle was lost to him.

"All right," he said. "I'll accept that as the truth. But it's not the only thing I need to know. You told me you had no knowledge of Mica's fate. But all the while you were allied to Davim. I assume you asked him what happened to my brother. What did he tell you?"

"That he had placed your brother in one of the Reduner tribes. He didn't tell me which one. Several years later he told me Mica died in an accident with a pede. That's all I know."

He went cold all over. Mica was *dead*? Only a few days earlier, back in Breccia, he'd talked to one of the invaders from the Red Quarter who'd known Mica and he'd begun to hope again that his brother was alive. "Was – was that the truth?"

"I can't think of any reason he would lie."

Jasper put down his drink, untouched, and stood up. He went to stand at the window, looking out yet seeing nothing beyond his memory of the day Wash Drybone Settle had been slaughtered. The fires, the blood, the screams, the dispassionate killing by men who simply didn't care. He remembered hearing Mica calling out to him as he was taken away.

I didn't believe he'd died, he acknowledged. *I never truly admitted it was even possible. Even now, I go on hoping.*

How long he stood there grieving, yet refusing to lose hold of hope, he did not know. If Taquar spoke to him, he did not hear. When he turned once more to face the Highlord, he said calmly, "Now, shall we see if we have any real basis for a partnership? I want to know if you can truly raise water vapour from the Giving Sea."

"Now?" Taquar appeared dumbfounded.

"Why not? I have no intention of staying here unless there is good reason. And cloudmaking is that reason. The only one." He put his drink down. "Do you have a stormquest room?"

Taquar drank the last of his amber. "Yes. Although it hasn't been used as that for as long as I remember. It's the library now." He rose to his feet. "Follow me."

The library had the elements Jasper had come to think of as essential to stormshifting: a view out towards the Giving Sea, lecterns suitable for looking at scroll maps and a large table for bigger maps. For the time being, though, he was unconcerned about where to send water. He just wanted to know if they could do it at all.

He walked straight over to the open shutters. He could not see the sea in the heat haze of the horizon, but he could feel it:

a vast expanse of water impinging on him as a vague presence just at the edges of his conscious thought. "Show me."

Taquar came to stand beside him. Without speaking he stared outwards. Jasper waited at his side, sending his water-sense seawards, concentrating to feel the first movement of pure mist wisping out of the salt water. It came, such a tiny spiral of vapour he almost missed it. Taquar gathered it together, controlling it with ease so it didn't escape and dissipate. Easy enough, especially when the amount was so small. He searched for other misty half-formed clouds typical of the coastal areas and started to pull them together. Not enough to form a rain cloud, he had to admit, but it all helped.

Jasper glanced at Taquar. The Highlord was sweating with the effort.

Pede piss, Jasper thought. *Is this the most he can do?* If a cloud hardly the size of a myriapede took this much effort, how were they ever going to create clouds containing enough water to supply even Scarcleft, let alone the whole of the Quartern? Impatiently, he tugged at the vapour, pulling it upwards away from the surface of the sea, dragging it out of Taquar's hold as fast as the Highlord created it.

"That's it!" Taquar said, gasping. "Makes it easier."

It was true. The set of Taquar's shoulders relaxed, his breathing steadied. The vapour eased out of the Giving Sea at a faster pace. The cloud thickened, billowed larger. It took time, but finally Jasper could feel the weight of its water.

But even so, he thought bleakly, *people are going to die all over the Quartern. Taquar hasn't as much power as Granthon, even when Granthon was at his most ill.* He swore under his breath, all the worst epithets he had learned down on Level Thirty-six.

Still, it was a start. It was a cloud. It held water and he could send it high enough over the Warthago to bring rain to the mother wells of one of the cities.

And, sunblast it, it meant he had to stay in Scarcleft Hall.

Then he smiled, a grim smile of determination. He had been Taquar's prisoner once, but this time things would be different.

7

Scarpen Quarter
Breccia City, Breccia Hall, Level 2

Kaneth is alive.

Ryka was consumed by the thought. He was alive. Injured, but standing. They had thrown him onto a pyre and burned his face, yet he was still alive. *Dear Watergiver.* She stopped that thought, fought her nausea, quelled the bile in her throat. *Don't think about that.* He was *here*; that was all that mattered.

Kaneth – his name an anguished whisper in her head – *we can get out of here, the two of us. And we can kill Ravard and Davim before we leave.* After all, Kaneth was a more powerful rainlord than she was, and a fine swordsman, too. If the Reduner sandmaster and his heir were dead, that would leave their forces in disarray, surely.

Leaning against the balcony railing, she willed him to look up. *Please love, see, I'm here. You always said you knew when I was near; you sensed my water.*

It was one of the quirky oddities of his unpredictable power and she was the only person he could recognise that way. The ability to identify people by their water was supposed to be a stormlord skill, and Kaneth was no stormlord.

But he didn't look her way. *No, of course, he wouldn't. He's too afraid to give away his identity.* Her next thought horrified her. *But Ravard said the burnt man can't remember who he is.*

What if that's true? For a moment she was back in the Breccia waterhall. A spear had creased Kaneth's head. He'd staggered and fallen, dragging her with him into the cistern. *So much blood* . . . He'd been conscious for a bit, then he'd drifted away to some place and she hadn't been able to call him back. For a moment she was paralysed with pain and grief and worry.

Get a hold of yourself, Ry. You need to eat to restore your power. She had to eat a lot. Drained by the battle, without food and rest, she wouldn't have sensed even a cistern two paces away. Ravenous, she left the balcony to fetch some food from the reception room.

She stuffed a slice of bab bread into her mouth, all of it at once, then followed it with a piece of unidentifiable meat and a boiled egg. Piling some more food into a bowl, she carried it out to the balcony. Overlooking the forecourt once more, she continued to eat greedily as she watched what was happening below.

When several more men were killed with casual efficiency because they refused to swear fealty, she almost vomited all she had eaten. Kaneth hardly seemed to notice. He swayed slightly as he stood, and several times Elmar reached out to steady him. Ryka's heart plummeted.

He looks ill, she thought. *And so hurt.*

She forced herself to eat more even though her appetite had gone. Gradually, she felt the dim stirrings of her power within her once more. Not enough to kill a man, but she thought she could move a drop of water. When they were all students at Breccia Academy, much of the flirting had involved moving drops of water. He would recognise that, surely, and think of her?

She separated a drop out from the onyx carafe on her food tray and sent it down into the forecourt. Carefully, she manoeuvred it to trickle down Kaneth's face, the unburned side, just as she had done so often when she had been a cheeky academy student, and he an exasperated senior. He batted absently at his face, as if brushing away an insect. When his fingers came away wet, he looked at them absently and wiped them down his tunic.

Ryka winced. *No . . . make it not true. He must remember. He must.* She brought out another drop from the jar. This time she danced it right in front of his eyes. At first he didn't seem to notice, then he caught the drop in his fingers, but made no move to look around. Instead he rubbed his forehead the way he always did when something puzzled him.

Thank the Sunlord, no one noticed. They all had their own problems. But, agonised, she wondered how he could be so . . . so . . . unlike himself.

The last of the slaves swore their fealty, Davim disappeared inside the Hall once more and Ravard gave orders to the guards. The slaves were marched out in the direction of the pede stables and all was quiet in the forecourt again.

Ryka returned inside and began to pace. She tried the outer door once more. Barred on the outside, of course. She raged with frustration, desperate to build her power and let it fly, to do something, anything.

Kaneth was acting a part. Of course he was. He had to be. If they thought he was half senseless, they wouldn't fear him, even if they found out he was a rainlord. He was waiting for the best moment to kill Davim and his immediate underlings, that was all.

And yet her fears niggled. Maybe he was as sick as he appeared. Maybe he couldn't remember who he was. Maybe he didn't remember *her*.

She paced some more, swallowing her fury at her situation, battling her frustration.

The woman delivered another meal in the late afternoon. The guard accompanying her, a man Ryka had not seen before, let the servant into the room and then leaned against the doorway watching. He was a gaunt man with bushy eyebrows as red as his skin, elderly, but a warrior nonetheless, with scars on his face and several fingers missing on his left hand.

She inclined her head respectfully in his direction and, using the Quartern language, asked him what his name was. He just stared at her.

"You are the son of a whore and you have the prick of a wilted sand-leech," she said with a pleasant smile. The woman's eyes went wide with horror, but the Reduner didn't react. Still smiling, Ryka spoke to the woman, waving a hand at the food as if she was merely thanking her for bringing the meal. "Don't worry, he doesn't understand. Can you tell me where the Breccians intended for slavery are being kept? The men and the boys?"

The woman paled, but fortunately did not look guiltily at the guard as Ryka had feared she might. "The pede stables," she said, as she stacked up the empty dishes from the morning's meal. "They took all the pedes away and they're using the stable to keep people." She glanced at the guard then, to see if he objected to the conversation, but he was gazing around the room, his look one of scornful contempt. "They're being taken to the dunes tomorrow morning. Early, like. The kitchens have to prepare food for the journey."

"Are the stables guarded?"

"'Course." She looked at Ryka, and the desolation in her gaze was almost beyond fear, or grief. "They say – they say all the rainlords are dead. The Cloudmaster and Stormlord Jasper, too. They even killed the priests. There's no hope for us. We either die now, or thirst to death later." She ducked her head and turned away. The guard didn't react.

Ryka, sick at heart, said nothing. She was one person, one rainlord.

Watergiver forgive me. What can we do? I can't save every-body; not even Kaneth and I together can do that.

She turned her back as the woman and guard left.

She ate again, forcing the food down, even though her anxiety made her nauseous. Her power was nearly wholly restored, and she wanted to keep it that way.

Come on, Ryka; you pride yourself on your mind. You need a plan, and you need it quickly.

Ravard had given her three nights to sleep alone. Could she trust him? He'd made a promise and something told her he took his promises seriously. He'd told her he preferred an acquiescent woman in his bed and she had no reason – yet – to think he lied. She was reasonably certain he would not come to Nealrith's quarters until the three nights were up.

She had to use the time alone to escape. Or at the very least, to arrange an escape. Leaving the room would not be difficult. She could tear bedding to make a rope from the balcony to the ground, for instance – but to remain unseen? The courtyard was never empty of Reduners.

She could entice the guard outside her room to enter, kill him, and escape that way. A better solution, perhaps, but there would be no going back from that. If she used her water skills, the Reduners would know they had a rainlord in their midst. They wouldn't know who, so they might well kill all the Breccians in the Hall just to make certain they had eliminated all possibilities. If she didn't use her water powers, she might die in a fight.

Once free of the room, she would still have to enter the stables, presumably by killing more guards. Then free Kaneth. Elmar too; he would be an asset in any escape. But how would they get out of Breccia Hall? Through one of the water tunnels? What if Kaneth was too sick to use his powers? And she was one of the weakest ever to have been granted the title of rain-lord. Yet she had to do *something*. She couldn't allow them to move Kaneth to the Red Quarter. In his condition, he might die. Unless he was faking it . . .

She grunted in exasperation. How could she plan anything when she knew so little about what was happening outside Nealrith's apartments?

Restlessly she prowled the rooms, seeking ideas or a fresh perspective. Just as the sun set, she realised she had over-looked the obvious. The room above had a small projecting balcony. She could climb to it by standing on the balustrade of her own balcony, with a good likelihood no one in the forecourt below would notice in the dark. She had no idea who was sleeping up there, if anyone, but she did know most Reduners did not favour sleeping indoors, enclosed by walls. From the room above, she might be able to make her way through Breccia Hall, using her water-sense to avoid meeting Reduner guards as she went.

While trying to picture what she knew of the layout of the Hall, she heard the door of Nealrith's bedroom opening, the one she had guessed led to Laisa's rooms. A moment later Kher Ravard was striding across the reception room towards her. His eyes flashed with anger; his whole stance radiated suppressed rage.

She took a hurried step backwards.

His anger, though, was not directed at her. He said, "Came t'tell you we leave for the dunes t'morrow morning." He grabbed her arm and pulled her into Laisa's room, his grip more urgent than rough. "Choose some clothes. Whatever you need. Bundle them up and I'll see they are put in a pede pannier."

She found herself gaping at him, and quickly closed her mouth. "Reduners are *abandoning* the city?" she asked. *Already?* Her heart lurched with hope. *Holy Watergiver, it can't be that Taquar or one of the other cities has come to our aid, can it?*

His lip curled in sardonic amusement. "Hardly. Just me and the men of my tribe. My father has ordered us t'take the new slaves for Dune Watergatherer back t'our dune."

"Oh." She kept her face a blank mask, but her feelings roiled – horror and hope entwined as she struggled to think how she could use this. "The men I saw in the courtyard today?" she asked.

"Them, plus some women. The sandmaster is humiliating me by sending me home," he added bitterly, "as you'll doubtless be glad t'hear." He grimaced. "'Cause I didn't kill you when he ordered it. He let me keep you, but a Master Son's defiance, however small, must be seen t'be punished." He shrugged. "So Tribemaster Ravard is dismissed back t'the dunes t'think on his lack of respect for the sandmaster. You cost me a cut to my pride, Breccian city-woman."

She snorted. "You have plenty left, Reduner."

He leaned against the bedpost, indicated the curtained wardrobes along one side of the room, and folded his arms. "Choose."

She pulled back the curtains and was faced with an array of silken dresses, many of them either embroidered or sewn with jewelled trimming. She sighed. Definitely Laisa's, and a complete contrast to anything Ryka Feldspar liked to wear. She abandoned the first cupboard and looked at the next. These were more to her taste – travelling clothes: trousers and tunics. There was also a fine cloak lined with the fur of the red desert fox. She selected that and chose a number of the other outfits, grateful she and Laisa were not too different in size. And the fine cloth was beautiful, the weave tight enough to keep out the dust and the sand-ticks.

"Take some of the dresses, too," he said when he saw what she was choosing.

"They aren't my kind of clothes."

"Maybe not, but I like them."

"Then you wear them!"

"You test my patience, woman!"

"And you mine, if it comes to that."

He flushed angrily and came across to her, seizing her by the chin and forcing her to look him in the eye. "Don't ever forget, Garnet, I'm the conqueror here, and you the conquered. I give the orders; you obey."

She returned his stare, unblinking. "You can't intimidate me, Ravard." A lie uttered in defiance, but she sensed it would be a mistake to give any appearance of total submission to this man with his odd mix of wilful youth and cruel warrior.

"Oh yes, I can," he snapped. "You wouldn't like the slave women's meddle, believe me. A different warrior every night? Two or three at a time, perhaps?"

"You can't fool me, Ravard. There is no way you can send me to the slave women's meddle now. Your men would laugh at you – a leader who accepted a humiliating punishment for a woman who wasn't even worth keeping?"

He glared at her and she glared back, stare for stare. Suddenly he started to laugh. "Gods, but you are a woman! Did your husband know what he had, I wonder? Let me tell you something, sweetling; you're mine when your three nights are up, and I'll never let you go for any man. Not even my father. But if you mock me, I'll make you regret it. I'll see you naked and beaten raw while the whole tribe watches, till you have no pride under that tough skin of yours. Now, choose four of those dresses."

Without a word, she turned back to the first of the cupboards and began to hunt out dresses which were neither too revealing nor too impractical.

"And call me Kher," he added as an afterthought.

I have to think of a way to kill him. But not yet. Now is not the time. She cursed silently. "As you wish, Kher," she said meekly, with just enough sweetness in her tone to have him wonder if she was making fun of him. She held up one of the dresses against herself. "I had not thought dunesmen dressed their women in city finery."

"We're not barbarians, as ignorant as Gibber washfolk!"

"No? Yet you come into our land and destroy and thieve like the barbarian tribes of our histories. I see little difference."

"We're a cultured people, with a love of the beautiful. As you'll see soon."

Ryka almost threw up her hands in despair to mock him, just stopping herself in time. *Watergiver help me*, she thought. *He is so damnably young, a puffed up sandgrouse cockerel, full of a cockerel's pride* . . . And dangerous, nonetheless.

"You will need sandals and undergarments. If this woman's do not fit you, tell me, and I will get others."

With heavy distaste, she continued to search through Laisa's things. When she unearthed some jewellery, he insisted she take that as well. She spared a wry thought for how much that would enrage Laisa if she knew.

When the pile of selected items was large enough, he gave a nod of satisfaction. "We breakfast before dawn t'morrow and head out before first ray. Choose something t'wear from this pile, and take the cloak as well."

She pawed through the selection, looking for the most practical and least attractive of the travelling clothes. *Damn Laisa, she couldn't have an ill-made garment in her whole wardrobe, could she? How the sweet waters do I calm down the passions of this silly man if I have to dress like a snuggery girl?* Even as the thought crossed her mind, she shivered in a mixture of exasperation and fear. The trouble was he was far from a boy in stature and body, and he had the power of a Master Son. She would have to deal with that. *Oh, Beryll, maybe yours was the easier route* . . .

No. Never think that. You have a son to think of!

"So, you're taking all those slaves who were down in the courtyard this morning," she remarked, pulling out a travelling tunic. "What was so special about that burnt man?" Her tone was casual, but her heart thundered so loudly, she wondered he did not hear it. "The injured one."

"Him? Ah, just a whim of the shamans. They think he's some kind of reincarnation of a mythical hero. He's as dumb as a neutered pede, but strong. Fortunately he hasn't the wits t'be disloyal."

That, she thought with grim satisfaction, *is what you think.*

Back in Nealrith's room and alone again, Ryka pondered her decision to seek out Kaneth that night. Their best opportunity to escape would be once they had left the city. There would be pedes they could use, and with the power of two rainlords and any other slaves willing to flee, their chances of success were high.

But what if she was kept apart from the others? What if Kaneth and Elmar didn't know she was part of the caravan? Best to let them know beforehand. She would try to reach the stables.

She slept a little in the earlier part of the night, and then followed her plan to climb up to the balcony above. First she tried to sense the air to see if there was any living water in the room above, but could find none. All was quiet in the courtyard below as well.

Hauling herself up was harder than she had thought it would be. She blessed the training Kaneth had insisted she undertake to strengthen her arms and shoulders after they had realised war with the Reduners was a likelihood, but still it took three attempts before she succeeded in scrambling to safety one floor up. Once there, she found the shutters were latched from the inside. She had expected that might be the case and had come prepared. It was the work of moments to slip the broken sword tip through the gap between the closed doors and flip the latch.

The room beyond was small and pokey and dark. She paused on the threshold, tasting the air with her water-sense. There was no one there.

Leaving the shutters open for light, she crossed to the door on the other side. It gave out onto a passage so narrow and dark she guessed this was part of the servants' quarters. No light, no sound. Still no one around. Making a guess at the best direction to head in, she felt her way along. The passage led to another, slightly wider, and a faint light ahead proved to come from an oil lamp at the head of a set of rough stone stairs heading downwards. Definitely servants' stairs.

She picked up the lamp and headed down to the next floor, but didn't linger there. A further set of steps beckoned her on to the ground floor. At the bottom, she emerged into the kitchens where a coal fallen free from the banked fire gave a gleam of light. A candle lantern, designed for outdoor use with shutters to protect the flame against the wind, was hanging on the back of the door. Just what she needed. She lit it from the other lamp and looked around.

The sense of water was overpowering: the kitchen cistern, water in pots on the hobs of the two huge fireplaces, water held in fruit, bab palm mash and other food in the pantry. A line of moving water marked the underground channel of a water tunnel. The only living water she could detect nearby was small and stationary – a cat asleep somewhere, she guessed. She edged the leaf-woven cover of the kitchen cistern back to expose the surface of the water.

Then she turned to the door in the outside wall. It was heavily barred on the inside. Quietly, she lifted the bars and eased the plank door open. She was looking out onto a walled kitchen courtyard. Oil jars were stacked two deep and three rows high along one side. A rat scampered over the top of them, but apart from that, she could detect nothing alive nearby. She left the door open so she could return the same way.

The courtyard was accessible through an archway, and when she moved quietly to the edge of the arch and looked out, she sensed people beyond. She cursed her inability to sense far, but thought she was safe enough from immediate detection. Better still, because she was aware of a number of prone bodies at the edge of her water-sense – the sleeping warriors in the entrance forecourt – she could place herself in relation to her knowledge of the layout of Breccia Hall. She needed to turn right to reach the stables. Shuttering the lantern so as to allow no light to escape, she waited for her eyes to adjust to the starlit world outside.

To her right was a narrow lane running between the main Hall building and some outbuildings, roofed by another storey of the Hall. She edged her way along this covered way to the end, her footfall silent on the paving stones.

When she peered from the archway at the other end, she could see the open rectangular courtyard in front of the main façade of the stables. The huge double stable doors, directly before her and large enough to allow the passage of a fully loaded packpede, were closed and barred from the outside. They were also guarded by two men, both squatting on their heels as they talked quietly. The sandmaster was wisely not taking any risks with his new slaves, sandblast him.

The right-hand side of the courtyard was formed by the wall of the main Hall. The left-hand side gave onto a large rutted road she guessed led between more outbuildings to Breccia Hall's main entrance and its main gateway, the only gateway large enough for the use of packpedes.

Ryka bit her lip, perplexed. How could she pass those guards unnoticed and enter the stables? Recalling the few times she'd been inside those doors, she remembered entering the main building from there. If she went back inside the Hall she may be able to locate that entrance. Or she could spend half the night searching, only to find it guarded as well.

She tried to conjure up memories of being inside the stables. Talking to a pede groom. A stablehand doing something. Shovelling manure. Now why was that important? Of course – he was throwing it into a muck chute. A muck chute to the right of the main door . . . but how was that possible? That side of the stable shared its wall with the main Hall building.

She frowned into the darkness. To the right of the façade, a patch that wasn't part of the brickwork showed up black as obsidian. An impasse, that's right. She remembered now. A short piece of laneway going nowhere, a delivery bay, where they brought the pedes to unload feed directly into the bins through openings in the stable wall. And a muck chute, where the dirty straw and pede manure were shovelled from the stables directly into a handcart. Those openings would probably be boarded over, but they weren't guarded.

Her problem would be to reach them without alerting the guards at the main doors. With a sinking heart she stared at the surface of the courtyard; it was covered a hand span deep in loose gravel, so as not to blunt the pointed feet of the pedes the way a smooth, hard stone surface would. And it was the noisiest surface in the world to walk across. Even if they didn't see her in the dark, they could hardly fail to hear her.

Diversion . . . she had to make a diversion. A noisy diversion to cover any sound she made. Something that would leave no trace behind. *Come on, Ry, think!*

She retreated down the passageway to the other end, until she was close enough to the kitchens to pull a brick-sized chunk of water out of the uncovered cistern. She was not Jasper, and it took her time to manoeuvre it and then to keep it moving through the air in front of her without spilling or having it flying off in all directions in countless little drops. The effort of maintaining it as a single entity made her sweat. She gave an irritated grunt, recalling all those hours of frustration in Breccia Academy as she had tried to learn the art of watershifting. She had never been much good then, either.

Facing the stables once more, she shifted the brick of water over to the left. Pressed up against the wall of the passageway so she would be hard to spot, she lowered the water into the gravel and then barrelled it through the pebbles straight down the centre of the road. The small round stones rattled and danced noisily as they were ploughed aside by the water brick. Both guards jumped to their feet and stood rooted, staring. The noise was uncanny; the cause invisible.

"A cat?" one ventured, his question tentative.

Ryka doubled the amount of power she was using and the gravel shot away, flung aside by the speeding brick. She eased herself out from the shelter of the passageway and skirted the wall to her right, keeping to the perimeter of the courtyard. If either of the guards turned his head, he would see her. Feeling exposed and vulnerable, she wanted to run, but curbed the desperation that prompted such risky behaviour. She flattened herself against the stones of the wall and slowly edged towards the murky darkness of the delivery bay. The gravel scrunched under her feet, but more quietly than the noise made by her water brick as she reversed it and then spun it around and around in the gravel.

"That's no cat," the other guard muttered in Reduner. "We'd better look." He unhooked a lantern that had been hanging on the outer stable wall and directed a beam of light towards the noise.

She swore silently, wondering if the water would glint in the light. Squeezing her eyes shut in concentration, she flattened and broadened the water into a plank instead of a brick, buried it just under the gravel and then moved it along broadside. The pebbles danced and clinked and jostled in a wave.

Ryka crept on, sweating with the exertion. Blighted eyes, it was easier to kill a man than do finicky things like this. The water brick wanted to weep its contents onto everything it touched. Never mind, she told herself, if she did leave some behind, it would be invisible in the dark and would soon evaporate.

The two guards followed it still, but were cautious about catching up. She slowed the water down, but when they approached it, she sent it furrowing through the gravel once more. She whisked it suddenly around the corner in the direction of the main gate. As soon as it was out of sight, she raised it high into the air and tossed it over the roof, deliberately splitting it into as many drops as she could and casting it wide enough not to be noticeable. At the same time she dashed into the dark bay along the side wall of the stables. Once there, she briefly cracked open the lantern shutter to cast a sliver of light on the wall.

She could just make out a wooden cover of some sort, projecting out of the wall at waist height, about a quarter of the size of a normal door: the muck chute. Next to it was the delivery door. Designed to be opened by someone standing on a pede, it was too high for her to reach. She cursed richly under her breath. Such a simple way to enter the stable, easy to unbar, out of sight of the guards, even if they returned to their post in front of the door, and she couldn't open it.

Ryka screwed up her nose at the muck chute. It smelled, even with the entrance closed. The cover was easily unbolted from the outside and lifted away from the opening, to reveal a short chute sloping upwards. She poked her head inside. Pede pellets were dry, so it was not slippery or slimy – but the smell was intense, reminiscent of dried antiseptic herbs mixed with ammonia. There did not appear to be a cover at the other end, but the stable beyond was in total blackness. Snorting sounds punctuated the darkness in an unattractive din. Not pedes, she decided. Men. Snoring, bless them.

Withdrawing her head, she propped the chute cover against the wall, then hooked the lantern onto the back of her tunic belt, took a deep breath and ducked down inside the chute again. It wasn't difficult to scramble upwards and a moment later she poked her head into the stable. She couldn't see a thing. She waited for her eyesight to adjust, but even then the darkness seemed total. Unhooking the lantern, she looked to see if the candle was still alight. It was, but guttering badly. She unshuttered one side and shone it around.

The stable floor was untidily scattered with straw and sleeping bodies. Stealthily, she hauled herself out of the chute and stood up. No one stirred, and the snuffling and honking and snorting helped to cover any noise she made. As far as she could determine, there were no guards inside the building.

She began to walk between the rows of sleeping men. It was hard to make out faces and, short of waking everyone up, it seemed an impossible task to find either Elmar or Kaneth. As she hesitated, though, she saw one of the stall doors open. A tall man stood in the doorway, looking her way. She didn't need to see him properly to know it was Kaneth.

He always did recognise my water, she thought, emotion bringing a lump to her throat. She began to thread her way through the sleeping bodies to his side. When she arrived, he didn't move, but just stood there, looking down at her. She raised the lantern to view his injuries, and the sight was enough to wrench her insides.

"Oh," she whispered, and her hand touched his cheek with gentle tenderness. "Your poor face . . ."

He gave a half embarrassed smile, and when he spoke, he sounded at a loss. "I'm sorry," he said softly. "I don't seem to know you. Who are you?"

8

Scarpen Quarter
Breccia City, Breccia Hall, Level 2
Foothills of the Warthago Range

Ravard had called him witless. Ryka had hoped he'd hidden his sharp mind along with his identity, so his words had the impact of a physical blow. She was unprepared for the sense of rejection, unprepared for the pain his inadvertent betrayal of their love would cause her.

She stepped away from him, and perhaps he glimpsed the horror in her expression because, whispering, he apologised again. "I'm sorry, I just don't remember. I don't even remember my own name." He pointed to the scar on his head. "I was hit here, I think. In a fight, I suppose. I don't recall."

"I do," she snapped, and was instantly contrite. It wasn't his fault. "I was there," she added more gently, lowering her voice. "It was a spear – you fell into the cistern." *And saved my life.* "You truly don't remember?"

He shook his head. "We knew each other?"

His polite disinterest was shocking. It was a moment before she could bring herself to reply, "You could say that." *Watergiver, how do you tell a man who can't remember his own name that he has a wife – and a baby on the way?* "I'm—"

She didn't finish. Elmar Waggoner stepped out of the shadows in the pede stall and grabbed them both by the elbows to pull them inside, away from the men sleeping in the common area. Already one or two were stirring and someone had roused himself to look around to see who was talking.

"Shh," Elmar said, his urgency intense. "You can't trust everyone." The look he gave her was meaningful, but she could not interpret it. She stared, uncomprehending, as he closed the door to the stall. They were alone, just the three of them, but her mind was appallingly blank. Elmar took the lantern from her and hung it from a hook on the wall.

"He *really* can't remember?" she asked Elmar, finding her voice at last, but it was belief which made her wretched, not doubt. She didn't need an answer.

"Not even me. I'm a metal worker from Level Twenty-five, by the way. Never been in the army and the only bleeding thing I know about a sword is how to craft one. Taken it upon meself to look after this great hulking lump here, even though he's missing half his wits. He needs someone to keep an eye on things for him. Doesn't remember a thing. Not even which side of the battle he fought on. Mind's as blank as a baby pede carapace."

She looked back at Kaneth, her breath coming in quick gasps. *Not remember which side—?* He smiled at her with a shining innocence that recalled to mind the words Ravard had used. Halfwit.

"What name do you go by here, lady?" Elmar asked politely, his gaze locked on her face. Lady, not lord.

When the silence threatened to become embarrassing, she said quietly, "Garnet Prase. Housewife from Level Ten, who can't find her husband. I am slave to the Master Son, Kher Ravard. We are all being taken to the Watergatherer Dune, setting off tomorrow morning, you two and me included. Did you know?"

Kaneth shook his head. "I didn't." He frowned. "Kher Ravard is a good man."

"He's a slaver," she spat back at him, aghast, not quite believing she had heard him correctly.

He wrinkled his nose. "You smell really odd. Did you know that?"

Nonplussed, she was speechless.

Once again Elmar intervened. He picked up two water skins from the floor and thrust them at Kaneth. "Go fill these. We will need them if we are travelling in the morning."

Kaneth frowned, baffled, but he took the skins. "It's too dark."

"Then take the lantern." Elmar thrust that at him as well, and he took it without comment, turned and went back into the main area of the stable. Elmar closed the stall door again, and they were plunged into almost complete darkness.

"Blighted eyes, Elmar – what the withering shit is going on here?"

She felt rather than heard his intake of breath. She was still whispering, but her tone and her swearing startled him.

"Watergiver forgive me, Lord Ryka, but he doesn't remember as much as a newborn babe about himself. He doesn't know he's a rainlord. He doesn't remember you, or me, or the fighting, or who he was. And the worst of it is – he doesn't seem to *care.*"

She wanted to call him a liar, to pound her fists against his chest in fury, but part of her knew her indignation was irrational. This wasn't Elmar's fault, and he wasn't lying. She took a deep breath. "How did you find him?"

"I managed to flee the waterhall. I didn't see what happened to the two of you. By the time I got down to Level Two, the Reduners had the main gate to the Hall open and the battle was over. I got rid of my sword, changed my clothes and tried to blend in with the servants. I was hauled off to carry bodies to the pedes. Ended up down in the groves, building pyres for the dead. I worked all day at it – fetching dry fronds, heaving the corpses into the flames. Sunlord save me, the stench! It was a horrible day. So many people I knew . . ."

Impatient to know what had happened, she choked down her dread and asked, "You saw him flung on the pyre?"

"No, no. I was collecting fuel. I didn't know he was among the dead until I saw him lying there, burned, coughing up his lungs, with people standing around. Reduners among them. I reckon he was out cold when they flung him into the flames, but – thanks be – being burned roused him enough to shout. Somebody pulled him out. He wasn't much burned anywhere except the face and his hair." His voice stumbled and grew hoarse. "It's not too bad, but he'll – he'll never be the handsome man he used to be."

"The Reduners – why didn't they kill him? Don't they know he's a rainlord?"

"No. No one knows who he is."

"But he's Kaneth! *You* recognised him! Others must have, too."

"Lord Ryka, most of the soldiers and the uplevellers – people who would know him well – they're *dead*." His voice was low and urgent. "If they survived the fighting, they were slaughtered afterwards. Don't you know that? Men, women, children! Sunlord save me, I probably tossed bodies of people from every villa on Level Three and Four onto the pyres. And I doubt there's a single priest or reeve left in the whole city. If you are looking for friends or family, forget it. They're dead and roasted. Their water not taken, no ceremonies, nothing."

She was glad the lantern was gone. She didn't want him to see her face. She didn't want to see his, either; the bitter horror in his voice was enough.

Elmar glanced at the stall door and lowered his voice still further. "As far as I can find out, just about everyone here is a downleveller, an artisan of some sort. If there are some who've seen him before, they don't know him well enough to recognise him when he's bald and half burned. You just saw his face. Besides, he doesn't *act* like Kaneth, or a rainlord. He even holds himself different. Humble, like. And if they do recognise him – or you, come to that – who are they going to tell?"

He continued, calmer now, "The only reason I'm alive is because the Reduners think me a metalworker, not a soldier, and it seems they need metalworkers. My brother owns a metal workshop and I do know a thing or two, fortunately."

"We can escape. With his power and mine, we can kill guards, seize the pedes, maybe even free the rest of the slaves. I thought perhaps our first night out from Breccia might be a good time—"

"Lord Ryka, Kaneth doesn't even *know* he's a rainlord."

"Then tell him! I'll tell him who I am! Remind him he is to have a child – anything! How can we bring back his memory, if we don't stimulate it?" Frustrated, she glanced towards the stall door herself, wanting Kaneth to return. Why had he left so meekly at Elmar's bidding?

"You're expecting a baby?" He sounded taken aback.

"Yes! We have to make him remember."

"No, we mustn't. Not yet. My lord, he is ill. His vision is blurred, his thoughts confused. His head aches, and he is in constant pain from the burns. He doesn't understand anything yet."

"But we must escape before—" She hesitated. *Before Ravard climbs into my bed.* "Before we reach the dunes. Before we cross the Warthago Range."

"Lord Ryka, he's not—"

The door opened then, and Kaneth stepped in with the lantern and the water skins, now filled. He smiled absently at Ryka, as if he had forgotten her all over again. She felt her heart break, all over again, in answer.

104

"Go," Elmar muttered. "Before you are caught here. Look after yourself and the child. It is all you can do."

She turned away from Kaneth to stare at him. "How can you ask that of me? I made a vow once—"

"Yes. I know. I was there, remember? But now your duty lies with your child. I am sure your man is in good hands," he said carefully.

"He is also a prisoner of his worst enemies." For a moment she felt as if she had lost her hold on the conversation, as if the words were flowing by her like water from a broken jar. There was so much to say, to find out, but shock had left her with no idea what she should be asking first. Or how to grasp the meaning of words as they streamed past.

Kaneth did not appear to be listening. He hung up the lantern again and placed the water skins back on the floor. "My head hurts," he said. "I think I will lie down."

"Good idea," Elmar agreed. The look he gave Ryka was full of meaning, and Ryka saw his unspoken, *You see?*

"This is insane." She lowered her voice still further. "Elmar, he is in such danger. If anyone gives them a hint of who he is, if he gives *himself* away, because he doesn't know his power—"

He snatched the lantern from the hook, grabbed her by the elbow and pushed her through the door, which he then closed. Her last glimpse of Kaneth was of his burnt face as he lay on his side in the straw. The fresh scar was still raw and ugly. *I wonder if I could quicken the healing*, she thought, *by drying it out . . .* Or would that make it worse? She didn't know.

Elmar handed her the lantern, then pushed her against the wall with an urgency she sensed rather than felt. "Lord Ryka, please heed me," he whispered in her ear. "He is not to be trusted. Do you understand? He doesn't know who he is. If you tell him your name and his name, he's likely to blurt them out to the first Reduner he meets. He's like a small child, with no sense of danger."

"He wouldn't," she protested, her anger surfacing. "He is *Kan*—"

He stopped the word by jamming his hand across her mouth.

"No. He's not. Not yet. He's a sick man who can't remember a thing. His thoughts go nowhere and his pain is intense enough to make a sane man act sun-fried. The less he sees of you the better at this point – for your own safety."

She pushed his hand away, the pain of his truth more than she could handle. "I'll never abandon him. *Never*. What kind of a woman would that make me?"

"A living one! What kind of a *mother* would it make you to stay in danger when you have the power to escape?" he asked.

Ryka's desire to slap him was intense and immediate, but she was also aware her anger was only so sharp because she knew he was right. And because she did not want to relinquish the man she loved into the hands of another who sometimes looked at him the same way she did. Yet it was her duty to guard her child. Kaneth's child. Her duty as a mother, as a wife – and, as a rainlord, to bring another water sensitive into a thirsty world.

"Escape now," Elmar whispered. "You know that's what your husband would want, if he were himself. If he regains his health, he will be able to get himself out of this. Me too, I hope."

She hesitated still.

"You cannot trust him," he repeated. "Trust me. You know I'll care for him."

Just then Kaneth called out petulantly, so unlike the man he was she could almost believe it was someone else, "Elmar! Where are you?"

She turned and walked away, back towards the muck chute.

* * *

Ryka retraced her steps back to her room without any trouble. The two guards at the stable entrance had returned to their post by the time she reached the edge of the courtyard again, but were easily distracted by more gravel scattering in front of another block of water – stolen from the prisoners in the stable this time.

No one had noticed the open kitchen door, the lamp from the passageway burning in the kitchen, or the missing candle lantern. She put everything back the way it had been. The climb down to her balcony proved easier than the climb up. She lay down on her bed – no, on poor dead Nealrith's bed – and surrendered herself to her grief.

An hour later, feeling no better, but more in command of her emotions, she roused and went to wash away the lingering smell of pede droppings and stable hay. Her dirty tunic she stuffed under the mattress in the centre of the bed.

Odd, she reflected, *for the first time in my life, I don't care about how much water I use.* It was Reduner water now, not the Scarpen's, and she felt no desire to conserve it.

Afterwards, she sat in the darkness of Nealrith's study and tried to come to terms with all that had happened. She had already made up her mind that any escape would be better achieved from the caravan with a pede under her. That way there was the possibility of making it to one of the other cities and freedom. What she had not yet made up her mind about was whether she would escape at all, if Kaneth wasn't prepared to go with her.

One by one she marshalled the advantages and disadvantages. With a cold dispassion, she examined her own motives. If she was going to choose an alternative based on emotion rather than her academic impartiality, she wanted to be aware of it.

Finally, she drifted into an uneasy doze.

*   *   *

An hour later, the same serving woman brought in her breakfast. Quickly, Ryka roused herself and dressed. As an afterthought, she selected a number of board books from the collection in Nealrith's study and tied up the bundle with bab string, giving a wry smile as she did so. Even in a desperate situation, she could still dread the horrors of having nothing to read.

She was just sitting down to eat something, when the door opened again and Ravard entered. She glanced up but did not rise.

"Pour me some tea," he said, indicating the pot. "I'll eat with you."

Silently she did as he asked, only then noticing there were two drinking mugs on the tray.

He sat opposite her at the table, dumping the small cage he carried down on a spare chair beside him. She smelled its occupants: ziggers. Sunlord, how she hated them! Their sickly smell, their greed for human flesh, the promise of pain in their dribbling saliva and their clicking mouth parts.

Oblivious to her distaste, he helped himself to a steaming bowl of bab fruit porridge. "Dunegod save me, I'm getting so sick of Scarpen food," he remarked. "At least there's one good thing 'bout going back t'the dunes. Decent game on the platter and damper made from root mash, not withering bab flour." He glanced across the table at her. "Why so silent?"

She shrugged. "I have nothing to say."

"What, no sharp words about my moral standards or my taste? Now that's a change!"

"You expect me to be brimming over with delight at being carted off to another quarter as a slave for the entertainment of a man who has just helped lead an invading horde into my country, an invasion that killed my family?"

"Why not? You'll share the bed of the Master Son, the man who will one day lead the dune that rules all others. That's a position some women of the tribe would kill for! 'Sides, I am young and virile, as older men are not. Bet your husband was old and lacking."

She took a bite of her bread to stop herself from saying something she would be made to regret.

"And remember," he added, spooning down the porridge in noisy gulps, "we have a bargain. You welcome me t'your pallet, I protect the child you carry, and keep the other men from you."

"It would be easier if you tried courting me," she snapped, "after a decent interval of mourning. And if you didn't come to my bed while I carried another man's child!"

He tilted his head, amused. "Maybe I would – if I loved you. But I don't. I *want* you. There's a difference."

"You've just told me there are plenty of others who would *like* the company."

"Ah, but I'm stuck with you now – for reasons of pride, aren't I?" He grinned at her. "'Sides, I like a challenge."

She gritted her teeth.

"Don't be so difficult," he said. "I gave you a choice, remember?"

"A *choice*? When the alternative is a piece of personal horror? You have a strange idea of choice, you Reduner barbarian."

Ryka thought he would match her fury with his own, but he shrugged with an indifference that was chilling. "I suggest you make it easy on yourself when the time comes."

"And just how do you recommend I do that?"

"By accepting the inevitable calmly. What you had is gone. So why not enjoy what replaces it? A roll around on my pallet each night could well be pleasurable." He stood up and spread his hands out. "Look at me. Am I so unattractive?"

She stared at him. Since she'd first met him, his hair had been washed and rebraided with red and black beads. His red belted tunic with its embroidered panel down the front accentuated his broad shoulders. Underneath he wore full breeks gathered in at the ankle. He moved with all the muscular power of the young and virile, yet his smile, revealing white, even teeth, was more boyish than manly. Even his reddish skin and hair were attractive. If he had not been a threat to her, she would have thought him appealing. And handsome. Instead, he represented a future she was dreading with a sickness deep in her gut.

"You appeal to me about as much as those ziggers in the cage." She waved a spoon to where one of the beasts had climbed up the bars and was gazing at her with sharp beady eyes – more like a bird's eyes than an insect's – smelling her with its waving antennae and slavering at her taste on the air. She thought of it burrowing deep into the soft tissues of her eye, spreading its acid as it went, feeding on her flesh.

"You'll get used to me, and them, too." He tapped the cage top and the zigger fell from the bars to the cage floor, where it spun on its back, legs flailing. For a brief moment it could have been just an ordinary beetle, but then it flipped right side up and snarled at her, as if blaming her for its indignity.

"They are as much a part of a Reduner warrior," Ravard said, "as the scimitar at our belts. Without ziggers, we are not warriors, and must have the status of a servant. On the Watergatherer, I own more ziggers than anyone but the sandmaster, as is my right."

Ryka snorted. "Owning those monsters is nothing to be proud of."

Once again he took no offence. He held out a hand to her. "Come," he said, "it's time we left."

She snatched up her bundle of books without taking his hand, so he grabbed her arm and pulled her towards the door.

"What are those?" he asked.

"Books," she said.

He laughed. "Books? You want t'take *books* with you? Woman, there are better things t'do with your time on the dunes than read."

"Like what?"

"Weaving and sewing and tent-making and cooking and fetching water. And sharing my pallet. Womanly things. Your job is t'look after my comfort." He looked contemptuous. "We don't have women warriors as you Scarpen folk do. It's unnatural. A woman is not built for such things."

"No? They cart water, bear children, dig for roots, cook over open fires in the heat while they are pregnant, and lots of other things suitable only for weaklings, eh?"

"You don't know the strength required for a warrior."

She looked at him brightly. "No, of course not. Funny, though – I did hear there was a Reduner woman warrior of considerable skill who has outwitted Davim himself. What was her name now? Redmane? Yes, that's it. Vara Redmane. Old woman, too, I heard."

She expected him to be angry; she didn't expect him to flush, but he reddened enough for her to be aware of the darkening of his cheeks and neck. *Embarrassment or anger?* She couldn't tell.

He changed the subject and asked snappishly, "What's in the books?"

"They are histories, myths of the past, that sort of thing."

He snorted. "We have storytellers for all that. You have no need of books." He pulled the bundle from her and tossed it on the floor. "Come."

"Just because you are an ignorant barbarian who doesn't know how to read or write his own name, doesn't mean there's no value in it!"

Without warning, Ravard slammed her up against the wall. Her head rang as it hit the stonework. He leaned in against her. His arm pressed her back as he snarled, "Don't you *ever* despise me for what I am," he said. "Being different doesn't mean being ignorant! Not reading or writing doesn't make me a fool. Just 'cause you read your bleeding books, doesn't mean you know a sand-flea's piddle about anything. You with your city upbringing have no right t'despise me 'cause I had a different life when I was a young'un. Y'understand me?"

Weakly, she nodded. She had feared him from the moment they had met, but this was the first time he had terrified her.

"Sorry," she said unsteadily. "You are right. It doesn't make me wise, or you stupid." *And that's the truth. Especially the bit about me being wise.*

He released her, opened the door and gestured her through to where the guard stood outside in the passage, but he turned back into the room. When he joined her, it was to thrust the bundle of books into her arms.

I don't understand you, she thought, surprised. *I don't understand you at all.*

Ryka rode with the female slaves, fifteen of them, all now belonging to Davim's dune and mounted on the same pack-pede. A Reduner drover guided the beast from the front segment, and another took the last seat at the back. None of the women were roped as the male slaves were. The men had their hands lashed together at the wrist, the rope then threaded through the handles screwed into every segment.

As they rode away from Breccia heading north, Ryka gave a sour smile. The Reduners didn't trust the men, but it had evidently never occurred to them that a woman among their slaves might not only know how to drive a pede, but had accumulated several years of desert experience doing just that. If she could steal a pede, she could drive it.

She knew none of the other women on the pede and none of them indicated that they had any inkling of who she was. Listening to their chatter as they rode, she gathered they were all women from the lower levels, all but one chosen for their looks and youth. The exception was Junial, a plump older woman, kidnapped, or so she said, for her baking skills. Nine of the younger ones were snuggery girls resigned to their fate; five others – inexperienced girls between fourteen and twenty – were dull-eyed with fatigue and the memory of horror, or weepy in their despair. Some bore the external marks of the abuse they had already suffered because they dared to resist: bruised faces, black eyes, cracked ribs.

Rage gathered in Ryka. *Sunlord forgive me, but if I had the power I'd kill every single warrior here . . .*

There were a hundred or so of them, every one a seasoned fighter, so it was hardly a sensible objective. And Ravard she could not kill with her water-powers, not if he had the usual water skills of a tribemaster.

The Escarpment dropped out of sight behind them as the pede caravan pushed its way up the track towards the Warthago Range. She glimpsed Elmar on the pede ahead of her and thought with vicious enjoyment, *Leaving him alive was another mistake you Reduners have made.* Her next thought was one she tried not to think about at all. What if Kaneth never recovered from his injury?

How the Reduners regarded him was puzzling. In the stable, he and Elmar had been given a stall to themselves. Now he was not roped and was being kept separate from the other slaves, including Elmar. He rode behind a couple of warriors on a myriapede. When they stopped to rest at midday, a bladesman brought food to him. Another gave him a water skin. Both men treated him with deference.

Ryka watched, mystified. *What the blighted eyes is going on?* She looked across at Elmar where he sat with the other men on the ground, still roped together. He shot an unhappy glance at her and she guessed he was aching to get to Kaneth's side. When Ravard strolled up to Kaneth and sat beside him to eat his own meal, Elmar appeared positively sick. Ryka didn't blame him. She looked away and tried not to think too much.

They travelled north from Breccia all day. Every now and then they passed one of the inspection towers, obese brick giants that strutted in lines across The Sweepings. Their midday rest lasted several runs of the sandglass, until the sun had settled lower in the sky and the burn had gone from its rays. The pedes then rose of their own accord, shaking the sand out of their segments and swinging their heads around in search of their owners as if to say it was time to move on.

Ryka saved some of her own food and, choosing a time when none of the warriors was looking, fed titbits to the mount she rode. She studied its carvings carefully so she could recognise it again, even in the dark. Then she spent the few moments before they mounted up rubbing the soft tissue where it's head joined the first segment behind. The animal rasped its purring approval of her touch and gazed at her in short-sighted adoration. You never knew when a friendly pede would be an asset.

Shortly afterwards, the beast's driver shooed her away, and they were on their way once again.

They passed through the first of the caravansaries without stopping, and it wasn't until the sun slipped below the rugged spur of the Warthago Range that they halted for the night alongside one of the inspection towers. In the shadows of dusk, the warriors untied the men and set all the slaves to work, the women to prepare the food and the men to unburden the packpedes, groom the animals and erect tents. To Ryka's horror, several of the warriors smashed the wooden cover and the iron grille over the shaft and bade the women haul up water from the underground tunnel. All her years as a Scarpen rainlord were assailed by their action. Hard-earned water – pulled from the sea by the sacrifice of Cloudmaster Granthon – now defiled, opened to the elements and stolen by invading travellers. They cared nothing for the damage they did, for the destruction they would leave behind. Breccian water meant nothing to them. As a rainlord, it was her duty to prevent both such thefts and any damage to the tunnels that would lead to silting. Having to stand and watch it happen galled her.

"Your second night alone," Ravard whispered in her ear as she stirred a cauldron of food over one of the fires. She didn't react and he walked on.

Her gaze sought Kaneth. Excused by his captors from the chores, perhaps because of his injuries, he sat alone on a rock, looking peaceably at the colours in the sky. No one seemed to care when she strode to his side, not even Ravard.

He looked up when she arrived and greeted her with a simple, "Hello."

She greeted him, feeling oddly uncomfortable as she sat down nearby. He looked weary and was, she suspected, in considerable pain. She said, "Have you thought of escaping? Of stealing a pede and riding to one of the other Scarpen cities?"

He blinked in a puzzled way. "Why?"

"Because here we are slaves!"

"Slavery is not allowed."

She curbed her frustration as best she could, striving for an even tone. "The Reduners don't follow our laws. I am a slave. So are you. They are taking us to the dunes. If you want to be free, you must escape." She looked over her shoulder. No one was looking their way. Ravard had his back to them, directing some of the slaves where to put his tent. Never having raised a tent before, they were clumsy and inefficient. Ravard was yelling at them.

Kaneth frowned. "I have a headache. I don't think I can

ride any more tonight. I want to sleep. And nobody's said I am a slave."

She hid her dismay. "The rest of us are, believe me. We Scarpen folk, I mean. Doesn't that worry you?"

His frown deepened, as if he was trying to work through a problem. "Slavery – I thought – I thought there was no more slavery. I don't remember there being slavery." He gazed at the Scarpermen. "That's why they were roped?" The question was as innocent as a child's.

She nodded. "We are all slaves. We folk from the Scarpen Quarter – as you are." When she looked around again, Elmar glared at her and then mouthed the words she had no trouble deciphering. *Don't trust him!*

Kaneth did not notice. He looked at her, troubled. "The drovers say they know me. That I was born of the dunes, a long time ago . . ."

"That's not true."

Watergiver's heart, Kaneth. How can you not know who you are? She desperately wanted to jog his memory. She wanted to tell him his name. She wanted to place his hand on her abdomen so that he could feel his son move under his palm. Instead, she said, hoping that she might be able to stir a memory, "Ravard wants me to share his bed."

Her heart sank still further as he smiled pleasantly at her. "That's good. He's a handsome man."

Ryka felt as if she'd been stabbed through and through. Speechless, she rose to her feet. He ignored her as he gazed at the sunset and the light fading from the sky.

"What are you wasting your time talking to him for?" Ravard's voice asked from behind her. "You won't get much sense out of him, y'know."

She turned, smiling faintly to hide lacerating pain. "So I discovered. You were right. His head's stuffed with sand."

"Come, have something to eat." He led her towards the

campfire, sat her down on one of the many boulders scattering the area and seated himself beside her. She was uncomfortably aware of his proximity. A woman came to push a bowl of food into her hands, and she toyed with it, but ate hardly anything. "Relax," Ravard said. "I don't bite." He nibbled her ear.

"Don't start what's not going to be finished tonight," she told him, keeping her voice low.

He shovelled some food into his mouth. "Don't worry. I don't break promises. But you seem so sad tonight. I shall keep you company. Would it not be good to fall asleep in my arms?" He nuzzled at her cheek. "Nothing more."

"I don't trust you."

"I don't break my promises," he repeated. "And my men expect to see you share my tent."

She glanced around, to see both Elmar and Kaneth watching them. Elmar looked away, frowning, either upset or angry; she wasn't sure which. Kaneth smiled at her gently with benevolent interest, and it was Ryka who looked away.

"It would be good to fall asleep in the arms of someone who loved me," she murmured. "But you do not."

"Never mind. Tonight you can lie next to me and pretend I am your lost husband, the father of your child. Another night after this one to grieve, and then you'll begin a new life on my pallet. You'll start t'be a dunes woman."

Nauseated, she glanced back at Kaneth, but he had already looked away, bestowing that same smile on everyone without discrimination. It devastated her, that smile.

She had never felt so alone.

9

Scarpen Quarter
Scarcleft City

On his second full day in the Hall, Jasper decided to test just how much freedom he had. When he left his room in the morning, the two men on guard outside fell in behind him, marching in step in silence. They followed him to breakfast. Later, they waited outside the stormquest room while he and Taquar cloudshifted. When he went outside to the roof gardens of the Hall, two more men fell in step behind. Four of them, discretely watching everything he did, listening to every conversation he had, even though the only people he spoke to were the gardeners and servants.

After lunch, he left the Hall for the streets of the city, and his escort expanded as four of the seneschal's water enforcers joined them. Jasper's previous experience with enforcers had been unpleasant and these strengthened his mistrust. The men formed a wall around him and gave him the impression they revelled in pushing people on the street out of his way with the shafts of their spears. "Just guarding you," one said with an ill-concealed sneer. "Looking after your security, your safety, your well-being, m'lord."

"There's no need to be so rough," Jasper protested, painfully aware of their contempt for outlanders.

"Stormlord," the overman among them replied, "we've

been told to make sure no one approaches you. In case of assassination, m'lord."

"*Assassination?* Who in their right mind is going to assassinate the only stormlord the Quartern has?"

"Reduners might, m'lord."

"And just how many Reduners are there in the streets of Scarcleft? If you see any, you have my permission to protect me. In the meanwhile, *my* orders to you are to treat the people in the streets with respect."

The man looked at a point somewhere over Jasper's head, his face impassive, and said, "Stormlord, it's the Highlord gives us the orders."

"Watch what you say," Jasper snarled. "Taquar is not the Cloudmaster yet. And he won't be until the Council of Rainlords agrees that he is. Is that clear? In the meantime, he may rule this city, but I am a stormlord of the Quartern. I would suggest you don't forget it!"

The man barely hid a smirk. "I serve Lord Taquar." There was a lengthy pause, long enough to be an insult, before he added, "My lord."

Painfully aware that he was friendless in Scarcleft, Jasper narrowed his eyes but said nothing. Jasper let the matter ride. It was between him and Taquar, not him and the enforcers. "All right, let's just walk. I want to see the damage done to the city by the earthquake."

"Of course, m'lord."

When he returned to Scarcleft Hall, it was time for the afternoon session of watershifting. When that was over, he headed back to his own rooms, accompanied by a different pair of Hall guards. Frustrated, he tackled one of them. The armsman was young and if his awkward manners were any indication, awed by being assigned to look after the stormlord.

"What's your name?" Jasper asked.

The man shifted his weight from foot to foot, rather like a child in need of an outhouse. "Dibble Hornblend, m'lord."

"Dibble?"

"A nickname, m'lord. My friends think it amusing. A dibble is used for boring holes."

"Your friends think you are boring?"

"Er, I think it was more they thought me good at digging holes for myself. Getting into trouble, that is, m'lord."

"Ah. What are your orders about me, Dibble?"

"To keep you safe, m'lord."

"How?"

In an apparent agony of embarrassment, Dibble grasped his sword hilt, then removed his hand, looked at it as if he'd never seen it before, and finally clasped both hands behind his back.

Jasper took pity on him. "Perhaps you should just recite your specific orders."

"To never permit anyone to be alone with you, to prevent the approach of strangers, to be at your shoulder with at least one other guard at all times within the Hall, and to have no less than eight guards outside the walls, m'lord."

"Would it be all right one day to go for a ride in The Skirtings?"

Dibble looked appalled. "Oh! Er, I shouldn't think so, m'lord. You could meet some of those marauding red bastards out there."

Of course, silly question.

"I would like to see the damage done to Scarcleft Hall by the earthquake, Dibble. I understand it was worst around the room where that waterpainter girl was confined. Can you show me the place?"

"No, m'lord. I don't know where it is."

"Could you find out?"

"Of course, my lord."

However, when Jasper asked him about it later on that evening, Dibble looked agonised, but finally said the damaged part of the Hall was still dangerous, and no one was allowed entry. It sounded logical enough and Jasper might have believed him, except Dibble was a poor liar and blushed red as he said it.

Jasper concealed a sigh. "Very well. Never mind," he said, and retreated to his room.

In the middle of the night, after lighting a lantern, Jasper ruffled his hair and flung open his bedroom door, the lantern clutched in his hand and an anxious expression fixed on his face. The two guards on duty outside his room immediately sprang to attention.

"I heard a noise at the shutters," he told them. "Take a look and see if anyone is there, will you?"

They crossed the room, opened the shutters and stepped out onto the balcony. While they were staring out into the darkness of the roof garden on the level below, looking for a non-existent intruder, Jasper formed water from the large jar in the water-room into a human shape, then whisked it out into the passage, out of sight.

"Can't see anything, m'lord," one of the guards said a moment later. "Likely a cat, or such."

"Probably." Jasper shrugged. "All right, never mind."

Before either guard moved, he swept the water down the passage past the door. In the dim light cast by a candle lantern outside, it could have been a person. The guards shot out of the room to investigate.

Jasper grinned. He had whisked the water out of sight through one of the passage's unshuttered window slits. When the guards disappeared around the corner, he pulled the water back inside and replaced it in his water-room. He then took advantage of the men's absence to head off in the opposite direction. By the time the guards returned they would find the door firmly shut and Jasper nowhere to be seen. If he was lucky, they would assume the stormlord had returned to bed.

He knew vaguely where he wanted to go. He'd asked the odd question, listened to servants and workmen, and from the outside he'd studied the damage to the Hall and matched it up with what he knew of the interior. Terelle had done the damage herself; he was sure of that, and it would have been greatest where she was imprisoned – otherwise how had she escaped? The thought amused him. Taquar had poked a stick into an ants' nest when he had imprisoned Terelle the water-painter, and he'd been bitten.

After one or two false forays into empty bedrooms, he found the room soon enough. As he shone the lantern around, he was surprised to find it looked as if it had not been touched since Terelle left. There was a gap in the outer wall. One of her paint trays lay upturned on the floor; the chair and desk were still toppled, a candle had rolled from its holder. A painting, freed from its tray, had rolled under the dust-blanketed bed, another was crumpled on the bed.

He righted the desk and put his lantern down. Then he picked up the painting from the bed and gently unrolled it onto the desktop. It was already torn, as if someone had roughly opened it prior to this, but the scene was still recognisable: the entrance to Russet's rooms down on the thirty-sixth level, with the profiled shadow of Terelle herself on the wall. Smiling to himself, he let the painting curl up again. He picked his way over the debris, dust eddying around his feet with every step, to the missing wall, and looked down on the starlit repair work.

Workmen had already cleared most of the tumble of mud bricks and rubble below. New bricks were stacked ready to put in place. He could see the shadowy outline of ladders and bab trunks lashed together as scaffolding.

As he gazed, he tried to imagine what it had been like the day Terelle had looked down on the destruction of the earthquake and risked her life to escape. He thought about her, the turn of her head, the scornful way she would look at him if he said something stupid.

I miss you, he thought. Sandblast, but her absence *hurt*.

He turned to go, then remembered the second painting sticking out from under the bed. It was a portrait of a woman standing outside a door down on Level Thirty-six. He recognised it; Terelle had shown it to him. She'd said Russet Kermes had painted it to show her the power of water-painting. He'd told her it was payment for the soul of an artist, payment for her. She'd thought he was mocking her, an unpleasant habit he had, but she'd changed her mind later.

That painting and the way it had changed had been the bait for the trap Russet had laid for her. It had intrigued her and she'd been snared. Jasper sighed and flung it away in distaste.

Just to make sure there was nothing else he'd missed, he knelt to look under the bed. And found another portrait, this one half dislodged from its now empty tray. It portrayed Taquar lying on the ground, his head at an odd angle like a broken doll. An ugly wound in his chest and an inordinate amount of blood made it clear she had intended to paint the Highlord dead.

But Taquar was still alive. Had her magic failed her? Or had she never tried to shuffle it up? He rolled the painting up, remembering her smile, her laugh. *I loved her,* he thought, and grieved as he tried to come to terms with the knowledge he'd probably never see her again.

"So," said Taquar, "you came here."

Jasper spun around, shocked. He had been so engrossed in his memories he'd been unaware of the Highlord's approach. "How did you find me?" he asked, gathering his scattered wits.

"My guards keep me informed. And as you know, it is easy enough for people like us to track a moving body of water. You are the only person up and about. You even have an added advantage over me. You can tell who a person is by their water." He looked around the room. "So you came here."

"Yes."

"Why?"

"Why not?"

Taquar stood, waiting for him to say something else, but he kept quiet. With growing certainty, Jasper knew his silence was a victory. There was nothing Taquar could do to him now, nothing. He smiled in the darkness, picked up his lantern and walked to the door. As he passed Taquar, he shoved Terelle's painting of him into his hands, saying pleasantly, "Perhaps she wasn't as fond of you as you like to think," and walked back to his room.

The next night, he was dismayed to see that the two sentries outside his room were not Hall guards, but enforcers.

"You're going to marry *Taquar*?"

Jasper stared at Laisa and then started to laugh. She had come to the stormquest room just after lunch on his fourth full day at the Hall and was now seated, swinging an elegantly crossed leg, in one of the upright chairs. He'd been looking at the chart Cloudmaster Granthon had given him, pinpointing all the water catchment sites and detailing how to recognise each using his water-sense.

"Is that so amusing?" she asked.

"Marriage to Taquar? I wish you joy of that!"

"It makes good sense," she said, defensive.

He thought about it. "Perhaps. I'd watch my back if I were you, though. Have you told Senya?"

"No, not yet. Why?"

"Nothing. She may be a little, um, dismayed." The side-long looks and flirtatious smiles Senya had been giving the Highlord since they had arrived in Scarcleft had not escaped his notice.

Her brow wrinkled. "She has a mild infatuation for him, it's true. She'll soon grow out of that."

"Not, I suspect, soon enough. When is the wedding?"

"We have asked Lord Gold to perform the ceremony next Sun Day. Nothing elaborate, given my recent widowhood."

Jasper stared at her. "Lord *Gold*?" he asked. "The Quartern Sunpriest – *that* Lord Gold? He's here? Someone told me he died in the fight for Breccia!"

"Oh, the old one. Yes, he did. But his underling escaped."

"Ah." He added flatly, "That would be the last High Waterpriest, I suppose. Lord Basalt."

"Yes. As the most senior of the waterpriests, he became the new Lord Gold when the old one died. He is making the Sun Temple here in Scarcleft the main seat of the one true faith. I believe he crept out of Breccia before the fighting started with all the regalia in his baggage. He says the old Lord Gold sent him. I wonder if that is true, myself. I suspect he fled the moment he heard Kaneth give the warning that the Reduners were attacking. As a rainlord, he had a good chance of avoiding the Reduners. He's a conniving, money-grubbing sneak if ever there was one."

"Takes one to know one, I suppose. A nasty little man, I agree."

She ignored the insult. "He's already insisting on donations from the faithful to make the temple on Level Three suitable as a place of worship for a Sunpriest." She snorted.

He grimaced inwardly. The man was a religious fanatic, lacking both compassion and tolerance. Worse, he loathed Jasper. In Breccia, he'd been tasked with Jasper's religious education, and had developed a deep – and justified – suspicion of the sincerity of the new stormlord's religious convictions. He was not a man Jasper had any wish to meet again.

When he didn't reply, Laisa added, "You and Senya must give some thought to your own wedding."

He nodded neutrally. "Oh, I will. I will. A lot of thought."

She gave him a sharp look, but changed the subject. "Where's Taquar?"

"I have no idea. After he has brought a cloud out of the sea, he leaves me to do the rest. I am moving a cloud as we speak."

"That's impressive skill – to do it without any signs of stress."

"Moving water is not my problem."

"Taquar has been very secretive about whether you are having any success. That's why I decided to drop by today and find out for myself."

"We have two sessions a day," he said, not seeing any reason why she should not know. "Whatever he can bring out of the ocean, I can shift. Unfortunately, it is about half of what Granthon achieved, even at his sickest. Taquar finds it exhausting. He really isn't a stormlord."

"Ah. That explains his bad temper, I suppose." She was examining her nails, as if they suddenly fascinated her. Without looking up, she said, "He told me he was insisting you fill the Scarcleft mother cistern before you send water elsewhere."

"That's right. He is quite vociferous on the subject."

Her sharp gaze stabbed at him. "Taquar may be too exhausted after your sessions to sense where you send the clouds, Jasper, but I am not. That cloud you are manipulating as we speak is heading off to the north-east, outside the Scarpen. At a guess, you are going to make it rain in the White Quarter."

Sandblast, of course she would feel the cloud; she's not a bad

126

rainlord. I should have thought of that. "Sometimes the clouds wobble across the sky in unexpected ways."

She dismissed that excuse with the contempt it deserved. "Are you mad? Taquar may not have sensed it, but he does have two rainlords in the city's employ, quite apart from waterpriests. True, they are old men, and not particularly talented, but they are experienced. And there's our new Lord Gold. Sooner or later they'll wake up to what is happening, especially if Taquar asks them to watch out for it. Anyway, his reeves will tell him the level of water in our waterhall is not what he expects. You, of all people, should know what he is like. You don't thwart Taquar with impunity."

"So? Without me, his clouds go nowhere. I am the only person who can move them, just as he is the only person who can make them, and only then if he has my help. He's hardly going to kill me. Or even risk making me so furious I won't cooperate."

Laisa gave another snort. "As if you would do that. He reads you like a scroll. You haven't the guts to cut off water to the people of the Scarpen by refusing cooperation."

"Exactly. I won't cut off water – to the people of the *Quartern.*"

She stared at him for a little longer, then shook her head. "Don't come running to me when you rile Taquar, Jasper. There is a point beyond which I won't risk my neck. You are playing a very dangerous game with a very dangerous man."

"Laisa," he said with a sigh, "there's a point beyond which you won't risk a broken fingernail."

Her eyes narrowed, but she didn't waste any breath on a reply.

After she had gone, he continued to work on sketching out a comprehensive programme of water distribution. His biggest problem was that Taquar could not raise much water vapour. He tired too quickly. Their clouds were small.

His second problem was what to do about Qanatend and Breccia, both now in the hands of the Reduner warrior armies. And he had to include Portennabar in the problem too; the port might still have its freedom, but it received its water via tunnels from Breccia. Just thinking about it all was enough to make him feel ill. If he sent storms to the Warthago catchments for those cities, the Reduners would benefit, continue their occupation and steal water to send back to the Red Quarter. If he didn't send storms, the people who thirsted first would be the Scarpen inhabitants, not the Reduners.

He sighed, regretting the limitations of even a stormlord's power. The only way to move large amounts of water, from a distance and over long distances, was through stormshifting clouds. Moreover, to change clouds into water was fiendishly difficult without cooling them first, and it was tough to send the clouds high enough to do that without being aided initially by the updrafts along the slopes of the Warthago Range. Even clouds for the other quarters had to be lifted over the Warthago first, then moved to wherever they needed to be broken.

Always the limitations . . .

If the Sunlord wanted to help us, why the withering winds didn't he just send us regular rain in the first place? The people from across the Giving Sea say it rains all the time there!

He was still mulling over the best course of action when he heard Senya's voice, shrill with indignation, arguing to be let inside.

"You can't go in there like that," Jasper heard a guard say. "The stormlord is cloudshifting – he needs to concentrate."

"*I* need to speak to him!" she snapped. "Is Lord Taquar there too?"

"He left some time ago. If you wait, the stormlord will attend to you when he has completed this cycle of rain."

"He doesn't know I am here!"

"He always knows when someone comes."

She took a deep breath as if to berate him still further, so Jasper opened the door. He inclined his head politely. "Senya. Please come in."

She entered, her ruffled feelings evident in the irritable way she tilted her chin.

"What's the matter?" he asked. He indicated the chair Laisa had vacated. "Sit down. Did you come for a lesson on how we go about cloudshifting?" He waved a hand to take in the shutter flung wide to display a distant view, the book spread out on a lectern close to the window and the table strewn with maps and instruments.

She looked at them vaguely with a complete lack of interest. "It's Mother," she burst out. "She's going to *marry* Taquar!"

He nodded. "Yes, I know."

"You *knew*? Why didn't you *tell* me?"

"It was up to your mother to do that – as I see she has."

"How can she do it? Papa is only just dead! And *Taquar*! If anyone should marry Taquar, it's *me*."

"He's a good deal older than you," Jasper said reasonably, "and your parents have always hoped you would marry me."

"But you're a *nobody* from the Gibber! And I'm the daughter of a highlord, from a long line of stormlords and highlords. Just as Taquar is."

"Actually, from what I understand, Taquar was a nobody from Breakaway. And his mother was from the Gibber. But that's not really the point. The point is that he's childless. The whole point of your marriage – or mine – is to produce water-sensitive children with the potential to be stormlords."

"There's nothing to say *you* would have stormlord children," Senya said. She looked him up and down. "I don't want to marry you. I think you're ugly and stupid and you behave like a – a – *lowleveller*. I *hate* you."

Expressionless, he considered her words. "And if the future of the Quartern depends on having more stormlords?"

She stamped her foot. "I *don't care*. Why should I care about what happens years hence? While you are alive, we are all safe. Why should I have a meddle of half-Gibber brats just in case one of them is a stormlord? Which may never happen?"

He inclined his head. "Good point." He stood up straight, his smile deliberately warm and encouraging. "Why don't we forget the whole thing then?"

Ducking her head, she looked at him through her eyelashes. "But Mama says I must – and so does Taquar—"

"No one can persuade me to marry if I don't want to," he said. "No one can force me to do anything. If I don't want to marry you, I won't."

"Can you talk to them?"

"I will. I promise. Don't worry about it, Senya. You may not get to marry the person you want, but I swear – you'll never have to marry someone you hate."

She blinked, and he suspected she was disconcerted. He went to the door and opened it politely for her to leave. "Thank you," she said in a small voice, as if she was wondering why she felt so dissatisfied.

Once she'd gone, Jasper went to the window and looked out. He stood very still, sensing the water in the sea, feeling its presence: overpowering, seemingly endless.

"Terelle," he murmured aloud. "Oh, blighted eyes, how I wish you were here!"

There was nothing he wanted to do more than ride after her, wherever she was. Nothing he would like more than to rescue her from Russet. He would even have killed the old man to do it.

But he held a secret inside, where it gnawed at him from within, eating away his esteem, his hope, his future. He had analysed his abilities, he had studied all Granthon, then Taquar, did when he helped them to raise clouds from the sea. And beyond all whisper of doubt, he knew the crucial foundation on which to build the ability necessary for that task was absent from his mind. Somewhere in his childhood he had missed the moment to develop the basis for the skill, and so it had atrophied and vanished. He could boost Taquar's power to affect the change but the technique – the magic – was all the rainlord's.

I am never going to be able to change salt water to pure water vapour.

Which meant he was forever tethered to a man he despised. *For the rest of my life . . .*

10

Scarpen Quarter
Scarcleft City, Scarcleft Hall, Level 2
Sun Temple, Level 3

Jasper had more time on his hands than he'd expected. He could have worked much harder and longer hours, but Taquar could not. Or would not.

He filled his spare time in a number of ways. His priority was to study all the documents and information Cloudmaster Granthon had given him on stormbringing until he knew it all by heart. To improve his fighting skills and keep fit, he asked Taquar's permission for some of the Scarcleft Hall guards to become his sparring partners.

"Practice your blade skills?" the Highlord asked, amused. "Think you'll be good enough to take me on one day?"

Jasper shrugged. "I doubt it. Anyway, we both know I will never be able to give you the death you deserve. You are too valuable to the people of the Scarpen. My sword practice keeps me fit and prepared for the day the Reduner hordes ride down on Scarcleft, that's all."

"Fine. Keep fit, by all means, but allow me to worry about Davim. He will not approach this city, never fear."

Even with the sword practice, the cloudshifting and his self-imposed studies, there was not enough to fill all his time, and it was therefore almost a relief when – after he had been in Scarcleft ten days – Jasper received a request from the new Lord Gold to present himself at the temple on Level Three. Almost. His memories of the man's ill-concealed dislike, his uncompromising religious pedantry and his hypocrisy were too fresh in his mind for there to be any real pleasure in the idea that the Quartern Sunpriest wished to see him. He thought of insisting, just to make a point, that Lord Gold come to Scarcleft Hall to meet him rather than the other way around, but decided it would be more interesting to visit the Sun Temple.

In the end, it was Lord Gold who made the point by keeping him waiting for half the run of a sandglass. Jasper didn't have the slightest doubt the withering petty bastard had intended it as an insult.

When an acolyte finally ushered him into the office on the top floor of the temple's tower, Gold was standing talking to a waterpriest, a man whose spine was hunched with the gnarling of old age. They stood beside a large desk and matching chair, all made of hardwood, itself an extravagance considering the scarcity of trees. The other chairs in the room were made of bab palm. The ceiling above had skylights, unglassed holes positioned to allow direct sunlight to beam in at different times of the day. The man Jasper had known from Breccia as Lord Basalt was now standing in a pool of light. The other man stood where he was untouched by the sun's rays.

He timed it, Jasper thought, incredulous. *Just so that when I entered, he'd be illuminated by the Sunlord's radiance.* He almost laughed. "Lord Gold," he said, inclining his head.

"Stormlord." Basalt nodded in turn. "I do not think you have yet met the High Waterpriest of Scarcleft City, have you? This is Lord Taminy."

Jasper murmured a greeting; the other man bowed. "It is a pleasure to know we have a stormlord once more,"

Taminy said. "Forgive me for not presenting myself at the Hall to welcome you, but Lord Taquar informed me you have been too tired."

Did he indeed? "Being the Quartern's only stormlord is an exhausting task," Jasper said blandly. "However, I am sure I will benefit from the walk down here today."

"I understand Lord Taquar is doing much to help you," Basalt said.

"He tries," Jasper said. "However, he is not a stormlord and cannot stormshift." *There, Taquar, you will learn it is unwise not to give me my due . . .* "Tell me, don't you feel a little unsafe using the tower in its present state? I understand the top was damaged in the earthquake. I notice there is still scaffolding around it."

"The Sunlord protects his own," Basalt said, his tone admonishing.

"He certainly protected you," Jasper agreed amiably. "I'm amazed you managed to escape from Breccia. There was so little time between the warning and the Reduner attack. You must have moved quickly."

"The previous Lord Gold and I had my escape planned. Just in case."

"Ah. A far-sighted man. It is a pity he did not arrange his own escape. I must admit, I am surprised you have taken on the mantle of his post without waiting for confirmation from other senior waterpriests of the Quartern."

He knew he'd hit a raw nerve when he saw Taminy look away uncomfortably.

"And just how can anyone obtain such confirmation?" Basalt asked, sour-faced. "There is hardly an open line of communication to the priests of Breccia or Qanatend at the present time, if any are still alive. There is, however, a need for continuity of prayer and worship and leadership. The other cities have been informed."

134

"Informed?"

"They were informed that I have taken on that mantle. It is, after all, normal for the High Waterpriest of Breccia to become the next Sunpriest. And the Cloudmaster assented. But there is no need to concern yourself with temple matters."

"The Cloudmaster? We have a Cloudmaster?"

Basalt blinked in surprise. "Lord Taquar is Cloudmaster!"

"It is my understanding that after the death of the last Cloudmaster, a new one needs to be confirmed by his peers. There has been no such confirmation. Lord Taquar is not yet the Cloudmaster. Nor was he the heir, either. Cloudmaster Granthon withdrew that post from him on evidence that he was a traitor to the Quartern."

"Without Lord Taquar there is no Quartern! He tells me we would thirst to death without his aid to you."

"You'd thirst to death without *me*, Lord Gold."

Taminy looked sick with worry. Basalt, however, was purple, with anger Jasper guessed, although he was managing to keep it under control.

"These matters are not your concern," Basalt snapped. "I asked you to come because your spiritual health concerns me."

"Just as your health – and the health of all the Quartern's people – concerns me. No one will be particularly healthy if there's no water."

"You cannot have a truly healthy body without a healthy spiritual life. And your spirituality has always been suspect. You are our only stormlord. You must be seen to be pious and devout. You should *be* devout."

"Oh, I am." *Devout about doing my job, anyway.* "I just feel it is more important I stormshift, than that I be seen at the Temple, spending my time in prayer."

"You have the power to stormshift only through the Sunlord and the gift of knowledge made to the Watergiver. You must be seen to give thanks for their gifts at the Temple.

And you should continue to receive spiritual teaching from me or one of my colleagues until you have a full understanding of the nature of our faith. I am sure Lord Taminy can arrange for a suitable teacher."

"I already have a deep understanding of your faith, Lord Gold. And I shall, of course, present myself at the Temple for festival days such as the Gratitudes. You have my solemn undertaking."

"The understanding of faith is a lifetime undertaking—"

"For a priest, such a lifetime undertaking is indeed a necessity. I hope you, for example, are indeed growing in your faith and piety. I trust you will pray for my spiritual well-being as I am sure I am not as steadfast as I should be. I shall have to rely on your prayers to guide me, in fact, Lord Gold, seeing as the Sunlord has seen fit to put me in a situation requiring constant use of power and its debilitating consequences, leaving me no time to attend to religious study. I feel sure you will be a great source of comfort and spiritual sustenance to me with your prayers. And now, if you will excuse me, I need to return to my more, er, temporal duties."

Basalt's face was dark with suppressed rage, but he inclined his head and said, "Lord Taminy will see you out."

As the High Priest escorted Jasper down the stairs, the rainlord waterpriest said neutrally, "Lord Gold feels you mock him and the one true faith."

"And you, Lord Taminy? Do you agree with him?"

"I do not know you well enough to say, Lord Jasper. Although Lord Gold informs me that you came under the influence of a person from Khromatis while living on Level Thirty-six."

Jasper's interest quickened. "Do you know anything about Khromatis, Lord Taminy? And what has my acquaintance with someone from there got to do with anything at all?"

"They are blasphemers, my lord, denying our faith,

usurping the story of the Holy Watergiver and making it their own. Contact with them is the reason the Alabasters are heretics! The people of Khromatis taught the 'Basters to deny that the sun is the outward manifestation of the Sunlord, pouring his beneficence down upon us. It is of concern to Lord Gold that you have come under the influence of such a blasphemer. They are anathema to our faith."

"I assure you, Lord Taminy, the man from Khromatis whom I met did not alter my faith by as much as a grain of sand."

"I think Lord Gold was referring to a woman, my lord."

"A *woman*? I know no women from Khromatis."

Taminy frowned. "I am sure he said a young woman."

"Perhaps he was thinking of a friend of mine, Terelle Grey. If so, he is mistaken as to her origins. She is Gibber-born and has never set foot in Khromatis, let alone been taught anything of their faith. She sacrifices to the Sunlord."

"I am relieved to hear it."

To Jasper's amusement, he did indeed appear relieved. They stepped out into the sun at the foot of the tower just then and the heat blasted down on them. *I could wish for a little less of the Sunlord's beneficence*, he thought wryly.

"My lord," Taminy said, clearing his throat in an embarrassed fashion. "I do know it is unwise to tease Lord Gold. He has a low threshold for insult, imagined or otherwise. I also know it is unwise not to give due respect to the Sunlord and his Watergiver. They are the bringers of life – without them there would be no sun and no water. They are to be adored, and are mocked at your peril in this life and the life beyond. Have a care, my lord."

"Indeed I shall. This land depends on my continued good health."

"You will have my prayers."

Jasper smiled. "I have an idea that yours will be more

137

sincerely meant than the new Lord Gold's. My thanks, Lord Taminy."

As he walked back to Scarcleft Hall, flanked by both guards and enforcers, he dismissed Lord Gold from his mind. The man was a small-minded bigot, and there was no way he could bring trouble to the only stormlord the Quartern had.

11

White Quarter
The Whiteout

As Terelle and Russet continued to descend from the highlands around Fourcross Tell, they made slow progress. They had left the caravan route to Samphire City, and there was no track the way they were heading. The pede picked its way, plodding along with a stoic refusal to be hurried.

The scenery around them was strange, alien. The creeping vegetation was something Terelle had never seen before: a plant of plump stems but no leaves, or nothing she thought of as leaves. It was purple and green, a sea of it drowning all other growth.

"Samphire," Russet said. "Grows at lake edge."

"Lake?" She looked up, but all she could see beyond the samphire was a plain of white. A breeze gusting in swirls on the dazzling flats also teased against her face, leaving its residue. She touched her cheek and looked down at her fingers. "That's *salt*."

"A lake sometimes, every ten years or so, in Time of Random Rain. Be so again, if that obstinate Gibberboy not bring back planned storms. Use your head. How ye think it like that, if not water once?" He waved a hand. "Great inland sea . . . saltier than Giving Sea. Birds be coming from everywhere to nest and eat pink shrimps."

"Shrimps? Aren't they like *fish*?" People raised fish in the grove cisterns, but never shrimp. She had heard, though, that the very rich imported salted shrimp from the coast. She stared in disbelief at the salt. "Out there?"

"So they say."

Terelle found it hard to believe, but conceded the Whiteout's beauty. "It is almost splendid," she said, considering the hard sparkle of it, the bobbled edge of purple and green a contrast to the purity of the glittering white. She'd expected it to be dirty-coloured, like the salt blocks arriving in Scarcleft always were, but this stretched as far as she could see, so bright it hurt the eyes, white without end. Only the edges were grubby, dragging in the dust of the bordering earth.

"It's so hot out there. The pede will need a lot of water. What if—"

"Worry, worry, worry! Why ye worry so much? We get safely other side! Otherwise, how my painting ever come true?"

She felt sick. His faith in his painting agitated her with its implications.

"Anyway, Whiteout salt mines have tunnels bringing water, just like Scarpen cities. The pede can be finding it for us."

Her stomach lurched in doubt. "Can you be *sure* of that?"

His injury had made no difference to his arrogance. He didn't bother to reply. "Harness pede. Eat bab fruit as we go."

A few minutes later, as he struggled back on to the pede, she saw the calf of his leg. Red and inflamed, the skin stretched tight over the swelling was shiny. She wanted to protest, to say something, but the look he gave her stopped the words.

"We go on, girl," he said.

The salt penetrated everything. It coated everything. Sometimes the air was so still even the intake of breath was an effort. At other times the winds came: hot, salt-laden winds playing across the surface of the dried-up lake, stirring the crystals into white eddies, bombarding them both with tiny splinters. No matter how well Terelle wrapped herself against the onslaught, the salt grains infiltrated every crevice. Her eyes were soon red and sore, her toes inflamed, her lips cracked. If she used pede fat on her skin to protect against the worst of the sun and the drying wind, then the salt stuck to her like a dusting of the powder Opal's handmaidens used.

She brushed the pede even more carefully than usual each time they stopped, but the beast was in misery. In between the segment plates, the salt irritated its skin until it bled. Pain made it trumpet its distress, turning its head this way and that, as if it sought to find its attacker. Terelle rubbed the worst places with fat, and wondered what they would do when the tub of ointment was empty.

Lit by the blue light of stars at night and sheened with a luminous glow, the saltscape had a raw beauty. It begged to be painted. Yet Terelle could think only that Russet's stubbornness was going to kill them both. True, they had not seen any Reduners, probably because no Reduner was sun-fried crazy enough to cross this vast salt pan.

At times, her thoughts drifted to Shale. To his promise of protection. She would smile softly at the memory, choosing to recall not the irony of his inability to uphold the pledge, but the nobility of his intention. When she thought of the Reduners riding south into the Scarpen, a tear trickled down her cheek, washing a track through the dusting of white.

Loneliness set her dreaming of what might have been – futile, silly visions of a world that never could be, at least not to a Gibber girl sold to traders for water tokens. She knew her thoughts were foolish, but let them wander anyway. What she wanted, she would never have: Shale's hand in hers, Shale seated behind her right now, his hands holding her by the waist, whispering promises in her ear.

She turned her face to the sky and silently sent her thoughts questing, not even sure what power it was she queried. *Was it too much to want?* she asked. *Just to have one friend?*

When Terelle woke early the next morning, she lay for a moment staring at the sky. In the east, the stars were fading, then vanishing as the dawn light crept higher.

Another day. There was no way it would be a good one.

And you, my girl, have to stop whining and whingeing and feeling sorry for yourself. It's no use looking back. That life is behind you. Now you have to make the best of what's ahead.

And the first thing was to stay alive in order to have a life. When they set off once more, she gave the pede its head.

Russet roused himself enough to complain after they had been travelling an hour or two. "We've swung too far south," he protested.

"I'm letting the pede choose the route."

"Why? Don't need water yet!"

"The pede needs more than we can give it. Besides, you need help. Getting me to Khromatis will gain you nothing if you are dead."

"I be not dying!"

"You will be if you don't get help. I want to find the tunnel. We'll follow it to the nearest mining settlement."

"Don't be stupid, girl. You *know* we get through this. I painted you there, in mountains!"

"You didn't paint yourself, old man." His painting had portrayed her next to running water on a green hillside. His clothing had been in the painting – but not him. A painter could not paint himself to ensure his own future. He tried to argue with her, but she didn't listen and he was too weak to offer any physical resistance. The pede plodded on.

142

They stopped during the heat of the day, but when Terelle went to groom the animal she was shocked at how hot the black carapace was under her touch. Even the underlying skin connecting the segments felt much too warm. Alarmed, she looked across at Russet where he sat lifting a water skin to his lips. "The pede is feverish," she said.

"Pedes don't get fever. Desert creatures," he said in scorn, but she wondered if he would really know something like that.

She said slowly, "The people of the White Quarter own white pedes. White reflects heat. Number Twelve is far too hot. It's burning up, and there doesn't seem to be nearly as much water in its tissues as there should be."

"Don't bother me," he muttered. "Stop worrying. I be painting you there . . ." He lay down in the shade she had erected and closed his eyes.

Troubled, she patted the pede's head, but it didn't seem to have enough energy to raise its eye mantle to look at her. Its feelers lay flat to the ground, unmoving. She wondered if she should give it more water, and was torn. If the pede died, they were doomed. To continue on foot would be ridiculous; she had glimpsed the peaks of the mountains as an unevenness along the horizon, but they were still far away. She had no idea in what direction Samphire City lay, and no idea where the salt pan's water tunnels were. They couldn't even retrace their route because the wind had teased away the footprints. Besides, Russet was hardly able to stand, let alone walk. They *had* to have the pede, not just to ride, but to find the water of the tunnel.

Wryly resolute, she took up one of the water skins and offered the spout to the animal, letting it sense the water through its mouth. It did not stir. She even poured a little of the precious liquid into its gullet, but it gave no sign of caring. It wasn't dead yet though; she knew that. It still made odd snuffling noises, and occasionally clattered its segments in a shrug.

Not knowing what else she could do, she lay down to rest. Whatever happened, they couldn't move until the heat was gone from the sun.

When she woke, late in the afternoon, it seemed no cooler – and the pede was dead. For a moment she couldn't absorb the enormity of that. It was impossible, surely. For that huge a beast to die so quickly, without her even being aware of it, without a struggle, without a sound. She reached out and forced up the mantle that covered its eyes, wondering if she could be mistaken. Begging that she was.

The eyes were sunken, unseeing, speaking of nothing but an absence of life. In shock, she struggled to maintain her resolution. The disaster was too huge, too fraught with dire outcomes, all of them now probably unavoidable.

After several deep breaths, she went to wake Russet, only to find him delirious. He called her Sienna, her mother's name, and shouted at her angrily, asking why she had hankered after an eel-catcher, why she had run away. "Ye could have been Pinnacle!" he cried out in anger. "Don't ye be knowing how much I wanted to be Pinnacle? But no – I be not good enough for them. I not be having Pinnacle blood in my veins . . ." And then the words disintegrated into meaningless syllables.

Terelle sat back on her heels, thinking. Russet could not possibly walk, yet if he didn't, they had no chance.

Unless his waterpainting had been powerful enough. If so, then it ensured she at least would reach the land of the Watergivers one day. All she had to do was wait where she was and she'd be rescued, possibly Russet along with her. But could she rely on that? She didn't know enough about water-painting magic to be sure. Maybe if he died, and the magic of the paintings with him, then she could die as well, without ever reaching the water of Khromatis. Even if he didn't die, maybe as he grew weaker, so would the effects of his water-painting. She tried to assess whether her drive to go towards the mountains had lessened, but couldn't be sure.

"Blighted eyes," she growled, "I hate magic."

Nonetheless, she rummaged in her pack and took out her waterpaints to have a look at them. She had everything she needed: paints, tray, the last of their water. Russet had once said you couldn't paint the impossible and expect it to happen. But she could paint something sensible showing Russet being saved. A party of Alabasters riding up to their camp? But if she did, could she be sure she did not hurt someone else? What if one of the people who came to save them died *because* they came? She knew in her heart there was no way she could ever be certain. When you messed with the future, you had to be prepared to change other people's lives as well, not necessarily for the better. It was *wrong*.

She looked down at the old man and shook her head in exasperation. Here she was, wondering how to save Russet, when she should have been taking the opportunity to rid herself of him. Here she was, in danger of dying a slow and torturous death of thirst because of him, and yet she couldn't just walk away.

Life definitely wasn't fair – but at least she no longer expected it to be. She gave a snort of sardonic amusement and said, "I think I'm going to die because of you, old man, and I don't even *like* you."

One thing she did know for certain, she was *never* going to give up.

For the rest of that day and for the entirety of the next, Terelle worked. She used Russet's knife to strip off some of the cara-pace from the dead pede. It was a horrible job, difficult and messy and smelly. Fortunately, the worst of the smell dissipated after a few hours as the flesh dried out, but it was hard not to feel guilty. They had asked too much of the animal, and it had suffered a cruel death.

Trying not to think of that, she separated two segment pieces from the carcass and cleaned out all the flesh, which she cut up and laid out to dry in the sun. The legs and the thick skin of the underbelly she discarded. She set fire to the remains of the pede, using the oil from its own glands to fuel the blaze. It made a pillar of black, greasy smoke rising straight up into the air, a signal to anyone within several days' journey. She had no confidence anyone would actually respond. Why should they? If they were Alabasters, they would probably think it a Reduner trap. If they were Reduners, they wouldn't be interested in someone else's troubles.

While it burned, contaminating the air with an unpleasant acridity, she placed the two cleaned segments inner side upwards, lengthways one behind the other on the salt. They were vaguely boat-shaped, flattish in the middle but then curved upwards into a broad prow at either end. They dried out quickly in the heat. Using the point of the knife, she punched holes in the ends of each and linked them with twine. The result looked vaguely like a two-part insect, over-turned and legless. She lined one of the segments with the two blankets they had, then made a harness out of some of their clothes so she could pull the segments along behind her, like a sled.

When she'd finished, she straightened up to look around. In the far distance white figures cavorted, coalescing and parting, shivering and stretching.

Look, Terelle, sand-dancers . . . No. Salt-dancers, that's what they are . . .

She laughed, finding her own thought hugely funny.

Then she sobered. During the day and a half of the prepar-ations, she had restricted her water intake as much as she

146

could bear. Now that she had finished the sled, she was light-headed and finding it hard to think straight.

Russet was in a worse state. He lay unheeding, drifting in and out of delirium. His leg was still red and swollen, although it didn't seem to be worsening. He drank when she gave him water, he muttered and moaned when she touched him – but no more than that. When everything was ready, she laid him inside the padded segment. The curvature meant it could not have been comfortable, but he wasn't conscious enough to complain. Surprised to find how light he was, she had the fanciful feeling he was just a husk, that the real man had long since gone.

Blown away on the wind, maybe. No, not the wind, the salt-dancers. Maybe they took him . . .

She shook her head and frowned. Sunlord, her brains were frizzled. Russet wasn't dead. Concentrating, she packed into the second segment the items they needed: the remaining water, food, the shade cloth and its support poles, cloaks. She picked up her waterpaints, but put them down again. *Wrong. It's wrong. That little boy who died in the earthquake . . .* Reality faded into dream. Her resolution remained true, but the reason for it was blurring. *Thirst. Sunlord help me, I am so thirsty.*

She would not risk any innocent lives for either Russet or herself. That was the truth. *Hold on to it. You can do this without magic.*

When she set off pulling the makeshift sled, it glided along on the salt as easily as a snake slithering across the plains.

Behind her, the pile of unnecessary items was a dwindling dark patch on a white background. Behind her, the wind blew and silted salt into the paint trays, while the pede still burned.

She walked all night into the dawn of the next day, taking only the occasional short break. At night, there were the stars to help, but after the first day, the mountain peaks dropped out of sight beneath the horizon and she couldn't tell which way she was heading when the sun was high in the sky. Once that happened, she rested, dozing fitfully, only to wake and start again towards sunset.

Every step was a struggle against the drag of the sled. Every step was a struggle against the urge she still had to head towards Khromatis.

Another day. Thirst, and more thirst. And heat. The temperature – even under the shade of a makeshift cover she constructed with the bab matting and the pede segments – quickly became unbearable. Her throat scorched, her skin shrivelled. Her exposed skin was red and sore, although she had done her best to protect herself. The water they carried became more than a temptation; it was a torture. She knew she had to make it last, but she also knew she needed it *now*. Worse as the day wore on. Burning. Skin on fire, loose over her bones like borrowed clothes that didn't fit. And Russet, so hot. Delirious.

As she lay there under the meagre shade, her mind drifted, focused and drifted yet again. She shook her water skin and assessed what was left. Enough for the next day if she was careful; after that . . . well, neither of them would last more than a day without water. Not in this heat.

Look, the salt-dancers are back. Undulating. Like Arta Amethyst. Once I was a dancer, too.

She dozed in uncomfortable snatches, sleep born of exhaustion, not normal need. In the evening, when it was cool enough to go on, she set off again, the segments dragging behind her.

Another night of walking. Salt coated her, rubbed her skin raw, gummed up her eyelashes. Her shoulders ached. The shiny surface of the pede segments wore away, and the sled no longer slid across the salt with such slickness. Her slow plod became the dragging steps of an old woman; her hope faltered further as she began to stumble.

Thirst, waterless soul, the thirst . . .

She thought of Shale. He wouldn't really give himself up to Taquar because of her silly letter, would he? And Taquar. The way he had touched her hair. She must never meet him again. Not ever, because he would never let her go. She knew that look he had given her. She'd seen it before, on the faces of some of the men who came to the snuggery: looks that coveted, on men who were consumed with greed. Like Huckman, the pedeman who'd wanted to buy her first-night.

The earthquake, had she killed Vivie in the earthquake? And Amethyst, who had helped her escape the snuggery – what of her? No, she was dead. How could she have forgotten that? The knife in her chest. Taquar had knifed her . . . *Was that my fault too?* She couldn't remember. *Oh, sand hells, my mind is wandering.*

The next time she stumbled, she fell. The effort it took to rise was nightmarish.

The following morning as she set up camp for the day, she staggered and fell several times, everything taking three times longer to do than it had the morning before. She looked at Russet through gummed lashes and cursed him. "I don't care if you are my great-grandfather, old man," she shouted. "What you did was not right and I despise you for it!" But her throat was so dry her tongue stuck to the roof of her mouth and the words didn't sound right.

He gave no sign he had heard her.

She knelt at his side to lift his head so he could drink. He took the water eagerly, and seemed to revive. As she went to move away, he grabbed her by the wrist. "Paint!" he admonished. "Paint for us."

"All right," she said, and hunted for her paints.

They weren't there. She sat back on her heels and remembered: she'd left them behind.

She had cut Russet off from the one hope of survival

he had. Even in refusing to use her skills, she could kill. Her stomach cramped and she threw up a dribble of precious fluid.

There was no more water left. None.

When Terelle could go no further, she set up the camp and lay down in the heat. Russet was quiet now. He no longer moaned or moved. He wasn't dead; she could still see the slight rise and fall of his chest, if she bothered to look. But she didn't bother too much now; her own pain consumed her. At times she seemed to float, drifting over the salt, borne on a wave of heat so intense it had physical dimension. At times she could hear voices: Madam Opal, her smile avaricious, telling her she would make a good whore; Vivie, annoyed, telling her she had to come back; Shale, upset, telling her she had to go to Breccia City; Taquar, smiling, his hand stroking her hair, telling her she had to come to his bed; Amethyst, her bodice all bloody, telling her not to dance; Jomat, fat and greasy, telling her to go back to the brothel where she belonged; Russet, gloating, telling her she had to go to the mountains. Everyone ordering her to do this or that, shouting at her, angry with her. She cried, weeping without water for tears, begging to be left alone. To have some choices. To have *any* choice.

Pain, so much pain. Abraded, salted fingers. Eyelids glued, having to be wrenched apart. Grit on the eyeballs, burning blistered skin, cramping stomach, urine so hot it burned – then none at all. Thoughts of Shale, trapped in another kind of cage, Taquar lusting after her. Or was that Huckman? Guilt as sharp as jabbing spears, blaming her. Russet asking why she had not used her waterpainting to save him. Deaths to be laid at her door.

Sand-dancers – salt-dancers? – gyrated at distant pools of water, to mock her. They bred along the horizon, doubling, trebling, shivering, but never allowed approach; the pools dried up when she stared at them, and re-formed the moment she looked away, to torment the edge of her vision.

White salt, glaring at her, hurting her eyes, white everything, everything white: sky, land, skin, sun, salt, eyes.

Whiteout.

And then little pinpoints of light, flashing and dancing like the glow-worms of a waterhall; colours so pretty she wanted to reach up and touch them. There were red lines snaking from one glow-worm to the next, runnels of blood, surely, and disembodied voices telling her to drink, drink this, sip that. And it felt so good. Water in her throat. Sweetness. Moisture on her lips, dampness on her eyelids, coolness on her forehead. Sparkles of light, dazzling in their brightness, making her blink and close her salt-sore eyes.

Salt-dancers are real, she thought. *And they sparkle. So beautiful.*

Water, all the water she desired. Whiteness. Voices in her head. White hands, bloodless faces. Rubbing her skin with something soft and moist. Bathing her eyes. Those red lines and sparkles: threads and mirrors. Alabasters. The white people of this white land of the White Quarter.

Something made her speak. "Scorpion". He was stung by a scorpion.

Voices replied, assuring, kindly.

A tear ran down her cheek, and she let herself slip away.

151

12

"Lord Gold tells me the clouds we raised this morning went to Breakaway, not to the catchment area for Scarcleft, as I ordered."

Taquar sat at his desk in his study, his long fingers playing with his knife, his thumbs rubbing up and down the carved hilt. His voice was heavy with suppressed rage; his grey eyes sharp as the blade. Laisa was sitting on the embrasure of one of the windows, neatly peeling an orange plucked from one of the potted trees on the balcony. She smiled pleasantly in Jasper's direction, as if to compensate for Taquar's abrupt words. Basalt was standing by the open shutters of the next window, his expression rigid with dislike.

Inwardly Jasper sighed. Perhaps it had been a mistake to rile the Sunpriest. *But words are all I have left.* "So?" he asked Taquar. "This city has enough to last for a while, if we are careful. My calculations tell me Breakaway must be dangerously low in supply, even if they have been frugal in their usage."

"I don't care about Breakaway!" Taquar's rage blazed at him.

Jasper quirked an eyebrow. "I thought that's where you were born?"

"What of it? It is an irrelevance! I want Scarcleft to have full cisterns before we start thinking about others. That's an order, Jasper."

"He is not going to obey you," Basalt said.

Jasper could glean nothing from his tone, but he nodded in agreement. "I'm the stormlord. I make the decisions with regard to the placement of our storms."

"I am not against Breakaway receiving water," Basalt said. "Indeed, it is your duty to supply all those who worship the Sunlord. But yesterday's rain went somewhere to the east. It certainly did not fall within the boundaries of the Scarpen."

"So, we only water those who follow the same faith?"

"The faith which gave us the knowledge of watershifting! The Sunlord himself gives us water sensitives our power. He gave *you* your power, Lord Jasper. Obviously, the Sunlord wanted *us* to survive. Those who scorn our faith must surely be a secondary consideration. If they were of concern to the Sunlord, then he would have ensured there are many more stormlords, which would enable us to consider the needs of the heathens in the Gibber and the White Quarter."

Jasper narrowed his gaze and regarded the Sunpriest with dislike he did not try to conceal. "May I remind you, my lord, that I – your only stormlord – was Gibber born and raised? Yet you dismiss my place of birth with such easy scorn."

There was a moment of silence, so still it seemed to Jasper that everyone had stopped breathing.

Basalt took a deep breath. "I apologise, my lord. It was not my intention to insult you, of course. The Sunlord has indeed blessed you, but you have assured me that you do not scorn our faith."

"Ah. You do feel, though, that it is the Sunlord's fault the Gibber and White Quarter thirst?"

"Obviously. What other explanation is there? It lay within

153

his power to make it otherwise, and he did not. Still does not."

Laisa interrupted. "Enough of theology, both of you. Keep it for your sermons, Lord Gold." She smiled in the Sunpriest's direction to take the sting from her words, and popped an orange segment into her mouth.

Taquar ignored her. "Jasper – is Lord Gold correct in what he said? You sent yesterday's clouds to the Gibber?"

It hurt him to ask that, Jasper thought. *He so hates having to rely on another* . . . "Yes, it is true," he said. "Are you accusing Lord Gold of lying?"

"Of course I'm not. Although he could be mistaken."

Jasper shifted his gaze back to Basalt. "He's a little disdainful of your abilities, isn't he, my lord?"

Taquar stood up, saying, "I will not create clouds in order to have you squander them on the Gibber!"

Laisa slipped down from her seat at the window and came to stand beside him. She ate the last piece of the orange and dumped the peel in a heap on his desk. "Dear me, both of you, this is not worth an argument. Jasper, be a little conciliatory."

Jasper gave a shrug of acquiescence and addressed Taquar. "No one in Scarcleft will ever die of thirst, I promise. Other than that, you are just going to have to let me be the judge of where water goes and where it doesn't. That is my job as stormlord, and Granthon and Nealrith tutored me well."

"Lord Gold," Laisa said, at her most charming, "I think it's time we took our leave. These men have things to discuss." Without waiting for any reaction from Taquar, she took Basalt firmly by the arm and headed for the door.

After the two had left, Jasper remarked, heavily sarcastic, "Laisa, being tactful and pressing for cooperation. What *did* you say to her?"

"I don't like your attitude," Taquar snapped. "You need to show respect for your elders."

"Perhaps I would, if my elders respected me. Still, Laisa is right. We need to work together. She has spoken of little else since I arrived. And I am willing to make this more of a cooperative venture, if you are."

"You will follow my directives, Jasper."

"Or what? You'll keep me prisoner somewhere?"

"It's an idea."

"Not one you'd have any success with, I feel. Firstly, I could kill any guard you sent against me with my water-powers. Secondly, you need my cooperation to keep your city supplied. Thirdly, you will need my help if the Council of Rainlords makes you the administrative Cloudmaster. Without my cooperation, it won't happen. We have to work together. You know it – accept it."

There was a long silence while they stared at each other. Taquar spoke first. "I'm guessing you have some conditions in mind."

Jasper flung himself down in the chair next to the table. "Let's start with my concessions. I am willing to tell you where I am sending the storms and why. I will listen to whatever reasons you have for disagreeing. Scarcleft will be the last to suffer real water deprivation. I shall try to be reasonable in my demands, if you do likewise. I won't go anywhere without the guards you assign. I will marry Senya eventually, if she wants. When she is more, um, mature. Otherwise I will marry the girl you brought back from the Gibber, the one Nealrith said was going to be a rainlord. She's being trained in Pediment, I think."

He forced down the lump in his throat. *I'm sorry, Terelle. I'm so, so sorry.* "Those are my concessions."

"And your conditions?" Taquar asked.

Jasper reached out, picked up a piece of orange peel and

started to make patterns on it with his fingernail without looking at the Highlord. "I want to meet the teachers. The men from Scarcleft Academy who sent me the lessons when I was locked in the mother cistern. I want to continue my learning."

"Very well. Anything else?"

"I want to go to a snuggery."

"*What?*" Taquar stared at him, his astonishment jerking him out of his anger.

"I want to visit a snuggery. I'm a man, yet I've never lain with a woman. There is no way Senya is ready for marriage yet; at least not to me. She has a great more growing up to do. But I have needs."

"What in all the dry dust do Senya's feelings matter? We must have more stormlords! Blighted eyes, Jasper, how long do you think I can keep this up? You've been here a bare fifteen days and already I am exhausted. I have no idea how long it will be before you are able to create water vapour from the sea without my aid. I am already looking at years of this horror, and you want to add to it by postponing a marriage that might produce another stormlord?"

Hearing the man's desperation, Jasper was torn between irritation and amusement. "If Senya hates the sight of me, we are not likely to achieve the aim of having stormlord heirs. She needs time. Oh, and by the way –" he sought and held Taquar's gaze "– you have considerable gall to require *me* to remedy a situation *you* yourself are responsible for. If you hadn't killed all the other potential stormlords of your generation, we wouldn't be in this predicament."

Taquar stared at him, his gaze as hard as flint. "I do not know what you are referring to."

"Yes, you do." Jasper met the rainlord's look calmly. "You seem to think you can lie to me, Taquar. You can't. Not any more. You killed young rainlords you thought were going to be stormlords and thus a threat to your dreams of power."

"Who told you that?"

"No one." When Taquar was silent, he added, "Sandblighted hells, you told me about those young men and women yourself – and you blamed *Nealrith* for their deaths! *Nealrith*? Once I had met the man, how could I possibly think that was true? How could I possibly believe even you *thought* it true? A kinder, gentler man never lived than Nealrith Almandine, and you must have known that. But I can believe *you* guilty of murder. Oh, I can believe it *so* easily."

"And on the basis of that you intend to accuse me? Just whose deaths are you accusing me of, by the way? Those who died in accidents? Or of illness? The one who committed suicide? The two friends of mine who perished in the desert at the same time I almost died?"

"Oh, I doubt you were in any danger. I reckon you killed at least four people, Taquar. Five if you include Iani's Lyneth. Iani certainly believed it once I gave him her bracelet. The one you so carelessly left in the mother cistern."

Taquar stilled, his usual bland expression swamped by one of shock. Finally he asked, "And just what is your purpose in telling me this?"

"To let you know you have very little chance of ever being credible outside of Scarcleft ever again unless I am at your side, supporting you. Otherwise, this is it, all the power you'll ever have. Me and Scarcleft. And without me, you will have nothing. And I don't like it any more than you do. I am assuming that at the moment you are biding your time. Waiting for Davim and the Reduners to withdraw before you make your move to assert your claim to be Cloudmaster."

"I could always leave instead. Live across the Giving Sea."

"If you want to risk the unknown. In the Gibber they say, 'Better the scorpion whose sting you know than the spindevil who twists in ways unknown.'" Jasper threw the orange peel back on the desk. His heart was beating uncomfortably fast, but he ignored that. "We were talking about me visiting a snuggery."

There was another pause before Taquar answered. "If you want a girl, I'll have one brought here for you."

"I prefer to choose my own."

"Then I'll have several brought here."

"Taquar, I am going to visit a snuggery. I am giving you advance warning so you can tell your sandblasted enforcers to allow me to do so. If they try to stop me, I will take action – and they will have to decide whether they want to die in your service or kill the nation's only stormlord. If they can." He frowned, as if that was an interesting puzzle. "I wonder what they would do."

Taquar eyed him as if he had suddenly realised he had a viper by the tail. It was not a look that reassured Jasper. A shiver of fear crept up his spine.

Suddenly Taquar smiled, relaxed and said pleasantly, "All right, if you must. The guards will go with you."

The salted bastard. Damned if his charm is not scarier than his anger! Aloud, he asked, "Is that necessary?"

"That's more for your safety. The city streets are dangerous. The less water available, the more dangerous they get and any rainlord is likely to be a focus of discontent."

Jasper capitulated. "Doubtless you are right." He rose to his feet. "As long as you remember not to treat me as a prisoner, I am sure we shall deal together tolerably well. Like it or not we are stuck with each other, at least until my powers develop more. Ironic, isn't it? Never mind, I work better when I am more content, so this will work in your favour, too. There will come a time when I will be able to raise clouds by myself, and you can confine yourself to ruling."

It was a lie, and he knew it. *But I dare not tell him I am not getting any better.* He needed Taquar even more than Taquar needed him.

As if he sensed Jasper's fear, Taquar said, "Don't push me too far. You think you have the upper hand here. You don't. You see, you care about whether the people die of thirst. I don't."

That sick, clenching feeling in his stomach . . . *Damn the man.*

Because he couldn't trust himself to speak, Jasper left the room without excusing himself or even uttering a farewell. Outside the door, he felt his knees buckle and had to turn it into a clumsy misstep. One of the guards caught his elbow and steadied him. "Thank you, Dibble," he said. "Clumsy of me. We can't have the nation's only stormlord breaking his neck, can we?" He patted the man on the back in a friendly fashion and then walked ahead.

He'd come to know Dibble Hornblend better since they'd been training together, and he liked the man. He was becoming a – no, not quite a friend. Not yet. A comrade, that was it. Fortunately, the man's social ineptitude was not reflected in his fighting skills. He could make a sword or a scimitar dance; he could wield and throw a pike or a lance with deadly accuracy and, in spite of his youth, he was a good teacher.

That weeping bastard Taquar, he thought as he continued on his way. *He's right. He as good as has my water in his hand, to save or throw away as he chooses. If he ever realises that I will never be any better at cloudmaking, he'll be gone across the Giving Sea . . . What the salted damn am I going to do?*

In his room, Taquar continued to sit at his desk, staring into space. He remembered a child, a boy, insecure, almost obliterated by grief. He remembered a boy who believed all he was told. A skinny child, unprepossessing, who never wanted to look him in the eye. How had that child grown up to be this man? Jasper was still slim, but he was as tall as Taquar. His brown eyes were steady, seemingly without fear. He spoke with an adult's assurance, not a prisoner's uncertainty. He treated Taquar as though he, Jasper, had the upper hand. As though Taquar *amused* him . . .

Taquar jumped to his feet and paced across the room. Watergiver *damn* the dirty Gibber grubber, it wasn't so long since he had been a prisoner in the mother cistern! Waterless skies above, how had the brat grown up so fast – and become so *strong*?

He slammed his hand down on the desk, furious with himself. He had left the lad too long in Breccia and this was the result.

"You'll hurt yourself."

He looked up to find Laisa had come back. She shut the door behind her and leaned against it, her head tilted and her eyes narrowed as she watched him. "The boy has grown," she said, echoing his thoughts. "He's clever. We need to have our wits about us. I've been chatting to him every day, trying to bring home the realisation he has to cooperate, but he's not a fool. He knows I have a vested interest. He doesn't trust me."

He snorted. "You can hardly blame him. Why didn't you tell me he found out Lyneth had been a prisoner in the mother cistern and then told the Breccian rainlords?"

Her eyes narrowed. "That was true, then? It doesn't matter, Taquar. Everyone he told is dead! Nealrith, Kaneth, Ryka, Granthon, Iani, Ethelva. Your secret is safe." She came across the room towards him. "*Did* you kill the other students as well?"

"Why do you want to know?"

"The thought is – intriguing. A multiple murderer. That lad who supposedly threw himself off the balcony after a love affair gone wrong? Did he get some assistance from you that night?"

His impassive expression did not shift.

"How did you ever get admitted to his room?"

"A man has ways. He thought I cared about him."

She came up to him, her eyes sparkling with excitement. "You started killing very young."

"Irrelevant, surely. What you should be worried about is whether I have finished." He placed a hand over her throat and ran his thumb up to her chin.

Her lips parted and she bit her bottom lip. "Hmm," she said. "I always did like the scent of danger. And I think I know you – murder for a purpose only. Not pleasure." She ran a hand up the side of his face, to tangle it in his black hair and loosen the leather tie at the back of his neck.

"Oh? Believe me, my dear, revenge can be very sweet."

He took her on the desk, his hand clasped across her mouth to stifle her squeals when his roughness hurt her.

Afterwards, as she lay next to him on the desktop and tried to draw the tattered remains of her gown over her naked-ness, he asked, "Laisa, if you wanted to gain ascendancy over an enemy too strong to be defeated in battle, how would you do it?"

She turned her head to look at him. *So cat-like,* he thought. *Bruised but sated.*

"That's easy," she said. "Take hostage what he loves most in the world: his lover, his child, his land, his wealth, his power, whatever. The trick is to find out what he values most. Then you will have your enemy in the palm of your hand."

A slow smile lifted his lips as her words seeded the begin-nings of an idea. "Of course. Why didn't I think of that?"

"The problem will be to find what he values."

"No, that's no problem. I already know him well enough to know *exactly* the sort of thing he values." He sat up, reaching for his trousers. *That Gibber grubber is going to understand that trying to thwart me is distinctly unwise* . . .

"Laisa, ask Senya to join us for dinner tonight, would you?

I gather she is not happy with the idea of our marriage and I think it's time I got to know her better if she is my step-daughter-to-be."

Laisa blinked in surprise, obviously wondering what the connection was. "As you wish. As for our wedding on Sun Day, I thought after the normal service?"

"Perfect," he said, and hid his enjoyment of her astonishment at his abnormal amiability.

The snuggery welcomed the stormlord, of course. It was an honour – unexpected, but an honour. Madam Opal, the owner, blossomed as she considered the opportunities that might arise if the lord was pleased with what he found. She soon had the establishment's most expensive imported wine, tastiest food and prettiest girls on display.

It was a pity the main recipient of all the fuss seemed unmoved. Jasper refused the wine, declined the food and looked at the women as if they were pedes going to the auction block. He asked each one her name and where she was from, but when several approached him to take his outer robe, to make him feel more comfortable, he waved them away. Seemingly at random, he pointed to one of the girls and said, "I'll take that one."

Opal gestured, the other girls, pouting, turned their attentions to his guards, and the girl he had selected led Jasper upstairs to the best room.

As she shut the door behind him, she pushed the latch across to secure it. Then she stood leaning up against the door as if reluctant to move. She was dark, beautiful and frightened. Viviandra of the Gibber. Terelle had always called her Vivie.

"There's nothing to be afraid of," he said. "I'm not going to hurt you."

"Who are you?" she whispered. "Opal said you were a rich

162

merchant from Level Three. But no mere merchant has enforcers among his guards . . ."

"I'm Jasper Bloodstone. The stormlord."

She shrank back against the door.

"Why are you so frightened?" he asked, puzzled. "Did Terelle ever tell you about me? I know she wrote to you sometimes."

She appeared confused; fear pooled in her eyes like an animal in a slaughter yard. "Did the Highlord send you?" she asked, still whispering.

"No, of course not. Why would you think so? Oh – I'm sorry! You would know me as Shale Flint, of course."

Her eyes widened. "You're *Shale*? Shale Flint is the *stormlord*? Jasper Bloodstone?"

He nodded.

"Oh! You don't really want to bed me, then."

He smiled. "Is it that obvious?" he asked. "I'm sorry. That must sound rude, I suppose. I'm not looking for—" He waved vaguely at the bed on the other side of the room. "I wanted to talk about your sister."

She didn't reply and kept her eyes downcast.

"Viviandra, why are you so frightened?"

"We – we don't get rainlords and such in here. They go to the uplevel snuggeries. Except when Taquar came – and – and he chose me, too."

"Oh! I didn't know that." In shock, he assessed the implications. Perhaps he had endangered Viviandra. *Like Amethyst.* Nausea rose in his gullet. "What did he want? When was that?"

"He wanted to talk about Terelle. Twice. The first time was before the earthquake, maybe, oh, thirty days before. The second time was just after it. That time he had me taken up to Scarcleft Hall and – and the seneschal questioned me there. Is Terelle all right? Do you know if she's safe?"

"I don't know." He searched her face, trying to find something of Terelle there; but there was nothing. Viviandra was wholly Gibber: short and slight, brown eyes, brown skin, dark hair. A beauty, although there were telltale smudges around her eyes that spoke of a lifestyle taking its toll. It was easy to believe she and Terelle were not related; that Russet had been speaking the truth when he had said Terelle was entirely something else. Watergiver, whatever that meant.

He said, "Tell me what Taquar wanted."

She shook her head. "He would kill me. I – I heard what he did to that dancer, up on the tenth level. And – I know those are Taquar's guards and the seneschal's enforcers downstairs."

Inwardly Jasper winced. Amethyst had died because he'd sought her help, just as he was seeking Viviandra's.

He undid his money belt, grateful Taquar had never bothered to take it away, perhaps because he had not realised how many tokens Highlord Nealrith had given to him before his escape from Breccia City. *Sometimes,* he reflected wryly, *Taquar's inability to think of the mundane was an advantage.* He counted out five gold water tokens, each worth a year's supply of dayjars. Viviandra's eyes widened as he gave them to her. "Take these, and leave this house. Buy your way free. Don't tell anyone where you are going. Leave the city. There are caravans going to Pediment or Portfillik."

"Stay hidden for the rest of my life? They say Lord Taquar has a long memory."

"That won't be necessary, I promise you. Trust me."

She stared at him and then at the tokens. "I've never seen so much money," she whispered.

"Let's sit down, and you can tell me what you know."

With trembling hands, she tucked the tokens into her purse and sat on the edge of the divan. He sat beside her and smiled encouragingly.

13

As dusk deepened along the floor of Pebblebag Pass, Ryka stood on the southern edge and grieved.

Behind her, deeper inside the pass, was a Reduner tent settlement that had existed since the drovers of the dunes had besieged Qanatend. Ravard had declared they would join the camp there for the night, and the slave caravan was already settled in. From where Ryka stood, pedes and men were black silhouettes in front of the cooking fires and shadows danced on tent canvas, but she did not turn to look.

She remained at the top of the slope they had climbed that afternoon, gazing back towards the south, torn with grief. Although she stood in the fast-deepening shade of one of the highest peaks of the Warthago Range and the sun had already slid out of her sight, the plains below and the sky above were still bright with sunshine.

I must remember that, she thought. *I am in darkness, but somewhere down there they can still see the sun.* There was still light in the world. And life, too, like the one she had once known. Somewhere below, past the foothills and the more gentle incline of The Sweepings rising up from The Escarpment, were the four escarpment cities still free of the drover warriors: Scarcleft, Pediment, Denmasad and Breakaway and, further away, the coastal cities of Portfillik and Portennabar.

There was freedom, but she – she had lost something precious the night before: the ability to say no. The grieving time she had been allotted had passed, and Ravard had come to her pallet and taken what he thought he had a right to take. She had not fought him, nor had she killed him afterwards as he lay beside her sleeping. She could have taken his scimitar, carelessly discarded in its scabbard, and slit his throat. She could have used her water-powers to escape, to steal a pede and thwart pursuit. She could have been halfway to another city by now. She would have been long gone – except for the deep-rooted fear – no, the *knowledge* – she had that Kaneth would refuse to escape with her.

Instead, she had lain in Ravard's arms and wept as she lost the last of her innocence.

And she would do it all again.

I will not leave without you, Kaneth. Because that's what loving is.

There was a sound behind her and she turned.

He was there, watching her, her husband who no longer knew her.

"Kaneth?" she breathed, hoping, always hoping.

"Why do I sense you in a strange way?" he asked, ignoring her use of his name as if he had never heard it before.

She wanted to rush into his arms. She wanted to say, *Because you love me. Because you are a very special rainlord and you know my water.* But she dared not. He no longer knew her, no longer knew his loyalties, no longer recognised his abilities. His expression was confused, his gaze lacked desire, his words betrayed his fuddled wits.

"Your memory will return," she said gently. "And you will know who you are, and what you are. Be patient."

"Sometimes there are flashes of myself as a child. Children

playing, but I cannot name them. Adults teaching, but I can't remember what they said. A building, a place of learning where I was happy, yet I do not remember why."

"It will come," she whispered. "It will all come back."

She stopped, aware of water moving through the shadows, reminding her of the danger of being overheard. Someone was coming through the gloom towards them, approaching from behind Kaneth to the right, treading the loose stones without sound. His stealth made the hair on her arms stand up. She stared short-sightedly, seeking him out, but he stalked them from within the darkest shadows clinging to the boulders and bushes lining the sides of the pass. There, even the twilight did not reach.

"Have you eaten?" she asked more loudly. "I am sure the slaves will have cooked by now. You should go back."

Stones rattled down a slope behind him, this time to the left and above. Another stalker. Kaneth didn't turn. He was still looking at her. It was she who shifted her senses from the still invisible watcher to the danger on the bluff above. She tilted her face upwards, straining to see. At first, nothing. Then the danger had a shape, leaping feline-shaped water. She saw its silhouette against the dying light in the sky and screamed a warning. The yowl of the horned cat came in answer as it plunged, front paws aimed to break the neck of its chosen prey: Kaneth.

Her power flashed outward to take its water. She thought to kill it in mid-leap. And in her panic, she misjudged. The blast of power flew past the animal, too high. Kaneth started to turn. And in the final splinter of time, just before the cat's huge paws – backed by the force of its leap and its powerful shoulders – could hit him and snap his neck, the animal suddenly curled in on itself. Already falling, its force fading, it slammed Kaneth with its body, not its outstretched paws. Kaneth sprawled on the ground at Ryka's feet, the cat motionless beside him.

Her heart had stopped, and now it beat again as Kaneth winced and sat up. She stared at the cat, at the horns on its forehead, sharp and straight, at the thick fur richly marbled with colour: brown, ochre, umber – and the scarlet splash of freshly spilled blood. It was dead, and the cause was easy enough to see. Buried deep into the side of its neck was the hilt of a knife. On its flank, a suppurating sore, remnant of an old injury.

Her rational mind made sense of that. Wounded and starving, its usual animal victims chased away or killed by guards from the camp, it had hungered more than it had feared, and its hunger had been fuel for its fury.

She raised her eyes to see who had thrown the knife and out of the darkness stepped Ravard.

"A horned mountain cat. Beautiful animal," he said. "I have always coveted a pelt of one of these."

Ryka, still breathless and trying to still the wild beating of her heart, gathered her wits. When she spoke again, she concealed the remnants of her terror with sarcasm. "And I thought you did it to save a life."

He had no patience with her. "I gave you no permission t'come out here, let alone meet another man. Get back to the camp."

"There was no meeting," Kaneth said, rising to his feet. "Or only an accidental one. That was a fine throw and I am grateful." He casually dusted off his knees, and smiled up at Ravard.

The innocence of his smile was breathtaking and Ryka's fear returned in full measure. This man who had replaced Kaneth had no sense of self-preservation. He spoke as if the truth was all that he needed.

Ravard stared at him, momentarily thrown by his simplistic sincerity. "You're a slave," he said, his tone scathing. "D'you think I need your thanks? Now carry the cat carcass back t'the fires, you witless waste of water. I want t'have it skinned." He snatched the knife out of the animal's neck, grabbed Ryka by the arm and pulled her with him towards the camp, leaving Kaneth to lift and carry the animal alone. She wanted to protest, to say he still wasn't well, but she quelled the desire. It would make no difference.

"What makes you so sure he won't escape?" she asked, both curious and trying to divert the anger she felt in him.

He laughed, his mockery clear. "Why should he? He was probably sand-witted before he was captured – a hulking labourer from one of your low-life city levels, at a guess. Such men always lead miserable lives without hope. Before this he worked for money and probably never had enough t'eat. Or drink. Now he works f'rus and he'll eat well. He's better off here and men like him know it. Folk like you, you despise slavery, think it unjust and cruel. Ask yourself if the poverty of your cities in the Scarpen or the settles of the Gibber is not far worse than any slavery. Sometimes seems t'me like freedom t'starve."

"You've been to the Gibber?"

"Oh, yes," he said grimly.

Watergiver help me, she thought, *he was one of the Reduner raiders. Probably been at it since he was old enough to own a pede.* One of the marauders who pillaged and razed Gibber villages and stole their youngsters for slaves and warriors. No wonder he spoke the language of the Scarpen so well.

"If this burnt man is a mere lowlife as you say, why do your men treat him as if he is somehow special? As though they are half afraid of him? Why is he not chained like the others?"

"None of your withering business," he growled. "And let me make one thing clear, woman. You have certain privileges 'cause you're my chosen bed mate. Abuse the freedom you got, then you'll be roped like the rest of the men till we get t'Dune Watergatherer. Understand?"

So much for the goodness of slavery. "What did I do wrong?"

His grip tightened on her arm. "If men see you wander off like that, they'll either think you want t'escape and they'll bring you back for punishment, and I'll have t'order your lashing. Or they'll think you're off t'meet a lover. And I'll have t'order your death. Understand?" He stopped dead, his grip swinging her into his chest. "I would have t'do it, or lose the respect of my men. I can't have you mock me."

She could feel the heat coming from him as clearly as she felt his need to hurt her. He was angry and he knew no other way to handle his ire. And side by side with the anger was a hot-blooded desire he found difficult to control. He lusted after her. He was so weeping *young.*

She nodded, placating, then wasn't sure he would see the movement in the dark, so she raised her hand and pressed her fingers gently to his mouth, as if she could keep his rage within. "I understand. I won't do it again. But remember this: to be a leader of men, you must first learn to lead your own passions, not be led by them," she said.

"Gods, woman, you're lucky I don't break your bleeding neck!"

"I meant to advise—"

"You are a slave! Slaves *obey,* nothing else. I am no child t'be *advised* by a woman."

"And I am no slave. You can put me in chains, but you can't make me a slave."

"I could break you into a hundred pieces and make you come grovelling t'my feet!"

"Perhaps, if you want the wreckage of a woman in your bed. But even so, my mind will always be free. You can *never* rope my thoughts, Kher Ravard. Or my spirit."

For a moment he stayed still and silent. Then, sounding more exasperated than furious, he asked, "You sun-fried female, have you *no* fear?"

"You gave your word. You said you would protect the child I carry. You may be young, but you are a man of your word." She had no idea if that was true, but something told her he was fond of the idea of honour.

He kissed her then, grabbing her and pressing her to him, his mouth roughly plundering, his hands roving over her back and buttocks. Her response was muted, poised somewhere between acquiescence and passivity.

Stung, he flung her from him. "Go get your meal," he snarled and strode off to join the other Reduners at the fires.

She sighed, wiped her mouth with the back of her hand, and went to join the slave women.

The following day they rode on towards Qanatend, what was left of it.

The small free-standing hill, separated from the last of the northern slopes of the Warthago Range by a mile or two of grassy plains, was covered by buildings. Qanatend: a city that tumbled down the slopes to the encircling bastion walls and its external ring of bab groves, liveries and iron works. Connecting Qanatend to its mother cistern in the Warthago, the water tunnel left its spoor of brick towers, one at each inspection shaft. The caravan trail ran parallel to the tunnel. Both plunged in straight lines into the bab groves.

Once inside the groves, the Scarpen slaves stared in horror at the sight of trees wantonly hacked to death. The ancient irrigation system was in ruins, deliberately destroyed. Patches of heaped bab charcoal scattered throughout the groves marked the remains of funeral pyres and when Ryka obtained a better look at one, it was to see charred remains of bones protruding from the ashes.

She thought of Iani, with his limp and his sagging mouth and crippled hand, of his wife Moiqa, Highlord of Qanatend, mother of the kidnapped Lyneth. She remembered other rainlords she had known who had served the city and who had probably perished when it had fallen.

These are their bones, she thought, her stomach roiling. *And they died knowing they were defeated and we Breccians had failed them.* How Kaneth had hated that! He'd longed to ride to help the rainlords of Qanatend, and only direct orders from the Cloudmaster had stopped him.

"The bastards. The bastards. The sun-blighted bastards," Junial muttered from behind her. "Watergiver save us, did they leave *anyone* alive?" Junial, the middle-aged woman chosen for her baking skills, was the plump widow of a baker from Level Fifteen of Breccia City.

As they rode through the gates, they saw much of the city had been fired. House gates hung on broken hinges, shutters and doors were burned, roofs had collapsed, mud brick walls were blackened where flames had licked upwards. Occasionally they glimpsed city dwellers going about their business: a fish-farmer selling his wares; a blacksmith sharpening Reduner scimitars; street whores with haunted eyes flaunting grubby bodies; an old woman spinning bab fibre on her spindle, her gnarled fingers sliding up and down the thread in unceasing labour.

"They all look hungry," Junial muttered. "The bastards, those bleeding red *bastards.*"

Ryka turned to whisper a warning. "Hush. The pede driver may understand you. Some speak the Quartern tongue, especially the ones who were trade caravanners before."

"Don't care if he does, the spitless wretch," the woman said, but she had lowered her voice.

Sandblast it, I too am so sick *of being careful,* Ryka thought as they entered the city and began to climb up the steep streets.

When she looked upwards, she could see that the windmills drawing water up to the highest levels were still operating, but if she glanced back at the roof gardens of the levels they had passed, she saw most of the potted trees and plants were dying. No one had enough water, then. Small wonder, with the whole system disintegrating, no storms being sent to the gullies around their mother wells, and the Reduners carting as much water to the dunes as they could load on their packpedes.

A diseased city, she thought. *Damn these Reduners to a waterless death!*

Ravard led them to the Level Three Sun Temple and the slaves were herded into what had once been the forecourt for public religious services. There was not much room, and the women and men were bunched together, the men still roped. Most of the guards retreated to the curved viewing balcony overlooking the court, with the exception of the two men doling out water to the slaves. Ravard disappeared altogether.

Ryka looked around for Kaneth. With a soft smile and gentle words, he was bandaging the arm of a man who had suffered a wound earlier. She let him be and sought out Elmar Waggoner. He was at the end of his row of roped captives and had managed to ease out a bit of slack to sit back comfortably, his back to the outer wall. She came and sat as close to him as she dared, but didn't look his way. When she spoke she turned her face away and barely moved her lips.

"Is he any better, do you think?" she asked.

"A little. At least he speaks more. And he has started helping, instead of being off in a fog of his own all the time."

"Sometimes – sometimes I can't believe it's him. He has no *passion* any more. Sandblast it, Elmar, where is Kaneth Carnelian?"

He shot an anxious look sideways to make sure no one had heard. "Listen, um, Garnet, his passivity is what keeps him alive. Look on it as a blessing. The real him would be dead several times over by now, and he'd have taken half the bloody Reduner bastards with him onto the pyre."

One of the guards up on the balcony had spotted her and was staring her way. She rested her head back against the wall as if tired and half closed her eyes. Stealing a few drops of water from the water jar the guards were using, she brought them over to where they sat, and wrote what she wanted to say by using her power to form wet letters on the stone paving. She placed them in between their bodies, where no one but they would see. The air was still and dry and hot, the stones warm, so the letters vanished almost as soon as each word was written.

Who they think he is? she wrote. *Why respect?*

Elmar leaned forward over his bent knees to disguise the movement of his lips. "I don't really understand it. They call him lord, and they use another name when they speak of him. Uthardim. At least I think that's what it is. But I don't understand much of their cursed tongue. They do seem to mention their dune god a lot when he is around."

Ryka stilled, shocked. *Uthardim?* She knew the name from her studies. He was mentioned in the old myths and legends of the dune dwellers. Uthardim, one of their ancient heroes. She remembered a description of him: *blue-eyed, with flowing locks of red-gold, he smote those who came upon him, his thews and sinews as strong as the trees of the rock plains . . .* Uthar. It meant iron in the language of the dunes. And "dim" was a common suffix, meaning son of the sand or sands. Uthardim: Iron Son of the Sands. She thought, but did not write the words, *Oh, Kaneth. What is it they would make of you?*

She cracked open her eyelids to make sure no one was taking an undue interest in her or in Elmar, before continuing to write. *Why Uthardim?* she asked.

"It started right after he was pulled off the pyre. There was a couple of Reduner guards there, and one of them kept saying 'Uthardim, Uthardim,' and a whole lot of other stuff

I couldn't understand. And then one of the head drovers pushed his way through with his underlings to take a look. The Warrior Son, I think. 'Uthardim!' one of the guards told him, and pointed.

"And right then, the pyre went out. One moment it had been blazing away, and then – whoosh – it was gone. And at exactly that same moment Ka—, *he* sat up, sudden-like, his face all red and peeling and said 'Uthardim'. Startled me, I can tell you, but what it did to those Reduners was just plain freakish. The drover leader went as white as a 'Baster. Couple of the guards fell to their knees like they was praying or something.

"Me – well, I reckon *he* was out of his head right then. He couldn't have found the sky if you'd told him which way was up. He was just repeating a word everyone was saying, probably wanting in his befuddlement to ask what it meant. And as for the fire, well, those Breccians had been throwing buckets of water around, and I reckon they'd wet the wood. When the dry stuff burned out, the fire went out. But that's not the way they saw it."

Then?

"The Warrior Son gave orders for him to be put on a pede and brought up to Breccia Hall, for the sandmaster to take a look at. He was in a sorry state, though, so I volunteered to look after him. Didn't let on I knew him, of course. Not long after we'd been settled into the stable, Kher Ravard shows up, to see what all the fuss was about. The Warrior Son *and* the Master Son, the bastards. What I wouldn't have done to have had my sword right then! They had a long conversation. I stood there, as confused as a spindevil, and *he* was drifting in and out of dreamland, moaning. As far as I could make out, Kher Ravard didn't like what he was told one little bit, but the Warrior Son stood his ground and kept referring to Ka—, er, *him*, as 'Uthardim'. Ravard questioned me too, but I said I'd never seen this Uthardim fellow before in my life and no one knew who he was. In the end, they left.

"Ravard came again when our friend there was awake, and spoke to him at length. The Kher did most of the talking, and our friend answered, smiling politely, mostly just 'I don't know' or 'I don't remember'. He was so blasted guileless, there wasn't much Ravard could do. Then on the day before we left Breccia, Davim asked to speak to him on the steps in front of the main door of the Hall. I don't know what they said, but Ravard wasn't happy with it.

"After that, though, 'Uthardim' got better treatment. They even gave me a sort of a lotion every night to wash his burn and wound with. Dunno what's in it, but I reckon it works. It's healing real nice now."

Elmar stirred restlessly, and Ryka risked a glance in his direction.

He looked around to make sure no one was taking an interest in them. "Does this name Uthardim mean anything to you?" he asked.

Mythical red hero. Old story. She stopped writing, aware someone was pushing their way through the crowd of slaves. She evaporated the last of the water and raised her head to watch the guard coming towards her.

"Kher Ravard," the man said, jerking his head in a gesture that was clear enough: Ravard wanted her.

Without looking at Elmar, she stood and followed the guard. They were halfway across the courtyard when a commotion along the side wall brought the guard to a halt. Another guard had one of the female slaves pinned up against the wall, her skirts rucked high. When she screamed and struggled, he hit her with his fist in the centre of her face. Blood spurted and the woman's head lolled. Half senseless, she sagged, all the fight drained out of her.

And then, suddenly, Kaneth was there. He wrenched the guard away and held him by the neck, feet off the ground, like a sandgrouse about to be plucked. The woman crumpled unheeded to the ground.

Ryka tensed, every muscle in her body screaming at her to go to Kaneth's aid even as her mind cautioned her against moving. She squinted around the courtyard, relying on her knowledge of water as much as on her eyesight: four Reduner warriors, including the guard who had come to fetch her. And above, on the viewing balcony, five or six others, several now grabbing up their lances. She touched her power, ready to kill the first who looked like trying to spear Kaneth.

He dropped the Reduner, who – half choked – fell in a heap at his feet. He looked down at the man and spoke to him. In the now hushed silence of the courtyard, his voice carried to everyone. His words contained no anger, but they were implacable. "A man does not take from a woman what is not his to plunder. He shares. And gives. And asks. A man who does otherwise is no man."

A ripple of open horror crossed the faces of the slaves. They expected Kaneth to die then. So did Ryka. Yet none of the Reduners moved. They stayed poised, as if awaiting orders, but no one gave them.

I wonder if they understood? Ryka asked herself.

And then Kaneth did something she had not known was within his capability. He repeated the words in Reduner. His grammar was poor, his accent atrocious, but the meaning was clear enough.

Oh blast, she thought. *Damn it all, Kaneth, you picked a wonderful time to remember what you know of the Reduner tongue.*

And yet still nothing drastic happened and it was Kaneth who broke the tension. He held out a hand to the Reduner at his feet. The man, his fear flaring in his eyes, refused it and scrambled up unaided. Ryka's guard stirred then and went to him. He murmured something to the man, who turned and left the courtyard without saying a word.

"What the shit's going on?" one of the chained slave lads asked Ryka, as if she could supply an answer. "They seem frightened of this Uthardim."

"I don't know," she replied. "But they are not exactly frightened, they are more, um, *respectful*."

The lad gave a half laugh of released tension. "So am I, lady, so am I."

The older man roped next to him scowled. "We should all have his guts! Watergiver be my witness, if I get me a knife, I'll kill one of them bastards, prefer'bly that spitless bastard Ravard."

"Keep your tongue behind your teeth, Whetstone!" the lad told him in alarm. He looked up at Ryka, anguished. "He's *mad*. Wants to attack everyone!"

The guard came back and gestured her to follow. As she left the courtyard, she glanced back over her shoulder at Kaneth. He smiled.

There was so much fear in her chest, it hurt.

Ravard had found a decent room in one of the Level Three houses next to the Sun Temple. The bed was made up with clean linen and the bath water was warm in the adjoining water-room. A hot meal was set upon the table, a bottle of bab amber open next to two glasses.

"I thought you'd like a bath after the travelling," Ravard said, having dismissed the servers, all Scarpen women. "And a little luxury. Which would you like first – t'eat or bathe?"

"Bathe, please."

He grinned at her, that flashing white smile of his turning him from a warrior to a young man of boyish charm.

I wish he wouldn't do that, she thought sourly. *It makes me forget to fear him.* She couldn't afford to do that. She'd end up dead.

"Shall I scrub your back?"

Under her breastbone the baby stirred, his little foot – or was it his head? – pushing up into a noticeable bump. She had been about to snap at Ravard, to refuse any concession, to continue her policy of cold disdain. To let him know that every time he would have to take, for she would never, ever, give. But the safety of her son? She placed a hand on her abdomen to feel him move beneath her palm.

He's all that matters. Not my pride. Not Kaneth's, either. And certainly not Ravard's stolen pleasures. *Remember, Ryka, since the beginning of time, women have done for their children what you are about to do for yours.*

"No," she said with a soft smile, and stifled the sigh rising within, in spite of her resolution. "No, thank you, I prefer to bathe alone, but I will scrub *your* back if you wish."

His face lit up.

Oh, blighted eyes, she thought. *He's such a child!*

And yet she wondered, for when she washed his back she saw what she had felt but not seen in the dark of the tent on the previous nights: the criss-crossing of the long scars of whippings too numerous to count. There was not one piece of skin free of scars or puckers. She stared in horror, unable to consider how much pain he must have endured.

A child? No one who had ever endured such pain could ever be anything but a man.

He pulled her into the bath to kiss her, swamping water everywhere, and laughed when she squealed in shock. And then, just before he covered her lips with his own, he whispered, "Love me, Garnet. Even if you do it just for your child, just this once, love me."

The youth was back, there, in his pleading. She thought

of Kaneth. Of his son. She turned away from her memory of love and kissed the man who held her now.

"Teach me how to please you," he said a moment later. "Show me how."

Forgive me, she thought, and it was to Kaneth she spoke, the grief savage inside her as she made her choice. She pushed it away, yet still heard the echo in her pain: *Forgive myself.*

14

Scarpen Quarter
Scarcleft City and Pediment

On the night Jasper met Viviandra, he also had a long conversation with Madam Opal. That conversation led him to visit several other snuggeries on other levels in the days that followed. Taquar would have been surprised – and worried – about just how chaste his visits were, but Jasper took care he never found out. He tried to emerge from the inner rooms looking thoroughly satisfied and always indulged in a little crude banter with his guards on the way back to Level Two.

The information he elicited from the contacts that started with Opal eventually took him to the Silvermesh Snuggery on the tenth level. He was, as usual, accompanied by heavily armed guards and enforcers, none of whom objected to the duty. The stormlord was a pleasant young man, they all agreed. Easy to talk to, never demanding, yet not standing any nonsense, either. You knew where you were with him. Treat him with respect, and he respected you. True, the Scarcleft seneschal, Tallyman, had made it quite clear they were not to lie with any of the girls while they were on duty, but lounging around downstairs in the common rooms while the stormlord enjoyed himself in one of the upstairs rooms was not onerous and it did have certain advantages. As one of the guards remarked to another, the scenery was well worth ogling, and getting to know it more intimately was not such a remote possibility once you knew the terrain.

When they entered the Silvermesh, the madam, Tourmaline, came waddling up like a pregnant pede, proud that her establishment had been chosen by the stormlord. None of the guards were at all surprised when she whisked him away from the common rooms and into her private parlour, though they would have been astonished if they had heard what happened behind that closed door.

"The Madam of the Marcasite on Level Twenty-eight sent me," Jasper said once he had bestowed the obligatory greetings. "She said you might be able to help me because many of the caravanners visit your establishment."

"Madam Verissal. Yes, she sent me a message. Said the stormlord was interested in sending messages through caravans to the Gibber. And that he was willing to pay for discretion as well as the service."

"That's right. Actually, I want messages to go to the White Quarter as well, which is why I visited her. I was told the caravanners for the White Quarter went to the Marcasite Snuggery for their relaxation."

"Well, they used to. But there's been no caravan to the White Quarter from anywhere in the Scarpen for the past cycle or so. Far too dangerous. And 'Baster caravans don't come here no more; nor do the Reduner ones." She sighed, her large breasts heaving. "We snuggeries suffer from the lack of custom, dear. Did no one tell you that?"

"Yes. Madam Verissal. She also said, though, that Scarpen caravans continue to run to the Gibber, and Gibber towns maintain contact with Samphire in the White Quarter."

"Yes. However, most of our custom came from 'Basters and Reduners. Men away from home have more use of our services than men who live here. Business is withering bad,

I can tell you, dear. Folk don't have water tokens for us no more." She tossed her head in irritation and the hanging folds of fat at her neck rearranged themselves like door curtains in a breeze. "But tell me, why did you come here to me instead of going direct to the caravanners themselves? This way, m'lord has to pay me a cut, too."

"A wise woman once told me snuggery madams know more about men and women than anyone on earth, and if ever I wanted discretion, a snuggery was the place to buy it. I thought if I went direct to a caravanner, it might be the very one who would report me to Seneschal Tallyman. A snuggery madam, on the other hand, would be able to tell me who to approach, or better still would take my message and pass it on to a reliable caravanner."

She laughed. "I know who told m'lord that – Opal down on Level Thirty-two. But a snuggery operates only because Seneschal Tallyman allows it to operate. No snuggery madam in Scarcleft wants to butt heads with Harkel Tallyman. He reports directly to the Highlord. Upset those two, that's maybe treason. And they have a real nasty solution for that."

"Ah, but think: I am the stormlord of all the Quartern. The only one. What could be the future rewards of having me in your debt?"

"Nice, if I was still alive, dear."

Jasper smiled. The words might not have been encouraging, but he saw the glint in her eye that betrayed her interest.

A soft knock at the door presaged the entry of a handmaiden carrying a tray of drinks and titbits. She knelt at the low table in front of Jasper with her offerings. He took a goblet, not even bothering to see what it contained. It was much easier to gaze at the handmaiden. The deep tan of her skin proclaimed a touch of Gibber ancestry, but the long hair tumbling down her back was blonde and her eyes violet. The exotic combination was alluring, as was the plunging V of her neckline.

"Silver," Tourmaline said, seeing his interest. "One of our more experienced handmaidens. Excellent teaching skills. Or, of course, there are other younger handmaidens more your age."

"I'm sure Silver would suit beautifully if I wanted—"

"Ah, of course. Business first. Wait upstairs," Tourmaline said with a nod to the handmaiden. Throughout this exchange, Silver had kept her head ducked, a picture of demure obedience, but in the doorway she glanced back over her shoulder to give Jasper a broad wink and a mischievous smile.

He waited until the door closed behind her before he pulled a handful of tokens from his pocket, gold glinting among them. "There is also the matter of immediate rewards for your aid in this matter, of course," he said, indicating the tokens. "However, if you are not interested, I am sure I could find someone to oblige."

She grinned at him, her lips almost lost in the plump folds of her face. "And I am sure we can come to some agreement, m'lord."

Even after saying that, it took them another half-run of the sandglass to agree on the details, but finally he had what he wanted: her promise to see that a reliable member of the next Scarpen caravan leaving Scarcleft would deliver an anonymous oral message to the reeves or headmen of as many settles or wash-towns as they visited. The price was higher than he liked, but he had little choice.

"Never mind," Tourmaline said, when he protested her fee, "I shall include tonight with Silver free of charge."

When he demurred, she laughed and refused to listen. She personally delivered him to the door of Silver's room, her bulk lending force to her invitation. In the end he acquiesced, deciding it was easier to let her have her way than to argue. And, in truth, the idea of gazing at Silver again was an enticement.

The handmaiden's room was luxurious to say the least, and she gave every appearance of being delighted to see him. Her enthusiasm left him unmoved; he had learned far too much from Terelle to believe anything except that Silver's smiles and coquetry were part of her job.

As Tourmaline waddled away, he gently disengaged the hand clutching his arm. "You don't have to pretend," he said.

"Pretend what?" she asked.

He flushed. "That anything about me – other than my money – is at all fascinating. I wouldn't mind listening to some music, though," he said. "Do you play the lute?"

She did, and she had a sweet singing voice, so he spent a pleasant run of the sandglass listening. Between songs they ate the delicacies Tourmaline sent up from the kitchens and, when he asked a question or two betraying his lack of even elementary knowledge of music, she was happy to explain. At the end of that time, she laid her lute aside and moved to untie his tunic.

He grabbed her wrist. "No," he said. "I do not want to bed someone who is only constrained to do so for tokens."

She looked at him in astonishment.

"Tourmaline needn't know I didn't lie with you," he added. "I just hate the idea of sharing an, um, intimate moment with someone who has no real interest in doing so."

For a moment she looked at him blankly. Then she said, "But of course I want to! You are the *stormlord*, my lord!"

"Oh, so you don't want to bed me for money," he asked, amused, "but because I am the stormlord?"

Her mischievous smile was back. "And why not? After all, men want to bed me for my face and figure; why should I not want to bed a man because he is both personable and important? And it's nice that you are young too!"

Jasper couldn't think how to reply. His heart raced. Salted damn, but she was beautiful. He grabbed at the wine and

187

took another gulp, as if that would help him control his own body.

She pushed her advantage, her expression thoughtful and her finger raised to her cheek as if she was assessing his looks. "My lord, if we were two people meeting accidentally in an inn taproom, I would be plotting how to entice you into my bed so I could revel in the idea I had lain with the land's only stormlord – who also happens to be a very *innocent* young man with a sweet earnestness about him and—" She made a vague all-encompassing gesture at his torso, but the look on her face flattered.

He laughed. "You," he said, "are very good at your job. But do you really *like* bedding strangers?"

She wrinkled her nose and shrugged. "It's a job. But, yes, sometimes I do and this is one of those times. And you will disappoint me if you leave without seeing what I have to offer. You will disappoint me if you leave before I see what *you* have to offer *me*."

He wondered whether all of that was just the patter of a handmaiden. "Not much," he said, running a hand through his hair. "I have no experience."

"You're scoffing me."

He shook his head, his embarrassment darkening his colour. "Er – no, I'm not, actually."

"Merciful heavens, we shall have to do something about that! If it worries you," she added lightly, "then take pity on me. If you were to leave now, all the handmaidens would tease me, saying I have lost my touch and that I am no longer able to entice a man to stay till dawn. And Madam Tourmaline will send some old wrinkled fellow who smells to my bed instead." She reached out and slid her hand up his arm and across his chest. "But if you stay, I shall have something to remember – that I, Silver of no particular importance, once bedded the most important man in the Quartern. And maybe even taught him something useful?"

He had to laugh, and she raised her face to be kissed.

It was her job, he knew that, but he also knew he was going to stay the night, and enjoy it.

On returning to Scarcleft Hall that morning, he had breakfast in his room, humming while he had his tea, and then went to the library where they did most of their storm-bringing. By the time Taquar arrived, he had the day's water allocations planned.

They moved to the large window with a view in the direction of the sea, and together they assembled the cloud and saturated it with water to change cloud to storm.

This weakness of mine, Jasper thought as he gathered the moisture Taquar enticed from the ocean, *it's the manacles imprisoning me more securely than any bars could ever do. Free of Taquar's bonds, yet snared by the need for storms. How ridiculous is that?*

A servant entered the room twice to invert the sandglass, but still the two men worked on in silence. Once the restless clouds over the sea were heavy with impending rain, Taquar asked, as he always did in the same half-mocking tones, "Can you manage the rest?"

Jasper nodded. Taquar inclined his head in acknowledgement and left.

It took Jasper much of the day to do exactly what he wanted with the clouds, first over the Scarpen Quarter, then the Gibber and finally to push what was left to the Border Humps so rain fell in the White Quarter. Eventually the water would feed the tunnels serving the Alabaster mines and the city of Samphire. By late afternoon, he was exhausted. And satisfied. He had finally achieved success in something he had been trying to do ever since he had spoken to Viviandra.

"The guards tell me you've been here since I left you this morning."

Jasper jumped, turning to see the Highlord standing inside the doorway. He tried to sound matter-of-fact. "I've finished now."

"Why so long?"

He shrugged, hoping Taquar would not notice his guilty flush. "It was a difficult stormbringing. White Quarter – that's the farthest I have to send clouds. It takes time. Then I have to be very precise about where the rain falls. Difficult when it is so far away."

Taquar scowled at the idea of precious water going to the White Quarter. "Lord Gold will be complaining to me again tomorrow about you watering the heathens, I suppose. You want to watch yourself, Jasper. It doesn't pay to upset the priesthood, especially not when a man like Basalt is Lord Gold."

Jasper shrugged.

"I came to tell you – Davim has sent a message. He informs me he is withdrawing all his men from Breccia City. In fact, from all the Scarpen on this side of the Warthago. He intends to hold onto Qanatend, I suspect until it runs out of water. He assures me he now believes I really do have you in my custody, so he is prepared to return to the terms of our original bargain, only the line of division will be the Warthago Range."

"With the nation divided like a bab pie. Tell me, Taquar – how long will an alliance last when it is made between two men who know nothing of honour and trust each other even less?"

Taquar smiled thinly. "Long enough. He is busy in the White Quarter, and I have already sent men, both bladesmen and administrators, into the Gibber. The largest of the Gibber wash-towns bow to my rule now." He chuckled. "All it takes is a handful of armsmen with ziggers in each town. Shall I tell you something amusing? I used the example of what happened to your settle as an illustration of the fate of people who don't have protection against Reduner attack. The kind of protection I can provide. What was the name of the place again?"

Jasper had to unclench his teeth to speak. "Wash Drybone Settle," he said. "One day I will have the freedom to tell Gibbermen just who arranged for my settle to be wiped from the face of the Wash Drybone. What will happen to you then, I wonder?"

Taquar shrugged. "It doesn't matter what you say, or to whom. Who would fight men with ziggers and pedes when they have no rainlords or water sensitives? You just concentrate on your storms, boy, and leave the politics to me."

"Oh, I do, Taquar. I do." Taquar's look sharpened, so he added quickly, "But I wonder what the Scarpen forces will do when they realise the Reduners have retreated?"

"Scarpen forces?" Taquar snorted. "What Scarpen forces?"

"The ones the other cities are assembling."

Taquar looked amused. "Whatever makes you think that is happening?"

"No city was going to sit still and wait for the Reduners to come; not once they heard Breccia City had fallen to Sandmaster Davim. They will have been arming and training, and they will have learned a lesson from the fall of both Qanatend and Breccia. They will realise they must unite."

"I think you overestimate the good sense of the unwashed, Jasper. Even if you are right, it is to the Highlord of Scarcleft they will look for leadership. I am better armed, with better guards and more pedes. My guardsmen will take over Breccia City. My power will spread. How can it be otherwise? Besides, I have you. I am the only one who can threaten anyone with water shortages."

"You can threaten. But if ever they called your bluff, you'd be in trouble because there's no way I'd deny others water. In fact, I'd be more likely to reward them! And don't forget, many people know about your unholy pact with Davim. You don't have too many friends."

Taquar smiled. "I have Lord Gold. He controls the rainlord priests. And he doesn't like you one little bit. Don't underestimate me, Jasper. That would be unwise."

"And if I defy you, what then? Will you punish me? How? Kill me? Hardly, I think!"

Taquar did not answer.

Jasper pushed past the Highlord as he left the room. The expression on Taquar's face was fleeting, but Jasper would not have missed the moment for all the water in the city.

As he walked back to his room, though, his pleasure died. The taunting might be satisfying, but it was childish and probably dangerous. Taquar was right: if Lord Basalt lent his support to the highlord, and if the priests voted to uphold Basalt as the new Lord Gold, then Taquar could command a lot of power when it came to a vote to confirm or deny his position as Cloudmaster. Half the rainlords of the Scarpen were waterpriests.

And waterpriests were powerful among the devout.

Jasper had promised the dying Nealrith that Taquar would never rule the Quartern.

Spindevil take it, is that yet another promise I can't keep?

Pediment was one of the five escarpment cities trickling from the top to the bottom of the scarp like spilled bab molasses. For the past half-cycle or more, the main topics of conversation in the city, from the guards on the northern wall restlessly scanning the distance for telltale signs of dust in The Sweepings to the humble piss-collector on the city's lowest level, were the lack of water and storms and the possibility of a Reduner invasion. Probably it was the same in the other four cities as well.

At the same time as Jasper and Taquar were sniping at each other, the Overman of the Guard on Pediment's northern wall was dashing away from his post with undignified speed to race into Pediment Hall on Level Two. Once admitted, he took the steps three at a time on his way to the Hall's large reception room. At the top of the stairs, after a minimal knock on the door, he burst in on the highlord, who was meeting with his rainlords. As the group of startled men and women looked at him, the overman flapped a hand at the open door to the balcony. "My lords, look! Look at the sky!"

When a staid officer of the guard behaved so erratically, it seemed a good idea to listen. The highlord rose to his feet and did as he was asked. The other rainlords crowded behind him as he stepped out on to the balcony, their faces turned skywards.

One of them wiped away the dribble of saliva escaping from the twisted corner of his mouth and said quietly, "I'll be salted."

The expression on his face might not have appeared pleasant to most people, but to those who knew the recently widowed Lord Iani best, it was clear he was smiling for the first time in a long while.

Far above them in the sky, thin white clouds had formed into recognisable shapes. Letters. *Cities of the Scarpen unite*, they read. *Prepare for battle. Stormlord Jasper Bloodstone commands you.*

"What do you make of that?" someone asked Iani.

"I think at last we have a stormlord who is man enough to lead us."

The Highlord of Pediment added, with a wry smile, "And one clever enough to find out how to tell us. Who would have thought it of a Gibber-born wash-brat? Lord Iani, I think we are prepared to give you – and all the other free Scarpen cities – the cooperation you have been asking for."

Iani smiled. His thoughts were grimmer. *Jasper, Taquar has his spies everywhere. He will soon know what you've done. Be careful!*

Jasper decided he would not return to the Silvermesh Snuggery again, although part of him longed to do so. *I have to marry Senya*, he thought, *but I don't have to betray what I feel for Terelle by going to see Silver again.*

Yet three days after making that decision and pushing away all thoughts of Silver, he had a dream involving her. They were in Opal's Snuggery, and Laisa was there too, telling him not to think, just to enjoy, it was better that way. So he smiled, enjoying the sensations rippling through him. There was something wrong about that enjoyment though, he knew. It would annoy Nealrith and Terelle, that was it. In his dream he ordered Laisa to leave, then told Silver she had to go as well because he couldn't use the money Nealrith had given him from the Breccian treasury to pay her. She vanished, her place taken by Terelle. That was better.

Then the dream faded, and the substance was suddenly tangible. He woke fully, to find the pleasure racing through his body. Real, not imagined. His eyes flew open, but he didn't need to see who was touching him. He recognised the perfume.

He sat bolt upright, struggling to heave her away. "Senya – *what the waterless hells are you doing*?"

"I would have thought that was obvious," she said, and did something to him he would never have guessed she even knew about.

Appalled, he pushed her away. "Sandblast it! Stop that!"

She took no notice, and to his embarrassment, his body continued to respond. *Salted damn, but that felt good—* "Senya—"

Her head came up. "Jasper, you were right, and I was wrong. We need to marry. We have to have children."

"All right," he agreed in desperation. "But *later*—"

She wriggled upwards, her naked body squirming delightfully across him, and covered his mouth with her lips. Her hand went to where her mouth had been a moment before. He clutched at her, wanting to throw her off him, but his protest muted and then ceased as he felt himself awash with her smell and his own arousal. Thoughts tumbled, confused.

She's not new to this. Blighted eyes, her breasts are so—
Stop her.
Why? Enjoy it while it lasts. You know you have to marry her anyway.
Her nipples—
This is so stupid, I know it . . .
Oh, salted damn!

But he let his scruples go and allowed himself just to enjoy, to be borne away on the crest of pleasure. And then he was the one taking charge, sucking her delightful breasts, twisting her over onto her back and pushing himself into her. Part of him knew he would regret it, but the rest of him? That part didn't care and refused to listen.

Afterwards, she rolled out of bed, and in the dawn light entering through open shutters he caught the look on her face. She pulled on her robe and went to the door. The guard there turned to see as she emerged from the room. Only then did she pause and turn back to look at him. Only then did she smile provocatively. And then she was gone. The guards closed the door.

Jasper collapsed back onto the bed. He lay still, staring at the ceiling. Feeling sick. All memory of pleasure evaporated, replaced by self-loathing as his thoughts coalesced. He rose, lit a lamp and by its light examined the under-sheet.

There was no blood. He was not sure whether that made him feel worse or better. When he considered what it meant, especially coupled with her obvious experience and lack of shyness, he didn't much like the answer.

Who would dare? Who would even have had the opportunity?

Only one name came to mind.

Taquar Sardonyx.

But why? What possible cause could Taquar have had for a relationship with Senya? To annoy Laisa? To annoy him, Jasper? No, whatever the reason was, it had to make sense. Taquar did not act on the spur of the moment, and he was not such a rampant hedonist he would seize a moment's pleasure without some design in mind. Nor would he seek such a petty revenge on Jasper.

No, what had just happened was something Taquar had plotted for a reason. He'd planned it and had tutored Senya in what to do. He and Laisa and Senya had been in Scarcleft only, what – thirty or so days now, but still, time enough for Taquar to have that silly girl, already infatuated with him, purring at his feet like a petted cat. The withering bastard. And he, Jasper, had not had the strength of character to throw her out of the door.

I wonder if this is what a whore feels like . . . used. You are going to regret this, Jasper. He felt it deep in his bones.

She had wanted the guard to see, of course, knowing the news of it would spread. She had bedded him at Taquar's instigation, and he had been stupid enough to let her do it.

As she'd left, she had looked so damn *smug*.

Jasper dreaded Taquar making some comment about Senya, but at the next morning's cloudmaking session the rainlord neither said nor did anything to indicate he knew what had happened. Jasper was not naïve enough to believe the man did not know. Of course he did. Senya would never have behaved like that without being told what to do. And as much as Laisa was a poor mother, Jasper didn't think she would have been instrumental in using her daughter that way. No, this was Taquar's devious fingers manipulating a girl to do his bidding, and teaching her how in his own bed. All Jasper had to do was find out *why*.

After the session with Taquar, he hesitated on the stairs for a moment, then made a decision. He went to visit Laisa. She had been entertaining some of her Level Three friends, but they were already on their way out when he arrived at the door to her apartment. Senya, fortunately, was nowhere to be seen. Laisa admitted him and – as gracious as she could be when she put her mind to it – she served him some wine from across the Giving Sea and asked a servant to prepare a meal for him. "You have been cloudshifting all day," she said, "and you must remember to eat. I don't think you take enough care of yourself, Jasper. You will do no one any good if you fall sick."

He nodded, knowing she was right. "I am hungry," he admitted. He took a sip of the wine and added, "But that's not why I came to see you. I wanted to talk to you about Senya."

She placed a bowl of nuts next to him. "What about her? She is rather annoyed with you, Jasper."

"Oh? Why?"

"Your behaviour of late has been less than discreet."

"She found out I've been visiting snuggeries?"

"Yes. And you should not mention such things in polite company."

"Oh, I don't."

She glared. "Don't poke me, Jasper. I can bite."

"You can try, certainly. But you brought the subject up, not me. And speaking of Senya, she did not seem particularly put out by my behaviour last night when she came to my room and climbed naked between my sheets while I slept."

Laisa was so startled it was a moment before she could speak. "May I assume you were not dreaming?"

"No dream, Laisa. What happened was not at my instigation and I wish it had not happened. However, it did, and it led me to another surprise: I was not the first."

This time Laisa was more shocked than startled, and the ensuing silence was long. Finally she said, "Are you trying to drive a wedge between man and wife, Jasper? Because, if so, you are wasting your time."

"Ah. Interesting we should come to the same conclusion. Laisa, I have no illusions about your marriage to Taquar. And I don't care anyway. What I do want to know is this: what is Taquar up to? I did – I think – make it clear I'll marry Senya, if she is willing, as it's in the interest of the Quartern and its people. I don't love her. The state of her virginity is of no interest to me. I find it hard to imagine he'd think I'd be annoyed by her behaviour, at least not until such time as we were married. Once wed, I'll try to be the best husband possible under the circumstances, and I'll expect her to do the same."

He paused, painfully aware that he sounded like a pompous sand-brain. Hurriedly he continued, "Nor can Taquar have done this to father children on her; I understand he has always been deficient in that area and he can hardly expect things to change now. So what is all this about?"

"You can hardly think I encouraged my husband to sleep with my daughter, or that I knew of it beforehand?" she said icily.

"No, but I am wondering why this occurred at all."

"Perhaps Taquar wants your wife to be loyal to him, not you, and engaging her affections before the marriage included bedding her."

It was barely possible, but her uneasiness told him she didn't believe her own words.

"You should court her," she added finally. "Teach her what you've learned from your snuggery women. Tell her the kind of thing young girls like to hear. Wean her away from Taquar. You don't want a disloyal wife in your household, do you?"

He suspected her advice was good, but something told him she was deliberately trying to lead him away from Taquar's real motives. He nodded non-committally. "Perhaps you might have a word with her as well? I don't want a repeat of last night."

"Oh, I shall. And I suggest you marry her soon, too."

The meal arrived at that moment and he stayed long enough to eat. They spoke of neutral matters. The latest news – that Portennabar and Portfillik were importing vast quantities of wine and water from across the Giving Sea, mixing them together and selling the result to supplement their water supplies – was much easier to talk about than Senya.

15

The Scarpen to the Red Quarter
Qanatend to Dune Pebblered

They stayed five nights in Qanatend.

Ryka, impatient and crotchety, was locked in her rooms at Ravard's orders. Nauseated with worry, she wanted to see Kaneth so badly her body ached, yet she didn't want to risk her fragile peace with Ravard. If he trusted her, he might eventually give her enough freedom to bring him down, even to bring his whole tribe to its knees. That idea was as fragile as a sand-dancer's mirage, so she obeyed his directives and kept her expression neutral when he gave her orders. She used his title when she spoke to him. In his bed, she was compliant and meek. It went against everything she was, and if she inwardly boiled with rage, she also shut that part of herself deep within, like a coiled snake in the darkness waiting for the moment to strike.

She strove to remember all she had read about the legend of a hero called Uthardim. It wasn't much. She had never thought it important. The actual history and the tribal myths of the Reduners were inextricably mixed, until no one knew which were an approximation of the truth and which just tales.

In her twenties Ryka had made her interest in Reduner stories known to merchants in Breccia, and as a result, a steady trickle of shaman scrolls had come her way. In the Uthardim story she'd read, Uthardim had been miraculously born already an adult, sired by a dune god, birthed by the divine immortal, Fire. At his birth, however, a jealous mortal lover of Fire had appeared and distracted her at the crucial moment of Uthardim's delivery. Instead of being caught in his mother's arms, he had slipped into the flames of her conflagration. His face had been badly burned as a result, and thereafter he had been known as Uthardim Half-face.

But ponder as she might, Ryka could not remember the rest of the story, except that he had become a warrior hero. *Damn it,* she thought crossly, *I can't even ask the guards, because that would mean speaking to them in Reduner.* That ability was still better kept a secret. She toyed with the notion of asking Ravard, but shied away from that, too. She didn't want him to think she was interested in Kaneth.

And so, when they rode out of the gateway of Qanatend, she was none the wiser as to why the guards treated Uthardim with such respect.

The caravan was larger now, and the pedes stolen from Breccia were loaded with more slaves from Qanatend. Her heart grieved as she scanned them; they were so young. Girls and boys of perhaps eight to twelve or thirteen, no more. Reduners preferred children; it gave them a chance to raise them to be wives and warriors who could forget their origins. Unlike older adults enslaved for their skills, a child was always given a choice after a year or two: slavery, or become a tribal member with all its privileges and responsibilities and loyalties. Most chose the easier route, and who could blame them? By then the sands would have stained their hair and their skin until they resembled their captors.

Ryka glanced at the line of pedes making up the caravan. Every seat on a pede was taken up, either with people or water or baggage. Several packpedes were piled high with roped bundles of dried bab fruit stolen from the warehouses. This time she rode behind Ravard himself, and behind her were Reduner warriors. Ravard was almost light-hearted. She scowled at his back. Didn't he care what his people had done to the city? Didn't he realise what their plundering would do to the people left behind?

As they rode through the groves and she once again saw the dying trees, the parched soil and the evidence of wanton vandalism, she allowed her bitterness to spill over. "You have stolen their food and destroyed their means of replacing it. Was it necessary to kill their trees and wreck the irrigation?"

He shrugged and turned his head to reply. "You should never have built a city on this side of the range in the first place; this is ours. The Scarpen should start with the Warthago."

"Why?"

"Once we lived all the way t'the coast! Once the whole Quartern was ours. *You* pushed us out! So now we take back all the land north of the Warthago." He waved a hand back at the city walls. "Once we have taken all the water the city has, Qanatend will be levelled t'the ground. Obliterated. Let all you Scarpen folk go back t'where you belong – the southern side of the range."

"These people will die getting there!"

"Perhaps. We don't care, just so long as they never come back."

"Is this what you will do to Breccia?"

"Breccia you can have. We have no interest in your cities. We certainly don't want t'live in them. We went there t'kill your rainlords and stormlords, that's all. 'Specially Cloudmaster Granthon. And we thought t'capture his replacement."

"You mean Jasper?"

"Yes, him with the fancy name. Jasper Bloodstone. Is it true he's a Gibber grubber?"

"So I heard."

He snorted in amusement, but made no comment. "It's time t'return to a Time of Random Rain. With him in our hands it would have been easy."

"You have no heart!"

"You Scarpen folk taught us well." The bitterness belonged to him now. She heard the acid in his voice and the grief in his tone, saw rage in the way his hands tightened on the reins. "You came t'our land and killed and plundered and destroyed. You made most of the Quartern yours. The 'Basters came and made the White Quarter theirs – well, now it's our turn again. You'll be the nomads, lookin' for water. We will be the hunters and drovers who know how t'live in this land, as you never did. All you ever had was magic."

"Are we – the people living now – guilty for what our ancestors did a thousand or more years ago?"

He twisted in the saddle to look at her. "No. You're guilty for what you did yesterday. I grew up in poverty so bleeding grim I counted meself lucky if I had water t'drink and a rough piece of bab sacking as a blanket against the cold. You – the people of the Scarpen and your rulers – you allowed people t'live like that, while you had enough water for your bleeding fancy bath houses! You could have granted us more water. Then we could have grown more bab, raised more animals."

"We didn't have sufficient stormlords. Cloudmaster Granthon did his best."

"You looked after yourselves just fine." He glanced ahead to make sure the pede was on track. "Anyhow, now we'll return to a time when we are dependent on no one – no one but ourselves – for water."

"A Time of Random Rain."

"We call it *Saren Jan Kai*. You people translated it as

'Time of Random Rain', but that's not really correct." He frowned, searching for the right words. "'Time of God-granted Rain' is closer t'the true meaning. We believe if we give the dune gods due respect, if we respect our dune, then they will see to it we get rain."

She waved a hand at one of the water-loaded pedes. "God-given random rain? You steal!"

"A temporary measure in place of having Jasper Bloodstone. 'Sides, maybe we don't have random rain 'cause Bloodstone takes whatever clouds start t'form natural-like."

He was probably right at that. She fell silent and they rode on, into country she had never seen before: the dry flatlands known as The Spindlings. By midday, they had reached the border of the Red Quarter. Beyond a rough gully marking the boundary, the land was red and sandy. In the distance the first of the dunes was a long red barrier across the plains, extending east and west as far as Ryka could make out with her inadequate eyesight.

She felt the dryness of the air like a physical assault, sucking moisture from all it touched. The Scarpen was an arid, thirsty land, but the Gibber was worse, and so was this. There were no trees; just low plants, grotesque in shape and vivid in colour, clinging to the red sand, creeping hither and thither in a desperate anxiety to find water. Many had leaves designed to collect dew or suck the juices out of desert insects and small creatures. A savage, killing land, baking under a devouring heat.

By evening they were camped at the foot of the first dune.

"Dune Pebblered," Ravard said, and helped Ryka down. He left her standing there and started to give orders to his men.

"Here, help me down, dear," Junial begged from her perch on another pede. "I don't have a handsome warrior waiting on me. My joints are on fire with all this sitting still and I hate being this high up. I cling onto that handle as if my life depends on it. Which it probably does, think on it."

Ryka gave a weary smile and obliged. The woman snorted as she looked about her. "So this is one of their precious dunes, eh? Just looks like a heap of red sand to me. Is this where he lives? Ouch, but my backside hurts. All the muscles are scrunched up." She rubbed her buttocks, wincing. "They'll be after me to cook in a moment, too."

Ryka envied Junial one thing: she was not molested by the Reduners, possibly because she was old enough to be un-attractive to them, or perhaps because no one wanted to upset a good cook.

"There are settlements on many of the dunes, including this one," Ryka told her. "But we are going to the one Sandmaster Davim rules, Dune Watergatherer. We have to cross a number of dunes to get there, I believe."

"Thought he ruled the lot of them?"

"Sort of – except wherever the rebels are. Vara Redmane and her followers. Dune Watergatherer is where Davim started, and it's where he lives now, as far as I know. Each dune has its own sandmaster, although nowadays they all bow to Davim."

"So how do they build cities on a heap of sand?"

"They don't. They live in tents, and move the encamp-ments from time to time. There are several tribes on each dune, all owing allegiance to the same dune sandmaster. So Kher Ravard heads his own tribe, but he lives on the same dune as Sandmaster Davim."

The older woman sighed. "Don't tell me, more lying on the ground instead of a proper bed. No tables, no chairs neither, I'll wager. I'm too old for this. And all because I cook a good loaf of bab bread. How's that for fate playing its sand-blasted tricks on a widow woman?" She gazed up at the slope of the dune. The sand was patterned with lines of creeping plant life, runnels flowing forth in random designs. "Pretty enough, I suppose. But where are the tunnels bringing water? We've seen none of them shafts since we left Qanatend."

"No tunnels were ever built here. I was told once that the Reduners regard each dune as sacred to a dune god, and not to be defiled by digging – or any permanent building for that matter. Besides, the dune moves. Difficult to build anything permanent."

"Then how ever do they get their water?"

"A stormlord can make it rain on the slopes of each dune near the waterholes. The most difficult of all the cloudbreaks, I believe, and possible because each camp is only a few hundred people, so they don't need much water."

Junial looked at her curiously. "How do you know all this stuff? There's more to you than meets the eye, seems to me!"

Ryka hedged. "I was a scholar once." She paused, then added quietly, "I suppose that has gone, along with the rest of my life."

Junial grimaced in sympathy. "I'm sorry. At least I'm not young enough for the men to want to climb under my shift. But y'know, you did get the best of the bunch, m'dear. Whose is the bread rising in the basket? His?"

"The bread . . . ? Oh. My baby. Blighted eyes, he's not the Kher's! He's my husband's." She touched her abdomen. "It really is obvious now, isn't it?"

"It is that. How far along are you? More than halfway, by the looks."

They were interrupted by a guard yelling at Junial. "Time cook!" he told her. "Work!"

Junial shrugged and trudged off to where the guards and slaves were starting the cooking fires.

Ryka lingered a moment to watch the changing colours as the sun slid below the horizon. Dark blood-red shadows accentuated the dips and hollows. The dying light blazed on the ridges until they glowed as if lit from within. *It's not pretty*, she thought. *Pretty is for sweet frilly stuff. This is stark, harsh, dangerous.*

But she couldn't help adding, *and magnificent.*

Even as she watched, the dune groaned, a deep moaning sound reverberating deep in the sand like a note plucked from the bass string of a giant lute.

"The dune god speaks," one of the Reduners said in his own tongue, and thumped his fist to his chest in reverent acknowledgement.

As they were eating, six men mounted on individual myria-pede hacks appeared on the horizon. Ryka felt them before she saw them. In the gloaming, they were no more than silhouettes against a deep purple sky, hard to see, but having sensed their water she knew where to look. Quickly she glanced away, not wanting Ravard, seated next to her on the matting and cushions by the fire, to realise her water sensitivity.

A few moments later he must have felt them himself because he stood hurriedly and called to his senior bladesmen, who sprang to their feet in instant obedience. They strode away from the camp, fully armed with scimitars, zigger cages and zigtubes. Ryka scrabbled to her feet to see better.

Ravard doesn't trust the Pebblered folk, she thought. *They bow to Davim and his heir, but once they were subject to no one. I wonder if they hate the tribes of Dune Watergatherer as much as we do.*

Kaneth threaded his way through the slaves to stand at her shoulder as she watched. "Ravard sent word to the closest Pebblered tribe that we were here," he murmured in her ear. "You cannot cross an inhabited dune without the permission of one of the tribes living on it. Of course they are far too frightened to stop Kher Ravard and his men, but apparently he observes the courtesies and pauses to ask."

She did not turn to acknowledge his presence. "How do you know that?" she whispered, hoping to prompt his memories. At least he sounded more rational now.

"I don't know. I remember the oddest things, without any recollection of where I learned them."

"But you still don't remember who you are?"

"No. Why don't you tell me more about who I am?"

"No. A little knowledge is dangerous. It is better you discover it for yourself. If they find out who you are –" she made a gesture towards the waiting men "– you would die before you drew another breath. You must be careful."

"I find it hard to think I was ever so dangerous to them."

"Believe me, you were. And you had better hope no one ever recognises you."

Kaneth gave a lopsided grin and tapped at the scabbing on his face. "I doubt I look the way I used to." In the dry air the scar was forming well, but his skin was puckering, drawing his face into a travesty of the handsome man she had known. Her breath caught, snagged on her desire to touch his cheek, to say how sorry she was. To tell him it didn't matter to her. She wanted him to assuage the ache in her heart by touching her in turn, but knew he would not. When he looked at her it was with a neutral interest, not desire, not friendship, not love.

Oh Sunlord, how can I bear this?

"You're a slave," she said. "Doesn't that enrage you? We are all slaves, to be used as our masters see fit. Women and boys to be raped, children taken from their families. There was a time when that would have roused you to a raging passion."

He ran a hand over his head in a troubled gesture. His hair was beginning to grow back in a short fuzz. Once it had been long and golden, shining and luxuriant. She had liked to run her hand through it. She pushed the thought away.

"I – I don't know. I feel as if I'm walking within the

wavering mists of a sand-dancer mirage. Nothing is real around me. There are voices speaking to me, but from so far away in the past I can barely hear the words. I catch glimpses – of people, of places, but I don't know who they are, where they are, or what they meant – mean – to me. When I try to catch hold of the images they dance away and my head throbs with pain. And inside me there is an emptiness that once was full, a hole of nothingness I don't know how to replenish."

Hope disintegrated, spilling out of her in tiny pieces, each one hurting. "Can't you – can't you remember *anything*?"

"Silly stuff – playing, squabbling with other children. Nothing important. And there are things I feel to be true from my adulthood. I know if I picked up a sword it would feel right in my hand, as if it belonged." He glanced away towards the dune. "I know I have been to the Red Quarter before. That I have ridden a pede across the sands. That I have a smattering of their tongue because I have mixed with them before. That there was a time when they were no enemies of mine." He looked back at her. "I know I have held a woman in my arms and loved."

Her heart pounded as if she had been running. "But you don't recall who?"

He shook his head. "I suppose I'd know her if I saw her. I have no memory of her face, or her voice. Just of the way I felt about someone. And sometimes I think there was as much grief there as happiness."

His words seared more than they comforted, reminding her of all they had lost. She swallowed away the pain.

She cast a glance about them to make sure no one was listening. Ravard and the Pebblered men were still talking, far enough away to be almost invisible in the darkness, as well as inaudible. In the camp itself, the only light was from the fire and there was not much of that. There was no one close enough to hear anything she or Kaneth said and no one even looking at them. The Reduners were passing around some skins of amber; some were singing – the noise level had risen.

"What do you remember playing with when you were little?" she asked, unable to resist the urge to prompt his memory, like a child who couldn't stop picking at a scab.

"Water," he said promptly, without apparent thought. Then repeated the word in astonishment, as if the memory had suddenly returned. "Water! Sunlord help me! I could once *move* water."

She hushed him with a finger to her lips.

He stared at her, shocked. "*That's* why you think I am in danger! I was a water sensitive!"

She smothered her joy at the fragment of returning memory. "They must not know."

"I don't remember—" He rubbed his forehead. "Withering spit. I remember *moving* water. I was a *rainlord*."

She nodded. "You are *still* a rainlord."

He considered that, his frown deepening. Then, "No. No. I'm not. Not any more. There's nothing there. Nothing."

And he stumbled away into the darkness. She stared after him, appalled. It couldn't be true, surely. She wanted to follow, but it was too risky and she dared not, no matter how much her heart ached for him.

The next morning, the pedes climbed the dune in single file, their pointed feet angled backwards to give them purchase on the shifting sand of the incline. Once again Ryka was seated behind Ravard, his proximity a reminder of the way he came to her each night, his gaze alight with anticipation. His desire to please her with his lovemaking was oddly touching, but the naïvety with which he tried to achieve her pleasure exasperated. In different circumstances, it might have been endearing; now the joy he took from the slightest of her smiles both puzzled and alarmed her. Nonetheless, as she rode behind him, seated cross-legged on the embroidered saddle cushion, any kindness she felt towards him was overridden by an abiding hatred of his assumptions, the assumptions of a conqueror.

I'm a slave, she thought. *I have no right to say no – and therefore this is rape, for all it is an agreement I entered into to keep my son safe.*

She glared at his back. *One day I shall kill him for it.* Yet when she thought of driving a blade into him, what she felt most was not triumph, but regret that it would be necessary.

Sandhells – why does everything have to be so complicated?

When they reached the outskirts of the Pebblered encampment, they halted. Some of the tribal elders, plus a number of Scarpen and Gibber slaves, were waiting for them in the cool of the morning. Ravard had apparently promised the tribe some of the water from Qanatend.

While the slaves hoisted the large family jars out of the panniers and carried them into the camp, Ryka stayed where she was, seated on the pede. Ravard stood a couple of paces away, holding the reins and chatting with the tribemaster, an elderly man, portly and unattractive, and to Ryka's eyes, obsequiously fawning.

The fellow is terrified of upsetting the Master Son, she thought. *Ravard may be young, but the men of other dunes fear him the way men fear Sandmaster Davim. I wonder if it is Ravard's reputation making them so scared, or simply because he is the sandmaster's heir?*

She shot a look at Kaneth where he sat alone on the slaves' packpede. The other male slaves had been unroped so that they could help carry the water; he had simply ignored the order. Bravado? Foolhardiness? That weird innocence he seemed to have now? She didn't know. *Oh, Kaneth, please get better soon. I am scared too, and so alone . . .*

From the back of her mount, she glanced across to where

the slaves, both the ones from the caravan and those from the encampment, were working together to unload the packpedes. Each water jar was tightly sealed with bab gum to stop spillage or evaporation. *Scarpen water*, she thought, her bitterness so raw she could taste it on her tongue. *And how many will die because it was stolen?*

Elmar was there and several others, including the slave who had threatened to kill Ravard if he had the chance. What was his name? Whetstone, that was it. A Scarpen artisan with enough rage inside him to make him a poor choice for enslavement. Even now, he sent periodic scowls in the direction of Ravard and the Pebblered tribemaster.

The sand-brained fool, Ryka thought. *Sooner or later someone is going to notice and decide he's more trouble than he's worth.*

She watched as Elmar and another man climbed onto a pede to extract a jar from the pannier and hand it down to Whetstone. The jar caught on a piece of bab-fibre rope used to secure the pannier to the pede and they could not unhook it. Whetstone reached up to help, but the cord had pulled tight and he couldn't budge it, either. The guard, seeing their predicament, stepped forward, sliding his scimitar out of his scabbard to cut the cord.

Ryka's mouth went dry as she saw Whetstone change. His slouch tautened. His scowl dissolved into an avid hunger. *Oh, blast*, she thought. *He wouldn't.* She sent a frantic look in Kaneth's direction, more out of habit than conscious thought. She jerked her head to indicate what had caught her attention, and he turned his head to look.

The cord cut, the Reduner guard prepared to put his weapon back into its scabbard. His grip, loose and casual, was no match for Whetstone's powerful wrenching grab. Before the guard had fully realised what had happened, Whetstone had leapt away. His face was a portrait of blind rage as he raised the scimitar over his head in a double-fisted hold, his teeth bared in an animal-like snarl. He raced towards Ravard, the blade poised for a savage downwards slash. Kaneth scrambled up to stand on the back of his pede.

Ryka's thoughts were lucid and fast. *Whetstone wants to kill Ravard dead. I could stop this.* She could jump on the man as he passed between Kaneth's pede and hers. She could save Ravard's life.

But why should I? This was their chance. She had a pede loaded with food and water under her, Kaneth was right next to her, Elmar nearby and none of them was tied.

In the confusion we can ride out of here— Even as the thoughts tumbled through her head, she acted.

She too stood up. As she straightened, she beckoned to Elmar. Her heart was beating wildly. He gave a pikeman's salute, telling her he understood, then he leaped from the packpede and raced – not towards her, but towards Kaneth's pede. Exactly as she had hoped he would.

At the same moment, the guard who had lost his weapon gave a belated screech of warning and took off after Whetstone. Ravard heard and began to turn, his hand dropping the reins to reach for the hilt of his scimitar. He would be too late to save himself, Ryka saw that much. She took a step towards the driver's seat on the first segment and bent to grab the reins where they looped across the saddle.

And the world shifted. An eerie sound throbbed into the air from beneath the dune, like the echoing beat of a drummer in an underground cavern.

The legs of Ryka's mount sank into the sand along one side. She panicked, the terror of the incomprehensible over-whelming her as the animal tilted. In startled shock the pede reared its head, its mouthparts clicking and sawing its alarm. She lost her balance and began to topple. She flung out a hand to grab the pede's segment handle and missed. As she fell, the scene she glimpsed etched itself onto her memory.

Elmar, arms pumping, raced towards them in answer to her call. In front of him, one of Whetstone's feet sank into the sand as if it was water. He went flying, to sprawl head-long a pace away from Ravard. The scimitar flew from his hand in an arc. Ravard and the Pebblered tribemaster both tumbled to their knees, the ground unstable beneath their feet.

In the background, the throbbing sound changed to a higher tremolo, hauntingly beautiful, spine-tinglingly eldritch. Through it all, Kaneth stood on the back of the packpede alongside her, his expression stark and intense, yet devoid of fear, as the reddish slanting rays of the rising sun captured him in a glowing halo of light. He looked godlike, resembling images she had seen painted on temple walls.

And then she hit the ground. All the breath in her lungs was forced out. Pain lanced through her torso. She screamed silently, *The baby*! She gasped for air, tortuously dragged it into emptied lungs. And all the while the sand beneath her slipped and slid like unstrung beads and the strange unearthly song issued forth from the depths of the dune.

When coherence returned, Kaneth was kneeling at her side, touching her face, begging her to say something. The ground beneath her still moved, gently now as trickles of sand flowed this way and that. A small fountain of sand grains inexplicably burst forth next to her shins to shower her legs.

Nearby, the Pebblered tribemaster was hauling himself upright and Ravard was struggling to rise. He was buried up to his knees. When he finally pulled himself free, he lurched across the still rippling ground to the man who had tried to kill him.

Whetstone, on his knees, had lost the scimitar, and was

groping blindly around in the sand for it. Ravard drew his weapon, his intention clear. Ryka wanted to move, but pain and fear of more pain kept her immobile.

Kaneth looked up from where he crouched beside Ryka, and said, "*No.*" The single word was commanding, spoken with an authority he did not have, not here. It stopped Ravard, that voice. It stopped the sands too, or so it appeared, for they ceased moving the moment he spoke, and the song from deep in the earth fell silent.

You're sand-crazy, Ryka told Kaneth, but her words must have only been in her head, because she didn't hear them.

Whetstone was still on his knees, his rage deflated. "Lord! Lord Uthardim," he cried. "The Kher killed my family. My parents, my brothers. I want justice. Kill him. Kill this murdering redman."

Ravard ignored him. All his attention was now focused on Kaneth. "Who are you t'command the Master Son of the Watergatherer?"

Perhaps to his men he sounded merely outraged, but Ryka knew him well. She sensed uncertainty in him.

"The man who just saved your life by moving the dune beneath our feet," Kaneth replied.

Watergiver above! He's saying he *did this? Moved the sand?* She tried to rise, but pain gripped her, holding her prisoner.

He added, "And now I ask you to spare this man."

His calm made her heart pound. She felt everyone present holding their breath, although many surely did not understand the Scarpen language. Ravard stared at him, shocked. No, more than that, he was outraged by Kaneth's claim. She struggled against waves of nausea, trying to make sense of what Kaneth meant. Of all that had happened.

Ravard paused. Not once did he look at the man he wanted to kill. He gave a snort of disbelief, aimed at Kaneth. "Your brains shrivelled along with your hair. The sand was doubtless moved by the dune god of Pebblered to save me, not by you! Why the pickled pede would I spare a man who tried t'kill me? And doubtless will again if he has the chance?"

And with casual grace, he swung his blade in an arc that slit Whetstone's throat. Blood spurted, drenching Ravard's trousers even before the body fell. Ravard took no notice. His gaze locked on Ryka's. For the briefest of moments she glimpsed something there that was close to panicked concern. For her. Then it was gone, and his face hardened.

"That man's actions prompted the dune god to rise up to protect me and his tribemaster," he said, addressing Kaneth.

Kaneth shrugged. "Believe what you will."

"Even if that weren't so, I don't owe you nothing! I paid for it in advance with a horned cat. We'd be even, if it was you halted this man – which I don't believe."

"See to the woman of your tent. She may lose your child if she is not well tended."

Ryka drew in a sharp breath of anguish. He thought their son was *Ravard's*? A shudder ran through her body. Pain wrenched her, and she wondered if she was bleeding. *Sunlord, save my babe. It's too soon for him to be born. Much too soon.*

Vaguely she was aware of Ravard laughing. "It's not *my* bastard, you fool. She's just a Breccian woman, one of the better spoils of war." He turned to the Pebblered tribemaster. "Get her a travel pallet. We'll load her onto the back of a pede when it's time t'move off."

"She's injured," Kaneth said angrily. "Can't you see she's hurting? Leave her here in the Pebblered encampment until she recovers."

Ravard looked genuinely puzzled. "She's a slave," he said, as if that explained everything. "And a woman at that. Live or die, d'you think I care? Women are plentiful." He turned back to the tribemaster. "Do as I ask."

"Kher," Elmar said respectfully as the tribemaster disappeared from Ryka's line of vision, "may I get Garnet's cloak from the pede to cover her?"

"Yes, do so. And when the pallet arrives, put her on it and strap it t'the back of my pede. She can travel behind me." In the glance he gave her then, she saw concern, but he said nothing. *Too damned worried about what his men would think if he asked how I was*, she thought.

He moved away and Elmar climbed onto the pede, leaving Ryka and Kaneth alone. "Withering hells, Garnet," he whispered, "I'm sorry."

"*Did* you do that?" she asked, struggling to understand. "Did you move the sand?"

His frustration at his ignorance burned deep into her senses. "Is it something I could once do?"

She shook her head. His powers had always been odd and unpredictable, but not *that* odd.

"Are you badly hurt?"

She wanted to answer, to say something that made sense, but no words came. She caught the muttered conversation of the two Reduner guards who had come to drag away Whetstone's body.

"The dune god obeys him," one said in awe. "Did you see? He glowed red, and the sands moved at his gesture and stopped with his spoken word."

"He is Uthardim," the other replied reverently. "He will be the saviour of our people."

No, Ryka thought, muddled. *That can't be right. He's Kaneth, rainlord of the Quartern. Father of my son.*

217

16

Red Quarter
Dune Pebblered to Dune Sandsinger

They crossed two more dunes the day they left Pebblered, but Ryka knew little about the journey. Griping pains seized her gut and she turned her senses inwards, not outwards. The blood was already seeping out between her legs and she knew of no way to stop it.

Come evening, the caravan halted at the foot of Dune Sandsinger, another inhabited dune. When Elmar and several of the other slaves unloaded her, still strapped to the pallet, they did not take her to Ravard's tent, but laid her in the open. They put up a cover against the dewfall, and built a fire of dried pede balls for warmth. The smell was sweet with herbs; better, she thought, than the seaweed briquettes used in the Scarpen.

The other slaves left, but Elmar stayed, sitting close and keeping his voice down as he spoke to her. "Are you comfortable?"

She hedged. "The pallet is well stuffed."

"I managed to get hold of that scimitar. The one Whetstone grabbed. I have it hidden in the supplies."

"That was good thinking."

"A risk, though. The owner was searching for it when we left. If they think one of us slaves took it they might search us all."

"They'll think it was covered up in that upheaval of sand. Elmar, what *happened*?"

He shook his head. "I don't know. I spoke to a couple of the slaves who were carting the jars to the encampment when the ground shook, and they never felt a thing, although they did hear the singing. The only folk who felt it were the ones around about us."

"Kaneth says he did it. Ravard thinks it was the dune god, protecting his tribemaster."

He looked uneasy. "The dunes sing and make sounds. And the Reduners say under each dune a god sleeps. Every now and then he wakes to speak to the shamans . . ."

"We are supposed to believe in the Sunlord, not dune gods. They don't exist."

"Don't know I believe in anything much. But something made the sand move." He shivered. "Uncanny, it was. I don't like these dunes. They move anyway, you know, swallowing everything in their path, like some kind of monster eating its way across the land. Put a pike in my hand and an enemy in front of me, and I'll enjoy a good fight. But sand that moves and sings? Gives me the shiver-shudders."

She smiled. "The dunes move very slowly, a few paces each cycle, and I suspect it is the wind sending them on their way across the plains, not any monster or dune god within. Elmar, I need to eat a lot tonight. Meat, if you can get hold of some, to bring my powers up to par. I'm losing blood."

He looked shocked. "You're *bleeding*?"

"Yes. I – I may be losing the baby." She tried to sound matter-of-fact, but the expression on his face told her she had failed.

"Sunlord help you. I didn't know. I'll get some food. And one of the women."

"Ask Junial. She told me she sometimes assisted the midwife on her level."

She rested, glad not to be jolting along on pedeback, but her peace did not last. Ravard came.

With sick apprehension, she wondered whether he would wonder what she had been doing standing up on the back of the pede just before she had fallen. She hoped he had not noticed. After all, Whetstone had been attacking him at the time . . .

He didn't appear to be angry. In fact he looked more uneasy than anything. "Are you comfortable?" he asked.

"Not particularly."

He fidgeted awkwardly. "The baby?"

"I am bleeding."

"Ah." He scratched his ear, once again hardly more than a youth trying to cope with a situation too big for him. Sunlord damn, he looked *anxious*. Worried, for her.

She wondered if he ever appeared that way to his men and decided it was unlikely. They gave him a healthy respect and she'd never heard them mock him even when he wasn't around. No, this boyish, vulnerable side occurred only with her. *Spitless damn.*

"I'm sorry. Shall I get one of the women . . . ?" he asked.

"I've asked someone to come. Junial. The cook."

He looked blank, but nodded anyway. "Food . . . ?"

"Also coming."

"Is it, um, serious?"

"Of course it's serious."

"Oh. I— oh." He looked down and fiddled with the handle of the dagger thrust through his belt, as if he was an embarrassed lad of twelve, not the heir to all the dunes of the Red Quarter.

Then she saw the dark patch of Whetstone's dried blood on his trousers and looked away. *Don't mistake the insecurities of youth for kindness, Ryka.*

"I'm sorry," he said finally. "I dropped the reins and the

pede panicked when the sand shifted. I feel responsible. I wish t'apologise."

Blighted eyes, she thought, *there are times when I almost like him.* "Kher, what happened back there? The sand, moving like that—"

He shrugged. "The sand shifts on the slopes sometimes, and sings. Perhaps it is the dune god, perhaps not. One thing for sure, it wasn't Uthardim." His voice was larded with scorn.

"What did the shaman of Pebblered say?"

He looked uncomfortable. "The man heard the singing, but admitted that he did not recognise the song." He stopped and changed the subject abruptly. "If there is anything else you need, send someone t'tell me." He walked away without waiting for her reply, and she let out the breath she had been holding.

Elmar returned shortly with a plate piled high with food and helped her to sit up so she could eat it. "What did that bastard want?" he asked.

"To apologise," she replied and told him what the Master Son had said.

Elmar started laughing. "He thinks it was his fault you fell? Because he let the reins fall? That's as good as a double dayjar ration!"

She wanted to chuckle, decided it would hurt too much and dampened the urge. Instead, she forced herself to eat.

"At least he has no clue the two of us were thinking of escape. It was a brave thing you did, m'lord," he said, keeping his voice low. "Weren't your fault it didn't work."

"There will be another attempt, I promise you. Perhaps when I am more sure Kaneth will join us."

The look he gave her was troubled. "I wasn't about to give him a choice this morning. I was going to seize the pede he was on."

"I know."

There was so much pain in his eyes. And something else. Love. Not for her, though. It shook her to see the tough warrior so vulnerable. "What *happened* out there?" he asked. "What made him say he had saved Ravard? Why would he *want* to save Ravard anyway?"

"I don't think he was trying to do so. The sand collapsed under us, who knows why. Kaneth was just trying to make Ravard think he did it. Because of being Uthardim. The other Reduners are buying it, even if Ravard doesn't."

"I hope you're right. Because that would mean the old Kaneth is returning, piece by bleeding piece. Oh, he doesn't remember much past his early boyhood yet, but his, no, *he* is coming back. The man. The cynical sarcastic bastard we used to know and love."

Relief suffused her. *Soon. Soon we'll be out of here. Ravard will die and then we can go after Davim.*

He continued to kneel at her side, his large restless hands pulling at his clothing as if he was looking for the scabbard he no longer wore. He said at last, "I gather he knows now he was a rainlord, but you didn't tell him you were, too. You don't trust him yet either, do you?"

"He is so confused," she said. "Weeping hells, Elmar, he can't remember a thing that has happened over the past twenty years – none of it! Not the way the young stormlords died, not what Taquar did to us all, not our search of the Gibber for talented children, not even Nealrith's death. Sandblast, he doesn't even *remember* Nealrith except as maybe a child playing skittles with him! He doesn't know Jasper exists. How could he have any loyalty to anyone?

"You were right, and I was wrong. If he doesn't remember his loyalties, how can he know where to place his honour? I am waiting for a sign that he cares about us. When I have that, I'll tell him. In the meantime, you must tell him as much as you can, but not all at once. Little by little. A reminder here, a reminder there. Start – start with things furthest away in the past."

"I don't have much opportunity now," Elmar said. "Most of the time I am tied up with the other men and there are usually guards within earshot anyway."

He paused, and when he spoke again it was to reminisce. "I first met him when I was ordered to be his sparring partner in the practice yard, did you know that? Cocky brat he was then, as full of himself as a puffed up sandgrouse and sure he could best anyone. We knocked the stuffing out of him as fast as we knew how. But he didn't resent it. I liked that. After that, we were a team, Lord Kaneth and me. At first, I was the teacher, him the pupil. In the end, he led, I followed – because he was worth following. We protected each other's backs. I always knew which way he'd move, and he knew he could rely on me. The best years of my otherwise useless life have been with him. M'lord, it's breaking me in two to see him like this, and to be so powerless to help him."

The grief in his voice was profound, confirming something she had long suspected. "You love him."

He was silent.

"Does he know?"

His laugh had a bitter edge. "Come on, I got better sense than that. Would change things, him knowing. He may have slept with every damned snuggery girl in Breccia, but he's never looked at a man. Don't let it bother you. You got his heart, and that's the way it should be."

"And lost it, it seems, because of a blow to his head. Watergiver take it, Elmar; we are a sorry pair, aren't we?"

His low laugh was devoid of bitterness this time. "That we are. He wants to see you, by the way. Asked me if I would ask you first."

"Maybe it's Kher Ravard you should be asking," she pointed out dryly. "He's the one who owns us both."

"You may be out of earshot here, but you're hardly out of sight with only this bit of canvas overhead. I don't think the Kher'll take exception. He saw me bringing you the food and he said nothing. But then, he's a touchy bastard. Watch him, m'lord. He's a powerful man on the outside, but the inside quivers."

"With what?"

"Who knows? Fear? Insecurities? Madness? Hate? Rage against the world? That young warrior is two people, not one."

She remembered the scars on Ravard's back, and wondered about his past.

"I'll tell Kaneth to come, shall I?" Elmar asked.

She nodded.

"Go easy on him. Ah, here's Junial. I'd better go and eat something myself, before they truss me up for the night like a bale of bab kernels in a burlap sack." His scarred face seamed in a smile as he left and Junial took his place at Ryka's side.

Junial's advice was to the point. "Move as little as possible. You want to water the plants, you do it right here beside your bed. Bed rest is the only thing I know that can save a babe. But then, maybe it's better to let it go. After all, what's the point of letting a child be born to slavery?" She cleaned up the blood, pronounced the amount to be small as yet, and then left, promising to sleep at Ryka's side for the night if allowed, in case she needed help.

No sooner had Junial left than Kaneth came and knelt at her side. "How are you?" he asked.

She studied his face in the firelight, the concern in his eyes, but could see nothing there that spoke of love. Disappointed yet again, she said bluntly, "I'll live. The baby may not."

"I can't apologise enough."

"For what?"

"You were going to stop that man from killing Ravard. If you'd jumped on him as he passed, you might have died. He had his scimitar over his head, ready to strike! I thought you'd impale yourself. All I could think was to stop you. And instead I hurt you."

A sign. She had wanted a sign that he cared, even a little. And now that she had it, she stared at him, incredulous. "I wasn't thinking to *save* Ravard! I was happy enough to see him die!" The irony stabbed at her, cutting deep. She tried to explain. "I stood up to move to the driver's saddle. I was going to steal the pede and ride away with you and Elmar in the confusion of Ravard's death."

He frowned, as if he had trouble taking in all she said. Finally he remarked, "They would have killed us with ziggers."

"They would never have released them. They would have lost every single slave for a start, not to mention any Pebblered Reduners not wearing the correct perfume – which might have been all of them. You do know that, don't you? That each dune uses a particular perfume their ziggers are trained to avoid?" *And I would have killed any that came after us . . .*

He nodded. "Yes, yes, I know that." He rubbed his forehead once more, a gesture she was beginning to dread. "Facts I recall. But I don't think very well sometimes. Was I always so witheringly slow?"

"You had a sharp mind once. You will again." *But what the blighted hell makes you think you can move the very sand beneath our feet?* "Would you – would you have come with us?"

To her dismay, he didn't give an immediate answer, and when he did reply, she wasn't sure she wanted the answer anyway.

"I would have wanted to," he said finally. "But it seems wrong to leave folk in slavery."

"A rainlord's skills are better spent elsewhere." *You hypocrite*, she added beneath her breath, and it was herself she meant.

"But that's just it, Garnet. I'm not a rainlord. Although I suspect I was trying to call on my water-sense when I tried to stop you." He made a gesture of frustration. "I'm not explaining this very well. When I saw you – as I thought – preparing to jump on the slave with the scimitar, I was too far away to grab you so I reached out for something to use. Water, I guess. I suppose what I did was instinctive because I certainly didn't think about it. I just felt something deep in the dune and reached for it. I touched it. But I don't think it was water. Then everything went horribly wrong."

"You really believe you made the sand move?"

"I think I did something to start the sand moving. And once it started I didn't know how to stop it."

"I think you just said 'No,'" she said dryly, "and it ceased."

He wasn't amused. "I can't explain it. And I feel so guilty. You were hurt. Worse, now you tell me I wrecked your chance to escape."

She didn't reply. In truth, she didn't know what to say.

"Ravard said your baby wasn't his."

"Of course it isn't!" Her rage bubbled to the surface, even though she knew she was being unfair. "It's only been what – ten days? – since I had the misfortune to meet Kher Ravard! I was looking through a pile of corpses for the body of my husband at the time . . ."

"Oh. Oh, I'm sorry. I had no idea."

She stared at him, trying not to feel the hurt he had not meant to give her. The concern was still there in his eyes; concern for a stranger who had crossed his path. She wanted to reach out, touch his scar, cup his face with her hand. She wanted to feel his hands on her body, touching their child.

226

He said, "I don't remember what happened in Breccia in the days before I was flung onto the pyre."

In his confusion, his hand went to his head again and she wondered if his headaches were bothering him still. *Or maybe it's just talking to me makes men fidget,* she thought with a touch of hysteria. She took a deep breath and calmed herself. "The baby is my husband's. Let's just leave it at that."

Kaneth was upset, that was obvious. Her thoughts were in turmoil, but one emerged from the murk, clear and sure: he would not betray her. That danger was past.

"But there is something you should know," she added. "I didn't tell you before, because I wasn't sure I could trust you. You were so . . . confused."

"Go on."

"I'm also a rainlord. We've known each other since we were children attending the rainlord academy in Breccia."

He sat back on his heels, eyes wide. "Weeping shit."

She waited for him say something else. Anything.

"Then why didn't you escape before now?" he asked finally.

"Because I wouldn't leave without you, you sand-brained idiot! We are rainlords! We – we help one another."

Another long silence, as if he was trying to puzzle something out. "Did you go to bed with that sand-tick because of *me*?"

She snorted. "Don't pride yourself! Why the waterless hells would I do that? I did it to get out of Breccia in one piece and save my child. My sister died in my arms in Breccia Hall because she wouldn't bed Davim, and I didn't want to end up the same way."

"Oh, sandblast it. I have to think about this. I – oh, sod the bastard. Ravard's staring at us with his hand on the hilt of his scimitar." He stood up. "I think I had better go before I embarrass myself by uttering any more inanities. Can I apologise again for being ten times a sand-stuffed fool? Garnet, is there anything I can do to help you now?"

"You could call me Ryka, when we are alone, at least. That's my real name."

Breathless she waited for something – some recognition, some indication that the name meant something. But there was nothing. His face was blank.

He hesitated. "I'd rather not. We knew each other once. I've known you for years, it seems. And yet . . . I don't know what you were to me. Family? Sister? Lover? Fellow comrade-at-arms? Friend? I don't know. And perhaps you are wise not to tell me. For now you are just Garnet Prase, and I start afresh even if you don't. The day I call you Ryka, you will know I remember you."

She watched him as he walked away, biting her lip to stop herself from calling him back. Only when he disappeared into the darkness on the other side of the cooking fires did she turn her senses inwards to concentrate on saving their child.

The man who thought of himself as nameless rose before the sun the following day. He walked through the outer perimeter of guards, nodding amiably to the closest of the sentries who made no move to stop him, continuing on till he reached the top of one of the dune hills. The sky lightened as he went; the stars began to fade, then died in the shimmer of the coming dawn.

From the crest he could see in all directions. The encampment was beginning to wake. Slaves were out collecting pede droppings for burning in the camp fires, the drovers were cleaning and polishing their mounts. In the other direction, the tent settlement of the sandmaster of Dune Sandsinger was also astir. Unlike the travelling tents of Ravard and his men, the settlement tents were lavish affairs, embroidered and fringed, with a porch and several rooms each, and sides that could be rolled up or lowered. Their kitchens were communal, shared between three or four families, roofed with jute canvas and furnished with tables and benches made of bab wood or stone slabs.

Why do I know things like that? he wondered. *I even know the Reduners grow jute around their waterholes and the Gibber folk grow it in their drywashes, while the Alabasters grow flax somewhere or other – and yet I don't know my own name?*

He turned his thoughts to Garnet. Ryka. She puzzled him because she didn't seem to fit. He had vague memories of nebulous women – a lot of them – in his past. Women offering themselves for money, or perhaps for fun. Women taken and enjoyed and forgotten. He couldn't put faces or names to the memories, but he sensed they had not been like Garnet, nor had she been one of them. When she regarded him, the look in her eyes was unsettling in its intensity. In her presence he had a feeling of familiarity.

He thought of her, of the woman she was now, Ravard's woman. Now that he knew how recently she had been widowed and enslaved, he was staggered by both her bravery and her dignity. She had gone from wife to concubine, from free citizen to slave, all in the space of a few days, yet she stood up to Ravard and she held her head high. Her courage astounded him. *I am in awe of her.*

And then he gave a grim smile. Perhaps she admired his courage too; if so the admiration was misplaced. Oh, he was brave, he knew that, but his bravery came from a lack of caring. Without a past, he had no fear, because he knew of nothing he wanted to live for. Paradoxically, without a past, he knew of nothing he cared to die for either.

"What thoughts go round in that head empty of memories?"

He turned to face the speaker, who stood fifteen paces or so distant. If he really had been a rainlord, he would have sensed the man's approach, or so he supposed; instead, he was taken by surprise.

"Kher Ravard," he said, inclining his head to the man, but not enough to indicate his slave status.

Ravard glowered at him.

"To answer your question – I was debating the nature of bravery. And also what makes a slave."

"Defeat makes a slave," the younger man sneered, and came several paces nearer. "A brave man fights t'the death rather than be taken by th'enemy."

"No. Defeat makes a *captive*, not a coward. Bravery is sometimes the decision to go on living. Tell me, who was Uthardim?"

"A hero of the past who had a burned face."

"You appear to scorn the legends of your people."

"Scorn them? No. I scorn *you*." Ravard approached, and his right hand fell to his scimitar hilt. He had a zigtube clipped to his shoulder, and the nameless man could hear the frenzied buzzing of the zigger within. "You're not Uthardim Half-face reborn. You're a Breccian nobody, and you were thrown onto a funeral pyre before your time, that's all."

"Perhaps, perhaps not. I asked one of your drovers who speaks a bit of the Scarpen tongue about Uthardim Half-face. Apparently the story is he was the man who gathered together the remnants of the original people of the Quartern and led them to a new life on the dunes, after the ancestors of the Scarpen folk came from across the Giving Sea and displaced them. They looked on him as a saviour, the founder of their culture, because in the dunes they found the pedes and the ziggers and they became Reduner drovers and caravanners and hunters as a result, instead of the impoverished herders of goats they had once been. When Uthardim was dying, so the story goes, he said he would be reborn out of the fire, to lead your people to victory against the invaders."

Ravard, now only a pace away, dropped his voice to a low

tone laden with threat and anger. "That's not you, for sure," he spat out. "Why would a reborn Uthardim come back as one of the enemy, rather than a drover of the dunes? You're no hero returned! If I had my way, you'd be thrown back on that pyre, and that'd be the end of it. You keep away from my woman, or that *will* be what happens t'you, no matter what the sandmaster wants."

The nameless man smiled. "That woman belongs to no one, and in your heart you know it."

Ravard reached out and grabbed him by the neck of his tunic, jerking him forward until his face was only a hand span away. "Garnet made her choice. I don't force her. Ask her the truth of that, if you like."

"I can hardly ask her anything. You just told me to keep away from her."

"You're like all wilting Scarpen uplevellers! You mock us by playing with words, thinking they give you power. Well, they don't. Power comes from this –" he gripped the hilt of his scimitar "– and this." He tapped the zigtube, then flung the other man from him.

The nameless man staggered, but kept his footing. He said, and the words were lies, "This morning, I spoke to the slave woman who is tending Garnet. She says it is unlikely she will live the day out. Not if you strap her to a-pede for another day's trek. Leave her here, if you want her to live. Let the tribal women of Dune Sandsinger care for her until she has recovered."

"One day you'll make a mistake," Ravard said, "and I'll be free t'kill you."

The nameless man shook his head, upset. Had the fellow even bothered to listen?

They exchanged a stare, each taking the other's measure. The nameless man, bent on irritating the other, allowed a slight smile to play at the corner of his lips. They were both

231

large men. He was broader in the shoulder, but the Reduner was all muscle and sinew. He was experienced, he instinctively knew that much about himself, but the Reduner had the quickness of youth on his side.

"You can *try* to kill me," he said. "I feel sorry for you. There's nothing you would like better than to slit my throat with that scimitar of yours. But your men look up to me and Davim has forbidden you to harm me. In fact, I suspect he has forbidden you to treat me as a slave. After all, that wouldn't be wise if I really was some sort of reincarnation of a mythical hero, would it?"

"You're no hero, let alone one from the past. You're just sand-witted dross, the leavings of a man who doesn't even remember his name. Half-face is a good name for you. Because that's all you are; half a face, half a mind and half-witted."

"Ah, but can you be sure?" He was amused, and felt an echo of the man he had once been. "Did you not see the sands obey my words? I owed you a life, Ravard. And yesterday I paid you; you are right about that. We are even now, you and I."

"The dune doesn't obey *you*, a non-believer! You blaspheme. It was the dune god of Pebblered who saved one of his tribemasters, and in so doing saved me!"

"Are you sure?" he asked again. Then he turned and walked back down the slope towards the camp. *And you'd better see to Garnet's well-being, you bit of waterless shit, or I'll—*

The thought, however, stopped there, because he couldn't imagine just what he *would* do. He was unarmed in a camp full of Reduner warriors led by a man who was fast coming to hate him. He heaved a sigh, aware that, even though he had little memory of his history, at times he wasn't the wisest of men.

Garnet. If it looked as if Ravard wouldn't leave her behind, he would do something, anything, to make sure he did. He just didn't know what yet. And he wasn't quite sure why. What was it in his past that tied him to a woman he couldn't even remember?

PART TWO

The Price of Escape

17

White Quarter
The Whiteout and Mine Silverwall

Terelle woke knowing everything was wrong. It was night, that much was certain. Overhead the Star River shone in a brilliant band across the depths of the black sky. And she couldn't move.

Panic, urgent and futile, drove out thought. She lay on her back, head higher than her feet, her body firmly bound. Turning her head was possible, but nothing else. Yet she was . . . shifting. At speed. She could feel the wind on her face, whipping at her hair. The swishing sound of movement filled the air around her.

In fear, her heart hammered against her ribs. She struggled, wanting to sit up, but her bonds wouldn't allow it. Tiny pricks spattered softly at her face; when she licked her lips, they were covered in fine salt.

On her left, a shape loomed, gliding, keeping pace, a ghostly silver outline against the starlit salt. She lifted her head and strained to see better. A white pede, its countless legs moving in waves like a curtain in the wind. The driver stood on its back, holding the reins in one hand, long prod in the other, perfectly balanced. An Alabaster: white-skinned, flowing white hair, silvered now to blend in with his world. But she was not high on a pede's back. She was gliding as smoothly as a hawk on the wind, yet she was only a couple of hand spans away from the salt of The Whiteout.

She turned her head to the other side. Another similar pede and driver, only this pede trailed a rectangular shape. A litter, that's what it looked like. Front shafts tied to the rear of the pede, the back set with small wheels.

Her fear dampened and she began to think again. *Alabasters, Watergiver be thanked, not Reduners. And Russet.* That had to be Russet, tied just as she was. They were being drawn over the surface of salt. She remembered now. Alabasters had given her water, smeared her skin with some kind of ointment. They must have tied her to the litter so she wouldn't fall off. She lay back, tired, wondering drowsily if they had drugged her. Never mind, she'd worry about it all later. She closed her hurting eyes and drifted pleasantly away.

A long time afterwards Terelle awoke again, in a tent.

The sides were rolled up, and it was bright daylight outside. And hot. Stifling. Beneath her was the softness of a quilt placed on colourful carpeting. For a moment she stared, wondering why the woven patterns of that carpet seemed familiar. As soon as she stirred to take a better look, someone came to her side to offer her a water skin. A tall Alabaster woman, dressed in the white clothing of her people, she was one of the largest women Terelle had ever seen. The cloth of her robe, adorned with tiny mirrors and red embroidery on the front panels, strained to contain the abundance of her buttocks, the unusual breadth of her hips and the solid bulge of her breasts. Even her long white hair, braided in a single plait that reached her waist, was copious. Not a young woman, Terelle decided; her face was meshed with the lines of age.

"I'm Errica," she said, "the physician of our mine."

Terelle made no sense of that, but nodded anyway. "Terelle," she said. "From Scarcleft." Her lips hurt when she spoke. They had been rubbed with pede fat, but were still cracked and sore. She drank, long and deep draughts. Vaguely she remembered waking earlier to drink, several times. "Russet?"

"Pardon?"

"The old man."

"Ah. He's very ill. Scorpion sting. We're treating that, but it has poisoned his system. He may not live."

"Oh." She tried to think about that, but her thoughts kept slipping away.

Errica smiled in understanding, and did not press her to talk. Instead she helped her to drink some more, to eat some food, and showed her where she could relieve herself. Then she left her alone again. Terelle dozed.

The next time she awoke, perhaps a couple of runs of the sandglass later, she felt almost normal. Errica, sitting cross-legged on the carpet at her side, was mending a tear in an Alabaster robe. She laid that aside as soon as she saw Terelle was awake.

"Feel like getting up now?" she asked. "I have a clean robe for ye to be wearing – one of our own, if ye don't mind that. At least it isn't stiff with salt like your own clothes."

"Thank you. That'd be wonderful." Terelle struggled to her feet, wincing. All her muscles ached.

"When we get to the mine, there might be enough water to be washing clothes," Errica added. "We'll see."

"Where are we now?"

"We were travelling east from Mine Emery on our way to Mine Silverwall, when we saw your fire. We detoured a bit to be picking ye up and then camped here this morning to be giving the pedes a rest. We will start travelling again soon, once evening brings the cool air. We should be reaching Mine Silverwall by tomorrow morning."

"Mine? Oh, salt mines! You – you went out of your way

to find us? Thank you. You saved my life. Maybe Russet's as well."

"Ye should never take a black pede onto the salt, you know. The black colour absorbs the reflected heat from the salt as well as the direct heat of the sun. Their blood boils."

Terelle shuddered, chastened. "I didn't know that." *But I did guess Russet didn't know what he was doing.*

The woman indicated some clothing laid on the carpeting. "Get dressed now, while I get my husband; he wants to speak to ye."

She rolled down the sides of the tent, then left and did not return until Terelle had dressed in the heavy robe with its intricate pattern of inlaid mirror discs, each a bevel-edged circle about the size of a man's fingernail. Perhaps in the interests of comfort, the mirrors were confined to the front and sleeves of the garment. The weight of it pulled at her neck.

When Errica returned, she was not alone. She indicated the tall, serious-faced man who ducked his head to follow her into the tent. "Messenjer," she said. "Manager of Emery. My husband."

"Happy to be seeing ye awake and refreshed, child. We're gratified to be of assistance, especially to Watergiver lords." He indicated the carpet with a wave of his hand. "Shall we sit?"

Annoyed at being called a child, Terelle sat, imitating his cross-legged posture. Errica lowered herself with surprising suppleness, given her large size.

"Lords? Russet, you mean?" She considered that. "I suppose he is a lord in Khromatis."

He laughed. "Yes, indeed. Who else would dress in that fashion, all wrapped up in cloth like a colourful parcel? Who else would carry waterpaints but Watergivers? We have the things ye left near your dead pede, by the way, including the paints."

"Oh." Her heart sank. She had not left her choices behind her after all. "Thank you. That was kind." *How does he know about waterpaints? And how does he know what lords wear in Khromatis?* She struggled to make her sluggish mind move. And why did he sound vaguely like Russet? The way he spoke. Saying ye instead of you, the heavy accent, the slightly odd way of using words. Russet, of course, didn't speak the language of the Quartern very well, and these people did, yet there was something . . . similar.

"And ye. Are ye not also a lord of Khromatis? A Watergiver from across the borderland marshes?"

"No. To me a Watergiver is the emissary of the Sunlord." Then she added doubtfully, "You *do* worship the Sunlord as Scarpen folk do, don't you?"

"No, indeed we don't! A Scarperman fallacy, that. We believe in God, certainly; God the Only, but He is just that: God. No more, no less. We don't worship Watergivers, either. Watergivers are mortal people, for all they're much blessed by God. We're the Guardians. Don't ye know this?" He looked at her, puzzled. "But why do ye ask questions of our faith? Surely it's known to ye! And what were ye doing out on the salt with a black pede?"

She let her confusion about his beliefs slide and said, "We lived in the Scarpen, but the old man wanted to go home to the place he calls Khromatis. He's my great-grandfather and says he's one of the Watergivers."

Messenjer blinked, his face blank. "And ye are not?"

"I was born in the Gibber."

"Ah."

The silence that followed dragged on until Terelle began to feel embarrassed.

"Well," Messenjer remarked at last, "it'll be many weeks before your Russet is able to be journeying again, if he survives. Ye're welcome to be staying with us in the meantime, of course."

"That – that's very generous."

Errica smiled at her. "Your people are our responsibility – how can we not treat ye with honour?" Messenjer made an abrupt movement of his hand, as if to tell her not to say anything else.

But what she'd said made no sense to Terelle. Alabasters certainly weren't related to Watergivers; they looked nothing alike, for all the echo of similarity in their speech. And how could Alabasters be responsible for another people who lived elsewhere?

She said, selecting her words carefully, "I'd like to know more about Watergivers, if you can tell me."

They exchanged worried looks.

"I don't know my own history," she explained. "I am Gibber born and Scarpen bred. I don't even know what – who – Watergivers are. The only Watergiver I ever knew about, until I met Russet, was raised into the glory of eternal Sunfire and sits at the side of the Sunlord. He once dwelt with men, and taught the rainlords and stormlords all they know about stormshifting and cloudbreaking." She was reciting words she had heard from street preachers. Once she had been confident of their truth; now the words sounded oddly hollow and pretentious.

Messenjer frowned, but all he said was, "Ah." He and Errica swapped another look, this one laden with warning, then he added, "I'll give it some thought. We don't tell our history to outsiders lightly. And it seems ye may be that."

"Perhaps if ye were to be telling us about yourself?" Errica suggested. "It may help us to be making a decision."

A decision on how much I should know. They still sounded friendly, but she'd felt a slight decrease in warmth nonetheless, replaced by a more studied formality. She repressed a sigh. If she was to cope with the danger of her future, she needed to know as much as possible. If these people could tell her something, anything, then it was worth an honest recital of her past. "Of course," she said.

It took her half the run of a sandglass, but at the end of that time, they knew her history: how she had been born to Sienna, Russet's granddaughter, how she had grown up in the Gibber and then at Opal's Snuggery in Scarcleft, how she had met Russet and been trained as a waterpainter. Fearful of being disbelieved, she said nothing of the power present in the waterpainter's art, nor how Russet had used it against her. She described her meeting with Shale, her imprisonment by Highlord Taquar Sardonyx and how she had fled. Once again she omitted to tell the whole truth, remarking merely that she had used the damage created by the earthquake to escape. Other than that, she painted Russet with words exactly as she saw him – the manipulative murderer of her father. She'd have to be sun-fried crazy before she'd make him sound like a man of integrity.

When she finished, Messenjer and Errica exchanged yet another glance. Terelle was becoming more than irritated by their silent conversation of meaningful looks.

"Thank ye for telling us," Messenjer said. "I think we need to be consulting others back in Samphire about this. In the meantime, we must start this caravan moving now, if we're to be arriving in Mine Silverwall in the cool of the morning. We'll put Russet back on the sledge, but ye can ride up behind our daughter-in-law. When we arrive in Silverwall, we'll talk about these other things some more."

It was a dismissal of a kind, and Terelle had to swallow it, along with her irritation. "Can I see Russet now?" she asked.

Errica smiled, as if relieved this question was one she could answer. "Of course, if ye want, but don't expect too much. He's an old man, and he'll not be walking anywhere for a long, long time."

* * *

243

By the time they rode on, Terelle had met all of the party: Messenjer and Errica's two ghostly-pale sons, Cullet and Sardi; Cullet's wife Delissal, a woman of about forty, with a face like a block of salt: dirty white and angular; and two other men who were apparently servants of some kind. Terelle shared a mount with Delissal, and as they rode, the woman taught her some of the finer points of pede driving.

She squirmed under the Alabaster's critical regard, which manifested itself in a mixture of amazement and self-righteous tolerance. Whenever Terelle admitted her ignorance of any facet of White Quarter life, Delissal would throw her hands up in the air, utter an amazed "Oh, my!" and proceed to do her best to dispel such ignorance.

Russet, pulled behind Cullet's myriapede, slept. Offered food and water, he took it; but gave little other signs of animation and had to be cleaned like a baby. He did not recognise Terelle when she spoke to him.

She found it difficult to care.

Just at dawn, they reached the rim of Mine Silverwall. It was early morning, and the shadows were long. Her first impression was of a hole opening up in front of them, dark and deep. Vast enough to have held half of Scarcleft, it was not yet lit by the sun's rays so it took her a moment to understand what she was seeing. Not only were the salt mines dug into the ground, but so were the houses.

Three steep-sided walls descended in giant steps to the bottom of a quarry. Each of these walls was pitted with entrances; some were doorways or windows giving out onto a ledge, others were more like cavern openings. The fourth side of the quarry was a slope with a zigzag road accessing every level on its way down into the depths, far, far below.

"Why not just take the salt on the surface?" she asked Delissal, puzzled.

The woman seemed distracted as she answered. "Surface

salt is just granules, bulky and difficult to transport. Further down it's compacted, so we just have to cut the blocks . . ."

Her voice trailed away and Terelle realised there was something wrong. Everyone was still sitting on their mounts at the top of the slope, not moving, their bloodless faces blank of expression. "What is it?" she asked.

"Where are the pedes? Where are the *people*?"

The unspoken horror behind the words scared Terelle.

Next to them, Cullet slid down to the ground. "Terelle," he said quietly, "get down, please."

When she obeyed he held out the reins to his pede for her to hold. "Wait here." Wordlessly she did as he asked and he mounted behind his wife. Messenjer had already jabbed his pede with his prod and the beast was flowing down the slope in fast-mode. He took the first of the ledges to the right and rode halfway along to a doorway. The others followed, almost as fast. Terelle, left alone with Russet, went to his side. He was conscious, so she gave him a drink.

"Where?" he asked.

"One of their salt mines," she answered. "Silverwall."

"Not dying," he said. "Not in this waterless hell. Be going home, we two."

"Khromatis is not my home," she said, trying to be glad he recognised her now.

Leaving him, she tied the pede's antennae together and walked down the slope to the first ledge, taking the left-hand side in the opposite direction to the others. The first doorway she reached was hung with a curtain made of beads of rock salt threaded on red-dyed flax string. She pulled the curtain aside and looked in. It wasn't a cave, but a room carved out of the ground, with more rooms beyond. A house. The first room contained a fireplace and an oven, table, chairs, benches. She called out, and when no one replied she took a step inside, peering around at the rock walls.

No, she thought, *not rock. Salt.*

The furniture, solid and chunky, was sculpted out of the rock-hard salt. Shelves were incised into the walls but much of what had been kept there was now broken on the floor or tossed aside, as if it had been pillaged. Picture-reliefs engraved on blank spaces glistened in the dim light, telling stories new to her. An oil lamp hung from the ceiling but it wasn't lit and felt cold to the touch of her fingers.

She shivered.

"Hello?" she called again. "Anyone here?"

There was no reply. It was eerily still. Although she had not long stepped through the bead curtain, it now hung without a shiver. Spooked, her feet leaden, she walked further in to peer into the room beyond. There was a woman there, lying on a solid divan of salt strewn with rugs. Her white robe was rucked up over her head, and her bloated, shapeless legs were sprawled apart and bloodied. There was dried blood everywhere, pale pinkish blood: on the walls, the floor, the bedding. A lingering smell, sour and unpleasant, hung in the air.

Terelle hastily clamped a hand over her mouth and backed out of the room, her heart now pumping fiercely enough for her to feel it in her throat.

She leaned against the wall next to the stove. *Deep breaths, take deep breaths . . .*

Time dragged, mired in these deaths, in what they meant. Reminding her of other deaths she had never wanted to think of again. But this wasn't an earthquake. This was murder.

She unpeeled herself from the wall and forced herself to look into the third of the rooms. Two children huddled together on the floor, plump little hands clutching each other. Their bodies ended at the neck, a coagulation of mess and bone – and then nothing.

Their heads weren't in the house. At all. She looked.

* * *

Terelle sat on the ledge with her back to the outer wall of the house, and watched the sun climb up over the rim of the mine. Messenjer and the others had dismounted and were running – running up and down the ladders that connected the different levels, calling out to one another, checking, checking, checking. Trying to find just one person alive. Just one.

It seemed a long time before they gathered together in front of one of the mine entrances and beckoned Terelle to join them. Errica had collapsed onto the rung of one of the ladders. She looked ill and her breasts heaved as she tried to catch her breath.

"We'll stay here a day or two," Messenjer told Terelle, his voice harsh and cold. "Long enough to bury the dead. Then we will ride for Mine Emery."

"There's – there's no one?" *No one alive?*

He shook his head. "Some missing. The best of our youth. They must have taken them for slaves. It's not unusual with Reduners. This is the first time we've seen them so deep into the Whiteout, though."

"Reduners did this? There were two children back there. Scarcely old enough to walk. One clutched a toy in his hand . . . but they . . . they didn't have any heads. Why would they do that?"

Messenjer nodded. "They want to be teaching us a lesson. This is what'll happen to us all if we resist. They want to be ruling our land, selling our salt, and giving us a few bab fruit in return. Minerals, pedes, samphire, salt, wild red flax from the marshes of the borderlands: that's all we have. The rest we buy or exchange: cloth, food, fuel, metal. We live simply, but our salt and soda, our saltpetre and gypsum, our mirrors – they're sold across the Giving Sea, as well as in the Quartern, so we survive. These Reduners would make us as poor as a Whiteout cat . . ."

He was rambling and seemed to realise it, so he stopped and took a deep breath. "Bring Russet down and attend to the pedes. Delissal, cook us a meal. Life must go on. The rest of us will collect the bodies . . . God grant them an easy crossing to the afterlife."

It was only afterwards that she realised there had been tears in his eyes and on his cheeks.

Tears.

Alabasters wept water. Just as she did.

18

White Quarter
Mine Emery

"Ye must use your waterpainting powers," Messenjer said, "to be saving us all."

Terelle, who was warming her hands by the fire that burned in Messenjer's kitchen on Mine Emery, looked up sharply.

They had arrived that morning, but Messenjer had been gone from the house all day to return only with the setting of the sun. Terelle had grabbed some rest, but apparently he had not. Deep lines of exhaustion furrowed his face and reflected the pain of the conversations he must have had that day, telling his people what had happened at Mine Silverwall. In the distance, through the open doorway, she heard someone crying – a desperate keening of loss that had shafted into her consciousness on and off throughout the day, even though she didn't want the awareness.

"What do you know about waterpainting?" she asked sharply.

"That it writes the future in the hands of the skilled."

How does he know that much? *Just who are you, you Alabasters?* She curbed her aggravation and asked quietly, "Do you know what that *means*, Manager Messenjer?"

He was silent, so she answered for him. "The painting does what it is fated to do, not necessarily what the painter wants.

The two are not always the same thing. It's therefore dangerous. I asked to get out of a prison, and it made an earthquake that brought down part of a city. People *died*, just so that I could be free." Maybe her waterpainting had done that; maybe Russet's. It didn't matter; the consequences were the same.

"Then it was God's will that they died, for waterpainting is surely a gift from God."

"No – it was a gift from my great-grandfather: that old man lying in the room behind you in your wife's care. He's the one who taught me. Don't give me that nonsense, manager. Who are you or I to say what's a gift from the Sunlord and what is not?" She was tired, so very tired, of people telling her what to do; she didn't want to argue about it. She was unused to the long hours of riding on the salt pan, but it wasn't physical fatigue that plagued her now; it was the weariness of never being in control of her own fate.

"A gift from God, not the Sunlord," he corrected. "There's no Sunlord."

She ignored that and gathered together the shreds of her strength. "I will not waterpaint again. You know why I ride with the man who murdered my father and hounded my mother into a situation that resulted in her death? *Because he imprisoned me in his paintings and I can't free myself.* Russet painted me in a place far from here – somewhere in the Watergivers' land – and I have to go there, whether I like it or not. My mother ran from Russet in terror and despair. I suspect she died because she tried to resist. And yet I have to ride with him, day after day. Tending him as if he were a child in my care. I loathe him. I loathe what he has done to me."

She stepped back from the fire and faced Messenjer across the kitchen. "You and your family saved my life. I am grateful for all your help, more than I can say. But once Russet is well again, we'll be on our way because it is what I *have* to do.

Russet has water tokens; he can pay you for a pede and an escort to the other side of the salt."

He didn't answer that but said, "I want to show ye something." She was beginning to know him and she recognised the tone he used now: firm, soft, reasonable – with no possibility of dissent. He had not reached the level of mine manager by being weak. She already knew it was a post given by election, not inheritance.

He took her by the elbow and steered her outside to the ledge, the roadway that had no outer edge running in front of his underground house. "Look," he said. "Look around and tell me what ye see."

She shivered slightly under the cut of the cold night air. Mine Emery was larger than Mine Silverwall, but the design was similar: tiered levels, each having houses built into the cliff sides. In the daylight, the greenish white of the quarried walls was haphazardly veined with other colours: orange and brown and umber. Now, the open doorways and windows across the mine were patches of yellow lamplight in the darkness. All of the mine must have been awake. When she looked down at the mine floor, she could see the silvery shadows of pedes in the twilight: tens of them, tethered there, feeding on piles of dried samphire fodder brought in from the edges of the Whiteout. Earlier, mounted messengers had left for other mining settlements, to Samphire itself, with the news: Mine Silverwall had been attacked and annihilated.

"It's beautiful," she said to Messenjer. The sound of children's laughter drifted up from a lower level, clear in the crisp air. The patterns of light on shadowed canyon walls were symbols of a town with a beating heart, its people. She wanted to paint it all, but she didn't tell him that.

"Compare it to Mine Silverwall. Remember the silence, the stillness, the unlit houses there. The absence of *life*. Children no longer play in Silverwall."

Terelle shook, either with cold or horror. She wasn't certain which. He guided her back inside to the warmth of the kitchen where she sat in one of the solid salt-block chairs and wished she could move it closer to the fire. Messenjer took the kettle off and poured her a hot drink. The whitish liquid was salty and sour, but she drank it gratefully.

"The excretion from the glands of white pedes," he told her. "Their way of disposing of excess salt."

Spluttering, she eyed the drink with less enthusiasm.

He didn't notice. "Would ye like to see the Reduners here with their tribesmen and their scimitars and their ziggers?"

She was silent.

"Ye can stop it from happening."

She looked up at him in amazement. "Me? By water-painting? I don't think you understand the limitations of the art! I can't bring about a future unless I paint accuracies!"

"Explain."

"I know the man who leads the Reduner tribes is a sand-master called Davim the Drover. But I've never met him. Therefore I can't paint him being killed, or dying. Nor can I paint his camp being wiped out in a – let's say, in a spindevil wind, unless I know what his camp looks like."

"Ah. Then it won't be as easy as I thought. But there is much we can do. It's just a matter of giving it some thought . . ."

"Easy? *Easy*? You think it's *easy* to kill people?"

"The Reduners find it easy," he said. "Remember the children ye saw, clutching each other? I don't suppose they put up much resistance."

She took a deep breath to stop her shaking. "Manager Messenjer, do we really want to be like them? Waterpainting can kill the innocent. I know, because I have done it. Besides, there is something evil about it anyway. I could paint a scene right now, and shuffle your dead image up into it – and you'd fall lifeless at my feet within a heartbeat. In fact a waterpainter could do that to you from the other side of the Quartern if they knew what you looked like! No one should have that kind of power. No one."

"It is a gift from God. How can it be an evil thing?" he said. "God forbid that either of us would say all Reduners are evil, but God gave ye waterpainting skills to be using against evil people like those who wield zigtubes and scimitars to kill children. He would never bestow His gifts without a purpose. And He would never bestow the talent on a person who would use it unwisely."

She wanted to scream at him: *What about what Russet did to me? Isn't that misuse? Was that the will of God?* But there was no point. He did not fully understand the horror of what Russet had done.

"Leave the girl alone, Mez." Errica entered the room from the adjoining bedroom and stood there, hands on her massive hips, shaking her head at both of them. "If God gave her the gift, then he also gave her the goodness to be using it wisely, when necessary."

Messenjer made a gesture of apology with one white hand and ducked out of the doorway through the beaded salt curtain.

"Be gentle with him, Terelle," Errica said. "He lost a younger brother and a niece and a nephew back there in Silverwall. And we never found the children's bodies. They were probably taken as slaves. The girl was a beautiful lass: but fourteen, with salt-white hair down to her waist and eyes the colour of the palest skies."

"That's awful, and I'm more sorry than I can say. But I still can't do it," Terelle said, then added, her stubbornness surfacing, "and he should not ask it of me."

"It is his responsibility to help his people. He had to ask. But go and rest now. Ye have travelled long and hard and need your sleep. God is good; trust Him and all will be well."

She indicated the room she had just left. "Take the pallet next to Russet. He won't wake for a while."

It was surprisingly easy to settle into the routine of the mine over the next few days.

Russet spent much of his time asleep, or feverish and raving. As her drive to travel east was lessening, Terelle thought his continued physical weakness was diminishing the hold his waterpaintings had over her. Occasional restlessness told her the power was still there, but it was easier to resist. Every now and then she thought uncharitably how much simpler her life would be if he was dead. She dreamed up ways to kill him, but in her heart knew she would never have the . . . what? Courage? Nerve? Malice? Resolution?

I'm the kind of person who doesn't have the guts to put a suffering kitten out of its misery, how can I possibly kill a man? If I couldn't shuffle up Taquar dead, how can I kill my own great-grandfather?

She thrust the idea away and spent her spare time exploring Mine Emery. No one limited her movements. Errica and Messenjer's more likeable and talkative younger son, Sardi, made a point of guiding her around, including taking her inside the mine itself. To her surprise, it was cool, dry and pleasant underground. The floors glistened and the austere, cold beauty of the walls was sometimes patterned by lines of colour, pleasing to the eye.

"Our salt goes everywhere throughout the Quartern," Sardi said with pride, "and even across the Giving Sea. Or it used to. Now?" He shrugged. "We did send a large caravan off to the south four days ago. We are exploring a new route through the Gibber and then west along the Edge to Portennabar in the Scarpen, where it can be shipped to the Other Side. A difficult route though, because of the lack of water."

Several days later, when she saw a caravan setting off, she

remembered those words and was puzzled to see it head out to the east across the Whiteout. It carried salt blocks, though she knew the only settlement further to the east was Silverwall, now devoid of people. When she asked Sardi about it, he prevaricated as though he didn't know what answer to give, then muttered that the caravanners were carrying empty jars to pick up the Silverwall cistern water. It was a logical thing to do, but Terelle didn't believe it. The white packpedes had not been carrying jars. Sardi had uttered an untruth, even though her impression was that Alabasters rarely lied and felt uncomfortable when they did.

So much is strange here, she thought. *They hide things.*

She determined to ask Errica about the caravan, but the following day everything was turned upside down once more and she forgot.

Terelle was helping Delissal in the family kitchen, chopping up samphire for a vegetable dish, when she heard several people frantically calling her name from outside. The urgency of the call made them both drop what they were doing and race out onto the ledge. People had gathered there, their excited chatter blending into an unintelligible buzz.

"There's a message for ye!" Errica cried as she bustled up, far from her usual calm self.

Terelle's immediate reaction was that the statement didn't make sense. Who could send a message when no one knew where she was? Then she realised everyone was looking up, clutching at one another, laughing, almost choking on their excitement.

Blinking in the bright sunlight, Terelle raised her eyes.

There was a small storm cloud above, dark and compact, heading for the Border Humps. But that wasn't where people were looking. They were staring more to the east, and much lower. She turned her head. Her jaw dropped. There was indeed a message in the sky.

A white line of cloud had formed itself into shapes, into letters, as if someone had painted them there. A wave of laughter rippled around the mine as others emerged to look. Children danced and pulled at their parents' hands, begging to be told why the clouds were such a funny shape.

Then the first word leaped out at her: *Terelle*. Staggered, she needed a moment to make sense of the rest. *You cheated at Lords and Shells. Help me,* she read, *I am in Scarcleft Hall. I need you. Come to Pahntuk Caravansary. Shale.*

"Oh, Watergiver take me," she whispered. Joy so intense shook her that she almost fell to her knees. He was alive! But her next thought was far darker. *Scarcleft Hall? He's not safe in Breccia? Oh, Sunlord save him, Taquar has him again. No. Oh, please not.* Highlord Taquar, running his fingers up and down a strand of her hair while he manipulated her through her fear . . .

"It's a miracle!" Messenjer was clasping his hands together next to her, his face uplifted and shining. "Terelle, it's a true message from God."

"Oh pebbles 'n' sand," she snapped crossly. "That's not God, that's Shale."

Several turns of the sandglass later, Terelle – feeling that her whole world had been turned on its end yet again – was deep in negotiations with Messenjer, Cullet and Sardi, while Errica bustled in and out of the kitchen carrying items to be packed, an intent expression on her face. There had been another message, not for her alone this time, and it had changed everything.

Written in large letters held together as they travelled across the sky, they had read, *People of Alabaster, people of the Gibber, the stormlord bids you unite against the treason of Scarcleft and the Reduner marauders. Bring pedes, warriors to Pahntuk Caravansary, Breccian tunnel. We fight for the stormlord and our water!*

"Let me see if I have this right," Terelle said, looking straight at the mine manager. Inside, her anger roiled. "Mine Emery will supply me with the means to return to the Scarpen in order to help the stormlord Shale, but only if I undertake to use my waterpainting?"

"Yes. It's not just for us. This is bigger than Mine Emery, Terelle. Bigger than Alabaster."

"I know. But that doesn't make what you ask any easier."

Cullet snorted at that. Terelle glanced across at him. Although the older of Messenjer's sons, he lacked his brother's courtesy. A short, narrow-shouldered man a cycle or two over forty, he radiated dissatisfaction, frustration and petulance. Right then he stood with his arms folded, fingers tapping on upper arms.

Terelle said nothing, waiting to hear all Messenjer had to say before she could trust herself to speak.

He said, "If ye don't want to help, then there's no point in ye returning to the Scarpen. We'll go, though, whether ye do or not." He paused, evidently sorting out what he wanted to say and how to say it. "When the White Quarter was first raided by the Reduners, we thought we could deal with it ourselves. Back then, they raided our caravans, not our settlements. They mocked us, saying that white pedes were no use to them except to be roasted over a camp fire." He choked. "Our pedes – they are our wealth, our pride, our lifeline. Without them, we die."

He turned away to clear his throat before continuing. "We fought back, of course. The men of Alabaster are all taught to fight from pedeback. At least the theory of it. We're Guardians, after all. But we have no ziggers, and no defences against them, and it'd been a long time since we'd fought for our lives. Generations. Skills were lost, fighters were inexperienced. Warriors and pedes died under their zigger onslaught. The Miners' Council and the Traders' Council in Samphire had a joint meeting and called upon the Bastion to be asking for help from the Scarpen—"

"The what? Bastion?"

"Our leader. Highlord, if ye like, elected for life. He rules in Samphire, with the help of the two councils."

Strange, she thought, *all those years living in Scarcleft and I never had any idea of how Alabasters governed themselves.* The thought made her uncomfortable. People gossiped about anything and everything in the common rooms of the snuggery; but she hadn't heard a whisper about anyone termed "the Bastion". And these people thought of themselves as Guardians? Of what? Something important enough to be protected by armed and trained men? Yet another secret kept from the other quarters. What did they have to hide?

A possible answer popped into her head. *Some kind of connection to Watergivers.* She looked at Messenjer. *He cries tears. Like me. When Alabasters speak the Quartern tongue they sound a little like Russet. They know about waterpainting. And the patterns on their carpets – they are familiar because they remind me of Russet's tattoos, and the colours are like those of Russet's clothes. Yet they themselves don't look like us, not at all. Aargh, I hate mysteries!*

Apparently unaware of her unease, Messenjer continued, "We didn't get the aid we asked for, as ye know. The situation worsened. We had to start guarding our tunnels, our samphire fields, our mines. What I haven't told ye is this: a few days before ye came, Gibber folk sent a message. They'd heard Reduners invaded the Scarpen and seized the northern city of Qanatend. Some say Breccia is next. Perhaps it has already fallen, but we just haven't heard because who's there to tell us? Traders are too frightened to be running caravans any more."

Nausea swamped her. "We saw Reduners riding down to

Breccia. Russet said he thought they were the baggage train of an armed force." The next words were hard to say. "If Shale is in Scarcleft, then Breccia has already fallen and the sandmaster has given Shale back to Taquar Sardonyx."

Cullet, frowning, said flatly, "Ye say this sky message is from him. Ye say he was being trained as a new stormlord. But the Gibbermen say the new stormlord is someone called Jasper Bloodstone."

"I've never heard of him. But it would be wonderful news – two stormlords instead of one!"

"Does it matter who it was?" It was Sardi who spoke, his face alight with hope. Cullet gave him an exasperated look, as if questioning his younger brother's rationality, but Sardi wasn't quashed. "It must be a stormlord. No one else could write in the sky."

"Only Shale knows I cheated at Lords and Shells," Terelle said.

"He needs ye, and God sent ye to us for a reason," Messenjer said.

"I don't even believe in your god! I worship the Sunlord."

"A tragic heresy."

She stirred uneasily. It was so much easier when things were straightforward and obvious. So much easier when you believed in something and didn't have to *think* about it.

"I think we have to be going to Samphire with this," Messenjer said finally, looking at Terelle. "The Bastion needs to hear all ye have to say. He will want to be talking about your waterpainting abilities, too. That talent of yours may be our saviour. I've no doubt he will ask ye to ride with us to Scarpen if we go. Perhaps ye will listen to him."

Errica, who had just re-entered the kitchen with a pail of fresh pede secretion milk, paused. He switched his attention to her, saying, "All our fighting men must ride for Samphire."

Cullet gasped. "But that would mean we'd have to abandon the mine! We couldn't leave people here without protection."

"What purpose is a mine if we cannot use the caravan routes to be selling our salt?" his mother asked him. "We are already overstocked. We will leave."

Sardi and Cullet exchanged shocked stares. "The mine is also our *home*," Cullet said, dismayed.

"At least the Reduners can't burn it," Errica said with a shrug. "It will still be here when we return."

"There is something else you are not taking into consideration," Terelle said. "I am not free to travel. Russet's paintings tie me to him."

"He will come with us to Samphire."

"Each step I take towards the Scarpen and away from Khromatis will tear me in two." She shuddered, remembering how ill she had been every time she had plotted to rebel against the future he had painted for her, remembering the hours she had spent doubled up in the communal outhouse of their lodgings in Scarcleft.

The mine manager leaned towards her, his intensity intimidating, although she knew he probably didn't realise it. "*Resist him.* Ye are a waterpainter, like him. A Watergiver, like him. When all people have power, who prevails? Ye have your own strengths. *Use them.*"

"Easy for you to say! My mother *died*, probably because she tried to resist!"

Errica gave a sigh of exasperation. "Messenjer, ye're as articulate as a newborn pede with brain rot!" She turned to Terelle, saying, "Lass, waterpainting is not evil, although abuse of power has ever been the way of some men, I agree. Bullies with muscles intimidate weaklings. The man with the stick threatens the man with none. But ye need not abuse your waterpainting power. What Messenjer is so clumsily trying to be saying is this: if ye withhold your help, then ye're no

260

different from the bullies. Ye can misuse your power simply by not using it. Ye'll kill just as surely, by doing nothing. It's what we call the passive sin."

Terelle didn't reply. How could she? What Errica said was right.

Messenjer turned to his sons. "Prepare the mine for exodus. We leave tomorrow evening in the cool."

Sardi smiled at Terelle. "We play Lords and Shells here too," he said. "Do you really cheat?"

Cullet gave a contemptuous snort.

Terelle's face turned hot. *Blighted eyes, Shale, couldn't you have found another way to tell me the message really was from you? Just you wait till I see you again!*

She had to shake Russet to wake him. He lay on the raised platform of salt that was an Alabaster bed. It was strewn with colourful quilts and blankets woven and knotted of dyed linen, just like his clothes.

He opened his eyes and stared at her, frowning, as if he had trouble remembering who she was. The room had no door, so the bustle of a house in the turmoil of preparations for a journey was audible and he cocked his head to listen. Then he asked weakly, "What's happening?"

"We are going to Samphire. Everyone." She outlined what had happened. "And so," she said, "you'll stay in Samphire."

His protest was lucid. "Ye can't go back! I painted ye into a future in *our* land."

"*Your* land, not mine. Right now Shale needs me, and that's enough for me."

He was aghast. "I spent years teaching ye! Anyway, ye can't just walk away. The magic won't let ye."

"Watch me," she said calmly. "And if you want me to return to you, you had better give me some good advice. I need to know how to resist the spell of your paintings." He clamped his teeth together in an expression of stubborn silence, so she added, "Vivie told me that my mother was always weak and ill. So now I'm wondering: was it because Sienna resisted the future you'd bound her into? She *died*, Artisman."

He stared at her, malevolence fading into dismay. "Ye be saying I killed her?"

"It's possible."

"I not wanted to be hurting her! I needed her!"

"Nonetheless, she died."

His rheumy eyes stared at her in denial. "Be not my doing," he muttered. He struggled to sit up while she watched dispassionately, unable to bring herself to help him. When at last he was erect, he leaned back on the cushions, his face ashen.

"Tell me what I need to know, Artisman. As you get better, my drive to head towards Khromatis will grow – but I can't return if I've died, now can I? Tell me, or you may lose me, too."

"Promise me ye'll come back."

"No. No promises."

His malevolence returned. "Only death can change a future that has already been painted. A strong painting would even stave off a death . . ."

She was relentless. "Your art was not strong enough to override Sienna's determination. It won't be strong enough to override mine, either. Right now I'd rather die than not go back to Shale."

That's true, she thought, surprising herself. *Oh, Shale . . .*

He gave a grunt of frustration. "One day soon, ye'll stand where I painted ye, beside that river. I still had my power when I painted it."

"Perhaps. But I've got to stay alive first. Tell me how to resist without killing myself, and maybe, just maybe, I will return."

With a suddenness that shocked her, he seemed to deflate.

"Ye can kill me," he admitted. "I told ye that. If artist die, magic of painting dies."

They stared at each other. She wanted him dead, but could not kill him. *And he knows it, the salted bastard. But then, anything he says could be untrue . . .*

"What if the painting is destroyed before the scene it portrays comes true?" she asked. "Do the people in it really die?"

"Maybe. Maybe not. Be in peril, definite. Painting destroyed, but future magic be trying to hold true. Like war." He gripped her arm tight, his bony fingers surprisingly strong. "Ye have those paintings?"

She didn't answer, still unable to tell if what he said was the truth. *If that is true, wouldn't he have taken better care of the paintings?*

"Old Ba-ba say Taquar's men took them."

"I have them. Taquar gave them back to me."

"Don't destroy them. Dangerous. Truly. If I paint true, then future win. If I weak, then ye be dying when painting die. Understand?"

She nodded sadly. Shale had destroyed her painting of Vato the waterseller by accidentally treading on it, and Vato had died under a falling building within a year. Coincidence – or was waterpainting withering dangerous? "So how can I fight the desire to return?"

Huddled into the bedding, shrunken and ill-looking, his body was small and negligible. Even his voice was weak when he finally spoke. "Decide now ye will return in less than a year. Promise me. Magic then leave ye alone. Girl in painting can wait a year. After that, too late. Ye'd be different, look older than I painted ye. Understand?"

She thought about it. "As long as I promise to return before I look older than the girl in the painting, the magic will not force me – if my honest intention is to be there."

He nodded. "Genuine intention. Understand?"

She sighed. There wasn't going to be any way out of this – unless he died. And she was no murderer. "All right. I promise. I will be back in Samphire less than a year from now."

19

Scarpen Quarter
Scarcleft City, Scarcleft Hall, Level 2
The Skirtings, south of Scarcleft

Seneschal Harkel Tallyman had his ways of finding out every-thing of importance occurring in Scarcleft Hall. He had been informed – even before Senya had left Jasper's bedroom – of her night-time visit to him. He had relayed the information to the Highlord in the morning, and the slight smile with which Taquar had heard it was enough to tell Tallyman the news was pleasing. He didn't understand why, which annoyed him.

He liked to know what Taquar was up to; not knowing could jeopardise his own future. He'd spent many days locked in one of Scarcleft Hall's tower rooms for his last mistake – allowing the eighteen-year-old Jasper to escape Scarcleft – and he didn't want to make another. He shuddered just thinking about the *boredom* of incarceration.

Even though he knew cloud gathering was an exhausting business for an ill-qualified rainlord, it worried him that the Highlord was always irritable. Senya made no more visits to Jasper's bedroom, and Jasper appeared to be making an effort to be friendly to her, but it bothered Harkel that the young stormlord continued to make the occasional snuggery visit, especially as it was so difficult to find out what happened inside snuggery walls. Jasper's visits seemed too . . . *calculated* to be merely part of the amorous adventures of a young man. Frustrated, he hauled the snuggery madams in for questioning but learned nothing.

"I do not spy on my girls in the rooms," Opal told him blandly.

"Of course you do," he snapped back. "Do you think my wits are so sand-blighted I would believe that?"

"All right," she conceded. "There are peepholes, of course, but I only use them if I think the girls are in danger."

He didn't believe her for a moment and contemplated locking her up in one of underground cells and threatening her, but in the end he let her go. Snuggery madams were not without influence, and he had a nice income from the money they supplied to his office every month in exchange for a lack of harassment by his water enforcers. Besides, Jasper would not be happy with Tallyman if he found out the madams were in trouble. And he would find out. Tallyman wasn't sure how it was happening, but people spoke to Jasper. He wandered through the city at will. He chatted to everyone from workmen to sellers in the market. Even Tallyman's own enforcers were not obeying the standing order not to talk to Lord Jasper Bloodstone.

The problem was, of course, he was a *stormlord*. And you didn't poke a stormlord in the balls, not if you were wise. For a start they could kill you. For a finish, well, without a stormlord, no one drank. You *owed* them respect. And it seemed, if everyone was to be believed, conversation.

Withering little shit, Tallyman thought, but he kept the sentiment private. Nonetheless, his opinion nearly became public knowledge when the Overman of the Hall Guards came to make a report a few days later.

Tallyman heard him out, took a deep breath and said quietly, "Say that again, Overman."

"The stormlord has gone, seneschal. He has left the city, and a number of guardsmen have left with him."

"How long ago was this?"

"Three runs of the sandglass since he went out through the South Gate, my lord." The overman was unnaturally pale.

As well he should be. We could both suffer for this. "You had better tell me exactly what happened."

"He walked down into the city, early. His usual guards went with him, of course. Ten men. I understand he asked another guard to take a message to the Highlord that he was too weary for stormbringing this morning."

Tallyman hadn't known that, but he nodded. "Go on."

"He walked straight down Southway to the gate. He told the guards – the ones on duty there as well as those who were with him – that if they wanted to stop him, they'd have to kill him and he would try to kill them and their ziggers first. It was their choice. Then he went out."

Tallyman was incredulous. "And none of them tried to *stop* him?"

"Seneschal, would you, when the outcome would be your own death and possibly the death of the land's only stormshifter as well?"

Tallyman gritted his teeth. *I would have thought of some way of stopping him peacefully.* "Did his guards follow him?"

"Oh yes. The original ten and four others from the gate. The other fools on gate duty didn't tell me. I suppose they were hoping he'd come back before you or I or Highlord Taquar found out."

"Go on."

"He went to the livery stable outside. He asked the owner to saddle up a myriapede. He actually *paid* for the hire of the bleeding thing. He bought a couple of full water skins and a bag of bab fruit. The man was happy to oblige him."

Tallyman gave a grunt of outrage.

"Lord – he's the stormlord—"

"Sunlord preserve me from fools," Tallyman said through gritted teeth. *"Where did he go?"*

"South. Six of the guards seized a myriapede and joined him."

"Where would their loyalties lie? Are they likely to spy on him and then tell us what is going on?"

The overman looked unhappy. "Seneschal, he's been clever. He's a whole sandstorm more pleasant than Highlord Taquar, you know. He's been talking to his guards. Getting to know them. Taquar keeps changing the men to stop any of them becoming too familiar, but word got around: the young stormlord is a fine man. There's been a lot of chatter in the barracks—"

"Taquar would have your sand-stuffed head for that kind of talk, Overman!"

"Yes, I know. But he's going to have it anyway. Seneschal, we've lost the stormlord."

"You have what?"

Tallyman and the overman both jumped. The pen in Tallyman's fingers spun out of his hand and the overman dug a hole in his palmubra with his fingers. Taquar stood in the doorway. His face was the colour of a dust cloud rolling across the Gibber.

Jasper had not often felt so happy. He was free, and in charge. The men who followed him did not question him; he was the one who told them what to do, where to go, how far to ride. They deferred to him. It was a new experience and he enjoyed it. He revelled in the feel of the pede beneath him, the leather of the reins in his hand, the touch of the wind whipping his palmubra on to his back when he urged the beast to fast mode. His experience as a driver was minimal;

Nealrith had started teaching him back in Breccia, but then the war had intervened.

When he rode, memories came flooding back. The day he and Mica had saved the life of a Reduner's pede by pulling it out of the flooded wash. Its owner had been angry because it had broken the tip of its feeler. His love of pedes had been born that day. The same day Citrine had been born . . . Then there was the day Nealrith gave him a pede of his own. The pride he'd felt then, his wonder that anyone would do that for him.

He stroked the livery pede between its segments with the prod, as Nealrith had taught him. In answer, the animal swung one of its long feelers back to touch him with its sensitive tip, establishing rapport.

Nealrith had died on Jasper's dagger. Citrine had died on Davim's spear. The pede Nealrith had given him was long gone, doubtless stolen by Reduners. And Mica . . . Poor Mica. Always wanting to stick up for his younger brother and never quite having the courage. Who knew where he was now? Or even if he was still alive.

Jasper refused to accept for certain that his brother was dead. Davim might have lied to Taquar. Taquar might have lied to him. Mica might be a slave somewhere on the dunes. Although, knowing Mica, he might not have lasted long.

The thought made him sick with rage. He wanted to pound Davim into pulp with his bare hands and toss Taquar off a cliff for good measure.

I will change things, he thought. *Soon*.

There had been a time when he'd wondered if he could bargain with Davim. Rain in exchange for Mica, but he'd ended up dismissing the idea. If he let Davim know how much Mica meant to him, and if Mica was indeed a slave on the dunes, then Davim would have a lever to control the stormlord. He couldn't let that happen.

* * *

He led the guards on their myriapede down the trail towards Portennabar. When the sun was high in the sky, he took them off the trail and into a gully nearby where they halted. He shared his water and the bab fruit, joking with the men. *His* men. He didn't find it easy to chat about inconsequential things, but he always tried and hoped he was more successful than he knew. Any conversational skills he had, he knew he owed to Terelle.

Thinking of her, he grieved. Always, always there was that same thought: he had to marry Senya, or someone like her. He had to bring more stormlords into the world. If he didn't, the Quartern had no future. None.

In the mid afternoon, he felt the water of a large body of riders passing along the track they had left – travelling far faster than a merchant or passenger caravan. After counting the number of pedes and men he smiled, knowing he had seriously worried Taquar.

When he was sure the pursuers had disappeared further down the track, he turned to Dibble, the driver of the second pede. "Let's go back," he said.

The guards exchanged looks of surprise, and he realised only then that they had not really expected to return; they had thought he was intent on separating himself from the Highlord of Scarcleft. Even though he had been endeavouring to undermine Taquar's hold over Scarcleft men, he was momentarily astonished. Every one of them had been prepared to follow him, Watergiver knew where, with no guarantees of anything. Perhaps they believed he was their salvation. Perhaps they just feared what Taquar would do if they let Jasper go while they remained behind to take the blame. Jasper wasn't sure why, but he knew they were his men now. The thought shook him more than any spoken expressions of loyalty could have done.

Oh, sandblast, who am I to deserve this?

"I will see to it that every one of you is in my personal guard from now on," he told them.

By late afternoon they were back at the gates of Scarcleft. Dibble called out in a ringing shout as they rode up, "Make way for Lord Jasper, Stormlord of the Quartern, and his men!"

Jasper flashed him a surprised smile. The men sat straighter on the saddle as they rode in – and the guards at the gate saluted them.

No sooner had they entered the forecourt of Scarcleft Hall than an enforcer overman appeared, politely but firmly informing Jasper that the Highlord wanted to see him.

Taquar sat behind his desk, and he was furious. "What game is this you are playing?"

"No game. I just wanted to make it clear that I will do what I want, when I want. We've already agreed there's nothing either of us can do about this unpleasant situation. I'm just taking my concept of this agreement one step further. I will have my freedom. You know I can't run away."

Taquar sneered. "We're chained to each other because you are a weak and incompetent stormlord. I have not seen any increase in your abilities as yet. Am I to be chained, for the rest of my life, by your incompetence?"

"Give me a further year of your services as a cloudmaker. At the end of that year, you will be Cloudmaster in practice, ruling the Quartern in all respects *not* to do with water, and I will be cloudmaking as well as cloudshifting. I've had a couple of minor successes with changing water to vapour," he lied. "Just on a small scale, and not reliably. But it is coming."

"I hope you're right," Taquar said. He was fiddling with his dagger, turning it over and over in his hands.

Ignoring the implied threat of the knife, Jasper drew up a chair to the desk and seated himself, casually lifting his right leg to rest across his left. "Perhaps you should consider yourself lucky. My weakness means you can be a powerful man. I know now that I can never rule this land and be a stormlord, too. You can be the legitimate Cloudmaster. I will support your claim before the Council of Rainlords as soon as you care to make your move. I assume you are biding your time, waiting until Davim completes his withdrawal from Breccia."

Taquar laid the dagger aside and regarded him with an unpleasant stare. "That's right."

Jasper nodded, unsurprised. "From now on, I'll choose my own personal bodyguard. And I come and go as I please."

For a long moment, Taquar held his gaze. Then he nodded. "If we do have to live with each other, it may as well be with a semblance of harmony. Let me warn you, if you betray me, I will stop at nothing. Neither you nor any friend of yours will be safe. You need me more than I need you and you have more to lose than I do, because in the long run, I do not care for the Quartern the way you do. The way Nealrith did. I am a rich man, and a rich man can build a life anywhere, even on the other side of the Giving Sea. You see, I do not really care about any of it – not even Scarcleft. It has only ever been *what it can offer me.* Anything else is irrelevant. If it doesn't offer me enough . . ." He shrugged.

Jasper glanced away. "Power, not people?" he asked, keeping his tone neutral.

"Exactly. Power – and all that comes with it. If living here becomes too arduous, I will leave. I have been making inquiries; I hear life on the other side of the Giving Sea is comfortable, especially for a man who has assets."

"Water tokens are not going to help you there."

"Jewels have value everywhere. I have ziggers and the skills of a rainlord. Be warned, I already find tedious your insistence on continual cloudmaking so you can water the whole Quartern. I do not appreciate my constant fatigue."

Jasper's mouth went dry. "Then would Scarcleft be prepared to subsidize the import of water to Portennabar and Portfillik from across the Giving Sea?"

"No. Why should I? Shale, rid yourself of the notion I have an interest in anything not bringing *me* a profit or benefit. And expect me not to do any cloudmaking every third day. Two days on, one day off. I need to rest."

"Benefit?" Jasper's laugh was bitter. "You almost single-handedly ruined the life of the Scarpen when you murdered the young stormlords. You mistook what would benefit you! Beware you don't do so again. What, I wonder, will the Scarpen forces being assembled do when the Reduners leave Breccia?"

"Scarpen forces? The imaginary army you once mentioned?"

"Oh, wash stones, Taquar. You can hardly expect me not to have heard. Everyone knows! Caravanners gossip. I heard the servants talking. And if it hadn't been them, it would have been someone else. If you want to keep me in ignorance about everything, you had better lock me up in the mother cistern again. The Scarpen is seething, as well you know. I under-stand forces are being raised in Breakaway and Denmasad and Pediment. There are even rumours that perhaps the Gibbermen will rise up in rebellion if their water falls too low."

Taquar chuckled. "An army of Gibber grubbers?"

Jasper shrugged and added, "I'll tell you another thing you probably assumed I didn't know: the Scarpen forces are led by Rainlord Iani Potch. Interesting, eh? That half-crazy old man is still alive. Now tell me, Taquar, what do you think Iani will do with all those forces he has gathered, or is in the process of gathering? Do you think he will tell them to go home if Davim leaves? Or will he, do you think, turn his attention to the man who killed his daughter?"

"I did not kill his daughter! And he can't threaten me,"

Taquar said. "I have you; our partnership is surety for the good behaviour of Iani and everyone else."

"Exactly. You need me. And if I were you, I'd give some thought to whether any attempt by you to leave the Quartern would meet with success. I've been chatting to merchants from the coast, and they tell me that it is difficult to buy a passage without a permit from the portmaster. I'm betting neither of the portmasters would issue one for you."

"Why you little—"

Jasper raised his hands, palms out, in denial. "No, not my doing, I assure you. But I suspect Iani is *very* keen to shove a blade into your heart." He smiled cheerfully. "Let's just assume for the time being that you are going to stay and we will be working together. Later, I'll see you have the choice to leave – if you still want to." He stood. "I am going to change and have something to eat. Shall we meet in the stormquest room in, say, half an hour? We have some storms to bring. Oh, and one other thing, my name is Jasper. Shale Flint died long ago."

Back in his own bedroom, Jasper sighed. Not exactly a victory. And he didn't much like telling lies, either. In fact, he hated it.

He stepped out onto the balcony to look towards the ocean. The feel of the water came to him, vast and tantalising. So much of it, all they could ever need – if only there were storm-lords to deliver it. Once again he reached out to that water, attempting to drag up a portion as vapour. And once again, he failed.

I have to work in tandem with a man who despises me, whom I loathe in turn. Blighted eyes, Terelle, you would say it wasn't fair. He gave a reluctant grin at his own foolishness. *As if anything ever said life had to be fair, you sandcrazy Gibber urchin.*

He raised his eyes to the harsh blue of the brilliant sky. Tomorrow he would send another message to Iani, written in the clouds, to ask him to warn the portmasters not to let Taquar leave the Quartern. He was only too aware he was gambling. He had no way of knowing if his sky writing was ever read by those he intended it for, no way of knowing if they were interested in the proposals he was making to them, no way of knowing if the verbal messages he had tried to send through the snuggeries were ever delivered. No replies had yet reached him.

And Terelle; how could he be sure she would see his message? That she would return if she did? Everything was riding on a hunch. A nebulous feel on the wind, a whisper of a touch as insubstantial as sand-dancers shimmering on the plains in the midday heat. He'd felt her. Sensed her water on his tongue. She had been there in the White Quarter. He'd looked at Granthon's maps, laid them on the brass stormquest table with its etched compass directions, and placed her somewhere east of Samphire, probably at one of the mines.

Or was he just sandcrazed? He'd long since known storm-lords could recognise individuals by their water, unlike rainlords. Nealrith had told him that; so had Taquar. He'd found it impossible at first, but not any more. Not since that night when he'd gone to the room where Terelle had been imprisoned and felt her lingering presence in a way he never had before. She'd gone, but she had left something of her water behind. After that, he always recognised who was on the other side of a closed door.

But no stormlord should have been able to sense a person as far away as the next quarter . . .

Jasper lifted his face to the wind. She was not where she had been any more. She was getting closer.

Please let that be true.

Still, he couldn't relax his guard. Any day now Taquar would hear about his messages. True, many of Taquar's agents in the other cities would have abandoned him now that they knew what he had done to bring disaster to the Scarpen, but Jasper was not so foolish to think he could keep his cloud messages a secret. Once Taquar knew, the crack in the dayjar would open up in earnest. Trouble was coming and it would have the power of a rush down a Gibber drywash.

He smiled, but without real amusement. *You may be clever, Taquar, and I may be weak, but you have still underestimated me. She's coming. And when she does, things will change. I swear it.*

20

Reduner Quarter
Dune Sandsinger
Dune Watergatherer, Ravard's encampment

Ryka sat on a stool outside her tent, warming herself in the early morning sun.

Nearby, a pede lay stretched out on its side, its relaxed breathing producing a rhythmic purr as one of the mouth plates gently vibrated. The beast belonged to one of Ravard's bladesmen, one of the two men left behind to guard her who was now whittling a picture story on a segment plate. Around the Sandsinger camp, women were cooking while men tended their pedes and goats and sandgrouse. The smell of bab-flour damper laced with goat's cheese, newly lifted from the ashes of the cooking fires, drifted through the air. There was a leisurely pace to life, a rightness about the way the people lived, as if they drew the measured nature of their existence from the orderliness of their dune's slow progress across the plains.

If she could have had her books and scrolls, if Kaneth had been safe, if the Scarpen wasn't in danger, if there were only stormlords bringing rain, Ryka might even have been content. She gave a snort, ridiculing the thought. None of those things were true. And she was bored. Apart from the few books of Nealrith's she'd brought, there was no reading to be had, and as far as she knew Davim was still in the Scarpen, although she hadn't heard he had invaded more cities. Sunlord only knew whether Kaneth had managed to keep out of trouble, or whether Jasper was even alive.

It was thirty-five days or so since Ravard had left her here, bleeding and too weak to even raise her head from her palliasse. Anything could have happened. And given her situation, how could she ever be content? The last time she remembered being anywhere *near* content had been – it took a moment to remember – well, probably at Gratitudes. However, she was better, the bleeding had stopped and she still had her baby.

When Ravard and the slave caravan rode away, he'd instructed the Sandsinger tribemaster, within her hearing, to ensure that the tribe care for her as if she was Sandmaster Davim's daughter. If she died, Ravard added with a scowl, they could be sure of his revenge. And then he had gone, leaving two of his bladesmen behind, but without so much as another glance at her. That, she assumed, he would have considered showing weakness to his men. It had been Kaneth who had looked back, who had raised a hand in farewell. Too weak to acknowledge his gesture with a wave of her own, she managed a smile.

She had worried the tribe's fear of Ravard's threats would mean she was going to be subjected to a plethora of remedies and shaman medicine ceremonies. Instead she was handed over to the care of Arielker, the tribemaster's wife, who recommended little more than lying prone, drinking plenty and eating well. It might have been boring, but the regime appeared to have worked.

And so now, anxious to be gone, she sat and watched; learning, always learning, as the tribe went about their business. Her enforced rest had meant that she had done little work around the camp, but she had absorbed as much as she could and helped when not too much physical effort was involved. She had learned to weave a patterned pannier out of dune grasses and to carve needles and clasps for a cloak out of pede chitin. She knew how to make a damper and she could polish gemstones for hair beads.

At the moment she was knotting a goat-hair shawl, pausing only to watch as Arielker led her chosen group of women down to collect water from the encampment's waterhole on the plains. As was customary, they led the pack pedes; driving a pede was a privilege reserved for men, yet fetching water was a woman's business. If there was one aspect of Reduner culture she despised, it was their rigid division into men's and women's labour. Still, they seemed happy enough, in a way she never would have been.

Ryka watched them go – and planned.

"The water won't last much longer," a soft voice said at her elbow. She turned to see the aging, portly tribemaster standing by her tent, watching her. Plump cheeked and long nosed, with straggly hair almost too thin to bead, he was a man easy to ridicule, especially when she remembered his obsequious grovelling to Kher Ravard. Yet she wondered, too. There was intelligence in his grey eyes. And unflinching respect in the way his tribesmen regarded him. And he spoke his language with a lyricism that sometimes touched her appreciation of the poetical.

And he had spoken to her in Reduner.

She glanced at Ravard's bladesman, but he was too far away to hear and too intent on his carving to bother. Even as she looked at him, he moved further away to the last segment of his mount.

"Tribemaster," she said in her own tongue, inclining her head with the respect due to his position. "I'm sure you know I don't speak your language."

"I'm sure you do," he replied softly, still speaking Reduner.

"I've been watching you these many days, and I've finally recalled where I've seen you before. Some fifteen cycles ago I travelled to Breccia City to sell pedes. You visited our camp outside the walls because you were learning our tongue and wished to practice it. You spoke it well, even then."

Fear grabbed her and her hand went protectively to the bulge of her abdomen. *Sandblast, does he know who I am?*

"Yes," he said in reply to her unspoken question. "I don't remember your name, but you are a rainlord. Does it amuse you to know we of the Sandsinger will soon thirst?"

Her heart plummeted. She might have to kill him, and the thought sickened her. Answering him in Reduner, she said, "You have the water the Master Son gave to you, stolen from Breccia and Qanatend. What of them, who now must thirst?"

He gave a snort of disgust. "I never asked for it. Besides, it's hardly enough to water the pedes for a quarter-cycle. What do we do when it's finished and the waterhole has dried up because the stormlord will not supply us any longer?"

"You should have thought of that before you marched to war on the Scarpen. The Cloudmaster who watered you died during the siege of the city. *Your* siege."

"It wasn't *my* sandblasted choice," he said. "Or the choice of anyone on this dune. We were friends to the tribes of the Scarmaker, who led the dunes well, until Davim came. The warriors of Dune Watergatherer wiped Scarmaker out, and so we grovel to Sandmaster Davim and that ill-mannered Master Son – whose bed you share."

"Not willingly."

"What else am I to believe? You're a rainlord. You could kill him with a nod."

She did not disillusion him. "And yet you speak to me of your antipathy towards him. You are a brave man."

"No. A brave man would not have grovelled to Davim. A brave man would be riding side by side with Vara Redmane, wife of the man who was sandmaster of the Scarmaker." In scandalised tones, he added, "A *woman* leads the rebellion against Davim, not this foolish drover standing here who bowed his head in fear to a ruthless marauding sandmaster."

He shook his head sadly and looked away from her down the length of the dune to where one of his tribe's guards was outlined against the sky. "But now – now I am a saddened man who aches for the future of his tribe. An old man who listens to his shaman who says the dune god speaks of a parched people dying of thirst in the cycles to come." Then, swiftly, he turned his head to meet her gaze. "A desperate man who has seen something in another woman to stir the burntout ashes in his soul, and so to uncover a spark of hope. Kill me now, or give me a hint of a future that does not include our death by thirst, my lord."

Ryka considered her reply carefully before answering. "You are right. Not quite with a nod, but I could kill Ravard. A moment ago I thought of killing you to save my own life. I still could."

"I'll not betray you. I owe him nothing, least of all a rainlord's life."

"I hope not, for now I have other plans. The rainlords of Scarpen are not defeated yet, I promise you. Keep your hope, tribemaster, and await word. We will call on you when the time is right, and you will have to fight to reclaim your future."

"Water?"

"I can offer you none. I am no stormlord. Learn to live with random rain. Tell your women folk to have no more children for a while, until you know how to live in a waterpoor world. The random rains will come and you must chase them as your people did in the past."

His fury surfaced. "Those shrivelled sand-heads who would return us to such a time have baked their brains too long in the sun!"

"How many other dunes feel the way you do?"

"Four or five. And there are several others who are divided."

"Would you tell me who they are?"

He gave a faint smile. "We each risk much in trust of the other, do we not? Dune Stonebreaker, Dune Wrecker, Dune Widowcrest and Rarketim's Dune were all Scarmaker allies who hate this Davim. Dune Ravenbreak I am not sure about, but it is possible. Dune Sloweater and Dune Agatenob are divided. The western tribes on those two dunes are for Davim."

"And where can I find Vara Redmane?"

He laughed. "Some call her Vara the Spindevil and say she travels the wind with the men she has gathered around her. Who knows where the wind blows? Others say she uses the sand-dancers as her warriors. All I know is she came here once, and when she left in the middle of the night, a number of my young drovers went with her, taking their pedes with them. Some say she has no home because there is no water out there where she can set up a permanent camp. Others say she found the Source."

"What's that?"

"The unending spring where water gushes into the world from the mouth of the Over-god. It is a myth. A dream. In truth, Vara begs from tribes like mine. She steals from tribes like Kher Ravard's. She robbed several of Davim's caravans full of water stolen from Qanatend. I did hear she is a water sensitive. That she can smell water. It is possible. There are such women, although they usually don't talk about it. Men don't like the idea of a woman being better than they are at something like that."

She almost laughed. She liked this man.

He shook his head in reluctant admiration. "If anyone can stay alive out there, she can. She's old and wizened and wise, that one. Killed one of Davim's warriors, you know, when she escaped. She's death to ziggers. I used to wonder what sandmaster Makdim could ever see in her. Now I know what my blind heart could once not see. Her face is as weathered as granite in the sun, but she has the heart of a sandmaster and the favour of the Scarmaker dune god watching over her. Folk say the dune god left the dune the day Makdim died and followed her instead."

He regarded her solemnly, and his podgy face contained a dignity she had not noticed before that morning. "You must leave, you know," he said. "Arielker tells me you are fit enough to travel and your baby is safe. I can do one of two things. I can give you a pede and you can go where you will. I will tell Kher Ravard you escaped and stole one of our animals. Or I can send you to his dune under the escort of his two bladesmen, as he asked me to do."

"He would punish you if I disappeared. He has the power to wipe your tribe off the face of your dune."

"I put my trust in our dune god."

Ryka just managed not to roll her eyes. She had no faith in his god, which meant she held the fate of his tribe in her hands. She sighed, but knew her decision would have been the same anyway. "I will go back to Kher Ravard," she said. "I have an unfinished matter that needs completion."

Ravard's encampment on Dune Watergatherer was much better guarded than any other she had seen. All the peaks of the dune tops had a sentry, and there were outposts at intervals along its foot. Pedemen rode between them on an irregular beat.

To stop slaves escaping? Ryka wondered. *Or to spot an attack from the elusive Vara Redmane?* Neither, perhaps. More probably because Ravard – much younger than the men he ruled – believed in keeping his men busy and well-disciplined.

She first saw the dune from the back of a pede, seated between the two bladesmen. They rode in past the tribe's waterhole, just ten minutes' walk from the first of the dune's red sands. The boulder-strewn waterhole was tucked into a rocky gully; wild jute plants and bab palms clad the sides, their roots intertwining and writhing across the rock face looking for patches of soil. A pulley system had been rigged to haul water up to the level of the plain.

The first dune guards were there at the winch. Without being asked, one of them drew up a bucket of water for the pede. "So the Kher's whore is back," he said as the animal drank.

He thought she wouldn't understand, of course. She schooled her expression to bland disinterest, but it was impossible to stop the flush spreading to her cheeks. Casually she looked away, shading her face from them with her palmubra and a hand to its brim. She was glad when they started off again, heading into the dune.

The sand dales twisted and turned and branched like the spreading gullies of a drywash rising towards a hilltop. Easy for a stranger to become confused and follow the wrong branch, but the driver knew his way.

On a flat valley floor, an orderly array of red tents and canvas privies spoke of discipline and system. The surrounding slopes were anchored tight by creeping vegetation buzzing with insects and ablaze with wildflowers – yellow, pink, scarlet, white, soaking the air with perfumes. Ryka blinked in surprise. It was astonishingly beautiful, even though her defective eyesight blurred the details.

She raised her head to look at the surrounding ridges of the dune. Sentries everywhere. *Like a trap . . .*

Before she had time to dwell on that, the driver halted their mount close to the open tract in front of the pede lines. A crowd of men had gathered there, a mixture of the slaves Ravard had brought in from Breccia and Qanatend, the Reduner warriors she already knew and older men of the tribe she didn't know. No women. Startled, she realised something unusual was happening. No one gave her a glance. All eyes were riveted on the two men in the centre of the tract. She squinted, trying to focus.

Kaneth and Ravard.

Her heart lunged against her ribs, thudding.

The two men faced each other like goats preparing to battle, motionless and tense, each waiting for the other to break. A playful skitter of wind whisked red dust into eddies across the area; neither of them even noticed. What the withering hells was happening?

She had stepped into the middle of a nightmare, and all she could do was watch.

At the other side of the open space, a boulder was half buried in the sands. It was decorated with a body. A living body, Ryka realised. A slave tied there, trussed belly down. A Reduner stood next to him holding a dagger.

The guard mounted behind Ryka slid to the ground. "What's going on?" he asked to the nearest Reduner in a mutter.

Ryka leaned down to catch the answer.

"The slave over there tried to escape," the other murmured, without even glancing around to see who asked the question. "About to be punished when Lord Uthardim stepped in. Wants to stop it."

No. This time her heart missed a beat. Several beats. *Sandblast him to a waterless death . . . Kaneth, you fool.*

Kaneth was saying, "You caught him, ended his dreams. Let it be enough." He was calm, apparently without fear. "And what you intend is not punishment; it is torture."

"You push me too far, Half-face. The rule of this tribe is mine." Ravard's voice was as rough as blown sand, his gaze steely. "The usual punishment is death. I am being merciful."

"He is weakened with thirst. Your men have already broken his ribs. He will die under the cuts of the knife."

Ryka's heart beat again, pounding a warning. She knew then what the punishment was. They called it "a small death" – the back of the victim was repeatedly cut with a dagger and coarse salt rubbed into the wounds. The salt stopped infection, but it also increased the pain and resulted in raised, ugly scars. She sat on the pede, motionless, her view of the drama unimpeded. The driver stayed where he was too, seated in front of her.

"Take his place," Ravard said suddenly, still staring at Kaneth, "and I will untie the man unharmed."

The pinioned man began to struggle, striving to look back over his shoulder, crying out, "No! Lord Uthardim! Don't!"

Kaneth ignored the slave and answered Ravard. "As you wish." He undid the ties of his robe at the neck and, with a shrug of his shoulders, he bared his back and allowed the garment to slip to the ground. Underneath, he wore the white pantaloons of a Scarpen pede rider, now stained red by the sands of the dunes.

Ryka went cold. As yet neither of the two men had noticed her; their focus so concentrated on each other that everything peripheral had become irrelevant. Her gaze focused on Kaneth, hungry for information. He was thinner now, broad shoulders all rippling muscle and sinew with the excess flesh stripped away. The burn scars were there, mostly on his face where they puckered the skin and changed his appearance, but with patches extending down his neck to his shoulder and back. *Oh, Sunlord, his back!* Ravard couldn't have him cut, surely, not when the scar tissue was so fresh. She felt sick.

She didn't think. She couldn't. "No," she said, and it was Ravard she addressed, her gaze steady, her voice without quiver. "It would cost you too much, Kher."

Both men whipped around to stare at her. She was vaguely aware she had become the focus of them all – the watching

Reduners and the slaves. Even the man tied to the rock twisted as best he could to see.

"The Kher is ever wise," she said, meekly dropping her gaze. She prayed he would understand what she meant: Kaneth was under Davim's protection. To scorn the sandmaster by harming a man he had favoured, especially one considered a symbol of heroic past by the tribes, was surely foolish.

When she risked lifting her head, Ravard's gaze locked on hers. She dared not glance at Kaneth. Even the sand crickets stopped their singing, as if hushed by the taut edginess of the atmosphere.

"Garnet," Ravard said at last, shattering the fragility of the silence with brittle politeness. "I trust you have recovered."

She slid from the pede and smiled, but it was an effort to speak. She had no breath. Her throat ached with fear. Each word was a separate agony as she let it slip. "I am well, Kher. Awaiting your pleasure."

They all heard it then: the deep-seated cry of the dune god, weeping beneath their feet. The pede stirred restlessly, its feelers swinging outwards, scattering men as they tried to dodge the serrated edges. Ryka ducked, falling to her knees. The rock under the roped man shook, and ripples moved outwards, shivering the sand as they passed. Men fell, unable to keep their footing on the shifting ground. Ravard went down on one knee. The cry changed to eerie music, twisting and keening under the ground, a sinuous serpentine thread passing beneath.

Kaneth stood, unmoved, unmoving. Around him, there was fear on men's faces.

Ravard struggled to his feet and rapped out a question to his shaman. "What says the dune god?"

The shaman rode the moving ground like a pedeman on his bounding mount, dancing his skinny shanks to shift his weight. "He says free them both; the punishment is his to make. And his is the justice to mete." There was no mistaking the hint of fear in his tone. As if in response to his words, the ground stilled.

No sooner had the last trickle of sand ceased than an ululation started on the dune crests around them. The sound was so unexpected, Ryka jumped in shock.

They all looked up, to see the sentries gesturing from their vantage points. Ryka had no idea what it portended, but the Reduners obviously did.

"To your posts!" The cry came from Ravard. The tableau around the flat space broke up into frenzied movement. Men ran towards their tents, and they had purpose. Even the slaves obeyed the call, racing to saddle pedes and ready them for their drivers.

"Get to my tent," Ravard snapped at Ryka. Then he turned to the bladesman still mounted on the pede. "Get that baggage off," he ordered the man. "I'm taking your mount. You can sit behind."

"What's happening?" she asked Ravard as the bladesman scrambled to the back of the pede to untie their belongings.

"A large caravan coming," he said and hauled himself up into the driver's saddle. "Could be a raid. Could be my father. Take your things and get to my tent and stay there."

The bladesman tossed everything down at her feet. She bent to sort through the bundle as Ravard turned the pede and rode rapidly away without a second glance.

Elmar detached himself from the bustle around the pede lines. Seeing him approach, Kaneth bent to roll up a trouser leg and retrieved a dagger strapped to his calf. He gave it to the pikeman, saying, "Cut Bartles down and get him to the slave tents. He should lie as low as possible for a few days and hope everyone forgets about this."

Elmar took the dagger, then glanced over at Ryka. "Welcome back," he said morosely and headed for the

288

pinioned man. She suspected he was battling a desire to ask Kaneth if he'd been out of his tiny shrivelled mind, trying to provoke Ravard like that.

She scowled at Kaneth. "You have no more sense than a senile sand-tick."

"Sense? *Sense?* And what about you? You *scolded* the Master Son in front of his whole tribe! You risked as much to keep me safe as I did to save Bartles. More, in fact. That was madness, Garnet!"

"Can't you call me by my name yet?"

His irritation fell away. He shook his head. "I – I remember a child I used to play with. She looked a lot like a younger version of you. I struggle to remember her name, but when I open my mouth to say it, the memory slips away like curds from the spoon."

"You were the bane of that girl's life."

"She was diabolical in her revenge. I remember the honey."

"Ah." She recalled a picnic and an incident that had involved trickling the remains of the picnic honey onto his clothes while he was dozing . . . and Scarpen ants loved honey.

She smiled at the memory; smiled too, because he remembered.

The encampment seethed around them, but in the bustle no one paid them any attention. Elmar helped a limping Bartles towards the camp. Warriors were already riding out; pedes bristled with their weaponry.

"Think we are under attack from one of the Scarpen cities?" Kaneth asked.

Ryka shook her head. She could sense the water in the approaching caravan, and she could feel the panniers full of looted water. "Reduner. It would be a good time to escape now if we could find a pede somewhere."

He risked reaching out to touch her face. She shivered,

feeling his concern. Not love. Not yet. *Kaneth, remember me . . . I don't know how much of this I can bear.*

"I can't," he said.

"Why not?"

"The slaves. I may not remember who I am, or who I was, but you were right in what you said about the slaves and slavery. It means something to me. I don't know where I belong, but I do know that they don't belong here and the way they are treated is wrong. They even look up to me, Sunlord knows why. If I leave, so do they. Every blighted one of them. I will not leave them behind. I don't quite understand why I feel that way, but I know I do."

"You are a rainlord. We were taught that all the Quartern is our responsibility."

"I am a rainlord no longer. Whatever happened to me took it all away. But it left something in its place. I cannot speak to water, but I can speak to the dunes."

She fluttered a hand at the patch of disturbed sand. "It was *you* who did that, just then?"

"Yes. As I did that other time and harmed you. Then, I did not know what I could do."

"No, you're not talking to the dune, Kaneth. It's your rainlord connection to the dampness deep inside the dune. You call to the water and the sand shifts. You are a rainlord still."

He shook his head. "I do not feel the water even in my own water skin. But I feel something there, beneath our feet. A soul, something living. It speaks to me, and I can make it answer."

"Are you saying there really is a dune god?" *Kaneth?* Kaneth the disbeliever? So utterly uninterested in Temple, he refused to go to Sun Day worship? She gaped at him.

"No. All I know is that inside every dune we crossed on our way here, I felt a – a presence. Something that I connect to. A god? I don't know that I believe in gods."

"You are a shaman then, like that man who interpreted what he heard?" Ryka tried to keep the scorn out of her voice, but wasn't sure she had succeeded.

He gave a laugh, raw and sarcastic. "He's a faker, playing on the weakness of men. A clever one though, and a frightened one now. He no longer understands the dune, so he fears there may really be a dune god. Little does he know it is only me, playing with the sand entity like a desert child chasing ant lions in the sand. I don't know what I'm doing. Or how I'm doing it. I just know I can." Something he saw in her face brought a gentler expression back to his. "Don't worry. I know I am neither the Uthardim of legend, nor a dune god nor a mythical hero returned. I'm just a man who sees something that has to be done. And someone who can feel the heart of a living dune."

"Kaneth, if there was anything alive under the sand bigger than a dune lizard, rainlords would have felt its water long ago. There's nothing there."

He shrugged. "I know what I feel. It's not an animal. It's the dune."

She abandoned the argument. "I'm worried about you," she said. "You are antagonising Ravard. You have no fear in you, and therefore I am afraid *for* you. Kaneth, a man who does not fear dies because he does not know when to turn from danger."

"Is dying so bad a thing? I have nothing to live for because I have no memories, no idea of who I am or why I should live. So I weave a worthwhile aim based on a future, not a past: freedom for these slaves. A purpose for this nameless man, this possessor of a past hidden in mists. When the mists tease apart to give me a glimpse of that past, it tantalises, but it's never enough. Sunblast it, Garnet, I'm like a flower that's been picked. I look as though I am alive, but in truth I am already dead."

His words were spikes into her heart, into her being. She wanted so much to take him in her arms, to murmur words of love. But to him, she was almost a stranger. She could do nothing.

"It is different for you," he said. "You have a reason to fear death. You have a reason to live growing within your body."

Her calm shattered, gone in an instant as his words splintered her control. "So do you!" The cry ached with her pain. "It is *yours*! Yours, you idiot! Your *son*."

The lump in her throat stopped her breath.

She turned from him to go, to run. Anywhere. Just to escape from the hurt. To be able to breathe again.

And came face to face with Ravard.

He stood close enough to have heard everything she had cried out in her final burst of unbearable emotion.

His stare, the darkness of his eyes depthless, swallowed her alive. His voice when he spoke was as toneless as the trill of a cicada, but his eyes said his tone lied. "I asked you to go to my tent," he said.

She stood still, hearing his words, yet unable to say what they signified, not caring what they meant. It was the look in his eyes that stopped the breath in her throat.

Watergiver have mercy, she thought, *one of us is as good as dead.*

She just wasn't sure if it was Kaneth or herself.

21

Scarpen Quarter
Scarcleft City, Scarcleft Hall, Level 2
Breccia City

When the disaster came, Taquar didn't recognise it as such. How could he? Of all the things he had thought Shale – no, *Jasper*, but still a bastard plains-grubber for all that – might do, fleeing Scarcleft was not on the list. After all, he had been given the freedom to come and go. Yet that was exactly what he had done. Fled the city.

At first Taquar assumed he'd gone for a ride in The Sweepings or The Skirtings with his guards, as he did often enough on one of the days they didn't shift storms. Certainly he had been accompanied by his guards. But this time none of them had come back by nightfall, nor the next morning. Laisa had searched Jasper's room and noted his warm night cloak and several outfits were missing. Taquar, the growing rage within him suffused with the cold panic of a deep-seated fear, had gone immediately to the stormquest room with its view over the city towards the distant ocean. Laisa followed him in, looking around with bright-eyed interest. He had to repress a desire to wring her neck.

Even the briefest of glances around told him many of the maps and notes Granthon had given Jasper were missing.

He took a deep breath and calmed himself. "The boy has

no way of creating a storm without me yet. None. And if there is one thing I know about him, it's this: he would never let any part of the Quartern thirst. Every blighted argument we've had lately has been on that very issue."

"Firstly," Laisa said acidly, "when are you going to acknowledge he is no longer a boy? He's a *man*, Taquar, and the life he's led has caused him to be a surprisingly resourceful one. Besides, he must be nineteen or twenty. Why are you always so blind to that? Secondly, I find it perfectly possible he has been deceiving you about the extent of his storm-raising ability."

He shot a withering look her way.

She said, "You must have considered that he is pretending to lack skills he actually has, just to keep you physically weakened."

He hesitated before replying. "Yes," he admitted. "However, he also knows that if life is too unpleasant, I will leave. Money will get me a passage on a ship, no matter what Iani orders to the contrary."

"So the truth is, you don't know what he is up to." She tilted her head in question. "What do you intend doing?"

"We should soon know if he raises his own storms. We'll be able to feel them. If he can do that, then he has enough power of his own to look after the Quartern's water and he's probably gone to join Iani's army. If he has, well, we have enough water to last to the end of this cycle, even without further rationing or rain. I have the pedes and the men and the ziggers to steal more if need be. We must build up our pedes and our groves to their former numbers. We will need food and transport to wage a war."

"Rather than leave?"

"That's a last resort. I don't like people to get the best of me."

She gave a thin smile. "Some would say your present difficulties are a just punishment for murdering your peers."

"You think that's *so* amusing, don't you?" He made no attempt to hide the loathing in his voice. Its intensity made her take a step backwards. "How was I to know there were to be no more stormlords born? Or that your Senya or Merqual Feldspar's two daughters were not going to be stormlords? My aim was merely to dispose of those around my own age – not to wipe stormlords off the face of the Quartern! I certainly never ever intended Lyneth to die."

Just then, when he thought things could not get any worse, Senya appeared in the doorway, her mutinous expression and down-turned mouth enough to sour his stomach.

"My maid said Jasper has disappeared! Is that true?"

"It seems so," Laisa answered calmly.

"He can't do that! He has to marry me. You said so. You both said so!"

"I shall leave you to deal with this," Taquar muttered, and left the room.

Turning to her daughter, Laisa ignored his departure. "I spoke to Jasper only two days ago, Senya. He made it clear – yet again – that he will indeed marry you, and soon. And I must say I am glad you have come to regard the marriage as desirable."

"Well, you married the only man I *wanted* to marry."

Laisa suppressed a desire to snap. Senya could occupy a powerful position one day, and it would be foolish to alienate her. "Senya," she said gently, "you have no idea of how easy it is to burn yourself on a man like Taquar. I hope you have been keeping out of his bed, and out of his way, because he is not renowned for his patience. Quite frankly, I cannot see what he is up to in all this, and I don't like it when I don't understand what he is doing. You would do well to wonder just why he has been pushing you from his own bed into Jasper's before a wedding."

Senya pouted. "You're just jealous."

"And you don't know just how *laughable* that notion is. Did Taquar ever tell you *why* he wanted you to seduce Jasper?"

"To make him want to marry me all the sooner, of course. Then we shall have children and they will be stormlords and Taquar won't have to make clouds all the time."

Laisa regarded her daughter with pity. "My dear, you have the critical thinking abilities of a sand-dancer in a mirage. You must learn to think things through, for your own benefit. It will be eighteen or so years before any child of yours is a trained stormlord and in a position to be of help. So I hardly think it matters to Taquar if you have a baby next week or next year. There has to be another reason."

Senya pouted and flounced out of the room, leaving her mother continuing to ponder how to benefit best from the situation.

After that, matters went from bad to worse for Taquar. A few more days passed, and there was no word from or about Jasper. They did hear that Sandmaster Davim's troops, having completed their evacuation of both Breccia City and its mother cistern, had withdrawn beyond the Warthago Range. Davim informed Taquar by messenger that, although the Reduners were leaving a force in the northern city of Qanatend while there was still water left there to plunder, everything south of the Warthago was Taquar's.

"Just don't trespass over the range. And remember, if we don't have regular rain, then we must have random rain, or I shall be knocking at the walls of *your* city," the message concluded.

The words galled him with their cheek, but also left him elated. Breccia City was within his grasp and he revelled in the thought. *It should have been mine years ago.* He almost forgot himself enough to rub his hands together, as gleeful as a carpet merchant about to make a sale. *Two* cities; Scarcleft and Breccia. It was a beginning.

The next day, he left for Breccia, accompanied by a force of pede-mounted water enforcers armed with ziggers.

When he gazed at the destruction the Reduners had left behind, though, he was appalled. The devastation and looting were more extensive than he had anticipated. Fierce fighting had left the interior of many buildings burned. Much of the bab grove would have to be replanted. There were no pedes in the city, not one. The metal works and the forges outside the walls were all in ruins. There was no food or oil or fuel briquettes or weapons to be had. Other, odder items were also missing. Carpets. Metal items. Pottery. Gemstones had been pried out of the gates.

Worse, from what he could determine, Reduners had either put many of the men of the city to the sword, or taken them as slaves. They had been particularly vicious towards the richer citizens of the upper levels. Many Level Three and Four families had been wiped out to the last child. The luckier ones had escaped only because they had taken refuge in the hidden tunnel and avoided the initial slaughter that had followed Jasper's escape from the city.

Although the fate of individuals did not interest Taquar, he *was* concerned about whether there would be enough labour to rebuild and replant. One of his first concerns was the water situation. When he checked, he found to his relief that the main cisterns were half full and water was still trickling in from the mother wells. With the population substantially reduced, the amount was adequate.

Over the next few days he set his men to locating all the city's water sensitives, rainlords and reeves. Their reports further dismayed him. There were no more Breccian rainlords. Ryka and Kaneth, as well as Ryka's father and all the ageing rainlords of his generation – they were all dead or missing, and so were all the rainlord priests. Even the priest who had hidden the people down in the tunnel had eventually been caught and killed. Taquar had half expected that, but he had not thought to find many reeves had been dispatched with ruthless efficiency as well. A handful of lowly water sensitives did report to Breccia Hall on his request, but he knew they were pitifully few to assert control of the city's cisterns and water distribution. Theft was already rampant.

Fortunately, the talented children he and the other rainlords had found in the Gibber had been scattered throughout the Scarpen just before the invasion, not that any of them had shown signs of developing stormlord talent.

None of that angered Taquar. His ire was directed at Jasper. How could he ever replenish Breccia's water if the little washrat had disappeared? The men he had sent out in all directions to hunt the stormlord down and persuade him to return had not yet reported back. In growing fury, he had to admit to himself how badly he had miscalculated.

With an effort, he replaced his anger with cold dispassion, and decided he had no choice in his next move. If he dispersed his men and his water sensitives and rainlords over two cities, they would be stretched pitifully thin. Better, he decided, to make sure he could hold Scarcleft, to develop his own city as the centre of Scarpen commerce and power. And hope that Jasper would never cut off the water because the people would suffer. Breccia would have to wait.

He spread the word that any man who wanted to join his armed forces would be welcome to return with him, and that artisans and skilled workers were welcome in Scarcleft. The number who answered his call was pitifully small. He knew why; he saw the fury in Breccian eyes as he passed in the street.

When he rode out of the city at the head of a disparate

selection of artisans and young men, a silent crowd watched, their collective gaze spilling misery and hate.

Taquar had left Laisa in Scarcleft. She was content to leave the rule of the city to Harkel Tallyman, who was more than capable of ruling without any recourse to her advice. When he came to her looking both shocked and at a loss, therefore, she was taken aback; when he told her what had happened, she stared at him in consternation.

"What?" she asked, wondering if she had understood his unusually garbled account. "Did you just say your contacts in Pediment and Portfillik have been seeing messages *written in the sky with clouds*?"

"That's correct."

"That's impossible. No one can have that much control over clouds!"

"Jasper?" he asked, and his tone indicated the question was a genuine one; he did not know the answer.

"Especially not Jasper. He cannot even draw vapour from salt water." *Or can he? No, of course he can't. We've seen no signs of storm clouds drawn from the sea since he left.*

"But he can manipulate clouds," Tallyman pointed out.

"Yes, but he doesn't have access to clouds without Taquar's help!" *And I wouldn't have thought it possible to have such finesse anyway, though someone obviously does.*

Tallyman was silent.

Laisa licked dry lips and felt a cold dread. It was Jasper. Of course it was Jasper. He had been deceiving them.

She had trouble forming her next words and Tallyman had to lean forward to hear them. "And these sky messages ask the cities of the Scarpen to unite under the banner of Stormlord Jasper and to march on Scarcleft and Breccia to free them from Highlord Taquar, the traitor who invited Davim to invade?"

"Yes. Not quite those words, but – yes. And they were signed 'Bloodstone.'"

How the pickled pede did Jasper know Taquar had gone to Breccia? The answer came as soon as she had framed the question. He'd felt their water, of course. The water of Taquar and his men. *He must be camped somewhere close enough for his powers to sense such things but just far enough away for other rainlords to be oblivious.* The little wash-rat, they had been underestimating him all the time. He was probably capable of watering the whole sandblasted Quartern if he put his mind to it. But how had he made clouds without other rainlords being aware of their formation? She'd had no idea, and surely Basalt would have said something had he sensed them.

Gathering together a semblance of her normal calm, she asked, "What's your reading of the situation in the other cities, seneschal? Will they take any notice of clouds spelling words in the sky?"

His thin face usually wore a cynical expression bordering on mockery. She saw none of that now. Harkel Tallyman was worried, worried enough to treat her with respectful seriousness.

He said slowly, "A quarter-cycle ago I would have laughed at the notion of the cities of the Scarpen achieving any sort of unity. They were each scrambling to keep their own rain-lords and their own guards to protect only their own cities, in case Sandmaster Davim turned his attention to them. But things have changed since then."

One by one he enumerated the changes, raising a finger with each new point. "First, the Reduners have left Breccia. Second, people are afraid of thirsting to death and they will examine any means of preventing that, even a war. Third, all of a sudden here is proof we have a real stormlord. He can arrange the very clouds in the sky to suit his own convenience.

That sends a powerful message. If he can do that, he can surely supply them with water. We might tell them differently – that Jasper needs Highlord Taquar – but will they believe it?" He raised his fourth finger. "Alas, Taquar now represents a target for them to throw stones at: the traitor who sold them to the Reduners and brought Breccia and Qanatend to their knees. Cloudmaster Granthon kept that dirty little secret while he was still alive, but too many people have heard about it since. The tale is out there now, the gossip is a wind-whisper everywhere." He waggled his thumb at her. "And what do you think the final difference is?"

"Iani," she said after a moment's consideration. "That dribbling old fool with his mad ramblings about his lost daughter."

"Iani," he agreed, showing her his five spread fingers. "A different sort of hero. Husband of a martyred heroine, driven half mad because he lost his daughter, murdered, so he says, by Taquar. A man now gathering an army from the cities of the Scarpen. I've heard wind-whispers saying people are looking to him for leadership. Lord Laisa, I think we may be in a lot of trouble."

She regarded him thoughtfully. "Harkel, are you perhaps suggesting we, um, desert our present pede foundering in sinking sand and – er, somehow find another?"

"If another mount were possible, I would definitely suggest it would be a good idea."

"I think I hear a 'but' coming."

"But there isn't going to be another mount for either of us, my lord, I regret to say. You became Highlord Taquar's wife *after* he threw in his lot with the Reduners. You can't plead innocence." He smiled faintly. "And me? There are too many people out there ready to rend me to pieces for what I have done in the Highlord's name. We ride this mount, my lord, because there will never be another for us."

He started to walk up and down as he spoke. "We were all

301

safe enough while we had Jasper on our side. But now?" He shook his head. "Our only hope is either to hold fast here, or hold Breccia and abandon Scarcleft. I doubt we have the resources to do both. Or we could flee and take a ship across the Giving Sea. There is something to being a small, well-fed mouse in a large city, as opposed to a very dead rat elsewhere. That should be your advice to Taquar. It is certainly mine. But he is not a man to take kindly to advice going against his dreams."

Especially not his dreams of far-ranging power, she thought, but she didn't say the words. "Send a message to the Highlord telling him of these cloud messages. And ask Lord Gold if he would be kind enough to attend me at his earliest convenience. Make it clear my earliest convenience had better be very soon."

He bowed and let himself out of the room.

She sat very still after he had gone, regretting her past decisions. *Yet . . . there must be a way out of this mess. There's always* something *one can do.*

When Lord Gold arrived, she had to repress a desire to grimace. She had never liked him. The previous Quartern Sunpriest had been a good man – irritatingly so sometimes, but one could always use a good man's scruples to manipulate him. This man was bigoted and vicious and had no scruples at all. Worse, he was sure he was right and treated any personal criticism as an attack on his religion. Which might have been laughable, except that it wasn't wise for a rainlord or a ruler to be seen by the populace as despising the one true faith. His disapproval of her was manifest; he even whisked the fabric of his robes away if it seemed the hem would be contaminated by the touch of her skirts. Oh yes, he could do her a lot of damage if he put his mind to it.

"Lord Gold," she said sweetly, "so good of you to drop by so soon."

"I am delighted to be of service," he said, although his expression implied anything but pleasure. "The spiritual concerns of my flock are always my immediate concern."

"It's not so much a spiritual problem that concerns me as one related to water-sensing ability. And I've called on you for aid, as I know you're a rainlord of considerable skill. And also that you've been monitoring – at Taquar's request – the storm clouds shifted by the stormlord."

His face took on a wary cast. "Yes."

"Have you noticed anything unusual since Lord Jasper left Scarcleft? I confess, I've not been paying as much attention as I should have been."

"No, I can't say I have, my lord. I was keeping track of where he sends the rain – that's what the Highlord wanted me to do – but there've been no new clouds since Jasper left. And so I told Lord Taquar before he left for Breccia."

Laisa frowned and muttered, more to herself than to him, "So what the sweet water is he up to?"

"Oh, well, he has been shifting the old cloud around. I can't imagine why. Practising, I suppose."

She pounced on the strangeness. "*Old* cloud? *What* old cloud?"

"Why, the one he and Lord Taquar kept over the Warthago. They used to add to it every day, to make it bigger. Lately, though, they – well, Lord Jasper, I suppose, shifts part of it to make it rain somewhere."

"Did you mention this cloud to Lord Taquar?"

"No. Why should I? Didn't he know about it?"

She was silent.

"Ah. I see. The cloud is large, or it was, and heavy with water. However, it is tucked down inside a valley. I suppose that makes it hard to detect. I knew it was there because I was following the clouds Lord Jasper moved." He made the comment sound like a reproof of her laxity.

She changed the subject abruptly, embarrassed to say she'd had no idea the cloud existed. But then, she had never bothered to look at the Warthago. "And Jasper has been accessing this cloud since he left the city?"

"Yes. In fact, he seems to have been sending bits of it all over the place, without actually making it rain. Or at least someone has. I have no way of being sure who, of course, although my understanding is he's the only one of us who can cloudshift."

"You're saying Lord Taquar helped him to *make* this cloud?"

Basalt looked bewildered. "Don't they always make clouds together, my Lord? I assumed—"

"But you never actually mentioned to Taquar that this particular cloud was oddly placed."

"Er – well, no. I assumed—"

"You never talked to him about parts of it being moved, either, did you?"

"Well, no. I mean, I assumed—"

"When he returns, I think Lord Taquar is going to be very angry about your assumptions, my lord. It seems Jasper has been saving a little every day to build up a reserve. And you never thought to mention it."

Basalt paled.

"Thank you, Lord Gold. That will be all."

He blinked at her abrupt dismissal and hesitated. In the end, he lifted his hand in blessing, then – his voice heavy with meaning – uttered a prayer to the Watergiver to accede on behalf of all sinners. When she glared at him, he bowed and left.

Spindevil take the blighted bastard of a Gibber grubber. He tricked us.

She was still considering what the consequences might be, when Seneschal Tallyman was ushered in with another message. "From the Highlord," he said, and handed it over. "He says he is returning to Scarcleft."

Quickly she scanned what Taquar had written. "Ah. So he has abandoned the idea of holding Breccia."

Tallyman gave a grim smile. "He has indeed. He told me to send out water enforcers and pedes to steal water from the Breccia tunnel."

Laisa stared at him. "Watergiver save them."

Tallyman gave a bark of laughter. "I doubt he will. Seems they have no rainlords to tell them if we steal their incoming water. Although I suppose rainlords in other cities might sense what we are doing?"

"Too far for a rainlord. You know, seneschal, mostly we water sensitives don't sit around trying to trace the movement of water throughout the land. Mostly we try to *ignore* water. It is too easy to become overwhelmed by all we feel otherwise."

"Ah."

Bastard has filed that bit of information for future use. "Stealing Breccian water – well, I am hardly going to object, not if Jasper fails to return or send rain to the mother wells."

"What is he up to?" Tallyman asked. She didn't reply, so he added morosely, "One would almost think he was in league with Sandmaster Davim, intent on returning us all to a Time of Random Rain. But who can read the mind of a Gibber grubber?"

I can. He's been using the cloud stored in the Warthago to send messages, that's what he's been doing. Because he still can't make his own clouds. Damn! There is something here we are not understanding . . .

There was a knock at the door followed immediately by the entrance of the steward. Obviously flustered, he had not waited to be granted leave to enter.

"Yes, what is it?" Laisa asked, annoyed.

"It's Stormlord Jasper, m'lord. The guards at the South

Gate sent a message to say he has returned and is on his way up here."

"Us, read Jasper's mind?" Laisa murmured to Tallyman. "Not a hope."

22

The Red Quarter
Dune Watergatherer, Ravard's encampment

Time slowed.

Or perhaps it was just that Ryka's thoughts speeded up and her heartbeat raced. But everything else seemed sluggish. And Sunlord knows, she needed the time. To save her life, to save Kaneth's, to kill Ravard – she didn't know which. Not yet, and she had that sliver of time granted her to decide.

Kaneth was staring at her, almost as if he had forgotten Ravard was there, as if he didn't care. Perhaps he didn't. His expression was all misery, a new misery burrowing deep into the man he now was. He didn't remember her, and that failure was devastating. He was father to a son he had forgotten, lover to a woman he could not remember – and the lack appalled him. His inability to change anything shook the foundations of the man he was.

She knew all that without being told. What she needed to consider was: would he leave with her now if she killed Ravard? She thought he would. No, she *knew* he would. They could escape. It would be difficult, though. She couldn't use her rainlord power because Ravard could hold onto his own water.

Those thoughts skittered at speed through her mind and were discarded as fast as they came. She couldn't ask it of Kaneth. If he escaped with her now, it would be a duty, and she didn't want to be anyone's duty. What he wanted to do was stay until he could free the slaves. Second, there were mounted men all around them not far away. Not the best time to kill the heir to the sandmaster.

Ryka concentrated on Ravard. "He has forgotten me," she raged, waggling a hand at Kaneth to make it clear he was the one who had riled her. "He said he'd love me until time ended. He seduced me away from my husband, took me to bed, got me with child – and now he doesn't know me from – from a street whore or a snuggery girl! Uthardim? *Him?* He's no hero! He's just a metal worker with a fine set of muscles to entice a woman from her husband and the will to cast her off like a sleeping shift discarded with the dawn." She spat on the sand at Kaneth's feet, the greatest insult a Reduner could offer.

She allowed her voice to soften, her gaze to mellow, her mouth to lift in a rueful smile as she spoke to Ravard. "We women are so foolish. We allow our glances to wander and our hearts to follow, forgetting that there is more to a real man than a fine pair of buttocks and the muscles in his arms and thighs." She gave what she hoped was a penitent shrug and lifted her hands. "I do not know where your tent is, Kher." *And if fear doesn't make me puke, this conversation will...*

She bent to pick up her bundle but a boy who had been standing nearby forestalled her. He was a lad of thirteen or so, old enough to have his hair braided, but not yet of an age to wear a weapon. "I'll carry it for you," he said in Reduner. She didn't dare reply for fear she'd give away her understanding of what he said, so she just smiled instead.

"Come with us," Ravard said roughly to Kaneth. He took Ryka by the hand and pulled her, without any semblance of gentleness, across the camp. He stopped in front of a large red tent, erected slightly apart from the others. At the back was a canvas privy, at the side a shade roof over the cooking area, both places standing free of the tent. The lad put the bundle down and scampered away, suddenly less a youth and more a child; Ravard pushed Ryka under the shade of the tent's canvas front veranda and turned on Kaneth, his look filled with rage and frustration. "You will kneel before the dune god's shrine tonight," he said. "All night, from sundown to sun-up, unmoving on your knees, praying for his forgiveness."

"Forgiveness for what, Kher?" Kaneth asked.

Ryka winced. *Sandblast you, Kaneth, can't you just keep your withering mouth* shut *for once?*

"If you don't, I'll kill you," Ravard snarled.

He believes it, Ryka thought. *He can't articulate it without sounding crazy, but he believes that Kaneth somehow manipulates the sands of the dune.*

Her next thought she directed at Kaneth, as if he could hear her. *Be careful, you irritating sand-tick of a man – one foot wrong and Ravard will slaughter you where you stand, his father's wishes be damned.*

Kaneth did not glance her way. He bowed and departed towards the slave lines. Ravard pulled Ryka into the tent.

"Are you well?" he asked again. "Do you still bleed? Does the baby still live? Blighted eyes, I have missed you!" He blurted this last out, then looked embarrassed.

"I am recovered. And the baby moves still."

He covered the curve of her abdomen with his hand. "I claim this child," he said. "He's a son of the dunes. He'll be raised t'take his place in this tribe. As he grows he'll deny the man who seeded him."

She felt a muscle twitch in her cheek. *I wonder if you will ever know how close you are to death at this moment.*

Then she saw the intent way he was looking at her, the concern in his eyes, she heard the fervour in his voice. She was reminded how young he was, and her anger drained away.

You're a researcher, Ryka. Remember your training. He had been raised in a tribal society where women couldn't even drive or own a pede. He was offering her all that he knew how to offer – clumsily, born as much of jealousy and ideas of ownership as they were of friendship or love – but still far more than most Reduner men knew how to give.

She smiled at him, and touched his arm. "Thank you," she said.

He jerked his head at the open flap of the tent. "This Uthardim, was he the one you were looking for in the heap of the dead in Breccia?"

She nodded. "More fool me." She heaved a sigh. "I knew my husband was already dead."

"You have no need of such a lover now. Or a husband. I am enough for any woman."

"Mmm," she agreed vaguely.

"Stay here until I return. Out of sight. I have to speak to the sandmaster when he arrives and I do not want him reminded of you."

"It's the sandmaster's caravan that's arrived? Is this his encampment?"

"No," he said with pride. "This is mine. I have led this tribe since I defeated the tribemaster in combat when I was seventeen. I am the youngest tribemaster in living memory. Sandmaster Davim's tribe is further along the dune towards the sunset. He's just stopping here tonight t'pick up his tribe's slaves." He kissed her gently, tentatively, as if he was afraid she'd slap him, then the kiss deepened. When he released her, he tapped her gently on the nose with a forefinger. "Tonight," he said and left the tent.

Sands, she thought, *he must drive some of the grey heads in the tribe insane. Were we like that, Kaneth, when we were twenty? Balanced between maturity and inexperience? Brave, stupid, thoughtless, generous, cruel, kind, all rolled up together?*

She thought back. *I think we were different. Although perhaps no wiser, in spite of being trained and educated . . .*

Ravard had been forced to do his own growing up. Pity stirred deep inside her. She knew it was dangerous. She knew there might come a time when she had to kill him – when she dared not hesitate.

With a sigh she grabbed up her bundle and looked around.

The tent had three, no, four rooms: the large reception space with its huge family jar of water, and three small separate sleeping rooms, each with its own wash stand and stuffed quilts for a bed. It was easy to see which was Ravard's room. It had lavish carpets, richly coloured woven wall hangings and four heavy carved wooden boxes, of the kind that were imported from across the Giving Sea and sold in the market places of the Scarpen. Ryka opened them one by one and looked inside: folded clothes, extra quilts and cloaks, weaponry, saddlery, onyx vials of perfume, decorative pede prods and bridles. Jewels, probably looted. Daggers, swords, scimitars. All for the taking.

You are far too trusting, Ravard . . .

She unstoppered one of the perfume vials, smelled the fragrance and replaced it where she'd found it. Closing the chests without touching anything else, she explored some more.

In the second of the bedrooms, she found her own clothes – or Laisa's, to be exact – neatly folded into a plain wooden chest. The idea of a wash and a change of clothes was appealing, but first she visited the privy built behind the tent. As she emerged, she caught a glimpse of Davim's battle-hardened warriors riding into the camp.

Her thoughts suddenly filled with the sharp memory of her father holding a blood-drenched sword in a bloodied hand, coming into the Breccia waterhall during a lull in the fighting to ask if she was all right. She'd kissed him, the salty taste of his cheek and the unshaven bristles on his chin biting into her cracked lips. That was the last time she had ever seen him.

Although she wanted to weep at the memory, she held back her grief. *No time for it,* she thought. *Perhaps when this is all over. When we are free again.*

There was no place for weakness, not now.

She washed in the Reduner way, using a wet cloth and a minimal amount of water, changed her clothes and went to kneel at the edge of the closed flap of the tent to peer out through the gap. Davim's men were making camp further down the small sand valley of the dune. To feed the pedes, slaves were bringing bales of vegetation harvested on the plains. Others were starting cooking fires.

Kaneth was nowhere to be seen. Directly in her line of vision on the crest of the dune to the side of Davim's temporary camp was a tall, narrow rock driven into the sand. The exposed part was as tall as a man. She'd seen the same thing on Sandsinger: a shrine stone to the dune god.

From her studies, she knew Reduners considered religious observance to be the duty of the tribe's shaman, and if the tribe was plagued by bad luck the shaman was likely to be sacrificed to the god. To find a new shaman, the men in the tribe ran one by one down the steepest slope of the dune until the dune god sang under the feet of a runner – who then was proclaimed shaman and expected to interpret the words of the god.

You know all that, don't you, Kaneth? Are you using their religion against them? You don't really believe in their dune god, do you? Oh, sand hells – what are we doing here? How long does this have to go on?

Ryka sat back on her heels and raised her hands to her face. For once, not even the thought of the child who stirred under her breastbone could make her regard the future with anything but dread.

A small voice interrupted her thoughts, calling to her from outside. She thought it must have been a girl, but when she drew back the flap slightly, she saw the lad who had so obligingly carried her bundle. He was panting as if he had been running.

"Kher Ravard—" he said, and then stopped as if he suddenly realised she wouldn't understand whatever message he had.

"Yes?" she prompted in Reduner.

Taking heart from her knowledge of that word at least, he burst out, "Kher Ravard said Kher Davim is coming."

She made a gesture with her hand, pointed inside the tent and raised her eyebrow in question. "Coming here?"

He nodded, looking over his shoulder nervously as if they were hard on his heels.

Blighted eyes. She went to step out on the veranda, thinking to go somewhere else but he pushed her back inside and vanished. She took the hint and retreated to her sleeping room. Once there, she untied the canvas door and unrolled it to the floor to close off the doorway. A moment later she felt the water of two people enter the main room, and blessed the nameless boy for his warning. She sat down quietly on the clothes chest. One of the two men lifted her door to peer in. It was Ravard. He did not speak, but raised a finger to his lips, bidding her be silent. She nodded, and the heavy cloth fell back into place.

"We're alone?" Davim asked. "I've private matters to discuss."

He can't sense me, she thought suddenly in surprise. And Ravard hadn't worried that he would. Why not? She was confounded. Wasn't Davim a water sensitive after all?

"The slaves are busy elsewhere, Sandmaster," Ravard said.

"I have given orders that they are to attend to the needs of your men and pedes."

She smiled and settled back to listen. Fortunately, it apparently hadn't occurred to Ravard that she might by now have picked up enough of his language to understand a conversation. They spoke first of the situation in the Scarpen. Davim's army had abandoned Breccia after stripping the groves of all the bab fruit and stealing all the water they could carry. There was still a token force in Qanatend, however, headed by the Warrior Son, Medrim.

"No point in abandoning that place," Davim remarked casually. "Not while there's still water coming in from the mother cistern. A nice supply for us to pillage without crossing the Warthago. The stormlord even made it rain up in the mother well valleys the other day." He chuckled. "That young fellow is as soft as pede milk curds."

Ryka sensed the shrug of Ravard's shoulders. "He doesn't want his water-plump city dwellers to thirst."

Davim laughed and the sound made the hairs on the back of her neck stand up. "Oh," he said, the smiling tone in his voice carelessly cruel, "we killed most of the dregs on our way through. Just left the useful ones to serve the men we left behind. So in truth, the stormlord is supplying us with water in plenty. With so few folk in the city, we'll do well, I think."

"I thought the idea was for us t'return to a Time of Random Rain." There was a faint edge to Ravard's voice and Ryka stirred uneasily. The last thing she wanted was the Master Son upsetting the sandmaster.

"And so we shall. So we shall," Davim said. "But it's shrivelling tough while this stormlord picks up any stray water vapour along the coast to make his blasted storm clouds."

"But they draw water from the sea!"

"Jasper's weak. Seems he gathers as much natural water vapour as he can to help him out. We have little chance of sufficient random rain to meet our needs if he does that. Taquar is using it as a threat, of course. If I upset his plans too much, we get no rain at all."

"Is he bluffing? Sandmaster, we need a long-term plan."

"I don't need you to tell me that, you insolent pup." The words conveyed annoyance, but Ryka was relieved to hear his tone remained mild. Even so, she thought she felt the tension spiral tighter.

There was a moment's silence Ryka could not interpret, then Davim continued, "We have to kill Taquar and young Bloodstone. There'll be a battle to end all battles, and soon. Which is something I wanted to talk to you about: the preparation of your men. Of all our men. I've sent messages to every dune, asking all tribemasters to gather at my encampment to discuss this."

"And Vara Redmane?"

"A sand-tick biting our arse. A nuisance, an itch, but no more than that."

"Every tribe has lost slaves to her cause. Not to mention disaffected warriors – many of the experienced older men who supported her husband's leadership. And her army is *behind* us – somewhere in the dunes."

"Army? They're rabble! They're also thirsty. Of what possible danger can they be to us?"

"How can we attack Taquar and the stormlord if we leave our bare backsides hanging out so someone can shove a spear up them? And if we're thirsty because random rain is far more random than—" But whatever he was going to say was broken off short in the sounds of a scuffle. Ryka drew in a sharp breath. Her water-sense told her both men had jumped to their feet, and one – Davim, she guessed – had grabbed the other and shaken him, none too softly, either.

"They have no waterholes!" Davim shouted. "Get that into

your sand-addled wits. That woman and her fellow traitors are dying *now*. Out there somewhere on one of the empty dunes. You're no bleeding blood son of mine, Ravard – don't make me regret choosing you as my heir. And don't ever forget that while I'm still alive, I can change my mind. I do have blood sons."

"What kind of a Master Son would I be if I didn't tell you what I think? Sandmaster, I'm not going to lie to you to make you happy! If that's the kind of Master Son you want, you chose the wrong man. And don't take me for a suncrazed fool: I know once your sons are grown, one of them will replace me as Master Son. I've always known that. I even know that besides the two born in your tent and acknow-ledged, there is another almost grown over on Dune Hungry One, who knows who his father is, even though he was born to an unpledged woman."

When Ravard spoke again, his tone was quieter, yet more impassioned. "I owe you everything I am, everything I have, so I'll serve you, and I'll serve your sons when the time comes, if they don't shove a knife in my guts first. And none of you'll get anything but the unpolished truth from me."

There was a silence, then a rustle. One of them had moved to touch the other.

"You're right; I'd not want a honey-tongued Master Son. I know we have a foe jabbing at our arses – but I also know that those forces are as weak as an old man's piddle. Sands, they're led by a woman with a shrivelled womb, what do you expect! I will deal with the Redmane bitch later. Right now, we have to stop a rainlord and a stormlord from stealing our random rain. And that's my final word on the matter.

"Let's speak of other things. This Uthardim fellow."

Ryka sat up straighter, her heart thumping.

"He's no reborn hero from the past."

"You're sure of that? One of the first things I heard when I rode into camp is that the dune gods listen to him. Protect him. Back on Pebblered, I heard their dune god rose up at Uthardim's command to save their tribemaster from an assassin."

"The dune god saved someone, certainly – but Half-face didn't ask him to do it. Not that I saw. It's just a rumour, as false as a sand-dancer's tits."

"And what happened here earlier today? Men are saying our dune god saved Uthardim from punishment."

"No. The dune god saved me from doing something foolish. I was annoyed by Half-face and his arrogance and nearly defied your orders to treat him with respect. The dune god serves our tribesmen, not that Scarperman city-groveller."

Briefly Rovard outlined what had happened, without any reference to Ryka's part. "Sandmaster, this man's appearance and his burning is no more than a coincidence. If the true Uthardim returned to us, he'd be born to one of our tribe, or at the very least a dunesman. But this fellow was birthed in the Scarpen – a street-groveller, walking on stones and sleeping without the cleansing light of stars. He champions our Scarpen slaves. Stirs up trouble among them. One of the women is bearing a child he fathered. Is this the mark of the true Lord Uthardim? *He* was known for adherence to our people's ways, and for his love of his wife, the Mother of his tribe."

"You are sure of all this?"

"I'm not the only one to notice the way the slaves turn to him. Older heads than mine have already spoken their warnings and voiced their doubts about his ancestry. Jordestid the pedeman, for example. And old Brudedim. You know him; nothing much escapes his eye, or his ear."

"No, that's true. In fact he's already said he wants to speak to me on the matter. All right – the man is not Uthardim. Kill him, but quietly. And soon. No corpse. No rumours. Understand?"

"Tonight he prays at the shrine on my orders. I can make him, um, disappear. And my shaman'll say the dune god came for him."

"Do it. No witnesses, Ravard. I made a mistake with the man, I'll admit. I don't want anyone to have to pay for that error."

"I'll do it myself. When the camp settles into sleep at the darkest hour of night. It'll be a pleasure."

In the other room, Ryka listened and sweated.

The two men continued to chat, a hundred different topics. They boasted of their battles, laughed at the ease of their victories in the Scarpen. Spoke of the continued raids into the White Quarter, of the death of a mine because Davim had wanted it so. Ryka, her mind racing, hardly heard. It wasn't until she realised that the two men had stood again that she concentrated on them once more.

It was well she did, because Davim was saying, "I want to nap before the evening meal." And someone's water approached her door. Davim's she assumed, although she could not differentiate one man's water from another's.

Without waiting to find out which one of them it was, she dived off the box and into the second sleeping room. Fortunately the canvas curtain was not tied open – but it swayed as she pushed past it. She bent to steady it and prayed he wouldn't notice.

It's the breeze, she thought insanely, as if she could influence him with the power of her mind. *Just think it's the breeze you made when you stepped in there . . .*

To her horror, she felt his water cross the room she had just vacated, heading for her. She spun around and leaped for the wooden chest in the room. Hauling it open with one sweeping movement, she threw the quilts it contained onto the pallet in an untidy heap. Panicked, she dived into the chest, curled up and closed the lid. She heard the rustle of the raised curtain door. She heard Ravard, further away, say something but could not make out the words.

"No, nothing," Davim said.

The body moved away from the door and then his water was supine. She let out the breath she had been holding. She was crushed into an impossibly small space. The chest was not made to hold a body, let alone a pregnant one. It was dark and airless. Every muscle screamed at her to get out of there, shrieking pain. But she dared not move. Not yet.

She waited.

Much later she edged the wooden lid upwards. A crack at first, until she heard the even, heavy breathing of a man asleep in the next room. She levered the lid open and unfolded herself. Standing by the chest once more, stiff and aching, she stared at it in disbelief. She had fitted inside *that*? In a saner moment she would never have even tried.

For a moment she hesitated, wondering if there was some way she could kill the sandmaster, but she had no weapons, and always, always, she remembered the danger to her child. In the end, she tiptoed across the room to the back wall of the tent. Once there, she peeled back the carpeting to reveal the sand beneath. Carefully, silently, she scooped sand to one side until she'd made a hole under the wall. She bent down and peered out. There was no one around; the back of the tent faced the privy and beyond that, the back of several other tents. She slithered out, filled in the hole, and pulled the carpet flat before letting the wall fall back into place.

Outside, she sank down in the shade of the tent, panting as if she had run a race. She doubted Davim would have been forgiving of either of them had he caught her eavesdropping on his conversation with Ravard. Especially if he remembered her from Breccia.

And now what was she going to do? She had to warn Kaneth, and soon. The sun was already low in the sky, and the shadows were long. He had to leave. With or without the other slaves, he had to go. She thought about the conversation she had overheard, wondering what was bothering her about it. Something to do with Ravard. It had been niggling at the edge of her consciousness as she had listened, but she couldn't decide what it was.

The trouble is I may think I speak Reduner well, but I don't really, she thought. *It's not my language. I missed something. Some nuance of something. And I don't know what it was.* She tried to capture the thought, but it skittered away like an ant lion sliding through sand. She turned to wondering about Davim, and why he hadn't sensed her water.

"So this is where you got to."

She jumped. Eyes closed, she had been so busy thinking she'd forgotten to pay attention to her surroundings. Ravard was looking down at her.

"It didn't seem a good idea to stay in there."

"It wasn't. I sent Khedrim t'tell you t'get out."

"The lad? He did try, but we have a language problem and there wasn't time."

He grinned at her, shaking his head half in mockery, half in reluctant admiration. "Me guts shrivelled, thinking the sandmaster would rip us t'pieces – and then you weren't there. I felt your water in the wooden chest, but I couldn't believe you'd fit inside!" He chuckled, pulled her to her feet and kissed her on the cheeks, then the lips. Then he sighed, exasperated. "I can think of a lot of things I'd like t'be doing right now, but you'd best be gone. Go down t'the slave lines and stay there till I call for you."

She was furious. He knew he was going to kill the father

of her child that night, and he could kiss her, pretend everything was normal?

He had spoken with Davim so blithely about Kaneth's death, not caring because he thought she understood none of it. *Well, I understood every word, you spitless horror,* she thought. In her anger, she wanted to claw his eyes out.

Instead, she asked, "Why didn't the sandmaster sense my water? Sandmasters and tribemasters are water sensitives, aren't they?"

He hesitated and she thought he was going to brush away the question, but in the end he said quietly, "You mustn't tell anyone that, Garnet. If you do, you'll die. He has some sensitivity, enough to feel a waterhole f'rinstance, but it is weak. It's why he made me the Master Son, so I could help hide his weakness. His shaman covers for him too. We do it 'cause he is a truly great leader and warrior, a man who will return the Red Quarter – no, the whole Quartern – to its former glory. He doesn't need t'feel water t'do that. He can have water sensitivities like me do it for him."

She shrugged, even as she wondered whether he was warning her or threatening her. "It's nothing to me." One thing about being around Ravard so much: she was learning to be a good liar.

After she left Ravard, she found Elmar without too much trouble. He was busy grooming pedes down in Davim's camp. None of the slaves was roped any more, or even watched. Escape was impossible without a pede, water and supplies; leaving the dune without alerting the ring of sentries would be hard and pursuit would be immediate.

But we'll do it, she thought with grim determination.

She grabbed a polishing cloth and a bag of beeswax and worked alongside Elmar while she talked.

"Do you know where Uthardim is?" she asked quietly.

"Someone came looking for him earlier. He's supposed to be a metalworker and they needed some weaponry sharpened." He grinned at her. "I reckon he'll be doing his best to thin some blades beyond what is wise."

"I've got to see him urgently." Quickly she outlined the conversation between Ravard and Davim.

"Withering *spit*," he snarled. "Listen, you had best look for Ka— Uthardim yourself. Look for the forge fire, that's where he'll be. Tell him I'm assuming tonight's the night for the escape then. I'll start telling our folk."

She nodded and slipped away. By the time she'd located the camp forge fire, the sun had almost set and most of Davim's men were heading towards the cooking pots in the main encampment.

Kaneth took one look at her face and barked, "Oh good – a pair of free hands. Can you work this for me?" He thrust a set of leather bellows into her hands and indicated where he wanted the air directed. "What is it?" he asked under the cover of the noise they made. He thrust a scimitar into the glowing coals.

"Are you supposed to do that?" she asked.

He grinned at her. "No, it weakens the blade. But no one is watching and the metalworker has gone off to eat."

She glanced around. The nearest Reduner warriors were picking through a pile of mended weaponry. Quickly she told him what she had overheard. "I've already let Elmar know. He thinks we should all leave tonight. He's telling the other slaves."

He gave her a long stare then, and withdrew the scimitar. She stopped the pumping of the bellows and the coals darkened. He took the weapon over to the worktable and started hammering at it with little concern for the health of the blade.

"Everyone goes," he said. "Or as many as we can take.

I'll kill Ravard when he comes to kill me. Then I'll bring the slope of the dune down on Davim's camp. That will be the signal. Tell Elmar that. Your job is to organise water and food and tell the women. I have to be up at the shrine in a moment."

He glanced upwards. The holy stone was a black shadow against a red sky, a finger of rock pointing upwards. Closer at hand, the Reduners at the pile of weapons walked away, talking among themselves.

Kaneth turned back to her, to say something further, but changed his mind as someone else approached.

Ravard's shaman stopped by them, his face shadowed by the hood of the cloak that he had pulled over his head. He spoke in his own tongue. "It's time. The dune god awaits your prayers."

Ryka glimpsed a fleeting expression of distaste on Kaneth's face and looked away. *He knows he is going to kill the man tonight.*

He laid down the scimitar and walked to where he had flung his cloak over a tent guy rope. The way he moved then told her he had snatched another sword from the pile of weaponry in passing, hiding the theft within a swirl of the cloak. The shaman was too busy glaring at her to see, too busy wondering what she was doing there, pondering whether he should scold her for it. He would pay for that mistake.

She could even feel the stirrings of pity as she began to walk away.

"Lady." She halted and turned back. Kaneth was standing there, his cloak hitched over one shoulder, his head tilted in the way she knew so well, the glow of the sky illuminating one half of his face, the unscarred half. For a moment she could pretend he was the handsome man she had once known. "I am so sorry," he said, his tone formal, the words laden with deeper meaning. "I profoundly regret that I do not remember

what ought to have been remembered and celebrated. I hope –
I hope you will not hold it against me."

By way of answer, she moved her hand to cover the bump
of their child. "Never," she said, and wondered why it sounded
far too much like a goodbye.

23

Scarpen Quarter
Caravanner route and Pahntuk cistern

Something was sparkling up ahead. Little twinkles of light, pinpricks in the still harsh light of a desert day just coming to a close.

"Alabasters," Sardi said with certainty, shading his eyes as he stared down the track. He was older than Terelle, but his youthful enthusiasm made him seem younger, at least to her. She'd shared his mount all the way from Samphire to the Scarpen, and sometimes she tired of his overt exuberance. Still, it was hard not to like Sardi.

She looked down at her clothing, a borrowed Alabaster robe. As they rode the mirrors flashed irritatingly. "I'm sure you're right," she agreed. "But where are they coming from?"

"The Bastion sent out spies to Pahntuk Caravansary as soon as the messages arrived. Just to check if it was a trap. They'll be coming to tell us what they found."

"Oh." She wasn't surprised; when she had met the Bastion she'd come away with the impression that he was an astute old man, not given to making impetuous decisions. Inwardly she sighed, remembering the city and the many questions she had that had never been answered. If she had come away with any impression of Alabasters, it was that they were secretive.

However, the Bastion had passed on the latest news

Samphire had received messages from the Scarpen via the Gibber. Breccia had fallen to the Reduners. The old Cloudmaster, Granthon, was dead. The new stormlord, Jasper Bloodstone, was now in Scarcleft. Other than that, they had not been able to tell her much about what was happening elsewhere, and they had been secretive about their own affairs. *There is so much I need to tell Shale. So much I want to ask.*

Sardi twisted in the saddle to grin at her. "Oh, good! Father has given the signal to stop for the day. There's a caravansary up ahead!"

A little later she was gratefully slipping off the pede and helping to set up camp outside the caravansary walls. There were pedes to clean and water, cooking to be done, mounts to be hobbled and set free to graze, water to be fetched. She was only halfway through her normal chores when Messenjer called her into the caravansary to meet one of the men who had ridden in from Pahntuk.

The man who rose from one of the daub benches in the public room was a tall, thin, middle-aged Alabaster with kindly eyes. "This is Feroze Khorash," Messenjer said. "A special envoy of the Bastion. He'd like to talk to you."

The name seemed familiar, although she couldn't think where she might have heard it. After they'd exchanged greetings, Messenjer left and for a moment there was an awkward silence until Terelle asked, "The stormlord who sent the cloud messages – is he in Pahntuk?"

"No. Just his army. Men and women from all over the Scarpen and some Gibber folk, too. They are being trained by some of the rainlords under Lord Iani Potch."

Her heart pitched, leaving a sick feeling behind. *Oh Shale, when do I get to see you again?* She had been dreaming of it, but it wasn't going to happen any time soon after all.

"Have a seat," Feroze said. He sat down watching her, concerned. "Ye don't look well."

"Where is he?" she asked, too agitated to be polite. *So sand-brained. We scarcely know each other* . . .

"In Scarcleft with Lord Taquar. Together they are stormshifting."

She paled. "I was hoping—" But she couldn't go on.

"I wouldn't worry too much. Lord Jasper is a very resourceful young man, and he is in contact with Lord Iani on a regular—"

"Lord Jasper? I meant Shale Flint!"

Feroze blinked. "I'm sorry. Who is that?"

"The – the person who sent the sky messages." *It must have been him. Only he knew I cheated at Lords and Shells* . . .

"Ah. Then I think he and Lord Jasper must be one and the same person."

While she was still trying to take that in, he added, "I looked for ye once, ye know. Least, I assume it was ye."

"For *me*? When? Where?"

"A few cycles ago. A caravanner once told us he had seen a Watergiver man and a girl. In the streets of Scarcleft. Do you remember seeing an Alabaster trader?"

The day she'd met Russet for the first time, an Alabaster man had bowed to her. Russet had said he recognised her by her tears. She had forgotten all about that. Now, as Feroze reminded her, she wondered, *Recognised me as what? A Watergiver?* "Yes, I remember."

"He told me about seeing ye. The next time I was in Scarcleft, I looked for ye – but I was attacked and had to leave in a hurry. I met Jasper on that visit. At least he said his name was Jasper. Is your Shale from the Gibber? About nineteen or twenty years old?"

She nodded. "There was an Alabaster he talked about. A salt merchant. Of course! That's where I've heard your name before! He helped you to escape Scarcleft. We were hoping you'd get word to the old Cloudmaster. When we didn't hear anything, we thought you hadn't made it. He was upset." *And he is the Scarpen's only stormlord after all . . .*

The man stared at his knees. "I failed him. I was injured and ill and suncrazy. The pede took me to Portennabar, on the coast. I was sick for a long time. A long story and some day I will tell it, but not now. In the end I did get to Breccia, arriving just in time to see the Reduners scaling the walls. I turned my pede and headed for Samphire, to take the news." He reached into his purse. "Look, I still have this. He gave it to me, but I kept it. It was far too valuable a present and I have looked forward to the day I can return it."

He was holding a gemstone in his fingers. It was the size of a sandgrouse egg, green in colour and flecked through with splashes of red. Still unpolished, it was rough and dull.

Had Shale mentioned that to her? She couldn't remember.

He changed the subject. "Terelle, why don't ye join me on my pede tomorrow? I am sending my companions back to Samphire to tell the Bastion and the councils what is happening, but I am riding back to Pahntuk with ye all. Messenjer says ye are troubled about your waterpainting powers. Perhaps it would help to be talking to me about it."

She accepted Feroze's invitation, and for the final two days' ride to Pahntuk Wells she mounted his pede. He used a driver, and sat with his back to the man, facing her. It made talking easy and she wondered why she had never seen anyone do it before. Sardi grinned broadly every time he glanced their way, so he thought it was a huge joke; his brother's sour face told another story, obviously thinking such behaviour was not appropriate for a man of stature. Feroze didn't care what anyone said. Terelle found herself liking him more and more.

When she told him her story, what Russet had done to her with his paintings shocked him so much there were tears in his eyes.

"I never thought I would hear of a Watergiver lord misusing his power like that. It is despicable! Are ye feeling ill now?"

"No. I followed his advice and it seems to work. I can feel the tug of my need to be in Khromatis, but it is more annoying than sickening."

"He's a wicked man. Or crazed."

"And yet you are all asking me to use my waterpainting powers to kill. How do I know if that's the right thing to do? Messenjer says the powers come from God and cannot therefore be evil."

He snorted. "Messenjer is a dear friend of mine, but he can also be a sand-brained fool. Any of God's gifts can be misused. Ye must indeed be careful, and use its magic sparingly. But it can also be a sin not to use it, too."

"That's what the Bastion said, too. And Errica. Everyone seems to ignore the fact that I don't believe in your God anyway! I have always offered water to the Sunlord."

"I don't know much about the Sunlord," Feroze admitted, "but I can tell ye that Ash Gridelin was only ever a Watergiver like your mother was, or Russet is, so I doubt the Sunlord has any validity except what men have made of him for their own ends."

"That's terribly blasphemous."

"To a Scarpen waterpriest, doubtless. To an Alabaster or anyone from Khromatis, the idea of Ash Gridelin being an emissary of the sun is laughable. It all depends on where you were born, really."

She frowned, thinking.

After a while he continued, "In Khromatis, everyone who can move water and anyone who can shuffle up a waterpainting is called a Watergiver. They are the Lords of Khromatis. Ash Gridelin was one of these nobles, not a Quartern man at all, as ye are taught. A restless man, an adventurer who dreamed of exploring the world. Against all laws, he strayed into the Quartern. He went to Alabaster along the way, which is why we know about him, then on to the Scarpen and Gibber. He is a historical figure to us, appearing in our histories as a real man. He met the Bastion of that time, upset several prominent families with his dalliances with their women. In fact, several Alabaster families – including my own – can trace back to him as an ancestor."

She stared at him, wide-eyed with shock, and he laughed. "He was just a man. Not a particularly good man. He stayed in the Quartern to be helping a land suffering because of its water shortages. He *taught* people to be rainlords and stormlords."

"That's withering spittle! You can't *teach* someone to be a stormlord. Even a water sensitive is *born* that way. Only the Sunlord can grant that gift!"

"Well, I have oversimplified things, I admit. Yes, one is born with the talent. In the Quartern, though, no one was born with *any* talent at all, until Ash Gridelin. The first stormlords and rainlords and reeves were all his descendants. That was the way he saved the Quartern. Until the first children grew up and he taught them how to manage their powers, he was the only stormlord."

She blinked, taken aback. "You're saying—?" She gave a bark of sceptical laughter. "He must have been prolific!"

"He was."

"That's ridiculous!" she said, exasperated.

He didn't look in the least offended, saying, "Ah, but we have proof of the origins of Ash Gridelin. Did Russet ever tell ye about the naming of people in his land?"

Terelle nodded. "He said they were—" She halted, then whispered, "*Oh.*"

"Ah. I think ye see the connection now, right?"

"He said people there are named for colours. Ash and Gridelin. They – they are both types of grey. I never thought

330

of that. All right, so he might have been from Khromatis. But the ancestor of *all* water sensitives? Sandblast it, how many children did he have?"

"Oh, about a hundred, I believe. His seed was known to be, um, effective. Most of those born were water talented to some degree or another."

"A *hundred*?" She was horrified. "That's – that's—"

He cut her short, which was probably just as well. She had been going to say *disgusting*.

"He saved the Quartern and its people from dying of thirst from his generation onwards. Most of his children were born to Scarpen folk, but there were Gibber and Reduner and Alabaster children, too. Your friend Shale must come down through the Gibber line."

"Surely that can't be right! How could such a person be revered as *holy*?"

"Well, he wasn't to us. Quite the contrary. In fact, he was rather an arrogant fellow by all accounts, not worthy of reverence by your priests and their faithful congregation. He failed to instruct his extended family in our faith, which was unforgivable. He gloried in the fact that women flocked to his door. He must also have been charming, I suppose. A man who genuinely loved the company of women. There is proof of his very human existence all over the place in Alabaster. Even in my family we have journals written by family members in which he is mentioned. He seduced my many times great-grandmother, and she wrote it all down afterwards in an excess of remorse. The language is archaic and the ink faded, but the scrolls are still legible. I've read them myself."

Upset, Terelle tried to reject what he was saying, but his honesty was obvious. He believed his words.

"He returned to Alabaster as an elderly man," Feroze continued, apparently oblivious to her inner turmoil, "to be dying among those of his own faith. He was quite unabashed and wrote down all his tales of life in the Scarpen and Gibber. Ye can read his stories in the Samphire library. Written in his hand. Although they are in the Khromatis script, so ye wouldn't understand them, I suppose."

"You mean – are you saying that the Alabaster faith and the Khromatis religion are *identical*? And that the Scarpen one true faith is all made up, probably to account for an ability that had its origins in – in – a man with the morals of a street cat?"

He nodded.

She felt a wave of dizziness, as though the pede had tipped, upsetting her balance. "I don't think you had better mention that aloud in the Scarpen."

"Believe me, I won't."

She tried to smile, but felt nauseated. *Have I really been believing a lie all this time? Wasting my water praying to a deity who never was?* Maybe there was no deity at all. Perhaps life was just as random as flinging leaves into the wind and watching while they danced and fluttered their way to the ground.

The idea was too big, too alien, for her to grasp. She wasn't sure she even wanted to know.

Messenjer, driving his own pede with several warriors seated behind him, halted the mount as he topped the rise over-looking the caravansary. He shook his head in bemusement at what he saw. "Who would have thought it? Gibbermen coming to the aid of Scarpen freedom."

Terelle removed her palmubra and fanned herself. Now that they had stopped the heat was ruthlessly desiccating. She was hot, dusty and tired. She looked over her shoulder. Behind them, the whole line of white pedes was slowing to a halt. *So many of them,* she thought. Myriapedes, packpedes, armsmen, supplies. She couldn't even see the tail end of the Alabaster caravan. *Surely enough men to rescue Shale from Taquar, even though they don't have ziggers.* The other thought niggling, though, was darker: *But not enough to defeat the Reduners. Not nearly enough.*

She dragged her thoughts back to Messenjer's words and stared at the pedes and people milling around outside the caravansary walls. *Gibbermen? How did he know?* Certainly the pedes around the caravansary were black, but then they could have been Scarpen beasts, couldn't they?

"Gibber pedes are not as robust as Scarpen ones," he said, answering her unspoken question. "They are lighter, narrower animals. There's a mix of both Scarpen and Gibber ones there."

"Those people behind us will catch us up at any moment," Messenjer said to Feroze. "The dust is closer." They had been watching a red dust cloud behind them all day, stirred up by unknown followers. At first, they had feared it could be Reduners. Now, close to the caravansary, the fear had faded.

"Whoever it is, they are pushing their mounts," Feroze remarked in answer, his tone heavy with disapproval. Like most Alabasters, he hated to see a pede abused or overworked. "How about moving on, Mez? My old bones need to get off this animal."

Messenjer, who was older than Feroze, grinned and waved a hand in acknowledgement as he urged the pede down the slope to the caravansary. Feroze winked at Terelle.

As they reached the outskirts of the crowd around the caravansary, the billow of dust finally resolved itself into twelve men on a single black packpede. Boisterous Gibbermen armed with an extraordinary selection of weapons – everything from a sledgehammer to numerous thatch-cutters and the poled knives used to harvest bab fruit. They were young, exuberant, undisciplined and noisy, causing Messenjer to stiffen with distaste, Feroze to stifle a laugh and Terelle to grin.

"Are you out to join the stormlord?" she asked them as they drew up alongside.

The driver on the first saddle flashed a smile. "'Sright! You read them sky-writin' words too?"

She nodded.

"We're all from Wash Kering Settle. Our reeve tole us what them sky words said. There's been messages of all kinds all over the Gibber, not just written in them clouds. Comin' out of the Scarpen from some stormlord called Bloodstone. Heard tell the old Cloudmaster snuffed it and this is the new fellow."

Feroze nodded. "Have ye seen many Gibbermen on the road answering the stormlord's call?"

The pede driver shrugged. "There's plenty who'd like to, y'know. But we're pissin'poor washfolk. Aren't many pedes in the Gibber, and fewer weapons . . . But he wrote up there on the sky he was washfolk like us, y'see. The new Cloudmaster! A Gibberman! When folk heard that, they was real eager t'help out. Everyone as could get hisself a pede's out there somewhere, on their way here. 'Strue he's a Gibberman?"

"Yes," Terelle replied. "I've met him. His name is Sh— um, Jasper Bloodstone, and he's from Wash Drybone Settle."

"Really?" one of the younger Gibbermen asked, awed. "We always thought them stormlords were gods, not *Gibbermen*. Even after folk tole us what them sky words said, we wondered if they was scoffin' us."

"And we heard Wash Drybone Settle was burned by them Reduners," the driver added.

"That's right, it was," Terelle said.

They pelted her with questions, which she did her best to answer. She was relieved when one of them spotted a group of Gibbermen making camp beside the track and they rode off to join them.

Feroze halted the Alabaster caravan and he and Messenjer started to organise a camp. Terelle made herself useful by grooming Messenjer's pede, but as she worked, she gazed around. With the arrival of the Alabaster caravan, the overflow of people and pedes outside the Pahntuk Caravansary stretched half a mile beyond the walls in all directions.

Sandblast, she thought, *Shale did this?*

Only then did the enormity of what was going to happen become real. There was going to be a battle. And the Alabasters, maybe Shale as well, were going to be looking to *her* to do something. People were going to die. They wanted her waterpainting to work miracles – and she still did not have the faintest idea how to do it.

Terelle's first impression of Iani Potch was not favourable. He stood up to greet her, but had to brace himself against the wall of the room, as if to give himself some stability. He looked sick and old, a Scarperman with dragging steps and sagging cheeks. His gaze found Feroze and his face lit up in a pleased smile – or so Terelle surmised. It was hard to tell when half of his face did not move at all and his mouth on that side drooped open at one corner.

His gaze shifted to her. "Would you be Arta Terelle the waterpainter?" There was a tremor in his hands, as if he had been drinking, but she could smell no amber on his breath. "In spite of your Alabaster robe?"

She nodded dumbly.

"Then I am truly delighted. I'm Lord Iani Potch. Otherwise known as Iani the Sandcrazy. You have heard of me, I believe, from Jasper." Without waiting for her acknowledgement, he turned to Feroze. "And would it be too much to hope you came back with your army?"

"Indeed I did. I met them two days out – one thousand armed men, several hundred support workers, another thousand armsmen to follow in a few days. I hope ye have water and food for them all, because we are running low."

Iani smiled, but his smile was little more than a sideways twist of his lips, and ended up more like a sneer. "Welcome. We're hunting and salting meat for everyone. As for water, the tunnel is still running. We found some of those treacherous Scarcleft enforcers trying to steal some yesterday down aways.

"But I am forgetting my manners. Please sit down." He waved to one of the men hovering at the door, indicating he wanted some tea brought. The room was typical of a caravansary: brown adobe walls several hand spans thick, window holes that could be shuttered tight in a dust storm, an adobe seat running all the way around the walls, strewn with threadbare embroidered cushions and faded rugs. Low tables made of polished pede segments were the only other furnishings.

Iani sat and patted the cushions next to him. "Sit here, Arta. Jasper gave me your description. Told me all about you. What you can do. He said he thought you'd come back because he sent you a sky message. We've had people looking for you everywhere."

She was astonished. "You've *seen* him? I thought he was Taquar's prisoner in Scarcleft! Jasper is Shale Flint, isn't he?"

Iani nodded. "He is. And in a way he is trapped. He needs to meet you, urgently. We're to take you to see him – apparently you're very important to his plans."

She blinked, trying to absorb that. "You mean, he's *free*?" Annoyance fluttered, threatening to grow larger. Shale had brought her back, not because he was in Taquar's clutches, but in order to *use* her?

He knows how hard that is for me . . .

Oblivious to her growing irritation, Iani said, "Not exactly. He still lives in Scarcleft so he can make it rain with Taquar's help. But he does come and go as he pleases. He'll meet you outside the city. You'll be safe, don't worry; Taquar won't know you're there."

Agitated, she stood and went to look out one of the room's windows. Below she could see a seething mass of people, mostly men; a swarm of would-be warriors scurrying about like wingless ants from a disturbed nest. They seemed disorganised, uncoordinated, undisciplined. She remembered all Shale had told her of Davim. Of the way his men had callously wiped out the village of Wash Drybone. What chance did these people below have against a ruthless Reduner warrior?

She turned away from the window. "How – how is he?"

"Perhaps I'd better tell you the whole story. Why don't you sit down, Arta, while I explain. We can have some tea . . ."

She did as he asked, curbing her impatience while the tea was brought in tiny hollowed-stone cups, accompanied by honeyed bab cakes as hard as desert rock, and Iani began to explain.

"Jasper sent me a sky message – no, let me begin before that. I met Jasper when I rode to Breccia to get help for Qanatend. Cloudmaster Granthon turned me down. So I rode back. The Reduners had Pebblebag Pass blocked of course, but I found a way through. By the time I got to Qanatend, it'd fallen. From what I could find out from the few folk who escaped, the rainlords there were all dead. Including – including my wife. So I rode to Pediment.

"They wouldn't help, either. I tried Denmasad and Breakaway as well. They all turned me down. Then Breccia fell to Davim and I managed to get all the cities talking to one another, planning for war, training men, especially when they found out the Cloudmaster was dead."

"What happened to Shale?" She corrected herself. "Jasper. When I left Scarcleft, he was in Breccia."

"Apparently he fled when the city fell, with Nealrith's wife, Laisa, and their daughter Senya. Laisa drugged him and handed him over to Taquar. Ironically enough, it was probably

337

just as well, because he and Taquar, working together, manage to make it rain." He paused to wipe away the spittle dribbling down his chin. "Rumours spread about what I was doing, and Jasper got to hear. He sent a sky message. We met out in The Sweepings."

"Is he – is he all right?"

Feroze's pale eyes flickered her way in interest.

"He's fine. I took him to Portfillik and Pediment, to meet the Highlords there. Then he returned to Scarcleft."

"He *returned*? By himself? But *why*?"

That memory replaying in her head: Taquar standing beside her, playing with her hair, the rapaciousness of his gaze eroding her confidence and her courage, while she wrote a letter to entice Shale back into his cage . . .

"To make it rain, of course." Iani dabbed again at his lip and tried to sip from the cup. "He'd grown since I saw him last. Got not just taller but . . . older, somehow. I hardly recognised him. 'I'm glad to see you got my message,' he said, as calm as you please. As if I could have missed it! Anyway, first thing Jasper told me about was his cloudmaking. He can only do it with Taquar. That's why he can't leave." His face suddenly changed, haunted by a fleeting expression of hate and despair. "Taquar killed Lyneth, you know. He might say he didn't, but he did." The words were as stark as sun-bleached bones and Terelle had to repress a shudder.

"So I can't kill him," he added. "I want to. But if I do, we thirst and die. Jasper wants to free Qanatend from the last of Davim's claws. Did you know some Reduners are still there? Under the Warrior Son. And they control the mother cistern of the city, too."

She was silent. In the face of his despair, any words she might have uttered froze on her tongue.

"Moiqa died there; my wife, you know. One day soon, I will kill Davim. Him, I can kill."

"Where is he?" Feroze asked quietly, speaking for the first time.

"Gone back to the Red Quarter now, along with the Master Son. That's his heir, man named Ravard. Jasper will take the battle to the Red Quarter one day. You'll see."

Shale? Shale would? Terelle was reeling. He was the same age as she was. He wasn't a warrior. How could he lead men to battle? It was all too much to take in, and Iani's conversation was as undisciplined as a sand-dancer. "Why would he want to do that?" she asked at last. "If they go back to the Red Quarter, why not let them go? Leave them alone?"

"What about us Alabasters?" Feroze asked her, gently chiding. "They won't leave *us* alone. Should we just wait for them to kill us all?"

Iani nodded grimly. "He has to be stopped. But Jasper says we have to deal with Taquar first. And he needs your help."

Terelle felt her heart lurch to the pit of her gut. He meant *her*, not Feroze.

"Davim killed my wife, my Moiqa." His voice became a wistful shadow of its former strength. "I never even got to tell her about Lyneth . . . I never saw her again. By the time I arrived back at Qanatend, she was dead." He dabbed once more at his lip. "I am getting together an army, men from the other Scarpen cities, from the Gibber and the White Quarter. Taquar – that withering traitor. I'll make him pay." Hatred welled up and spilled over, pulling at the ravages of his damaged face, dragging his expression into the same hell-hole his soul had occupied for so long.

"I want to go back to Qanatend," he whispered.

Terelle swallowed, not knowing what to say to this man, so obviously balanced only precariously between sanity and madness. "How can we fight Taquar? We have no ziggers," she said, "and Taquar has thousands. And if we can't kill him anyway . . ."

"We have rainlords. Mostly very old ones, it's true, but skilled enough to kill ziggers. Moiqa's dead, you know. Did I tell you that?"

Terelle felt herself lost, so disoriented she might as well have been whirled away by a spindevil. Here was a rainlord of the Quartern talking to her as an equal, as if she was someone important. As if she could make a difference. She wanted him to sound competent and rational, but he was far from either.

She shot a despairing glance at Feroze, who then asked, "How can you fight a man whose strength is needed to bring storms?"

Iani was silent for a long time. Finally he whispered, "I want him dead so badly. They call me sandcrazy because I searched for her for so long – I never gave up hope, and all the while—" He choked. "Now I just want him dead. But I'm frightened, I'll admit that. If Jasper makes a mistake, we all die – slowly, of thirst and starvation. But he has a plan. Something to do with you, Terelle.

"He can be harsh, Jasper, when he needs to be. I told him the Highlord of Breakaway wanted guarantees before the city would help him. The next day, Jasper sent a sky message. 'Ouina,' he wrote, and he didn't bother to call her lord, 'I'll give you a guarantee: if you don't send your forces to support me, Breakaway will always be the last place to have its cisterns filled.'

"I told him that was harsh. 'It was meant to be,' he said. 'But not, I think, unreasonable. These are harsh times. Somewhere, Iani, there has to be a smooth middle road. Somewhere between weakness and abuse. It's just a matter of finding it. I don't want to be either Nealrith or Cloudmaster Granthon. It was their weaknesses, their lack of understanding of evil, that brought us to this point. But I don't want to be Laisa or Taquar, either – for they are not fit to rule.' Then he told me to train the men who came to this caravansary while I waited here for you. Which I have done. And we aren't the only ones, you know. Jasper sent sky messages to all the other cities. People are gathering in other places, waiting for his orders."

Terelle gave a snort of laughter. "And Taquar doesn't know Shale is sending messages all over the place?"

He shrugged, indifferent. "He must know by now, I would think."

She took a deep breath. "So, when do we leave for Scarcleft?"

His lips moved, a twisted travesty of a smile. *Poor Iani*, she thought. *Crippled and heart-wounded, full of hate and aching for revenge, and Shale's asking him to wonder if his moral rights to that revenge are worth the risk to the water supply of a nation.*

Waterless soul, help me. Shale thinks I can solve this problem. What do I know?

24

Red Quarter
Dune Watergatherer

On the surface, it seemed a stupid time to plan a mass escape of slaves. There were one hundred more pedes and five hundred more seasoned warriors in camp than usual, the latter all heavily armed and outnumbering Ravard's men. In addition there were countless camp followers with them to serve the warriors, look after their pedes and care for their weapons.

However, Ryka soon realised they could not have chosen a better night. With so many extra men in camp, nothing was normal, and therefore anything unusual went unnoticed. Slaves came and went; when masters called they were busy elsewhere and no one thought much of it. When women slaves went missing, the men who usually slept with them made sour remarks about "Davim's bleeding randy drovers", but did nothing. When water skins went missing and water levels in camp jars were low, when a particular pede couldn't be found where it was supposed to be, if food seem to vanish as soon as it was cooked, if the encampment was unusually noisy with the buzz of whispered conversations, if slaves seemed extra busy and always carrying things from one place to another, if every look exchanged seemed heavy with meaning, well – what else did you expect? There were so many extra people, all of whom were tired – you had to assume there would be a muddle.

Ryka turned to Junial for help. The baker was delighted to see her again, happy to explain both the workings of the camp and what had already been done to prepare for the escape.

"You know," she added at the end of her explanation, "Kher Ravard doesn't have any slaves of his own, or didn't until we arrived. I believe we all belong to the sandmaster, not Ravard. Except maybe you. Apparently the Master Son doesn't much like slaves."

Ryka's eyebrows shot up. "You could have fooled me."

"Me too. But everyone here when we arrived was a Reduner. Or an outlander who had adopted Reduner ways and a Reduner name, even becoming warriors, some of them. So we've trusted no one but ourselves. Uthardim and Elmar and a couple of the others have been organising this escape for ages. Everyone knows what to do, believe me. All we have to do is pass the word that it's tonight."

After she'd made sure that Ravard and Davim had left the tent to join the feast down in Davim's camp, Ryka returned to the tent and extracted the two perfume vials from the box in Ravard's room. She passed one to Elmar and the other to Junial, after using it herself. "It's the zigger perfume," she explained. "Just in case someone sends ziggers after us."

She joined the women then, finding and filling water skins and dayjars, cooking and packaging food, tying up the bedrolls and travelling tents. She herself spirited away two packpedes and a number of panniers into the dunes, and women took their pilfered items out there to be stowed.

Elmar had stolen a myriapede for himself, Kaneth and Ryka, and showed her where he'd hidden it in a hollow away from the camp. Asked by a Reduner where he was going,

Elmar blandly told him he had been ordered to stake it out for grazing. Ryka found a set of saddle bags and tied it onto one of the rear segments, full of all the food she could pilfer, plus a couple of water skins, several warm blankets and three knives taken from the chests in Ravard's tent.

All the while, she was as tense as a pebblemouse aware it was being stalked by something big and hungry. She feared for them all. *If Kaneth has lost a rainlord's power, then he has no water-sense. He won't sense when Ravard comes to kill him.* Tension teased out into numbing fear. *If he gets taken by surprise . . .*

One part of her said Kaneth was more than capable of looking after himself; another that he was handicapped. He couldn't wear a sword openly, he had to face at least two men, not one, because the shaman would be there. And he had to do it quietly. On the other hand, Ravard, for all his youth, was a man raised as a warrior, a man who had fought in battles starting with those waged against other Reduner tribes when he was fifteen, or so he had told her.

She fretted for herself, too. She'd seen the way the Kher had looked at her. A man hungry in a way that might have delighted a woman in love, but that disturbed her because it was the look of a man who wanted to possess a woman in a way that gave no thought to equality. He *owned* her.

He came for her, as she knew he would. Davim's men had begun to drift back to the valley, settling into their tents, if they had them, or wrapping themselves against the cold in their bedrolls if they didn't. The fires began to die down, the songs faltered and then ceased. In the distance a horned cat howled and spat. Ravard found her finally grabbing something to eat from what was left of the feasting. The sand-master was nowhere in sight.

He slipped his arm around her waist and licked her ear. "Come," he said, and she went.

This is the last time, she told herself. *It doesn't matter.*

And then another thought: *This is his last time, ever.* She felt a stab of compassion, and had to remind herself that when this night's lovemaking was over, he intended to kill Kaneth.

She swallowed, and spiralled her dread down into a tight coil within. She would do this, and she would do it well. And because she did, perhaps when he walked up the slope to the shrine, he would miss the first signs that someone was waiting to kill him.

Once in the tent she slipped her arms around his neck and pulled him down to kiss her, opening her mouth to his probing tongue.

As Ryka lay in his arms afterwards and Ravard drowsily nuzzled her breast, he seemed in no hurry to leave. "Why d'you wear those awful trousers," he asked, "when you have the dresses we brought from Breccia? T'morrow I want you t'wear that green one. I want every man here t'envy me for what I have."

"The sandmaster too?" she asked. "I thought you wanted me to be inconspicuous."

"He doesn't have t'know I'm still bedding you." He smiled and hugged her tight. "I have a surprise for you t'morrow."

"What's that?" she asked, and wondered what he would think of the thudding of her heart.

He didn't seem to notice. "Half-face dies tonight."

Even though she knew it was coming, she stiffened in shock.

"My present t'you," he said and idly traced a finger over her breasts from one nipple to the other.

She was silent even as she sought for a response, any response.

"Aren't you pleased?" he asked. "The man got you with child and then abandoned you. Now he doesn't even remember."

"He – he's still the father," she said.

"No, he's not," he replied, his anger hot and immediate. "I am. I told you. He is mine now." He touched the bulge of her belly. "And will be so always. My son, bearing a name of my choosing. Or my daughter," he added as an afterthought. "The child is never to know the name of the man who sired him, ever. He – or she – is never t'know. That is my gift t'you tonight."

"You – you are going out to kill him now?"

He chuckled. "No, I have better things t'do tonight. You've been out of my bed too long, sweetling. I sent a couple of my men t'take care of him instead." He laid his head on her naked shoulder, and in spite of his promise, within half a dozen breaths he dozed.

She waited, still and silent, hardly daring to breathe. Gradually his breathing deepened. Still she waited. When she was sure he wasn't going to wake, she edged out from under him.

Stealthily she picked up her clothing, stole another dagger and a sword from his chest, and left his room. She dressed in her room and tied some of Laisa's ribbons to her belt in a loop to carry the sword; not the best way to carry a blade but at least it left her hands free. She took her cloak and blessed the pockets sewn into the lining. They were big enough for some extra items, including the dagger. Finally, pulling up the hood, she left the tent.

Ravard slept on.

Outside, she raised her eyes to the crest of the sand hills surrounding the encampment. They were silhouetted against the sky, and occasionally the stars beyond them disappeared and reappeared a moment later. Sentries, walking to and fro along the sand ridge, doubtless cold and bored. Not yet sensing anything wrong. *It all seems too easy*, she thought. So many things could have gone wrong, so many ways they could have made a mistake. And none of it had happened.

At least . . . not yet.

A glance at Davim's encampment showed her only darkness. She caught muffled sounds of whispers and shuffling and hoped it was some slaves sneaking away. A number would already be hunkered down by the pede lines, waiting for the moment to snatch as many beasts as they could for transport and to scatter the others. They would be waiting for the signal – Kaneth's signal.

She struggled up the loose sand of the dune towards the crest where the shrine stone was. She couldn't see it, but as she climbed closer she could feel the presence of water there. Four bodies, one alive, three dead. *Three.* She had no idea which, if any, was Kaneth. Could he have killed *three* people?

Her cloak snagged on the prickles of the low bushes dotting the dune, jerking her back. She took it off in irritation and impatiently started to unhook it. And felt someone else's water. A man, stealthily climbing up behind her. Ravard?

She hesitated, torn. Reach out with her power and kill him, whoever it was? But what if it was Ravard? He'd feel the attempt and be warned. *Damn.*

Turning her senses upwards again, she knew that whoever was alive at the shrine was not moving. If it was Kaneth, what was he waiting for? She wrenched at her cloak, tearing it away from the prickles to drape it around her shoulders, then crouched.

When the follower came up to where she was, she shrugged off her cloak and rose up in front of him, scimitar in one hand, dagger in the other. "Stand," she said, and then said it again in Reduner.

"*Ryka?* Thank goodness! I thought you might not be able to get away from that bastard."

Elmar. Ryka let out the breath she had been holding and lowered her weapons. "What are you doing up here?"

"I came for Kaneth. I thought maybe something had

gone wrong. And he doesn't know where we've got our pede stashed anyway. Everything's ready. Where is he?"

"At the shrine. I hope. There's one person there – and three bodies."

"That will be him then, the live one," he said with confidence.

And it seemed as if he was right, for no sooner had he spoken than the sand started to sing. This time it was a glorious sound, a stringed harmony threaded through with a poignant wandering melody that could have been played by a master piper. Then the hillside near the shrine began to rip with a tearing noise that challenged, then overwhelmed, the earth music. The slope rumbled, and the ground beneath Ryka shook and shifted slightly, so she staggered.

"Sunblast it," Elmar snapped, "I hope *he's* not falling down with that lot."

She broke into a smile. *He was alive.* "No, he's well away. Walking towards us. Jogging, in fact. Or someone is."

The sound grew, the rumbling became a scream, as if every grain of sand was scraping against another and combining their individual sounds into a single cry of a land cleaved and shattered.

"Salted Sunlord," Elmar said, in awe. "I'll go meet him. Stay here."

He started up the path to the shrine; she turned to pick up her cloak. It was caught on thorns again. Cursing, she bent to unhook it. No thought of anything but to get out of there as fast as possible. No thought of any other danger.

It happened so quickly there was nothing she could do. Nothing anyone could do. The ground beneath her feet sheered away and dropped. She flailed, but there was nothing to clutch save her cloak. Her screams were lost in the ululation of sand on the move, the pain of a hillside as it died.

Kaneth had reached into the soul of the dune, too deep, too far, with too little understanding.

Elmar whirled and stared. Where Ryka had stood a moment earlier there was nothing, not even the ground she had been standing on. And then, while he still stared at the dark empty space, jaw dropping in disbelieving shock, dust bellied upwards from below, dense and choking, great billows of it curdling the air. All that was left of a hillside now surged skywards on the wind its fall had created.

He backed away from the still crumbling edge. Backed, because he could not tear his gaze from what was no longer there.

Coughing, choking, he bumped into Kaneth, who grasped him by the shoulder. He jumped in shock and almost fell.

Kaneth grinned at him, his teeth a gleam in the dark. "Sorry," he said. "Seems I got carried away. Still, no harm done. Let's get going."

Elmar opened his mouth to speak, but no sound came out.

"Waterless soul, you're shaking all over! Come, let's go."

But Elmar stood rooted, speechless.

"Come on, my friend. Get a grip on yourself. We have to move!"

"Are you – are you all right?"

"Yes, of course! Let's get off this hillside. It could be unstable. Besides, we have to get off the dune before the Reduners organise themselves. I've no idea how much damage I managed to do. Probably not as much as I hoped – most of Davim's men were more to the other side of the dip, I think." He grabbed Elmar's arm and began to drag him down the slope. "Where's Garnet? Is she safe?"

"She – she—" His mouth opened, but the words wouldn't come out.

"*Elmar!*" Kaneth sounded more exasperated than alarmed.

The words came in a rush. He didn't consider them. They came unasked, unthought, hard on the heels of the thought that he had to save Kaneth and he wouldn't be able to if the man started searching for Ryka. And Ryka was *dead*. The words reached his ears as if someone else was forming them. "She gave me a message for you."

"Which was?"

"She – she decided not to go with us."

Kaneth stopped abruptly. "*What?*"

"Because – because of the baby. She said she couldn't risk it. Too dangerous. If she stays the baby will be safe. Reduners are good to babies. She said she'll escape later. When the baby is born. She's very close to the birth, you know."

Kaneth stared at him. The twisted scar of his face appeared dark and ugly in the starlight.

His stillness, his silence, was unnatural. Elmar groped for more words. More lies. Anything to get him out of there. "She asked you to understand that the child comes before anything."

When Kaneth spoke again it was so softly Elmar hardly caught the words. "I see."

He continued on down the hill, and this time Elmar had to run to catch up.

"One day, I will kill that man," Kaneth said through clenched teeth. "He has no right to any child of mine."

Elmar had never been so heartfelt sick in all his life.

25

Red Quarter
Dune Watergatherer

Ravard woke from a deep, contented sleep, to find himself naked but standing, holding his sword in one hand and a dagger in the other. The transition from slumber to the stance of an alert warrior was disconcerting and in his momentary bewilderment, he tensed.

What had woken him?

His bed was empty. He turned his head, sensing for the water of another body. There wasn't one. Garnet was gone. Common sense told him she had merely gone to the privy. Her pregnancy meant she was up and down all night . . . yet something had startled him, prompted his warrior instincts. He dropped his weapons, pulled on and tied his breeches, shoved the dagger into the belt band and picked up his sword again.

And then his question was answered.

The dune god. The wrenching cry skirled over the camp, louder than Ravard had ever heard it. The pain of a ravaged god.

He strode to the tent flap and out into the night. He ignored the bite of the cold on his bare chest and arms. The darkness filled with sound: shouting, panicked voices, screams, the wail of the god, and more. A rushing, rolling noise like a thousand pedes thundering down a rocky slope. The ground shook beneath his feet. A woman emerging from a tent nearby turned her frightened face towards him. In the gloom, her eyes were large dark holes of terror in her face.

"Torches," he snapped at her. "Organise the women to light every bleeding torch in the camp!" He didn't wait to see if she obeyed. She was a dune drover's woman; he knew she would.

Running now, he headed towards the worst of the sounds. And then slid to a halt. The vale in the dune where the sand-master's men had camped, which should have dipped down in front of him, was not there any more. It was filled with a dark moving mass billowing skywards. The dune god was silent now. In place of the earlier agonised cry came a soft slithering sound. Trickles of sand on the move. The dune shifting as if the god had roused and rolled over. The air was thick with dust, the surge of it reaching out to him, sliding over and around until he could see nothing. Sounds muffled and he choked. He clamped a hand over his mouth and nose, trying to shut out the worst. Behind him, torches sprang into life, flames forming eerie globes of light in the dust.

He turned back to grab one from a woman and then ran on. He coughed, spluttered, thrust the burning brand high to see what was happening. A pede loomed up and disappeared behind. There were people on its back, but he could not make out who. He narrowed his eyes, shaded them with his hand to keep the dust out and wished he had a shirt he could tear off and use to cover his face. His mind caught up with the rest of him. A sand slip, that's what had happened. The face of the dune had slid into the valley. And yet the slope had not been steep and it had been well anchored with bushes and snake grass. It should not have fallen.

Uthardim.

That weeping *bastard* of a city-dweller. He'd done this,

Ravard *knew* it. Shaman Voraliss and the two warriors he had sent to kill the man had botched the job, stuff their shrivelled brains! He should have done it himself . . . but there had been Garnet and he hadn't seen her in so long.

He went cold all over as his thoughts made connections he did not want to whisper even to himself.

One of Davim's pedemen stumbled out of the cloud of dust. Choking, he managed to gasp, "The slope came down on the tents!"

"Have you seen the sandmaster?"

The man shook his head.

Ravard pointed towards the tents of his own tribe. "Tell everyone you meet to bring whatever they can find for digging – anything at all!" He ran on, disoriented, no longer able to see where Davim's camp had been. He stopped for a moment, probing with his water-sense to locate people. Another pede emerged out of the whirling dust, head lowered, feet churning. Coming right at him. He glimpsed men on its back – two of them. The beast was bridled. It shouldn't have been. No one should have been going anywhere at this hour of the night.

He could have flung himself sideways out of the way. Instead he dropped the brand and leaped for the heavy metal ring at the edge of the mandibles where the bridle threaded through. He glimpsed the horrified face of the driver, blurred by the dust still hanging in the air. As the fingers of one hand gripped the ring, his body was flung back along the side of the pede. He slammed hard into the carapace of the first segment, then dropped so his feet dragged. His other hand grabbed at the bridle, yanking. The pede was forced to dip its head, but it churned on through the dust-thickened air nonetheless.

When he still didn't let go, it slowed and flung its head up, clacking its irritation and flicking its feelers. He went with it, feet and body swinging outwards, only to thunk down again. The breath whooshed out of his body. His arms felt torn from their sockets. One hand jerked loose when his fingers were nipped hard between one of the pede's mandibles and the chitin of its face.

He grunted in agony. The pede crashed its front end down to the ground and ran on. The driver, snarling at him, tried to pull the bridle free. When that didn't work, he drew his scimitar.

I recognise him. A bleeding slave. Ravard stretched out his mangled hand to grab the bottom mounting handle screwed into the first segment. Agony from his crushed fingers shot up his arm. He ignored it. Nothing was broken; pain was an irrelevance. He let go of the bridle to move his other hand up beside the first. His feet flailed and found the lowest of the mounting toe-slots. At last he could take the weight off his arms.

The bridle, suddenly freed of his weight, jerked up under the pull of the driver. The man lost his balance and the slash of his weapon at Ravard's hands went wide. His body slipped from the saddle and he was forced to drop the scimitar to grab for the saddle handle in front of him.

As the scimitar slithered past, Ravard made a desperate snatch at the blade. He cut his fingers but secured the weapon. He swapped his hand to the hilt. Dripping blood, he hauled himself one-handed up to the next mounting handle. The driver was now hanging from the saddle handle, his body dangling on the far side of the mount. He scrabbled to heave himself back on top. Ravard grinned at him over the curve of the pede's back. *My friend, you are about to die.*

He raised the scimitar in one hand to slash it sideways into the slave's neck.

But he had forgotten about the second man. He'd been well behind on one of the rear segments, obscured by the dust and darkness. The uneven jumps of the pede as it ploughed its way up the dune slopes and plunged downwards into the hollows had kept the fellow off-balance and slowed his progress forward, so Ravard had dismissed him as an immediate threat. Now he was within a sword's length – and armed.

By now, the pede had borne them away from the dust, and in the starlight he saw who it was. *Uthardim.*

Ravard's heart thumped, relishing the moment. He abandoned his idea of slashing the driver and swung at Uthardim. The blade didn't connect as the pede rocked and swayed. The driver leaped upwards to grab the place on the top of the first segment. Ravard was quicker. He jammed one foot under the saddle handle for stability. The other foot he raised and smashed into the man's face. At the same time, he raised his scimitar to catch Uthardim's downward stroke. The driver grunted and fell. His body vanished into the darkness.

Ravard and Uthardim faced each other on the back of the lurching pede. Uthardim widened his stance and bent his knees, striving for balance. Even as the man lurched forward in a clumsy lunge, Ravard could not help thinking this was a ridiculous way to fight. It was hard to see in the dark what the other was doing. The pede was weaving, careening out of control. Both of them were more likely to fall and break their necks than run the other through with a blade.

He held the scimitar near his body, his left hand against the blunt side of the blade to brace it when he parried. He hoped to entice Uthardim in close, then slip under his defences, the move covered by his own body, the turn of his arm and the darkness.

He didn't get the chance. The man was good.

No mere metal worker, he realised, cursing as he accepted this was a fight he might not win. *The man's a trained warrior. Garnet lied. The city-born bitch. I have to think of something else.*

He disengaged his foot from the handle and attacked, driving Uthardim back in a ferocious series of slashes. Then, before the man could take advantage of his over-extension, he dropped to one knee, drew his dagger and stabbed the pede between the segments with his dagger. It wouldn't do much damage to the pede, but it would make the beast angry. Uthardim was starting his lunge as the pede feelers came whipping back. Ravard ducked. The pede trumpeted its pain. A feeler caught Uthardim across the arm and curled like a whip around his back. The sharp-edged spines and hooks ripped his clothing and tore his skin; the force of the blow sent him flying. He held on to his sword, but fell awkwardly. He clawed at a saddle handle, missed and disappeared over the side.

The pede faltered, but didn't stop.

Ravard let out the breath he'd been holding. It hurt. He was bruised over the ribs where he had been slammed into the carapace. His left hand, dripping blood, was a mass of pain and swelling fast. He returned to the first segment, sat down on the saddle cross-legged, and grabbed up the reins. He slowed the beast and turned it. *I want that bastard dead. God, how I want him dead.*

He felt living water behind him. Close. *Close enough to touch.*

That was all the warning he had. Uthardim had made no sound, nothing. He had not fallen at all; he had been clinging to the side of the pede all along. Now he was back on the rear saddle once more. Ravard was aware of a hand already raised behind him. Probably about to lop off his head . . .

He did the only thing he could to save his life.

He threw himself off the pede.

As he plunged to the ground, rolling over and over, he saw the sword bite into the chitin of the carapace. Then pede, man, sword – all were swallowed up by the gloom.

They did not come back.

Shakily, Ravard climbed to his feet.

He was a Reduner warrior, tribemaster and the Master Son of Dune Watergatherer – yet all he wanted to do right then was weep with rage.

As Ryka fell, as the sand vanished from under her feet, she felt no fear. It happened too quickly. She still clutched the cloak in both hands as she dropped, battered by sound and numbed by shock. What flashed through her head, woven through with disbelief, was a poignant appreciation of the moment. She had come to the red dunes to save Kaneth; and in the end he had killed her. He had killed his own son. *I hope he never knows*, she thought in the splinter of time it took for her to fall.

But she didn't die, not then.

After a fall of about twenty paces her arms were wrenched upwards and her descent was abruptly halted. At the same time she was slammed sideways. Sand poured down on her, an avalanche of it battering her. Her arms, extended over her head, still gripped the cloak. It had snagged on something, and the folds blanketed her head, protecting her upper body from the barrage of sand that went on and on and on. Even so, the air thickened and she choked.

And then the rush stopped. She dangled, swaying slightly, gulping for breath. Her shoulders ached. Terror stopped her from moving for a long time; she knew she was hanging over emptiness. Her muscles protested. She tried to climb higher, hand over hand. She kicked with her legs and touched sand and plants somewhere to one side. A steep cliff of sand and plants. But that didn't make sense. There never had been a cliff; just a slope.

She couldn't see it. She couldn't see anything. She couldn't find a toehold. Her hands slipped, and the cloak started feeding through her fingers as she tried to hold on. Her feet flailed in empty air. She had no idea how far she would fall. Probing for water, she caught the feel of two people on top of the cliff, but they were moving away from the edge, fast. Elmar and Kaneth? She screamed then, for the first time, calling them by name, begging them to help. The two moving bodies of water didn't even falter.

Horrified, she realised her voice was just one of many. Voices shouted and cried and screamed below her. Worse still, in the thick air, the sounds were muffled, indistinct, confused. No one was going to answer. No one was even going to hear. She saved her breath, concentrated on holding tight.

It was impossible. *How long can I hold on like this?*

She tried screaming again. No answer. She shouted for Kaneth, for Elmar. Nothing. She shouted in the Quartern tongue, in Reduner. No one answered. *Just be glad they survived. Elmar saw what happened – they are coming down to look for you below, of course.* Her fingers slipped still further, and her head emerged from the folds of her cloak. She looked down into darkness, unable to see how far the ground was below. She stared at the wall at her side, just a few hand spans away. In the starlight, it was a dark blanket with many tattered holes, the areas in between littered with tangles of threads and bits of plants. Every now and then, sand slithered and the dune god groaned.

She looked up. Her cloak was dangling from a small bush stuck on the blanket. It looked like the same bush the cloak had been hooked on next to the path. Except now it was growing out of a cliff. Nothing made sense. The world had tilted?

Sunlord help me, she whispered, begging. *I must not lose this child. I must keep him safe.*

Something tore and she jerked down another half body length, only to be brought up short again. Her shoulders

358

screamed their pain. Her front teeth went through her lip and she tasted blood. When she looked upwards again, the black shape of the bush now hung upside down. Its network of spreading roots kept it precariously suspended. The cloak, hooked on its thorns and sinuous branches, was well snagged – but the bush was not. As she squinted, trying to see better, more roots ripped and everything shifted again, dropping her a little lower, showering her with sand.

She moaned, knowing time was running out. How long had she been like this? A tenth of a sand-run? Longer? Or did it just *feel* that long? She yelled some more. No reply.

Carefully she reached out with one hand and touched the tangled threads of the cliff. Not threads at all. Roots. Too fragile to offer a hold. Withdrawing her hand, she clutched at the cloak again.

She thought she knew what had happened. Kaneth had started a landslip. The land had become unstable at the base of the slope, starting a slide. But the top of the dune was a blanket of small plant life, connected just below the surface by intertwining roots. Those had kept the surface together as the dune was hollowed out beneath. The sand had broken through on the slope below her somewhere, to cascade down into the vale. Left hanging, the blanket of the slope surface had flopped vertically down, refusing to be ripped apart.

Forcing herself to look down again, she strained to see what she was going to land on if – no, when – she lost her grip. And that was her last thought as the bush split from its remaining deeper roots.

She fell without a sound.

Almost immediately, her feet hit a slope of sand so steep she was pitched forward onto her face. The cloak and the bush came down on top of her and she was tumbling, head down, feet up, feet down, head up, cloak tangling, branches scratching, sand moving in streams around her.

And then, at last, all was mercifully still. She was bruised, bloodied, shaken, half-buried – and still alive. The baby gave an indignant kick.

Fearing the rest of the sand cliff would slide again at any moment, she crawled and clawed her way out of the sand, then struggled to her feet. She had lost her cloak and her weapons. Staggering away, she put as much distance as she could between herself and the unstable cliff. Her feet sank into the loose sand, making her stumble. The dust began to clear and she could see better. People were now running to and fro carrying flaming torches, but she was disorientated; everything had changed. The dune looked as if it had been roughly sliced with a giant sword; the slope had flowed down into the valley, leaving the open cut exposed as a cliff, ending in a scree of debris. And there, the top one-third of the cut was still covered by the hanging plant life.

As far as she could make out in the darkness, one of the pede lines had vanished; so had some of the tents and fires belonging to Davim's men. Someone was organising a rescue to dig out the tents. She had to circle around wide to avoid them, even hiding once or twice until guards had passed by. Kaneth and Elmar were nowhere to be seen. Limping, she headed to where their pede was hidden. In the dark, the hollow was difficult to find, especially when she had to dodge so many people and had no torch herself. When she did find the place, it was empty. The pede had gone.

Kaneth would have waited, she thought. *I must have the wrong hollow.*

She circled around, and returned to the same spot. Her heart plummeted. There, stuck in the sand, was the pede-tallow candle she had used for light when she had been packing the myriapede.

Someone must have found the pede, she thought. *One of the other slaves, perhaps . . . Kaneth would never have left without*

360

waiting for me. Anyway, they need me to find water on the journey . . .

Then she began to wonder: maybe he had been killed in the landslip after all. Maybe Elmar had, too. Maybe it had been someone else she'd sensed.

Fear encroached, then overwhelmed her. She started shaking again. Sinking to her knees, she bent down and rocked, as if that would help the pain. *Let him be alive, let him live, please let him come back for me.*

She was tired of it, tired of always being scared for herself, for her child, for Kaneth, for the Quartern. Sandblast it, was there never to be an end to this horror?

When she was calmer and quite sure neither Kaneth nor Elmar was coming, she trudged back to the encampment. By then, sunrise was staining the cloudless vault of the sky. The ruined section of Davim's camp had been largely dug out and the Reduners were reviewing the damage. She heard one of the women of Ravard's camp telling another there were ten men dead and fifteen still missing, and no one had any idea how many pedes were dead, how many had run off and how many had been stolen by the slaves.

Ryka tried to be inconspicuous as she surveyed the camp, looking for any sign of Kaneth. A group of slaves, about twenty or thirty men and women, sat on the ground guarded by several drovers with ziggers. Neither Kaneth nor Elmar was among them. Wondering what to do, she was still dithering when someone come up behind her and grabbed her arm. Ravard.

For a moment they stood staring at each other. He was just as battered as she was, she could see that much, and he was furiously angry, although he had himself under tight control.

"I thought you had gone with the rest," he said.

She thought it best to feign ignorance. "Gone where? The rest? What rest?"

"You knew about this!"

"About what?"

"About the slaves escaping!"

"The slaves? I thought you meant the landslip!"

"Don't play games, Garnet. When I woke up you weren't on my pallet. Where were you?"

She gambled. "I was in the privy when the dune god screamed. You know I can't sleep the night through, not with this baby—"

"Where have you been since then?" he shouted.

"Helping with—"

Fortunately for her ingenuity, just then Davim approached them, backed by ten or twelve of his own men. He strode up to Ravard, his expression wild with fury, an emotion matched by those with him. Without any other warning, he lashed out with a fist and hit Ravard on the cheek. Ryka scuttled out of range. The blow was savage enough to send the Master Son flying. He landed flat on his back, a dazed look on his face.

Ryka expected him to scramble to his feet and defend himself; instead, once he was upright again, he just stood before his adopted father, his arms dangling loosely by his sides. She continued to move away, slowly edging backwards, step by step.

"This is your tribe," the sandmaster raged at him. "I came to pick up my new slaves and be on my way. And what do I find? An encampment riddled with a lack of discipline and carelessness! So lax that slaves escaped – riding *our* pedes, with *our* stores and *our* water! How could you let this happen?"

He struck out at Ravard again, the powerful open-handed blow catching him across the ear. Once again Ravard fell. This time he rose only to his knees, his head hanging in submission.

Davim waved one of his men forward. His next words,

though, were still addressed to Ravard. "Your punishment is one hundred lashes. Fifty today, fifty when the first have healed." He turned to the man at his side. "Arvegir, I am going to leave you here to guide this idiot son of mine until he knows how to be a proper tribemaster. Your first task will be to see that he has the wisdom of a true warrior whipped into his outlander hide. Make a *man* of him!" And he walked away, calling for his other men to follow. They could, he said as he left, take any pede of Ravard's tribe they could find if they needed to replace their own.

By this time, Ryka had retreated under the veranda of one of the tents where several of the tribal women and their children were grouped. Junial, the baker's wife from Breccia, was among them. None of them said a word, but Junial slipped a hand about her shoulders and squeezed.

Ryka stared at Arvegir as the light in the sky strengthened. He was an older man with a deeply lined face and scars on his arms and hands that spoke of past battles. The look he now gave Ravard was one of utter contempt and burning resentment.

Sand hells, Ryka thought, *Ravard is in real trouble. And where does that leave me?*

Arvegir snarled, "Your withering foolishness cost me my best pede and three slaves! Not to mention having to stay in your bleeding camp. You displeased the dune god and his anger has killed our dunesmen. Now I have to live under his sway because of you, sandblast your weeping hide. Get up and let's get this done, you salted bastard."

Ravard stood and walked towards the punishment stone. Within moments word of his sentence had spread through the tribe, and the tribesmen gravitated to the edge of the camp, the place where Kaneth had stood up to Ravard and prevented the cutting of a slave. Ryka stayed where she was with Junial.

"Have you seen Uthardim? Or Elmar?" she asked the older woman, desperate to know.

"They escaped."

"Are you positive?"

"Yes. One of the others saw them go. Kher Ravard tried to stop them, but later he came back walking, alone and without the pede, so the two of them must have made it."

Ryka drew in a deep breath that was nine parts relief and one part fury. *Damn the two of them.*

"Why didn't you escape?" Junial asked.

"I was caught up in the landslip. By the time I reached the meeting place, everyone had gone." *Kaneth . . . how could you?* "What about you?"

Junial shrugged. "The way the wind decides, I suppose. One of the redmen took me to his pallet. One of them fellows of Davim's, not our lot. The spitless bastard. First time it's happened and it had to be last night. I couldn't get away. My rotten bleeding luck, I suppose. At least I'll be here for your babe's birth. The wind blows both good and ill. What do you reckon they'll do with the slaves they nabbed trying to escape?"

"I don't know. Nothing good, I imagine."

"You look weary. And battered. You all right?"

Ryka nodded, but she felt less than certain. She hurt, inside and out.

"You should get back to your tent and rest up. Not a good time to be mixing with the tribesmen anyways. Everyone is in a foul temper at the moment." She smiled unpleasantly. "In fact, just to see their sour faces is almost worth missing the escape."

Wearily, Ryka made her way back to Ravard's tent. Behind her, Davim's Reduners were taking their pick of whatever pedes were left; ahead she could see a large crowd gathered around the rock. She paused under the veranda of Ravard's tent as the sun rose above the crest of the dune and sent its light to stretch long shadows out from the foot of the canvas. In the quiet of dawn, the only sound was the crack of the whip.

She stood motionless, her imagination freezing her in place, as each crack etched a visual horror into her mind. *No one deserves that. No one. And he has endured this before.*

She waited, dreading hearing him scream, believing no one could endure fifty lashes without screaming, surely – yet she heard nothing. The crowd was silent and still, evidently taking no pleasure in Ravard's punishment. Perhaps he moaned, but if so she didn't hear. The whip cracks seemed unending.

A Reduner woman approached her with a clay jar and placed it at her feet. She hardly noticed until the woman spoke. "Honey ointment," she said in her own tongue. Ryka stared at her, her mind refusing to work.

The woman pried off the lid and showed her the paste inside, then made a gesture of rubbing with her palm. "Rub it into his back. It will be painful because it has salt in it, but it stops infection. You understand, city-dweller?"

Ryka blanched and nodded. Blighted eyes, she could hardly imagine the pain of salt in such wounds. *Fifty lashes. Watergiver save him.*

The woman turned and left, and Ryka listened.

Somewhere in the low shrubs a bird sang, but that she did not hear. There was only the whip cracking, slicing the air, slicing his back.

Crack. Crack. Crack.

PART THREE

Freedom's Battle

26

Scarpen Quarter
The Sweepings
Scarcleft City, Scarcleft Hall, Level 2

Several tents, erected out of sight of the escarpment track to the Gibber Quarter, sat in a drywash that probably hadn't seen water since the Time of Random Rain. The largest was pleasantly opulent inside, complete with carpets, cushions, wooden chests and a brazier for warmth once the sun set. Sentries ringed the area, but their Scarcleft uniforms bore an insignia Terelle did not know until one of the Scarpermen accompanying her said it was Jasper's personal emblem, a representation of a piece of bloodstone jasper. Shale himself had not yet arrived.

The man in charge of the camp introduced himself as Dibble, Jasper's personal aide. He bowed and called her Arta, which only served to make her feel a fraud. He indicated she should make herself comfortable inside the tent and brought her tea and sweets made of bab sugar. She felt off-balance. Everything seemed wrong. She was just Terelle, a snuggery girl trying to make her own way in the world; Jasper was just Shale, a Gibberman with a talent. Yet now he was a storm-lord named Jasper Bloodstone, some even said he was Cloudmaster, and people called her Arta and bowed.

Halfway through the afternoon, through the open side of

the tent, she saw him arrive with more of his guards. He was mounted on his own myriapede, dressed in the fine linens of a Scarcleft upleveller. He was different. Taller. So much older. Which was strange; it hadn't even been a full cycle since she'd seen him last.

When he entered the tent, she stood, awkwardly tongue-tied.

"Terelle," he said. His face told her nothing.

"Shale. It's – it's good to see you again."

"It's good to see you, too. I was worried."

Were they really going to be so stupidly banal? She couldn't stand it. And yet when she opened her mouth, angry words ripped from her. "You said you were a prisoner in Scarcleft," she accused. "In the sky message you sent. That's why I came – have you any idea how *hard* it was for me to come back? Every step I took was a step in the wrong direction, with something tearing at me to turn around and go back. And now, when I get here, I find you don't need me at all! You are free and you have a whole sand-blasted army at your disposal."

Immediately the words were spoken, she regretted them. They were an exaggeration, born of her frustration and longing, designed to make him feel guilty. She ached to take them back, to unsay them, but didn't know how.

He opened his mouth, then closed it again. Finally he said, "I do need you. The Quartern needs you."

"And what about what *I* need?"

"If it will solve anything, I will send someone to kill Russet. I can give the order right now."

Her mouth went dry. He *had* changed. Blighted eyes, but he had changed. "He's the only family I have," she muttered to give herself time to think.

"He's a terrible old man who doesn't care one drop of water for anyone but himself, least of all you."

"Killing him before I have fulfilled the prediction of his last painting may result in my death, too."

"Did he tell you that?"

She shook her head. "No, just the opposite. Several times. But I don't trust him. Do you?"

He considered that. "No, I reckon not. But it's more likely he'd lie to give you a reason to keep him alive than the other way around."

"He knows me well enough to know I would never kill anyone if I could help it."

For a long moment they stood staring at each other in silence. *This is not the way I wanted it to be*, she thought, and bit back the desire to weep tears.

A guard interrupted from the tent flap. "Is there anything else you require, m'lord?"

"Tea would be fine," Shale replied, and then added in a whisper as the guard bowed his way out, "I can't do anything without a guard at my elbow, hovering like a hawk about to pounce. It's so hard to find time for myself."

"They are from Scarcleft! They are *Taquar's* men?" she asked. Her head was beginning to ache, as if her mind couldn't cope with the magnitude of the changes.

He laughed, but there was little amusement in the laughter. "They *were*. Mine now, I think. Fine men, but they can be tiresome sometimes . . . Terelle, what happened after you ran from Russet's rooms that day?"

Sitting down on one of the cushions, she rested her back up against a wooden chest. He sat opposite her, his gaze on her face. "Time to swap stories, eh?" she asked. "All right then, I'll go first, but believe me, Shale – you had better have a good explanation for bringing me here."

She'd thought she had little to say, but once she started, all the things she had never been able to tell anyone came pouring out: how she felt about Amethyst's death; the darkness of her fear of Taquar; her revulsion at the devastation of the earthquake and the boy who had died. The way she was haunted by those memories; the despair of her journey to the White Quarter; the horror of nearly dying of thirst. She told him about Mine Silverwall and Feroze. She told him about what she had learned of the Watergivers and the origins of the religion of the Sunlord. The guard came back with the tea but neither of them noticed. Somewhere along the way, Shale moved closer to take hold of her hand.

"I'm so sorry," he whispered when she finished. "About everything. About leaving you in Scarcleft. I made a promise with the very last words I ever spoke to you, and I didn't keep it."

She shook her head. "It wasn't your fault. And I'm sorry I shouted at you just now. How did you get away to Breccia City in the first place? And after that? You didn't take any notice of that awful letter I wrote, did you?"

"I was so glad to get it! It meant you were still alive . . . I don't think I ever felt worse than when I heard the seneschal give the order to kill you that day in Scarcleft. As if you didn't count, as if you weren't a human being. I never knew for sure you *had* escaped until I got your letter."

As he detailed all that had happened to him, she found it hard to think of him as the nation's Cloudmaster; this was just Shale, who had caught her cheating at Lords and Shells. He was a little older, a little wiser, a great deal sadder, but he was still Shale – Gibber-bred, maybe not yet twenty, caught up in a world too big for him. Coldly calm, thoughtful, serious. And somewhere inside was something only she knew was there: pain.

She heard it when he spoke of Rainlord Nealrith's death. She heard it when he spoke of Cloudmaster Granthon's betrayal in naming Taquar his heir. She heard it when he mentioned his brother, Mica. She heard it when he told her of Laisa's betrayal. She heard it most when he spoke of the people who'd died because he had not surrendered himself to Davim. Taquar, the sadistic bastard, had told him the details he'd learned of that on his visit to Breccia.

Her heart stirred and she blinked away her tears.

At the end of his recital he said, "Terelle, I can't even begin to say how glad I am you are alive. That you are here. I need you. I – I think I always did. You're the only person I've ever been able to talk to, really talk to, since Mica was taken. I was so alone, for so long . . . and then there was you. And then I lost you again." He shook his head, as if he could not find the right words. "I'm scared, Terelle. You're the only person I can admit that to. I was only ever a dirty little Gibber kid with a father who was always slurped and a mother who never seemed to care much for any of us, at least, not until the moment of her death. I was just Shale nobody. And now everyone looks up to me – people three times my age – as if I have all the answers! Well, I don't. And I'm so scared I'll make a mess of things . . ."

She held his hand a little tighter. "So am I. Scared, I mean. I promised the Alabasters I would use my waterpainting to help, but the last time I used my skill, I killed innocent people." She licked dry lips. "Shale, Lord Iani says if you leave Taquar the Quartern has no water. What are we going to do?"

"Our best, I suppose. At least – at least you are here." He gave a half laugh. "And the tea has been here for ages; it must be cold by now." He poured a cup, added honey and seeds and handed it to her. "You have to use your water-powers, Terelle. I know you don't want to, and I understand why. But if you don't, there will be more deaths than if you do. If I've learned anything lately, it's that sometimes there are only bad choices. What you have to do is choose the least damaging."

She dropped her gaze. "I guess I knew you were going to say that. I'll – I'll help as best I can." *I just don't want to kill any more children . . .*

He squeezed her hand and changed the subject. "You know, I think I hate Taquar more because of what he did to Lyneth than because of what he did to me. She was six years old when he took her. I know how awful it was to be imprisoned at the mother cistern for almost four years, but she was so much younger, and she came from a loving family, and she was there just as long. It must have been so much harder for her. For that alone, Taquar deserves to die. But even if I find another way to make clouds, I can't kill him. Who knows when I might need his skills again?

"Nor do I want to attack the city and have people die just because they are from Scarcleft. I have ideas about how to free myself from Taquar and bring him down, but first I have to find a way to make the clouds without him." The look he gave her then was telling.

"You think *I* can help you? But I can't shift water!"

"Yes, you can. You do it when you shuffle up. Last time we talked about it, you mentioned doing a painting of it raining. But I think we were looking at things the wrong way round then. What you *can* do – you can paint me having the power to make clouds from sea water all by myself. With the power of your painting to aid me, I won't need Taquar to make it possible."

She looked at him doubtfully. "You think that will work?" Something inside her shrivelled. Power, her power. It mattered.

"I don't know. I just think it's worth trying. You aren't drinking your tea."

"I'm not thirsty."

He set his own cup aside. "Can we try now, then? I've got to know."

Soberly, she held his gaze. "What do you want done?"

"A painting of me, looking as I do now, but sitting outside, with dark black storm clouds coming in from the south."

"Paintings don't always work the way I expect or want."

"What can go wrong this time? Terelle, there are no other clouds anywhere in the Quartern. If this produces one, then your magic made it possible. It won't be stolen from somewhere else. No one will suffer, but a lot of people will benefit because I can move it and break it and bring water to the places that need it."

It was the first time she'd painted him. She tried not to put too much of herself into the portrait, tried not to paint that odd feeling she had every time she looked at him, of something awakening, stirring, a personal storm promising much if ever she unleashed it. She tried not to gentle his expression to the way she would like him to regard her. She tried, in fact, not to feel too much at all.

They'd moved away, out of sight of the camp. He sat a few paces from her while she captured his posture, his clothing, his surroundings, the warm light of The Sweepings. He was concentrating at the same time, she knew. Trying to lift water vapour from the distant sea.

She thought back to the time when, from the flat roof of the snuggery, she had seen a stormlord's cloud travelling towards the Warthago Range. Long before she had ever met Shale . . . Her waterpainter's memory brought back every detail. Carefully she reproduced that cloud, every nuance of its colour and shape and turbulence. At last she was done. She sat very still, regarding the painting. Then she took a deep breath and focused. She shuffled up the colours as Russet had taught her to do, pulling them from stasis to living reality, changing the passivity of a painting to the promise of a future event. The shift shuddered across and through the water, through the paint, through herself.

She felt the transformation and knew she'd altered the destiny of that day in some small way. And part of her hated what she'd just done.

By all that's water holy, she thought, *please don't let this hurt anyone.*

"Sands 'n' dust!" Shale cried, his face suddenly shining with an intense joy. "You did it!"

Startled, she looked back at him. "How do you know?"

"I can feel it. I took the water up into the sky! It is pouring upwards . . . clouds of it . . ." He jumped up and grabbed her in a hug, his exuberance so out of character she gaped at him. He didn't appear to notice. "Thank you, Terelle!"

"You'd better sit down again as you were, otherwise the scene won't be right," she told him.

He grinned and obeyed. "It will be a while before I get it here," he said. "Terelle, do you realise what this means? I don't have to go back to Taquar! We can make rain – you and I, together. Without him. *Together we are a true stormlord!*"

He gazed at her wordlessly for a moment longer then said softly, "Thank you."

Terelle should have been happy, but she knew she wanted more than just his gratitude.

When the clouds were well on the way to their destination, Shale returned to the tents and called for Dibble. "We will be joining Lord Iani's army instead of returning to Scarcleft," he told the armsman. "I want you to send two of your best riders with a message for Lord Iani at Pahntuk Caravansary, telling him to start south as soon as he can, with all his men."

As the man moved away to follow the instruction, Shale turned back to Terelle, who was packing up her painting things. "I'll use part of this cloud we've made to send a sky message saying the same thing, just to make sure he gets it.

We'll ride north to meet him. When we return to Scarcleft, it will be with an army behind us."

His joy was so intense he didn't seem able to contain it, but Terelle shivered. She had painted a picture, but the immensity of the implications was out of all proportion to the artwork. And she suspected she had not even begun to understand them all. She said, "Waterpainting you as a stormshifter is not all you want of me, is it?"

His grin faded and he hesitated before replying. "No," he admitted. "I have to tackle Taquar. He's a traitor, a murderer and totally untrustworthy. I have to bring him down. And I need his trained armsmen and his pedes, because then I can confront Davim."

"You want to go to war?"

"I hope it doesn't come to that with Taquar. But against Davim? Yes. It's inevitable. You saw what he did to Mine Silverwall."

"You can't rely on me, Shale. I have to go back to Russet in less than a year."

"Then we'll have to do this within a year. It'll be tough. I have too few rainlords at my disposal, and no stormlords at all. Without them, winning a war with Reduners is . . . unlikely. Unless we can think of some way to kill ziggers using your water skills."

"I've been thinking of little else ever since we left the White Quarter and I haven't come up with anything. I had a long talk with Russet about different ways to use waterpainting, but no matter what, you can't change the limitations: you have to paint accurately for it to work. I know all ziggers look alike, and I could paint pictures of ziggers dead in their cages, for example – but it wouldn't work if I didn't know what each cage looked like, and how many ziggers there were inside each one."

They looked at each other soberly. "We'll think of something," he said, "because we must. Otherwise Davim will come after us. I'm a stormlord, and for him that's reason enough."

She stared at him then turned away, her thoughts turbulent. *In the end, I am going to be a prisoner again. Not Taquar's, or Russet's, but a prisoner of my own conscience. If Shale needs me to make storms, how can I leave him to go to Khromatis? I will have to be always at his side, every day for the rest of my life, painting the storms, keeping the land alive.*

Somewhere deep inside her, she felt the tug of Russet's waterpainting like a dagger under her breastbone. Just thinking about not returning to Russet was enough to start the pain. *I may have to live with that.*

But what if it killed her?

It killed my mother . . .

Courage. I must have courage.

"My lords, there's another sky message." The servant who'd admitted the seneschal to the dining room had scuttled away, leaving Harkel Tallyman to confront the three rainlords: Taquar, Laisa and Senya.

Taquar looked up from the stewed goat on his plate. Ever since the wretched Gibber grubber had disappeared yet again, he had not bothered to hide his messages and Taquar was sick of hearing about them. "Harkel, can I not even have a meal without one of your accursed interruptions?"

"You did ask to be informed."

Taquar lowered his spoon and fixed the seneschal with a look that would have reduced any lesser servant to stuttering terror.

Laisa scrambled to her feet. "Sandblast that boy! Is there no way to stop his insolence?" She strode out onto the balcony to have a look and Senya, after an interested glance at Taquar, followed.

"Seeing as he is doubtless doing this from miles away –

probably not," Taquar said, loud enough for her to hear. He didn't bother to follow. Instead, he reached out to help himself to some more fried bab rolls.

"Aren't you going to dissipate it?" Tallyman asked.

"Has anyone else read it?"

"By now I would think half of Scarcleft has."

"Then there is little point to my ridding the world of the words. The half of the city who did not read it will certainly hear about it from those who did." Taquar dipped the roll into his stew and continued to eat.

"Lord, these messages are very damaging."

"Yes, Harkel, I know. However, I find it difficult to spend my whole life up on the roof waiting for the next message to manifest itself, just so I can disintegrate the cloud before anyone gets to read it. I am not a stormlord, Tallyman. There is a limit to my skills and I have reached it. I need to rest."

It was the closest he could come to admitting he was exhausted. Waterless soul, what he could not have done had *he* been granted the kind of power generating these sky messages!

Somehow Jasper was not only controlling clouds with careful precision, but he was using clouds of his own. Or maybe he had found another rainlord with the power to help him. Now that Taquar was no longer expending his energies on sucking up vapour from the Giving Sea, he could feel rain falling in the Warthago Range and across the Border Humps, feeding the mother wells of all the cities and washes and mines, with as much success as Granthon had been able to achieve alone. Not as much as there should have been, but more than Jasper had been able to do with Taquar's help.

I don't understand it. Who is helping him? Who is that strong? Taquar did not enjoy being mystified.

"So?" he asked Tallyman. "Is that clear enough for you?"

"Yes, my lord. However, you should be aware that yesterday fifteen of the Scarcleft guard deserted and left the city. I have been told they are searching for Jasper and his army. To *join* them."

"*Army?*" Laisa entered the room once more. "Note that, Taquar. They are calling it an army now."

"So it would seem," Taquar said. "I have heard he has met up with Iani and some malcontents." He made a dismissive gesture. "We are better off without the disloyal, Harkel. So if you intend to desert your post, I suggest you do it sooner rather than later."

"I'm not a fool. I know who puts water in my jar. I would not last long here if Jasper ruled; he heard me tell the guards to kill that snuggery runaway of his and I saw the look on his face then – and I've seen the same expression since whenever he could actually bear to look at me. He'd see me dead and feel it was a good day's work done."

"Then you had better strengthen our defences. That is your job. Please do not waste your time telling me mine."

"No, my lord. But I think it might pay you to read this particular message." He hesitated, fidgeting.

"You have something else to say?"

Tallyman blurted out, "There is nothing to say any member of the guard, or even any water enforcer, would raise his scimitar or tap his zigtube against the army of a stormlord. Any stormlord, least of all one elevating himself by his actions to Cloudmaster." He waved a hand at the open window and the sky beyond.

"Remind them I will take the water of any man who disobeys an order!" Taquar growled through gritted teeth. "Leave me, Tallyman, and do not come back until you are the bearer of *good* news."

"He is becoming insolent," Laisa remarked after the seneschal had turned on his heel and left the room. "You should discipline him. But he is correct about one thing; you do need to read this."

"I think I am having quite enough trouble with the servants and guards as it is, Laisa, without alienating Tallyman as well." He dabbed at his lips with his napkin, rose, and went to join Senya on the balcony. Once there, he raised his eyes to look at the cloud-made message. It was a list of names: *Rainlord Emilissa Moonstone, died aged 13. Rainlord Tareth Kissad, died aged 15. Rainlord Prethi Stoneman, died aged 15. Rainlord Firth Emerald, died aged 17. Rainlord Lyneth Potch, died aged 10. Arta Amethyst Lyman, died aged 45.* Underneath there were the words: *Murdered by Rainlord Taquar Sardonyx.* And underneath that another sentence: *Cloudmaster Jasper's forces approach to free Scarcleft from tyranny.*

Taquar's face paled. "Damn him to a waterless hell! When I get my hands on him, I will *drown* the little grubber!" He took a deep breath of pure rage and sent his power outwards. The effort left him staggering, and he had to grasp the balustrade to keep himself upright. A minute or two later, the cloud edges above began to wisp away into the blue of the sky.

The message was just the last in a series, each planting its insidious doubt in the minds of Scarcleft citizens. The first had asked the question: *Do you want to kill the Quartern's only stormlord?* Others had told of Jasper's imprisonment by Taquar and mentioned Taquar's alliance with Davim.

"No one will believe all these stupid lies," Senya said. "Jasper is so dumb. Who's going to believe a Gibber grubber over the Highlord of Scarcleft?"

"Stones and dust, Laisa! What is her head stuffed with?" Taquar asked, still holding himself upright. Slowly the clouds above lost their definition and merged into one another.

Senya pouted and her bottom lip wobbled. "Don't be rude," she said.

"You stupid child," Taquar told her. "Can you not even see the truth when it is written in the sky above your head?

Although Jasper did miss one – I talked Miriene Copper into killing herself as well. And I didn't kill Lyneth!"

Senya gaped, her eyes wide – first with disbelief, then horror. Finally she turned on her heel and ran, hand over her mouth, from the room.

"Well, Laisa?" Taquar asked. "What about you? Are you also going to abandon the crumbling edifice? You married the wrong man, it seems. You should have fluttered your eyelashes at Iani."

She remained where she was, her face showing no emotion. "Life is ever a gamble," she said at last. "Are you going to wait calmly for Jasper and this army of Iani's to arrive?"

"Oh yes. There aren't many alternatives, and who knows – I may get the opportunity to surprise him yet."

She rolled her eyes in disparagement.

"Do you have a better suggestion, my dear?"

"Leave. Go across the Giving Sea. I am sure there are ways, Iani's portmaster notwithstanding."

"Odd, now I am face to face with the necessity of leaving, it does not seem so palatable," he admitted. "I prefer to stay. Perverse of me, I know. I need to find out how he is creating those clouds or who's helping him. And once I know, I can work out how to use that knowledge. In fact, my position could well be better. I could be free to live as I damn well please instead of spending my energies drawing water out of the ocean. I just have to work out how to get Jasper back under my control, and I have already started on that."

"How?"

"That is my secret. Apart from that, I know my enemy. He is weak, like Nealrith, always worrying about killing the innocent. He will be reluctant to loose an army on this city, you'll see. He will not want me to use my ziggers either, because he knows they'd kill as many innocent city dwellers as they would his armsmen. So he will come prepared to bargain, and in bargaining I have a wealth of experience."

"And absolutely no honour."

"Exactly."

She stared at him as if she had more to say, but then thought better of it. "I think I will retire to my room with a bottle of that very good imported wine you have, if you don't mind. Just in case Scarleft Hall is invaded. It would be a shame to have it go to waste."

He gave a cynical smile and gestured as if raising a glass to her. "This is your fault as much as mine. You were the one who said you could control the Gibber brat. I'll make you a promise. Jasper Bloodstone will one day soon be back under my heel. And once there, he will never escape again. His power will be mine until one of us dies of old age. I swear it."

"I hope, for my sake, you are right."

Taquar stood still until she had gone and the door had closed behind her. Then he dropped to his knees, his hands sliding down the supports of the balustrade as he strove not to fall. He lay his forehead against the brick support and closed his eyes, willing his power to pour back into his body.

Blast you, you little Gibber bastard. Blast you to waterless damnation. You will regret this.

27

Scarpen Quarter
Scarcleft City, outside the walls
Scarcleft Hall, Level 2

The sound of the drums brought back memories of Terelle's childhood. Of settle weddings. A family celebrating the birth of a healthy son. The twice a year festivals of the water rush. Most of these particular drums had been hurriedly and imperfectly fashioned in the past few days out of old pede segments, yet they could return her so easily to her past.

"Scared?"

The word was almost lost in the drumming. Something inside her chest reverberated with the sound, leaving her with a peculiar, breathless feeling. Or was it just terror?

"Petrified," she replied, in a weak attempt to sound as if she was joking. "I keep expecting ziggers to come shooting at us over the walls."

"So do I. And I wouldn't hear them coming either, with all that drumming. It's effective though, isn't it? Intimidating. And loud enough to hurt." Shale grinned at her. "Hurt us, anyway."

She was sick with apprehension. Together with Iani, Feroze Khorash and Ouina, the sour-faced, argumentative Highlord of Breakaway, they headed the group that sought entrance to Scarcleft. Seated on myriapedes, with nothing between them and the city walls, she felt as exposed as a pebblemouse out of its hole. Behind them, Breakaway forces and Shale's Scarcleft guards, many still wearing the city's uniform with Shale's bloodstone insignia hastily drawn on their tunics, waited in silence. Flanking them all were two rows of Gibbermen on foot, many with a hand drum, and further back two rows of Alabasters, well armed, dressed in their red-embroidered robes, mounted on their white myriapedes. As the sun caught their mirrors, they flashed and glittered. Altogether a thousand people headed towards the Scarcleft gateway.

Several thousand more armed men and women led by rainlords ringed the city, within sight, but further away. They had orders to stay there. Although there had been some grumbling from the more bellicose, Shale had made it clear he expected to be obeyed. He didn't want all his forces trapped within the city if something went wrong, and he didn't want the Scarcleft watchers to realise just how badly armed much of his army was. Most of the Gibbermen only had knives, or grove implements – hardly a sight to impress the trained guards of Scarcleft.

They continued on at walking pace and the gate ahead remained open. Terelle glanced up at the sky. Shale's latest message was still there: *Open the gates for the Cloudmaster of the Quartern, Jasper Bloodstone, Stormlord.*

"Bleedin' pretentious lil'git, that Gibber grubber, innie?" Shale had cupped his hands to his mouth to yell the words in a thick Gibber accent, but fear made her incapable of a light-hearted response.

She shouted back a reply. "He wouldn't really set the ziggers on you, would he?"

"Who knows? He's wilted if he does, and withered if he doesn't . . . I'm gambling, Terelle. I'm gambling his men won't do it even if he orders it. Everyone needs water."

"Doesn't look as if they are going to shut us out," Ouina

mouthed at them, not even trying to make herself heard. She was a scrawny middle-aged woman who treated the storm-lord with a mixture of deference and suspicion, as if she could not make up her mind whether he was the legitimate Cloudmaster, or a Gibber grubber who had overstepped his level in life. Terelle she ignored, her ill manners stopping just short of sufficient rudeness to prompt Shale into doing something about it.

"Good," Iani shouted back. "Let's hope it's not a trap."

As they reached the gate, an officer with the rank of half-overman stepped out to make a sign of abeyance. Shale – Terelle still couldn't think of him as Jasper – dipped his head in return and indicated to his Gibbermen escort they were to stop their drumming.

"Welcome back to Scarcleft, lord," the half-overman said into the ensuing silence. He sounded both flustered and nervous. "Would your men prefer to leave their mounts at the livery?" He waved an agitated hand in the direction of the stables outside the walls.

"Perhaps later," Shale replied, his face bland. "I expected the Highlord to be here to greet me."

"He's, um, in Scarcleft Hall, my lord. He has all the city's ziggers with him, but most of his men have left him. They have made it clear they are loyal to you, my lord."

"Ah. And who might be there with him?"

The man shuffled, looking embarrassed. "His wife and step-daughter. The Overman of the Hall Guard. He felt it was his duty. Some other guards who remain – er – obedient to his rule. Maybe two hundred or so men, all told. Seneschal Tallyman, of course, and most of his water enforcers. That's another hundred or more. Even not counting the ziggers, they're well armed. The Highlord said he'll release ziggers if you threaten him, and he doesn't care who the victims are."

Iani gave a grunt of contempt. "Watergiver above – he is pitiable!"

"How many ziggers do they have?" Shale asked.

"There must be close to five thousand. Some of my men say he's been starving 'em. We hear them whining . . ." The half-overman cleared his throat uneasily. "My men are safe enough against the ziggers that belonged to the guards. We all have the correct perfume to wear, and there are more bottles of the stuff in the stores. There's plenty for you and your men, at least . . ."

Shale snorted. "Who has had access to those stores lately, Half-Overman?"

The man paled as he realised what Shale was asking. "You mean – you mean the perfume's been replaced with something else?"

"Or contaminated. Distribute it by all means, but I would suggest you place no faith in it."

"I – yes, my lord. We don't have any protection against the water enforcers' ziggers anyway. They have always kept theirs separate, training them to a different smell."

Shale gave a terse nod. "Order the city's citizens to shutter their houses and stay inside. Anything else I should know?"

"Several days ago the Highlord sent two of his men out. Rumour has it they were to go to Sandmaster Davim to ask him for help."

Shale laughed. "Well, well. I suppose I should have expected that. Thank you, Half-Overman – Wendel, is it? I want to write a message for the Highlord. We will remain here until we have an answer."

"Yes, my lord." Wendel turned away, snapping out orders to the group of guards who were standing to attention just inside the gateway.

Shale turned to his own men. "Dibble, have a few men remain here at the gate, just to make sure it stays open.

Send messengers to the rest of the army to tell them everything said here. Your men can stand down outside the gates. They can find some shade in the groves, but tell them they are to remain on the alert."

As Dibble relayed the orders, Shale slid down from his mount, then helped Terelle to do the same. "I'm sorry – so much is going to depend on you," he murmured.

She had rarely felt so miserable. Now it was time to put their plan into practice, she was appalled at their temerity. *This can't work. We're mad.* And if they failed, the consequences were unthinkable. Worse still, in the days since she had met him again, she had been seeing a side of Shale she had never seen before. He had grown, leaving her behind. He was a Cloudmaster; she was still a snuggery girl striving to find her place in a world that wanted no part of her.

I expected too much, she thought sadly. *There was a time when we were beginning to fall in love, I know there was. He was too shy to talk about it then, and now it's too late.* It wasn't her fault, or his either. It was just the way life was for a stormlord.

He turned away, asking for pen and paper. He and Iani stepped into the guardhouse to use the table there. Terelle stayed outside with Ouina and Feroze. Ouina glowered at her.

"You shouldn't be here," Ouina said suddenly. "You're a distraction to him, and this is no time for distractions."

Behind Ouina's back, Feroze pulled a face. "I guess she's scared," he said to Terelle, his voice pitched just loud enough for Ouina to hear. "Nervy people get that way sometimes."

Terelle stifled a giggle.

"Now perhaps is the time to pray," he added.

"Thanks to you, I'm not sure I believe in the Sunlord any more."

"God exists, Terelle. He just wasn't what you thought."

"Why should your God be any more real than the Sunlord? Perhaps you are just as deceived."

"We have written records," he protested, "going back to the time when God walked among us."

"How do you worship your God?" Ouina asked, her eyebrows snapped together into a thunderous line. She uncorked her water skin and ostentatiously poured a libation onto the ground to honour the Sunlord.

"Not by wasting water," Feroze said mildly. "We have a daily act of worship. Each day, we do one act of deliberate kindness outside our normal routine. Helping someone less fortunate than ourselves in some way, not necessarily with money. That is our form of worship. The recipient knows he or she is participating in the giver's worship, and is therefore also blessed. And as for our prayers? We can pray wherever and whenever we want. Prayers of thanks or forgiveness, prayers for wisdom in our actions. Which is the one I am going to be performing now." He closed his eyes and bowed his head. Ouina edged away as if she thought he was defiling the air around him.

She doesn't like me, Terelle thought. *And yet she scarcely knows me. It's because someone told her I was a Watergiver by birth, and that sounds sacrilegious. I wish the lords of Khromatis called themselves something else . . .*

She turned her thoughts away to the more practical plans she and Shale had rehearsed – and sighed. There was so much scope for things to go wrong. *It's all very well for him. He just gets to die if this fails. I'll be the one that has to live, knowing it was all my fault, knowing I could have killed Taquar simply by painting him dead.*

If Shale died, Taquar would be alive and she would have to face him alone. She remembered his touch and, in the heat of the sun, she shivered.

* * *

Laisa stood on the balcony, looking at the sky. The message was fraying away at the edges, teased into nothingness. *Waterless hell*, she thought. *He's so strong he thinks nothing of wasting water.*

"Mother, you made a mistake. A big mistake." Senya, sitting on the balcony divan, glared at her. "Taquar is doomed. He can't stay walled up in this place forever. But you *married* him. So now we're stuck here, and Jasper's out there somewhere with an army of barbarians. We could all be *killed*."

Laisa swallowed the ire that Senya's childishness aroused and said calmly, "If there is one thing Jasper won't do, it's kill you. He's sensible enough to know the two of you have to marry eventually."

"*Does* he have to marry me? One of those Gibber grubber children you brought out of the Gibber shows promise of being a rainlord. Taquar told me that. He heard she's over in Pediment."

Laisa frowned. She knew that, but she wondered just what he was up to, telling Senya. "You have bedded the silly young man, so you have the advantage, or at least I hope you have. I trust you were pleasant enough to make an impression. Is there any chance you are pregnant?"

Senya looked sulky and said evasively, "It's too early to say."

Before Laisa could point out that that was hardly true, they were interrupted. Taquar strode into the room, carrying a letter in one hand. Laisa scanned his face, looking for some signs of tension, and found them, as obvious as the element of sardonic amusement lurking in his gaze.

"There has been a more *normal* communication from the Gibber grubber," he said. "Delivered by a guard. Jasper is inside the city, with a portion of his ragtag army, and he wants to fight me in single combat." He laughed.

Laisa looked at him in disbelief. "He wants to *what*?"

"You heard me."

She was puzzled. "Using water-powers? He knows you won't accept such a challenge. He would win with his head stuck in the sand. He's a stormlord and you're a rainlord. Although he might find it hard to kill you using water-powers."

"Even I can hold on to my water," Senya said.

They both ignored her. "It wouldn't be so very one-sided," he said. "I am a very skilled rainlord, and he is a weak stormlord."

Involuntarily Laisa glanced up at the sky. "That last has escaped my notice lately."

Taquar snorted. "He's only making clouds with help. I'm sure that's the case. But irrelevant anyway. He's offered to fight with swords. The winner gets to state his unconditional terms afterwards. If the loser is still alive."

Senya laughed and clapped her hands. "Swords? You'll win then!"

Laisa's eyebrows shot up. "It's a trap. He can't possibly expect to defeat you in a duel, even if Nealrith did insist on lessons and your guards have been tutoring him since. All that amounts to nothing against your experience."

"Perhaps he thinks that is enough. You told me Kaneth said the lad was good."

"Good for the amount of training he had, yes. But it still wasn't much. And he's not stupid. He knows there's a difference between being a good student and being a good bladesman. This has got to be a trick to get close enough to use his water-powers."

"Possibly. At first I thought he just wanted to get me outside the walls where he might have an archer to pick me off. So I sent back a reply, saying it had to be the Hall forecourt. He can bring a few witnesses. Everyone except himself to be unarmed. I made the same concession – no armed guards on the walls or with me. He has answered saying that would be acceptable only if you, Laisa, went out first and could guarantee he would not be attacked by ziggers or anything else. He wants you to give him that assurance first."

"He's mad. Even if I said that and thought I was being honest, what guarantee has he that I know what *you* intend?"

"You're my wife. He's going to take you hostage. I think he's assuming that would make a difference to my integrity." He chuckled.

She glared. "Maybe he's just stupidly romantic enough to believe that, but I suspect Iani is there at his shoulder to disabuse him of that notion. Anyway, it still doesn't tell us what the trap is."

"No. It has to be something to do with his water-powers, because that's the only advantage he has. But what? And how can I thwart it? I certainly have enough power to stop him throwing water at me or stuffing it down my throat! Yet somehow I don't think he intends obvious treachery – a hidden bowman, for example. He has an odd idea of honour, for a start. Yes, an interesting conundrum."

"You're not going to *accept* this challenge, are you?"

"What choice do I have? My guards have already opened the city gates to him."

"What about Davim?"

"Don't be ridiculous. It might be weeks before he arrives. I sent for him because I envisaged Jasper mounting a siege, and I would *have* weeks. I did not think my own guard would turn on me. I was hoping all the disloyal ones had already left. I was over-optimistic, I will admit."

"Jasper will be scared of what you can do with the ziggers. You could still hole up here on Level Two and wait to be rescued."

"That did cross my mind. I did think of using the ziggers to kill as many of them as I could, and too bad if the nation's only stormlord was among them. I had lost anyway – might as well take them all with me." He reached out and cupped her chin, smiling unpleasantly. "My pretty wife and step-daughter included."

"You're sandcrazy."

"No. Just vengeful. But I think perhaps that Gibber brat has my measure very well. He has presented me with a challenge. He knows I can't resist because what he proposes also presents me with a chance, just a chance, that I can still win. And he has to take that risk, because if he does not, I will loose five thousand ziggers into the streets of Scarcleft the moment he attacks the walls of Scarcleft Hall."

"It's a pretty problem for you, isn't it?" Laisa said, lacing her words with sarcasm. "If you win and kill him, then you also lose because the nation's one and only stormlord will be dead. If you win and somehow regain control over him, the problem will be how to maintain that control."

"He can kill me, yet I can't dispatch him to the hell he deserves for his insolence. But if I can win without killing him, I can turn Jasper's value to my own advantage. If I put a sword to his throat his allies will back off. It is probably one reason he has conceived this plan. He knows no matter what, he will not die." He snorted his contempt. "He owes me everything, the ungrateful little sand-tick. I taught him. I rescued him from an abusive father. He was half starved, beaten, ill-clad, illiterate and didn't even know he had power. He owes *everything* to me. What he doesn't know is that I have one piece of gold to offer him, and it is irresistible. If I win, I have him forever."

Senya looked from one to the other, her eyes bright with interest.

Laisa looked dubious. "I have no idea what you contemplate."

He turned to look at Senya. "Go to your room, girl. Make yourself look pretty. You have a fight to witness and I need you to look your best."

After Senya left, Laisa asked, puzzled, "She can't be your piece of gold, surely? Jasper regards marriage to her as an unpleasant task he has to undertake, rather than a jewel in his future."

"I am aware of that." Taquar bent towards her, dropping his voice. "This is the last game, Laisa. And then we will see if you chose the right player, eh?" He kissed her on the lips, holding her chin firmly so she could not turn away. When he released her he added, "And I think – before I answer this latest missive – I shall partake of my wife's charms. It has been a while and I cannot say the last of the kitchen maids appeals."

Laisa was more resigned than pleased.

The small door in the main gate to Scarcleft Hall opened and Laisa walked out, as cool and as beautiful as ever. She walked alone across the square in front of the Hall and down the steps into Temple Street on Level Three. Here, out of sight of any of the Hall windows, Jasper waited with Iani, Ouina, Feroze, Terelle and a mix of Scarcleft guards, Gibbermen and Alabasters. Lord Gold hovered behind in full ceremonial garb, accompanied by a bevy of nervous waterpriests.

When Laisa reached Jasper, she knelt at his feet and said, without the slightest emotion, "Lord Laisa Drayman asks for forgiveness for past transgressions, and pledges loyalty to the Cloudmaster, Jasper Bloodstone."

Jasper nodded and held out a hand to raise her to her feet. "Can you offer any proof of your change of heart?"

"Hardly. I *can* tell you Taquar will fight you but does not intend to cause your death. He believes you intend to trick him, but he doesn't know how."

"So he doesn't intend to attack me with ziggers the moment I set foot inside the Hall?"

"Not to my knowledge. He wants to win by legal means.

Before the fight begins, he wants you to proclaim in front of witnesses his legal right to rule the Scarpen as Cloudmaster if he wins. Administrative ruler, separate from the position of stormlord."

"If said stormlord is still alive," Jasper said dryly.

She inclined her head. "He can't kill the only stormlord, as you well know."

"Your allegiance is accepted. As for the rest – we will see. I expected Senya to be with you."

"Taquar insisted she stay."

"As hostage for your lies perhaps?" These words came from Iani.

"And it's lovely to see you again, too," Laisa said.

"He has a point," Jasper said.

She shrugged. "She will be there, watching the combat. Taquar did not ask me to lie. I do not think he saw the need for lies – he is certain he will win this fight, no matter what trick you have in mind."

"I am relying on his certainty," Jasper said with a smile. "Let's get on with this."

He turned to the other two rainlords. "Iani, you are in charge here. If I don't come back, do what you will. Laisa will stay here. Ouina, you will come with me as witness. So will Terelle. Dibble, I want two Gibbermen and two Alabasters and two Scarpen guards with me, all unarmed. Half-Overman Wendel – you will take orders from Rainlord Iani if anything happens to me."

"I demand to go with you."

Jasper turned, surprised at the imperious tone. Lord Gold. He might have known it. "Pardon?"

"I am the Quartern Sunpriest. And a rainlord. The people in the Hall, Lord Taquar included, are all part of my flock. I have more right to be there than *her*." He nodded coldly at Terelle.

"I doubt that Taquar would be happy to find I was taking two rainlords with me."

"Then leave Lord Ouina behind."

Jasper glanced at Ouina. She shrugged, as if to say the priest had a point.

"It is also my duty to make sure Lord Senya is not harmed," Lord Gold added.

"No one is going to harm Senya," Jasper growled, but he capitulated anyway. "Very well, take Ouina's place. Iani, be ready to enter the moment the gates are opened afterwards." He shouldered the bag containing Terelle's painting things and his own water skin. "Let's go."

As he and Terelle walked quickly across the open square towards the Hall gate, putting some distance between them and the others so they could speak privately, Terelle said in a small voice, "I can't believe this will work." She held her water skin far too tightly; her knuckles were white.

Jasper noticed and touched her arm in comfort. "It will. I know how to unbalance Taquar, and he's going to be looking in all the wrong directions for the trick."

"What if he has heard about the magic of waterpainting?"

"How? No one in the Scarpen knows. Waterless skies, Terelle, they used to ask Russet to paint artworks for their entrance hallways! No one dreamed there could be anything strange about it."

"They knew about it in the White Quarter."

"But you yourself said they don't talk about these things to outsiders. Don't worry, everything will be fine."

"You *are* the only stormlord: do you have the right to risk yourself this way?" He heard the love in her voice and it almost unmanned him. *You have to marry a rainlord,* he told himself. *You have to.*

He faced her then, allowing nothing to show on his face, stopping in front of the gate. "I am so fed up with people telling me I must not risk myself. Have you any idea what it is like to know *every person* in this nation depends on *me* for life? I am risking my life for them – and they have to be prepared to die, just as I am. If I don't subdue Taquar, rainlords and stormlords and Gibber folk will never be safe from him. If I confront him in battle or siege, he will loose his ziggers on this city and on those who have followed me here. I know that. He knows that. I cannot compromise, hide myself and say it's fine if a few thousand people die because most of the people of Scarpen will live. Do you understand, Terelle? I will rule this land my way, or I won't rule at all. *It is the only way I can live.* In the long run it is the only chance we have where we can *all* live."

Even as he said the words, the gate opened. He turned away from her worry and walked inside.

28

Taquar could not hide his surprise at seeing Terelle.

Jasper smiled to himself, knowing he had scored a small victory just by having her there. He uttered no greeting, nor did he allow the Highlord time to collect himself. "I have brought Lord Gold along as a witness," he said. His heart was thundering in his chest and only total concentration could keep him outwardly calm.

He looked around as he handed Terelle her painting bag. Two of Taquar's guards were closing the gate again. The only other men of Taquar's he could see were the Overman of the Scarcleft Guard, Seneschal Tallyman and two more guardsmen. None of them appeared to be armed and Jasper could neither smell nor sense any ziggers. The only other person from the Hall was Senya, who smiled brightly at him as though she was delighted to see him. He gave her a brusque nod and dismissed her from his mind.

"You have something to say, I believe?" Taquar reminded him.

"Ah, yes. If I am defeated at your hands here today, I will recognise you as the Cloudmaster, the legitimate administrative ruler of the Quartern, while I work as the stormlord."

Behind Taquar, the overman and Seneschal Tallyman exchanged glances.

Taquar drawled, "I have been the legitimate Cloudmaster since Granthon's death, and you know it."

"Disputable," Jasper said. "And irrelevant."

"Well, irrelevant, at least." Taquar frowned in Terelle's direction. "What are you doing?"

She was filling a water tray she had placed at one edge of the forecourt. He had to repeat the question before she realised she was being addressed. "Jasper wishes there to be a painted record of what happens here," she replied, without looking at him. Her voice shook. "Should you win, doubtless it will be yours to dispose of, however you will."

He was openly suspicious, but could not seem to decide whether what she did was some sort of trick, or merely a diversion. Careful not to turn his back on Jasper, he walked over to where she was and examined the items she'd pulled from the bag: paint pots, a spoon for each, cleansing sand. There was nothing there to arouse his distrust. She took no notice and was already sprinkling the undercoat onto the water in the paint tray.

"I still have the painting you did of me riding my pede," Taquar said loud enough for Jasper to hear. "A fine piece of work. A shame it became detached from the water during the earthquake. When this is over, you shall do some more for me."

She didn't answer or look his way but worked on.

He walked back to Jasper. "I would like to see your sword," he said.

"And I would like to see yours." Iani had warned of poisons that could be placed along the blade to ensure even a small cut was either fatal or at least debilitating. With a smile Jasper took his sword from its scabbard and gave it to Taquar.

"I know this weapon," Taquar said, "it is Iani's." He took

it, held it up to the level of his eye, scanned it thoroughly from that angle, then wiped it with a cloth before handing it back, along with his own.

"That's right. He said he wanted it to taste your blood."

Jasper wiped Taquar's blade carefully, and then his own, using his own dampened cloth. He unbuckled his scabbard and walked over to lay it on the ground close to Terelle. "All right?" he asked softly.

She nodded. The motley base was already finished and she was now painting in the background: the adobe walls of Level Two surrounding Scarcleft Hall, the steps up to the massive front doors, the stone brickwork of the walls, the way the shadows fell. "So far. Just give me the time I need."

"I'll try." The timing was their main problem; they both knew that. There had been no way she could paint anything beforehand, nor could she rush her artwork now. The background had to be accurate. He walked back towards Taquar, but stopped short, still keeping his face as bland as he knew how to make it. "Before we begin, there is one more thing. A request from Iani."

Taquar inclined his head. "The man is mad; I suppose you realise that."

"He wants to know what happened to Lyneth. The details."

"Ah. That troubles him still, eh? She died."

Jasper quelled his anger. "Did you kill her?"

"No, of course not. She was my hope for power. She would have been a damn sight better stormlord than you. I treated her well. She had good food, toys. I came often to teach her."

"You kept her in the mother cistern alone?"

"Hardly! She was only five – or was it six? – at the start. I found her a nurse. A kindly nursemaid who loved her dearly. Unfortunately, however, the woman was not all that young, and one night she apparently died in her sleep. As luck would have it, it must have been just after I'd visited. Lyneth was alone for several weeks with the body of a dead woman. As you so astutely guessed, she was ten at the time. I suspect she killed herself by removing her own water. As I say, she was extraordinarily talented. Believe me, her death grieved me deeply." He shrugged. "She was brave to the last."

Pulsating anger welled up inside Jasper, but he pushed it back down. This was not the time for rage.

"Lord Taquar," Lord Gold said in a shocked voice, "you will have to atone for this crime. Your confession is but a beginning. I shall—"

Taquar looked annoyed. "No more nonsense. Let's begin." He took off his sleeveless jacket and flung it aside. One of his guards handed him a water skin and he took a sip.

"A moment," Jasper said. "I wish to pray."

Once again he had disconcerted Taquar. The rainlord made an irritated gesture with his sword. "What possible interest could *you* have in prayer?"

"An admirable desire," said Lord Gold, with a glare in Taquar's direction, "and not one anyone could object to."

"Nealrith made sure I was instructed in the proper observance of rituals," Jasper said, scrupulously polite. "As we both know, the chances I will emerge from this alive are not certain. Allow me to make my peace with the Sunlord."

"Don't be absurd. Of course I'm not going to kill you." Taquar's suspicions were thoroughly aroused now. He paused, still looking for a trick, some reason for the delay, even as Jasper laid his sword aside on the ground and poured a libation from his water skin, his lips moving in prayer.

Jasper felt rather than saw the moment when the Highlord made his decision. Terelle wasn't ready; she hadn't shuffled up the magic. And Taquar moved. He came at Jasper with the assured stride of a man used to fighting. Jasper dropped the water skin and grabbed up his weapon.

Taquar stopped and raised his blade in the standard salute,

waiting for Jasper to cross blades. Instead, Jasper back-pedalled, fast. Taquar was left standing, ready to fight – but his opponent was no longer anywhere near.

Nealrith had told Jasper several times that Taquar was the best sword fighter the Scarpen had, and Jasper's lessons had been desultory at best. If Taquar crossed blades with him, he was doomed, and he knew it. While Taquar was still staring after him, nonplussed, he turned and jogged across the forecourt to the other side.

"What the salted wells do you think you're doing?" Taquar roared at him. He was shaking with anger.

"You want to fight me, you have to catch me first," Jasper called back.

Taquar strode after him. Jasper waited until he was a couple of strides away, then darted back the way he had come. When he reached where Lord Gold and Senya stood side by side, he stopped.

"You're a coward," Senya said.

Intent on what Taquar was doing, Jasper took no notice. The Highlord was following him, but this time his gait was different, telling Jasper that next time he intended to forestall any rush across the forecourt. This time he started moving while Taquar was still some distance away. He tore towards the gate, as if seeking a way out, and Taquar took off after him, rapidly catching up because he travelled the shorter distance. When Jasper reached the overman, he grabbed him in passing, then whirled around the man and raced back the opposite way. Taquar was caught unprepared, and lost ground as he reversed direction to follow. One of Jasper's Gibber guards muffled a laugh and Taquar reddened in fury.

Terelle wasn't watching.

Good, Jasper thought. She had to get her painting finished. And he had to get himself – and Taquar – to the place she had painted . . . *Oh, sand hells, please let her finish and shuffle up before Taquar skewers me.*

Taquar hesitated.

That's right, my friend, worry about your dignity, Jasper thought, guessing that Taquar was afraid he'd look a fool if he chased his opponent all over the forecourt. Jasper didn't care for his own prestige – let everyone in the Hall think he was a coward, running away from a fight, it didn't matter. He just had to stay alive.

As Taquar came at him again, Jasper raced behind Terelle, sparing a glance at what she had done as he passed. The background was detailed, but plain. She had painted it as if looking from above; that way most of the background was simply the packed earth of the forecourt. Against this, she was filling in the smudgy outlines of two men. Taquar and himself. Jasper continued on, to pause on the far side of the forecourt. He knew now where the real action of the fight was going to be.

Taquar moved towards him. "What the hell do you think you're doing, you cowardly wash-rat?" he snarled. "You intend to spend the whole day running from me?"

"He's a Gibber grubber. What else do you expect!" Tallyman said. "And this is the youth who wants to lead the Quartern? We'd be better off with a sun-fried idiot missing half a brain than a coward!"

"What's so brave about a talented swordsman who agrees to fight a novice?" Jasper asked. "Doesn't sound like bravery to me."

Taquar said, "Come on, Jasper, let's get this over and done with. You know you can't win and you know I am not going to kill you."

Jasper shot a look at Terelle. She was still painting. Taquar took a couple more steps forward and Jasper sidled away, circling the forecourt once more. Taquar made a dash, not at him, but to cut him off. Jasper raced away to avoid being boxed in against the corner of the wall, his feet scudding across the forecourt, racing for the open area near the steps to the Hall building. It was a close thing. Taquar thrust out his sword to trip him up. Jasper took a flying leap over the top of the blade to slip past. The tip of the sword caught the leather heel of his sandal and he stumbled – but didn't lose his footing. By the time Taquar had whirled around, Jasper was several paces away, heading for the centre of the court.

And Terelle shuffled up her painting.

She raised her head, looked straight at him, and nodded. And Taquar caught the exchange. He must have sensed something then, because he faltered. He stared hard at Terelle, trying to make sense of the silent signal.

And Jasper ran towards him, waving his sword and yelling.

The look of alarm on Taquar's face was comical. Jasper guessed it wasn't fear of him but rather fear it was going to be difficult to avoid killing him. But at the last moment, Jasper threw himself into a forward roll, tumbling *past* Taquar, not at him. Taquar, about to strike at Jasper's sword, had to hold back for fear of slashing his unprotected back or neck instead.

As he came out of the roll, Jasper slashed upwards and sideways. It was an awkward blow, but it hit Taquar behind the knee, slicing the tendon. His leg collapsed beneath him and he went down with an expression of appalled disbelief on his face. As the rainlord fell, Jasper knocked his sword from his hand.

Jasper stood and pointed his sword at Taquar's throat. Unfortunately his hand no longer seemed steady, and he unintentionally pinked the Highlord's neck. "You've been hamstrung," he said quietly. "Stay right where you are."

Taquar lay still, but his eyes blazed his fury. No, more than that. An emotion Jasper had never seen in them before: hate. "You can't kill me," he said, his gaze never leaving Jasper's face. "You *dare* not waste someone whose power can help keep this land watered. I don't know how you managed to find the power to cloudshift, but I do know you dare not rely on it. You have to keep me alive and well."

The bastard. He knows that's true. Jasper did not reply. Fear prickled his skin. *I ought to kill him right now. If I don't, he'll find a way to bring me down, I know it. And yet I can't.*

Dibble ran to open the gate again, to let in more of his men.

Senya, who had been sobbing ever since Taquar had fallen, now ran to kneel at Taquar's side. "Are you hurt?" she asked him, her voice tremulous.

"Of course I'm hurt!" he snapped. He was rocking to and fro, clutching the sides of his upper leg above the knee with both hands.

She glared at Jasper. "How could you! Are you going to kill us all, you horrible Gibber grubber?"

"No one is getting killed," he replied, suppressing a sigh. "Your mother has sworn fealty to me, and you will return to her care. Both of you will have plenty of opportunity to show where your loyalty lies, and I suggest you avail yourself of it, Senya, because my patience does have a limit and it's not very far away from where you stand right now."

Fortunately for his patience both Iani and Laisa came up then, with Lord Gold trailing behind, wearing his usual supercilious expression. Laisa grabbed Senya by the arm and pulled her away, whispering advice as they went.

"Harkel Tallyman, the Overman and the rest of the Hall guards are being rounded up," Iani said. He nodded in Taquar's direction. "I'll take care of him, too."

Taquar looked horrified. "Don't be ridiculous!" he yelled at Jasper. "The man will kill me as soon as he gets me alone!"

"Do you think I would wait *that* long?" Iani asked him.

"Lord Iani!" Lord Gold admonished. "That is not a joking matter!" He sprinkled some water on Taquar, saying, "I will see to your comfort, my lord, never fear."

"Take good care of him, Iani," Jasper said, ignoring Taquar and trying hard not to roll his eyes at Lord Gold's words. "He needs a physician as soon as possible."

Iani called to Dibble to bring a litter, then looked down at Taquar. "Dear me, that injury looks nasty. I doubt you'll walk properly again. Looks like the duffer's stroke, too. Don't you remember? Old Shamsir used to teach it to the dummies in the class – the boys who were novices or who had no aptitude for fighting. Roll and slash. You get one chance, and only one. Fail and you're dead because you'll come out of that roll as vulnerable as a pebblemouse about to be gutted for the pot. Fancy you falling for that one."

Jasper left them and walked over to Terelle. His knees felt weak. He looked down at the picture she had shuffled up: Taquar lying on the ground, blood pouring from the back of his knee. Jasper standing over him, sword in hand. "Thanks," he whispered. "It was you who did that, not me."

With a rough gesture of her hand, she destroyed the picture and stood. Her face looked drawn, hollowed out with stress, yet she managed to smile at him. "We did it together," she said.

29

Red Quarter
Northern dunes
Dune Watergatherer

Elmar licked dry lips and said, his voice cracked and husky to his ears, "We need to find water."

Kaneth, taking his turn driving the pede, didn't bother to turn around as he answered. "That's a superfluous remark if ever I heard one. Do you want to say something about your cracked ribs while you're about it?"

The rainlord had been in a foul mood ever since they had left Dune Watergatherer some twelve days earlier. The reason wasn't hard to figure out. Kaneth was furious with Garnet. Ryka. Elmar gritted his teeth, then winced. Ever since the fight with Ravard one of his teeth had been loose and painful. Not to mention the cracked ribs he'd received falling from the pede.

Kaneth might not be able to remember his own wife, but Elmar was not sandcrazy. He knew one part of the man was still in love with Lord Ryka, even when he thought she was Garnet the slave. And the thought that she had voluntarily chosen to stay behind on the dune – probably still sharing Ravard's bed if the tribemaster hadn't broken his neck taking that dive from the pede – with his son growing inside her, riled Kaneth beyond measure. To make his feeling of betrayal even worse, Kaneth believed her decision had endangered all of them. Without a rainlord to find water or to sense warriors hunting them, he and all the escaping slaves were mired in trouble. Kaneth blamed her, not knowing she was blameless, not knowing she was dead.

Elmar, sick with guilt about his lie, still couldn't find the courage to confess. How could he burden Kaneth with the guilt of knowing he had caused the death of his own wife and child? Yet if he hadn't uttered the untruth, Kaneth would have insisted on trying to dig Ryka out and they never would have escaped. And she was *dead*. Elmar had seen the whole slope disappear into a thundering billow of sand. If the fall hadn't killed her, being buried would have. So Elmar had given voice to the one lie that would save Kaneth's life, and now he didn't know how to undo the damage.

If he finds out, he'll never forgive me. Weeping shit, how did I ever get into this mess?

They rode on in an oppressive silence, their pede leading a line of animals over the sands of yet another red dune, the escapees huddled behind them in the misery of thirst. Hot winds gusted, sending bursts of dust into their faces to abrade their skin. Grit insinuated through their hair to the scalp, trickled down their necks to lodge under their clothing as irritating as hot sparks from a fire. *I don't think I'll ever be clean again,* Elmar thought. *Or comfortable.*

To take his mind off his misery – and that all-pervading gnawing thirst – he let his thoughts drift to the past. Elmar Waggoner, twenty-eight years old. Unsentimental, tough, a brawling pikeman with his origins in a downlevel blacksmith's house, sent to teach a few classes in handling a pike at the Breccia Academy. His favoured watering hole at the time had been an all-male snuggery on Level Twenty, his favourite pastime indulging his lust; his most profound belief that love didn't exist. Not for him. And who cared anyway? He didn't need it.

Until he had fallen – tumbled like an amber barrel rolled down the North Way steps – head over heels, for one of his eighteen-year-old students. Worse, he had never changed his mind. It was a bitter irony that the man who had captured his heart proved to be a serial lover of women, a nipple-chaser unable to keep out of female beds, at least until his marriage to Ryka.

Do you know, Kaneth? Did you ever guess? Do you ever see something in this scarred old face of mine to tell you I'd bleeding die for you any time you asked?

Once he'd thought not. But now he wasn't so sure. Kaneth wasn't Kaneth any more. He was Uthardim, and Uthardim was a mystery, even now that he was sensible. He still didn't remember much, but at least he did know which side he wanted to be on. And he craved information. About Taquar, and Shale, who was Jasper, and all that had happened in Breccia leading up to the fall of the city. Except about Ryka. He never asked Elmar to tell him about Ryka.

I liked her, you know, Ryka Feldspar. If I couldn't have you, reckon she was the next best thing that could have happened to you. But I couldn't let you stay behind for her, not when she was withering dead.

He had liked Lord Ryka, but he had been jealous, too. Sun-fried stupidity, he knew. But love was like that. You couldn't tell it what to do. And so now he ached with the knowledge she was dead – and he couldn't speak of it. Served him bleeding right.

Apart from that, they'd been lucky. Kaneth had found him in the dark on the night of the escape. In spite of the confusion, they had gathered together the slaves who had escaped. Come sunrise after that first night of riding, they'd been safely off the open plain and into the first of the dunes to the north of the Watergatherer. There'd been no sign of followers. Part of the reason had been obvious: the escaping men and women had taken many of the pedes and scattered the rest. And some Reduners had been killed in the sand slip, of course. Either Davim or Ravard would have managed to reorganise the tribes eventually, but with the camp in such a mess, men dead and injured and pedes gone, if they had indeed set out to find the missing slaves, it had been too late.

None of that had stopped the other escaped slaves with them from complaining at first. Sand-blasted bellyaching mob, these Breccians. Had it too easy in their water-sated lives.

One hundred and two people had absconded with them, mounted on fifteen pedes, and they wanted to go home even though "home" probably didn't exist any more. They'd wanted to go south, but Kaneth wouldn't have it. He said that's where Davim's men would be looking for them, and without Ryka to feel their water, they'd be caught right quick.

So Kaneth had driven them relentlessly north, one dune after another, hiding by day in sand hollows, riding by night, urging them on by the sheer force of his personality. Not to mention the bleeding mystique of the man that was Uthardim. It had been his idea to give the pedes their heads when they had run out of water. The beasts had headed for the nearest waterhole. In the dark of night, they'd stolen the water, and so it was, dune after dune. And the eeriest thing was the way they never left tracks when they crossed the dunes. Out on the plains, yes, but on the dune sands – never. It gave Elmar the creeps. Somehow the sands shivered after they passed, and the tracks just . . . disappeared. At first he'd thought it was the wind. Not any more.

The journey was slow. What could you expect from people who had never driven pedes, whose first ride on pedeback had probably been the day they were forced in bondage from their home city? And now some of them were expected to drive pedes at night over unfamiliar terrain, dodging encampments yet raiding waterholes. Several times they were seen and chased, only to have their pursuers deterred when Kaneth made the sand move under their feet.

When Kaneth stated that their destination was the hideout of the Reduner rebel army under Vara Redmane, Elmar had worried himself sick. These people they were leading to freedom weren't armsmen. They knew salted damn-all about fighting. Half of them were women, for pity's sake!

Elmar thought their complaining was going to be a problem, but it didn't happen. Kaneth was looking more like his old self now, with his hair growing out and covering the scar on his head, and the rumour began to circulate that he was actually the rainlord Kaneth Carnelian. Although Kaneth neither confirmed nor denied it and among the slaves there were no uplevellers or armsmen who had known him previously, there were several who had seen him before. The initial grumbling faded away. It was replaced by a wary awe, especially as many now believed he could subvert the Reduners' very own gods to do his bidding.

Still, Elmar worried that their respect might not last if their thirst continued. They were so far north now they seemed to have run out of inhabited dunes. They no longer sighted the smoke from encampment fires, and the plains between the dunes were strewn more with rocks than with vegetation. Even the pedes were hungry and sluggish. Worst of all, they had no more water.

"Just when are we going to stop?" Elmar asked. The sun was already perched on the horizon and they had been riding all night.

"Something's out there," Kaneth said. "We'll ride to the top of the dune and look."

After all their care to stay hidden, this was a change. Elmar said nothing, and attempted to subdue his unease. Sometimes he could not see Kaneth in Uthardim. This new man had an added aura of power he had never seen in Kaneth. That, Elmar

411

figured, was an improvement; what he wasn't sure about was the added layer of . . . something. Elmar was used to Kaneth's rainlord abilities. An alert rainlord was always aware of the world around him. He had seen Kaneth navigate his way through the dark of a steep-sided valley at night without a moment's hesitation, simply because he could sense the water in plants. Now he said he had lost his rainlord abilities, yet he seemed to know other things in their place. Like how to move the sand of a dune. And odd things, like how he, Elmar, felt about something. It was uncanny, and Elmar wasn't sure he liked it.

Once on the crest, they stopped. Kaneth stood up on the carapace of their pede. Behind them, the other mounts ploughed their way to the top. He looked to the north, where yet another dune crossed the plains from east to west. Between their dune and the distant one was an outcrop of red rocks, like bab puddings turned out of different-shaped moulds of different sizes. Fat and short, tall and thin, smooth or pleated or nubbed. They were at least as tall as the dune they stood upon. Taller maybe. *Tits and dicks and buttocks,* Elmar thought.

The pede waved its antennae and shuffled its numerous legs as if stimulated by something it smelled in the air. *I hope that's water.* Then Elmer looked to the horizon behind him, to the south. In the sky, there were clouds. Pink clouds, lit by the sunrise. A string of them, fashioned into weird shapes. "Why are they *carved* like that?" he asked.

Kaneth, spotting them too, started to laugh. "I may not remember this Jasper Bloodstone, but I begin to like him. I'll bet he's stirring up a dust cloud among the rainlords."

Elmar gave him a sharp look. "You remember the rainlords?"

"I remember the feelings they gave me of being inadequate."

Kaneth had felt inadequate? Why? He had been one of the Scarpen's best bladesmen! He decided not to pursue that thought. It was rainlord politics, and he wasn't going to understand. "Why would Jasper make patterns in the clouds, and why send them here? And what in all hell's dust holes are clouds doing way out here where nobody lives?"

"Someone does live here," Kaneth replied as the first of the other pedes arrived beside them. "I don't know her, but I suspect it's Vara Redmane. She's out there in that rocky outcrop." Losing interest in the scenery, he sat down on the saddle again.

"How the withering winds do you know that?"

"I haven't the faintest idea. I just know there is someone very old there, with fine wrinkles on her skin. I think it's a woman, although I'm not sure what gives me that idea."

Elmar blinked, absorbing that. "Er – is she alone?"

Kaneth shrugged. "I don't know. I can't feel any others. It's the wrinkles I feel, not her water."

"Weeping shit!" For a moment Elmar was rendered speechless, then he asked, worried, "So what are those clouds?"

"The patterns spell out Reduner letters. Jasper is writing in the clouds, Elmar. He's just sent a message to Vara Redmane."

"You can *read* it?"

"No. 'Fraid not. But I do know what the Reduner script looks like."

"I doubt Jasper does."

"If he escaped Breccia to one of the other cities, he would have help. I hope Vara Redmane can read. Not all that many Reduners can."

Elmar lowered his voice to make doubly sure the others could not hear. "None of this makes sense. You should be able to sense water, not – not *wrinkles*."

"Weird, isn't it? I can no longer sense the large, but the minuscule suddenly makes sense."

"What the waterless hells is minu-whatever-you-said?"

"The small things. A full water jar means nothing to me any more. I wouldn't know it contained water unless I opened the lid and looked inside. But if you were to wet your fingertip with dew, the dampness would burn its message into my brain like a bee sting. I feel the crease lines on someone's forehead if he frowns, because it changes the arrangement of water in his face. I know when someone is upset by the way their muscles tense up. I can feel a grain of sand deep in the dune and know its importance."

"Is it you who's been altering the sand behind us? To obscure our tracks?"

"Of course. That's easy. What is hard to understand is why and how I can do these things." He gave a snort, half amusement, half exasperation. "Was I always so unfathomable?"

Elmar gave a bark of laughter. "No, m'lord. You were once as transparent as water in a cistern. Show you a snuggery lass and you were like a tomcat on heat. Put a sword in your hand and you ached for a fight."

Kaneth turned to look at him, a peculiar expression on his face. "Is that true? You know, I'm not sure I like this Kaneth fellow very much. I'm not certain I ever want him back."

"You did change after—"

"After what?"

"After Ryka. Garnet."

"Did I marry her, Elmar?"

"Er – yes. You did. I was at your wedding."

"Ah. I have a vague memory. Bleeding hot day, and that stupid priest going on and on . . ."

"Basalt."

"Pompous fellow. And a woman. Wearing an awful dress. But I can't picture her face. I can't remember the feel of her." The grimace he made then was one of pain, as if the thought broke his heart.

Oh, spindevil take it – how am I ever going to tell him?

Kaneth turned to the others gathered around on their

pedes. "The end of the journey," he said. "Down there, among those rocks. Freedom, my friends!"

He prodded the pede and it leaped forward.

Behind him, Elmar made a grab for the mounting handle. *I hope there's more than Vara out there,* he thought, and licked his dry lips. *We could do with some water.*

"Ouch! Is there any need t'be so rough, woman?"

"Perhaps you can enlighten me as to why a man who can take a vicious whipping without the slightest whimper squawks like a babe when I put honey on his cuts?" Ryka smiled sweetly at Ravard where he lay on his pallet and applied some more of the balm the women of the tribe had given her.

"Aargh! Because it *hurts.*"

"And you don't mind being a babe in front of a mere slave?"

He pushed her away and sat up, pale-faced and wincing. "Enough, enough."

He was in a foul mood, as usual. In one night his tribe had gone from being the one most favoured by the sandmaster to the poorest on the dune. All of the slaves that remained after the escape had been taken by Davim. Pedes killed or missing from Davim's meddle were replaced by those taken from Ravard's tribe. Davim himself had taken Ravard's myriapede, and that she knew rankled. In an unguarded moment Ravard had told her he'd coveted the beast for years before being able to afford to buy it from its owner.

In the aftermath of the landslip, he ordered as many of his men out as could be mounted to search for the missing slaves and pedes, but they had returned empty handed. He'd then sent them out again, this time to hunt and capture wild pedes. He'd not been able to go himself, because of his flayed back. For several days he was even feverish, and it had fallen to Ryka's lot to nurse him. As his wounds closed and healed, his temper had grown worse, not better.

"You'll open up the cuts again," she said as he objected to her ministrations, "not of course that I care. I'll be perfectly happy if you rip the scars open and get them horribly infected."

He glared at her, but lay down again. "All right, all right. I know it makes you happy t'cause me pain."

"*I* didn't whip you," she said. "And whoever gave you those very first scars was a monster. You were no more than a child when that was done."

She didn't expect an answer, so was surprised when he said, "I was fifteen."

"What could a fifteen-year-old have done to deserve that?"

"Who says I deserved it?"

He was silent while she continued to apply the ointment, and once again she did not think he was going to say anything more. Then he added quietly, "I refused t'kill someone. The sandmaster wanted me t'prove m'loyalty to the tribe. He said he'd kill me if I didn't."

"And you refused?"

"Yes."

"That was brave. Foolish, but brave. Are we talking about Sandmaster Davim?"

He nodded. "He had me whipped instead. Till I couldn't stand the pain. Till I said I'd do the killing. They tied Chert to a boulder and gave me a knife. Told me t'cut his throat. He just stood there looking at me, not trying t'pull away or struggle. Waiting t'die."

"Who was he?"

"Just a lad. I'd hated him once, but then things changed and we grew up and I liked him. We swore t'look after each other's backs, y'know? I'd never had a friend like that before, and in the end he died 'cause we were friends. He hadn't done nothing, 'cept refuse t'serve the tribe."

There was another long silence while he remembered.

Several beads of perspiration ran down his neck to pool in between his shoulder blades.

"You killed him?" she prompted, stilled by his words. Imagining. *They were just children. Half-grown boys who should have been ogling the girls and trying to pluck up enough courage to steal the occasional kiss.*

"You know what the worst thing was? Chert told me t'do it. I thought I'd rather die. But he looked at me and said, 'Do it. I'd rather you killed me than those bastards did.' He was still looking after my back, y'see. So I took the knife and tried. But I didn't know how t'slit someone's throat. I stood in front of him and slashed. But it didn't kill him. He moaned in pain. There was blood. All over me, all over him, everywhere. But he was still standing, and trying t'say something."

He closed his eyes and banged his forehead into the cushion under his head, as if he could rid himself of the memory.

When he took up the story again, it was in a whisper. "Davim and the other men, they were *laughing*. Laughing, 'cause I'd done it all wrong. It was horrible, horrible. But to them it was *funny*. In the end one of them yelled, between his guffaws, 'Do it from behind, y'sand-brained grubber!' So I got behind Chert and pulled the blade across his throat."

Oh, Sunlord save him, she thought. She wanted to weep but wasn't sure if it was for Ravard or his friend. *What kind of world is it that Davim would have us live in where men laugh when a boy is forced to kill his best friend?*

He rolled onto his side to look at her.

"You know what I learned that day, Garnet? That there are some things worse than death. Before that I was scared of everything. Of being beaten. Of dying. I was always shaking and shivering, trembling like dune sand on the move, too scared to be anything but a coward. Always too frightened t'stand up t'anybody. I've never been afraid of death since, or of being whipped. They call me 'The Dauntless Kher', d'you know that?

It took Chert's dying t'make me that way, and they got it wrong, of course. It's not bravery; it's just there's nothing can hurt me that badly again, so what is there t'scare me?"

He looked her straight in the eye. "Don't push me too far, ever. 'Cause I could kill you as easily as cupping a pede for a zigger feed. And walk away from it afterwards without a backward look."

"No," she said, "not yet, you wouldn't. You promised to keep my babe safe, and it's a promise you will keep."

"You so sure I am an honourable man?" He gave a harsh laugh. "Your head's stuffed with sand."

"I'm sure," she said, her voice steady. "Your honour is all you have. You won't throw it away so easily."

"You *lied* to me. You told me Uthardim was a metalworker, a nobody, but he wasn't. He's a bladesman. That lie cost me more than you could possibly know. You helped them escape. Afterwards I saw that some of the perfume vials and weapons were missing from the wooden chest over there. For all of that, you deserve death, yet you expect me t'honour my promise to you?"

The tone of her reply was implacable. "Yes."

He stared at her, then scrambled to his feet. He pulled on his tunic, every move exaggerated as he attempted to avoid the pain, and left the tent. Outside he walked tall, as if nothing bothered him.

Men, she thought.

She'd thought him so simple to understand, and she had been so wrong.

Uncomfortable, she shifted position. She already felt ungainly; how was she ever going to cross the dunes like this? *But, oh, I want to leave this place so badly. And I will, I swear.*

Steal a pede, water and food, defend herself against ziggers, dodge people sent to hunt her down – she could still do those things. She was not guarded or confined. Apparently it never occurred to anyone she would try to escape on her own. They would never think she might dare to cross the Warthago and The Spindlings alone.

But what about her son? Since her fall in the sandslip, she'd had some blood spotting. She rested as much as possible, horribly aware a long journey on pedeback would probably be the worst thing she could do to the child.

Now that she'd had time to think about what had happened, she was more inclined to forgive Kaneth for leaving her behind. Elmar, she decided, had seen her go over the edge. He would have told Kaneth. The two of them had believed her dead. It was unrealistic to think that Kaneth would have cared enough to grieve deeply; he didn't remember her, not really. He even had to take it on trust that the baby she carried was his, because he had no remembrance of the act that had created it.

And that, perhaps, was the knowledge that gave her the most pain. Illogical, but it *hurt* that she had been forgotten. Silly, but it shattered her heart.

30

Scarpen Quarter
Scarcleft City, Level 10 and Level 2
Foothills of the Warthago Range

The snuggery on Level Ten was called Suzur's. The original Suzur was long since dead but, as tradition demanded, the present owner answered to the name. That much Terelle knew as she tugged at the bell pull and waited for the doorman to answer the summons. What she didn't know was just how Vivie had ended up there. When Terelle had gone to Opal's and asked about her sister, the handmaidens had told her sourly that Viviandra had decided she was too good for Level Thirty-two and had gone to the tenth instead. To Suzur's.

Terelle ran a finger along the patterns of purple amethyst inlaid in the woodwork of the gate while she waited for someone to answer the bell; by comparison, the white quartz designs on the gate at Opal's Snuggery were dull. Vivie had moved up in the world.

When she was ushered into her sister's room a little later, Vivie was still wearing her night robe and her eyes were heavy with sleep. She stared at Terelle blankly. "I'll be waterless," she said finally. "It really is you. I didn't know whether to believe the maid when she said my sister was here. Though I did hear that Stormlord Jasper was back and Highlord

Taquar's been imprisoned. Was that something to do with you? I've been puzzling and puzzling as to why two such important men would both be interested in *you*."

Terelle had been about to hug her, but resisted the urge. Vivie didn't sound particularly pleased to see her.

"I paid back everything you owed Opal," Vivie went on, "if that's what's worrying you. The bitch wouldn't let me go until I paid everything."

"Shale said he gave you enough to be free of this kind of life."

Vivie shrugged. "And what would I do? Where would I go? I prefer this." She waved a hand around the room and brightened. "See this, Terelle? Silk sheets, no less! Changed every day. Look in my jewellery box over there. It's full of corals from the Giving Sea and opals from the Gibber. I have one customer a night, and I get to choose who. You know what happened? When people heard both Lord Taquar and Lord Jasper had sought me out, men – rich men – came asking for me. They wanted to know what was so special about me. Then Madam Suzur heard about it and made me an offer. And now – now men line up for a night with Viviandra! Who would have thought it?"

"Are you happy, Vivie?"

"Of course! How can I not be? Terelle, you haven't come to – to *spoil* things for me, have you?"

Terelle stared at her, not comprehending. "How could I do that?"

"I don't know. I thought maybe Lord Jasper wanted his money back or something. Or maybe now that you mix with all these fancy people, maybe you're ashamed of having a sister who's a handmaiden . . ."

Terelle shook her head, at a loss for words. Vivie really did *want* to be a handmaiden. "Don't worry about it, Vivie. You do what you like."

Viviandra looked relieved. "Are you staying in Scarcleft?" she asked politely.

Terelle shook her head. "No. I'm leaving with Shale. Jasper. He is going to join the rest of his army. We are going to reclaim Qanatend."

Vivie's relief disappeared under a worried frown. "I did hear rumours Scarcleft was in danger from Reduner attack. Is that true? Are they going to try to take this city the way they did Breccia City and Qanatend?"

"We are going after them first. Shale thinks he can stop them before they cross the Warthago Range again. Better that than waiting for them to arrive here and having to defend the city, the mother cistern and the tunnel."

"But . . . isn't that dangerous? I mean, for you to go with Lord Jasper? Why don't you just stay here?"

Terelle looked at her sister in silence. She wasn't going to explain that she had to paint a picture for Shale every day just so he could make clouds. "Shale needs me," she said finally.

Vivie's puzzled look dissolved into a knowing smile. "Oh! Really? Pebbles and sand, you have done well for yourself, then, haven't you? But you know, you ought to call him Lord Jasper, like everyone else does. Men *like* that kind of thing." She grinned cheerfully, having at last reduced Terelle's situation to something she understood. "You *are* the lucky one. He's nice, Lord Jasper. D'you know, he wouldn't sleep with me? Although I did offer. I've often wondered why not. I mean, he'd paid for me and all."

"I think he probably had other things on his mind," Terelle said kindly. "I'm sure it had nothing to do with your charms. Vivie, I have to go. He's expecting me back in Scarcleft Hall. We have a lot to prepare before we leave. If – if there's anything you ever want, you can find me through him."

Outside again a few moments later, Terelle paused to lean against the gate while she took a couple of deep breaths.

Her armsman escort, supplied by Shale, politely looked away.

There I was, she thought, *worrying myself sick over my sister, who is perfectly happy with her imperfect life. While I, the companion and assistant to the Quartern's only stormlord, surely now more respectable than I ever thought I would be, feel trapped.* She pushed herself away from the wall and headed up to Level Two. Irony was so very, very irritating.

"I don't understand why I have to share a myriapede with *her*," Senya said. She was speaking to her mother, but her gaze was for Terelle, already mounted on the first segment of a hack from the Scarcleft stables.

"Perhaps because she knows how to drive one, and you don't," Terelle told her sourly. "Frankly, I don't relish the idea of riding seated in front of a spoiled, whining brat. So just mount up and stop whingeing."

"How dare you!" Senya snapped.

"Easily. Believe me, after all I've been through, I'd dare almost anything."

"Just mount up, Senya, dear," Laisa told her daughter wearily.

"But I don't understand why she has to come anyway," Senya continued. "She's not a rainlord. What use is she going to be when we go to battle? Who is she? She's just a nobody."

"A nobody who is getting very sick of being discussed as if she wasn't here," Terelle snapped. "Just plonk your rear end onto that saddle before I really lose my temper!"

This time it was Laisa who took umbrage. "You would do well to remember whom you are addressing," she told Terelle.

"Oh, I remember. The traitorous daughter of a traitorous mother. Believe me, I am wondering why *you* are here, Senya. I can understand why Lord Laisa may be of use as she has sworn fealty to Lord Jasper and he has need of all the rainlords he can get – but you? What possible use are you?"

"Not another word!" Laisa snapped. "There is an odour about you that I don't like, Terelle Grey. Rumour has it you started life as a snuggery handmaiden, so maybe that explains it. And I have an idea I have seen you before somewhere. I suspect you must be lying about some aspect of your past."

Terelle shrugged, unworried. She thought it unlikely their paths had ever crossed, but she didn't trust Laisa, and had chided Shale for being overly trusting. She'd also asked him why he wanted to bring Senya along. Pressed for a reason, he'd said, "I promised her father I'd take care of her." And he'd flushed as he said it.

Senya tossed her head. "Oh, you're just jealous because Jasper has been in *my* bed and he's going to marry *me*, not you. I've seen you looking at him with your tongue hanging out like an ant sipper."

Terelle, speechless with shock, stared at her. When her brain started working again, she thought bitterly, *She's not as dumb as I thought. Or as harmless.*

Senya, looking past her, halted her spiteful tirade, but only because Shale had ridden up. He was dressed in the finest of clothes, looking like an upleveller of wealth and power. Around his neck he wore his piece of bloodstone jasper, now polished and mounted on a gold chain; Feroze Khorash had returned it to him and he'd taken it to a jeweller. He looked like the lord he now was – but he'd obviously overheard Senya, because he was flushing a deep red.

He looked at Terelle and said woodenly, "Climb up behind me. Senya, you share your mother's hack. We'll leave this one to some of the Gibbermen; they could do with another mount." He signalled one of the guards to come and take the reins.

Terelle couldn't speak, and her thoughts were in turmoil.

Is it true? Did you—? Senya? No, surely not! Not that piece of useless frill.

Wordlessly, she climbed down and mounted behind him. He swung his mount around towards the Hall gate and – still in silence – they began their journey north to meet up with the joint Quartern army being assembled in the Warthago.

She wondered if he could feel her glare boring into his back as they rode. He must have heard what that stupid girl had said; wasn't he going to say anything about it? Sandblast him! She'd be weeping waterless before she'd start the conversation. *She* wasn't the one who had some explaining to do . . . *Oh, how* could *you, Shale!*

They'd left The Escarpment and the walls of Scarcleft behind them and were climbing up through the drylands of The Sweepings, the peaks of the Warthago ahead of them, before he spoke. He turned his head sideways so she could hear and said, without looking at her, "I'm sorry—"

So it's true, she thought. *He did bed her.* She interrupted abruptly. "Whatever for? You don't owe me an explanation."

"I owe you more than that. And I *am* sorry."

"Perhaps it is Senya you should be apologising to, not me."

"Perhaps. But I didn't want you hurt." His face flushed even redder as he said the words. He still wasn't looking at her, and all she could see was his profile.

"Hurt? Who says I'm hurt? I'm snuggery-raised, remember? I am used to what men do. It doesn't matter. You never promised me anything beyond friendship anyway." *So why do I feel as if I have been gutted?*

He looked over his shoulder then, his expression wretched. "Please try not to argue with her, Terelle. She's very young and silly yet. And she has been through so much. First she lost her father and her grandparents. Then she lost her home and her city. Then her mother married Taquar.

And now – now, she has lost Taquar and all the security he offered. She is much to be pitied."

She pressed her lips into a thin line to stop the tears collecting behind her eyelids. She was damned if she would cry.

What the sandhells does he see in her?

The answer was obvious, of course. Senya was as pretty as her mother was beautiful. They deserved each other, Shale and Senya.

That thought was followed quickly by another: No, Shale deserved better, for all that he carried his brains between his legs. No one deserved that little bitch. *I'm just jealous. How stupid is that?* She was wise enough in the ways of the Scarpen, surely. When would she ever learn? She was a lowleveller, born in the Gibber, brought up in a snuggery, and his beginnings might have been humble, but he was Cloudmaster now. They stuck together, these rainlords. All uplevellers at heart, and they didn't like it that a nobody from a downlevel snuggery was close to the new Cloudmaster.

And of course, none of them knew why she was so important. She had insisted on that and he had agreed. They both knew Shale had to have stature to rule. He was young and inexperienced, yet he was putting himself forward as the Quartern's Cloudmaster. The Council of Rainlords had yet to ratify him in the position. It wouldn't have been wise for anyone to know he still couldn't shift clouds without another's help. So she had only herself to blame that all the rainlords around Shale, including that awful Lord Gold peering down his priestly nose, looked askance at her. They all knew she had been raised in a snuggery, Laisa had made sure of that, and their scorn and contempt were on their faces every time they looked at her.

He bumbled on. "I made a mistake," he said. "I was stupid. I botched things, and it has been horrible. Please, Terelle, don't turn away. I don't think I could bear it."

"A few words of apology doesn't mend broken things, Shale. Are you telling me you are free to marry whomever you please?"

He was silent.

"Let's not talk about it," she said when it was clear he had nothing to say. "Because I'll be sandblasted if I have anything at all to say to you."

It's not fair. I could love him so well . . . Sweet water save me, this is going to be an interminable journey.

"You can't do this to me!"

Jasper tilted his head. "Pardon?" he asked politely.

Horrified, Taquar was staring at the scattered stones of a ruined building and the grille set into the cliff slope behind the ruins. For three and a half days he had been drugged with festin root to make sure he didn't use his water-power on his captors. Strapped to a transport pallet, he had been man-handled like a sack of bab fruit on and off a pede. The effects of the drug were wearing off, and the rainlord was now sitting upright on the pallet where Jasper and Iani had unloaded it.

Jasper knew what the drug was like. Not only had Laisa used it on him, but so had his Reduner kidnappers when he was a boy taken from his village at Taquar's instigation. It had been an unpleasant, terrifying experience for a lad who had just seen his family murdered in front of him, and he had little sympathy for Taquar now.

Dispassionately, he contemplated the scene. The ruins had once been a caravansary on the main route between Breccia and the Pebblebag Pass in the foothills of the Warthago; the grille barred the entrance to what had been the caravansary's cistern cave. The whole complex had been abandoned when a landslide further along had swept the track into a ravine, making the route permanently impassable. Few people even knew of its existence any more.

Iani had selected the place and shown Jasper, and only the two of them were there now with Taquar. Together with Terelle and the guardsman Dibble, they had parted company with the army over a day earlier, leaving their destination a mystery. Terelle, deeply reluctant to have anything to do with Taquar when he wasn't drugged out of his mind, had gone with the guardsman to explore the ruins while the two men dealt with the rainlord.

Jasper handed Taquar a crutch; then he and Iani helped him stand upright. Taquar's left leg was healing well, but doubtless it still hurt too much to put it to the ground. He staggered, and had to lean against the pede for support.

"We thought it appropriate," Jasper said. "I spent nearly four years locked behind a grille like that one there. So did Lyneth. Eight years, between us, and Lyneth was only a child. You're an adult. Eight cycles should pass quickly enough, don't you think?"

"Eight *years*?" Taquar stared at him, aghast. "Why? I didn't hurt you!"

"Didn't you? Oddly, that escaped my notice. Still, we have no intention of hurting you, either. Physically, that is. You will have adequate food, just as I did. All the water you can drink. We have refilled the cistern. We've supplied furniture, clothes, blankets, books. A rainlord will personally deliver your supplies every thirty days, just as you did to me. If it happens to be Iani, I wouldn't rile him if I were you. He hasn't exactly forgiven you for Lyneth's death, or Moiqa's for that matter. Take my advice and be extra polite. He is the new Highlord of Scarcleft, did he tell you that?"

Jasper took Taquar by the arm and guided him firmly into the cavern. Most of the wide cavern opening had been blocked with solid metal bars, still sound after several centuries. The entry grille door was narrow. The single long cavern beyond was about a hundred paces deep, the back of it lost in darkness.

428

Iani, limping on Taquar's other side ready to catch him if he fell, said, "It goes without saying we have devised several locks for the grille that don't depend on moving water. And, by the way, this whole prison thing wasn't my idea. I wanted you dead. Still do. At the very least, I wanted to put you in an underground room without light and feed you on bab mash for the rest of your life. Jasper has said I can only do that if you don't behave here. He also said I had to tell you that. And so now I have, but believe me, there won't be a second warning."

He didn't have to say why it was impossible to imprison Taquar in Scarcleft. How could you keep a rainlord behind bars when he could threaten to kill any water-blind person within range of his powers? When he could move water in other parts of the building to do whatever mischief he wanted? He had to be isolated.

Taquar looked from one to the other. He was pale-faced, but he managed defiance. "Davim will bring you down, Shale."

Shale, not Jasper. The blighted bastard. "He will try, certainly. When I have his head on a trencher, I will send it to you." He looked across at Iani. "Let's get on with it." As he took Taquar's other arm, he added, "Davim is already on his way back into the Scarpen, by the way. He's still north of the Warthago Range, but he's heading south from Qanatend."

"How the hell could you know that?" Taquar growled.

"I can sense his water. Or rather the water of an army as large as his, and it is huge. But other than that, I sent for him, in a manner of speaking. After you did, I will admit, but I have a quicker way of communicating than sending a messenger on pedeback. Either way, Davim might think he is riding to your aid, but I intend his defeat on a ground of my choosing."

Taquar looked at him blankly.

"I don't like our chances if we ride deep into the Red Quarter," Jasper explained. "Yet I dislike the idea of letting

Davim loose once again in the Scarpen. So I am enticing him into a trap. By the time I finish, there will be no Sandmaster Davim and I intend to wipe the scourge that is his dune and his marauders off the face of the Quartern." He steadied Taquar as the man stumbled.

"You sent him sky messages."

"That's right. Signed by you, of course. Handy skill, I find."

"He's not going to believe they came from me."

"He might – because you so obligingly asked him for help anyway. In my messages, I just increased the size of the bait. Myself. Delivered up, supposedly by you, to do what he wants with."

Taquar snorted. "We shall see, shan't we?"

"Jasper is soft-hearted," Iani added. "He says we might consider letting you out after eight years. I say you deserve to die several times over. We haven't resolved that question yet." He walked to the back of the cave to pump some water from the cistern into the pede trough outside the cavern entrance. The pede ambled up to the trough to drink, and Iani went out to unload it.

"We have already supplied you with some of the basics," Jasper said, waving a hand at jars and barrels and boxes arranged along one side of the cavern. "Seaweed briquettes for fuel, oil, candles, preserved food. And these are your first fresh supplies," he said, as Iani brought in the first of the sacks. Jasper knew better than to ask him if he needed help. Iani's pride made him resent any suggestion that his weakened arm and leg curtailed his ability to do normal tasks.

Taquar lowered himself onto a chair with a barely concealed groan. Jasper, remembering the painful effects of being tied to a pallet for hours, guessed he was aching all over. Iani went to get another sack.

Taquar lowered his voice. "I want to speak to you alone."

"No chance," Jasper said. "If you have anything to say, you can say it in front of Iani."

"I have something of value you want." He spoke so softly, it was unlikely Iani would hear anyway.

"I doubt it."

"A bargain is best discussed in private."

"There cannot be anything you could offer me that would change a single grain of sand beneath my feet."

"Not even Mica?"

Jasper felt himself go utterly still. There was nothing he wanted to do more than seize Taquar by his neck and throttle him until there was no more life in him. Instead, he asked, "What about him?"

"He's alive. I know where he is."

"And *now* you tell me?" He smiled faintly. "You know, I can't think of a single reason why I should believe you. Not one. You'll have to do better than that."

"Give me my freedom. Freedom to leave the Quartern. Undertake to put me on a ship for the other side of the Giving Sea. And in exchange I'll tell you everything I know about him and where he is to be found."

"Convince me you know where he is."

"You don't think I would have allowed Davim to kill him, do you? Rainlord talent runs in families. Even if he had no talent himself, he might have sired a stormlord. Anyway, he was to be our lever, should you refuse to cooperate."

"Then why did you allow Davim to kill Citrine?"

When Taquar looked blank, Jasper's rage boiled to the surface. His hands curled into fists, but he kept his arms by his sides. "My sister," he said. "Why did you let Davim slaughter her – in a *game*?"

"Oh! I had forgotten her name. He wasn't supposed to kill her. He was supposed to take them both. But you lied to him and he didn't like it. He thought he had to make you fear him."

Once again, that ache. The agony of the knowing. Of never being able to undo the past. His action – a childish attempt to hide who he was – had resulted in Citrine's death. He'd been too young, too ignorant, too innocent. He said, "At the time you denied knowing what had happened to Mica. You *didn't* in fact use him as a lever for my good behaviour."

"It wasn't necessary. Had you proved recalcitrant, we would have produced him quickly enough."

"You still didn't use him later. You threatened Terelle instead."

"If that failed, I was going to tell you about Mica."

"I think you didn't use him because you didn't have him. In fact, you told me after the fall of Breccia you knew Mica had died. That Davim had told you so. Did he?"

"No. I *know* Mica is not dead. I know where he is."

"Then why did you tell me he died in a pede accident?"

"Because I didn't want you going to look for him."

"Gabbing pebbles and nonsense, Taquar! If you'd had him, you could have had him brought to me. You can't think I will believe this. I don't think you have him at all. I think, if he is still alive, he's in Davim's hands and that's why you used Terelle."

There was a long silence, then Taquar capitulated. "All right, it's true. He *was* in the Red Quarter. Still is. I was worried you'd want to rescue him and end up caught by Davim. I *can* tell you where to find him. I can tell you which tribe guards him, and on which dune."

Jasper shook his head. "You are pathetic. We are on our way to war against Davim and his men. Soon I will indeed be able to look for Mica myself. I don't need your information. And I don't believe you've actually seen him, even if he is alive. All you have is what Davim tells you, and you have no way of knowing if that is the truth."

Mica, oh Mica. I don't know what's the right thing to do . . .

Iani brought in the last sack and nodded to indicate he had finished. Together they left the cavern and closed the grille door. Taquar sat where he was, watching Jasper lock it from the outside, using a conventional system of iron padlocks, six of them fixing the door on all sides. Six metal plates meant none were accessible through the bars from the inside.

"With a little luck, I shan't see you again," Jasper said. "Ever."

As he and Iani walked away, leading the pedes back to where Terelle waited with Dibble at the ruins, Jasper said, "When you come to bring his supplies, be very careful, my friend. He's a clever man, and his water skills surpass yours. Never open the grille. Pass the food in through the bars. Never have the keys on you."

Iani looked back at the grille. "I wish I could be certain he can't break out of there."

"I'm sure he'll try. I want him to try. I want him to try, again and again. The padlocks will hold him unless someone comes with a sledgehammer or something similar to deal with them. You need to maintain a general watch in the area, men who will keep their mouths shut about what they are doing. Well-paid, loyal men who have a grudge against him, like the men you got to mend the grille and bring in the furniture and supplies. Men who have suffered at his hands and will never tell anyone he is here, but don't let them anywhere near him. He could threaten to seize their water to force you to release him."

Iani scratched his cheek. "Secrets are hard to keep. Tough to know who whispers pillow talk to a wife or lover."

"I know. I do have a – a back-up plan to keep him where he is just in case. Better you don't know about that, I think. But then, who would want to help him? The Reduners won't, not now he has nothing to offer them. That alliance is long gone.

And anyone else will know he is a traitor who brought us to thirst by his murders. Who would want to free such a man?"

Still, he would have preferred Taquar Sardonyx dead. Instead, he needed him alive, just in case he ever needed the man's help to stormshift. In case he and Terelle couldn't find a way to bring rain to the Quartern while she rejoined Russet.

He mounted his pede and they rode the rest of the way, pulling up a few minutes later in front of Terelle and Dibble. "Let's go join the army," he said, smiling at her.

He reached down to pull her up behind him, while Dibble mounted behind Iani. "Did you have a look?" he asked her quietly as they rode away.

"Yes. I could paint it with my eyes closed."

"Eight paintings," he said. "One for each year. With him slightly older in each. Every year, Iani will paint a number on the rocks outside the entrance, starting with number one, then two, and so on. Your paintings should reflect that change. That way I hope he will be tied to that place, his future determined for the next eight years. He won't be able to escape."

She didn't reply.

"Will it work?" he asked over his shoulder.

"I don't think it's wise to do paintings so far in advance. Once they are done, the artist can't change them to unmake the future. What if you need to release him so he can help you make storms again?"

This time, he was the one who was silent.

She leaned forward to speak quietly into his ear. "I'll do it, but not like that. I'll paint it as it looks now, but with the grille open and Taquar standing free outside, back view, alongside several guards wearing Scarcleft uniforms and a man wearing the robes of the Sunpriest. I'll do all those people from the back, identifiable only by what they are wearing. And I will paint something on the large rock to the left of the entrance. The word 'Shale', that'll do."

He frowned, trying to follow her line of reasoning.

She explained, "The word is irrelevant. The important thing is it's not painted there in reality until just before you are ready to release Taquar. That will mean *you* control the means of his release, not Taquar. He will only be free if there are Scarpen guards and a Lord Gold present, surely something he could not arrange."

He twisted in the saddle to speak urgently in a low voice. "But Lord Gold could! And such a painting might ensure he decides to do it for some obscure purpose of his own. I loathe the man, you know. Why not paint me there?"

"I chose guards and the Quartern Sunpriest because they have recognisable clothing. It means I don't have to bother with their faces, or how much they age, and I don't change the fate of a specific person. But I have guarded against this happening without your permission anyway. Only you and I will know about the name on the rock."

"Ah, I see. But if we do it that way, you have just ensured Taquar will one day be free."

"Yes."

"Why?"

"Shale, you know what it was like locked in there. And yet you want to do it to someone else?"

"He had my sister killed, and my village."

"You can let him out and shove him back in again."

Just then Iani rode up alongside, so they fell silent. Iani fingered the gold bracelet he had just pulled from the water token pocket of this tunic. "Who was it once said, 'Revenge is balm to the injured soul'?" he asked Jasper.

"That was Edicus the Evil, Cloudmaster about five hundred years ago," Jasper said dryly. "It has also been said – probably by a much nicer person – that 'Revenge blackens the suffering heart.'"

"Hmm. I think I prefer the first."

"I prefer to think of it not as revenge, but as justice."

And the two men exchanged grim-edged smiles as they rode on to rejoin their army, not far ahead of them now, in the Warthago Range.

Terelle, troubled, was silent.

31

Red Quarter
Dune Watergatherer

The blood spotting soon stopped altogether, much to Ryka's relief. She forced herself to rest and eat well, wryly amused at how difficult she found the first, and how easy the second. She had developed a fondness for deer baked in heated sand beneath an open fire, for the delicious desert beans always in plentiful supply, for sandgrouse eggs boiled and stuffed with wild garlic served with a sauce of spicy beka seed pods, for sliced melon flavoured with a tangy sweet paste from powdered vine seeds.

It's odd, she reflected, *I hate being here, but there is something seductive about the life. Now, if only they had books, or I had my own pede to ride out on a hunt . . .*

And Kaneth at her side, loving her. *Damn the louse of a man.*

No, don't think about that. Not now. Kaneth is gone, changed into Uthardim. And he doesn't know you. Or care, not really. Think instead about how you love the desert nights. Think about all the things you appreciate.

That feeling of openness she'd never had within the walls of a city. The kindness of the women, their wisdom and the way they passed it on from one generation to the next. The way the tribespeople gathered around the fires at night to sing or dance or listen to the storytellers among them. (How she longed to have parchment and pen to record that wisdom, those tales!) Beyond the encampment the night-parrots boomed and the crickets sang; above the Star River passed in a blaze of light.

Early evening, before the light was gone from the sky, the women would mend and embroider while the men sharpened or oiled their weapons, or made needles and brooches from bone to give to their womenfolk, or sewed leather into sandals or water skins and other items. Children played hide and seek in and around the tents.

And then there were the days. The gloriousness of the dawns and the way the dune shadows sped miles across the plains as the sun came up, shadows trying to drape the landscape – in vain – with the last vestiges of the dark. The way the hawks hung in the sky as if they had been pinned there. The way the dune sang deep inside as the sand shifted, or the way tiny spin-devils whispered as they played their games along the crests.

She'd even made a friend, of sorts – the lad, Khedrim. For some reason he'd taken a liking to her, and whenever he had any spare time he became her shadow. With his strange mix of bright intelligence and a clumsy lack of social skills, she couldn't help but like him as he chatted away, impervious to her supposed lack of understanding.

Blighted eyes, she thought, *why did these Reduners have to spoil it all with their schemes of war and dreams of a Time of Random Rain?*

Fortunately Ravard was no longer so inclined to take her to his bed. His anger and suspicion simmered. He watched her, his glower a mix of rage and pain. Mostly, though, he was too concerned with the tribe and the morale of his men even to speak to her. Once his back allowed it, he pushed his men hard and himself even harder, often disappearing for days while they chased the meddles of wild pedes and brought in some of the immature beasts for taming.

438

When in the encampment, the men spent their days encouraging the animals to accept saddle and bridle and rider, equipping them with handles and mounting slots, persuading them not to panic at the sound of ziggers in cages. It was hot, back-breaking work, and usually at the end of the day, after eating a meal and drinking amber around the fire, Ravard would tumble onto his pallet and sleep the night through, exhausted.

Or maybe, she thought, *it's just that a woman as pregnant as I am lacks allure to a man as young as he is.* Whatever the reason, she appreciated the result.

In the meantime, she planned her escape, even though she was not sure when to risk it. The return to the heart of the Scarpen would take her possibly twelve days or more, riding hard and direct and resting little. Along the way, she would have to bypass Qanatend without being seen, because Ravard had told her Davim still had a remnant force there, under the Warrior Son, holding both the city and the mother cistern up in the Warthago Range. At least Breccia was free again.

But first she had to steal a pede, more difficult now there were fewer of them around. She needed to pilfer enough food to last for the journey. Even feeding her mount would be a problem. A pede could graze on plants, of course, but the grazing time needed for a beast to obtain enough nourishment was substantial, and for a fugitive time would be in short supply.

Night after night, she slipped out under the walls of the tent, easier now she slept alone, to filch food, one small theft at a time. Families made it easy because they kept their food stored outside their tents, usually in half-buried earthenware jars shaded by a woven grass canopy. Stealing was unknown within the tribe, unnecessary even because food and water were freely shared. She found petty thievery was simple: a handful of pede kibble here, a few strands of dried pede meat there, some salted eggs from a jar, dried bab. fruit originally stolen from Qanatend. No one expected it; no one took any precautions against it; no one noticed.

She wrapped all of it carefully in cloth she cut from her bedding, then stored it under the carpets in her sleeping room, in holes she dug then salted to keep the grubs and ants out. It was a slow process, but at last she decided she had sufficient food for herself for the journey. The pede kibble, though, was not enough. She would have to achieve a more audacious theft on the night she left. Water she could take from the waterhole on her way off the dune, using her rainlord skills. The panniers and jars to carry it would be more difficult.

The pede presented a problem, too. The one she had befriended on her journey into the Red Quarter had been taken by Kaneth. The new ones were semi-wild and only just beginning to bond with their trainers. The old, tamer ones were now tethered close to the tents. Stealing one of those would be fraught with danger, as pedes being saddled tended to be restless, noisily snuffling and blowing, or clicking their mouthparts.

Finally she settled on one of the three youngest of the newly caught beasts. They were corralled together in an enclosure at the foot of dune not far from the waterhole. They were all five or six moults away from maturity, and of no interest to warriors looking for a mount now. Pedes entering moult were useless for half a cycle until the old chitin had been shed and the new hardened. Khedrim, not yet old enough to be granted his own myriapede, had been told to look after them, and he'd gratefully accepted an offer of help from Ryka.

"This one," he told her the first time she came to the yard, pointing out the larger of the three, "is going to be mine. I've called her Redwing. My brothers laugh and say she is too young to train, but already she comes when I call. That one there

440

I call Blackwing. And the third one is Skite, because he likes to show off."

Talkative and trusting, both character traits making him the butt of jokes and teasing from his peers, Khedrim was happy enough to escape the camp as often as possible in order to tend to the three young pedes. Ryka, mixing sign language and horribly broken Reduner mangled by a terrible accent, made him laugh, and she soon had him following her lead without even knowing he did so.

She started by coming with him when he led the pedes to water every evening at the waterhole and helping him collect feed. Fortunately, Reduners thought nothing of women working physically hard until their confinement, so no one remarked on her activities. She trained the one he called Blackwing to come when she called, to associate her presence with delicious treats and delightful rubs between the segments. She asked Khedrim to carve mounting slots and screw a saddle handle onto the animal.

"The chalamen say that's stupid," he said. "After they moult you have to do it all over again when the new chitin grows in."

"What matter?" Ryka asked with a shrug. "Khedrim, Garnet, ride now can, eh? Young," she added, pointing to both pedes, "learn quick. Easy teached."

He looked shocked. "Women don't ride pedes!"

"Blackwing, Redwing not proper pede," she said hurriedly. "Baby only!"

He still looked dubious, but she persuaded him to do it, then impressed on him that it was probably better he didn't tell anyone she intended to ride. By the time he had second thoughts, he was already complicit and it was in his interest to keep quiet. Inwardly she felt guilty. He was so gullible, and she was using him. One day he would get into a heap of trouble because of it.

Apart from a couple of times with Khedrim when no one

was around, she mounted Blackwing only at night. She'd wait until the sentries were on patrol in the opposite direction – easy enough for her to determine with her water-senses – and would ride the pede round and round the corral. When the sentries returned, she would duck down behind the young pedes and wait for them to pass. It did not take her long to teach Blackwing to put up with her on its back, to obey the bridle and to respond to the prod.

In her life around the camp, she was careful never to upset Ravard or any other Reduners. She was helpful, pleasant and hard-working. She had no great skill as a cook, so she made a point of doing much of the other work for Ravard's servants, and once the slight bleeding had stopped, she never let her pregnancy be an excuse for shirking. It was hard to make any friends other than Khedrim, though, when she had to pretend that her language skills were pathetic.

Most of all she missed Junial, who had been claimed by one of Davim's men. *One day, Junial,* she promised, *you will be free again.*

In the meantime her problem remained: should she risk her own escape at all? Blackwing was small and would not have much stamina for a long journey. She was carrying a child; what right did she have to risk his life? In the end, it was Junial's absence that decided her. She wanted a Scarpen woman with her when she gave birth.

Sunblast you, Kaneth, why in all the waterless hells aren't you here to help?

"Kher?"

Ravard looked up from his midday meal. He was sitting on the carpet in the main room of his tent, helping himself to the array of dishes Ryka had placed in front of him. Once she would have eaten with him, but no longer. Now she knelt a short distance away and waited.

"Blast," he muttered. "First time I've sat down today and I'm interrupted."

Khedrim stood hesitantly outside the open entrance. "Yes?" Ravard asked. "What is it?"

"There's a messenger from the sandmaster, Kher."

Ravard's face didn't change. "Bring him here." The lad ran off. Ravard pushed his plate away. "It'll be about that message we saw written in the clouds at dawn."

Ryka gaped. No one had told her about any message in the sky, and she had not seen it herself. *Jasper?* she wondered. *It has to be.* She hid a grin of appreciation at his ingenuity.

"What did it say?" she asked Ravard.

"I can't read, can I?"

The messenger appeared in the doorway a moment later, but Ravard did not rise. He didn't send Ryka away, either. "You have a message for me?" he asked.

"Yes, Kher." The man, grimy with dust and sand, launched into the memorised wording. "Sandmaster Davim wishes to tell you the following, Kher. He says: 'I have had word from the Scarcleft Highlord, Taquar. The first message, by pede, arrived last night. It said Scarcleft was surrounded by rainlord forces and asked for aid. The second message arrived earlier this morning, written with clouds in the sky. It said Taquar agrees to give the Stormlord Jasper Bloodstone to the sandmaster in return for our aid against those who besiege Scarcleft.'"

Ryka's eyes widened. She turned her head away so neither of the men would see her surprise and realise she understood. *Taquar? Taquar can't send clouds sailing across the sky, let alone fashion letters out of them first. He couldn't even hold on to that storm he stole from Granthon, sandblast it! Which means the words can't be true. I hope.*

"Is that all?" Ravard asked, when the man stopped to catch his breath.

"No, Kher. The sandmaster says we are riding to seize Stormlord Jasper. He says the remaining fifty lashes due to you are repealed. He orders you, and as many warriors and pedes and supplies as you can muster, to come to Qanatend as soon as possible. All dunes have the same instruction. He says the sun soon rises on the day we hold the last of the stormlords. That is the end of the message. And Kher, I am returning your personal pede to you, at his request. I have left it at the pede lines."

Ryka's thoughts raced. Jasper had somehow come into his own and was now a cloudmaster powerful enough to send such a message? Was Taquar really involved at all? Maybe Jasper was still free and trying to entice the Reduners out. Which seemed foolhardy, to say the least.

Blighted eyes, not knowing was frustrating.

After the man left, she decided to risk asking Ravard what the messenger had said, but he forestalled her, and told her everything anyway, his satisfaction obvious. "You see?" he concluded. "The Scarpen'll be on its knees before us soon."

"You're all sun-fried," she said. "If you don't know why, then go and take a look at how much water is left in the encampment's waterhole. How the waterless heavens are you going to survive without stormlords?"

"Ah, but we'll have one. Didn't y'hear what I said? Taquar's giving us this Jasper Bloodstone. The sandmaster has no intention of killing him! At least, not yet. The stormlord'll be forced t'bring us water till we're ready for the Time of Random Rain. Then, when all the rainlords are dead, and no one's collecting the random clouds along the edge of the Giving Sea, some will come inland to us, and we'll go back t'being true nomads."

"That idea is as daft as a legless pede. What was the matter with the way of life you had before? Davim is leading you to disaster and death. Can't you *see* that? How many of you are going to die first? What loyalty do you owe him anyway?

He had you whipped as a boy! Forced you to kill your friend. That's *sick*, Ravard. You are a greater man than that."

"I owe him everything. I grew up as poor as a pebble-mouse in a sand patch. My father spent any tokens he could get us t'earn for him on raw amber. He was slurped nine days in every ten. My mother was the settle whore, sleeping with any caravanner who passed through—"

She stared at him. "Settle? You are *Gibber born*?"

He stared back, his surprise evident. "Of course! Surely y'knew that? How else would I speak the Quartern tongue so well? And I reckon I don't sound like you city-dwelling fancy-hats from the Scarpen neither."

"I thought you must have been taught by a Gibber slave. Davim certainly collected enough of them."

"Taught by a Gibber slave? I *was* a Gibber slave!"

"Davim *enslaved* you and yet you *still* serve him?"

"In the Gibber I starved! I was cold and hungry, or thirsty and hungry. He took me and made a *man* of me. He taught me t'fight. T'stand up for meself." He stood, agitated, and waved a hand around at the tent and its contents. "Look at all this. I'm *comfortable*, Garnet. In the Gibber, we froze at night. Froze with rumbling bellies. I'm somebody now. I own things. People respect me, fear me—"

"You think all this is what makes a *man*? Davim just had you whipped, scarred you for life, and you bore it. He made you kill your friend to prove your loyalty when you were a child. And probably the only reason he not only didn't kill you, but made you the Master Son, is that he needed your water sensitivity because he had so little of his own. Is any of that the mark of a man to look up to? You want to be like him?"

"I'm the sandmaster's chosen heir. Davim wouldn't give such a place of honour to a man unworthy of his respect. Had he died in the siege of Breccia, I'd be sandmaster now. If I live longer than he does, that's what I could become."

"Don't be a sun-fried fool, Ravard. Do you think you'll still be Master Son once his own sons are grown? I hear he has several. If any of them are water sensitives, Davim'll have half a dozen spears plunged into your back the moment it suits him. If Chert had been the one who had water talent, he'd be the one sitting in this tent, not you."

That name, she'd heard it somewhere before. Presumably on the rainlord search through the Gibber to find water-sensitive children . . .

And then memory hit her like a slap in the face. She lumbered to her feet, staring at him, searching his face. "Dear pools within! Chert . . . That was the name of the palmier's son. Oh, what a sun-shrivelled *fool* I am. Sunlord save us all, you're Shale Flint's brother! *That's* why Kher Davim made you so loyal to him, not just because you are water sensitive!"

He was silent then, his speech stolen by her words.

"Why didn't I see it? There's even a bit of a resemblance! Your skin and hair are so red that I never dreamed you weren't born Reduner, dryhead that I am." No wonder something had puzzled her when he'd been speaking to Davim. His accent. And Davim had called him an outlander. She'd been stupid to be sidetracked by his colour; even her own hair and skin showed signs of a reddish stain.

"Shale Flint," she continued. "Shale Flint of Wash Drybone Settle. He had an older brother, older by about a year, called Mica."

The wary look he gave her then was a mix of worry and outright shock. Again, she was reminded of how very young he was. Young, and surprisingly vulnerable. *Pedeshit*, she thought, dismayed. *I've been bedding Jasper's bleeding brother. Oh, Sunlord's balls. How will I* ever *explain that?*

"What's it matter now who I was?" he asked at last. "Yes, I had a brother. He's probably dead. You knew him? Shale?"

"That's Jasper's real name."

"Whose—? You mean *the stormlord*? You truly are sun-shrivelled!" He laughed again, but the laugh soon faltered and died. "You're lying."

"No. Why should I?"

He stilled. The venom in his next words made her shrink away from him. "You *lie*. Shale was no stormlord!"

He whirled away from her to where his scimitar hung in its scabbard from the central tent pole.

She jumped to her feet, her heart pounding. *Sunlord save me from this sun-fried idiot of a man!*

He slid the blade out and grabbed her by the waist, twisting her back up against him so the blade lay against her throat. "Say you're lying!"

She eyed the family-sized water jar in the corner of the tent. It was closed tight. No help there. She said, "The way I heard it, you weren't a water sensitive as a child, either. Shale was – is – now more than he was. So are you."

"I'll kill you!"

"I've seen him, Ravard. Mica. I've spoken to him. He told me how Davim killed Citrine, pitted her on a chala spear—"

"Shut *up*!"

She twisted in his grasp, pushing his arm and sword away, and he let her go. She stood facing him, her arms crossed protectively over her abdomen. "You can't run away from the truth forever, Mica. You know what happened. You were *there*. You know what Davim did. What you didn't understand was why."

When he didn't reply, she risked continuing, even as she edged closer to the water jar. "He and the Highlord Taquar planned it. Taquar came to your settle with the other rainlords, remember? He tested Shale—"

"He didn't! He didn't! Shale was never tested."

"He was. And Taquar did it in secret and realised what

447

he was. He told Davim and the two of them planned for you and Shale to be taken. Taquar took Shale, Davim took you. I suppose he wanted to use you to force Shale to cooperate if need be, but then he realised it would be even better if you were on his side. Shale would do anything to save you."

He struck her then, the blow coming out of nowhere, the flat of his hand slamming into her cheek. She staggered back against the water jar. The lid jabbed into the small of her back. She turned to lean into it sideways and, even with her head ringing, managed to ease the lid off as she clutched at it for support. At least now she had access to water.

"You're lying," he said, the words, thick with venom and contempt, ripping out of him. "How could you know any of this anyway? You're just a Scarpen woman who cheated on her husband with the first handsome bladesman who passed her way."

Briefly she considered telling him she had been there, in his settle, the day Shale had been tested. *No, too risky,* she told herself. *It might jog his memory, or he might guess I am a rainlord and I want that to be a nasty surprise when I need it.*

She said nothing.

He raised his hand again. She refused to shrink from him, saying, "You can hit me all you like. You don't scare me and it won't change a thing. Davim *used* you. Taquar told him he had found a boy who had a good chance of being a stormlord, and it amused him to turn a stormlord's brother into the supposed heir to the Scarpen's worst enemy."

He heard her, and she knew her words hit home. He wasn't stupid. He was thinking the same thoughts, but just didn't want to listen to them. Waggling his scimitar in her face, he growled, "Don't say another word, or I'll kill you. Baby or not, I'll kill you."

Ryka, she thought, *take the hint. This is the moment when it would pay you to keep your mouth shut.*

He stared at her a moment longer, recognised she was not going to say anything more, then plunged out of the tent, shouting orders. She listened, and heard him give the instructions to prepare for a dawn departure.

So be it, she thought. *And I will be right behind you, Mica Flint.*

32

Red Quarter
Dune Watergatherer and further south

Ravard was busy most of the afternoon and night, supervising preparations for the journey. About three sandglass runs before dawn, he entered her room. He was carrying an oil lamp and placed it on the box. Then he sat down on the lid beside it.

She made no pretence of being asleep. "There was no need to hit me," she said, her contempt undisguised. "No *man* of stature ever does such a thing." She rolled over and sat up to stare up at him. "You go to kill or capture your brother. He spoke of you with nothing but affection. He worried endlessly you might have died. What kind of man are you?"

He refused to meet her gaze. Then, after a long silence, he said, "I'll speak to Sandmaster Davim 'bout this. We'll bring Shale back with us, to the dunes. He'll become one of us – a Reduner Kher. He'll be our stormlord, if indeed that's what he is. We can still have our random rain and yet know we need never thirst if things go wrong."

At least he was openly believing her now.

"Have a care, Mica. Davim has his own plans and if he thinks you will thwart them, he will have you killed." *And you know nothing of your own brother if you think he would join you in such a plan.*

With an unwitting similarity to her thoughts, he said, "You know nothing of our ways. Nothing!"

"*Your* ways?"

"Yes. *Mine*. I lived in hell once, son of a sot and a whore, starved and thirsty – and did any Scarpen lord care then? Did any stormlord send us more water? I *hated* that life. We were *worse* than slaves. Here on the dunes, when I was a slave, I had food in my belly, water in my skin, and a chance t'better myself. A chance t'become a man, a warrior, not some water-less scum living on the fringe of a settle begging for drink. Davim gave us a new life."

"No, he didn't. Whatever he gave you was for himself, not you. But Chert he killed and he made you do it for him. That is not the work of a man who cared for either of you."

"You know nothing! And how d'you know so much about Shale anyway?"

She stayed close to the truth. "I'm a teacher. When he came to Breccia, he needed schooling. I was one of his teachers."

He came and knelt beside her. "Garnet – Mica is dead. He died right here on the dune."

"No, he didn't. He's you. He's still there inside you."

"What d'you know about it? Mica died of ill-use as a slave. He was whipped and kicked and humiliated." He took hold of her face in both hands and held it steady, a hand span from his own. "You know what that's like? A lad of fifteen, passed around like a skin of amber, for everyone to do what they liked with."

She tried to look away, but he gripped her tighter, his thumbs digging into her cheeks. "A slave, used up the backside till there was nothing more left of him. Oh, nothing special. In Davim's tribe the warriors do it with everyone when they are new – men, women, children. And then they stop. And you're grateful 'cause they stop."

Words jerked out of her in revulsion. "Oh, waterless soul."

451

"I don't need your pity. 'Cause that's when Davim came and took what was left, and made *me*. Ravard. Warrior. Kher. He taught me t'be a Reduner; t'have pride in who I am. If Shale comes looking for Mica, he won't find him. And I reckon if I go looking for Shale, I won't find him in this Stormlord Jasper, neither. Reckon once you start sleeping in a bed under a roof and eating all that fancy fodder, you become one of them. Scarpen folk, water-soft flesh and flint-hard hearts."

She raised a hand to cup his cheek, as gentle as he was not. "And yet in *your* tribe you do not have slaves."

He shrugged. "If folk don't want t'join us, I don't want them. Other tribes can have them if they like, but not here. That's not weakness; that's strength." He pulled her hand away from his cheek.

"I don't want any more conversation from you t'night. Nor do I ever want t'hear the name Mica again, on your lips or anyone's. I am Ravard." He bent to kiss her and she acquiesced, opening her mouth to his probing tongue.

No more than what thousands of women have done through the ages, she thought. *Selling our bodies in exchange for safety. Or to avoid something more unpleasant.*

It could have been far, far worse.

But still: Jasper's *brother*?

In her heart she couldn't even bring herself to hate him, or even to hate what he did to her. He was a tormented man, and she thought in the end perhaps she suffered less than he did.

Later, in the bustle of the impending pre-dawn departure, Ryka took advantage of the lack of guards around the camp to dig up her stash of food and take it down to where the young pedes were corralled near the waterhole. The transport water jars for the war party had already been filled, and the camp guards had long since been called in to help, so there was no one to question her about where she was going or what she was doing.

She had to make several trips carrying the things she would need: panniers, water jars, bridle and saddle, blankets. She used her senses and avoided people as much as she could, but no one cared what she was doing anyway. The women were both busy and silently grieving with the knowledge their menfolk were riding to war. The men thought it beneath them to concern themselves with the affairs of women.

The war party left before it was light.

Ryka watched them go, then sought Khedrim and told him in execrable Reduner she would look after the young pedes that day. Better, she told him, that he help around the encampment because all but the very young and the very old men would be gone. He nodded, yawning, and went back to his pallet.

She slipped away in the dark to the pede yard, where she finalised the packing. Once everything was done, she rode Blackwing down to the waterhole. Keeping an anxious watch behind her, she used her power to fill the water jars, then headed south, her shadow springing into existence as the first ray of the sun tipped over the horizon onto the plain.

Blackwing flicked his antennae this way and that, sometimes reaching back to touch her in protest. It was the first time he'd been ridden any distance, the first time he'd carried a load, the first time he'd been separated from his litter mates.

"Ah, Blackwing," she murmured, "I'm not sure you are really big enough for what I am asking of you, you poor little thing."

The animal stopped then, and turned a questioning head, as if to say, "Do I have to go on still further?" Ryka gave a rueful laugh. She jabbed him with her prod, aware they mustn't drop too far behind because she had to bypass the

Reduner forces while they were in Qanatend. If she was too slow, they would reach the pass through the Warthago first.

The journey was not going to be a dew-coated stroll, not on a young pede with no idea of what it was supposed to do, and with a baby who could decide to be born any time at all. She was probably being foolish. She told herself she was taking the risk because Jasper needed to be warned an army was on its way. Just in case he hadn't been responsible for the messages. But in the end, she couldn't fool herself.

Be honest, Ryka. This journey of yours has nothing to do with warning the Scarpen and everything to do with wanting to see Kaneth. You want him to be there when his baby is born. You don't care if he is Uthardim still, you don't care if he left you behind, you want him there.

Mid-afternoon on that first day she felt a body of moving water behind her. Painfully aware of her inadequacies as a rainlord, she'd made a deliberate effort to be alert to her surroundings. Usually her concentration ended up telling her useless things like the presence of an eagle in the sky above. This time, though, it wasn't a bird. She'd just passed over the first dune south of the Watergatherer and the next was still a red line breaking the skyline ahead. She stopped Blackwing and turned to look back, but could see nothing. Her shortsightedness annoyingly blurred the line of the last dune into an amorphous mass of shades of red.

About the length of a sandglass run later, Blackwing became restless, slowing down and balking if she prodded him. When he battered at her with his antennae, expressing his annoyance, she was forced to stop. He turned his head behind, his feelers swirling in the air. She guessed he scented another pede and was rebelling at any notion she had of keeping ahead of whoever was following.

Looking back herself, she could now see a puff of dust

rising up into the air. She was being followed. Her water-sense told her only that it was a single pede, but she had no idea how many people were on it.

She gave Blackwing a piece of dried bab fruit, hoping to put him into a good mood so he would move on, but he was stubborn. *Spitless damn*, she thought, *you idiot lump of chitin! I might end up having to kill someone because of you.* She dismounted and tried leading him, but he just dug his legs into the red soil and clicked his mouthparts at her in annoyance. Worried he might take it into his head to pull the reins out of her hands and flee, she clambered up again, cursing the sheer *bulk* of her pregnancy. He still wouldn't move.

He *was* willing enough to wait, so they sat there in the sun and gradually the puff of dust grew larger and changed into a single figure on pedeback. Her eyesight was such that the rider was almost on top of her before she recognised him or his mount: Khedrim on Redwing. *Sunblast the boy.*

He drew up alongside and stared at her.

With a sinking feeling in her stomach she saw he was clutching a zigger cage full of the murderous beetles keening their hunger. Her heart flipped over.

"Khedrim, what do you think you're doing?" she asked.

"You're escaping," he accused, apparently not noticing her Reduner had suddenly improved to almost faultless diction. "And you *stole* a pede. I went to help you and you weren't there."

"So? Just go home, lad."

"Grandfather told me to come after you. He's in charge now the tribemaster and the others have gone. Redwing showed me the way – she wanted to follow Blackwing. It was easy."

"And they sent a single boy after me? Do they expect me to calmly return with you?"

"What can you do?" he asked scornfully. "You're just a woman, and a slave. And you're having a baby. There's nothing you can do. Besides, I have ziggers." He waved the cage at her. The beetles screamed in anger. "And a scimitar."

"Your grandfather told you to *kill* me?"

"No. That's just to threaten you with."

"And if I still say no?"

An astonished look spread over his face. "But you wouldn't want to die!"

"No, I wouldn't. However, I *am* refusing to go back with you. The question remains, then, are you willing to kill by releasing a zigger? Or several ziggers?"

Astonishment turned to confusion. It had obviously never occurred to him this could be the outcome. "You're scoffing me," he said at last.

"No, I'm not. I'm not going back with you. I am riding on."

His reply was a wail. "You can't! I'd have to let a zigger out!" He looked as if he was about to weep.

"Khedrim," she said as kindly as she could, "I am wearing the correct perfume."

"You're lying. No one gives the perfume to *slaves*."

"Maybe not, but I stole some of Kher Ravard's. Look, why don't you go home and say you couldn't find me."

"That's not *true*. Besides, I have to stop you. Otherwise you might warn the Scarpen folk our warriors are coming."

"Ah. Then we are at a . . ." She tried to think of a Reduner word meaning impasse, couldn't, and changed what she had been going to say. "I don't think we can find a solution then, at least not one that will suit you."

She glanced at the ziggers in the cage and sucked the water out of them, one by one, taking care not to hurt Khedrim in the process. "Sorry about this, but I think it's the best solution."

He didn't understand at first. Then he realised the ziggers were silent and looked down. Water dripped out of the cage. The dried up husks looked no more harmful than the curl of a dead leaf.

He gaped, his jaw sagging, as he struggled to comprehend what had happened.

She didn't wait for his realisation, but jabbed her prod into the gap between Blackwing's head and thorax. Startled, the pede leaped forward.

Unfortunately, Redwing, now she had caught up, wasn't about to let her litter mate disappear again. She sprang after him without waiting for any signal from her driver. Khedrim jerked in shock and the zigger cage went flying out of his hands. He grabbed for the reins.

Ryka cursed. The lad was not trying to rein the animal in; he was urging it on. "Witless boy," she muttered. "Surely he knows now what I am and what I can do to him."

Redwing was the stronger animal and she was soon streaming along level with Blackwing. Khedrim yelled at Ryka to stop. Redwing, apparently convinced this was a fascinating game, paced herself to match Blackwing's speed perfectly. Her nearside feeler entwined with Blackwing's in a playful caress.

"Go home! Go home before I kill you," Ryka roared at Khedrim. "I'm a rainlord, you stupid sand-tick! I can dry you up like those ziggers . . ." She wondered briefly if she could blind the pede to stop the lad. *Oh, blast it, if I disable the beast, how will Khedrim get back to camp? He could die out here . . .*

Khedrim glanced away, bending down, struggling with something strapped to Redwing's other side. Almost too late, Ryka realised what he was doing. The silly boy had brought a chala spear with him. And he intended to use it. On her. Even as she absorbed that, he had leaped to his feet, perfectly balanced on the saddle, feet hooked under the segment handle and his arm drawing back, preparing to throw.

The waterless little shit, she thought, with more exasperation than rancour. So typical of a boy's game, endlessly practised, now turning deadly with such ease. She dragged back on the reins. Indignant, Blackwing threw up his head, but his feeler was still locked with Redwing's and the two young animals slowed together.

In the split second left to make a decision, Ryka dismissed the idea of throwing herself to the ground as too dangerous, declined to blind the lad as too cruel and rejected the obvious alternative, of drying the flesh on the hand that held the spear, as too crippling. Instead, she drew out the water from one of the bare toes poking out of his sandal.

He screamed in agony, lost his balance and fell from the still-moving pede.

The two animals parted. Redwing, freed of the weight of her rider, came slowly to a puzzled halt. Ryka pulled Blackwing around in a wide circle to return to where Khedrim lay, unmoving, on the ground. Quickly, she hobbled Blackwing's feelers together with the reins to prevent the pede from wandering and slid off to run to the boy.

Even before she reached him, she knew he was dead. His neck was broken, his eyes open, unblinking and lifeless. She fell to her knees, keening.

Khedrim, oh Khedrim.

The day before he had been happy and obliging. Today, blood seeped sluggishly from his nose and ear, spreading a dark red stain on bright red soil.

So needlessly dead.

She rocked to and fro beside him, cursing, trying to make it not true. She cursed Davim and Taquar and Ravard and their senseless dreams of vanquishing the rainlords. She cursed their cruel vision of returning to a Time of Random Rain.

And tried, in vain, not to curse herself for making a mistake. *A boy dead. Was it worth it, Ry?*

Then, because she was Ryka – pragmatic, unromantic Ryka Feldspar the historian – she took Khedrim's water. When she left him, he was no more than a dry husk, bones and teeth wrapped in sinew and parchment skin all draped with red cloth, his skull adorned with red-stained hair and shiny agate beads tumbling around his face.

She rode on, stony faced, with her load evenly spread over two young pedes.

33

"They are here." Shale's – no, *Jasper's* – pede prod jabbed at the map spread out on the ground. Terelle had to remember he was Jasper now, among these people. He was Jasper to himself, too. She had to let go of the person he had been and the name he had used. Jasper, the stormlord, that was how she had to think of him.

She glanced around at the people gathered around him under the canopy strung up outside Iani's tent. Eleven of them – seven rainlords representing all the Scarpen cities, two Alabasters, two Gibbermen. Light and shadow danced crazily when Messenjer joggled the lantern hooked on the roof pole over his head.

"That's the cavern of the mother cistern of Qanatend," Iani muttered, identifying the map symbol under the point of Jasper's prod. "Those red bastards are camped at the city's water source." He shook his head. "Poor Moiqa. How will she cope if she knows that?"

As everyone else believed Moiqa was dead, no one knew quite what to say.

Terelle, at the back of the group, frowned and came in closer to see. "And where are we?" she asked.

It was Iani who answered her question, kneeling to place

his finger on a point still further south from Qanatend and its mother cistern. "Here. We're at the northern end of Pebblebag Pass. We're way above the cistern. From here it's more or less downhill all the way, until you get to Qanatend. Beyond that, flat lands, then the Red Quarter. And Davim. One day I will kill him."

"The trail?" asked Feroze, who now knew Iani well enough by now to ignore this last.

"It follows the dried-out floor of the wash. Narrow, enclosed by steep valley sides. In front of the cavern of the mother cistern, it opens into a huge flattish area divided by the stream bed. Reckon that back in the days of random rain the gully got blocked and it filled up with soil until it was as flat as a griddle. Not much vegetation anywhere – nothing that would offer any cover to either side. After that, the trail narrows again all the way to the bottom. To Qanatend. Moiqa's city, you know."

"The cavern?" Jasper asked. Like Feroze, he ignored Iani's deviation from the matter at hand. "What's it like?"

"The holding cisterns and inlet and outlet pipes are all inside. The cavern itself is set in a cliff. Rather like the Scarcleft mother cistern. There is a narrow gully coming down from the catchment area higher in the mountains. It ends directly above the cavern, hanging there. Once, when an extra large rush came down after a cloudbreak, the water fell over the cliff like a lace curtain in front of the cavern." He gave a snort. "Real waste, that was. Usually the water is piped directly into the cistern from a pool above, through some cavities and a couple of small caves inside the cliff."

Feroze scratched his face thoughtfully. Mirrors twinkled in the lamplight as if he was covered with fireflies. "Can we attack them through that hanging valley?"

"It's inaccessible except by climbing the cliff near the cavern opening."

461

"Didn't I hear that when the Reduners attacked Breccia City they found another way through the Warthago besides Pebblebag Pass?" That was Ouina.

"So Kaneth told us," Jasper agreed. "Iani?"

"My scouts found that route. It starts not far from here, right inside the Pebblebag. They used it because the Breccian forces were watching the southern entrance to the pass. It was no more than a way of bypassing the watchers. I've made sure they won't be going that way again, but it's of no use to us." He stabbed at the map. "If Davim's forces are moving up, and we assume they are, tomorrow night they will camp here. And the night after that, they should be just below where we are now – about here." His finger jabbed again.

"How do we know where they'll camp?" This time it was Messenjer who asked. "And why so slow?"

"Because that's what they did last time. Tent poles and pede lines and fires leave marks. Besides, those two places have the only flattish land between the cistern and here. And you don't move a large force up a narrow, steep track as if you were running a race." Iani looked around the group, wiping away the dribble from his chin with the back of his hand, before he scrambled clumsily to his feet. "They are a much larger force than us, but they'll lose the advantage because they will be squeezed into the narrow drywash."

"How can ye be so certain where they are now?" The question came from Feroze.

"They're a large enough force for me to feel them," Jasper said. "I can't estimate numbers, though I suspect Davim has at least two thousand more men than we do. Because of the narrowness of the valley, that will not necessarily be an advantage. Fortunately for us, too, they will have no reason to think themselves threatened. We hope they expect to fight Taquar at Scarcleft." He looked around the group. "Iani knows this country, and he's fought the Reduners. He's our Overman.

However, we need someone with more experience with pedes and knowledge of fighting from pedeback. Envoy Feroze will be that man, answerable only to Iani. In the battle, I will be responsible only for the deployment of my own stormlord powers."

Clever, Terelle thought, *to divide the command like that.* It wasn't easy to please everyone.

Feroze straightened up, a smile deepening the rifts on his salt-white face. "It would be an honour to my people. We shall spend some time in prayer for our endeavour before we sleep tonight."

"There is one question I have," Jasper added, addressing Feroze. "You use spears in battle. So do Reduners."

"That's right. Each warrior is expected to be riding with two spears, the first for throwing and the second for stabbing and lancing. The balance is different."

"Who makes them?"

For a moment the salt merchant froze. "What do ye mean?" he asked after a pause far too long for such a simple question.

"Those spears of yours, and the Reduner ones too – they're made of wood. Straight poles of wood. We have bab wood, certainly unsuitable for such shafts. Our other trees are gnarled, their wood twisted. The Red and the White Quarters have no wood at all. The Scarpen and the Gibber buy good wood, if they want it, from over the Giving Sea. Where does yours come from?"

"Ye have a reason for asking besides mere curiosity?"

"Indeed I do," Jasper snapped, beginning to lose his patience. "Reduner marauders have been fighting you and the Gibbermen for several years now. They mounted an attack on Qanatend and Breccia. I can only assume many of their spears have been broken in all that fighting. The spearheads they may have been able to salvage and sharpen – but the hafts? They will need replacing. *So where will they get their wood?*"

"Ah. I see. Stormlord, this is not something for public discussion—"

"We are allies, Feroze! It's not a time for secrets!"

The Samphire gate, Terelle thought, suddenly remembering. The gateway to the Alabasters' city had been hung with two huge wooden doors. The thick planks must have come from trees that were too large for her to even imagine. *We don't have anything remotely like them in the Scarpen or the Gibber.*

Feroze swallowed uneasily. "They used to be buying their spears from us. A few years back, Dune Watergatherer bought a great many. They told us wood beetles had burrowed into their armoury tent and ruined those they had. And they needed many more tent poles for the same reason."

"You supplied just the wood?"

"Er, no. The spearheads as well. I understand the Red Quarter does not have fuel for much ironworking."

"And I assume tent poles could be whittled down to make a replacement haft for a chala spear?"

"I suppose so."

Jasper held the Alabaster's gaze with a hard look. Terelle expected him to ask where the Alabasters obtained their iron and wood and fuel, but he said merely, "What's your assessment of the Reduner preparedness with regard to weaponry?"

"I would say it is not a problem for them."

One of the two Gibbermen in the group glared at Feroze, teeth bared in a snarl. "You salt-heads got what y'withering deserved when the Reduners turned on you, eh?" A rock collector from Wash Gereth named Lourouth, the speaker was a grizzled, lanky man who had spent most of his life traipsing the plains on the hunt for gemstones. His pragmatic ability to manage, even when he was without resources, had earned him the leadership of the disparate band of Gibber folk. What he was not renowned for was his tact. "Thought you could sell them red m'rauders spears and not get 'em back in your arse one day, huh?"

Hurriedly Jasper interrupted. "Iani will now brief you all on the plans for the next two days. If you have any comments afterwards, feel free to voice them." He nodded for Iani to take over, and then retreated from the group. As they turned their attention to the rainlord, he beckoned to Terelle.

When she joined him, he murmured, "We need to talk."

She had not seen much of him since they'd joined the rest of the army. There was always another storm to bring, another problem to solve, another argument to settle, another decision to make. And no matter what else was happening, somewhere or another the Quartern needed to have water supplied.

He had even stopped openly posing for her paintings. She painted one each day, distinguishing it from the previous ones by introducing a new object, such as an item of clothing or weaponry lying on the ground where he was to conjure up his cloud. Each day he surreptitiously matched his surroundings to the painting already done. That way they avoided any association between her paintings and his stormshifting. "After all," he told her with one of his rare grins, "I don't want to get a reputation for an unhealthy need to have my portrait painted every day."

As for Terelle, if anyone disturbed her while she was painting, she covered the tray with a cloth and said she preferred no one to see her unfinished work. In fact, although she was careful not to harm a shuffled-up painting *before* it came true, she destroyed each after Jasper had successfully acted on it.

They continued to hide her power and cultivate the notion she was just an artist who recorded the stormlord's history in paintings. She would not have minded this, except that her lack of stature allowed Senya to spread the rumour Terelle was of dubious lineage, the product of a snuggery liaison and – as to be expected from such a mongrel mix – unbalanced and strange. The snuggery girl had been lost in the Whiteout too, for days, Senya added. Perhaps that explained things . . .

Terelle simmered with the injustice of it all. She doubted Jasper had any idea how often she woke in the night doubled up with cramp. She knew why: although her mind knew she had to return to Russet, she longed to stay with Jasper. Every time she felt nauseous and in pain, she had to spend time thinking of how she would travel back to the White Quartern and then on to the land of the Watergivers. After a while, she would feel better. For a time.

And always there was that other hurt: Jasper had bedded Senya. She knew she had no right to be so pained; his promise to her had been nebulous at best. She now knew that he had been told, over and over, that he had to marry a rainlord. What right had she to be hurt? And yet it rankled. No, more than that. She felt brutally betrayed. *Senya.* So pretty and shallow and *dumb.*

As they headed towards his tent, she asked, "Why didn't you press Feroze to tell you where the Alabasters get the wood for their spears?"

"Because he didn't want to tell me and I didn't want to upset him. Besides, I think I know."

"Khromatis."

He nodded. "Where else?"

"They keep a lot of secrets." Briefly she told him all the things that had puzzled her when she was in the salt mines and Samphire. The lack of any evidence of how they worked their metal or made their mirrors, the huge gates of Samphire, the salt caravan that had gone eastwards, the way they called themselves Guardians, yet wouldn't explain what they were Guardians of, their knowledge of Watergivers and the power of waterpainting.

"They have so many secrets," she said. "If I asked questions, they either lied or dodged answering."

"Tell me about the Bastion."

"He's an old man, but sharp still. When I met him, he was surrounded by council members, and it was all very formal. He said he would arrange to send an army, even though the Scarpen under Cloudmaster Granthon had not helped them when the Alabasters asked for it. He told me I had to use my waterpainting powers. He promised to see that Russet was cared for. And then I was dismissed."

"Did you speak to many other people?"

She shook her head. "I had the feeling that they were keeping an eye on me to make sure I didn't. Messenjer and his wife and sons were with me all the time. D'you know – I never saw a single person in Samphire who wasn't an Alabaster. It's not like a Scarpen city."

"What do you think they are Guardians of?"

"The border to Khromatis? I don't know. I'm just guessing."

"Could be right. But best we don't ask, I think. Not yet. They are our allies, and I don't want to upset them. Anyway, that wasn't why I asked you to come with me." They had reached his tent by then, and he raised the flap for her to enter. "I want to show you something."

His was the largest tent in the camp – in fact most of the men had no tents at all. It had been an Alabaster tent originally, roomy and furnished with their colourful rugs and blankets. She thought, *They make themselves comfortable when they travel, these Alabasters.* He waved her over to sit on one of the wooden chests next to his pallet, then pulled the cloth from a small cage to show her the contents.

"Ziggers," he said. "I had them brought from Scarcleft."

She had a flash of memory, Donnick the gateman dying at her feet, the zigger crawling on his cheek . . .

"I'd heard you refused to bring them. That you weren't

going to let our people use them." She meant to sound impartial, but the distaste in her tone was obvious.

"I'm not. These are for you to study, so you can paint them. Paint them dead. I wanted you to have a look at them alive first."

She quelled her revulsion and bent to look. Mindlessly, the ziggers flung themselves at the bars, trying to get to her, their drilling mouthparts whirring obscenely as they slavered. She jerked away, remembering that night in the snuggery. Remembering the blood. Remembering the death of a youth with a kind heart and simple mind.

"I have an idea," Jasper continued. "From something a man said to me while I was in Breccia City, just after the Reduners came. He said ziggers are attracted to lantern light . . . and later I saw it myself. Dead ziggers, burned against the hot glass of a lantern, or seared by candle flame and sizzling in the candle grease. My idea won't kill all the ziggers, but it might get rid of a great many of them, without the slightest danger to our men. I'll kill a few of these later, so you know what they look like after hitting the lantern. Tomorrow you'll come down the wash with me, to a point just above where I think the Reduners will camp two nights from now. I want you to be able to paint the place accurately."

She nodded but didn't speak.

He grimaced wryly. "We need all the help we can get, Terelle. Nothing will change the fact that the Reduners have more warriors than us. Seasoned warriors. While our men are salt traders, or potters, or gem cutters, or grove croppers."

He's scared, she thought. *But he'll never show it.* "How much painting do you want me to do?"

"An awful lot by the day after tomorrow."

At Jasper's request, and using his money, she had scoured the Scarcleft markets before they'd left, buying all the painting materials and ingredients she could find. He'd been planning ahead, of course; being the Cloudmaster when she just wanted a friend; being a stormlord, when she wanted someone to put his arms around her, and tell her he cared.

"Terelle," he said after she'd been silent a while, "we don't seem to talk any more. What's wrong?"

She settled her expression into bland indifference. "Well now," she said thoughtfully, "that might have something to do with the fact you're always so busy. Or not around. Or it might have something to do with your apparent preference for that spoiled brat of a Senya." *Oh, Watergiver take it, I never meant to say that.* Her face felt hot in spite of the cold night air. She stood up abruptly and left the tent.

Behind her, Jasper was wrestling with himself, wanting to call her back. But to say what, exactly? "Terelle, I didn't want to bed Senya." "I only did it once." "I know I bedded her, but I don't like her, not really." "I'd much prefer to take you to bed, but you've got to understand, everyone says I have to marry Senya."

He sighed. At least he hadn't been stupid enough to give voice to any of those sentiments. He didn't know much about women, but he had a fair idea not one of those excuses would have been well received.

Damn it all to waterless hell. I'm the Cloudmaster, and I still can't have what I want.

"Can you tell if they've already moved from the cistern?" Terelle asked. It was a strain keeping the conversation neutral, but they were both doing their best. She sneaked a look at Jasper where he stood, holding the reins of the myriapede, looking down the wash. She wondered what it would be like to fit the curves of her body to his . . . and stopped the thought abruptly.

"I have them in my mind," he said. "I feel them coming,

like a horde of – of bugs tramping their way up the stem of a plant. A long line of them coming up the wash towards us. They will camp just around that bend there tomorrow night. You'll have to finish the paintings before their first scouts arrive, probably around mid-afternoon tomorrow. We'll need to be gone by then, but we'll leave everything in place. I will come back at night with some of the Gibbermen and rainlords to light the lanterns. Their sentries will spot them."

She nodded again.

He walked over to unload the pede, extracted a lantern and placed it on a rock, well away from the trail. "There's your first one."

"Won't their scouts notice any of these?"

His smile was playfully artless. "I'm assuming they won't find them because your paintings will have ensured the future is that they don't."

Unable to joke about waterpainting power, she went to fetch her painting things and begin to prepare the first of the trays, blessing the extravagance of buying thirty of them in Scarcleft.

"I can do all the motley bases now for the trays I have," she told him, "but I won't be able to paint until I see what everything looks like at night. Jasper, are you *sure* the ziggers will be attracted by the lanterns?"

"Ziggers use their sense of smell as well as their eyesight, especially at night, or that's what the Scarcleft guards say. Someone will have to be here to provide the enticing smell to bring them in first. A few rainlords and me. Live bait. We'll wait beyond the lanterns. With luck, they'll be confused by the lights before they ever find us."

"If they do like to sizzle themselves on lanterns, won't the Reduners know that and not use them at night?"

"They used ziggers the night they attacked Breccia, so I think they will here, too. They'll expect to lose some, but I reckon they think most would rather find something to eat than butt heads with a lantern glass."

She shuddered just thinking of him being bait for ziggers. "Tether a pede here," she said. "It'd be safer. I think someone once told me that they feed off pedes in the wild."

"Yes, and a few ziggers wouldn't harm them. But there won't be just a few, there'll be thousands. I won't kill pedes. If any get past the lanterns, we rainlords can deal with them."

"You shouldn't risk yourself. This land depends on you. We all depend on you."

"I can't ask people to do what I will not do myself."

"You're more important than they are."

"I know that."

"Then—"

"Forget it, Terelle." His tone implied he would not listen to anything else she had to say on the subject. She suppressed a sigh as she squinted up at him from where she knelt in front of her tray. "How many ziggers do you think they'll release?"

"Believe me, there's no way you can paint as many as they have. Just portray as many as you can. However many die will mean less for them to use elsewhere."

She nodded and started to fill her trays while he watched. "Sh—, um, Jasper," she said after a moment, "I've been meaning to ask you, did you ever hear from the rebel Reduners in answer to your sky messages?"

"Vara Redmane? No, but then how would they reply anyway?"

"Can you feel them, the way you feel those forces coming towards us?"

He smiled at her. "I wish I could say yes. But at that distance, it's tough. There are waterholes and camps – those have enough water for me to locate and they don't shift, either. But people moving from place to place?" He shook his head. "Not unless they were really bunched together like Davim's forces. I sent the message for her to the area that she was supposed to be hiding in, far to the north. I heard that much about her ages ago, before Breccia fell. Oh, and I did send another message visible to all the dunes once Davim was on his way."

She looked up, interested. "What did you say?"

"That Davim's warriors were on the move, coming to attack the Scarpen and now would be a good time for rebels to try to attack him from the rear if they wanted their freedom. If they wanted me to bring water to their dunes."

"But Davim will have seen those messages, too."

"Perhaps. Though I did wait until he was already on his way up the wash." He made a gesture of irritation. "It's so difficult to know what to do, or what effect any of it has had. I can't even tell if they have read the messages! Not all that many Reduners ever learn to read." He shrugged, summing up his inadequacies. "I miss Lord Ryka. She knew so much more about them than anyone else. In the end I sent out messages in the Quartern tongue as well as Reduner. I thought if Vara Redmane, or any of the tribes, had contact with Scarpen slaves, there would be a chance of one of them understanding and passing the message on."

"So we just have to hope someone in the Red Quarter is stirring up trouble for any forces Davim left behind."

He nodded. "I have to go back to the camp. I am leaving a couple of guards with you. If you need anything, ask."

She nodded and smiled a farewell.

As he turned and walked away, wind whistled up the drywash, scurrying the dust along like the sweepings of an invisible broom, but it wasn't the wind making her shiver. It was fear, and the knowledge that she was twisting the future of the men coming up the wash to suit those waiting for them at the top.

*　　*　　*

She painted all night and into the next morning. Each time she completed a picture, she checked it carefully to see if she had the details right: the exact way each lantern or lamp sat on the ground, the configuration of the stones at its base, the scratches on that particular lantern. Then she shuffled up the ziggers into the heart of the suggestive blotches she had already sketched in: hundreds of them in each picture. Dead or dying ziggers, grouped around each lantern, their wings frizzled against the heat of the glass. And then she moved on to another tray. When she had finished a number of them, she came back and cut the picture from the first ones, their purpose already defined, their power already stamped, for better or for worse, on the future. And so on to a different lantern, in a slightly different place – and another picture.

All morning she was aware of people coming and going up and down the wash. Scouts to watch for the arrival of Reduners. Jasper, to check on her progress. Feroze the Alabaster, Lord Iani and Lourouth the Gibberman, to check on the terrain – those three passed her by, discussing the positioning of their men, and hardly noticed her presence.

Laisa came once and watched her with shrewd eyes. She knelt by the tray Terelle was working on, staring. Then she said, "You're not what you seem, are you?"

"I don't know what you mean, Lord Laisa."

The rainlord used her forefinger to turn Terelle's face until their gaze met. "No one paints the same thing over and over – dead ziggers at that – just to record a history that has not yet happened. What are you hiding?"

Terelle jerked her head away. Sandblast it, she hated the way the woman tried to make her feel like a child. "Not as much as you, at a guess. Tell me, my lord, are you on the side of the Scarpen and Jasper now, or is it just a temporary thing? Will you betray him the first time someone offers you something better?"

Without answering, Laisa left in her usual swirl of silk and clink of jewellery, trailing her perfume behind like the lingering musky scent of a horned cat.

Sometime around midday, Jasper laid a hand on her shoulder. "The first of their scouts is not far away," he said quietly. "I want us to be out of here soon."

She sat back on her heels and nodded. Shuffling, she decided, was exhausting. She finished the picture she was working on and stood, stretching aching muscles. Salted damn, but she was hungry!

"You've drawn thousands of ziggers," he told her. "Far more than I thought was possible. Congratulations." He gathered up the paints and trays. "Let's get you back to camp. You've done your bit; the rest is up to other people now."

It's not enough, she thought. *No matter how many are killed here, it still won't be enough. They'll have more.* In spite of the heat of the sun and the warm blast of the wind, she felt cold, shrunken. Tomorrow, led by a handful of rainlords, Jasper's ill-prepared men would have to face a large army.

He cradled her as he rode back to their camp. It should have felt good to be there, safe. His arms were strong, his muscles hard, his hold secure. Yet when he took a hand off the reins to brush hair away from her cheek in a gesture of care and concern, she would have liked to turn her face into his tunic and cry.

"You have tears on your lashes," he said.

"That happens to me sometimes," she mumbled. "So silly. Shale, be careful, won't you? Not because you're a stormlord and we need you, but because – because I don't want anything to happen to you. Please."

She'd forgotten to call him Jasper, but he didn't seem to mind because he grinned, that rare grin of his which lit up his face from the inside. "I don't want anything to happen to me, either." He bent his head and she knew he was about to kiss her. She wanted it so badly, she hardly knew herself. And then he withdrew. "Damn," he said softly. "We have company."

Feroze and Iani rode up with a group of their bladesmen, wanting to discuss more details of their plans for the next day, and it wasn't long before Jasper was suggesting she ride back to their camp in the pass without him. "Do you want me to send someone with you?" he asked.

Still reeling from her exhaustion, she was tempted to say yes. Instead, she shook her head. "No, I'll be fine. Really. You – you take care."

He nodded and changed before her eyes from Shale to Jasper, stormlord. He seemed suddenly regal, greeting the men, giving orders, overriding her assurance she could ride back herself, and sending her on her way seated behind Iani's driver. As she looked back one last time to see the group listening to his every word, she knew they would never again sit on the floor side by side to play a game of Lords and Shells. They would never again feel young.

Tomorrow he would be a man who led his people to war.

34

Red Quarter and Scarpen Quarter
Dunes and Warthago Range

Ryka had never been so weary. Long days on the saddle under a hot sun had merged into one another, each spent dodging dune encampments and driving the two young pedes out of the way to avoid groups of riders. The quarter was alive with warriors on the move, riding between dunes and along dunes and across dunes to assemble at their agreed meeting point. She was always tense: straining her inadequate eyesight to glimpse riders, straining her unreliable water-sense to track approaching pedes and men so she could evade them, straining her own cumbersome body with too many hours on pedeback.

Finally – how many days was it? She couldn't remember – she crossed the southernmost dune undetected. Ahead was the Scarpen; ahead somewhere was safety. And Kaneth. But her backtracking and detours had delayed her far too much. And so she rode on towards the Warthago Range, knowing that for her, the sand was running too fast through the glass. She bypassed Qanatend at night, stealing water from a pede livery outside the walls as she rode by. She hoped somewhere within were Ravard and Davim and their men, but she knew it was more likely they were still ahead of her, already pushing their way deep into the Scarpen.

The track upwards was hard on the young pedes. They had

never encountered such a steady climb and they fussed and clicked their anxiety. Whichever one she was riding would swing its feelers behind to flick her in irritation, sometimes grazing her skin with their spines. She found herself bribing them with treats more and more often, just so they would keep going. The second day past Qanatend was even worse than the first because she wasn't feeling well. She'd lost her appetite. Her back ached. No matter how she wriggled or squirmed, she couldn't find a comfortable way of sitting on the saddle.

And then the reason struck her. *Oh no. Not now.* Then, aloud and even more anguished, "Nooooo." Her baby was on its way. And she was still short of the mother cistern. Blackwing, sensing her inattention, ambled to a halt and turned to look at her. She raised her head, pulled a face at him and gave him a prod between the segments. When he'd started up again, she turned her senses upwards. Water, a lot of it. The cistern was only a couple of hours further on. Her powers were not sufficient to tell her what she would find there, not from this distance and not against a background of so much water. As hard as she tried, she couldn't sense people or pedes until she was dangerously close to them.

You have no choice, Ryka. Push on – and hope there are no Reduners there. Hope they are all still back in Qanatend. And perhaps you had better consider turning religious as well because a prayer or two might be in order . . .

A little voice that had been bothering her thoughts ever since she'd left the Watergatherer whispered, *Do you really think the Reduners in Qanatend would leave their water supply unguarded?*

You're a rainlord. You can do this, Ryka, she told herself, *you know you can.*

She shouldn't listen to the little voices in her head; they never said cheery things, blast them.

* * *

It never occurred to her that Kaneth had not stuck to their original plan. It did not cross her mind that, once he realised his group of escaping slaves was without a rainlord to tell them when they were in danger, he would decide it was safer to trek north to join forces with a woman fast becoming a legend: Vara Redmane.

It was just after sunset, but there was still light in the sky as Jasper, Laisa and Lord Ouina of Breakaway silently led a group of Gibbermen down the slope from where they'd left their pedes, to the lanterns. Overhead, Jasper amassed waiting clouds to cloak the sky until the night had an eerie sombreness. The lack of star-shine reduced the normal exuberance of the Gibbermen to wide-eyed silence.

"A black sky," one of them had muttered earlier, eyes wide with fear. "Whoever heard of such a thing?"

"It's unnatural," his companion whispered. "It's like walkin' down an adit after your lamp blew out."

Even after Jasper had explained, they weren't any happier. Spooked by a darkness they had never known, they were like pebblemice caught out in the open, startled at every little sound, jumping at the sight of a scraggy bush looming up out of the shadows.

To Jasper's surprise, nothing went wrong even though the men were jittery. They dispersed to light the lanterns and camp fires. When they returned, he sent them back to the Scarpen camp, leaving the three rainlords behind.

"Now I know what it is like to be a decoy mouse, set in the windhover trap," Laisa said in Jasper's ear as they waited for the Reduners to react. "You had better be right about this, Gibber boy, because there is no way two of us can dry up thousands of ziggers."

"You won't have to," he said, trying to express a confidence that suddenly seemed absurd.

She asked, "Are you going to explain just what that little snuggery girl of yours had to do with all this?"

"No," he said. "I'm not. There's nothing to tell. The Reduners will see the lamps and fires, they'll think it's our camp. They will loose their ziggers, we will stand here on the far side of the lamps. The ziggers will home in on our smell, but be distracted by the light. They'll fry themselves. Once they start coming, we move away."

"Sounds ridiculous to me," Ouina said with a scornful snort.

"To me, too," Laisa agreed.

Both women then proceeded to raise all the same questions that Terelle had, plus a few of their own, to ridicule the idea that the Reduners would release their ziggers.

Jasper listened patiently, and wondered what they would say if he said he knew it would happen because Terelle had painted it that way . . . It did sound ridiculous when you put it like that.

In the end Laisa did in fact ask, "And what the hells was that girl of yours painting dead ziggers for?"

"She's superstitious, that's all. She believes painting dead ziggers means all the ziggers will die."

"That's absurd!"

"Yes, isn't it?" he agreed, smiling blandly. Underneath his cheerful exterior, he wondered how long it would be before Laisa began to put two and two together and came up with an approximation of the truth. He had a horrible idea that if and when she did, it would mean trouble for Terelle.

"What's happening?"

"The dark is eating the sky!"

Fear surrounded them on all sides. It was there in the whispers, in the eyes raised upwards, in the harsh curses and the soft-spoken prayers, in the way men crowded together as if there was safety in proximity. Ravard was exasperated.

These were the same men who displayed no fear when facing the reality of death in battle?

He and Davim and Medrim, the Warrior Son, moved among them, trying to dispel the fear and calm the mounting panic. "The stars are still there. Nothing is eating them, it's just a cloud blocking your view of the sky."

"You afraid of a cloud now? What, you reckon it will come and eat you, too?"

Embarrassed, the men began to disperse as the word spread. Ravard, still carrying his burning pitch torch, returned to where their tents were erected, to find Davim had already arrived back and was now in conversation with Medrim and a Reduner whom Ravard didn't know. "This chalaman was on sentry duty up the gully to the south," Medrim was telling Davim. "There are lights and fires on the hillside above us, apparently a large camp. He reckons the Scarpen army must have come down just after dark and settled in for the night."

"Damned quiet about it they were too, but they aren't trying to hide the lights, so they can't know we are so close," the chalaman added.

Ravard grinned, touched by an unexpected excitement. *War.* Battle: the promise of it was there in the shine of the sentry's eyes, in the anticipation of his tone.

"Show us," Davim ordered. "How many men do you estimate?"

"Several thousand, maybe? There must be a couple of hundred lamps at least, and a number of cooking fires. It's too sandblasted dark to see much, though, with the stars gone, and no way a scout can get close, not without making a racket."

Ravard knew Medrim's estimate was probably accurate. He was an experienced warrior. He was also Davim's uncle and he'd held the same position under the previous sandmaster. He would keep it, Ravard guessed, until one of Davim's sons was old enough to fill the role. *I just wish he was a wiser man. We could do with some wisdom now. Experience is not everything . . .*

Uneasily, he looked up. Half the night sky was still blotted out. *Why?* he wondered. *So we don't have starlight to see when they attack? But then, how can they attack if they can't see either? They'd be stumbling all over the place and we'd hear them coming.* It didn't make sense, and Ravard didn't like things that didn't make sense.

Some time later, when they rounded a turn in the gully where the last row of sentries was posted, they had a view up the wash to the Pebblebag Pass. On the hill slope there were scattered lights and flickering camp fires.

"You're right, Medrim. That's not a scouting party," Davim remarked, keeping his voice low even though they were too far away to be heard. "Too large by far. This is an attack force."

"Not Taquar's, surely?" Medrim asked.

"Hardly. This is the stormlord's trap for us."

Ravard struggled with that. "The message was from him, not Taquar?" *The bastard! Davim knew all along. But he was worried the other tribes might give us trouble if they knew we were riding into a trap.*

"Did you doubt it? Seems they are bringing the fight to us." He smiled. "I've been expecting something like this ever since I found out there have also been sky messages for that old bag of bones, Vara Redmane. As if the sandcrazy old bitch could read them! I hadn't expected they would set the trap so far down the gully, but I am glad they have. We will teach them the folly of their leadership."

"We attack?" Ravard asked, trying to sound nonchalant. His heart beat faster in his eagerness. And yet another niggling thought refused to be cast out entirely: what if Garnet wasn't lying? What if Jasper Bloodstone and Shale Flint were one and the same person – and Shale was up there somewhere? *Shale,*

*always being beaten down by Pa, and yet so bleeding stubborn
he never gave in.*

"Ever the warrior, aren't you, Ravard! I know you'd rather
wield a sword than a zigger, but there are better ways of
winning a battle than poking your nose into a scorpion's hole
and getting it stung." Ravard couldn't see the sandmaster's
smile, but he heard it in his tone as the man clapped Medrim
on the back. "Let loose some ziggers up there – they'll do a
better job than we ever could."

"How many?" Medrim asked.

"Make a thorough job of it. Send five thousand. We
wouldn't want any of the Scarpermen to miss out, would we?"
His tone told Ravard he was wearing that feral grin of his,
that glint in his eye only ever fuelled by blood lust. Davim
loved ziggers in a way Ravard never had.

"Five thousand?" Ravard was taken aback. A zigger that had
gorged on human flesh was sated and useless for three days.
A third of their ziggers would be out of action. And only Dune
Watergatherer had that many.

Medrim warned, "We'll lose quite a few. They'll fly into
the flames or sizzle themselves on the lantern glass."

"Some, yes." Davim didn't sound worried. "But once those
men start screaming and running, they'll be better targets
than a lantern, believe me."

Ravard rubbed irritably at the back of his neck as they
returned to the camp, leaving the sentry at his post. So many
things seemed to be bothering him lately. He hadn't liked the
idea of returning to the southern Scarpen in first place. While
he approved of the idea of being free of the power of stormlords and returning to a Time of Random Rain, Davim's quest
for power and his hatred of all Scarpen folk smelled dangerously passionate to Ravard. Passion was fine in a warrior, but
in a leader? A man wanted to feel he was being led by someone
who used his head, not his temper, to make decisions.

482

When he arrived in Qanatend, Ravard had tried to counsel caution, but Davim had not been in the mood to listen, especially not when the usually bold Master Son preached prudence. Davim then asked him, with considerable asperity, if Ravard had lost his guts. Medrim, the sunblasted old bastard, had laughed.

"So what if it is a trap?" Davim had asked. "We will prevail. The rainlords of the Scarpen are doomed. Jasper Bloodstone will either die or be in our hands. Either way, we win."

Ravard's unease was with him still as he and Medrim ordered the zigger assault. It wasn't a simple matter; each dune used ziggers attuned to a different perfume. With their appetites satisfied, they were happy to return to their cages and ignore anyone else around, but until that moment it was essential only warriors doused with the correct perfume were anywhere in the release area.

They thought of giving everyone the Watergatherer scent, but a look at the stores convinced him there wasn't enough of it. Instead, Medrim pulled back everyone except the men of Dune Watergatherer and sent them down the gully. Only Watergatherer ziggers were released, and he insisted that only cages with inbuilt zigtubes were to be used. This made the beetles crawl down a tube pointed in the right direction, one after another. They then tended to keep flying in a straight line. Haphazard release through an open cage door often meant more aimless flight as they hunted for a victim that smelled right. The last thing anyone wanted was fatalities among Reduners from other tribes.

Once he and Medrim had everything moving smoothly, and the first batch of the ziggers were on their way, Ravard didn't wait to hear the screams. He returned to the camp to report to Davim.

He ducked his head inside the flap of the sandmaster's tent.

Davim was there, and so was a Qanatend slave women, crying softly in the corner of the tent.

"You want me to get rid of her?" Ravard asked neutrally.

"No need. She doesn't speak a word of our tongue, and I shall have more need of her before the night is over. You can avail yourself of her reluctant services if you like. We will doubtless be fighting tomorrow, and this could be your last night on earth. What better way to spend it? The bitch bit me though, so be careful."

There had been a time when he would have taken up the offer without a second thought, but now, since Garnet—

God, what had that woman done to him?

He thought of her wistfully. And wondered, not for the first time, why he hankered so after a woman who must be ten or fifteen cycles older than he was, and who was probably still in love with another man.

She looks me in the eye, he thought, *as if she is my equal.* A strange reason to like a woman, when he came to think of it. *Maybe she is my equal.* He didn't pursue that thought. It made him uncomfortable.

"All done?" Davim asked.

"The ziggers are on their way. Do you want to follow with an attack by the chalamen?"

"No. Not until we see in the morning what happened. Come in, come in. Have some amber with me. Best brew I could find in Qanatend." He held out a drink skin.

Ravard withdrew his head and glanced around. Down in the dry stream bed, rows of warriors were trying to get some sleep wrapped in their bedrolls against the cold; small fires of pede droppings glowed between the prone bodies, helping to take the cold cutting edge from the air. On the higher flat ground, the tents – belonging mostly to the sandmasters of other dunes and all the tribemasters – had their flaps laced shut. Ravard knew without being told that many of them contained other slave women, or men, brought upwash to use, just as Davim had used the girl now shivering in the corner.

Where men were still up, they were quiet, chatting around a fire perhaps, or eating a late meal. Everything was as it should be. It would be at least half a sandglass run before the first ziggers returned. There was nothing to do but wait, so he entered the tent, accepting the skin as he sat. He tossed a blanket to the girl before lifting the skin to his lips.

Davim gave a mocking smile. "You are too soft, tribemaster," he said.

Ravard shrugged. "Not where it counts."

"Don't disappoint me tomorrow."

"Do you expect me to?" He handed the skin back to Davim. He wasn't interested in drinking and had taken little more than a sip. If he died in the fighting to come, he didn't want it to be because he was slurped. He didn't like drunkenness; it reminded him too much of his father, Galen the sot. *Dune god save me, I hate the bastard even now.*

"No, I don't think you will. I made a man of you. You were *nothing* when you came to the dunes. Nothing but a snivelling Gibber grubber scared of his own shadow." Davim took a long drink. "I beat that out of you. In fact, I beat the fear out of you. You're not afraid of anything now, are you?"

He grinned and said, "I have a healthy fear of my sand-master."

"Here, drink up." Davim handed the skin back and lay down on his pallet, hands behind his head. The girl watched him fearfully, but he drifted off into a doze.

Ravard wanted to see whether the ziggers were already returning, but decided to wait a little longer in case Davim woke. He ignored the girl, now wrapped in the blanket in the corner, and stared at the sandmaster instead. Asleep, he looked almost benign.

Those unwelcome thoughts intruded again. What if the

sandmaster had known who Mica was right from the beginning? What if Davim was the one who had killed Citrine just to teach Shale a lesson?

Ravard's memories of that day were blurred by the terror of the event, muddied by the intervening years. If Davim was the man who had come and spoken to them outside the huts, who had seized Citrine, Ravard was unaware of it. The Reduners had all looked the same to him then – redmen, heads and lower faces wrapped in red cloth, red tunics, red breeches, every one of them armed, merciless and terrifying. He had no recollection of anyone in particular. He'd been so scared he'd pissed in his breeks, he remembered that much.

The rest was just one horror piled on the next. Citrine first, then his mother, then his father. Shale starting to scream like a desert cat caught in a trap, screaming and clawing like a wild thing, until one of the redmen had punched him in the stomach. The air had gone out of him, the redman had picked him up like a sack of bab fruit under one arm – and Ravard had never seen him again. He hadn't turned up among the slaves, so he must have been killed, like so many others that day. Another grief he'd had to bear. Or so he'd thought.

He'd never spoken about it to Davim. Never asked him why he had chosen that settle. He'd just assumed it was one of many attacked by the Reduners in their desire to end the dominance of the Quartern.

But Garnet had said the sandmaster had gone there to find Shale . . .

Because Shale was a stormlord.

She'd said he was still alive. A wave of nausea swept over Ravard.

No. Garnet was a liar. He couldn't bear to think what she had told him was true.

What if he, Ravard, was just a weapon to be used as Davim willed, when he willed, and discarded when it was convenient?

Used, manipulated. A hostage for Shale's good behaviour, if ever that became necessary. Davim had two legitimate sons. The eldest was not old enough to braid his hair yet, but when he was – what then? Would he be named Master Son in Ravard's place?

Shale, his enemy. The ziggers he'd just ordered released – one of them right now burrowing into his little brother. An agonising death.

No.

No. He wouldn't believe it. He wouldn't.

Outside, someone screamed. A hideous, jagged sound, scarifying furrows of panic through his mind. He shot out of the tent, scimitar drawn, Davim right behind him flinging on his tunic as he came.

A chalaman raced past, his eyes wild with shock.

"What is it?" Davim shouted.

"Ziggers!" the man screamed, the whites of his eyes large in the dark of his face. "Tens of them!"

Davim grabbed Ravard by the arm and wrenched him back into his tent with him. Then he closed the tent flap. Ravard automatically began checking to see there were no gaps or holes anywhere. The girl watched them, wide-eyed.

Davim gave a half laugh. "Now, there's a good idea!" He reached out a hand and ripped the blanket from her to expose her nakedness. Opening the tent flap just wide enough to accommodate her, he made her crawl out on all fours, but kept a hold on her ankle. Then he yanked at her so she fell flat just outside the entrance. Still clutching her foot, he tightened the tent flap around her ankle and tied it tightly. "There," he said, "that should save a few lives at least."

Ravard, disgusted, tried to keep his expression neutral. "If these are the ziggers we released, they are all from Watergatherer. You and I are in no danger." He didn't need to ask if Davim wore the perfume; no one ever neglected to do so, even when they were at peace.

The foot wriggled, but Davim kept a tight grip. The girl continued her wailing, not understanding, but knowing something bad was about to happen. "Blasted female," Davim complained. "She never would stop that hideous noise of hers."

A moment later the crying melted into a sound of pure terror and the sandmaster grinned at Ravard. Gulping sounds followed, as if she was experiencing pain so severe she could not even scream. The noises continued for five or six minutes before she was quiet.

"In the end she proved herself useful after all," Davim said carelessly and released his hold on her ankle. He pushed her foot outside the tent.

Ravard swallowed back his bile. *She's only a slave.* He didn't know her. It shouldn't worry him, but it did.

In the distance, they could hear other cries of anguish. *Withering hells,* Ravard thought, *it takes a lot to make a Reduner warrior shriek like that.*

Davim asked, "Now tell me why, if they are our ziggers, they would return without having fed?"

"If not ours, then whose? *Taquar's* after all? Scarcleft's the only city that has any number of them."

Davim didn't answer.

The screaming outside subsided, but Ravard dreaded what he would find. Most of the Reduners did not have tents. If the ziggers were Watergatherer ones returning unsated, then only those from other dunes were vulnerable. If they were Taquar's, then everyone was at risk.

"Why did you attack Wash Drybone Settle?" he asked suddenly. The question startled him. He hadn't thought about asking it; he'd just blurted it out. He didn't even know what he would do with the answer when it came.

Davim stared at him is if he was mad. "What?" he asked. "Where?"

"Wash Drybone. Where I was born."

"What has that to do with anything? Are you sun-fried?"

"I need to know."

Davim threw his hands up in the air. "I heard there was a boy there who had water-powers."

"Did you find him?"

"Does it look as if I found him? Can you see him anywhere? I counted us lucky we found you. Although who would have thought then that you would become a water sensitive with enough water skill to be a tribemaster?" He pointed at the tent flap. "Now get the sand hells out there and see what's happening. Let's hope they were Watergatherer ziggers, eh?" The glare he gave was a challenge. He'd given an order and he expected obedience, knowing it could mean Ravard's death if there were stray ziggers from another place – and not caring.

I mean that little to him. Garnet was right. Burning with anger, he went. No warrior defied a direct order, ever.

He took a lamp with him. As Davim retied the tent flap behind him, he stepped over the girl. She was dead of course. Blood oozed sluggishly from the ruin of an eye. It looked as if she had been attacked by only one beetle. It still sat on her chin, cleaning the flesh from its wing cases with its back legs. When it had finished, it opened the cases displaying its gauzy delicate wings in a rainbow of shimmering colour and flew away.

Ravard looked around.

One of his own bladesmen came up, his face haggard, his gaze still glassy with shock. He was holding his zigger cage. There was only one zigger inside. It sat quietly, cleaning itself.

"What happened?" Ravard snapped.

"Those that came back were hungry. So they burrowed into some of the men from Dune Sloweater."

"They were our ziggers? You're sure?"

The man nodded. "They didn't touch any of our sentries on the way in. None of our dune men here have been killed as far as I can see."

"How many others died?"

"Not that many. Maybe twenty or so."

"There were thousands of ziggers out there!"

"They – they haven't returned."

"Then *what the bleeding hells happened to them*?"

They looked at each other, unable to offer an explanation for the inexplicable.

"They couldn't just disappear!" Ravard protested.

"Kher, they've had more than enough time to fly there, gorge themselves ten times over if possible, and fly back. It has been more than two runs of a sandglass. We waited and waited. And then a few trickled in. But they hadn't fed. They were *hungry*!"

"The rest are dead?"

"Either that, or captured. Not one that came back had fed. Not one."

Ravard thought about that, his face grim.

"They say rainlords can kill ziggers with a glance," the bladesman remarked.

"Thousands of them? I doubt it. Where's Medrim?"

"Talking to the other tribesmen. Their sandmasters are furious, Kher. They don't like losing men to our ziggers. And our men aren't happy, either. They don't like losing trained ziggers."

"I'll go tell Sandmaster Davim what happened. He'll have to talk to the other sandmasters." He ducked back into the tent.

"I heard," Davim said irritably. He was strapping on his scimitar. "I'll speak to the sandmasters and tribemasters, although why I should have to is a mystery. Did they expect to fight a war without losing a man?"

"What do you think happened? I mean, where are all the missing ziggers?"

"Don't be pissing waterless! Dead, of course. It was a trap.

Maybe the camp was full of rainlords waiting for them to fly in. Maybe it wasn't a camp at all. Maybe it was just the lights. You know what they're like around lights – moths to candle flame if they don't have anything else to distract them, like people to eat."

"Taquar—?"

"Taquar's no fool and he knows ziggers." Davim paused, and when he spoke again, his rage was more under control. "But Taquar *needed* us. It can't have been him. We have been tricked, Ravard. Go organise the burials while I calm down the dunesmen."

It was much later when Ravard finally lay down to sleep in his own tent, tired, irritable and besieged by worries he could not shape into any sensible plan of action. He woke at the hour of deepest night to a sound he had never heard before. For a moment he lay absolutely still, listening to the impossibility of hundreds of fingertips pattering on the tent top. And a feeling of being surrounded by water.

God, he hadn't had that feeling since he and Shale had played in the water that came in that unexpected rush down the drywash when they were boys . . .

He sat up, listening, his overwhelmed senses muddled. The pattering changed to a battering, and water dripped on to his face. *Water.*

He stood up and touched the ceiling of the tent. A trickle of water ran down his arm. The tent sagged as a pool formed on the roof.

Water dropping on us. The thought was ridiculous. The stormlord must have broken that cloud over their heads. But why? The *waste*! He straightened his clothing, grabbed up his scabbard belt and scimitar and ran outside.

The darkness was profound. He wasn't used to that, so he immediately ran smack into a panicked chalaman who had come to wake him. Water was falling on them, wetting their hair, their clothes, running into their eyes and ears. It was *cold*.

The chalaman blurted out, "Kher Davim wants to see you, Kher Ravard!"

Ravard pushed him away and ran on. Davim was standing outside his tent. "Why would the stormlord want to do this?" Ravard asked. He had to shout to make himself heard above the noise of the rain.

"I don't know," Davim yelled back. "One thing's for certain, Taquar is not controlling him. I should have known that bleeding boy was going to cause us trouble. Smart-mouthed little wretch he was, even back when Taquar kept him caged. Tried to mock me – me! – by holding a ball of water over my head!"

As he was speaking, a tribemaster's tent next to them collapsed in on itself as tent pegs loosened in the deluge, and the jute canvas absorbed too heavy a burden of water. It had been a long time since Reduner tents were made to shield occupants from more than the sun, the night-dew and wind. *Pedeshit,* Ravard thought. *If we ever do return to a Time of Random Rain, we are going to have to rethink how to make a tent.*

The rain pelted down and Ravard was both appalled and impressed – water, wasted as if it was no more precious than dust on the wind. Water just flowing away, unused, sucked into thirsty, useless soil. "What should we do?" he asked. He was stunned, at a loss, wanting leadership. He wasn't the only one; the other sandmasters and tribemasters were gathering around. Several men were trying to funnel as much water as they could into their dayjars; others were ineffectively trying to shore up their tents.

Davim singled out Medrim. "Make sure the sentries stay alert. Double their number. I shall talk to the men."

* * *

Ravard returned to his tent to snatch a short sleep. He dropped off quickly, but soon woke again to another sound, and to a hauntingly familiar feeling of unease. A murmur in the distance, getting closer; that mutter becoming a roar—

A rush down a Gibber wash.

For the first time in a long while he felt the starkness of terror. Not fear for himself, but for others. He dove out of the tent and began to run, not to safety, but down the slope towards the warriors still in the wash. Slipping and sliding, he fell down on one knee, rose with his trouser leg heavy with water and his arm covered in mud up to the elbow. He ran on.

Dune god save me, save the men, why didn't I remember the rush, why didn't I think, Wash Drybone after rain . . .

Most of the men were now huddled among the rocks trying to keep out of the rain, or attending to the pedes still pulling at their lines and bucking in nervous spasms as they felt rain on their backs. As he ran, he bellowed at the top of his voice: "Out! Out of the wash! Out! *Run!*"

He skidded to a stop just in time: just before the plunging wall of water slammed down the gully – and obliterated everyone there as if they had never been. In the darkness, he couldn't see much; above the thunderous roar of the flood he couldn't hear much, either. The water lapped around his ankles where he stood on the slope. Someone brought a lamp and he grabbed it, raising it high. They stared into the darkness. There was no one. No men, no pedes, no packs.

Gods, but it was dark! A black void overhead, disgorging water as if the stars were pissing on them. Perhaps there were survivors out there he could not see, perhaps there were pedes that would ride the waters down – yet, somewhere inside his reasoning mind, he knew they had just lost five hundred men and who knew how many mounts. He lowered the lamp. This was not war. A real man fought with a scimitar or a spear or a knife. But with water? What could you do against water?

Against rainlords and stormlords? This was cold-hearted murder.

Shale. Blast him to a waterless death.

At his shoulder someone asked in bewilderment, "Where is everyone, Kher? Faldim was camped here, with all his brothers. And Karidar – you remember Karidar? He was the fellow with the ridiculous nose . . ." His voice trailed off. There was no one to find.

Shrivelled damn, Ravard thought, *will this nightmare never end?*

He stood where he was, mind-sick. Water rolled from his chin, to sputter on the heat of the lantern glass. Some irrational part of him blamed Uthardim for all their recent ills, and he couldn't rid himself of the idea. The bad luck had started, or so it seemed, the moment that strange man with the scars entered his life. *He turned the dune god against us, and our luck has gone.*

He was relieved to see Medrim arrive, giving orders to some of the men around him, bidding them find a couple of pedes and ride downwash to search for anyone who needed help.

Ravard plodded back up the slope to where Davim waited. "I can't see anyone," he said, "and very few appear to have climbed out of the wash in time. There may be some on the other side of the water, though."

"But you think most of them will have died," Davim finished for him.

He nodded. "What should we do?"

"Break camp. We will move back to the cistern."

"In the dark?" Medrim asked, astonished, speaking for all the gathered sandmasters and tribemasters awaiting orders.

Wither it, Ravard thought, *there'll be water in the wash.* The ground was slick with mud, and it rained still, blinding men and beasts.

494

"In the dark!" Davim confirmed in a temper. "We are vulnerable here. What better time for them to mount an attack? At least at the cistern we will have our backs protected by a cliff wall, and we have the supplies. *I* will pick the battle ground, not some half-grown, brown-skinned lowlife!"

Ravard tried to think rationally. Jasper Bloodstone. Shale Flint. But what sort of army could he have? Breccia was defeated, and Taquar's men would not follow him, surely.

"I'll skin him alive one day, along with every rainlord and reeve I can lay my hands on," Davim said, his voice choked with rage. "Reduners will *never* kneel to the blackmail of stormlords, not ever again." He looked up the wash, into the terrifying blackness of a rainy night. "We will go back to random rain," he whispered. "I swear it." And he shook his fist at the darkness blotting out the stars, at the clouds that were manifestations of a stormlord's power.

Ravard shivered at the vicious hate he heard. Then he turned to find his own tribesmen, to find out who lived, and who had died.

35

Scarpen Quarter
Warthago Range

Iani's voice spoke into the darkness. "Lord?"

Jasper jumped. Would he ever get used to a man of Iani's age and experience calling him "lord"? He sighed. Maybe it was just as well they all did. It reminded him he wasn't Shale the Gibber grubber any more and, spindevil take it, he still needed to be reminded. Often.

"Are the men in position?" he asked, wondering if anyone would hear the waver in his voice. The panic. Probably not. He was good at hiding his feelings. An expert at displaying a cool calm to the world. His father and Lord Taquar had done that much for him.

He smiled at the thought and felt better.

"Feroze says we're all ready," Iani said. Near him, there was laughter as Gibbermen on pedeback teased one another as if the thought of death was far from their minds.

The timing of their attack would be all wrong, though. They had wanted to hit the Reduner camp immediately after the flood passed down the wash, but he'd miscalculated the speed of the floodwater build-up. His fault – he was the stormlord, yet he had not expected the hill slopes to drain off so quickly. The surge had followed hard on the heels of the zigger attack, instead of later, at dawn, as they'd intended.

The men had not been in position, and now the scramble down the wash after the Reduners would be a nightmare of slipping and mud and falls and bruises. Iani and Feroze had pressed to go ahead, feeling that it was better to attack while Davim's forces were still reeling from the effects of the water rush, before they had a chance to regroup at the mother cistern. "We have to grab every advantage," Iani had said, "because they outnumber us and are better armed and more experienced. And right now they are confused and suffering."

Jasper swallowed his reservations and nodded to Iani.

"On your signal," the rainlord said.

Around him, his personal guard mounted their pedes, their excitement and their fear tainting their water with the same sweaty sourness he smelled on himself. He turned his attention to the remnants of cloud overhead, forcing them a little higher. A light shower was to be the attack signal to his troops scattered on both sides of the wash.

He swallowed, still nauseated, as the rain started again. He didn't expect any more ziggers, but some of his men could die soon anyway because he asked them to fight. They were no match for seasoned Reduner warriors. You couldn't make an armsman out of an artisan in a matter of days.

Men dying at his request: it seemed an obscenity, a disaster compounded by his mistake with the timing of the flood. He pushed back the doubt as Dibble turned their mount down the slope towards the remains of the Reduner camp. He was Jasper Bloodstone. Stormlord. Cloudmaster. He knew what he was doing.

Mind you, it was so dark he doubted Dibble had any idea where the pede was putting its feet, but never mind, the beast seemed to know. Its flow down the slope was as smooth as wine from the calabash and surprisingly quiet. Those on foot were far less comfortable with the descent. Behind him, Jasper heard the slither of stones, the sounds liberally studded with only half-subdued curses.

Irritably, he pushed away the rain drifting into his eyes and directed it to where the Reduners were. From every side now, he could hear his men and their pedes pouring downwards into the wash, rivers of men and beasts taking the easiest course. He reduced the cloud cover to allow the starlight to shine through, and a little later he spotted the camp, or what was left of it. To his chagrin he realised all of the Reduners were already mounted – apparently they'd decided to leave without waiting for the morning.

Hearing their attackers, the Reduner pedemen whirled the beasts around with flicks of their reins and goaded them into fast mode. Their feet slashed through the mud as they flowed away into the darkness, back down the gully towards the cistern.

With whoops and yells, Jasper's pede-mounted men followed, leaving those on foot behind. Dibble pulled back into the middle of the pack, not wanting to expose Jasper to the dangers inherent in being among the leaders. Even so, for a moment they were racing at breakneck speed among the rocks and the mud of the wash. Jasper gripped the segment handle to the front of his saddle pad, something a more skilled rider would never have done.

The rush ended abruptly in a swirling mass of pede bodies, of screaming men and the clash of weaponry as the Scarpen leaders caught the slowest of the Reduner pedes. Jasper drew his scimitar. His personal guard, on their own myriapedes, tightened the circle around him, beating off any mounted Reduner who came near. Someone screamed.

Sunblast! What's happening? In the darkness, it was hard to grasp the larger picture. Everything was fragmented, immediate, imminently dangerous; small pieces telling him nothing of the progress of the larger battle. He glimpsed a pede laden with six or seven of his men ride down a slow-moving Reduner pede with a single driver. Gibbermen attacked the man with a mishmash of implements and makeshift weapons. The Reduner pedeman impaled the driver with his chala spear and slashed the man behind him with his scimitar, opening up a bloody gash on his leg. Jasper gripped his own blade tighter and yelled at Dibble to guide their pede closer. When the guardsman was slow to obey, Jasper in frustration gathered a ball of water from the pools left by the rain and flung it in the face of the Reduner. The warrior faltered, blinded. One of the Gibbermen took advantage of the moment and stabbed him with a bab cutter. As the man fell, another Reduner driver came to his aid. His pede carried six chalamen, and several Gibbermen disappeared from the back of their pede with spears in their bodies.

Jasper gave up trying to follow the fight and concentrated on his small part. He grabbed clean water from wherever he could find it, shooting it like darts into ears and eyes and open mouths. Dibble, grinning, controlled their pede to keep his stormlord on the edge of the battle.

The pre-dawn air was filled with sound, every cry and clash grating along Jasper's heightened nerves. The screams of men in intolerable agony. The wailing ululations of terrified pedes. Shouted orders no one could hear or understand. The rolling scream of ziggers released from a falling cage. Howls of desperation from men who knew they were about to die. Cries of triumph from others who knew they were about to prevail. Absurdly, Jasper wanted to yell, to tell them all to stop, to be silent so he could think. So he could *do* something more than just fling water around.

And then, above it all, the boom of an Alabaster horn, signalling a retreat. "Oh, Watergiver's mercy," Jasper thought. "We've lost." And he hadn't even used his scimitar.

He looked around to sort out what had happened. Someone had a lighted brand. A few of the slow Reduners had been killed and their pedes captured, but – from the look of it – only after they had inflicted casualties out of all proportion to their numbers. Jasper drew in a sharp breath. The death of such experienced marauders came only at a high price.

He could hear Iani shouting orders and cursing at the top of his voice, his anger directed at those mounted Scarpen forces who were following the Reduners escaping down the wash. Even though Feroze had sounded an immediate retreat, many of those exhilarated by their supposed victory had not obeyed.

As light crept into the valley, Jasper surveyed the bodies of the men who had died where he had been fighting. They looked so young, so vulnerable. So very, very dead. Limbs and guts and organs and clothes in a horrible bloodied mix, like a knacker's offal heap. Scimitar slashes. They were *messier* than swords, or spears.

And these had been people he knew. He felt his stomach constrict, radiating pain. Those who had followed the Reduners did not return. Their missing water, the empty spaces they left behind, were further wounds to Jasper's soul.

This was what it was to lead men to war.

Surprisingly, the pain was bearable. It was the intensity of the pressure, not the pain, that made Ryka groan and drive her nails into the palms of her hands. The effort involved was so concentrated she wondered how she could ever survive it. How any woman ever survived it. When she said as much, in between the spasms, one of the slave women tending her laughed and patted her hand.

"Every one of us is here because our mothers pushed us out into the world. You'll survive this. You'll even do it again one day in all probability."

"*Pedeshit!* Never!" she cried as the next crushing wave came to submerge her.

When that one was over, and her head collapsed back onto the sacking, the same woman – what was her name again? – said with added satisfaction, "The next push will do it, I think. The baby's head is ready to pop into the world, poor wee mite."

Sunlord damn it, she just wanted this over. Anina, that was her name. And the other woman was Maida. Ryka concentrated on feeling grateful that not only had the only people at the cistern been slaves from Qanatend, but that two of them were women who had delivered babies before. She hadn't quite understood why they were there and the Reduners not, but they were part of the Reduner army. Davim and his forces were ahead of her, invading the Scarpen. And they had dragged slaves along in their wake, then left them behind at the cistern. Camp followers, Anina had called them. Something about being there if needed. As whores. Or to nurse the wounded. Or something. Ryka tried to feel grateful, and she was, truly grateful. But right then it was hard to think of anything except how she would survive the next surge.

When it came to consume her, she cried out – in real pain this time, and then was lost in a torment-lacerated world where the war didn't exist.

A boy, one of the women said. Ryka was too tired to care, let alone be glad. He lay curled in the crook of her arm. Red and squashed-looking and not really much like a person. More like a kitten without fur. And tiny, although she supposed he was larger than a kitten. He'd certainly *felt* larger than a kitten.

Am I supposed to love him? she wondered. *Watergiver help me, I wish I had paid more attention to – to all that domestic stuff.* It had always seemed so boring in comparison to her books, or to a ride into The Sweepings, or talking to the outlanders in the foreigners' market.

Her lack of attention had caught up with her. Taking a closer look at his crumpled face, unexpectedly she found herself smiling.

She was stroking her son's tiny cheek with a finger when she heard a sound she could not identify. Loud, rushing, frightening. She had heard it before, somewhere. Here, it felt out of place. What *was* that? She wanted to jump to her feet, to run out of the cistern cave where they lay, but everything hurt when she tried to move too much.

Beside her Anina sat up, her eyes wide in the lantern light. The noise outside became louder, more invasive. Growling its way down the wash in the dark like a runaway meddle of pedes. Or a hillside on the move. Or—

"What is it?" the woman asked, her fear a tangible thing, reaching out for comfort.

Ryka felt a fleeting amusement. She was as weak as a day-old pede wobbling after its mother, and the woman was coming to her for assurance?

"Water," she said, lying back down and holding her son against her body. She could feel it in her mind now; water on the move, tumbling, bucking, churning. "Water on its way down the wash."

"How do you know that?"

"I've heard it before. In the Gibber. I hope there's no one out there."

The woman shook her head. "No. None of us, anyway. We were all asleep here in the cavern. But why would there be water in the wash?" She shook a puzzled head. "The Cloudmaster never sends water this way. Qanatend rain falls in the valley behind the cistern, much higher in the mountains. The water seeps down into caves. The cistern intake pipe taps it there. I know that because we've all been looking for a way to escape the valley without those red bastards seeing us. Haven't had any luck because the caves don't go anywhere. I doubt there's been water in this wash since, oh, since the Time of Random Rain."

Ryka forced her mind to think. "Perhaps the stormlord has just drowned a lot of Reduners."

They stared at each other, thinking about the implications. Outside, dawn was beginning to tinge the sky and simultaneously they turned to look. Nothing visible moved, but there was no doubt that water was tumbling down the gully; to Ryka, the roar was unmistakable.

When Anina spoke again she said softly, "Garnet, I think we had better get a hiding place ready for you and the babe, just in case. Unless you want to give up on the idea of running away."

"No, of course not. I just need time to rest."

"I will fix a pallet for you behind the oil jars in the storeroom. If any Reduners return, you can hide there. You will have to keep the baby quiet, though."

"Storeroom?"

"Not a room exactly. It's just another cave off this cavern. A small one, over there." She pointed. "You'd be less obvious in there, and the Reduners never fetch and carry the stores. They leave that to us."

Ryka was overwhelmed with a surge of fierce protectiveness, laced with intense rage. No one must hurt her child. She would not allow it. Shaken by the rawness of her response, she tried to joke. "Maybe it's just as well he sounds like a mewling pebblemouse. No one would think it a baby's cry. I'll be gone as soon as I can, though."

"Where?" the woman asked. She pushed a lock of hair behind one ear. She was forty years old and still beautiful, except for the bruised look in her eyes that spoke of recent tragedy endured and survived – and still raw. "Don't you think we'd all be gone from here if we could? But the sandmaster's army is up there somewhere in the gully, and below us there are only more of the bastards in Qanatend. You can't leave the gully, you know. The Warthago is too rugged."

"I have the pedes. In fact I could take some of you. Oh – the pedes! The Reduners mustn't find them. Can they be hidden?"

"Where? If the Reduners return, they'll be crawling all over the place. I'll just say they belonged to a Reduner who left them behind because they were too small. If that doesn't make sense to them, we can all plead ignorance. Slaves aren't expected to know stuff. And if they think they belong to someone, no one will touch them." She brought the lamp close to look at the sleeping child. "Have you thought of a name for him yet?" she asked.

"Khedrim," Ryka said.

Anina stared at her in surprise. "That's a Reduner name!"

"Yes. He – he is named after a lad who died."

A child who was sent after me by those who thought I was just a pregnant woman who would never fight back.

"I botched the timing," Jasper admitted to Terelle after he returned to camp to do the day's stormshifting. "I guess I did a good job of throwing water, though."

His tone was flat, but she knew the depth of his self-inflicted pain. It was there in a tightening around his eyes, in a remoteness in his gaze and a drop in the register of his voice. Most people might not have noticed his moods, but she read him as well as she could read her waterpaintings.

"It was your first battle," she said cautiously.

He cut her short. "It was the first battle for many of us. But I am the stormlord and the only thing that passes for Cloudmaster, thanks to you. I am not supposed to sit dumbly on a pede like a block of salt and do nothing except chuck water at the enemy."

"No. You're right," she told him with rising ire. "You are a stormlord. *The* stormlord. You are supposed to stormshift and sit in Breccia City governing this land. You aren't supposed to rush about waving a scimitar, especially when you don't really know much about using it. If you do more good throwing water about, then that is exactly what you ought to do. I am sure it is safer. You are too important to risk your life. Dibble was quite right not to allow your pede into the heart of the fighting."

"That's such – such a *girl* thing to say. You don't understand."

They glared at each other.

"To most people in the Quartern," he said at last, "I'm too young to rule. To them, I'm not another Granthon. I don't even have the validity of Nealrith either, even when they considered him weak. They might not have liked Taquar, but they respected him. Me – I'm too young. A Gibber urchin at that. I have to *prove* myself worthy. Otherwise, how can I rule? And today I made a mistake of timing. I saved a few lives chucking water about, it's true, but my mistake cost more lives."

"And rulers prove themselves worthy by acting like idiots with a sword?" she asked, throwing her hands up in exasperation. "Such a *boy* thing to do. It is Iani and Feroze who are supposed to be in charge of the fighting. And have you also considered how many people you saved with our deception that killed so many ziggers? Anyway, I don't understand why you *want* to fight, or rule, for that matter. Your value is in your stormbringing abilities. Why not let someone else govern?"

He stared at her, amazed. "You don't understand, do you? Yet you just said it yourself – I am a valuable commodity. Don't you see, Terelle? Whoever rules would also gain control of me and of my power – by law. I've endured years of not being my own person. I didn't like it. I'd rather do the controlling myself."

"What about if someone like, oh, Iani, for example, ruled?"

"Wash stones, Terelle, he's half mad. He used to be obsessed with Lyneth. Then Taquar. Now it's Davim. To get revenge for Moiqa's death."

"Well, one of the others, then."

"They are all playing their own politics. If Nealrith were alive . . ." He sighed. "Yes, I would have served him, gladly. Or Lord Ryka. Because they were wise and they had a way of seeing all the facets of something. Yet others thought Nealrith weak and Ryka headstrong, so maybe I'm not much of a judge of people."

"Never mind." She grinned at him. "I am. And I would follow you anywhere if that's what you wanted."

Her grin was so infectious he couldn't help laughing. "You must be biased. I use your skills to cover my weaknesses and hide your talents from everyone while I take the credit, and you can still say that?"

"Sun-fried idiot." She said it fondly enough for him to have no doubt of her affection.

"No. The wisest thing I ever did was—" He stopped short, flushing.

She felt sure he had been going to say, "to love you". *Oh, Shale, can't you just say it?*

He looked so tired, so dejected, she changed the subject. "What happens now? About Davim, I mean."

"We think he will have hunkered down at the cistern. He knows he can't get past us without losing a lot of men, so he'll wait for us to go to him. Of course, he could head for the Red Quarter too, but we all think his pride won't allow that. If he looks weak, more Reduners will join Vara Redmane's rebellion."

"Are you sure there is no other way through the Warthago? They found a route before – could they do it again some-where else?"

"I'm here this time. If they do that, I will know."

"By sensing their water?"

He nodded. "Luckily, Iani knows this track to Qanatend better than anyone. He agrees Davim means to make a stand at the cistern. He will have all the water he needs there, and although we will be attacking from above, which has got to be an advantage, he will have his back to the cliffs behind the cistern. No one can come in from behind, or the sides."

"Could he ambush you on the way to the cistern?"

He grinned at her. "Not a chance."

"Oh. Rainlord power again. I keep forgetting. Where are our forces now?"

"Down where Davim's were. I just came back here to see if you had done a waterpainting for today's stormbringing. And to tell you – and the rest of the camp here – to move down the wash after us." He raised his eyes to meet hers. "I need you, Terelle."

She knew he wasn't referring to her help with his storm-bringing. He meant he needed her to fight.

After the day's cloudbreaking, Jasper sought out a group of the wounded who had earlier been brought up the wash to the flatter land at the top of Pebblebag Pass. *I may not know what orders to give,* he thought, *but at least I can show I care.*

To his surprise, one of the wounded greeted him with effusive thanks. "You saved m'life!" he exclaimed. The Gibberman turned to others lying beside him. "Look!" he said, holding up his roughly bandaged arm. "There I was with a witherin' useless arm, 'n' m'scimitar dropped, with this hulkin' Reduner fellow about t'spear me through, and all of a sudden he gets squirted in the mouth with a stream of water. He chokes, can't see an inch in front of his arse-red nose, and is scared witless as well. So all of a sudden I had time t'get me bab blade outta my boot and slide it 'tween his ribs 'stead of him gutting me! M'lord, that was a sight I'll remember the rest of me life!"

Jasper smiled at him and wondered if that was really what a battle was all about. Saving the life of the men around you, by doing the best you could. Throwing water about might not be the stuff of heroic stories to be told around a camp-fire, but it meant everything to that man.

He had done something after all. He walked away, his shoulders straighter. Without thinking, he headed to where Terelle was painting, his renewed sense of hope prompting him to seek her out. Halfway there, he stopped. How could he give her hope – or himself hope – when there was none? Not for them. She had to leave to rejoin Russet. He had to marry the right person to produce a new generation of stormlords.

I have no right to seek her out when I can offer her nothing.

Struggling against his desires, he went to join Senya and Laisa for a meal. He sat there, hating himself for the hypocrisy of his polite conversation, for the false smiles he bestowed on Senya, for the empty lies of their every interaction. And when later he saw Terelle pass by, glance at them and then turn away, he grieved.

When they rode further down the wash after the Reduners, they found the bodies of the men who had disobeyed the signal to retreat. They had been beheaded and disembow-elled, left to bloat in the sun. The heads were missing. Insects crawled on the coagulated blood of their necks. Most of them wore the garb of Gibber folk.

Jasper swallowed back his vomit and gave the order for two of the rainlord priests from Breakaway to stay behind and extract their water in homage. He wanted to stop his imagination, halt his memories, but instead he heard the echo of laughter, the bravado of young men before battle pretending they were immune from death. They had been *giggling*, by all that was waterholy. Perhaps these were the very same men.

Perhaps not. Either way, his decisions had brought them to this moment.

He rode on, staring straight ahead.

They camped that night at the lower of the two Reduner camp sites and the next day most of them rode on to camp within sight of the Qanatend mother cistern. In the evening, they found out what had happened to the missing heads. They were being used as balls in an impromptu game of chala played in front of the cavern that held the water cisterns.

Jasper, lying concealed with Iani, saw the beginning of the game. As soon as he realised what they were using for a ball, he rolled over onto his back and looked at the sky instead. Did Davim organise the game to remind him of Citrine? Probably.

Sandblast the sick bastard.

Faintly he heard the laughter of the players, wafted to their ears on an updraught. *Warriors who can laugh at what they do. To teach me a lesson. Oh, pedeshit, what sort of men are they?*

And then, just when he felt there was nothing worse that could be done to him, he felt it. The familiarity of water he recognised.

Mica. Mica was one of the players.

And his world fell apart yet again.

"Men are dying, Terelle. Ziggers. We have to do something, and soon." Which was why Jasper had brought her here to look, of course.

It was her first glimpse of the cistern. She was lying on a slope, just below the ridge. She'd cautiously raised her head over the rise to peek down at the scene below. From where she lay, the ground sloped steeply downwards in a tumble of grey scree. The thousands of loose stones were inert enough now, but the whole slope looked unstable enough to slide down to the flatter land in front of the cistern if a single pebble was disturbed by as much as the scampering of a mouse, although Jasper assured her it wasn't as precarious as it looked.

She and Jasper were on the right-hand arm of the crescent-shaped slope. The left arm was a steep cliff cradling the mother cistern of Qanatend. Terelle could see the entrance, far below. The grille had been smashed and pedes and people – small enough to be unrecognisable – came and went through the cavernous gap, carrying dayjars and water skins for refilling.

The large flat clearing in front of the cavern filled the valley from one side to the other. Split by the gully of the wash, which also cut back into the slope, the flat area was cupped inside the base of the crescent. Right then it was cluttered with scarlet awnings, pedes, cooking fires, a few tents – and armed tribesmen. The men wore their deep red robes, the hems to mid-calf, over trousers of red. She knew these same men had played a game of chala with the heads of the men they had killed, just two days earlier. Jasper hadn't told her that, but she had heard it nonetheless.

She turned her attention to the drywash. Water still lurked in rocky crannies of the gully, where the curves of the valley sides offered partial shade. The rest of the flood had long vanished down the slope towards Qanatend. Downwash, the valley sides were not so steep, and many warriors were camped on the slopes as well. A glance was enough to see that it would be hard for warriors to climb up the wash unseen; Jasper's men could ambush them from both sides.

The Reduners went about their daily business as if they did not know they were being watched, but their spears were never far away, their scimitars swung at their sides, their daggers remained thrust through their belts. A few guards stood around, apparently with nothing to do, but they spent their time looking upwards. Terelle didn't need to be told that they were waiting for the first sign of a Scarpen charge.

"Could a rainlord kill the Reduners from here, by taking their water?" she asked, as if it were an everyday thing to speak so casually about how to take the lives of men.

Jasper shook his head. "Too far. And even then – it is the hardest of all water abilities. People don't want to die. They hang on to their water simply by the act of living. I'm told it's very exhausting to kill that way." After a moment, he added, "It might possibly be less tiring to do it my way, I suppose."

"What's that?" she asked.

"To hold water over their nose and mouth until they die. Or stuff it down their noses. I can shape water and I can push water. I can push it into a man's open mouth with such force he cannot close his mouth to stop it. Or I can push it against his eyes or into his ears. I've learned a thing or two in the past couple of days when we met some advance scouts. The trouble is, it takes concentration. I can only kill one man at a time, focusing everything I have on a single man, not wavering as I watch him die."

She felt the colour rush from her face.

"There's nothing nice about what's going to happen here. There's nothing nice about what they'll do to us if they win."

"No," she whispered, "I know." She reached out and took his hand in hers. For a moment they lay in silence, neither of them looking at the other. "What about taking all the water in the cistern?" she asked. "You can do that, can't you? Leave them to thirst or surrender or retreat."

"Wouldn't work. The cisterns just keep filling up from the mother wells, through pipes deep in the hillside."

"And you're saying we're within their zigger range."

"Yes. They release a few every now and then. No pattern to it. Hard to detect them. People are dying."

Something in her chest tightened at the thought.

"They are testing our courage, to see how long we can remain here without flinching." He sighed. "At least they won't send them our way at night any more. They learned their lesson there. But we are at an impasse now: they can't use the drywash trail to Scarcleft and we can't take the fight to them unless we are prepared to lose a lot of bladesmen – there's no cover on the slope. The moment we come down over this rim, they'll throw every zigger they own at us. I could gamble they don't have many left, I suppose. If we come down through the wash, the moment we emerge at the base, they will be waiting for us. We'd walk into a wall of spears—" He stopped and swallowed. "I find it hard to ask men to die, Terelle."

"And yet you ask me to kill them."

"Yes." He stared at her, expressionless. "You, and everyone here. This is an army. This is a war."

She met his stare, but in the end it was her gaze that fell. His message was clear. *No exceptions.*

He slid back down from the crest and dusted off his clothes. "Let's go back to the camp."

"Why not just stay here, blocking the way?" she asked as they walked back to the tents. She had to lengthen her stride to keep up, realising once again how tall he had become. "Sooner or later he'll give up. Let him go, Jasper. All the way back to the Red Quarter. After all, wasn't that what he was going to do as part of his bargain with Taquar?"

"The game has changed now. He knows who challenges him. He knows I can't let him go back to the Red Quarter. He would be a spear in our side, just waiting for his next chance. He would conquer the White Quarter and raid the Gibber Quarter. Besides, he needs to kill me. I can control the water of the whole of the Red Quarter . . . how can he let me live? I can stop him getting random rain, and he knows it. He knows Taquar has lost control of me. If I don't go down that slope after him, he'll just wait until he has the opportunity to attack us, if not here and now, then later."

"What about waiting to see if Vara Redmane turns up?"

"She is more likely to attack those warriors he left at home. It always was a long shot, and I'm guessing she won't care about us. I reckon she'll try and take back her own dune, the Scarmaker, while his men are here."

"Will his men be short of food?"

"They are hunters, Terelle. And these ranges are full of mountain goats and deer. Truth is, I don't know what to do."

"Sneak down the slope at night?"

"You can't *sneak* on scree. And if we went down the wash, it would have to be in a narrow column. We'd be killed too easily emerging at the foot. We don't have anywhere near the training or experience his men have. We may have killed a few hundred the other night with our trickery and rainlord power, but they still outnumber us by far. Waterless hell, Terelle, I'd *beg* you to draw Davim dead, if you knew what he looked like."

"Archers?" She was desperate.

"We do have a couple of hunters who can pierce a windhover at a couple of hundred paces – but they have less than fifty arrows between them."

She wasn't surprised. Bows and arrows were rare throughout the Quartern because there were no suitable trees to make them, and the taboo against cutting down a tree was formidable anyway.

They reached the camp and Jasper flung himself down on the mat under the shade of one of the awnings. A bladesman came to offer him a drink, but he waved the man away irritably and said, "Davim has a weapon that could bring me to my knees like nothing else could."

She waited for him to explain, but he said nothing. The bleak look in his eyes told her what he meant. She'd seen that look before. "Oh, blighted eyes. Mica. You think *Mica* might be down there?"

He shook his head. I don't *think* so, I *know* it."

She stared at him, her stomach churning in shock. "How?" she asked in a whisper.

"I can sense his water, of course. Oh, he's changed, and I can't sense him as well as I can sense you, but I am aware of his presence. Of his water. That's really the only way I can describe it."

"But they are tribesmen in that camp, not slaves," she protested. "They wouldn't bring slaves, surely, to fight a war – they couldn't trust them."

"He's not a slave. He's one of their warriors."

"You can't know that."

"He was playing a game of chala, down there, in front of the cistern, with other Reduner warriors."

Her eyes went wide with shock. "You mean with the heads? He—? Oh, Shale."

"I don't suppose Davim could be sure I was watching, but it was a message for me anyway. He was hoping I'd recognise Mica. I didn't, of course, not his face; he was too far away and he's a man now anyway. I couldn't even work out which of them he was, but he was there. I – I recognised his water, moving back and forth." He picked aimlessly at the mat under his feet. "Funny, when I was a boy in the Gibber, I didn't realise I was beginning even then to know people by their water, but I was. And his – the feel of it, rather than the shape – it came back to me."

She continued to stare in horror. He said it with an unemotional flatness, as if it didn't matter. But oh, it did. She knew the last time he had seen his brother they had stood side by side and watched as Sandmaster Davim played chala with their baby sister.

"You think – you think he did it deliberately? *Mica*? To hurt you?"

"I hope not. I would not have thought he would become so – so *cruel*. But Davim? *He* knew there was a good chance

I was watching. He sent me this, through a messenger under a wrapped sword of truce, the same day." He fumbled in his belt pouch and extracted a piece of parchment which he handed to her.

She unfolded it and read the words. They were written in a rounded childish hand, in ungrammatical Quartern tongue. *To Stormlord Shale Flint. Come down. Mica Flint go up. Same time. Pass each by. Then no war. Reduner go dunes. You stay Scarpen. So swear Sandmaster Davim, Dune Watergatherer.*

You not come, Mica die.

Terelle shook her head as she read it. "That's, that's *vicious*!" She raised her eyes to look at him. "You can't do that. And he knows you won't. You go to him, he'd kill you and then we'd all die of thirst."

"And the Reduners would emerge as the survivors. Yes, I know."

"He's just trying to hurt you by tormenting you."

"He's succeeding."

"You said Mica wasn't a slave. Davim's not going to kill one of his men just to spite you."

"Of course he would, if he wanted. He killed my sister to teach me a lesson. The people of Wash Drybone are just so many Gibber sand-leeches to Davim, to be slaughtered or enslaved. He's never thought of any of them as people."

She was silent, unable to think of anything to say to help him. She felt cold all over. If Jasper led an attack down the slope, he could end up killing his brother.

He stood up and began striding about under the shelter, crumpling his palmubra, fiddling with a pede prod, refusing to look at her.

Terelle felt something rip inside her; what had once been a certainty tore from its shelter to become doubt. *This is what we are fighting . . . a sandmaster who deals in humans as if they were salt blocks, to be bought and sold and used – or discarded*

*or destroyed at a whim. A whole land is at stake. We have to
do something, anything at all to stop this . . .*

Aloud she said, "How could Mica go from slavery to being
a Reduner warrior?"

He shrugged. "He proved his loyalty. Somehow. I don't
want to think how." He paused before continuing.

"When I was younger, I had a daydream. The same dream,
all those years I was Taquar's prisoner, and all the time I was
in Breccia, too. I was going to rescue Mica. I believed Mica
would *never* become one of the Reduners, he was too kind,
too gentle. I knew he must be a slave, and one day I could
save him, and we'd be together again. But now I know he's
down there, I remember other things. How he didn't always
stand up for me against our father. That he often took the
easiest way out. That he kept silent. And I've thought maybe
the easiest thing for a slave to do is to join his master."

His voice garnered roughness with every word. "If that
happened, how can I condemn him for it? He was only fourteen or fifteen when he was taken. It doesn't make me love
him any less. It just makes it so much harder for me to . . .
fight *them*."

Tears came into her eyes. *Sandblast it*, she thought. She
wanted to ease his hurt, but had no idea how. Inside her, doubt
corroded the validity of her past decisions, making them seem
childlike.

He sat down next to her again, arms resting on his bent
knees, hands fiddling with his palmubra. "Terelle, I don't
know how I can win this one alone. I know you don't like
using your waterpainting power, but I don't see we have any
choice. And I'm not talking just about killing ziggers."

She shied away from consideration of the ruins of her moral
certitude and spoke instead of practicalities, of what was – in
theory – possible, or otherwise. "I don't know what to suggest.
If I've learned anything, it is that I have to be very careful.

I have to provide the means to make the painting real – otherwise the water-power may use a method I don't like. For example, if I painted all those Reduners lying on the ground down there dead, without also making it clear what killed them, the reality might be some catastrophe horrible enough to kill us all." *Like an earthquake.*

He nodded. "I understand. The lanterns were the means to destroy the ziggers, and so those paintings worked exactly as they should."

"And if we paint something that is simply impossible, then it won't happen."

"So it's no use painting my fifteen hundred men killing all of theirs in battle? It's just too remote a possibility – unless the painting also supplies the means."

"Even if I *would* do it, I don't think I *could*," she said. "I'd need to sketch an approximation of every one of your men. The Reduners wouldn't be so bad – wrapped up like that they all look alike." She frowned suddenly, deep in thought. "I wonder if we are looking at it from the wrong direction."

"What do you mean?"

"Maybe we need to be more – more *creative*. Think of new ways to – to – win." *To kill.*

Before she could tease the idea out into a more coherent thought, they were interrupted. An Alabaster man came riding down to the camp from the rim. Sunlight twinkled off his mirrors, blinding Terelle. She raised an arm to shield her eyes as Jasper leaped up and the rider cried out, "More ziggers! Help!"

The pede rattled to a halt, segments compacting. Jasper held out an arm to the Alabaster, and in one fluid movement the man had pulled Jasper up behind him and the pede was prodded into motion again. Terelle remained seated, taken aback by the suddenness of their departure.

Her thoughts jumbled, remembering dancing lights in Russet's rooms, remembering the glare of salt.

A glimmer of a smile began to play around the corner of her lips. "Now that's an idea," she said.

"What is?" a voice asked behind her, honeyed tones laced with something much more nastily pungent.

She jumped to her feet. "Lord Laisa. Just a – a thought. About how to fight Reduners."

Laisa came a step closer. "I am still trying to puzzle you out. Tell me, were you ever tested for water sensitivity?"

"Hardly necessary. Believe me, a snuggery madam would have spotted a water sensitive and sold her to the rainlords in less time than it takes a single sand grain to run through a sandglass." Which was true enough.

"Doubtless." Laisa's mockery was overt, nasty. "Yet there is something about you that troubles me." She shrugged. "I'm sure I've seen you before. You are certainly out of your true element here. Enjoy it while you may; it will not last."

She turned and walked away in her usual swirl of silks and subtle perfumes. *How the salted damn does she do that? Even here! The best of clothes and the best of smells. The bitch.*

36

Scarpen Quarter
Warthago Range

"So are you going to marry her?"

Terelle stood facing Jasper in the privacy of his tent. It was dark outside, but a lamp illuminated the interior. She wasn't sure what had prompted her to ask that question right then. They both had so many more important things on their minds. *Stupid. I'm such a child. I still want the world to be fair and just and right.* But she wasn't able to help herself. Seeing him and Senya together like that, talking, laughing even – it had hurt her, a deeply visceral hurt that had no sense to it; it just was.

He said, level-voiced and apparently calm, "I'm sorry, Terelle. I can't lie to you about this. I won't marry Senya against her will, but I have no high expectations she will refuse when the alternative is a lower social position for her, less comfort, fewer servants."

She was silent, hearing part of what she wanted to hear: he knew exactly how shallow Senya was. He knew exactly what sort of woman she was becoming. And also hearing something she hadn't wanted to hear at all: he was still going to marry her.

"There's only one woman I want to marry," he said at last. "And she's not Senya. But I can't ask her because people demand I have stormlord children. If I don't, future generations will die."

Terelle stared at him, eyes widening as she finally understood. "Is *that* what all this is about?"

He was confused. "Pardon?"

"I thought it was some sort of silly Scarpen stormlord custom. 'Don't marry beneath you. Marry some upleveller rainlord's daughter because she'll make a regal consort. You can't possibly marry an outlander whore who was raised in a Scarpen snuggery.' I thought you were drinking at that scummy trough. And all the time it was just so you can father the right kind of children?"

He exclaimed, wounded, "Terelle, I don't give a sand-flea's piddle about uplevellers' daughters! I'm a Gibber brat from the poorest village on the Gibber Plains, spindevil take it! I care about *you*. Surely you know that."

"You haven't exactly said it—"

He was really riled now, and shouted at her. "Well, I'm saying it now: I love you! Is that plain enough?"

The silence following was as deep as the velvet darkness of a water tunnel. They both stood still, rendered immobile by the passion behind his words. "Oh," she said weakly.

"Well?"

"Well what? You've just this minute told me the way you feel means nothing!"

The look he gave her almost broke her heart. "It means everything," he whispered. "Everything. But I can't do anything about it."

"You idiot, of course you can, *if* we really want to marry each other! What's Senya's pedigree, compared to mine?"

Once again he was bewildered. "Huh?"

"How many stormlords and rainlords are there in her ancestry? One stormlord grandparent. Rainlords for parents. But me – from what Russet tells me, my whole family on his side are either stormlords or waterpainters. That's *stormlords*, not rainlords. He doesn't use that word, but that's what they are. Water-powerful, the whole lot of them, including my mother and her parents. Sounds like a better lineage than your sulky brat Senya."

"You're a waterpainter, not a rainlord or a stormlord."

"So? Russet hasn't told me nearly enough, but he did tell me the Watergivers of Khromatis, such as he was once, are just as powerful as stormlords in their own way. Anyway, I think I could do by painting much of what a stormlord does. I already do, don't I? I could do things without working through you, too. I could paint a storm cloud bringing rain to the correct part of the Warthago Range. Or to anywhere else. Unlike you, I'd have to visit every place first, to get the picture fixed in my mind, and I'd have to return there often, in case the place changed, but it could be done." She hesitated. "Although I'm just not sure what the larger results would be. If I made it rain here, using my magic, how would I know the water I used didn't come from, say, someone's cistern?"

He stared at her, and for once the thoughts warring in his mind were written on his face: hope, chagrin, delight, worry.

"I've been exceptionally stupid," he said at last. "I've been torturing myself, when the answer was under my nose all the time. If there are plenty of stormlords in your family, I don't have to marry Senya, or the other rainlord girl the rainlords found in the Gibber!" He grinned, but his grin faded when he saw her face. "You – you do *want* to marry me, don't you?"

The expression on her face didn't change.

"Terelle, I want to marry *you*. Terelle Grey. Not the waterpainter, just you. But I don't have a choice. I have to marry where I have a chance to have water-talented children."

She considered him seriously. "Jasper, I know most girls marry at my age. But I'm not most people. I don't want to marry so young. I certainly don't want to be forced to have a meddle of brats just to satisfy the nation's need for storm-lords. I'd like the – the luxury of time. And anyway, I'm not sure I want to marry someone who sought solace in Senya Almandine's arms the moment my back was turned."

"Pede piss! Are you going to throw that back at me for the rest of my life?"

"Probably."

"Ah." He pondered, then said, "I'd – I'd like to think you'd be around for the rest of my life so you could. Throw it back at me, I mean. I don't know what to say about what happened with Senya. I am not going to make excuses for myself. Is it – is it enough to say I don't want it ever to happen again? Terelle, could you at *least* say you love me?"

She tilted her head and considered him. "Well," she said at last, "you mean more to me than anyone else I've ever met. I can't imagine ever wanting to marry anyone else. I know when I think of Senya I want to wring her neck. I know I don't want to leave you. I know I will miss you while I'm gone. I know I missed you before and worried myself sick about you. I know when I look at you I want all kinds of things one is not supposed to talk about in public. Is that loving someone?"

He let out the breath he had been holding. "It sounds good to me. More than good." He ran a hand through his hair in a gesture of frustration. "I've made a muck of this from begin-ning to end, haven't I? I don't know the right things to say. You're the last person I'd ever want to hurt, and yet I managed to do just that."

"Yes."

"Does it help if I say I wish I could undo it? That I wish it had never happened?"

"Not really. Senya, of all people – that *hurt*. More than you understand. I tried to tell myself I was being ridiculous. That we'd made no promises to each other. That we were just friends, and therefore I had no rights. I tried to be sensible about it, but sometimes being sensible doesn't seem to cure pain."

He desperately wanted to say he hadn't gone to Senya, that she had crawled naked into his bed, but he thought better of it. Trying to excuse himself would sound so . . . pathetic. Besides, he was hardly guiltless. There had been Silver, too. He didn't think he wanted to mention her at all. "What – what do you want to do?" he asked finally. "I want to marry you. I don't want you to leave."

"I have to go back to Russet."

"I hate that man. I don't trust him."

"I don't care about him either, not after what he did to me. I don't care if he is my great-grandfather. But it makes no difference, does it? If I don't go back in the end, I think I'll die the way my mother did. And I'll be damned if I want that. But how do we make sure that my absence doesn't pitch the Quartern back into a Time of Random Rain?"

"You're just as trapped as I am, aren't you? Terelle, I'm so, so sorry." The pain in him tore at her, and involuntarily she moved closer to him. She tried to speak, but was overcome with her own raw emotion.

Jasper did the one thing that could help her, enclosing her in his arms and holding her tight. She felt safe, so safe she didn't want to move. When she lifted her head, he bent to kiss her. And something inside her awakened, something so profound she almost lost her sense of what was real.

She felt his water against hers. The rush in her veins, the shivering in her heart, the weaving and curling through her blood. His water singing in greeting. Every part of him reaching out to her, her body responding. Music made in the harmonies. Intertwining, plaiting, enmeshing. For the first time in her life, she was aware of herself as a being of water. For the first time, she felt herself, her connections, her place in the world, her desires.

The tug of Jasper's water was a force against her own. She felt the swelling in him pressing against her and cupped it with her thighs when he lifted her higher in the strength of his muscled arms. His tongue met hers, water to water, desire to desire, passion seeking – and finding – an equal passion. She knew if she let go she would be changed forever, her body no longer just hers, her life no longer just hers. She would be putting her life in his hands. He could kill her, just by the act of loving. Or they could unite in a way most people never knew. Already part of her was lost in a rush, deliciously lost, no longer just one person but two, poised on the brink of discovery.

And something made her draw back, take a shuddering breath. *Not now. Not here.*

He was the first to speak. "I didn't – I didn't know it could be like that." His chest was heaving as if he had been running.

Terelle knew what he was trying to tell her: *Senya could not do that to me.*

Her smile was deliberately sly. "It seems there may be . . . compensations in our trap."

He laughed out loud, rare for him. "Sandblast, Terelle, I love you. Will you marry me?"

Raising a finger to his lips, she said, "One day. How could I not? But not now. Not yet. Not with Russet's water magic pulling me away." She stepped away from him, straightening her tunic and tactfully looking away from the more obvious sign of his arousal. "You know, I didn't actually come to your tent for this. I wanted to tell you I've thought of some things that might help."

The expression on his face didn't change, but she sensed his withdrawal nonetheless. He was in command once more: the stormlord was back, the more openly passionate Gibberman banished. "You have an idea," he said, breathing deeply. "About ziggers?"

"Not exactly." She sighed. "I wanted simple solutions, but that's just stupid. There aren't any. You told me if I withheld my skill, I'd hurt even more people than I would by using it, and you were right. I know I have to do this and do it well, so we can start to build a peace. Does that sound a very . . . *girl* thing to say?"

"No. It sounds a very *wise* thing to me."

"When we were in Russet's rooms one day, you were playing with your water-skills and there was a shaft of sunlight hitting the water in a certain way. It shone into my eyes, blinding me. Do you think you could do that – on a larger scale? Shafting sunlight through water, or bouncing it off water, down onto the Reduners below, so they couldn't see what we were doing up here?"

He understood immediately. "Yes! Oh yes . . . When the sun is high overhead . . . I wonder how thick the water would have to be? And how wide . . . have to angle it just right. I'll have to think about this. And experiment. But to do it long enough and well enough to hide the descent of our men to their camp? Difficult. They would still hear them. And they would know something was up and release their ziggers anyway." He began to pace to and fro, thinking.

She continued, "My idea was to do this in order to cover some other tricks. You can move a large block of water, at least for a short time, can't you?"

He stopped pacing and nodded. "Clean, fresh water, yes, certainly. As long as it's not too far away."

"There's a lot of water in the mother cistern down there."

"I did think of dumping it on them. But the effect won't last. Wetting people is hardly warfare."

"Ice might hurt more than water. When I was in the White Quarter, Russet told me about ice falling from the sky. All by itself."

"*Ice?* How is that possible?"

"Apparently the higher you go into the sky, the colder it gets, or so he said. If you were to send water very high, it would turn into ice."

The glance he gave her was dubious. "Ice might have more impact than water, I suppose. I'll try."

"I've thought of another way in which you could dump a whole lot more than just water on their heads. Something somewhat heavier . . . Rocks." She swallowed, pushing away her distaste. Her reservations. *People would die . . .*

"I can't move rocks," he protested.

"No. Water can, though."

"Lord Laisa?"

Laisa had been asleep, but Terelle's words in her ear woke her instantly. She propped herself up on one elbow and gave her a sour look. "What is it?" she asked, sharp-voiced.

"I have a request to make of you."

"And that gives you the right to enter my tent in the middle of the night?"

"I don't care much about your rights. Any rights you had, you lost when you betrayed Jasper and married Taquar. I came to ask you for some sinucca leaf."

The older woman stared at her in stupefaction. "*What?*"

"You heard me. I need some, and I thought you were the most likely person to carry such a thing around."

"How *dare* you insinuate—"

"Oh, don't give me that outrage. You aren't the kind of woman to remain faithful to a man who could spend the rest of his life a prisoner. And you'd always carry something, just in case. Nothing wrong with that."

"If I did, do you think I would give *you* some when the man you've been eyeing like a pede in heat is the man my daughter will one day marry? You have the gall to ask such a thing when Senya is asleep in the next tent!"

"Look at it this way – if I become pregnant to Jasper, you are going to find it even harder to marry him off to Senya. It's in your interest to give me some sinucca."

Laisa stared at her as if she couldn't believe her ears. "Well," she said at last, "the sauciness of a snuggery whore, I suppose." She dug around in her travel sack and produced a pot. "Here," she said. "Take it. It's already ground, ready for use."

Terelle smiled pleasantly. "Thank you. I knew you'd see it my way."

"One of these days Senya will have to deal with you. And I have no doubt she will."

Terelle, unworried, shrugged. "Thanks for the sinucca."

She ducked out of Laisa's tent and headed for Jasper's. His lantern was still lit, which didn't surprise her at all. She lifted the flap and entered without indicating her presence; she knew he would have sensed her anyway.

"Is anything wrong?" he asked. He was lying flat on his back, hands behind his head.

"Yes," she said. "You should be asleep."

"I think you know why I'm not."

It could have been any one of several things: he was planning for the next day, he was worried they would fail, he was wondering if the Reduners would have time to release ziggers, it could even be because he was thinking of her – but she knew it was none of those things.

"Mica. You are afraid what we are going to do tomorrow will kill him, too."

He gave the slightest of nods. "Terelle, until you came along, he was the only person, ever, who stood up for me. The only person who *cared*. You know what that's like. You only ever had Vivie."

She came to sit by his side on the rugs.

"How can I do something that is probably going to kill

the last member of my family?" he asked. "I've thought and thought, trying to find a way to protect him. If I knew exactly where he was, maybe I could . . . make sure he was all right. But my feelings are so nebulous . . . it's been too long. I doubt I can pinpoint precisely where he is in the middle of a battle. And so there's nothing I can do. Nothing. Tomorrow there's a fair chance someone is going to kill my brother."

"Send him a sky message," she suggested.

"He couldn't read. And I don't imagine that has changed."

She was silent, unable to offer him any comfort, let alone a solution.

"Why did you come?" he asked. "Is there something wrong?"

A hot flush crept up her neck. "I came to make sure you sleep well tonight, because . . . because tomorrow you will need all your strength."

"Sleep? I can't sleep—"

"You will," she said, and bent to kiss him full on the lips. Once more there was that wondrous feeling of water recognising water belonging to the same vessel, of the desire to join the two parts of the whole.

When they parted Jasper said huskily, "But I thought you weren't certain – that you weren't ready—"

"You know what?" she said. "Being ready for marriage and ready for *this* are two different things." Her fingers found the ties of his tunic and deftly undid them. He reciprocated, but his fumbling at her clothes was tantalisingly clumsy.

The water within her responded so that her whole body sang. *I bet the snuggery girls never felt this.*

He was naked, and so was she. Tiny shudders skimmed her skin. He pulled her down, clasped her tight. A moan of pleasure escaped her. After that, she was incapable of a coherent thought for quite some time.

* * *

She was right; Jasper slept very well indeed that night. Terelle lay awake for a long time beside him, caught in the muscular curve of his arm. She felt as if every sense she had was sated, every particle of her body warmly glowing. Nothing she had ever learned from snuggery girls had prepared her for this. Jasper and she had something special and she knew for the rest of her life she would always be aware of him, through his water. She would always know where he was. She would know if he died. At the same time as she was suffused with the joy of it, she felt a wrenching sadness.

She still felt the tug of the mountains, she still felt the power of Russet's last waterpainting.

I'm still trapped, she thought. *Our cage has no visible bars, but they're there nonetheless. But I swear it, I'll break them somehow, because this is where I belong.*

Ryka awoke in the morning, lying in the small store cave off the main cavern of the mother cistern. Tucked into a small space between the rock wall of the cavern and the smooth earthenware oil jars, she found her world had contracted to this space, hardly large enough for her to lie straight. If she stood erect, she was in danger of being seen, and she had to be careful. Fortunately, the slaves, all Scarpen folk, knew she was there and were prepared to keep one of their own hidden at a risk to their own lives.

At first, she was glad of her inactivity. She was exhausted. The arduous ride and giving birth had left her wanting no more than rest and copious amounts of sleep and food and water. And so she stayed hidden and quiet. Besides, she was prepared to do almost anything to avoid Ravard. The thought that he might find her, that he might claim her child as his own, made her gorge rise. *Never. I will not allow it. Not now, not ever.*

Fortunately, Khedrim was content to eat and sleep most

of the time. She lay gazing at him for long periods, enjoying the little moues of his lips, the way his tiny lashes lay against his cheek as he slept, the perfection of his toes, his fingernails, the delicate curve of his ear. This was her child. *Hers –* and Kaneth's, if he ever came back to claim him.

Oh, Kaneth, I wish – I wish you could see him. I wish you could feel what I feel now. I never knew it was possible to feel like this about another person, never. So protective. So utterly consumed with love.

Khedrim. A Reduner name for a Scarpen baby. He's our future, she thought.

When he cried, it was usually in a fretting, irritable way, rather than bellowing, and she was grateful because it meant no one heard. Anina brought food and water from time to time. Ryka managed her body wastes, and Khedrim's, by extracting the pure water and putting the dry residue in a pot for Anina to take away when she had the opportunity. She'd had to explain to the bemused woman that she was a rainlord, then reduce her expectations because Anina's immediate idea was that a rainlord could rescue them all with a minimum of trouble.

After several days of enforced rest, Ryka grew more fidgety. Her frustration boiled deep inside her, but she could not give it a voice, nor quell it with activity. Anina had told her the Scarpen forces were now arrayed around the rim of the crescent slope surrounding the flat area in front of the cistern cave. Kaneth would be there, surely; so near – yet he might as well have been on the other side of the Quartern. He didn't recognise her water any more, let alone remember her.

She was a rainlord, able to help in the coming battle, but surrounded by Reduners, how could she do anything and survive longer than the first few minutes? And there was Khedrim to think of. He changed everything . . .

I will get out of here. With my son. I will take him to safety.

I swear it. I just have to wait for the right moment. Maybe during the battle. If there is a battle.

Patience, Ryka, patience.

She sighed. Ryka Feldspar had never been known for her patience.

Early that morning, Ravard took over the task of cleaning his own pede, much to the surprise of the slave whose job it was. He found a measure of peace in the rhythmic polishing and brushing. And he needed to calm the tumult of emotions, the way his thoughts bucked and churned, refusing to focus on ordinary tasks.

It wasn't the thoughts of war that unsettled him. They excited rather than unsettled. No, it wasn't the coming battle. It was the playing of chala with the heads of their enemies. Not the game itself, but that Davim had asked him to play in the first place, in full view of any watching Scarperfolk.

He wanted Shale to see. He wanted to remind him what happened to Citrine. *I wonder if Garnet is right?* Perhaps the sandmaster had been the one who had caught Citrine on his spear, all those years ago. The thought made him sick. He hadn't thought about it in years, yet now it all came flooding back, and he didn't like it. He didn't like the idea he had been used.

No, Garnet must be wrong. Davim came t'admire my courage. He saw I could be a warrior. He saw I had water talent that I didn't even know about and that I could be a tribemaster, even a sandmaster. It wasn't just 'cause I was Shale's brother. It wasn't.

She was wrong, and yet he thought of her all the time, unsettling, restless thoughts. He didn't know why. She was a slave. She was a lot older than he was. She wasn't particularly beautiful, although he loved her thick wavy hair and – ah, the sheer arousing sensuality of her long legs . . .

531

But she only lay with him to protect her baby. That hurt. He'd thought it wouldn't matter; now he found he wanted more. Sometimes he ached with the need to see a certain look in her eyes – fondness? Pleasure he was near? Something other than anger or pity or resignation. She had tried to escape with the other slaves, with Uthardim, he was sure of it. Something had brought her back, but he wasn't sun-fried enough to think it was her affection for him.

As he turned his attention to brushing out the grit from the softer flesh under the overlap of the segments, he pondered his mistakes. If he could have, he would've turned the sand-glass over and gone backwards in time to undo those errors.

I should never have made the safety of her child a reason for her t'come to my pallet. I should have given her and her babe protection and waited for her t'come to me.

What he had done was wrong. It made him . . . *less*, not just in her eyes, but in his own. He knew that now, when it was far too late to undo the damage. Frowning, he wondered how he knew. Everyone around him took the slaves whenever they wanted. Just as men had come to Marisal the stitcher, his whore of a mother, when they had wanted to lie with a woman. They had paid her, it was true, but their attitude had been the same. She was available and they thought a few tokens bought them the right to do what they liked with her body. He remembered their unpleasant contempt. He remembered that all his father cared about was the tokens. He remembered the times they had been told to leave the hut so she and her customer could have a semblance of privacy. Growing up he'd thought nothing of it; why then did he now feel distaste for her situation, rather than contempt for *her*?

Garnet, it was all Garnet's fault. She had twisted his world somehow with her refusal to be cowed. Her refusal to bow to fear or defeat, her courage – and not least her way of making him think.

Sandblast her, he thought.

"Kher?"

He turned to see one of the chalamen from his own tribe. He forced a pleasant smile. "Havelim? What's the problem?"

"I'm not sure it is a problem, exactly. You haven't seen that young son of mine about, have you? Khedrim?"

"No. Why? He shouldn't be here at all, surely? The lad's hardly old enough."

"I agree. That's just it, he shouldn't be here, but I just saw that his pede – one of those youngsters we brought in, remember? – is down on the pede lines. In fact, two of those young ones are. Which strikes me as strange. Would be unlike the lad to be disobedient, and I can't find anyone who's seen him, but who else would bring in an undersized runt from the dune? Right mystified, I am, Kher."

Ravard's heart started to pound under his breastbone. "Who owned the second one?"

"Don't rightly know anyone had claimed it. That slave of yours was looking after it."

"My slave?"

"The woman. Garnet."

The withering bitch. He could hardly believe it. She had *followed* him, he knew it. She was here somewhere. But why? Not because she missed him, that was for sure. God below, she must be ready to drop her babe any time and she had ridden across the dunes and The Spindlings just to escape? Was she weeping sandcrazed?

"You haven't seen her here, I suppose?" he asked dryly.

"No, Kher."

"I want the whole area searched for her."

The man blinked, puzzled. "For who, Kher?"

"The slave!"

The man looked at him as if he truly was sand-witted.

"You heard me. Organise a search. Use our tribesmen,

and look for anyone who shouldn't be here. Especially Garnet. I don't think you need worry about your son."

The man bowed his head slightly and moved off to organise the search.

Ravard stood still beside the pede, the pede brush he had been using dangling from his hand, his task forgotten.

Terelle rose early that morning, at sunrise. Even so, Jasper had already disappeared from the tent. She dressed, then stepped out through the flap yawning and stretching, smiling in joy at her new memories – only to come face to face with Lord Gold. He must have been coming to see Jasper; instead he caught her in what could only be a compromising situation. She was snuggery-trained and it meant nothing to her, but the expression on Basalt's face told her he had a different opinion.

His cheeks purpled in anger and his eyes blazed. She was taken aback at the ferocity of his stare and retreated a step. Sandblast him, the man had never even spoken to her and he was acting as if she was a Reduner about to impale him on the end of a spear.

But no, I won't let you spoil anything, you stupid scrawny-spirited priest . . .

"Whore!" he said. "Have you no shame?"

There had been a time when she would have slunk away, apologetic, but that was long past. "Actually, no," she replied. *Ashamed? Of what happened last night?* With effort, she stopped herself from laughing in his face. "Not with regard to this, none."

"You belong in a snuggery! You should have stayed there. How *dare* you corrupt the stormlord?" He stepped forward, thrusting his face into hers, spittle spraying. "It was bad enough when I thought you were a Gibber grubber, but I've heard you are actually an outlander, one of the blasphemers who call themselves Watergivers. Your very presence here corrupts. How dare you defile one of our lords?"

She stared at him, more in astonishment than outrage. The sun had risen on a day of battle. By the time the sun set, many of those in this camp would lie dead – and this pompous fool of a priest wanted to single her out for his ignorant diatribe?

She placed her hands on her hips in deliberate provocation. "You don't even know me and you condemn me? What kind of a religious example do you set for the rest of your followers, Lord Gold? And you don't even know what you are talking about. May the spindevil winds preserve me from the stupidity of waterpriests in general, and you in particular!"

He gaped at her. "You ill-mannered *slut*," he hissed. Before she could think of an appropriate reply, he turned away and stalked off.

"Not the wisest of moves, my dear – making an enemy of the Quartern Sunpriest."

Terelle turned. Laisa, of course, who else. Blighted eyes, the woman was always listening, spying, poking her nose into Terelle's business. "Maybe not, but it felt good." That was true; it had felt *marvellous*. She gave the rainlord a broad smile.

To her surprise, Laisa favoured her with a conspiratorial grin. "Nasty, pompous old bore, I agree," she said. "But take my advice anyway and watch your back. Shall we go find some breakfast?"

"My lord!"

She had been dozing, Khedrim lying sated and content in the crook of her arm, but the urgency in Anina's voice jerked her wide awake. She sat up, still holding her son, to see the slave woman's head peeking over the top of the jars.

"They are looking for you! They'll be coming any minute!"

"Who? Who's looking?"

"Ravard and the men from his dune. They are doing a thorough search, and they mentioned you by name." She didn't need to say the hiding place would not survive a proper search; Ryka knew it.

She handed Khedrim to Anina, stuffed the pot and the extra cloths into a gap between the jars, and grabbed up the padded coverlet she had been using in place of a pallet. When she scrambled out from her hiding place, she took that with her; dark and dingy in colour, it was ideal for what she had in mind. Once she was standing beside Anina, she took Khedrim and then wrapped herself in the coverlet, covering the both of them.

"I'm going to hide under the water in one of the cisterns," she said in answer to the woman's questioning look.

Anina's worried look intensified.

Ryka peered around the corner so she could see into the main hall of the cave. It was dim, lit only by sunlight from the entrance. There was the usual bustle: slaves bringing in the pedes to be watered or filling dayjars and water skins, others taking food from the stores to the camp fires out in the open. Outside, though, there was a group of Reduner warriors standing in the sunlight. One of them – or so she deduced from his gestures – was dividing the group up to send them in different directions. She swore under her breath.

"Anina, you will have to tell me when it is safe to come out. Look for me in the far corner of the last cistern at the back of the cave."

Anina stared, bewildered.

"I'm a rainlord, Anina. I'll be fine. *We* shall be fine. What I want you to do now is walk to the entrance of the cave and then pretend you see a zigger coming. Scream, yell 'zigger' and point – but just make sure you point away from the back of the cave. I want everyone looking the opposite way. Now go, and don't look back. Go!" Ryka gave her a push.

Anina hesitated only briefly, then nodded. Ryka watched her go and waited.

Her scream when it came was blood-curdling. Ryka didn't wait to see every head swing the way of that sound; instead she walked rapidly to the back of the cave to the echo of the frantic shrieks of "Zigger! Zigger!"

The cisterns – there were two – were gouged out of the rock of the cave floor. The rim was flush with the floor and the water started about a hand span below. As far as Ryka could judge, it was deeper than she was tall, but not by much. The back one was fed by the inlet pipe, a system engineered so long ago in the past that no one knew who had been responsible. There was a constant flow from one cistern to the other, and the mountain water was always cold.

Ryka knelt by the back cistern, in the darkest corner where little sunlight reached, still clutching the dark mottled coverlet around her. Ignoring the commotion at the entrance to the cave, she pushed the water aside and dried the floor. Then she let herself down to stand on the solid stone of the floor. The air was damp and cold and dark. Khedrim stirred against her making sucking noises, and she wrapped him deep in the coverlet.

She lowered herself to sit, then gingerly allowed a layer of water to close over her head, except for an open funnel of air about the width and length of her arm. She kept the coverlet over her head, and hoped if anyone happened to glance into the cistern they would not notice anything.

As she settled down to wait, praying Khedrim would not start crying, she remembered that other time when she had found safety in a cistern – the day on which her world had disintegrated into pieces she'd never find again. Even if she rebuilt a life worth living, it would be different, with pieces for ever missing. She remembered the last words she had spoken to Kaneth as she watched the spreading stain of blood in the water around them: *Live, live for the three of us.*

She bent her head over Khedrim's. "Live, little one," she murmured. "Live, and we will build a new life, and it will be good, I promise."

37

Scarpen Quarter
Warthago Range

Terelle lay just below the crest of the hill and waited.

Everything was in place. They had spent the better part of the day preparing for this moment, for the precise time when Jasper decided the sun was high enough in the sky for the angle to be right. When everything matched her painting.

It hadn't been a good day. The Reduners had intensified their zigger assault, and the rainlords were hard-pressed to stop them all. Men and women had died. Terelle had never been so frightened. Several times she'd heard the buzzing whine and looked up to see men fall, screaming, clutching at their eyes, or ears, or throat.

In spite of the fear of zigger attack, the men had worked hard most of the night at Jasper's request. They were following the plan based on Terelle's ideas, first cutting as many pede segments as they could from the pedes that had drowned in the rush, then scraping out the flesh. Thoroughly mystified, they filled them with all the sharp-edged stones they could find.

In the meantime, Jasper used the drinking supply to make a block of water several paces each way and a pace deep, to check if Terelle's main idea was workable. Halfway through the night they had the first loaded segment floating easily on top of the water. Jasper, elated, asked them to fill as many pede segments as they could find.

By noon the next day, all was ready. The men were fully armed, waiting quietly for the word. Some even dozed.

Jasper had not answered the sandmaster's message, and as far as he and Terelle knew, Mica was still alive. But they had no way of knowing. When you called a man's bluff it paid to know him, and they didn't. Not really. The thought made her ill, that Mica could die just to make a point. Not so much because she cared for a man she had never met, but because she hated seeing the drawn, haunted look on Jasper's face.

Around her, tension was building. Men woke until everyone was alert – and edgy as they waited. They had been told that the attack would take place when the sun was high in the sky.

She looked around, her waterpainter's eye absorbing the scene, etching it permanently into her memory whether she wanted it that way or not. Ranged just below the south rim of the slope, out of sight of the Reduners, the undisciplined Gibbermen were scattered in small groups, hefting their unlikely selection of weapons. They were noisy still, laughing, teasing their friends, covering their nervousness with banter and jokes and crudity.

Twelve of them waited closer to Jasper, strapping young fellows he had personally selected as capable of handling heavy weights. The pede segments were now lined up in front of them, each laden with stones the size of small oranges. Iani remarked they looked like a line of miniature barges along a portside quay.

The waiting Scarpermen were more serious than their Gibber allies. They sat quietly for the most part, alone with their thoughts – of family and the homes they were defending, perhaps. Waterpriests, including Lord Gold, moved among them, dispensing blessings in the form of tiny waxed sachets of blessed water that could be tied to the upper arm. Even Jasper was wearing one, although Terelle doubted it meant much to him. When Basalt had reached the place where Terelle sat painting, he had passed her by without offering her one, his contempt mirrored in his expression.

A little later another waterpriest, apparently knowing nothing of his superior's prejudice, had noticed she had no sachet and offered her one. She took a petty pleasure in refusing it and felt defiantly unrepentant afterwards. And strangely bereft, too. Hollow inside. Her belief in the Sunlord was now so shaken that it offered no comfort. Once she'd been able to sacrifice a little water and feel warmed inside, less troubled. She'd been able to believe in something larger than herself and be comforted. Now there was just emptiness.

Scattered, too, were the rainlords: Iani, Ouina, Laisa and the others who had joined Jasper from Breakaway, Pediment, Denmasad, Scarcleft and the two port cities. Some twenty altogether. Many lay peering over the rim's edge, even Senya, staring down on the scene below, alert for any zigger attack.

The Alabasters had stayed together, a solid line of white, four deep, their pedes with them. Most were praying. Their mirrors sparkled in the sunlight. *To their god who isn't the Sunlord* . . .

Earlier on, Jasper had passed through the waiting throng, halting briefly to offer a few words of encouragement here and there. Only Terelle and Iani knew he saw victory also as a potential personal tragedy.

How does he stand it? she wondered. *He doesn't want to kill people any more than I do, not really.* He was a man who wanted to rule using his head, not his sword arm – or his killing water-power.

As he looked down on the cistern, his calm was comforting. Davim could choose to launch a zigger attack at the lone figure outlined against the sky, yet Jasper appeared unconcerned. Every now and then he glanced down at the waterpainting at his feet, to check how close the scene she had painted was to what he could see below. "I spoke to Feroze this morning," he said to her suddenly. "About what he knows with regard to Watergiver powers."

She looked up at him in quick interest, even as she wondered how he could talk about it right then. "What did he say?"

Without taking his eyes from the scene below, he said, "He confirmed what you said – Watergivers have two kinds of powers: waterpainting and water moving. I also got the feeling there was something he wasn't saying. They know more than they tell us, I think."

She nodded. "That's what I thought, too."

"Apparently, they don't have to stormbring in the mountains; did they tell you that? In fact, he had some tale I found hard to believe, all about how there was too much water and they directed their talents more to *preventing* clouds from breaking, but—" He broke off, then shouted, "Zigger! Duck!" She buried her head deep under her cloak, which she had brought with her just for this purpose.

A moment later he added, "It's been dealt with. You can come out now."

As she emerged, he reverted to the previous conversation without even sounding ruffled. "Sounded odd to me, and of course Feroze hasn't been there. In fact, from what he said, I don't think anyone from the Quartern ever has except Ash Gridelin."

"And they say he was a Watergiver explorer from Khromatis."

"Yes." He squatted, still watching the sky and the Reduners below. "Lord Ryka once told me the Reduners have a slightly different version, about a paradise beyond the White Mountains where gods deliberately hide their land from greedy mortals to prevent anyone visiting. Their minions manifest themselves as sand-dancers to confuse those who try. According to the

Reduners, these gods are responsible for random rain. Some say the gods' green land is where you go when you die, if you have given proper worship to your dune god."

"So that's different again."

"Feroze said the Watergivers are not gods, but he agrees they hide their land and refuse to let anyone from the Quartern approach it. However, he admitted they do mingle with Alabasters on the edges of the White Quarter."

Terelle snorted. "Yes – mingle. I heard. And leave babies behind."

"I don't think they do that any more, or the Alabasters would be awash in water sensitives, which they are not. Terelle, all these years of hunting for another stormlord and none have been found except me, and I'm flawed. You and I can bring enough water for the Quartern for the moment – but what happens if one of us dies? What happens if I die before the sun sets today?"

He finally looked away from the scene below and met her eyes in a steady stare. "You have to go with Russet, we both know that. Initially, I thought when you reached the place he painted, you could turn around and come back. I thought of sending people with you, to make your return easy."

"And now you've changed your mind?"

"There's a hidden land there somewhere beyond the White Quarter, apparently full of people who can help us. Some of whom can shift water. But they deliberately keep knowledge of it from us. You, however, have a great-grandfather who wants to take you there."

She looked at him, her jaw dropping. "I'll be withered. You want me to go there *and bring some of them back.*"

He nodded. "To be stormlords. Until there are more Scarpen stormlords. Or to be the fathers or mothers of more storm-lords, if that's what it takes. It's the only way I can think to free you from painting storms. It's the only way the Quartern's future can be certain. It's the only way I can ever have any life of my own. But it also means sending you into the heart of a land we know nothing about with the very man who imprisoned you with his painting. And it's just a chance anyway. They might think it's a rotten idea to come here. It's certainly a rotten idea to ask you to go there – but it's the only idea I have for a long-term solution."

She sat quietly, pondering. In pain, yet unable to determine the origin of her sorrow.

"I think," he said slowly, without looking at her, "that this is the hardest thing I have ever had to ask of anyone. I want you here, with me. I want you to be happy, content, safe – and by my side. Instead, I am asking you to leave. To be hurt. To surrender yourself to someone who does not have your best interests at heart. To go into danger." He looked at her then, his eyes a mirror to his misery. "I love you. I always will. And I am asking you to do this, not just for the Quartern, but also because I think it may be the only way we will ever find something for us – a life for us and our children. You are right, Terelle. Using waterpainting, even the way we are doing now, is no solution. It could go horribly wrong at any time. It could have effects we know nothing about. And it would tie you down to a lifetime of repetitive work, or even continuous travelling to the most arduous places in the Quartern. I don't want that for you. I really don't want—" But he couldn't go on.

Terelle intertwined her fingers into his and squeezed his hand. Her thoughts were in such turmoil, it was a moment before she could reply. "I have to go anyway," she whispered. "If ever we can work out a way for you to stormshift without me."

"There'll be a way." He lifted their clasped hands and brushed the back of her fingers with his lips. "We'll work on my using your paintings, even when you are not here. Or I'll find a way to use the power of other rainlords, more than one of them, perhaps, to boost my own power. The way I used Taquar's. We'll find a way. Because we have to. And you'll find a way back to me. I won't let you go alone, you know."

She smiled her gratitude, but it wobbled on her lips. Tears trembled, but would not fall. "You realise that bringing Watergivers here will upset the waterpriests, to say the least? Especially if Watergivers from Khromatis are at all like the Alabasters, and preach what they believe – that Sunlord worship is a heresy based on a distortion of history."

"Wouldn't priests rather find the truth of history than believe a lie?" Jasper asked.

"Are you scoffing me? No, they wouldn't. This is their *faith* we are talking about. Besides, people believe the silliest things at the best of times, even in the face of evidence to the contrary. In the snuggery, the girls used to use an expensive cream to make their skin fairer. It never made the slightest difference, but they kept on using it. They thought anything that cost that much must be good."

He sighed. "You're right. Basalt taught me about the one true faith, and he believed all sorts of stuff that sounded like dubious nonsense to me." He looked back at the sky and his face changed. "The time is right," he said.

"Take care," she said, her heart leaping with fear.

He signalled to the waiting men and they mounted their pedes. Dibble came forward with the pede he was to drive for the stormlord. Jasper smiled at her as he mounted. "Dibble and my guards and Laisa are all pledged to bring me through this alive."

Laisa? She wanted to ask him if he trusted her, then decided she was probably a wise choice. Laisa liked her comfort, and if Jasper was the only way they were ever going to return to plentiful rain, then she would do her best to make sure he lived.

The bladesmen on foot assembled behind the pedes,

checking their rudimentary armour, their weapons. Those on pedeback took up their spears and loosened their scimitars in their scabbards. All of them – bar Dibble and Jasper on their pede – stayed behind the rim, out of sight of the Reduners.

Terelle edged up to look down on the Reduner camp and cavern. She saw the water the moment it left the entrance. A long snake, the thickness of a pede, it slithered out of the cistern above the heads of Reduners, and swung up into the sky. She shivered. This was the crucial moment. If Davim ordered the release of thousands of ziggers now, all their plans would falter and probably fail. Jasper had to work quickly.

She glanced to where he sat, cross-legged on his saddle. His face was impassive, giving no hint of the turmoil of his thoughts, or the strain on his body. She felt it, nonetheless. His water was turbulent inside him.

The great snake looped across the Reduner camp, still dragging its tail out of the cistern opening. Jasper parcelled out some of the water from its head, moulding it, curving it, keeping it smooth to give it the mirror-like qualities he wanted. At the same time he was splitting the rear end of the snake up into great rafts of water. The mid-section he made into a cloud, which he then pushed skywards, controlling its passage so as not to block the sunlight. He was hoping to send it high enough to make ice.

He moved the water-mirrors into place and angled them towards the sun. Almost simultaneously light dappled the cliff opposite. Jasper tilted the mirrors more, shafting reflected sunlight downwards at the camp. Terelle saw Reduners fling up their arms against the brightness, or look away. She saw some of them running, and her heart sank. They were going for their zigger cages. They must have received the order to release them.

Jasper didn't notice. He'd already brought the first of his

water-rafts down towards the rim and held it there, a block of water with no obvious boundaries to stop it flowing away, hovering a hand span in front of where he stood. The men around him were ready and waiting. They seized the pede segments at their feet and floated them on the water-raft. They worked fast, silently, focused.

He did that, she thought. *Jasper.* With the force of his personality and the briefest of training, he had moulded a group of undisciplined Gibbermen into a unified, efficient team. By the time the first raft was crammed with segments, the second raft was already in place to be loaded and Jasper was manoeuvring the first one away from the rim. It sailed across the Reduners, water sloshing a little when he briefly failed to keep the integrity of an edge. Men looked up, faces reflecting their wary incomprehension.

The first row of Scarpen and Gibbermen fighters, led by Iani and the rainlords on pedes, started carefully down the scree. Before long, though, the descent degenerated into a slithering rush as men fell, pedes sped up and loose shale cascaded. Noise crescendoed as men and rocks and pedes rampaged down the slope together. Jasper and his personal pedemen guard, Lord Laisa, Senya and Terelle stayed where they were. So did the Alabasters under the leadership of Feroze.

Below, men ran and shouted, loading their zigtubes. It was going to be close. Too close. One man lifted his hand to gesture at the sky. Others aimed their zigtubes in the general direction of Jasper and his men, then winced as they were blinded by sunlight. More men poured from the cavern carrying zigger cages. Terelle fixed her gaze on the first of the rafts where it hovered over the middle of the open ground in front of the waterhall. She saw the moment when the entity of it fractured as if it was torn asunder from beneath. Water cascaded. The pede segments, filled with thousands of pebbles and sharp-edged stones, toppled. As they fell, tumbling over and over, they spilled their lethal cargo.

To Terelle, it appeared to happen in slow motion. She watched as water and stones showered the men below. Reduners gazed upwards, realising the danger too late. She saw that frozen moment when no one seemed to understand the reality of the coming rain of death. Then the scene broke into a chaos of anguish and pain and screaming. Men collapsed: dead, injured, unconscious, she couldn't tell which. Pedes bolted for the safety of the cavern, ramming people aside as they fled.

Emotion crushed the air out of Terelle, making breathing difficult. Fear and sadness gripped her chest tight. The horror had arrived.

Near at hand someone screamed, "Ziggers!" She heard the buzzing whine, yet could not drag herself away from the horrible fascination of what she was watching. The second, third and fourth rafts were over the Reduner camp now. Rocks spilled on the people below. Reduners toppled as they raced for the safety of the waterhall. She saw zigger cages smashed and hoped desperately that the freed beetles would be wiped out by falling water. Next to her, one of the men who had been loading the rafts clutched at his eye and fell screaming to the ground. It was Laisa who killed the zigger burrowing deep into his eyeball, but the man went on screaming until one of his companions could stand it no longer and clubbed him behind the ear with a rock.

Terelle vomited her last meal.

"Wait here till it's over, Terelle," Jasper yelled. *What if he never comes back?* The thought made her want to throw up again, but she could not stop herself watching.

Jasper turned from her towards the Alabasters under Feroze, and at his nod, they sent their mounts over the rim. Dibble prodded their mount and they plunged downwards with the Alabasters in a moving tide of dust and sliding scree, Laisa's beast close on one side. Senya had remained behind, where she pointedly ignored Terelle.

Just as the riders reached the bottom, arriving immediately behind those on foot, the rainlords combined their power to throw the water from the mirrors at the Reduners regrouping in front of the broken cistern grille. As still more Reduners poured out from the cavern, Jasper shattered the last two rafts. A shower of pede segments, rocks and water struck the ground in front of the entrance to the mother cistern, the sound as loud as anything Terelle had ever heard in her life. The last of the tents were flattened. People were knocked flat. Tethered pedes curled tight into balls, legs tucked away, eyes shuttered and heads deep within the curvature of their bodies. The Reduners who survived the assault from above advanced to meet the first men to reach the bottom of the scree.

The ziggers stopped coming. Terelle looked up in the sky. More clouds were forming, far above her head: black, angry storm clouds. *Stormbringer,* she thought. They used to call stormlords stormbringers. She scanned the ground. So many dead. So many injured. *I never wanted to do this. I never wanted to have to hurt anyone.*

She had painted the mirror and the rafts. She had painted the stones falling. And if asked, she would do it again.

Hidden under the water of the cistern, Ryka could not understand what was happening. The water was moving. Not the gentle flow as it drifted sluggishly from one cistern to the other, but *fast*. As if there was a massive hole in one end of the cistern, sucking out the water. She leaped to her feet in a panic, Khedrim in her arms, and pushed water away from them both. What was going on?

Anina had not returned to tell her the search was over,

even though the Reduners must surely have had time to search the entire cavern and surrounding hills half a dozen times over. Khedrim had woken and been fed, and it had taken an age to get him back to sleep. He'd fretted and cried and squirmed, and she had been afraid someone might hear.

But no one had come. And now, with the baby asleep again at last, the water was being pulled out of the cistern. Panic subsided almost as soon as it began. If water was moving in unexpected ways, then it had to be at the very least a rain-lord who was responsible. And more likely the stormlord.

She widened out her air space, placed Khedrim gently on the floor, and clambered up the rough edges of the cistern until she could peek over the edge.

What she saw took her breath away.

A long whirling tress of water emerged from the cavern and climbed steeply. Outside in the sunlight, men were gathering, fully armed, many of them with their pedes. Most of them were looking upwards and shouting. It was enough to tell her no one would be worrying about her for a while.

Jasper, when you do something, you don't do it by halves, do you!

She nodded in approval as she picked Khedrim up and tucked him into her clothing. A moment later she was back in the store cave. The jars had all been moved around as if the place had been thoroughly searched. She laid Khedrim down on the floor out of sight, still wrapped tight in the coverlet, and then ventured out once more into the main waterhall.

Reduners milled around just inside the entrance, but none of them glanced her way. Some were intent on what was happening outside; others were filling their zigtubes from the zigger cages stacked along one wall. She had an almost overpowering urge to run back to Khedrim, to cower down behind the jars with him in her arms. She was a mother and it was her job to protect her child. Kaneth's child.

Without rain, there is no future for your son, her sensible, reasoning side said in her head. *You're a rainlord. It's your duty to fight Davim to stop what he's doing because, if he wins, the Scarpen is doomed. Not to mention the Gibber and the White Quarter. And your son.*

"Oh, shut up," she muttered, but in her heart she knew the rainlord side of her was right. Fortunately for her own peace of mind just then, she saw Anina sneaking into the cavern and signalled for the slave woman to join her.

"The Scarcleft's forces are attacking?" Ryka asked.

"Yes!"

"Where are the rest of the slaves?"

"They're up in the small cave where the water inlet is. You have to climb up the cliff a bit to enter."

"Can I get up there?"

She shook her head. "Not without being seen. And there's no way out. The water is funnelled in through the roof from the valley above."

Ryka dithered. Risk joining the others? Or was there more of a risk in staying? What if her hiding place was discovered? Even as she wavered, she hated her indecision. *Sunlord blast it, does being a mother turn you into a shilly-shallying sandbrain?*

"Where's the baby, my lord?" Anina asked.

She made up her mind. "Back in the store cave. He's just been fed. Can you lie there with him? If this goes badly, if the Reduners win and I don't make it, try to pass him off as your own."

Anina nodded, her eyes wide with apprehension.

"My real name is Lord Ryka Feldspar of Breccia. Remember it. If the Scarpen forces win, go to any of the rainlords and mention that name."

"Yes, my lord. Just – just in case." For a moment they stared at each other, in a silent sharing. Neither of them mentioned how Anina was to feed a newborn if Ryka died. There was no point.

As Anina turned away, Ryka pushed her maternal instincts into the back of her mind and crept along the wall, still unnoticed by any Reduner, towards the zigger cages. When she was close enough, she grabbed up a cloth covering one of the cages and wrapped it around her head and lower face. Then she edged away and sat huddled against the wall as if she was just another slave woman, scared out of her wits by all that was happening.

Sunblast it, there are so many of the little bastards. She reached out with her senses and began to draw out their water, one by one. The moisture she removed from the cage, so that the manner of their deaths would remain a mystery.

A short time later, just outside the cavern, light flashed, then steadied. She blinked in surprise. The area was lit up, suddenly bright. More puzzled than frightened, she stood to see better. The Reduners outside, half-blinded, were ducking their heads or raising their hands to shade their eyes.

Blighted eyes, what is going on?

And that was when the skies opened up and water, rocks and pede segments came crashing down. When she recovered from the shock, she wanted to rejoice, to laugh at Jasper's ingenuity, but part of her also saw the blood, and the broken bones, and the slaughtered young men.

Oh, Jasper, she thought. *Your brother is out there somewhere. I wonder if you know it?*

38

Scarpen Quarter
Warthago Range

Jasper, amazed, found himself still on the back of the myriapede when he reached the level ground. Gripping the
mounting handle until his fingers ached, he'd muttered, "I
will not fall, I will not fall," all the way to the bottom. The
slide of scree built up as they descended, and they arrived in
a welter of rock and choking dust.

Not everyone fared well. At the base, a young Gibber youth
was sitting on the scree, rocking to and fro, clutching the top
of his shin with both hands. A bone poked out through torn
flesh. At least one white pede had lost its footing and tumbled,
spilling men from its back like bread from a basket. One man
had died, impaled on his own spear. The pede thrashed, scattering stones and bellowing in pain.

Jasper wrenched his gaze from those around him to the
scene in front. On the flat land the first warriors down were
holding their own, just. Some of the Reduner forces had taken
shelter in the waterhall, others were dead or wounded. Even
so, Jasper stared at the number of men attacking and was
appalled. From the bottom of the scree it looked like a solid
wall of steel and men waited for them. But no ziggers. *Be
grateful for that.*

He needed to see better.

"I'm going to stand," he shouted in Dibble's ear.

Dibble nodded.

Jasper grabbed up the extra spear racked along the pede's side and stood. With his feet hooked under the segment handle and the spear haft slotted into the groove carved into the carapace for the purpose, he had some stability and he could see better.

There was water everywhere, most of it too muddy for him to use. He cursed his limitations and left the puddles for the rainlords. He was forced to reach further away for the clean water trickling into the cistern.

The fighting was frenzied. Ignoring it as best he could, he pitched water balls, hard, into faces. A moment's inattention, a hesitation – on a battlefield, men died for that. Dibble and other members of his personal guard knew what to expect this time around. Thrusting spears jabbed, scimitars swept the air in brutal savagery, metal clashed on metal. Pedes reared and keened. Feelers whipped through the air distributing indiscriminate carnage. Injured men screamed and moaned. Maimed men died under pede feet. Jasper didn't kill, but knew more men died on the battlefield because of him than any other single warrior could have dispatched.

The screams. Ah, sweet water, those *screams*. He would hear the echoes of them for the rest of his life. The blood – it was everywhere. His scimitar was clean, yet he was spattered.

A Reduner tried to climb up the pede to slice at his feet. He panicked and threw so much water at him the man had to drop off in order to breathe. A red-robed bladesman on foot leapt for Dibble's reins and yanked. The animal objected and, before Dibble had time to react, opened up its mouthparts and squeezed the attacker's head in the vice of its feeding pincers. Jasper watched, horrified, as the Reduner's skull was crushed. And then his personal horror just became part of the swirling, chaotic hell around him. Blood, smells, screams and fear – all merged into a single, featureless coalescence of revulsion and terror. He fought on in his own way. Manipulating water. Throwing it. Saving lives sometimes, causing death often. Until he was beyond terror, beyond horror, without thought or humanity or reason. *Don't think. Don't care. Don't feel. Not now.*

Still later – moments? A sand-run? Two? – he looked about and saw more of his own men than Reduners. The invaders were being beaten back towards the waterhall or further down the gully. Simultaneously, the knowledge appeared to hit them like the shudder of wind through a grove, and Reduners turned and fled. Those left behind fought on for several more minutes until the whir of a bullroarer sounded. Pedes wheeled, men on the ground scrambled to pull themselves up behind the drivers, all of them racing back to regroup across the cavern front, the cliff at their backs.

"Are you all right?" he asked Dibble. "You saved my life a couple of times back there."

The man turned to grin at him. He dabbed at a cut on his hand, saying, "That's my job, my lord."

"You did it well."

He searched for the water of those who remained. Iani, Feroze, Laisa, yes – somewhere Mica was still alive, too. A moment's relief coursed through him, but hard on that joy came confusion.

He felt something wrong, botched, water falling where there should have been none. Water bizarrely deformed. Panic rose in his throat.

Not water. Ice.

In shock, he remembered the clouds he had sent so high.

Yelling for help from the rainlords, he strove to bring his powers into play. They nudged the falling ice in the right direction so that it fell in front of the cavern and further down the gully, smashing into the bulk of Davim's forces.

Rounded chunks of ice, each half the size of a man's fist, crashed down on the Reduners without stopping.

Jasper blinked, distressed. Some of his own forces were caught up in the edges of the ice fall, too. He saw three or four Alabasters fall from their pede, their bodies blossoming blood. A handful of Gibber men, too slow to separate themselves out from the retreating Reduners, dropped to the ground. A Scarpen pede screamed as its feelers were broken.

Why had he forgotten? He'd sent the clouds as high as he could command them and waited for the ice to fall, but that had been much earlier. When nothing had happened, he'd decided the ploy had failed. He hadn't realised it would take so long.

He looked around. His army and the Reduners were now separated. Davim's men – as many of them as could fit – had crowded into the cave. Those still outside had either run down the gully or sought shelter huddled alongside the pedes, or flattened themselves against the cliff. Ice still fell on that side of the cleared area, the balls sometimes bouncing harmlessly off pede carapaces, sometimes cracking segments and breaking feelers. And sometimes killing men.

Pedes. They didn't deserve this.

Scarpermen, Alabasters and Gibbermen were scattered over the southern half of the flat land and on both sides of the gully running down the middle. The whole area, including the drywash, was littered with the dead, the dying and the injured.

"'Ware ziggers!" Iani yelled, bringing him back to reality even as the ice continued to fall, smaller pieces now. "There's no reason now why those bastards in the cave don't loose the last they have in this direction." He stood up on his pede, ordering bladesmen to heap the dead, face up, as bait, hoping the beetles would not sense much difference between the recently dead and the living. Men raced to obey.

Still keeping track of the falling ice balls to make sure they fell only in front of the cavern, Jasper turned his attention to those around him. He searched out the rainlords with his water-sense, dismayed to find there were six dead, their water lifeless. One part of him thought, *We can't afford to lose so many;* another part simply grieved.

In front of him, Dibble twisted a torn sleeve around a bleeding wrist. Laisa sat on the back of a myriapede behind her driver, looking as if she had just stepped out of her tent. She had partially veiled herself to keep the dust out of her hair and nose; her riding clothes were immaculate still. Looking at her, Jasper was uncomfortably aware of his sweat and dirt and blood. Next to her, Feroze was standing on the back of his great white pede, directing men to carry the wounded to the back. On the ground nearby Jasper saw no less than eight white-clad bodies, and when he glanced over the battlefield he saw many more.

The worst affected, though, were the Gibbermen. Inexperienced and badly armed, they had fought with heart but little skill. The results were horrendous. Their ranks had been thinned. Pedes which had once carried a dozen riders now settled down to rest, legs tucked under their bodies, riderless. One animal was running its feelers up and down a Gibberman's body, grieving. Jasper looked away; each and every death added a scar. Each scar was a burden he would bear.

I'll make it up to them one day. Somehow. But how was it possible to compensate for even a single death?

He searched for others he knew and could not find them. There were a number of suspicious gaps in his own guard he didn't want to think about. Oddly, he found himself thinking of Ryka. He'd never believed in ghosts, but for a moment her presence was there with him, so real he relived his grief at her death. She had taught him so much.

He looked up at the sky. The dark storm clouds were localised directly above. Over to his left, the bottom rim of the sun was resting on the horizon, the light bleeding out over the land and bruising the turbulence of the black clouds with purple. Blighted eyes, the whole afternoon had gone, vanished into the hell of battle. He probed with his senses to see what ice or water remained. Entranced, he paused: the clouds were full of ice balls, rising and falling in the turmoil . . . but how to use them? He gave it a moment's thought, then drew the clouds downwards, sucking the water in all its forms towards him.

Already, as he looked back towards the cavernous entrance to the waterhall, he could see Reduners busying themselves with zigger cages, passing them outside to the armsmen sheltering beside the pedes. They wanted to release them on the edge of their forces to diminish the chance of accidents to their own men.

Around him, Jasper felt the shiver rippling through his army. Facing a warrior was one thing, but a normal man quailed before ziggers.

"Don't run," he yelled. "Whatever you do, *don't run*! Trust me." He continued to drag the storm cloud towards him, pulling it as fast as it would come, hoping he would be in time. "Rainlords, spread out! Concentrate only on the ziggers flying towards your section."

"Down!" Feroze yelled from further along. His white robe was spattered with blood, but none of it seemed to be his. "All you men, crouch down. Put your head between your legs. Keep your nose, ears and eyes covered! Quickly now. Pack in close as you can to one another – that's it! Closer. Closer still."

"You too, Dibble," Jasper said. "This time I can look after myself."

The man nodded and dismounted, pausing only to give the pede the signal to contract its segments to close up the gaps, and then to hunker down to protect its underside. With the pede taken care of, he joined the other armsmen. They all knew it was a temporary measure at best; few wore cloth thick enough to repel a determined and hungry zigger. Between them and certain death were the rainlords – and Jasper.

The buzzing whine, when it came, sent shivers across his skin. Not one, not ten, but fifty or so ziggers, homing in, and behind them, the Reduners in the entrance to the waterhall were already reloading their zigtubes for the next wave. Jasper redoubled his efforts to bring the storm cloud.

Iani looked at him briefly, his palsy accentuated by his fatigue. His face sagged in lopsided weakness, his left hand shook. "Pedeshit," he muttered and killed the first half a dozen ziggers heading his way, "I hope you know what you're doing, Jasper."

The sight of the water cloud tearing through the air, a compact mass of dark fury, was as unnerving as the sound of ziggers, even to Jasper. Momentarily distracted, he missed an approaching beetle and had to whirl around to pinpoint its direction as it zoomed down on the huddled men. He shot a piece of ice, and it disintegrated, shedding chitin and wing cases and soft flesh harmlessly onto someone's back. Further along, several ziggers had penetrated through the rainlord's line and men were screaming with pain as the vile things burrowed in. The rainlords scrambled to deal with the beasts, before they dug into their victims too deep to be shrivelled.

The second wave approached. *Blighted bastards,* Jasper thought, staring at the sky to concentrate on his cloud. Further along the line of rainlords, Laisa sat on her mount, no longer so cool and unruffled. "You conceited Gibber grubber!" Agitated, she waved an arm at the turbulence descending on them from the sky. "You'll kill us all with this kind of pretentious bragging!"

"I doubt it," he said calmly, even though his heart hammered at his ribs. "You hair might be messed up a little, though. Which could be a new experience for you, I suppose."

"You could have killed us all with that ice!"

Jasper whipped the cloud closer, twisting it as it came, moulding its shape into a long tube. And he sent it straight into the opening of the waterhall, sweeping up the remaining freed ziggers and all the zigger cages on the way. He turned to Iani and Feroze. "Now's the time to move closer."

Feroze stood up again and gave the order. Others passed it along to those behind.

The Reduners in the entrance saw the cloud only at the last moment; their view had been blocked by the cliff above them. No sooner had they looked up than the cloud hit them, a whirling maelstrom of ice and mist. The wind tore their zigtubes from their hands and hurled the cages to the back of the cavern. It wrenched the wings from the bodies of ziggers, blew men to the floor and flung them against the rock walls where they were unable to rise against the gale of ice-laden air. Water drenched their robes; hail battered their bodies, bruising them under a barrage of ice. And it didn't stop. The wind Jasper created by hurling the cloud into the cavern had nowhere to go; it hit the walls and hurtled on, its turbulence whirling unabated.

One by one the men in the cave sought the walls and clung there. The ice hit them again and again, bouncing from walls and roof or buffeted in random directions by the wind. It hurt. It blinded. It knocked men unconscious. Sometimes it killed. It brought strong dunesmen to their knees, weeping for respite. Others hauled themselves towards the entrance, terrified, wet, bleeding and confused.

And then Jasper collapsed. His power trickled away, replaced with profound exhaustion. He panted, gasping for air. Unable to stand, he collapsed to his knees. Dibble dug into the saddle bags and hauled out a handful of bab sweets for him. He hardly had the energy to chew, but he stuffed several into his mouth.

The wind abruptly died. Silence came, so precipitate they

were all taken unawares. Then, almost as suddenly, noise overwhelmed. Pedes keening in pain and clicking their distress, the appalling screaming of men overwhelmed by their agony. Men moved and groaned, pedes skittered and shuddered. And the sandmaster's army, what was left of it, began to emerge from the cavern.

"We'll ask them to surrender," Jasper said to Iani as the rainlord rode up with Feroze not far behind him.

"Iani can ask," Laisa said. "You stay here, Jasper. I don't want you going anywhere near those bastards."

"She's right," Iani said, even as Feroze grunted in agreement. "All it would take would be one aggrieved redman to take it into his head to throw a spear . . ."

Jasper nodded, understanding the reasoning, yet irritated, and a moment later Iani rode forward alone with his scimitar wrapped in cloth and held high in his good hand. Jasper guessed that was the accepted way of asking for a parley.

A moment later a man rode out from the Reduners with his scimitar similarly wrapped. Jasper recognised the pede immediately: Burnish, the sandmaster's beast, and Davim was riding it. While he and Iani spoke, Jasper scanned the lines of waiting Reduners, trying to figure out which one was Mica, but in the crowd it was impossible to pinpoint one person's water from another's.

I can feel him, though. He is safe. The joy he felt sifted through him. *Soon we'll meet again, and everything will be all right . . .*

Iani returned almost immediately. He was glowering.

"He said no, I assume," Jasper remarked.

"Actually he said he doesn't care if they lose, as long as you die in the battle. He also said that if you personally surrender now, he will allow Mica to go and he will take all his men back to the Red Quarter. Including those in Qanatend." He gave Jasper a hard look. "He'd kill you, you know."

Jasper sighed and looked once more at the Reduners. They were battered, but there were still enough of them to be a formidable force. They stood silent, armed and ready.

Blighted eyes, he thought. *We have to fight again. All because I have to live.*

"Are you all right, my lord?" Iani asked.

"Exhausted," he said. "I've eaten something, but at the moment I have no powers to offer."

"What answer shall we give them?"

Forgive me, Mica. "We fight."

"Then stay back," Iani said. "That's an order, my lord. We don't want to have to worry about you when we should be fighting."

He nodded, knowing that made sense, and yet felt the heat of a blush in his cheeks. *Shame.* Shame at his relief. Silly, he knew, but felt it anyway.

Iani turned to Dibble and said, "You and your men stay with the stormlord. He is your responsibility. You too, Laisa." He then turned to Feroze and smiled. "Shall we advance on these drowned rats and put an end to this?"

Ryka had no idea how many ziggers she disposed of before the first of the battles began, but it was certainly in the hundreds – enough for several of the Reduners collecting the cages to comment on the number of dried-up beetle husks in worried tones.

"It's those devils of rainlords," another man said. "They're killing them, those skyless dwellers. Damn them to the dune god's hell!"

Not one of them bothered to look at the slave woman huddled against the wall of the cavern with a dirty rag over her head. And then they stopped fetching the ziggers, the stones and pede segments stopped falling from the skies and the battle on the flat clearing in front of the cistern started in earnest. It was horrible to watch, yet there was a sick fascination about it, too.

Too tired to continue killing ziggers, Ryka checked on Anina and Khedrim and raided the food for a meal. Then she crept back to the broken grille at the entrance. She recognised Davim and guessed at the identity of Medrim, the Warrior Son, standing on the back of their pedes, stabbing with spears, swinging scimitars, leaving a swathe of destruction behind them. Ravard fought the same way, except he didn't use a driver. He'd taught his mount to respond to spoken commands; she knew that much from riding mounted behind him. His pede was ferocious. It augmented his forays with weapons of its own – cutting down anyone who did not wear red with the whip of its feelers or the crunch of its mouthparts. Together man and mount were formidable.

As she watched, she tried to come to terms with the relief she felt that he still survived, then gave up. *He's Jasper's brother; that's good enough reason. I personally don't care if he breaks his neck.* And yet she remembered the last conversation they'd had when she'd found out who he was, and been touched by grief at his tragedy. It didn't change anything; he was still the enemy. He and Davim and the Warrior Son – the three of them seemed invincible, damn them.

She scoured the battle for any sign of Kaneth but couldn't see him. Or Elmar, either, blast it. But then, with her poor eyesight, what could she expect? She thought she glimpsed Iani once, using his sword with a killing passion, but she couldn't be sure.

She wanted to fight, damn it, but the thought of Khedrim, her own fatigue and the way in which her cycsight limited her in a large area like this battleground kept her where she was.

Then, when a ball of water came flying past her out of the cistern, she changed her mind. She watched as it smashed into a Reduner face. The man jerked his head in shock, and in the aftermath, as he sat half stunned and half blinded on his pede, a Gibberman stabbed him with a spear.

She grinned and decided even her meagre skills could do that much; it was easier than drying out ziggers or drawing water from men. She sent ball after ball of water into the battle area. *Withering hells*, she thought, *why didn't we think of this during the battle for the Breccian waterhall?* She knew the answer, even as she asked the question. After a lifetime of always saving water and never, ever wasting it, the idea of flinging it at someone was almost blasphemous. It had simply never occurred to them to do it, let alone that such a harmless tactic could be so effective.

Still, even throwing water around was tiring to her in her present state, especially as she had never been a particularly strong rainlord anyway. Fatigue soaked her, dragging at her limbs, miring her thoughts until they were almost incoherent. She slipped back into the smaller cave to check on Khedrim again. Her gaze softened as she cuddled him; it happened every time. Sunlord damn, what was happening to her? So absurd – she'd become as soft as a bowl of bab mash. Here she was, in the middle of a battle, wanting to smile at a baby or feel the tight grip he gave when she put her finger into his palm.

He was restless, so she fed him briefly and he soon dozed off once more. She forced herself to eat some more, pilfering bab fruit and dried apricots from the jars stored in the cave.

When she returned to the main cavern, she had an even better idea. Now that no one was looking, she grabbed up as many of the zigger cages as she could carry and held them one by one under the water of the cistern until the beetles inside had drowned. Then she returned them to where they had been stacked. Each cage had ten ziggers, so she'd disposed of several hundred beetles before she had to stop – or be caught doing it.

The battle had changed. The bullroarer was sounding and the Reduners were retreating in an orderly fashion towards the waterhall.

"Pedeshit," she muttered. "Now what?"

She hunkered down against the wall once more, still with her head and face wrapped in the cloth from the zigger cage. She could hear the sandmaster shouting, ordering the men to regroup in front of the cistern. And then Ravard's voice, yelling for the last of the unfed ziggers to be brought out. Hastily, she retreated to the store cave, but continued to peer around the corner. Anina was hiding behind the jars, begging her to do likewise.

Something crashed down on the ground, shearing the nose from a Reduner warrior on the way down. It was white and hard, but that was all Ryka could see. A heartbeat later, more white rock-like objects followed. Some shattered harmlessly on the ground, others felled men, even killing them. Pedes bolted for the waterhall, fighting men in their frantic fear to get under cover.

Blast, the place was going to get crowded. She dived for her hiding place behind the oil jars.

It was cramped sharing the space with Anina and stuffy under the coverlet. And nerve wracking. They could not risk talking and had to sit still and in silence. There were soon men inside the alcove, helping themselves to water and food or resting while they spoke of the battle and how this one had died or that one had killed a rainlord. And all the time Ryka watched Khedrim for any sign he was going to choose to cry. He snuffled once or twice, a small sound drawing no attention, and slept on.

When you are older, I shall laugh about this with you, she thought, *and tell you what a brave boy you were.* She touched his cheek with her fingertip and added a moment later, *Please let that be true.*

They had no way to tell how much time had passed, but suddenly there was the sound of hurried movement, shouted orders from outside, followed by silence. She waited a while longer, then peeked over the top of the jars. The small cave was empty, and although she couldn't see anyone in the water-hall, she felt sure there were people there, crowding at the entrance. She could no longer feel the presence of the pedes, so she guessed they had pushed the beasts outside, the better to accommodate themselves.

"I'm going out to see what's happening," she whispered to Anina.

The woman nodded, but her face was a portrait of a fear so deep-rooted, Ryka wondered if she could even speak. She patted her arm and left.

The waterhall was still crammed with warriors, but now they were only at the front, standing in rows, facing away from her. Preparing to advance, she assumed, as soon as they were given the order.

And then the picture splintered as though they had all entered the heart of the spindevil wind. A huge rope of water, twirling and howling, touched down in front of the cave to scatter men and zigger cages and pedes, shooting out slivers of white as it passed. One of these shot into the cavern and came to rest near Ryka's feet. She bent to touch it. It was *ice*. For a moment she crouched, unmoving, staggered by the thought anyone could do this. Outside, the sun, now low in the sky, was still hot; the land still burned with the heat of the day. How could it happen? She'd seen ice before; in the deep of the desert at night sometimes the dew froze, or the stopper in a dayjar iced up. But never in the heat of the day.

There was no time for thought. The wind and water entered the hall, blowing men before it like grass seeds in a gale. She turned and plunged back into their hiding place, drawing Anina and Khedrim into her arms, wrapping them all in the

566

cloth and the coverlet. Khedrim started to wail in earnest, but that was the least of their worries. No one was in any condition to hear him or, if they did, to care.

Men crowded into the store cave again, screaming in terror and pain. Ice hit the walls over Ryka's head, shattering and sprinkling them with shards. The wind rocked the row of jars, and several of the empty ones smashed. Fortunately half of one of these broken vessels came flying through the air, only to wedge firmly between a full oil jar and the wall, forming a shelter protecting them from the worst of the other flying debris. Ryka dragged up some dregs of power and used it to ward off flying ice and water.

Anina sobbed endlessly, and Ryka could hardly blame her. *Jasper,* she thought, *if I ever get out of this alive, I will wring your neck for scaring me to death.*

Just when she thought they might live through the storm-lord's version of a spindevil wind, a ferocious gust made a man stagger into one of the oil jars, sending it reeling into another to create a chain reaction. Several jars smashed and suddenly there was bab oil everywhere.

Ryka leaped up, Khedrim clutched to her chest, to save him from being drenched in oil. She slipped almost immediately and sprawled, flinging herself onto her side to avoid crushing Khedrim. He immediately started bawling with surprising volume. And at that precise moment, the wind stopped. It didn't die away, it simply vanished. People began to pick themselves up off the floor. Into the sudden silence, Khedrim cried, the insistent squalling of an outraged newborn. Heads swung her way, disbelieving stares sought her out.

She scrambled up, horrified. The more she tried to quieten Khedrim, the louder he yelled. Someone came pushing through the crowd of armsmen, and Ryka found herself looking up at Ravard.

For a long moment he was speechless, with rage or surprise she couldn't tell. She stood, joggling Khedrim to quieten him, but he would not oblige. He was dripping with oil, and so was she.

"What the sandblasted withering *shit* are you doing here?" Ravard asked at last.

"Running away from the Red Quarter?" she suggested. "And having a baby."

He opened his mouth to say something else, but no words came out.

Outside, people were calling for him.

Finally he said through gritted teeth, "Stay here. I'll deal with you later." He turned and was gone.

Ryka loosened her clothing and gave Khedrim the breast to quieten him, even as she looked for Anina. To her shock, the woman was lying as still as death in the oil. A pointed shard of pottery jutted from her breast. Her eyes stared sightlessly upwards, an expression of surprise on her face.

Ryka cursed, long and hard. The woman could have been safe, hiding with the other slaves, but she had come back to help.

Oblivious, Khedrim sucked hungrily until, sated, he fell asleep again. There was nothing she could do for Anina, so she walked away with him in her arms into the main cavern. The Reduners – at least those who were alive and relatively unhurt – were all gone. Injured warriors were sprawled on the floor, some unconscious, some with broken limbs, along with many bodies. There was nothing left of the zigger cages, or the ziggers.

Outside, after some sort of lull, the battle had been rejoined. Keeping close to the cavern wall, she peered out. A glance told her it would not be easy to sneak away. The fighting surged immediately outside the cavern, with the Scarpen forces pressing the Reduners closely. If she did venture out, she would be in danger of being trampled by a pede or cut by a stray antenna, not to mention killed by someone from the Scarpen forces. Her oil-saturated clothing was a travelling tunic of Laisa's, but it had long since been stained red by the sands of the quarter. Her skin and her blonde hair were red. The middle of a battle was not the place to start arguing your allegiance.

Damn, she thought. Wearily she slid down the wall into a sitting position. She ached everywhere, uncomfortably aware she was still bleeding from the birth and that her exhaustion was worse after using her water-powers.

Jasper, you had better win this battle, because I don't want Ravard to come for me . . .

And where the blighted hells was Kaneth? *Please let him be all right.*

It was every man for himself. Ordinarily the Reduners would have made short work of an army of shopkeepers, bab pickers and resin collectors, but Davim's men were no longer the proud, undefeated marauders they had been a day or two before. The Scarpermen and their allies smelled victory and fought with a tenacious spirit. Jasper, far from being safe at the far side of the flat ground, found himself imperilled by the ferocity of the fighting around him.

Sandblast them, he thought, *they are out to kill the storm-lord.* He had taken advantage of the lull during the parley to eat as much as he could force down his throat. He could manipulate water again, but he suspected his renewed power would not last long.

He stood up on the back of his pede and tried to keep himself above the worst of the fighting. He plucked water from the cistern and threw it at those who came at him, leaving their destruction to the guards around him. Laisa, next to him and still giving the appearance of being coolly unruffled, blinded men by sucking the water from their eyes.

Aghast, he saw Dibble fall, and then another of his personal guard, and another. His pede, driverless, reared in anger when a Reduner thrust a spear between its segments. Jasper tumbled and sat down hard on the saddle. He saved himself from a further fall to the ground by grabbing for the mounting handle. Someone cut the man down from behind, and the spear was dislodged.

A Reduner driver on pedeback, tall and well muscled and young, fought his way towards him. The man wielded both spear and scimitar, and wreaked havoc among the bladesmen and pedemen tasked with keeping Jasper safe. The ordeal inside the cavern had not cowed this warrior. His robe was wet. His face was bruised and bleeding. His nose was broken. Yet he manipulated his steed with a finesse not many could achieve in normal circumstances. He alternated between scimitar and spear, slashing and stabbing with grim intent. When he wasn't using the scimitar, he held it in his mouth, blunt side inwards. When he wasn't jabbing with the spear, he used it as a stave to ward off attack. Both weapons were red with blood; men died under the feet of his mount. He was terrifying.

They had not crossed weapons, though Jasper had first glimpsed him earlier through the shambles of battle. Now he was close.

Jasper threw water at him. The warrior appeared to sense it coming. He ducked and the water splashed harmlessly across his shoulder. When Laisa turned her attention to him, he spoke to his pede and a feeler whipped through the air in her direction. She saw it coming and threw herself sideways. The serrated edges of the feeler tore through her clothing and she fell to the ground.

The Reduner reared his pede, throwing himself forward until his face was cheek-down on the beast's head. He yanked hard on one of the reins and yelled something to his mount. The animal pivoted on its back feet, and as it turned, its feelers swung out in a wide slashing arc, ripping at everything within range. Men fell, Scarpermen, Gibbermen and Reduner alike; pedes scattered.

Jasper and the man were left alone in the centre of a cleared space.

I'm going to die, Jasper thought. *Unless I think of something quick.* He raised his scimitar into a defensive position and drew as much water as he could from the cistern with what remained of his power. *I'll throw the lot at him, knock him from his pede . . .*

The response was sluggish. He felt as if he was hauling a recalcitrant pede, not water. He panicked. He was tired, so tired. *No, this is more than that. What the salted wells is he doing?* And then realisation: *He's a reeve. He's fighting me with water skills.* The man couldn't move water, but he could resist it.

When the pede whipped its feeler around at Jasper, fear clogged his thoughts. He jerked back, thinking he was going to be sliced open, but the animal stopped short of hitting him, and gently touched his face with the tip. Only then did Jasper notice the feeler on the other side was broken. He looked into the animal's myopic eyes. It was stroking him, a pedeic sign of welcome to a friend.

Jasper jerked his head up to look at the rider and was overwhelmed with a sense of recognition. It wasn't Mica's face he recognised, but his water. The features were those of a hardened Reduner marauder: sharp-chiselled, calculating, stained red – that man he did not know. But the inner self? That was Mica; that hadn't changed.

And he was swinging his scimitar in a sideways slash that was about to remove Jasper's head from his shoulders.

Worst of all was the recognition in those cold, dark eyes. Mica Flint knew exactly who he was going to kill.

39

The battle swirled back and forth. Attack, retreat. Retreat, attack. Slash, parry. Parry, slash. Reduner killed. Alabaster triumphant. Scarperman killed. Reduner victorious. A patterned chaos; a chaos with patterns of life and death. Deadly, desperate and bloody. Always bloody.

And always ugly.

The ugliness of the smell. The stink of voided bowels, of urine, of vomit, of guts spilled and trampled. Pede shit, pede piss. The sweet, strong stench of human blood. The ugliness of the noise of battle. The grating scream that wouldn't stop. The harsh sobbing of human beings in pain. The bubbling gasps of men without lungs trying to breathe, the animal grunting of men without guts trying to go on living, the whistling breath of men with pierced windpipes. The guttural horror of the death rattle, that awful final sound of air expelled, never to be replaced. Each sound distinct, whether soft or loud, and each layered in its own special abomination.

And now, for Jasper, another ugliness. His brother was going to kill him. Mica. Mica who had loved him. Worried about him. How could it ever have come to this?

It was the pede that saved him, Mica's pede. It brought a feeler down hard across Mica's arm and the stroke went astray.

"*Mica!*" Jasper cried. "It's me – Shale!" And to make sure he was heard, he shut out the battle. He enclosed them in their own little world: he ringed them with water, a wall of water, with just Mica and him and their pedes inside. Sounds muted, and the men outside drew back, fearful. Yet the wall was nothing more than water, easily breached.

Mica recovered from the pede's blow and, cursing, swung his scimitar up again for another murderous slash.

Jasper grabbed up his spear to parry the blow that was coming. "You used to protect me," he said.

The words were inane, yet they penetrated, and only then could he see the boy that had been Mica in this man, this Reduner. There, on his face, a brief look of worried uncertainty, once so typical of Mica, as his resolution wavered.

Yet when he spoke, his voice was firm, the words those of an adult. Jasper recognised the voice, heard the slur of the Gibber accent, although it was no longer so pronounced. "I know. And you have t'die. I'm sorry, young'un. But that's the way it's got t'be. We have t'go back to random rain. And my name is Ravard now," he said. "Kher Ravard." He lowered his scimitar slightly and Jasper read a brief flash of compassion in those dark eyes, even though the line of his mouth and jaw told him there was no wavering of determination.

Still, it was hard to believe he was in danger, so he ignored it. "I almost didn't know you," he replied. And it was true. Without the pede, would he have ever recognised this tall tribesman with the red face and hard eyes? The effect was accentuated by the newly broken nose, still bleeding, and the bruises on his cheekbone. "You've grown . . ."

Sand-brain. Can't you think of anything sensible to say? He blurted out what was uppermost in his mind. "How could you, Mica? How could you join Davim's marauders? After what he did to us?"

Mica stiffened. "Did to us? What did he do to us that hadn't

574

already been done by our own? Beaten, starved, going to bed thirsty night after night, licking the dew off palm leaves just t'get enough water."

"Davim killed Citrine," Jasper snapped, outraged. "He threw her up into the air and caught her on his chala spear—"

"I remember. So what? One less snivellin' brat, what did it matter? She was a third child. She wasn't even s'posed t'have been birthed. She should never have been born!"

Jasper stared at him, appalled. "She was our *sister!*"

"She was thieving our water, when we didn't even have enough for ourselves. Soon enough she would've been sharing our food. A half-starved, snot-nosed, half-wild animal like th'other waterless brats of Wash Drybone. She would have growed up t'be another gormless bitch like Marisal, watching and simpering while her husband-pimp beat the hell out of his son. She was better off dead." He looked at Jasper in scorn. "And so you're the stormlord now. What have you done for the waterless of the Gibber, Shale? You going t'change it so bastards like Rishan the palmier don't steal the riches of the grove from those who work it?"

"Give me time—"

"Ah, yes, time. The rainlords and stormlords ruled in Breccia City 'fore we stood up to piss, Shale, long before. And they did dry-boned *nothing* for the likes of us in the hundreds of years they had power." He leaned across from his pede to insert the point of his scimitar under Jasper's chin.

Jasper thought of lowering the water wall, of calling for help. But that would mean Mica would die . . .

Inside he ached.

Mica continued, apparently unworried about his own safety. "The poor of the Gibber won't get any richer while water-soaked priests and rainlords sit on their well-watered bottoms and sip their sweetened drinks. I've been t'waterless hell and back since we were parted, you stupid tick. I've dragged myself up through the ranks t'what I am now – the Master Son of Dune Watergatherer. *I* did that, not any water-sated bleeding stormlord."

They were interrupted briefly then. One of Jasper's guards and his Reduner attacker smashed through the water wall in a shower of droplets. They were so intent on their own fight, they didn't even seem to see the two men and their pedes. A moment later they splashed back out, grunting and panting, with their scimitars still clashing.

Jasper hardly spared them a glance. "Mica, think! What about those innocents killed by Davim's men? The children? The women raped? Countless people died in Qanatend and Breccia City just because they were outside their houses! Ziggers don't choose . . ."

"Where were those innocents – or their parents – when us two were growing up half naked and starving and thirsty in Wash Drybone? Shivering all night long 'cause we didn't have nothing but a sack t'cover us? Tell me that! *They* didn't give a pede's piss then." His hate spewed out, hot and angry and twisted, all the more potent for its basis of truth. "Scarpermen came and took our resin, but what did we ever get back for it, you and me? Marisal sold her 'broidery for a pittance in tokens and never made enough t'feed us. She sold her body for water, a whore used by the Reduner cara-vanners and 'Baster salt traders. They used her and all the while they mouthed their pious sayings to us kids. And in the end the only time the rainlords came t'see how well we did under their benevolent rule was when they wanted t'rob us of our talented brats." The point of his scimitar forced Jasper's chin still higher. "I will *never* be at the mercy of rain-lords again, Shale. They doled out just enough water t'keep the tribes of the villages from dying, but never enough for us t'be *free*."

"You think it's easy to bring the whole of the Quartern

water? I'm only one man! The old Cloudmaster was only one man! How the—"

Mica scowled and dug the blade point a little deeper. Jasper jerked back and pushed the blade aside.

He opened his mouth to speak again, but Mica interrupted. "Sandmaster Davim has showed us how. If we can't control a stormlord ourselves, then we go back to a Time of Random Rain – and so will everyone else. We'll see who heads the meddle then, won't we? Will it be a Reduner, d'you think? – or a Scarperman, used t'living inside his walls, with a roof over his head and a fancy 'broidered pillow under it?"

"You're not a Reduner, Mica. You're a Gibberman."

"That's where you're wrong. I've *earned* the right t'be a Reduner. And I'm not giving it up."

"You'll have to kill me to go back to a Time of Random Rain."

"You could join us, urchin."

Was the offer made in all seriousness or did he do it to mock? Jasper didn't know. He felt an overwhelming despair. Where was his brother? Where was the child who had cared for him as best he could? Where was that person in this man with the hardened soul and scornful words? "Mica—"

"Mica's dead, Shale. This man here in front of you? He's Ravard. And he has no heart, no compassion, no place for affection for a long-lost brother. This –" he tapped his own chest "– is what you got in Mica's place. This is all there is: Tribemaster Kher Ravard, Master Son of the Watergatherer. Reduner with his own tent and his own woman and his own tribe." He grinned, and there was nothing pleasant there.

Jasper knew then he ought to kill this man. He ought to pour his water on him and then stab him with his spear while he was blinded and startled. But he couldn't. For all his words, this was Mica. He had Mica's mouth, Mica's voice, Mica's memory of their shared childhood.

He didn't know what to do, and his indecision twisted his guts with nausea.

"Who's the fastest, d'you think, brother?" Mica asked softly. "Can I plunge this sword into your throat quicker than you can hit me with that water, d'you think? You can't take my water, y'know. I am water sensitive enough t'stop you."

He knows, Jasper thought. *He knows I will never do it.*

And then he was forcibly reminded again that he and Mica were not the only two people in the world. A pede came crashing through the water wall, its rider crouched on its back, bloodied scimitar in his hand, his robes almost torn from his reddened body. Jasper recognised the beak-like nose and close-set eyes: Davim the Drover. Instantly, while Jasper was distracted, Mica had the blade back at his brother's throat.

"So we meet again, Gibber boy," Davim said, and his voice was almost a snarl. "Leave him be, Ravard. This one's mine."

"If my sword falls away from his throat, he'll act," Ravard warned, and his eyes never shifted from Jasper's.

"He's *mine!*" Davim cried, and brought his pede closer to face Jasper's, on the other side from Mica.

Jasper flicked his gaze from Mica to Davim. The brightness of the glitter in the sandmaster's eyes was fuelled by contempt and hate.

Because I'm a stormlord. He needs no other reason.

Mica shrugged and gave a slight quirk of his lips as if to say: *what does it matter?* He dropped his sword and moved out of the way. Jasper exploded the wall of water into Davim's face.

And Iani, appearing out of nowhere, flung his dagger straight and true into the sandmaster's back. "No," the rainlord said as the blade thunked home, "*you* are mine, Davim. For Qanatend and Moiqa."

For a moment, nothing changed. Then Davim's scimitar dropped from his hand and he fell forward, toppling towards Jasper. Instinctively, Jasper raised his spear. Unseated and spewing blood, the sandmaster fell against the point, impaling himself. Soaked in blood and shuddering, Jasper pushed him away. Davim slipped from the steel of the spearhead and, his eyes wide in shock, crashed to the ground. He lay there on his back, looking up at Jasper with an expression of disbelief on his face as his life dribbled away.

"Look, Lyneth! He's dead. I told you, m'dear. I told you I'd do it." Iani lifted his head and tried to grin in Jasper's direction, but his twisted mouth drooped on one side, producing an ugly scowl instead.

"For Citrine," Jasper said.

Davim heard the words, but they made no sense to him at all.

By the time Jasper thought to look around, he was surrounded by Alabasters and Scarpermen. Mica had gone, melted away into the fight in front of the cavern. A bullroarer sounded a moment later, and the sound was taken up in ululations uttered by the Reduner warriors.

The scene was confused. Reduner bladesmen on foot were sprinting away. The fight was abruptly broken off all over the clearing. The Reduners were retreating on the run, their pedes with them. And everywhere Jasper's men, exhausted and wounded as they were, let them go.

Feroze rode up, holding a piece ripped from his robe to the side of his head. His ear had been half torn off. He looked down at Davim. "Isn't that the sandmaster?" he asked.

"Yes," Iani said. He jabbed the body over with his foot. "He's dead." He looked up at Jasper. "I think we should go after them. We need to free Qanatend, and if they are allowed to reinforce the men they already have in the city—"

"Iani, they still number more than we do. We won because we had a stormlord and rainlords. And we are all exhausted. Look at you – you couldn't raise a drop of water from a cup in your hand. If our men go after the Reduners with us in this state, more of them will die."

"More of us will die when we free Qanatend if we wait," he returned.

Feroze shook his head. "If we follow them now, there's not much we can do. They can block the whole wash with a few men while the main force gets clean away. We should follow with the main force tomorrow once we have recovered our water-powers."

"Feroze is right," Jasper agreed.

"Who was that ye were chatting to in the middle of the battle just then?" Feroze asked, wincing as he pressed the cloth to his ear.

"The new sandmaster of the Watergatherer," Jasper replied. "He was the Master Son until a moment ago."

"And is he likely to be a thorn in the foot in the future?"

When the long silence threatened to become embarrassing, Jasper forced the words out, trying to conceal the anguish behind them. "Yes. I rather think so. He also believes in a return to a Time of Random Rain. I'd like to say I could persuade him otherwise, if we were to meet again – but I suspect I would be lying."

Oh, Mica. It should never have been like this.

Feroze heaved a sigh, then grimaced at the pain of his wounded ear.

The sun had set, but there was still enough light in the sky to see by now that the storm cloud was gone. Some of the more resourceful men were already pillaging the cavern for torches and lanterns.

Jasper, so fatigued his hands shook and he had to clench them into fists, took a moment to look around, but his head was having trouble understanding what he was seeing. The ground was littered with bodies of the wounded and the dead, their allegiance now irrelevant. Lord Gold was directing men to carry the injured into the cavern. One of the waterpriest rainlords from Pediment was methodically checking each body to see if they really were lifeless. Her clothes were torn and the whole side of her face was bruised. Several Gibbermen were walking behind her, collecting all the weapons. Off to one side, Messenjer held the corpse of Cullet, his eldest son – the one Terelle had never liked.

She'll be glad it isn't Sardi, Jasper thought.

Dibble was anxiously hovering at his elbow, inquiring periodically if he was injured. He shook his head. "Not as badly as you are," he replied, taking in Dibble's bleeding shoulder, cut wrist and bruised face. "Waterless skies, man, get a physician or a waterpriest to look at that shoulder. That's an order. And get someone to do a count of all my guard. I want to know how many are still fit, and how many dead."

As Dibble left, Jasper turned to Iani and Feroze. "I'd like figures from everyone."

Iani nodded. He spared another glance for Davim's body as he turned to go. "So much damage and sorrow," he said sadly. "And for what? Moiqa is still dead." He looked back up at Jasper. "And I don't know why I'm still alive. I never wanted to be. So many good men dead, and this stupid husk of a man with his dribble and his limp lives on. I've lost the only woman I ever cared for and the only child I ever had. Why would I want to go on living?"

"I need you," Jasper said simply. "Maybe that's why."

Iani grunted. "Maybe. Maybe. Lyneth, oh, my little Lyneth. Four years in the hands of that monster . . ." His mumbling faded as he walked away with Feroze.

Jasper headed towards the waterhall, knowing he had to see what was left of his pitiful army who had fought so well. Knowing he had to see who was dead and who was alive.

The first person he came across inside the cavern was Laisa. Her clothes were torn, her chin was badly grazed from her fall, and she had a scimitar slash across the back of her arm. A physician had sewn it up for her, and now Terelle was bandaging it with a piece of cloth torn from a dead Reduner's sleeve. They were arguing as she worked, Laisa snarling and cursing Terelle between gasps of pain, Terelle growling back, telling her to keep still. It was plain they loathed each other; it was equally plain, at least to Jasper, that each had developed a wary respect for the other that had nothing to do with esteem.

As Jasper stood and watched, his need of Terelle swamped him. How could he ever do without her? And yet, he must. If the Quartern was to have stormlords, she would have to bring them. If she was ever to be free of her waterpainted future, she had to live that future.

As she tied off the bandage and leaned back away from Laisa, he heard her say, "Just keep your brat of a daughter out of my way. Or I might be tempted to paint her, and believe me, she wouldn't like the result." Then she looked up and saw him. She came across to him, both hands held out to take his. They stood like that for a long moment of silence and need.

"What are you doing down here?" he asked. "You should have waited up at the camp."

"I stayed there until I saw the Reduners leave. I worried," she said. "I lost sight of you in the battle. And Senya was worried about her mother. For once we found we had something in common, so we came down the slope to find you both."

"Senya's here? That surprises me. She doesn't like unpleasant things."

"Well, she saw Laisa was all right and then sat on a boulder at the edge of the wash and refused to look at anything. She's probably still there. I can't say I blame her."

He opened his mouth to try to tell her how he felt. To say how much the idea of the dead and dying devastated him.

To say his meeting with Mica had left him shattered, not knowing how to pick up the pieces. As usual, the words wouldn't come.

Terelle understood. She put her fingers across his mouth, stopping the words he was trying so hard to voice. "No, Jasper," she said. "I know how you feel. I helped to paint it, remember? Watergiver help me, these – these are my deaths, too. And we will learn to live with them, you and I, in time." She took a deep breath to steady herself.

"We won," he said, and knew he sounded foolish. "If you call this a victory."

"It was," she said firmly. "They won't be back."

He might. The thought was terrible. Too awful to ever put into words. How could he fight his brother? What had he ever done to Mica that he had been prepared to kill him? He knew the answer even before he formed the question, for Mica had told him. His brother saw him as joining the people responsible for their miserable childhood: the wealthy Scarpermen. The enemy of the Gibber, of the poor and wretched and waterless.

Terelle watched him, head to one side. "You found Mica."

"Yes. He knew who I was. He wanted to kill me. Might have done so if his pede and then Iani hadn't intervened."

She stared at him, horrified.

He looked away, adding, "All these years I dreamed of seeing him again, of rescuing him. And when we met, he didn't want to be rescued. He wasn't a slave, but an heir. Worse, he wanted me dead. He sees me as an enemy. I owe my life to a pede, Terelle. A pede with a long memory. I once pulled it out of a flood rush down a wash. How the salted damn Mica obtained that particular beast, I have no idea, but I'll bet it isn't a co-incidence . . . I'm babbling, aren't I?"

"Oh, Shale. I – that's awful."

He searched for hope in all that had happened. "In the end he didn't kill me when he could have. Maybe – maybe he found he couldn't. But I am not sure it's ended. He's the new sandmaster, and he wants to return to a Time of Random Rain. The fighting is not over."

She was silent. There was, after all, little she could say.

"Terelle," he said, "I'm sorry. So terribly, terribly sorry."

"For what?" she asked.

"For asking you to waterpaint this. For taking away your choices, yet again. For not protecting you in the first place. For – everything."

The smile she gave was both sad and knowing. "Neither of us had much choice, did we?" She made a gesture at the carnage around them without looking at the dead. "Make me another promise, Shale. Promise me you'll build something decent out of this."

"I promise I'll try."

"I keep forgetting to call you Jasper. Do you mind terribly? Jasper is the stormlord. Shale – he's the person I care about."

"You can call me whatever you want, and I'll like it. Although you could try, um, 'darling' or 'beloved' or something." He reached out and touched the tear hesitating on her cheek and a smile twitched at the corner of his lips. "Don't leave *too* soon, Terelle. Please."

She shook her head and what Jasper read on her face made him pull her roughly into his arms. She clutched at him, her embrace as desperate as his own, her needs matching his, as potent and passionate, containing all the wretchedness he felt himself, and all the hope he dared to dream might be theirs.

They stood like that for a long time, two people loving each other, surrounded by horror, trying to make sense of it all and hoping that at the end, they would still have their love, even if all else had gone.

"Mother!"

Senya's outraged tones cut through Laisa's pain and brough

her back to the present. Sighing, she gripped her elbow in a futile attempt to contain the agony of her throbbing arm. "What is it?"

"It's that horrible snuggery girl!"

Laisa stared at her daughter in incredulous disbelief. "We are in the aftermath of a battle and you want to complain about Terelle Grey *now*? Can't it wait?"

"She's hugging Jasper, and he seems to like it." Senya's face was sour as she pointed at the subject of her ire.

Laisa glanced that way and sighed. "So?"

"He can't *marry* her, can he?"

Laisa forced herself to coherent thought. "There would be plenty of objections. Jasper needs to have stormlord children, and your offspring offer a chance of being that, at least. You are the logical mate for him, but preferences don't carry the weight of law, you know. We can attempt to persuade him, but we can't force him."

"I'm going to have his baby."

"Oh." She wasn't surprised, but she had trouble grappling with the implications. She was hot and thirsty, exhausted and hungry. She needed rest and pampering, and Sunlord knew when she would get any of that. *Damn you to a waterless hell, Taquar. You brought us all to this.* "Then I think we shall have to make sure he will marry you, shan't we?"

"Can we force him to?"

"Oh, for Watergiver's sake, Senya, why would you want a husband who has been forced into marriage? No, we will *entice* him to do so. Easy, with someone who has an overdeveloped sense of duty. You *might* try being more pleasant to him, you know. If anything more is needed, we won't do it." Senya pulled a face at that, so she added, "If any further *encouragement* is needed, someone else will do it, not us."

"Who?"

"Lord Gold and the Sun Temple do have their uses.

For now, you can make yourself useful and get me a pede and a driver. I want to get back to my tent."

"Lord Iani and that awful 'Baster man are saying the pedes are for the wounded."

"Am I not wounded? Just go get one, Senya, and leave the conversation for some other time." Left alone, she glanced over to where Terelle stood within the encircling arms of the stormlord.

Laisa's eyelids began to droop with fatigue, then snapped open. *I'll be waterless*, she thought. *I know where I've seen that face of hers before.*

Not in person, but in a painting. A waterpainting, in the hallway of her own home, Breccia Hall. That strange old outlander artisman had painted a girl riding a black pede across a white saltscape. Laisa had been annoyed, because it hadn't been quite what she expected when she'd asked for something unusual, unlike the artwork he had done for others. Now that she recalled the painting, it was obvious that Terelle had been the model.

She frowned, trying to make sense of that. *Sometime, I must work out what this whole waterpainting thing is about. There's a mystery there, and that girl knows what it is. But not now, not now . . .*

Tired, she closed her eyes and lay back against the cavern wall.

She had no idea that just over two runs of the sandglass earlier, Ryka Feldspar had done exactly the same thing in the same spot.

40

Scarpen Quarter
Warthago Range to the gates of Qanatend

Ryka, almost unbalanced by fatigue, tried several times to leave the cavern while the battle was raging outside. The first time, she was threatened by a Scarperman who almost ran her through before he realised she was a woman with a baby; the second time she came close to being knocked flat by a blinded Reduner warrior and then trampled by a pede. Both times she retreated and watched for another opportunity. She couldn't tell who had the upper hand, and as the battle continued, she grew more desperate.

She tried again when the sun was low in the sky, the shadows long. Nothing much had changed. The fighting was still ferocious, the thickest of it directly in front of the entrance. She edged out past the grille, flattening herself along the rock face of the cliff, her arms wrapped protectively around Khedrim. Her chosen route was interrupted almost immediately. A Gibberman pulled a Reduner from his mount and both men thudded to the ground at her feet. They'd lost their weapons and rolled across the ground like a pair of schoolboys in a fight. Only this was deadly. The Reduner had his hands around the Gibberman's throat and was choking him. The Gibberman was trying to knock him out with a rock. Ryka settled the argument by kicking the Reduner between the legs. She leaped over them both as the Gibberman finished what he had started, but she still didn't progress.

Ahead a wounded packpede with a spear thrust into one of its eyes thrashed around in a frenzy of pain, attacking anything in sight. She took one look and retreated again. She knew she had built up a little more power after eating, but she was loath to use it on a pede. She wanted something in reserve for emergencies.

Just then, the nature of the fight changed. At first she wasn't sure what had happened. Someone shouted, but she didn't catch the words. A cry went up, a mix of victorious elation and wails of despair. It was followed by the rhythmic thump of a bullroarer. A heartbeat later, every Reduner seemed to be moving.

She paused, trying to make sense of it, hesitating about which way she should run. The Reduners were congregating in front of the cavern, cutting off her retreat in that direction; behind her the maddened packpede had just impaled a Reduner with a mandible and now, crazed with pain, it was tossing him into the air. When it flung the body aside and lumbered in her direction, she turned to flee.

And came up against the body of a myriapede, deliberately pulled in front of her.

The driver was Ravard. Quietly he gave the order for the other six or seven Reduners on the rear to kill the wounded pede. One of them stood and launched a spear into the beast's other eye. It reared, lashing its feelers through the air.

Ryka backed up against the cliff side. Carefully she sent her power to tease water out of the cistern. A single ball of water might be enough to confuse Ravard at a crucial moment . .

"Get up on the pede," he told her. "We're leaving."

She cursed silently, every foul word she could remember. If she'd stayed in the cavern, she would have been safe.

You withering sand-brain, Ryka. You should have had more faith in Jasper.

"You may be, but I'm not," she told him levelly. "I'm staying here, with my own people."

"Get up, or I'll haul you up."

"Ravard, go away. You don't want a reluctant woman in your bed, or another man's child. You are young yet, and there are other women out there. Just leave me be."

"I am the sandmaster now," he said. "You'll be my wife, and your sons will rule if they are water sensitive, I swear it. You're worthy of being a sandmaster's consort."

"I haven't the faintest wish to be a sandmaster's anything! And you, sure as the sands are hot, don't want me in your encampment. You wilted idiot – I'd kill your warriors given half the chance and dance on their bleeding graves!" The ball of water was in the air above him now; she resisted the temptation to look up. Instead, she glanced around to assess the surroundings.

And stared, rigid with shock. The man sent to kill the packpede had only made things worse. The now blind animal took a flying leap and hit the cliff beside her head on. The force of its charge, the weight behind that leap, broke its head open, spraying liquids and chitinous pieces into the air. And its great body, towering over her, began to topple in her direction. She released her hold on the water and turned to run, knowing she was too late to escape. It was huge, several times larger than any myriapede. It would crush her, and Khedrim as well, as if they were made of paper.

Ravard was showered with water. He didn't appear to notice. With one fluid movement, he leaned down and grabbed her arm. He swung her upwards, her upper arm clamped tight in his grip, yanking her away from danger. The Reduner behind him on the myriapede reached out to help him take her weight and drag her onto the back of their mount. Terrified for Khedrim, she clutched him to her breast, with one hand, and let it happen, even as her shoulder was wrenched and her body bruised.

Their pede was already moving, itself panicked. The falling packpede crashed into it. The myriapede keened its distress and bolted, but not before several more Reduners had leaped to take hold of mounting slots on the other side.

Ravard yelled for one of them to take the reins and drive. He himself pulled Ryka up into his arms and placed her in front of him on the second segment, his arms wrapped around her and the baby to stop her from falling. Khedrim screamed and screamed, his little body tense with instinctive terror. Ryka sobbed, ripped through with pain, her shoulder shrieking, her stomach cramping.

Oh, pedeshit, she thought, aware of the blood between her legs. *This is not good.* She bent her head over the baby and tried to soothe him, but he would not stop. Ravard was yelling, ordering his men to put as much distance between them and the Scarpen forces as they could before nightfall.

The pede was already in fast mode, feet whirring as it churned through sand and over rocks on its way down the gully. All around them there were other pedes, each packed with warriors. They plunged down the drywash in bucking lines, as frantic as a stampeding wild meddle. It wasn't yet dark, but the light was fading. Neither the beasts nor their drivers hesitated or curbed the headlong rush to escape. The animals jostled one another, feelers swinging, mandibles clicking, segments brushing the boulders. Wounded men fell and were left behind.

Ryka, thrown from side to side, lurching backwards and forward, was in constant pain. She couldn't believe this was happening. After all she had gone through to escape, and now she was retracing the ride that had cost her so much to make. She was being returned to slavery.

And she could not stop Khedrim crying. She touched his face in concern. Two days old, and what had he known but war and confusion? *I am so sorry, little one. You chose one sandblasted awful time to be born. And when I meet Kaneth again, I'll kill him, I swear. And this great hulking lout Ravard as well, I promise.*

Then she thought of a world where Kaneth was dead and her heart sank within her. Why had she seen no sign of him in the fighting? Nor of Elmar? In fact, of none of the other escaped slaves. *Where did they go?*

Kaneth had to be alive. Somewhere.

Later, much later, she was aware of being lifted down from the pede. Every bone, every joint, every muscle screamed with pain. At least Khedrim had finally fallen asleep, more with exhaustion than anything else.

Someone folded a blanket several times and placed it on the ground for her to lie down. It was dark and bitterly cold, and when she shivered, several cloaks were thrown over her. Under their cover she drew out the cloths between her legs and discarded them. They were saturated. She tore some pieces off the blanket and used them instead. Khedrim whimpered unhappily, so she fed him. Someone handed her some water and she drank deeply.

At least there was plenty of water; they were following the Qanatend tunnel and the men had broken into it through a maintenance shaft. What would once have assailed her rain-lord's soul, she now regarded with gratitude. She knew if she was dehydrated, she would have no milk for Khedrim. A little later Ravard appeared and gave her a handful of dried bab fruit. She took them wordlessly, ate every one and asked him, coldly, for more. He gave her his share. She took them without a word of thanks. Afterwards she slept.

They had left sentries behind, and when no one came after

591

them, they stayed where they were until the sky started to lighten in the morning. Ryka felt a little better when she awoke, glad to find her bleeding had lessened. She rose, wondering if she should escape now or later. When she reached for her powers, though, she realised her weakness. She could move water, but doubted she could kill in the rainlord fashion. Now was not the time to rebel.

Listening to the conversation of those around her, she gathered they intended to stay in Qanatend for a few days to rest the pedes and give the wounded a chance to recover. If the Scarpermen came, well, they would fight there. And win.

She had to eat well and rest herself so her powers would return. *Soon,* she told Khedrim in a whisper into his ear, *soon they will learn what it is to cross a rainlord.* She was fed up with being constrained by circumstances. Her rage was growing by the hour and it was all she could do to stay quiescent when Ravard approached her with his peace offerings – a water skin, something to eat scrounged from the little they had.

Fortunately, he was fully occupied with his men. Warriors from outside Ravard's tribe were not happy at being led by a man so young, who had ordered them to retreat from a battlefield where almost two thousand of their warriors lay dead. Ravard had to act now to consolidate his position, and she saw little of him.

They reached Qanatend in the mid afternoon under a blazing sun.

When Ryka saw the city walls ahead of her, ringed by bab groves, she could only feel relief. Sunlord, how she needed some rest! The southern gate was directly ahead of them at the end of the track, and the gates were closed. Towers on the walls were tall enough to overlook the bab groves, and beyond them the city rose to the top of the conical hill where the city's waterhall and its windmills for raising the water were located

Immediately below was Qanatend Hall, where Moiqa had once lived with Iani and Lyneth.

As they rode the last of the track, the gates swung open. Ryka, sitting behind Ravard, holding Khedrim, had to peer around him to see what was happening. To her mild surprise a group of Reduners rode out towards them, some sort of welcoming party, she assumed. Simultaneously, the walls came alive as tens of men lined up behind the daub parapet.

Ravard jerked in surprise. "What the—" he began and hauled on the reins to halt his mount.

Kher Medrim, the Warrior Son, who was riding next to him looked across uneasily and said, "They must have every man we left behind up there on the walls!"

"And some," Ravard muttered, frowning.

Ryka squinted to see better. The wall bristled with spears as if they were making it clear they were well armed. Even more odd was what she noticed next. The person in the lead of the group coming towards them appeared to be a child. When she stared harder, Ryka realised she was actually an old hump-backed woman, small in size because she was wizened and shrunken with age.

"Who the sands is that?" Kher Medrim asked. "There are no Reduner women in Qanatend!"

"There certainly weren't a few days ago. Go back through the men," Ravard said quietly. "There is something odd here, and I can't smell what it is yet. Warn everyone to be on the alert. Weapons at the ready. Put a watch on all sides and tell the rear guard to scatter through the trees in case anyone comes at us from behind."

Medrim nodded. The others on his pede dismounted at his request, and he rode back through the column. Ravard gestured the men now on foot to line up on each side of him. He then turned to Ryka. "Get down and stand over there at the side of the track. I think there's trouble, and I don't want either of you hurt."

She nodded and did as he asked.

The riders from the city continued to approach. Four pedes headed the group, each with only the driver. Thirty bladesmen and chalamen followed on foot. When they were within twenty paces, two of the riders detached and rode ahead another ten paces. The woman and a tall man.

Ryka shaded her eyes with a hand, squinting in her attempt to recognise them. The woman she didn't think she had ever met. Strangely, she rode a packpede, not a myriapede, and it dwarfed her, accentuating her small stature. The man . . . his red hair was short and lacked the braids and beads of a Reduner warrior. His face was scarred.

Deep within Ryka a sob swelled but was not voiced. *Kaneth*

It was Kaneth. Emotion warred with astonishment Disbelief. He was with the Reduners? *No, wait. That wasn' possible. Then—?*

The old woman: she must be Vara Redmane, of course Which meant Kaneth had not tried to head south for the Scarpen but had sought Vara's rebels, and then together they had taken Qanatend. *I'll be withering waterless. That rangy bastard of a husband of mine, he always does like to do the unexpected.*

Hope went to her head like the strongest of amber taken on an empty stomach. She could hardly contain the bubble of laughter, or joy, that begged to explode from her lips. She wanted to say aloud to Khedrim, "Look! That's your father!"

She edged off the track back into the first line of bab trees and while Ravard was still in shock, she took a few steps closer to the rebels. Towards Kaneth.

And then another thought, less happy. *Or is he still Uthardim Please remember me, love. I am bringing you your son.*

He had not noticed her, or rather perhaps he'd made

othing of the Reduner woman with an anonymous bundle
n her arms.

There was a time when you knew my water, she thought
numbly.

"Kher Ravard," Kaneth said in Reduner, and his voice held
authority. "You are not welcome here. This city is returned
to the Scarpen. The warriors you left behind are either dead
or gone back to their dunes. As you must go now. We are
several thousand strong, all well armed. We have ziggers.
Release those you have, and ours fly from the walls to you."

His Reduner had improved considerably since she had last
heard him use it, but still she wondered: several *thousand*
men? Was he getting his numbers mixed up?

Without waiting for Ravard to reply, he continued, "We
are fresh and our men—"

"And women!" Vara added in Reduner.

"—are spoiling for a fight." He exchanged a grin with
the old woman and switched to the Quartern tongue. "You
may have more men but our armsmen want to end the
Watergatherer's dominance of the dunes. And seeing you are
here, I guess you have lost the battle against the stormlord. I
don't see the sandmaster. Is he dead?"

"*I* am sandmaster of the Watergatherer!" Ravard snapped
in Reduner. "I rule the dunes now."

Kaneth continued in his own language. "If you mount a
siege here, how long before the stormlord and his men appear
behind you? You would be the insect crushed beneath our
feet. Go, while you still can."

*Why is he giving them a chance? They are tired and wounded
and demoralised. Perhaps he doesn't know how badly they have
been defeated . . .* Her thoughts jumbled, Ryka edged further
and further away from Ravard and unstoppered the water
skin she carried. *No, he's not an idiot. He has a reason for not
attacking. Or Vara Redmane does. Don't bother with that now,*

you sunfried woman. Just get out of here! She poised herse
to run to him.

Ravard yelled at her. "Garnet! Stop where you are!"

Kaneth's head jerked her way. And he tensed in the saddle
his spine rigid, his hands tight on the reins. His eyes bore
into hers. Astonishment – no, *shock* – drained colour fror
his face. He appeared to be rendered speechless, incapable c
movement.

Ryka whirled to face Ravard. Drawing herself up, holdin
her chin high, she spoke in the Reduner tongue, wanting hir
to know exactly what she was. "This ends here, Mica Flint.
am no slave of yours. I am Lord Ryka Feldspar, of Breccia
She pulled the water out of the water skin into the air an
kept it hovering in the air between them.

"No," he whispered, aghast, the sound strangled in the bac
of his throat. "That's not possible."

"Uthardim is my husband and he will pull the earth from
beneath your feet if you lay a hand on me again. Remembe
what he did to Davim's tents in your encampment."

Colour drained from Ravard's face, then rushed back, dark
ening his features. Fury flashed in his eyes. He leapt to h
feet on the back of his mount, his spear poised to throw
Instantly she sent the water to hover at his cheek. When h
tried to bat it away with a hand, his fingers ran through
without effect.

A murmur of fear and anger swept the Reduner rank
Men hefted their spears, awaiting the word to kill. To kill he
To kill Kaneth. Uthardim.

Behind Kaneth, his men edged forward, closer to him an
Vara. A mix of ex-slaves Ryka knew and Reduners she didn
She recognised Elmar on the pede that moved up to Kaneth
side.

"You're a single breath away from death," she yelled, st
in Reduner so his men would all understand. She touche

he water to his cheek. "Think before you move a finger. I an smother you with just this much water, and I can take ne water of any man who thinks to spear me."

He swallowed, then looked from her to Kaneth and back. The moment stretched taut, every warrior poised on the brink f explosive action. Ryka's gaze never shifted from Ravard's. f he gave the order to kill her, he would probably succeed, although he would doubtless die as well.

He moved first. He lowered his chala spear. "I will never est until I have killed you," he rasped, and it was to Ryka he poke. She was the focus of the unrelenting blaze of his stare, ut the words were for Kaneth as well because he added, "Until *both* of you lie dead at my feet." He snapped an order o one of the men on the ground and the men lowered their pears and sheathed their scimitars.

Ryka felt her power drain away. The water splashed on the roadway. She was shaking, trembling in reaction.

Ravard turned his mount away from the gate, and the column began to follow. Under the watching eyes of the men n the walls, they started to circle the city to the east in order o head towards the dunes. In front of the gate, no one moved ntil Ravard and those at the head of the column were out f sight.

Then Kaneth, still seated on his mount, leaned towards Elmar. He swung his pede prod and struck the pikeman with blow that would have sent Elmar sprawling to the ground he hadn't saved himself by grabbing for the segment andle. He swayed and righted himself, but made no move o retaliate.

Ryka blinked, bewildered. Watergiver's heart! What was all hat about?

Kaneth moved then. He urged his mount forward to her de and slipped down to the ground. Ryka didn't move. She asn't sure she could.

His hair had grown, covering the worst of his head scars, and the burn on his face was fading. With a hesitant hand, he reached out to part the coverlet she had wrapped loosely around Khedrim to protect him from the sun. He touched the tiny chin with a fingertip. Then he looked back at her.

"Ryka," he said. "Oh, *Ryka*."

41

How long had he been there? He was no longer sure. Already he had lost track. Watergiver help him, how would he be able to tolerate this? To tolerate the *powerlessness* of it! No one to command or respect him. No one in fear of him. No one anticipating his whims.

Just endless days of boredom, stretching out ahead . . . Eight *years*! And no guarantee he would be freed even then. Using his crutch, he paced the floor, dragging his injured leg. Up and down, up and down.

When he read, the books only reminded him of what he had lost. When he slept, he dreamed of women now out of reach. When he dreamed of Terelle, of her body, he could never carry the dream to fruition. Frustrated, roiling with anger – yet he had nothing to vent it on. If he shouted at the world, there was no one to hear.

He'd locked Shale up like this. The Gibber brat hadn't gone sandcrazy. But then, the mother cistern had been luxury to a dirty Gibber urchin. He, on the other hand, he was a rainlord!

But Shale had escaped . . . *There must be a way for me to do the same* . . .

Davim. He had to rely on Davim. Davim would come, Shale would be punished, and he would be released . . .

That Gibber brat would never be clever enough to bring down the sandmaster, the idea was laughable. Davim would come. And if he didn't, Laisa would. Senya would make sure of that.

Senya, of course. She must be his hope. The sand-brained brat was in love with him; she'd made that clear enough.

It was just a matter of time. Of patience. And he had always been a patient man. He had prided himself on his patience. Besides, he still had one more arrow already fitted to his bow. One more way to control Shale. All he needed was to get out of here.

When he sensed water approaching, he rushed to the grille. Visitors . . . He didn't care who it was. His desperation to see someone, anyone, was overwhelming. And it could be Davim and his men. Hope rushed into his throat spasming, choking him with anticipation.

But it was the last person he wanted to see.

Iani rode over the hill alone. He approached the grille, and then sat watching Taquar impassively from the back of his pede. "I have a present for you," he said. He took a parcel wrapped in bab matting and threw it onto the ground so it rolled up against the grille. And then he turned his mount and prodded it back the way he had come.

"No!" Taquar called. "No – wait!" He gripped the bars of the grille. "Iani – please, come back—"

Iani did not even bother to glance over his shoulder.

Taquar took a deep breath. How could he lose control like that? He was the Highlord of Scarcleft. He would be strong. He *was* strong. He would *not* beg.

He stood erect, his hands clutching the grille, a spider caught in an iron web not of his own making, and watched the man ride away.

He knelt at the grille and tried to pull the parcel inside. was just too large to fit through the squares of the grille, s he put his hands through and started to unwrap it. As the last wrapping fell away, he sat down on the ground with a thump, his heartbeat skidding violently in his despair. A stench of rotting meat tainted the air.

"No," he moaned, "*Nooooo—*"

Davim's head stared back at him, mouth grinning wide to mock the man behind the bars.

GLOSSARY OF CHARACTERS AND TERMS

(Note: Characters and terms introduced for the first time in this book are not included.)

ALABASTER
Name given to the White Quarter by its inhabitants. Also the name given to the white-skinned, white-haired people who live there. The Reduners call the Alabasters "the Forbidden People".

ALMANDINE FAMILY
see GRANTHON, NEALRITH, LAISA and SENYA.

AMETHYST, Arta
Dancer and friend to Terelle. Killed by Taquar after she had aided Shale's escape from Scarcleft.

ARTA (f) or ARTISMAN (m)
Title given to professional artists (dancers, painters, singers, musicians, etc.).

ASH GRIDELIN
The Watergiver's real name.

603

BAB PALM
Palm tree grown extensively in the Scarpen and Gibber; also found in small numbers around waterholes in the Red Quarter. The trunk is the main source of wood for the Quartern; the fruit, shoots and roots are edible; the leaves are used for thatch and weaving baskets, mats.

BASALT, Lord
Rainlord and High Waterpriest of the Quartern, second only to Lord Gold in the religious hierarchy.

'BASTER
Derogatory shortening of Alabaster.

BERYLL FELDSPAR
Ryka's younger sister; water-blind.

BLOODSTONE
See MARTYR'S STONE.

BRECCIA CITY
Scarpen city, traditional seat of the Cloudmaster.

BURNISH
Name of Sandmaster Davim's myriapede.

CHALAMEN
Spear-carrying Reduner warriors.

CHERT
One of the sons of Rishan the palmier, the head of Wash Drybone Settle.

CITRINE FLINT
Shale's baby sister; murdered by Sandmaster Davim.

CLOUDMASTER, The
A stormlord who also rules the Quartern through his fellow stormlords and a Council of Rainlords. The temporal power of a Cloudmaster is limited largely to water matters, maintenance of trade routes and taxation, achieved through consensus with his or her water-sensitive peers.

DAVIM, Sandmaster
Sandmaster of Dune Watergatherer and acknowledged leader of the Red Quarter by virtue of his charismatic leadership and armed campaigns.

DAYJAR
A container which holds exactly the amount of water gifted as a free daily ration to those entitled to such an allowance.

DROVER
Colloquial term for a Reduner, originating in their herding of pede meddles.

DROVER SON, The
Title given to the sandmaster's pedemaster. Not necessarily a blood son of the sandmaster.

DUNE GOD
Each dune of the Red Quarter is believed to have a god who lives at the heart of the dune.

ELMAR WAGGONER
A pikeman, friend and battle comrade of Lord Kaneth Carnelian.

ERITH GREY
Terelle's father, killed by Russet Kermes before she was born.

ETHELVA, Lady
Water-blind wife of Cloudmaster Granthon Almandine, mother of Highlord Nealrith, grandmother of Lord Senya.

FEROZE KHORASH
An Alabaster salt trader who also acts as a spy for the Bastion of the White Quarter. Escaped death by the Scarpen Enforcers thanks to the intervention of Shale Flint.

GALEN FLINT (also known as GALEN THE SOT)
Shale, Mica and Citrine Flint's Gibber-born father, husband of Marisal the stitcher. Killed by Reduners in Wash Drybone Settle.

GIBBER QUARTER
One of the four quarters of the Quartern. Gibber folk live mainly in settles in the drywashes, eking out a living from bab palm cultivation and fossicking.

GOLD, Lord
Name given to the Sunpriest, the most senior of the Quartern's priests; always at least a rainlord.

GRANTHON ALMANDINE, Cloudmaster
Highlord Nealrith's father; recently dead of apoplexy and exhaustion suffered when Breccia was attacked by Reduners

GRATITUDES, The
Yearly religious festival of thanksgiving in the Scarpen Quarter

HANDMAIDEN
A female sex worker in a snuggery.

HARKEL TALLYMAN, Seneschal
Seneschal of Scarcleft Hall and head of the Highlord Taquar's Scarcleft Enforcers.

HIGHLORD
A rainlord or stormlord who rules one of the eight cities of the Scarpen Quarter.

HOUSE OF THE DEAD
Religious building where water is extracted from the dead for re-use, as part of the funeral service.

IANI POTCH, Rainlord
Rainlord, husband of Highlord Moiqa, father of Lyneth; partially paralysed by apoplexy and somewhat deranged by grief and guilt at the disappearance of his daughter.

JASPER BLOODSTONE
Name used by Shale Flint after his arrival in Breccia.

KANETH CARNELIAN, Rainlord
Bladesman and rainlord, close friend of Highlord Nealrith, husband to Ryka Feldspar, comrade of Elmar Waggoner.

LAISA DRAYMAN, Rainlord
Widow of Nealrith Almandine, mother of Senya Almandine.

LORD GOLD, The
See GOLD, Lord

MARISAL THE STITCHER
Shale Flint's mother; killed by Sandmaster Davim while defending her daughter Citrine.

MARTYR'S STONE (also known as BLOODSTONE)
Name given to a type of green jasper flecked with red droplets; particularly valued by the priesthood, as it is supposed to have been stained with the blood of the Watergiver when he was attacked by nonbelievers in the Gibber.

MASTER SON, The
Title given to the heir of the sandmaster of each dune; not necessarily a blood son of the sandmaster.

MEDDLE
A herd of pedes.

MICA FLINT
Shale's older brother. Disappeared, either killed or taken prisoner by the Reduners during the raid on Wash Drybone Settle.

MOIQA, Highlord
Highlord of Qanatend, wife to Lord Iani, mother of Lyneth, believed to have died during the siege of her city.

MOTHER CISTERN
A cistern, supplied by mother wells, that in turn supplies water to a city through tunnels.

MOTHER WELL
Wells dug down into the water table, from which water runs into a mother cistern.

MOTLEY, The
The multi-coloured mixture of paint powders that forms a base coat for a waterpainting, necessary to fix the future of the scene depicted.

MYRIAPEDE

The smaller of the two species of pedes. Has six segments behind the head/thorax, three pairs of feet per segment; can seat five to six riders if there is no baggage, but manages better with only two to three riders. Feelers are as long as the body.

NEALRITH ALMANDINE, Highlord

Cloudmaster Granthon's son, rainlord, Highlord of Breccia. Died by the hand of Jasper after being severely tortured by Davim.

OPAL, Madam

The owner of the snuggery where Terelle was raised.

OTHER SIDE, The
OTHER SIDERS

Anywhere across the Giving Sea. Other Siders visiting the Quartern are mostly traders and seamen. They are not encouraged to stay long because of their waterless status.

OUINA, Highlord

Middle-aged Highlord of Breakaway, widow, mother of six children, none having more water talent than a reeve.

PACKPEDE

Length variable, three to five times the length of a myriapede, with eighteen segments and fifty-four pairs of legs. Feelers generally no longer than a myriapede's.

PALMUBRA

Sun hat used in the Scarpen, woven from the leaves of the bab palm.

PEDE

Large desert herbivore native to the Red and White Quarters. Black pedes now used throughout the Scarpen, Red and Gibber Quarters, and white pedes in the White Quarter, as personal hacks (*see* MYRIAPEDE) and beasts of burden (*see* PACKPEDE). Tearing, cutting and crushing mouthparts masticate food externally. Poor eyesight, excellent sense of smell.

PEDEMASTER

Man given responsibility for the care of a stable (Scarpen Quarter) or a meddle (Red Quarter) of pedes.

PINNACLE, The

Ruler of Khromatis. Always a Watergiver.

QANATEND

The Scarpen city closest to the Red Quarter, taken and held by the Reduners.

QUARTERN, The

A loose confederation of four distinct quarters (gibber plains, sand dunes, stony drylands and salt plains). Ruled by a Cloudmaster who has limited powers, each quarter largely independent except for water matters and matters involving trade routes, for which they are centrally taxed.

RAINLORD

A water sensitive who can sense the presence of and move small bodies of water and who can kill in the "rainlord way", i.e. take a person's water from their body. Addressed as "Lord".

RED QUARTER

That section of the Quartern consisting of lines of red sand dunes, peopled by Reduners.

REDUNER

A person born in the Red Quarter, or adopted by a tribe of the quarter. Anyone who has lived long enough on the dunes to be stained red, and to have adopted dune culture.

REEVE

A water sensitive who can sense but not move water.

RUSSET KERMES

A waterpainter born in Khromatis, great-grandfather of Terelle Grey. Murderer of Terelle's father before she was born.

RYKA FELDSPAR, Rainlord

A short-sighted Breccian rainlord of limited water-power, a scholar and teacher. Married to Lord Kaneth Carnelian.

SAMPHIRE

The only city in the White Quarter.

SANDMASTER

The ruler of a dune, commanding all the tribes found on that dune. Usually a water sensitive.

SCARCLEFT

The Scarpen city ruled by Highlord Taquar Sardonyx.

SCARPEN QUARTER

The most prosperous of the Quartern's four quarters. Consists of five stepped cities of the Escarpment, two port cities and one northern city on the other side of the Warthago Range.

SENYA ALMANDINE, Rainlord

Adolescent daughter of Highlord Nealrith and Rainlord Laisa. An unskilled rainlord.

SETTLE
Gibber village, usually located inside a drywash.

SHALE FLINT, Stormlord
Gibber-born son of Galen and Marisal, identified and trained as a stormlord by Taquar Sardonyx, then by the rainlords of Breccia and Cloudmaster Granthon. Also known as Jasper Bloodstone. His claim to the rank of stormlord or the title of Cloudmaster is debatable.

SHUFFLE UP, To
The process that changes a waterpainting from a mere artwork to a work of magic, fixing the future of the scene and people portrayed in it. It entails the use of the motley by a water-painter of talent.

SIENNA
Terelle Grey's mother, a woman of Khromatis who died in a Gibber settle after running away with her lover, Erith Grey. Granddaughter of Russet Kermes.

SINUCCA
A plant, the leaves of which can be made into a contraceptive paste.

SNUGGERY
Higher-class brothel (with either manservants or hand-maidens as sex workers).

STORMLORD
Water sensitive with higher powers than a rainlord. Can move fresh water or water vapour over long distances in larger quantities than a rainlord. Can make and move clouds.

TAQUAR SARDONYX, Highlord
Highlord of Scarcleft City. Unmarried and childless.

TERELLE GREY, Arta
Great-granddaughter of Russet Kermes. Born in the Gibber Quarter, but apparently related to the ruling family of Khromatis. Waterpainter.

TIME OF RANDOM RAIN
Period before the rise of water sensitives, about a thousand years ago, when rain was uncontrolled and scarce. Reduners were the major force in the Quartern during this period.

TRIBEMASTER
A man who leads a tribe of any dune of the Red Quarter; usually a water sensitive.

VARA REDMANE
Elderly widow of the Sandmaster of Dune Scarmaker and now apparently leading a rebellion against Sandmaster Davim's leadership. Whereabouts unknown.

VIVIANDRA (VIVIE)
Terelle's "sister", actually unrelated, sold to Opal's Snuggery with Terelle by her father. Now a handmaiden.

WARRIOR SON, The
Title given to the sandmaster's warrior leader on each dune. Not necessarily a blood son of the sandmaster.

WASH DRYBONE SETTLE
Gibber village where Shale Flint was born.

WATER-BLIND
Lacking any water sensitivity, i.e. not able to feel the proximity of even nearby water.

WATERGATHERER, The
Now the main dune of the Red Quarter, as the home dune of Sandmaster Davim and his tribes.

WATERGIVER, The
Believed by the Scarpen pious to be the intermediary of the Sunlord who taught men and women to manipulate water, thus bringing the Time of Random Rain to an end. His actual origins are disputed, even among the waterpriests. Real name believed to have been Ash Gridelin.

WATERGIVERS
Name sometimes used by the people of Khromatis to describe the water sensitives of that land. Includes waterpainters and those who can move water.

WATERHALL
A cistern room where the flow of water in and out is controlled by reeves.

WATERLESS, The
Anyone who is not entitled to a daily free water allowance. In the Gibber and Scarpen Quarters, anyone born to a waterless father, or deemed to have no regular employment, is one of the waterless.

WHITE QUARTER
The section of the Quartern closest to Khromatis. Peopled by the Alabasters. Produces salt, and related mineral products.

Samphire is the one plant that grows well. Native pedes are white in colour.

ZIGGER

Winged flesh-eating, blood-drinking beetle, native to the Red Quarter and now used as a weapon. Can be trained not to attack their owners. Excellent sense of smell and eyesight.

ZIGTUBE

Tube used to release ziggers, useful for determining their direction of flight.

extras

extras

about the author

Glenda Larke is an Australian who now lives in Malaysia, where she works on the two great loves of her life: writing fantasy and the conservation of rainforest avifauna. She has also lived in Tunisia and Austria, and has at different times in her life worked as a housemaid, library assistant, school teacher, university tutor, medical correspondence course editor, field ornithologist and designer of nature interpretive centres. Along the way she has taught English to students as diverse as Korean kindergarten kids and Japanese teenagers living in Malaysia, Viennese adults in Australia and engineering students in Tunis. If she has any spare time (which is not often), she goes bird watching; if she has any spare cash (not nearly often enough), she visits her daughters in Scotland and Virginia and her family in Western Australia. Visit the official Glenda Larke website at www.glendalarke.com

Find out more about Glenda Larke and other Orbit authors by registering for the free monthly newsletter at www.orbitbooks.net

if you enjoyed
STORMLORD RISING

look out for

THE DROWNING
CITY

by

Amanda Downum

1229 Sal Emperaturi

CHAPTER 1

Symir. The Drowning City.

An exile, perhaps, but at least it was an interesting one.

Isyllt's gloved hands tightened on the railing as the *Black Mariah* cleared the last of the Dragon Stones and turned toward the docks, dark estuarine water slopping against her hull. Fishing boats dotted Ka Liang Bay, glass buoys flashing in the sun. Cormorants dove around them, scattering ripples as they snatched fish from hooks and nets.

The west wind died, broken on the Dragons' sharp peaks, and the jungle's hot breath wafted from the shore. Rank with brine and bilge, sewers draining into the sea, but under the port-reek the air smelled of spices and the green tang of Sivahra's forests rising beyond the marshy delta of the Mir. Mountains flanked the capital city Symir, uneven green sentinels on either side of the river. So unlike the harsh and rocky shores of Selafai they had left behind two and a half decads ago.

Only twenty-five days at sea—a short voyage, though it didn't feel that way to Isyllt. The ship had made good time, laden only with olive oil and wheat flour from the north.

And northern spies. But those weren't recorded on the cargo manifest.

Isyllt shook her head, collected herself. This might be an exile, but it was a working one. She had a revolution to foment, a country to throw into chaos, and an emperor to undermine with it. Sivahra's jungles and mines—and Symir's bustling port—provided great wealth to the Assari Empire. Enough to fund a war of conquest, and the eyes of the expansionist Emperor roved slowly north. Isyllt and her master meant to prevent that.

If their intelligence was good, Sivahra was crawling with insurgent groups, natives desperate to overthrow their Imperial conquerors. Selafai's backing might help them succeed. Or at least distract the Empire. Trade one war for another. After that, maybe she could have a real vacation.

The *Mariah* dropped anchor before they docked and the crew bustled to prepare for the port authority's inspection; already a skiff rowed to meet them. The clang of harbor bells carried across the water.

Adam, her coconspirator and ostensible bodyguard, leaned against the rail beside her while his partner finished checking over their bags. Isyllt's bags, mostly; the mercenaries traveled light, but she had a pretense of pampered nobility to maintain. Maybe not such a pretense—she might have murdered for a hot bath and proper bed. Sweat stuck her shirt to her arms and back, itched behind her knees. She envied the sailors their vests and short trousers, but her skin was too pale to offer to the summer sun.

"Do we go straight to the Kurun Tam tonight?" Adam asked. The westering sun flashed on gold and silver earrings, mercenary gaud. He wore his sword again for the first time since they'd boarded the *Mariah*. He'd taken to sailor fashions—his vest hung open over his scarred chest, revealing charm bags around his neck and the pistol tucked into his belt. His skin was three shades darker than it had been when they sailed, bronze now instead of olive.

Isyllt's mouth twisted. "No," she said after a moment. "Let's find an extravagantly expensive hotel tonight. I feel like spending the Crown's money. We can work tomorrow." One night of vacation, at least, she could give herself.

He grinned and looked to his partner. "Do you know someplace decadent?"

Xinai's lips curled as she turned away from the luggage. "The Silver Phoenix. It's Selafaïn—it'll be decadent enough for you." Her head barely cleared her partner's shoulder, though the black plumage-crest of her hair added the illusion of more height. She wore her wealth too—rings in her ears, a gold cuff on one wiry wrist, a silver hoop in her nostril. The blades at her hips and the scars on her wiry arms said she knew how to keep it.

Isyllt turned back to the city, scanning the ships at dock. She was surprised not to see more Imperial colors flying. After rumors of rebellion and worries of war, she'd expected Imperial warships, but there was no sign of the Emperor's army—although that didn't mean it wasn't there.

Something was happening, though; a crowd gathered on the docks, and Isyllt caught flashes of red and green uniforms amid the blur of bodies. Shouts and angry voices carried over the water, but she couldn't make out the words.

The customs skiff drew alongside the *Mariah*, lion crest gleaming on the red-and-green-striped banners—the flag of an Imperial territory, granted limited home-rule. The sailors threw down a rope ladder and three harbor officials climbed aboard, nimble against the rocking hull. The senior inspector was a short, neat woman, wearing a red sash over her sleek-lined coat. Isyllt fought the urge to fidget with her own travel-grimed clothes. Her hair was a salt-stiff tangle, barely contained by pins, and while she'd cleaned her face with oil before landfall, it was no substitute for a proper bath.

Isyllt waited, Adam and Xinai flanking her, while the inspector spoke to the captain. Whatever the customs woman told the captain, he didn't like. He spat over the rail and made an angry gesture toward the shore. The *Mariah* wasn't the only ship waiting to dock; Isyllt wondered if the gathering on the pier had something to do with the delay.

Finally the ship's mate led two of the inspectors below, and the woman in the red sash turned to Isyllt, a wax tablet and stylus in her hand. A Sivahri, darker skinned than Xinai but with the same creaseless black eyes; elaborate henna designs covered her hands. Isyllt was relieved to be greeted in Assari—Xinai had tutored her in the native language during the voyage, but she was still far from fluent.

"Roshani." The woman inclined her head politely.

"You're the only passengers?" She raised her stylus as Isyllt nodded. "Your names?"

"Isyllt Iskaldur, of Erisín." She offered the oiled leather tube that held her travel papers. "This is Adam and Xinai, sayifarim hired in Erisín."

The woman glanced curiously at Xinai; the mercenary gave no more response than a statue. The official opened the tube and unrolled the parchment, recorded something on her tablet. "And your business in Symir?"

Isyllt tugged off her left glove and held out her hand. "I'm here to visit the Kurun Tam." The breeze chilled her sweaty palm. Since it was impossible to pass herself off as anything but a foreign mage, the local thaumaturgical facility was the best cover.

The woman's eyes widened as she stared at the cabochon black diamond on Isyllt's finger, but she didn't ward herself or step out of reach. Ghostlight gleamed iridescent in the stone's depths and a cold draft suffused the air. She nodded again, deeper this time. "Yes, meliket. Do you know where you'll be staying?"

"Tonight we take rooms at the Silver Phoenix."

"Very good." She recorded the information, then glanced up. "I'm sorry, meliket, but we're behind schedule. It will be a while yet before you can dock."

"What's going on?" Isyllt gestured toward the wharf. More soldiers had appeared around the crowd.

The woman's expression grew pained. "A protest. They've been there an hour and we're going to lose a day's work."

Isyllt raised her eyebrows. "What are they protesting?"

"New tariffs." Her tone became one of rote response. "The Empire considers it expedient to raise revenues and has imposed taxes on foreign goods. Some of the local merchants"—she waved a hennaed hand at the quay—"are unhappy with the situation. But don't worry, it's nothing to bother the Kurun Tam."

Of course not—Imperial mages would hardly be burdened with problems like taxes. It was much the same in the Arcanost in Erisín.

"Are these tariffs only in Sivahra?" she asked.

"Oh, no. All Imperial territories and colonies are subject."

Not just sanctions against a rebellious population, then, but real money-raising. That left an unpleasant taste in the back of her mouth. Twenty-five days with no news was chancy where politics were concerned.

The other officials emerged from the cargo hold a few moments later and the captain grudgingly paid their fees. The woman turned back to Isyllt, her expression brightening. "If you like, meliket, I can take you to the Silver Phoenix myself. It will be a much shorter route than getting there from the docks."

Isyllt smiled. "That would be lovely. Shakera."

Adam cocked an eyebrow as he hoisted bags. Isyllt's lips curled. "It never pays to annoy foreign guests," she murmured in Selafaïn. "Especially ones who can steal your soul."

She tried to watch the commotion on the docks, but the skiff moved swiftly and they were soon out of sight. A cloud of midges trailed behind the craft; the drone of wings carried unpleasant memories of the plague, but the natives seemed unconcerned. Isyllt waved the biting insects away, though she was immune to whatever exotic diseases they might carry. As they rowed beneath a raised water gate, a sharp, minty smell filled the air and the midges thinned.

The inspector—who introduced herself as Anhai Xian-Mar—talked as they went, her voice counterpoint to the rhythmic splash of oars as she explained the myriad delta islands on which the city was built, the web of canals that took the place of stone streets. Xinai's mask slipped for an instant and Isyllt saw the cold disdain in her eyes. The mercenary had little love for countrymen who served their Assari conquerors.

Sunlight spilled like honey over their shoulders, gilding the water and gleaming on domes and tilting spires. Buildings crowded together, walls of cream and ocher stone, pale blues and dusty pinks, balconies nearly touching over narrow alleys and waterways. Bronze chimes flashed from eaves and lintels. Vines trailed from rooftop gardens, dripping leaves and orange blossoms onto the water. Birds perched in potted trees and on steep green-and-gray-tiled roofs.

Invaders the Assari might be, but they had built a beautiful city. Isyllt tried to imagine the sky dark with smoke, the water running red. The city would be less lovely if her mission succeeded.

She'd heard stories from other agents of how the job crept into everything, reduced buildings and cities to exits and escape routes, defenses and weaknesses to be exploited. Till you couldn't look at anything—or anyone—without imagining how to infiltrate or corrupt or overthrow. She wondered how long it would take to happen to her. If she would even notice when it did.

Anhai followed Isyllt's gaze to the water level—slime crusted the stone several feet above the surface of the canal. "The rains will come soon and the river will rise. You're in time for the Dance of Masks."

The skiff drew up against a set of stairs and the oarsmen secured the boat and helped Adam and Xinai unload the luggage. A tall building rose above them, decorated with Selafaïn pillars. A carven phoenix spread its wings over the doors and polished horn panes gleamed ruddy in the dying light.

Anhai bowed farewell. "If you need anything at all, meliket, you can find me at the port authority office."

"Shakera." Isyllt offered her hand, and the silver griffin she held. She never saw where Anhai tucked the coin.

The she stepped from the skiff to the slime-slick stairs and set foot in the Drowning City.